Mrs. Frisby and the Rats of NIMH

by *Robert C. O'Brien*

illustrated by Zena Bernstein

SCHOLASTIC BOOK SERVICES

NEW YORK · TORONTO · LONDON · AUCKLAND · SYDNEY

To Catherine Fitzpatrick

ISBN: 0-590-10228-1

Copyright © 1971 by Robert C. O'Brien. This edition is published by Scholastic Book Services, a division of Scholastic
Magazines, Inc., by arrangement with Atheneum Publishers.

12 11 10   1 2 3 4 5 6/8

Printed in the U.S.A.

01

Contents

The Sickness
of Timothy Frisby

Mrs. Frisby, the head of a family of field mice, lived in an underground house in the vegetable garden of a farmer named Mr. Fitzgibbon. It was a winter house, such as some field mice move to when food becomes too scarce, and the living too hard in the woods and pastures. In the soft earth of a bean, potato, black-eyed pea and asparagus patch there is plenty of food left over for mice after the human crop has been gathered.

Mrs. Frisby and her family were especially lucky in the house itself. It was a slightly damaged cinder block, the hollow kind with two oval holes through it; it had somehow been abandoned in the garden during the summer and lay almost completely buried, with only a bit of one corner showing above ground, which is how Mrs. Frisby had discovered it. It lay on its side in such a way that the solid parts of the block formed a roof and a floor, both waterproof, and the hollows made two spacious rooms. Lined with bits of leaves, grass, cloth, cotton fluff, feathers, and other soft things Mrs. Frisby and her children had collected, the house stayed dry, warm, and comfortable all winter. A tunnel to the surface-earth of the garden, dug so that it was slightly larger than a mouse and slightly smaller than a cat's foreleg, provided access, air, and even a fair amount of light to the living room. The bedroom, formed by the second oval, was warm but dark, even at midday. A short tunnel through the earth behind the block connected the two rooms.

Although she was a widow (her husband had died only the preceding summer), Mrs. Frisby was able, through luck and hard work, to keep her family—there were four children—happy and well fed. January and February were the hardest months; the sharp, hard cold that began in December lasted until March, and by February the beans and black-eyes had been picked over (with help from the birds), the asparagus roots were frozen into stone, and the potatoes had been thawed and refrozen so many times they had acquired a slimy texture and a rancid taste. Still, the Frisbys made the best of what there was, and one way or another they kept from being hungry.

Then, one day at the very end of February, Mrs. Frisby's younger son, Timothy, fell sick.

That day began with a dry, bright, icy morning. Mrs. Frisby woke up early, as she always did. She and her family slept close together in a bed of down, fluff, and bits of cloth they had gathered, warm as a ball of fur.

She stood up carefully so as not to awaken the children, and walked quietly through the short tunnel to the living room. Here it was not so warm, but not really cold either. She could see from the light filtering down the entrance tunnel that the sun was up, and bright. She looked at the food in her pantry, a hollowed-out space lined with small stones in the earth behind the living room. There was plenty of food for breakfast, and lunch and dinner, too, for that matter; but still the sight depressed her, for it was the same tiresome fare they had been eating every day, every meal, for the last month. She wished she knew where to find a bit of green lettuce, or a small egg, or a taste of cheese, or a corn muffin. There were eggs in plenty not far off, in the hen house. But hens and hens' eggs are too big for a field mouse to cope with; and besides, between the garden and the hen house there was a wide sward of shrubs and grass, some of it grown up quite tall. Cat territory.

She climbed up the tunnel, emerging whiskers first, and looked around warily. The air was sharp, and there was white frost thick on the ground and on the dead leaves at the edge of the wood across the garden patch.

Mrs. Frisby set off over the gently furrowed earth, and when she reached the fence, she turned right, skirting the border of the forest, searching with her bright round eyes for a bit of carrot, a frozen parsnip, or something green. But there was nothing green at that time of year but the needles on the pine trees and the leaves on the holly, neither of which a mouse — or any other animal, for that matter — can eat.

And then, straight in front of her, she did see something green. She had reached the far corner of the garden, and there, at the edge of the woods where it met the fence, was a stump. In the stump there was a hole, and out of the hole protruded something that looked a little like a leaf, but was not.

Mrs. Frisby had no trouble at all going through the cattle-wire fence, but she approached the hole cautiously. If the stump was hollow, as it seemed to be, there was no telling who or what might be living in it.

A foot or so from the hole she stopped, stood still, and watched and listened. She could hear no sound, but from there she could see what the green was. It was, in fact, a yellowish-brownish-green: a bit of corn shuck. But what was a corn shuck doing there? The cornfield was in a different part of the farm altogether, away beyond the pasture. Mrs. Frisby hopped closer and then, carefully, crept up the side of the stump and peered inside. When her eyes got used to the dark, she saw that she had found a treasure: a winter's supply of food carefully stored and then, for some reason forgotten or abandoned.

But stored by whom? A racoon perhaps? Not very likely, so far from the stream. More likely a squirrel or a ground hog. She knew that both of these felt free to help themselves to the new corn each year, and that they were strong enough to carry ears away and store them.

But whoever had done it, why had he then abandoned the store? And then she remembered. Back in November there had come from near that edge of the woods the sound that sends all of the animals in the forest shivering to their hiding places — the sound of hunters' guns shooting, the sound that is accompanied, for someone, by a fiery stabbing pain. And then he never needs his stored food again.

Still, since Mrs. Frisby did not even know what kind of animal it had been, much less his name, she could not shed many tears over him — and food was food. It was not the green lettuce she had longed for, but she and her children were extremely fond of corn, and there were eight large ears in the stump, a noble supply for a mouse family. Down under the corn she also could see a pile of fresh peanuts (from still another part of the farm), some hickory nuts, and a stack of dried, sweet-smelling mushrooms.

With her forepaws and sharp teeth she pulled off a part of the husk from the top ear of corn and folded it double to serve as a crude carrying bag. Then she pulled loose as many of the yellow kernels as she could easily lift, and putting them in the shuck-bag she hopped off briskly for home. She would come back for more after breakfast and bring the children to help.

She backed down the tunnel entrance to her house tail first, pulling the corn after her and calling cheerfully as she went:

"Children! Wake up! See what I have for breakfast. A surprise!"

They came hurrying out, rubbing their eyes in excitement, for any kind of surprise in food was a rare and festive thing in the cold dead of winter. Teresa, the oldest, came first; crowding close behind her was Martin, the biggest, a strong, quick mouse, dark-haired and handsome like his poor father. Then came Cynthia, the youngest, a slim, pretty girl-mouse, light haired, and, in fact, a little light-headed as well, and over-fond of dancing.

"Where is it?" she said. "What is it? Where's the surprise?"

"Where is Timothy?" asked Mrs. Frisby.

"Mother," said Teresa, concerned, "he says he's sick and can't get up."

"Nonsense. Martin, tell your brother to get out of bed at once or he'll get no breakfast."

Martin ran to the bedroom obediently but came back in a moment alone.

"He says he feels too sick, and he doesn't want any breakfast, even a surprise. I felt his forehead, and it's burning hot."

"Oh, dear," said Mrs. Frisby. "That sounds as if he really is sick." Timothy had, on occasion, been known to think he was sick when he really was not. "Here, you may all have your break-fast—save Timothy's—and I'll go and see what's wrong."

She opened up the green carrying bag and put the corn on the table, dividing it into five equal shares. The dining table was a smooth piece of lath supported on both ends by stones.

"Corn!" shouted Martin. "Oh, Mother. Where did you ever get it?"

"Eat up," said Mrs. Frisby, "and a little later I'll show you because there's a lot more where this came from." And she disappeared into the little hallway that led to the bedroom.

"A lot more," Martin repeated as he sat down with his two sisters. "That sounds like enough to last till moving day."

"I hope so," Cynthia said. "When is moving day, anyway?"

"Two weeks," said Martin authoritatively. "Maybe three."

"Oh, Martin, how do you know?" protested Teresa. "What if it stays cold? Anyway, suppose Timothy isn't well enough?"

At this dreadful thought, so casually raised, they all grew worried and fell silent. Then Cynthia said:

"Teresa, you shouldn't be so gloomy. Of course he'll be well. He's just got a cold. That's all." She finished eating her corn, and so did the others.

In the bedroom Mrs. Frisby felt Timothy's forehead.

It was indeed hot, and damp with sweat. She took his pulse and dropped his wrist in alarm at what she felt.

"Do you feel sick to your stomach?"

"No, Mother. I feel all right, only cold, and when I sit up I get dizzy. And I can't get my breath too well."

Mrs Frisby peered anxiously at his face, and would have looked at his tongue, but in the dark room she could see no more than the dim outline of his head. He was the thinnest of her children and had a dark complexion like his father and brother. He was narrow of face; his eyes were unusually large and bright, and shone with the intensity of his thought when he spoke. He was, Mrs. Frisby knew, the smartest and most thoughtful of her children, though she would never have admitted this aloud. But he was also the frailest, and when colds or flu or virus infections came around he was the first to catch them and the slowest to recover. He was also—perhaps as a result—something of a hypochondriac. But there was no doubt he was really sick this time. His head felt as if he had a high fever, and his pulse was very fast.

"Poor Timothy. Lie back down and keep covered." She spread over him some of the bits of cloth they used as blankets. "After a while we'll fix you a pallet in the living room so you can lie out where it's light. I've found a fine supply of corn this morning, more than we can eat for the rest of the winter. Would you like some?"

"No, thank you. I'm not hungry. Not now."

He closed his eyes, and in a few minutes he went to sleep. But it was a restless sleep in which he tossed and moaned continually.

In mid-morning Mrs. Frisby, Martin, and Cynthia set off for the stump to carry home some more of the corn, and some peanuts and mushrooms (the hickory nuts they would leave, for they were too hard for mouse jaws to crack, and too tedious to gnaw through). They left Teresa home to look after Timothy, whom they had wrapped up and helped into a temporary sickbed in the living room. When they returned at lunchtime, carrying heavy loads of food, they found her near tears from worry.

Timothy was much worse. His eyes looked wild and strange from the fever; he trembled continuously, and each breath he took sounded like a gasp for life.

Teresa said: "Oh, Mother, I'm so glad you're back. He's been having nightmares and shouting about monsters and cats; and when I talk to him, he doesn't hear me at all."

Not only was Timothy not hearing with his ears; his eyes, though wide open, were not seeing, or if they were, he was not recognizing what they saw. When his mother tried to talk to him, to hold his hand and ask him how he felt, he stared past her as if she did not exist. Then he gave out a long, low moan and seemed to be trying to say something, but the words would not form properly and made no sense at all.

The other children stared in frightened silence. Finally Martin asked:

"Mother, what is it? What's wrong with him?"

"He is terribly ill. His fever is so high he has become delirious. There is nothing for it—I will have to go and see Mr. Ages. Timothy must have medicine."

Mr. Ages

Mr. Ages was a white mouse who lived across the farm and beyond, in a house that was part of a brick wall. The wall lined the basement of what had once been a large farmhouse. The farmhouse itself had burned down so many years ago that nobody could remember what it had looked like nor who had lived there. The basement remained, a great square hole in the ground; and in its crumbling walls, protected from the wind and snow, numerous small creatures lived. In summer there were snakes, dangerous to Mrs. Frisby, but there was no need to worry about them in winter.

Just the same, it was a long, hard journey and could be risky unless she was extremely cautious. It was so far, in fact, that Mrs. Frisby would not ordinarily have set out so late in the day, for fear that the dark would catch her before she got back. But Timothy obviously could not wait until the next day. So only five minutes after she announced that she must go, she was gone.

If she had been able to follow her nose, that is, to take the shortest route to where Mr. Ages lived, her journey would have been easy enough. But since that would have led her close to the farmhouse and the barn, and since the cat stalked those grounds relentlessly, she had to plot a much more roundabout way, circling the whole wide farmyard and sticking to the fringe of the woods.

She loped along briskly, moving in the easy, horse-like canter mice use when they are trying to cover ground. Her progress was almost completely noiseless; she chose her path where the earth was bare, or where grass grew, and she avoided dead leaves, which would rustle and crackle even under her small weight. Always she kept an eye out for hiding places—logs, roots, stones, things to scurry under if she should meet a larger animal who might be unfriendly. For though the cat was number one, there were other things in the woods that chased mice.

And as she did all this, she worried about Timothy and hoped that Mr. Ages would know something that would help him.

It was more than two hours later that she saw

she was getting close to the brick wall where he lived. Though her husband had been a great friend of Mr. Ages and had visited him often, Mrs. Frisby herself had been there only once before, and that had been in summer. Still, she remembered the place clearly. It was an odd sort of clearing in the woods. Long ago, when the old house had been lived in, before it had burned, there must have been a wide lawn around it. Over the years this clearing had grown over with a strange mixture of high, rank grass, tall weeds, berries, and wild flowers. In the summer it was a wild and beautiful place, bright with blooms and full of the smell of blackberry blossoms and purple clover. There were harsher plants as well—spiked jimson weeds and poisonous dark pokeberries, and bees droning everywhere.

But in winter it had a bleak and almost ghostly look, for the blossoms and the green leaves were gone, and only the dry skeletons of the weeds stood, hung with stalks and seeds and pods that rattled in the wind. It was from these seeds and others, and from the flowers and roots beneath them, that Mr. Ages made the draughts and powders that could sometimes save the sick from dying.

The time she had been here before—that was for Timothy, too, when he was only a baby, scarcely bigger than a marble. He had wandered, while playing with the other children, a little way from them and had been bitten or stung by something poisonous. They did not know what. When the others found him, he lay curled in a ball, paralyzed, and scarcely able to breathe.

That time her husband Mr. Frisby had been alive, and between them, taking turns, they had managed to carry Timothy to Mr. Ages' house. It was a sad and frightening journey, and when they arrived they had been afraid he might already be dead. Mr. Ages looked at him, examined his tongue, felt his pulse, and found a small red lump near his neck. "Spider," he said. "Not a black widow, but bad enough." He had forced a few drops of a milky liquid into Timothy's mouth and held him upright so that it could trickle down his throat, for Timothy could not swallow. In a few minutes his small muscles had unlocked, and he was able to move his arms and legs. "He'll be all right," said Mr. Ages, "but weak for a few hours."

The trip back home had been a happy one, and the other children were wide-eyed with joy to see Timothy alive. Yet Mrs. Frisby thought that this had been the beginning of his frailness. From that time on he tended to stumble a little when he walked, especially when he was tired;

he never grew as big or as vigorous as his brother Martin. But he thought a great deal more, and in that he resembled his father.

Now she reached Mr. Ages' house, a hole in the brick wall where one end of heavy floor beam had once rested. It was about two feet below the top of the wall, and one reached it by climbing down a sort of rough stairway of broken brick ends. She knocked on his door made of a piece of shingle. "Oh, let him be in, *please*," she thought, but he was not. There was no answer, so she sat down to wait on the narrow ledge of brick in front of his door.

Half an hour passed, the sun sinking lower in the west all the time, before she heard a slight scratching noise up above, and there he came, carrying a cloth sack bulging with some kind of lumpy material. His fur was a soft gray-white, and so glossy he seemed almost to glow. Mrs. Frisby had heard that Mr. Ages was not truly a white mouse; that is, he had not been born with white fur, but had turned white from old age. Whether this was so or not she did not know. Certainly he *seemed* very old, and very wise; yet he walked nimbly enough.

"Oh, Mr. Ages, I'm so glad you've come," she said. "I don't suppose you remember me, Mrs. Frisby."

"Of course I remember you. And I was sad to hear about poor Mr. Frisby. How is your young son — Timothy, was it?"

"It's about him I've come to see you. He's taken terribly sick."

"Has he? I was afraid he might turn out to be not as strong as the others."

"I hoped you might be able to help him."

"That may be. Come in, please, so I can put down this sack."

Mr. Ages' house, somewhat larger than a shoe-box but about the same shape, resembled the house of a hermit. It was bare of furniture except for a bit of bedding in one corner, a stool made of a piece of brick, and another piece of brick worn smooth from use as a pestle on which he ground out his medicines. Along one entire wall, ar-ranged neatly in small piles, stood the raw mate-rials he had collected: roots, seeds, dried leaves, pods, strips of bark, and shriveled mushrooms.

To this row he now added the contents of his sack. It held a number of small plants, all of them the same kind, with stringy roots and dark, veined green leaves that looked like mint.

"Pipsissewa," said Mr. Ages. "Botanically, *Chimaphila umbellata.* It stays green all winter, and makes a very useful spring tonic. Most people use only the leaves, but I have found the roots even more effective." He arranged the plants in an orderly pile. "But that's not what you're here for. What's wrong with young Timothy?"

"He has a very high fever. He's delirious. I don't know what to do."

"How high?"

"So high that he feels burning hot to the touch, runs with perspiration, and yet he shivers with cold at the same time."

"Keep him wrapped up in a blanket."

"I do."

"And his pulse?"

"So fast that you cannot tell one heartbeat from the next."

"His tongue?"

"So coated that it looks purple."

"How does he breathe?"

"He breathes very rapidly, and the air rasps in his chest. He said, at first, that he could not get his breath."

"But he does not cough."

"No."

"He has pneumonia," said Mr. Ages. "I have some medicine that will help him. But the most important thing is to keep him warm. And he must stay in bed." He went to the back of his house, and from a ledge formed by a projecting brick he took three packets of medicine, powders neatly wrapped in white paper.

"Give him one of these tonight. Mix it in water and make him drink it. If he is still delirious, hold his nose and pour it down his throat. Give him the second one tomorrow morning, and the third the next morning."

Mrs. Frisby took the packages. "Will he get better?" she asked, dreading to hear the answer.

"He will get better this time. His fever will be less on the second day, and gone the third, after he has taken all the medicine. That does not mean he will have recovered; his lungs will still be terribly weak and sensitive. If he gets the least bit cold, or breathes cold air—even a breath or two—the pneumonia will surely come back worse than before. And the second time he may not recover. This will be true for at least three weeks, and more likely a month."

"And after that?"

"Even after that he should be careful, though we may hope by then the weather will be warmer."

By now the sun was getting low in the west, settling into the high mountains beyond the woods. Mrs. Frisby thanked Mr. Ages and set out for home as quickly as she could go.

The Crow and the Cat

Mrs. Frisby looked again at the sun and saw that she faced an unpleasant choice. She could go home by the same roundabout way she had come, in which case she would surely end up walking alone in the woods in the dark — a frightening prospect, for at night the forest was alive with danger. Then the owl came out to hunt, and foxes, weasels, and strange wild cats stalked among the tree trunks.

The other choice would be dangerous, too, but with luck it would get her home before dark. That would be to take a straighter route, across the farmyard between the barn and chicken house, going not too close to the house but cutting the distance home by half. The cat would be there somewhere, but by daylight — and by staying in the open, away from the shrubs — she could probably spot him before he saw her.

The cat: He was called Dragon. Farmer Fitzgibbon's wife had given him the name as a joke when he was a small kitten pretending to be fierce. But when he grew up, the name turned out to be an apt one. He was enormous, with a huge, broad head and a large mouth full of curving fangs, needle sharp. He had seven claws on each foot and a thick, furry tail, which lashed angrily from side to side. In color he was orange and white, with glaring yellow eyes; and when he leaped to kill, he gave a high, strangled scream that froze his victims where they stood.

But Mrs. Frisby preferred not to think about that. Instead, as she came out of the woods from Mr. Ages' house and reached the farmyard fence she thought about Timothy. She thought of how his eyes shone with merriment when he made up small jokes, which he did frequently, and how invariably kind he was to his small, scatter-brained sister Cynthia. The other children sometimes laughed at her when she made mistakes, or grew impatient with her because she was forever losing things; but Timothy never did. Instead, he would help her find them. And when Cynthia herself had been sick in bed with a cold, he had sat by her side for hours and entertained her with stories. He made these up out of his head, and he seemed to have a bottomless supply of them.

Taking a firm grip on her packets of medicine, Mrs. Frisby went under the fence and set out toward the farmyard. The first stretch was a long pasture; the barn itself, square and red and big, rose in the distance to her right; to her left, farther off, were the chicken houses.

When at length she came abreast of the barn, she saw the cattle-wire fence that marked the other end of the pasture; and as she approached it, she was startled by a sudden outburst of noise. She thought at first it was a hen, strayed from the chickenyard — caught by a fox? She looked down the fence and saw that it was no hen at all, but a young crow, flapping in the grass, acting most odd. As she watched, he fluttered to the top wire of the fence, where he perched nervously for a moment. Then he spread his wings, flapped hard, and took off — but after flying four feet he stopped with a snap and crashed to the ground again, shedding a flurry of black feathers and squawking loudly.

He was tied to the fence. A piece of something silvery — it looked like wire — was tangled around one of his legs; the other end of it was caught in the fence. Mrs. Frisby walked closer, and then she could see it was not wire after all, but a length of silver-colored string, probably left over from a Christmas package.

22

The crow was sitting on the fence, pecking ineffectively at the string with his bill, cawing softly to himself, a miserable sound. After a moment he spread his wings, and she could see he was going to try to fly again.

"Wait," said Mrs. Frisby.

The crow looked down and saw her in the grass.

"Why should I wait? Can't you see I'm caught? I've got to get loose."

"But if you make so much noise again the cat is sure to hear. If he hasn't heard already."

"You'd make noise, too, if you were tied to a fence with a piece of string, and with night coming on."

"I would not," said Mrs. Frisby, "if I had any sense and knew there was a cat nearby. Who tied you?" She was trying to calm the crow, who was obviously terrified.

He looked embarrassed and stared at his feet. "I picked up the string. It got tangled with my foot. I sat on the fence to try to get it off, and it caught on the fence."

"Why did you pick up the string?"

The crow, who was very young indeed — in fact, only a year old — said wearily, "Because it was shiny."

"You knew better."

"I had been told."

Birdbrain, thought Mrs. Frisby, and then re-called what her husband used to say: The size of the brain is no measure of its capacity. And well she might recall it, for the crow's head was double the size of her own.

"Sit quietly," she said. "Look toward the house and see if you see the cat."

"I don't see him. But I can't see behind the bushes. Oh, if I could just fly higher . . ."

"Don't," said Mrs. Frisby. She looked at the sun; it was setting behind the trees. She thought of Timothy, and of the medicine she was carry-ing. Yet she knew she could not leave the foolish crow there to be killed — and killed he surely would be before sunrise — just for want of a few minutes' work. She might still make it by dusk if she hurried.

"Come down here," she said. "I'll get the string off."

"How?" said the crow dubiously.

"Don't argue. I have only a few minutes." She said this in a voice so authoritative that the crow fluttered down immediately.

"But if the cat comes . . ." he said.

"If the cat comes, he'll knock you off the fence with one jump and catch you with the next. Be still." She was already at work with her sharp teeth, gnawing at the string. It was twined and twisted and twined again around his right ankle, and she saw she would have to cut through it three times to get it off.

As she finished the second strand, the crow, who was staring toward the house, suddenly cried out:

"I see the cat!"

"*Quiet!*" whispered Mrs. Frisby. "Does he see us?"

"I don't know. Yes. He's looking at me. I don't think he can see you."

"Stand perfectly still. Don't get in a panic." She did not look up, but started on the third strand.

"He's moving this way."

"Fast or slow?"

"Medium. I think he's trying to figure out what I'm doing."

She cut through the last strand, gave a tug, and the string fell off.

"There, you're free. Fly off, and be quick."

"But what about you?"

"Maybe he hasn't seen me."

"But he will. He's coming closer."

Mrs. Frisby looked around. There was not a bit of cover anywhere near, not a rock nor a hole nor a log; nothing at all closer than the chicken yard—and that was in the direction the cat was coming from, and a long way off.

"Look," said the crow. "Climb on my back. Quick. And hang on."

Mrs. Frisby did what she was told, first grasping the precious packages of medicine tightly between her teeth.

"Are you on?"

"Yes."

She gripped the feathers on his back, felt the beat of his powerful black wings, felt a dizzying upward surge, and shut her eyes tight.

"Just in time," said the crow, and she heard the angry scream of the cat as he leaped at where they had just been. "It's lucky you're so light. I can scarcely tell you're there." Lucky indeed, thought Mrs. Frisby; if it had not been for your foolishness, I'd never have gotten into such a scrape. However, she thought it wise not to say so, under the circumstances.

"Where do you live?" asked the crow.

"In the garden patch. Near the big stone."

"I'll drop you off there." He banked alarmingly, and for a moment Mrs. Frisby though he meant it literally. But a few seconds later—so fast does the crow fly—they were gliding to earth a yard from her front door.

"Thank you very much," said Mrs. Frisby, hopping to the ground.

"It's I who should be thanking you," said the crow. "You saved my life."

"And you mine."

"Ah, but that's not quite even. Yours wouldn't have been risked if it had not been for me—me and my piece of string." And since this was just what she had been thinking, Mrs. Frisby did not argue.

"We all help one another against the cat," she said.

"True. Just the same, I am in debt to you. If the time ever comes when I can help you, I hope you will ask me. My name is Jeremy. Mention it to any crow you see in these woods, and he will find me."

"Thank you," said Mrs. Frisby. "I will remember."

Jeremy flew away to the woods, and she entered her house, taking the three doses of medicine with her.

Mr. Fitzgibbon's Plow

When Mrs. Frisby went into her house, she found Timothy asleep and the other children waiting, frightened, sad, and subdued.

"He went to sleep right after you left," Teresa said. "He's waked up twice, and the second time he wasn't delirious. He said his chest hurt and his head hurt. But Mother, he seemed so weak—he could hardly talk. He asked where you were, and I told him. Then he went back to sleep."

Mrs. Frisby went to where Timothy lay, a small ball of damp fur curled under a bit of cloth blanket. He looked scarcely larger then he had when she and Mr. Frisby had carried him to Mr. Ages as an infant, and the thought of that trip made her wish Mr. Frisby were alive to reassure the children and tell them not to worry. But he was not, and it was she who must say it.

"Don't worry," she said. "Mr. Ages gave me some medicine for him and says he will recover." She mixed the contents of one of the packets, a gray-green powder, in water, and then gently shook Timothy awake.

He smiled. "You're back," he said in a voice as small as a whisper.

"I'm back, and I've brought you some medicine. Mr. Ages says it will make you all right." She lifted his head on her arm, and he swallowed the medicine. "I expect it's bitter," she said.

"It's not so bad," he said. "It tastes like pepper." And he fell back to sleep immediately.

The next morning, as predicted, his fever was lower, his breathing grew easier, and his heartbeat slowed down; still, that day he slept seven hours out of each eight. The next day he stayed awake longer, and on the third day he had no fever at all, just as Mr. Ages had said. However, since Mr. Ages had been right in all that, Mrs. Frisby knew he was sure to have been right in the other things he had said: Timothy was not really strong yet. He must stay in bed, stay warm, and breathe only warm air.

During those three days she had stayed close by his side, but on the fourth she felt cheerful enough to go for a walk, and also to fetch some more of the corn from the stump so they could have it for supper.

She went out her front door into the sunshine and was surprised to find a spring day waiting for her. The weather had turned warm while she had stayed indoors; February was over and March had come in, as they say, like a lamb. There was a smell of dampness in the air as the frosted ground thawed, a smell of things getting ready to grow. It made her feel even more cheerful than before, and she walked almost gaily across the garden.

And yet despite the fine warmth of the day— indeed, in a way, because of it—Mrs. Frisby could not quite get rid of a nagging worry that kept flickering in her mind; it was the kind of worry that, if you push it out of this corner of your thoughts, pops up in that corner, and finally in the middle, where it has to be faced. It was the thought of Moving Day.

Everybody knows that the ground hog comes up from the deep hole where he has slept away the winter, looks around, and if he decides the cold weather is not over, goes back down to sleep for another six weeks. Field mice like Mrs. Frisby are not so lucky. When winter is over, they must move out of the garden and back to the meadow or the pasture. For as soon as the weather allows, Farmer Fitzgibbon's tractor comes rumbling through, pulling the sharp-bladed plow through the soil, turning over every foot of it. No animal caught in the garden that day is likely to escape alive, and all the winter homes, all the tunnels and holes and nests and cocoons, are torn up. After the plow comes the harrow, with its heavy creaking disks, and then the people with hoes and seeds.

Not all the field mice move into the garden for the winter, of course. Some find their way to barn lofts; some even creep into people's houses and live under the eaves or in attics, taking their chances with mousetraps. But the Frisbys had always come to the garden, preferring the relative safety and freedom of the outdoors.

Moving Day therefore depends on the weather, and that is why a fine day set Mrs. Frisby worrying, even as she enjoyed it. As soon as the frost was out of the ground, the plow would come, and that could happen as much as a month earlier (or later) one year than the last.

And the worry was this: If it came too soon, Timothy would not be able to move. He was supposed to stay in bed, and moving meant a long walk across the field of winter wheat, up and down hill to the brook's edge, where the Frisbys made their summer home. Not only that—the home itself would be damp and chilly for the first few weeks (as summer homes always are) until early spring turned to late spring and the nights grew truly warm. This was something that Mrs. Frisby and the children did not ordinarily mind; Moving Day, in fact, was normally a gay time, for it marked the end of the gray weather and the frost. It was like the beginning of a summer holiday.

But this year? Now that Mrs. Frisby had faced the problem, she did not see any answer except to hope that the day would not come too early. In another month (according to Mr. Ages), Timothy would be strong enough. Perhaps she was only borrowing trouble. One warm day, she told herself, does not make a summer. No, nor even a spring.

She walked on through the garden and saw ahead of her a small figure she knew. It was a lady shrew, a tiny thing scarcely bigger than a peanut, but with a wit as sharp as her teeth. She lived in a simple hole in the ground a few yards away; Mrs. Frisby met her often and had grown to like her, though shrews are generally unpopular, having a reputation for short tempers and extremely large appetites.

"Good morning," said Mrs. Frisby.

"Ah, Mrs. Frisby. Good morning indeed. Too good is what I'm thinking." The shrew was holding a stalk of straw, which she now thrust into the earth. It went down easily for two inches or more before it bent in her hand. "Look at that. The top of the frost is gone already. Another few days like this, and it will be all gone. Then we will have the tractor in here again, breaking everything up."

"So soon? Do you really think so?" asked Mrs. Frisby, her worry returning in a rush, stronger than before.

"He plows when the frost is gone. Remember the spring of sixty-five? That year he plowed on the eleventh day of March, and on a Sunday at that. I moved down to the woods that night and nearly froze to death in a miserable hollow log. And that day came after a week of days just like this."

Mrs. Frisby did remember it; her family, too, had shivered through those chilly nights. For the fact was, the earlier Moving Day came, the colder the nights were likely to be.

"Oh dear," she said. "I hope it doesn't happen this year. Poor Timothy's too sick to move."

"Sick is he? Take him to Mr. Ages."

"I've been myself. But he was too weak to get out of bed, and still is."

"I'm sorry to hear that. Then we must hope for another frost, or that the tractor will break down. I wish someone would drive a tractor through his house and see how he likes it." So muttering, the lady shrew moved off, and Mrs. Frisby continued across the garden. The remark was illogical, of course, for they both knew that without Mr. Fitzgibbon's plow there would be no garden to live in at all, and there was no way he could turn the earth without also turning up their houses.

Or was there? What the shrew had said was meant to be sympathetic, but it was not helpful. It meant, Mrs. Frisby realized, that she, too, could see no solution to the problem. But that did not mean that there was none. She remembered something her husband, Mr. Frisby, used to say: All doors are hard to unlock until you have the key. All right. She must try to find the key. But where? Whom to ask?

And then, as if to make things worse, she heard a sound that filled her with alarm. It came from across the fence in the farmyard, a loud, sputtering roar. It was Mr. Fitzgibbon starting his tractor.

Five Days

The sound of the tractor did not necessarily mean that Mr. Fitzgibbon was getting ready to plow. He used it for many other things — hauling hay and firewood, for instance, and mowing, and clearing snow in the winter. Mrs. Frisby reminded herself of all this as she hurried over to the corner post.

That was a very thick fence post at the corner of the garden nearest the farmhouse and the tractor shed. She had discovered long ago that it had, a few inches above the ground, a convenient knot hole with a hollow place behind it in which she could hide, when she had reason to, and watch what was going on in the yard. The cat, Dragon, also knew of its existence, so she had to look sharply when she came out.

She came up carefully behind the post, stared this way and that, and then darted around it and up into the hole. All clear.

Mr. Fitzgibbon had backed the tractor out of the big, cluttered shed where he kept it. Leaving the motor idling, he climbed down from the seat and called to the house. In a moment his older son Paul came out, closing the door carefully behind him. Paul, at fifteen, was a quiet, hardworking boy, rather clumsy in his movements but strong and careful about his chores. In a few seconds he was followed by his younger brother Billy, who at age twelve was noisier and had an annoying habit of skimming rocks across the grass at anything that moved. Mrs. Frisby did not much care for Billy.

"All right, boys," said Mr. Fitzgibbon, "let's haul it out and see about that linch pin."

"It was just about worn through last fall, I remember," Paul said. The boys disappeared into the shed, and Mr. Fitzgibbon remounted the tractor; he turned it around and backed it slowly toward the shed, so that the rear end was out of Mrs. Frisby's sight.

There was some clanking and clanging inside the shed while Mr. Fitzgibbon, looking over his shoulder, worked some levers on the side of the tractor.

"All set?"

He shifted gears and eased the tractor forward again. Hitched behind it, clear of the ground, was the plow.

Mrs. Frisby's heart sank. Surely he was not going to start *now*?

But as soon as he had the plow out in the sunlight, Mr. Fitzgibbon turned the tractor's engine off. It died with a sputter, and they all gathered around the plow-hitch.

"Sure enough," said Mr. Fitzgibbon. "She's just about ready to shear. Paul, I'm glad you remembered that. If I order it today, Henderson's will have a new one in three or four days."

"It took five days last time," Paul said.

"Five, then. That's just about right anyway. It's too wet to plow now, but five days like this ought to dry the ground out. Let's grease up while we've got it out. Billy, get the grease gun."

In her hiding place, Mrs. Frisby breathed a sigh of relief, and then began to worry again immediately. Five days, although a respite, was too short. Three weeks, Mr. Ages had said, would be the soonest Timothy could get out of bed, the soonest he could live through a chill night without getting pneumonia again. She sighed and felt like weeping. If only the summer house were as warm as the cinder block house. But it was not, and even if it were, he could not make the long journey. They might try to carry him—but what was the use of that? Only to have him get sick again after the first night there.

She might, she thought, go back to Mr. Ages and see if he had any ideas that would help. Was there some medicine that would make Timothy get strong sooner? She doubted it; surely, if he had such medicine he would have given it to her the first time. She was thinking about this when she climbed out through the knot hole and slithered to the ground below—not ten feet from the cat.

Dragon lay stretched out in the sunlight, but he was not asleep. His head was up and his yellow eyes were open, staring in her direction. She gasped in terror and whirled around the fence post to put it between her and him. Then, without pausing, she set out on a dash across the garden as fast as she could run, expecting at any instant to hear the cat's scream and feel his great claws on her back. She reached the shrew's hole and considered for a fraction of a second diving into it, but it was too small.

Then she glanced back over her shoulder and saw an amazing sight. The cat had not moved at all! He was lying exactly as before, except that now one of his eyes was closed. The other, however, was still looking straight at her, so she did not pause, but raced on.

Finally, when she was a safe distance away—two thirds across the garden and nearly home—she stopped and looked again more carefully. The cat still lay there and seemed to have gone to sleep. That was so odd—so unheard of—she could hardly believe it. Feeling quite safe, but puzzled, she looked for a vantage point from which she could see better. By rights, she should be dead, and though she had escaped by what seemed almost a miracle, she scolded herself for having been so careless. If the cat had killed her, who would take care of the children?

She saw a dead asparagus plant, stiff, tall, with branches like a small tree. She climbed it and from near the top looked back to the farmyard. Mr. Fitzgibbon and his sons had finished greasing the tractor and gone on somewhere else. But the cat still lay on the grass, seemingly asleep. Why had he not chased her? Was it possible that, close as she had been, he had not seen her? She could not believe that. The only explanation she could think of was that he had just finished a very large meal and was feeling so stuffed and lazy he did not want to take the trouble to get up. But that was almost as unbelievable; certainly it had never happened before. Was it possible that he was sick?

Then, on what had already been a day of oddities and alarms, she noticed something else strange. Beyond the cat, quite far beyond, between the barn and the house, she saw what looked like a troop of dark gray figures marching in columns. Marching? Not exactly, but moving slowly and all in line.

They were rats.

There were a dozen of them, and at first she could not quite see what they were up to. Then she saw something moving, between them and behind them. It looked like a thick piece of rope, a long piece, maybe twenty feet. No. It was stiffer than rope. It was electric cable, the heavy, black kind used for outdoor wiring and strung on telephone poles. The rats were hauling it laboriously through the grass, inching it along in the direction of a very large wild rosebush in the far corner of the yard. Mrs. Frisby quickly guessed where they were taking it, though she could not guess why. In that rosebush, concealed and protected by dense tangles of fiercely sharp thorns, was the entrance to a rat hole. All the animals knew about it and were careful to stay away.

But what would the rats want with such a long piece of wire? Mrs. Frisby could not imagine. Even more curious, how did they dare to pull it across the yard in broad daylight when the cat was right there? The rats were bigger than Mrs. Frisby, and could be, when necessary, dangerous fighters, but they were no match for Dragon.

She watched them for quite a long time. It was obvious that they knew exactly what they were doing, and they looked as well drilled as a group of soliders. They had about twenty-five yards to go to reach the rosebush; as if at a signal (which, however, she was too far away to hear), they would all pull together, moving the wire about a foot. Then they would pause, rest, and heave again. It was about twenty minutes before the first rat disappeared into the bush. A little later the last bit of wire disappeared behind them like a thin black snake, and Mrs. Frisby climbed down from the asparagus bush.

All that time the cat had slept on.

A Favor from Jeremy

In her worry about Moving Day, in watching the tractor, the cat, and finally the rats, Mrs. Frisby had forgotten that she had set out originally to get some corn for supper. Now she remembered it, so instead of continuing to her house she turned toward the far corner of the garden and the stump at the edge of the woods beyond. She was a little tired after her dash from the cat, so she walked along slowly, feeling the warmth of the sun and the smell of the breeze.

This mild breeze, carrying the moist essence of early spring, caused a dead leaf to flutter here and there, and across the garden near the fence it moved something that sparkled in the sunlight. This caught the corner of Mrs. Frisby's eye; she glanced at it, saw that it was only a bit of tin foil (or aluminum foil) blown from somewhere, and she looked away again. Then she looked back, for at that moment a black object plummeted from the sky, and she recognized her friend Jeremy the crow.

A thought crossed Mrs. Frisby's mind. She changed direction again, and, moving more quickly, ran across the earth to where Jeremy stood. He was hopping around the shiny piece of foil, eyeing it from one direction and another.

What had occurred to Mrs. Frisby was that although Jeremy was not the brightest of animals she had met, and though he was young, he knew things and places she did not, and one had to begin somewhere. As she approached him, he had picked up the foil in his beak and was spreading his wings to fly off.

"Wait, please," she called.

He turned, folded his wings, and then replaced the foil carefully on the ground.

"Hello," he said.

"You remember me?"

"Of course. You saved me from the cat." Then he added, "What do you think of this piece of foil?"

Mrs. Frisby looked at it without much interest.

"It's just a piece of foil," she said. "It's not very big."

"True. But it's shiny — especially when the sun strikes it just so."

"Why are you so interested in shiny things?"

"Well, really, I'm not. At least not very. But I have a friend who likes them, so when I see one I pick it up."

"I see. That's very thoughtful. And would the friend be female?"

"As a matter of fact, yes. She is. How did you know?"

"Just a guess," said Mrs. Frisby. "Do you remember saying once that if I needed help, I might ask you?"

"I do. Any time. Just ask for Jeremy. Any of the crows can find me. And now, if you will excuse me . . ."

He bent over to pick up the foil again.

"Please don't go yet," said Mrs. Frisby. "I think perhaps you can help me now."

"Ah," said Jeremy. "What kind of help? Are you hungry? I'll bring you some seeds from the barn loft. I know where they're stored."

"No, thank you," said Mrs. Frisby. "We have enough to eat." And then she told him, as briefly as she could, about Timothy, his sickness, and the problem of Moving Day. Jeremy knew about Moving Day; crows do not have to move, but they keep a close watch on such activities as plowing and planting so as to get their fair share of what's planted, and with their sharp eyes they see the small animals leaving before the plow.

So he clucked sympathetically when he heard Mrs. Frisby's story, cocked his head to one side, and thought as hard as he could for as long as he could, which was about thirty seconds. His eyes closed with the effort.

"I don't know what you should do," he said finally. "I'm sorry. But maybe I can help even so. At least, I can tell you what we do when we don't know what to do."

"We?"

"The crows. Most of the birds."

"What do you do, then?"

"Over that way," Jeremy nodded in the direction of the deep woods and faraway mountains that rose beyond the fence, "about a mile from here there grows a very large beech tree, the biggest tree in the whole forest. Near the top of the tree there is a hollow in the trunk. In the hollow lives an owl who is the oldest animal in the woods—some say in the world.

"When we don't know what to do, we ask him. Sometimes he answers our questions, sometimes he doesn't. It depends on how he feels. Or as my father used to say—what kind of a humor he's in."

Or possibly, thought Mrs. Frisby, on whether or not he knows the answer. But she said:

"Could you ask him, then, if he knows of any

help for me?" She did not think it likely that he would.

"Ah, no," Jeremy said, "that won't do. That is, I could ask him, but I don't think the owl would listen. Imagine. A crow come to ask for help for a lady mouse with a sick child. He wouldn't believe me."

"Then what's to be done?"

"What's to be done? You must go yourself and ask him."

"But I could never find the tree. And if I did, I don't think I could climb so high."

"Ah, now. That is where I can help, as I said I would. I will carry you there on my back, the way I did before. And home again, of course."

Mrs. Frisby hesitated. It was one thing to leap on a crow's back when the cat is only three jumps away and coming fast, but quite another to do it deliberately, and to fly deep into a dark and unknown forest. In short, Mrs. Frisby was afraid.

Then she thought of Timothy, and of the big steel plow blade. She told herself: I have no choice. If there is any chance that the owl might be able to help me, to advise me, I must go. She said to Jeremy:

"Thank you very much. I will go and talk to the owl if you will take me. It's a great favor."

"It's nothing," said Jeremy. "You're welcome. But we can't go now."

"Why not?"

"In the daytime, when the sun is out, the owl goes deep into the hollow and sleeps. That is, they say he sleeps, but I don't believe it. How could anyone sleep so long? I think he sits in there, part of the time at least, and thinks. And that's why he knows so much.

"But anyway, he won't speak in the daytime, not to anyone. And at night he's out flying, flying and hunting . . ."

"I know," said Mrs. Frisby — and that was another reason to be afraid.

"The time to see him is just at dusk. Then, when the light gets dim, he comes to the entrance of the hollow and watches while the dark comes in. That's the time to ask him questions."

"I understand," said Mrs. Frisby. "Shall we go this evening?"

"At five o'clock," Jeremy said, "I'll be at your house." He picked up the piece of foil in his bill, waved goodbye, and flew off.

The Owl

Jeremy appeared as promised when the last thumbnail of sun winked out over the mountains beyond the meadow. Mrs. Frisby was waiting, her heart pounding in her ears, and three of the children were there to watch—Teresa and Martin standing beside their mother, and Cynthia, who was afraid of the crow, just a pair of round eyes peering out the round doorway. Timothy was down below, taking a nap, and had not been told about the expedition lest he worry and blame himself for the risk his mother must take. (Indeed, the words Moving Day had not been mentioned in his presence.) Even to the other children Mrs. Frisby had explained only a part of the problem; that is, she had not told them that there were only five days left, nor anything about Mr. Fitzgibbon and the tractor. She did not want them to worry, either.

Jeremy landed with a *swoosh*—a bit dramatically, perhaps—and nodded at the children and Mrs. Frisby.

"Hello," he said. "Here I am."

Mrs. Frisby introduced Martin and Teresa (and Cynthia's eyes). Martin, who wished he were going on the trip himself, asked Jeremy in excitement:

"How high can you fly?"

"Oh, I don't know exactly," Jeremy said. "A couple of miles, I guess."

"Mother, did you hear? You'll be two *miles* up in the air."

"Martin, it won't be necessary to go so high on this trip."

Jeremy said cheerfully: "No, but I can, if you'd like."

"No, thank you. I wouldn't think of your taking the trouble." She was trying hard to hide her terror, and Martin had not helped matters at all. But Jeremy suddenly saw that she was trembling and realized that she must be afraid.

"It's all right," he said kindly. "There's nothing to be nervous about. I fly over the woods a dozen times a day."

Yes, thought Mrs. Frisby, but *you're* not riding on your back, and *you* can't fall off.

"All right," she said as bravely as she could. "I'm ready. Teresa and Martin, take care of Tim-

othy until I come back, and be sure you don't tell
him where I've gone." With a small leap she was
on Jeremy's back, lying as flat as she could and
holding tight to the glossy feathers between his
wings, as a horseback rider grips the horse's
mane before a jump. Martin and Teresa waved
goodbye, but she did not see them, for she had
her face pressed against the feathers and her eyes
closed.

Once again she felt the surge of power as the
crow's broad wings beat down against the air;
this time it lasted longer for they were going
higher than before. Then the beating became
gentler as they leveled off, and then, to her

alarm, it stopped altogether. What was wrong? The crow must have felt her grow tense, for suddenly from ahead she heard his voice:

"An updraft," he said. "We're soaring. There's usually one over this stretch of woods in the evening." A current of warm air, rising from the woods, was carrying them along. So smooth was the motion that they seemed to stand still, and Mrs. Frisby ventured to open her eyes and lift her head just a trifle. She could not look straight down — that was Jeremy's back — but off to the right, and a bit behind them, she saw a gray-brown square the size of a postage stamp. She realized with a gasp that it was the garden patch, and Martin and Teresa, if they were still there, were too small to be seen.

"Look to the left," said Jeremy, who was watching her over his shoulder. She did, and saw what looked like a wide, fearsome snake, blue-green in color, coiling through the woods.

"What is it?" she asked in wonder.

"You really don't know? It's the river."

"Oh," said Mrs. Frisby, rather ashamed of her ignorance. She had heard of the river, of course, but had not known that it looked like a snake. She had never been there, since to reach it one had to cross the entire width of the forest. There were advantages to being a bird.

In a minute more they had left the updraft, and Jeremy's wings resumed pumping. They went higher, and Mrs. Frisby closed her eyes again. When she opened them, the garden patch had vanished far behind them, and Jeremy, searching the trees below, began a long, slanting descent. Eventually, as he banked sharply, Mrs. Frisby saw off his wing tip a gray-brown patch among a stand of tall green pines; from so high it looked like a gnarled gray bush, but as they circled lower she could see that it was in fact an enormous tree, leafless, skeletal, and partly dead. One huge branch had recently broken off and fallen, and three pine trunks lay bent double under its weight. It was a gloomy and primeval spot, deeply shadowed in the gray dusk. Jeremy circled over it one more time, looking at a certain mark three-fourths of the way up the towering main trunk. Just below this spot another great branch, itself as big as an ordinary tree, jutted out over the tops of the pines, and on this at last Jeremy fluttered gently to rest. They were some ten feet from the main trunk, and Mrs. Frisby could see, just above the place where the branch joined the tree, a dark round hole as large as a lunch plate.

"We're here," Jeremy said in a low voice. "There's where he lives."

"Should I get down?" Instinctively, Mrs. Frisby spoke in a whisper.

"Yes. We've got to walk closer. But quietly. He doesn't like loud noises."

"It's so high." She still clung to the crow's back.

"But the limb is broad. You'll be safe enough."

And indeed the limb was almost as wide as a sidewalk. Mrs. Frisby gathered her courage, slithered down, and felt the solid wood under her feet; still she could not help thinking about how far it was to the ground below.

"There he is," said Jeremy, staring at the hole. "It's just the right time."

They inched their way along the limb, Mrs. Frisby gripping the rough bark tightly, being careful not to stumble; and as they came closer, she could dimly perceive a shape like a squat vase sitting back in the hollow of the tree. Near the top of the vase, wide apart, two round yellow eyes glowed in the dark.

"He can't see us," Jeremy whispered. "It's still too light."

Perhaps not, but he could hear, for now a deep round voice, a voice like an organ tone, echoed out of the hollow trunk:

"Who is standing outside my house?"

Jeremy answered:

"Sir, I am a crow. My name is Jeremy. And I have brought a friend. I hope we have not disturbed you. My friend needs your advice."

"I see. And can your friend not speak for himself?"

"Sir, my friend is a lady, a lady mouse."

"A mouse?" The sonorous voice sounded unbelieving. "Why should a crow be a friend to a mouse?"

"I was trapped, sir, and she set me free. She saved me from the cat."

"That is possible," said the owl, "though unusual. I have heard of such a thing before. We all help one another against the cat."

"True. And now, sir, my friend herself is in trouble."

"I understand," said the owl, moving closer to the round entrance of his hollow. "Mrs. Mouse, I cannot see you, for the glare of the daylight is too bright. But if you will step inside my house, I will listen to what you have to say."

Mrs. Frisby hesitated. She knew something of the dietary habits of owls, and she did not much like the idea of being trapped in his house. Finally she said timidly:

"Sir, I would not want to intrude. And I can hear you quite well from out here."

"Mrs. Mouse, please understand that I have no

interest at all, as a general rule, in helping mice to solve their problems. If you have indeed saved a bird from the cat, I will spare you a few minutes. But I do not discuss problems with people I cannot see. Either come inside, or tell your friend to take you home again."

Behind her, Mrs. Frisby heard Jeremy whisper, very softly, "It's all right. He wouldn't harm you in his own home."

She whispered back, "I hope not." She walked up the limb to the hollow, climbed over the sill and stepped inside.

Up so close, the owl looked very large. Each of his feathery feet was tipped with five gleaming talons an inch long. His beak was curved and sharp and cruel. He blinked his yellow eyes and said:

"Please step across the room, away from the light."

Mrs. Frisby did as she was told. As she grew accustomed to the dimness, she looked around her. The chamber into which she had stepped was spacious—at that level, almost half of the huge trunk was hollow—and clean, but the floor was extremely rough. It was not really a floor at all, but only the jagged ends of dead wood sticking up from below, like stalagmites in a cave, so that Mrs. Frisby had to climb rather than walk as she crossed the room. In the back the walls narrowed to a corner, and there she saw that the owl had built himself a nest, as big as a water bucket, of twigs and leaves; from the top she could see protruding some wisps of the feathers with which he had lined it.

When she got near this nest, she stopped and faced the owl, who had turned from the light of the doorway and was peering at her with his great yellow eyes. Jeremy was nowhere to be seen. She could only hope he was still waiting on the limb outside.

"Now," said the owl, "you may state your problem."

"Go to the Rats"

Mrs. Frisby began nervously, trying to arrange her thoughts:

"It's about my youngest son, Timothy. He is sick, too sick to leave his bed. And Moving Day is only five days off."

"Wait," said the owl. "Moving from where? Moving to where?"

"From the garden patch, where we're living, to the edge of the pasture by the stream."

"Which garden?" It had not occurred to Mrs. Frisby until now that a bird, flying freely over miles of countryside, would look down on many gardens.

"It belongs to Mr. Fitzgibbon."

"The one with the large stone?"

"Yes. My house is near the stone."

"What makes you so sure Moving Day will come in five days?"

Mrs. Frisby told him about the tractor, and

what Mr. Fitzgibbon had said: five days until plowing. "Of course," she added, "it might turn cold again, and freeze, or even snow . . ."

"No," said the owl, sounding quite sure, "it will not. The wild onions are already up in the pastures." He asked her then what kind of house she had, and exactly where it was in relation to the big stone; apparently he knew the spot well.

But the more she talked to him, the more Mrs. Frisby became convinced that he would produce no solution to her problem. It had been foolish of her to think he could, foolish of her to come at all. Because, she thought, there really *was* no solution. At last she fell silent, and the owl asked no more questions. Finally he said:

"Lying where it does, your house will inevitably be turned up by the plow, and probably broken to bits in the process. There is no feasible way to prevent this. My only advice to you is this: if you stay in the house you will surely be crushed and killed, all of you. Therefore, it is better to take your chances with moving. Wrap your son Timothy up as warmly as you can, help him as much as possible on the journey, and hope for warm weather on Moving Day. That way you are at least sure to save yourself and the other children."

The owl paused, turned away from her and

looked again at the entrance to his hollow; the patch of light it admitted was growing steadily dimmer.

"And now, if you will excuse me — the night is falling, and I have no more time to spare. I regret that I can not give you a more satisfactory solution to your problem. Good evening, Mrs. . . ." he paused. "I don't believe you told me your name."

"Mrs Frisby." The poor mouse spoke with a sob in her throat, for the owl had said exactly what she feared he would say. And she had no real hope for Timothy. The owl had said, in effect: Either Timothy alone must die, or they must all die together. Even if Moving Day should be extraordinarily warm, the nights were sure to be frosty, and that would be the end of him. Still, one must be polite, and she added sadly, "I thank you, sir, for listening to me. . . ."

But at the mention of her name an extraordinary change had come over the owl. He turned back to face her again and stared at her most intently. Indeed, he gave an agitated flutter of his wings and half flew, half hopped closer to her, bending forward until his great sharp beak was only a few inches from her face. Mrs. Frisby shrank back in fear. What had she done wrong?

"Did you say Mrs. Frisby?"

"Yes. You asked my name."

"Related to Jonathan Frisby?"

"Yes. He was my husband. He died last summer. He was Timothy's father. But how did you know about him?"

"That is not important," said the owl, drawing back a little and looking at her in a new way— almost as if with deference. "I will say this: His name was not unknown in these woods. And if you are his widow, that puts matters in a different light."

Something in the way he said this caused Mrs. Frisby's hopes to lift a little.

"What do you mean?" she asked.

"I mean, madame, that there *is* a way that your son's life might just possibly be saved. I did not mention it to you because I saw no way you could conceivably do it, and I did not want to arouse false hope. But if you are Jonathan Frisby's widow—then perhaps it can be done."

"I don't understand at all," said Mrs. Frisby. "What is this thing?"

"It is not a thing that I can do myself. You must go to the rats."

"To the rats? But I don't know any rats. They have nothing to do with me."

"I don't doubt that. They have little to do with anyone except themselves, and will have less as time goes on. Nonetheless, I think they will help you, and if they will, they can."

"But what can they do?"

"They must move your house to a place where it will be safe from the plow."

Now Mrs. Frisby's spirits fell again, and she said, almost bitterly:

"You are joking, sir; you are not serious. No rat could move my house. It is far too heavy, much too big."

"The rats on Mr. Fitzgibbon's farm have — things — ways — you know nothing about. They are not like the rest of us. They are not, I think, even like most other rats. They work at night, in secret. Mrs. Frisby, do you know their main entrance?"

"In the rosebush? Yes."

"Go there. You will find a sentry guarding the door. His name is Justin. Tell him who you are, and that you come at my request. Tell him that you want to see a rat named Nicodemus. I think they will let you in, though they may insist on swearing you to secrecy. If they should ask that, you must of course use your own judgement; but my advice would be to do as they ask."

Mrs. Frisby was close to complete bewilderment.

"Secrecy," she said. "Secrecy about what?"

"That I cannot reveal. I, too, have agreed to it. Also, there is much I do not know, though I have given advice on certain aspects of their—projects."

"Well," said Mrs. Frisby, "I don't understand at all. But if it might save Timothy, I will try to do what you say."

"Tell them," added the owl, "that I suggest moving the house into the lee of the stone. Remember that—the lee of the stone. Also, do not forget the names: Justin and Nicodemus."

"Justin. Nicodemus. The lee of the stone," repeated Mrs. Frisby. "I will remember." She was now so entirely puzzled that she did not think to ask what the phrase meant. Presumably the rats would know.

"And, Mrs. Frisby," said the owl, moving again toward the entrance to the hollow, "please understand: I was an admirer of your late husband, though I never met him in person. I wish you well. I hope your son's life can be saved. You see, I can understand your particular need, for I face a similar problem."

"You?" said Mrs. Frisby. "But you have no Moving Day."

"I have lived in this tree, in this same hollow," the owl said, "for more years then anyone can remember. But now, when the wind blows hard in winter and rocks the forest, I sit here in the dark, and from deep down in the bole, down near the roots, I hear a new sound. It is the sound of strands of wood creaking in the cold and snapping one by one. The limbs are falling; the tree is old, and it is dying. Yet I cannot bring myself, after so many years, to leave, to find a new home and move into it, perhaps to fight for it. I, too, have grown old. One of these days, one of these years, the tree will fall, and when it does, if I am still alive, I will fall with it."

With this sad prediction the owl stepped through his doorway, spread his great wings and was gone, soaring silently downward into the shadowy woods below.

Mrs. Frisby followed him out onto the limb. To her relief, Jeremy was still waiting where she had left him, though not very patiently.

"We must hurry," he said. "It's almost dark.

I'm not supposed to be out so late." Mrs. Frisby, who had the same feeling, climbed on his back, much less afraid now for two reasons: First, she was getting used to air travel; second, since the woods below them were dark, she could no longer see how far away the ground was.

"He talked to you for a long time," said Jeremy as they flew. "Did he tell you anything that will help?"

"I don't know," said Mrs. Frisby. Since the owl had brought up the matter of secrecy, and had, in fact, been secretive himself, she was not sure just how much she should tell Jeremy.

"Why don't you know?"

"I mean, he told me some things, but I don't know whether they'll help or not." She decided to counter with a question of her own. "What does 'in the lee' mean?"

Jeremy, being like all birds knowledgeable about the wind, knew the answer to that. "It means the calm side, the side the wind doesn't blow from. When there's a strong wind, you fly up to the barn from the lee, so you don't get bashed into the wall. My father taught me that."

"I see," said Mrs. Frisby, and she became more puzzled than ever. What had the wind to do with it?

"He told me," she said finally, deciding it

could do no harm, "to go and see the rats."

"The rats?" Jeremy was startled. "But they don't have anything to do with us."

"I know. But he thought they might help."

"What could they do?"

"He thought they might move my whole house. But how they could do it, I can't imagine."

"Oh, I don't doubt that they *could*," said Jeremy. "Everyone knows—at least all the birds know—that the rats can do things. They're up to something; nobody is quite sure what. For one thing, they're building themselves a new house, way back in the woods, over the mountains. They've even made quite a big clearing near it. I'd show you, but it's too dark now.

"They used to carry food, like the rest of us. But now we see them with other things—pieces of metal, and bits of machinery, and things I can't even recognize. They take them into that rosebush, and what happens to them I don't know. But the owl knows more than most. I expect he's had some dealings with them. Just the same, I've never heard of their helping anybody but themselves."

"Neither have I. But I'm going to ask them anyway. There isn't anyone else to ask."

By the time they reached the garden, it had

gone almost completely dark, and Jeremy could not linger.

"Good night, Jeremy," said Mrs. Frisby, feeling almost affectionate toward the crow. "Thank you for taking me, and for waiting to bring me back."

"You're welcome," said Jeremy. "If you need me again, just ask. After all, if it weren't for you, I wouldn't be here to ask." And he flew off into the darkness, the last crow to get home that night.

In the Rosebush

When Mrs. Frisby got home, Teresa, Martin, and Cynthia were eating supper, as she had told them to do if it got dark before she returned. Coming silently down the tunnel, she could hear them talking in the room below, and she paused a moment to eavesdrop on their conversation. Obviously Cynthia had been worrying, and Teresa was reassuring her.

"She couldn't have got back sooner than this, Cynnie. Don't you remember? The crow said it was a mile to the tree. It might even be farther."

"Yes, but crows fly so fast."

"But if he went two miles high"—that was Martin—"it would be three miles altogether."

"Six," said Teresa. "Two up, two down, and one to get there and one to get back."

"That's right. No wonder she isn't back yet."

"But what about the owl? You know how owls are."

"It was still light when they got there. He couldn't see."

"But it's dark now," said Cynthia. "Oh, I *wish* she'd come back. I'm scared."

"Not so loud," Teresa said. "Timothy will hear."

"I'm home," called Mrs. Frisby, hurrying the rest of the way down.

And now it appeared that they had all been worried, for they ran to her, and even Martin, who ordinarily avoided such displays, threw his arms around her.

"Oh, Mother," cried Cynthia, near tears. "I was so worried."

"Poor Cynthia. It's all right."

"How high did you fly?" asked Martin, recovering quickly.

"High enough so the trees looked like little bushes, the garden like a postcard, and the river like a snake."

"Did you see the owl? What did he say?"

"I saw him. Later, I'll tell you about it. First I want to see Timothy. How is he? Why didn't you move his bed out here?"

Teresa said: "I wanted to, but he said he'd rather stay in the bedroom. I think he's feeling worse again."

But when Mrs. Frisby went to see him, she

found him sitting up, and his forehead felt not at all feverish.

"I'm all right," he said. "I stayed in here because I wanted to think about something."

"Think about what?"

"About Moving Day."

"Moving Day! But why? What about it?"

Had he, after all, overheard her talking to the others? Heard about her flight to the owl? But no, he was explaining.

"I haven't been outdoors since I got sick, so I don't know what it's like. I mean the weather. But today, this afternoon, I noticed something."

"What was that?"

"A smell in the air, a warm, wet smell. If you sniff you can still smell it, though it's not so strong now."

Mrs. Frisby had noticed this, of course, both indoors and out.

"It's the smell of the frost melting," Timothy went on. "I remember it from last year. And after that, it wasn't long until we moved. Mother, when are we going to move this year?"

"Oh, not for a long time yet." Mrs. Frisby tried to sound as casual as she could. "It's still much too cold, too early to think about it."

"I have to think about it," said Timothy. He sounded serious, but calm and unworried. "Because if it comes too soon, I don't know if I can go. I tried walking a little bit today, in here, when the others were outside."

"Timothy, you're supposed to stay in bed! You'll make yourself sick again."

"I know, I know. But I had to find out. And I didn't walk much. I couldn't. I only went a few steps, and I got so dizzy I had to lie down again."

"Of course you did. You haven't really recovered yet."

"I guess I haven't. That's why I wanted to think."

"Timothy, you must not worry about it. That will only make you worse."

"I'm not worried at all. I thought I would be, but I'm not—or maybe I think I should be, but I can't. What I really think about is how nice it is there, in the summer beside the brook, and it's true, I want to go. But I'm not scared. I was afraid you might be, or that you might think I was. That's really what I wanted to tell you. I'm just going to wait and see what happens. So you shouldn't worry about it, either."

Mrs. Frisby realized that he had somehow switched their positions. He had seen the danger he was in—guessed, somehow, that Moving Day was near, and that he was very likely to die. And yet here he was—reassuring her. She wanted to tell him about the owl and the rats, tell him that something still might be done. But she decided she had better not; she did not really know if they would help. It would be better to wait until she had seen them.

So instead she said, rather lamely: "Timothy, don't think about it any more. When the time comes, we'll see how you are and then decide what to do."

The next morning at daybreak she went to see the rats. She had never been in the rosebush before, never even really close to it, and now, the nearer she got, the more nervous she became. No one had ever told her—nor, as far as she knew, told any of the other animals—to keep away from it. It was just something one knew. The rats on Mr. Fitzgibbon's farm kept to themselves. One did not prowl in their domain.

She had, before coming out of the garden, looked around carefully to be sure Dragon was nowhere in sight. But even Dragon, though he would chase a rat up to the edge of the bush, would not follow him into it.

The thorns, of course, helped to discourage trespassers. Mrs. Frisby had never realized until that moment, standing next to it, how very big the bush was, how dense, how incredibly thorny. It was bigger than the tractor shed, and its branches were so densely intertwined that as small as she was, Mrs. Frisby could find no easy way to crawl into it, though she walked all the way around it looking. She remembered approximately where she had seen the rats go in, and she studied that part of the bush carefully. How had they done it?

Then she saw that on one branch, close to the ground, the thorns had been scraped off, and about a half-inch of it—just big enough for a handhold—was worn smooth. She put her hand on this and pushed timidly. The branch yielded easily, rather like a swinging door, and behind it she saw a trail, a sort of tunnel through the bush, wide enough so that she could walk into it without touching thorns on either side. When she went forward, she released the branch, and it swung back silently into place behind her. She was inside the bush, and it was dark.

She walked forward, peering into the dimness and following the small trail which wound in a curving course toward the center of the bush, its earthen floor packed firm by the pressure of small feet. Then, straight ahead of her, she saw the entrance.

She had expected—what? A round hole in the dirt, most likely, but certainly nothing like what

she saw. First, a sizeable clearing — about five feet across — had been cut from the center of the bush. Branches overhead had been cleared away, too, not quite to the top of the bush but almost, so that the sunlight filtered through easily, and soft moss grew on the ground. In the middle of this bright green cave rose a small mound, eight inches tall, in the end of which was an arched entrance neatly lined with stone, like a small doorway without any door. Behind the entrance a tunnel, its floor also lined with stones, led backward and downward.

Beside the entranceway, looking at her with dark, unblinking eyes, stood the biggest rat she had ever seen.

Brutus

"Stop where you are," said the rat. "How did you get in here?"

"I walked in," said Mrs. Frisby, keeping her voice calm with an effort. "I found a branch with the thorns smoothed off. I pushed it back, and found . . ."

"I know," said the rat, rather rudely. "And now, walk out again. You aren't allowed in here." He moved a few inches toward her, placing himself between her and the entrance. She noticed how powerful his muscles looked under his glossy coat. He would almost be a match for Dragon — almost, but not quite.

"Go on," he repeated.

"But I have a reason . . ."

"I don't care what you have. Go away. You're small. I wouldn't want to hurt you."

"Are you Justin?" Mrs. Frisby inched back as the rat inched forward.

"I'm Brutus. Justin's not here." That was reasonably obvious, Mrs. Frisby thought. The rat named Brutus added: "You know Justin?"

"No," said Mrs. Frisby. "That is, not exactly."

"If you don't know him, how do you know his name?" Brutus sounded puzzled, and Mrs. Frisby observed that although he was greatly oversized and muscular, and his eyes were bright enough, he looked very young.

"It was told to me by a friend. Can I see him?"

"Justin? No. He's at a meeting. I'm taking his place. They're all at a meeting but me."

Bad luck, thought Mrs. Frisby. He's a substitute. She said:

"Then I'll wait for him."

"No," said Brutus. "You can't stay here. I've got orders. Now go, or I'll have to take you out myself." He moved forward again.

"My name," said the mouse desperately, "is Mrs. Jonathan Frisby. I want to see Nicodemus." It did not work.

"I don't care what your name is, and you can't see Nicodemus, that's sure." Brutus now looked both puzzled and annoyed. "Move on, and be quick."

"All right," said Mrs. Frisby. "You needn't force me. I'll go." She turned slowly and walked back the way she had come. She felt like crying—after coming all this way, after flying to see the owl, to be turned back so abruptly at the end. She thought, as she walked into the darker part of the bush, maybe she could just wait for an hour or so, until the meeting (what kind of a meeting could it be?) was over and then go back, and perhaps the rat named Justin would be at the entrance then. But would Justin pay any more attention to her than Brutus had done? She had a feeling that he would.

But when she stopped she heard footsteps behind her. She looked back and saw that Brutus was following her, so she started again, hurrying to keep out of his sight. After a while she paused again and listened. This time there was no sound. He must have gone back to his post. She sat down on the ground.

Then, ahead of her, in the direction of the place where she had entered the bush, she heard a rustle, a faint scraping noise. It was the branch she had pushed to get in. Someone else was moving it. Someone was coming in, walking along the narrow path toward her. It must be another rat. Suddenly she was terrified. What would he do, meeting her unexpectedly here?

She shrank to one side, as close as she could get to the wall of thorns, hoping that whoever it was might go on past, not seeing her.

Then he came around the curve, and she saw him. It was her old friend, Mr. Ages, the white mouse.

He was moving extremely slowly, and she realized that he was limping badly. One of his legs was injured; it was wrapped up in splints and bandaged.

"Mr. Ages," she called softly, "it's Mrs. Frisby."

"Who?" He peered into the shadow. "I can't see you."

"Mrs. Frisby." She moved into the middle of the path in front of him.

"Why, so it is. Mrs. Frisby. How do you do?" He sounded cordial enough, but he was startled. "I didn't know that you . . . How do you happen to be in here?"

"It's a long story."

"Then tell it to me while I rest. I'm supposed to be at a meeting, but I'm late already, and a few minutes more won't matter. As you can see, I had a bad fall and broke my ankle."

"I'm sorry to hear that. I hope it doesn't hurt."

"It is mending. But I can walk only slowly and need to rest frequently." He sat down with a sigh. "Now tell me what you're doing in the rats' bush."

Mrs. Frisby (who was wondering the same thing about him) told him as briefly as she could about Timothy, Jeremy, the owl, and Brutus. Mr. Ages listened in silence, interrupting only once.

"You went *into* the owl's tree?"

"Yes. But I was afraid."

"I should think so. That took courage."

"I had to do it."

When she had finished her story, Mr. Ages sat quietly for a minute, considering it.

"Poor Timothy," he said at last. "I should have thought of that myself. But, of course, when I gave you the medicine, the weather had not yet turned warm. Then I fell and broke my leg, and I forgot all about it." He stood up.

"I think," he said, "that you should come with me back to the entrance."

"But I can't. Brutus will still be there."

"Mrs. Frisby, having done all that you have

done, you are not going to give up now. I'll talk to Brutus."

"You know him?"

"I have known him since he was born. He's not very old, you know. I think he will do what I ask." From the way he said this, Mrs. Frisby could tell he did not merely think it, he knew it. But how?

"All right," she said doubtfully. "I'll try again. But I don't understand. How do you know Brutus?"

"We had better move along." They started back toward the entrance at Mr. Ages' slow, limping pace. "As to how I know Brutus—that's a much longer story than yours, and I doubt that I'm the one to tell it to you. It is for Nicodemus to say.

"But I will tell you this: if we go in the entrance—as we will, if you are to ask for help— you must promise that you will never tell anyone anything at all about what you see and hear."

"I will promise," said Mrs. Frisby. Again, she thought, she had no choice. "The owl told me that, too."

When they approached the entrance again, Mrs. Frisby saw that Brutus stood at his post as before, but that another rat had joined him. Two of them, she thought. I hope Mr. Ages knows them both. The new rat saw them coming. He looked alert, dark gray in color, and extraordinarily handsome, though not so huge as Brutus.

"Mr. Ages," he said. "How's the leg?"

"Better. But it will be a while before I can run again."

"Justin," said Brutus, staring at Mrs. Frisby. "There she is. That's the one I was telling you about."

"Is she now." Justin looked at her casually. He did not sound particularly alarmed.

"Mrs. Frisby," said Mr. Ages formally, "may I present my friends Justin and Brutus?"

"How do you do?" Brutus sounded doubtful.

"Mrs. Frisby?" said Justin. "Not Mrs. Jonathan Frisby?"

"She is Mrs. Jonathan Frisby," said Mrs. Ages. "A widow, as you know."

"Madame," said Justin, bowing politely, "it is an honor to meet you."

Brutus now looked astonished. "You both know her? Who is she?"

"Brutus," said Mr. Ages gently, "don't you remember Mr. Jonathan?"

Brutus wrinkled his brow. "Mr. Jonathan? You mean the one Dragon . . ."

"Yes," said Justin quickly. "And this is Mrs. Jonathan."

"Oh," said Brutus. Then, to Mrs. Frisby: "Why

didn't you *tell* me. I wouldn't have chased you off."

"Well," said Mrs. Frisby, "I did try. But it doesn't matter."

"No," Mr. Ages added. "Because on the way out she met me coming in. She needs to talk to Nicodemus—and quickly."

Brutus looked doubtful again. "Nicodemus? But can she? I mean, how about the rules? What about the Plan?"

Mr. Ages said: "That has been taken care of. She has promised secrecy, and she is to be trusted completely. That I, myself, guarantee. After all, consider who she is." As an afterthought he added, " . . . and who her children are."

Who am I then? Mrs. Frisby asked herself in wonder. I suppose that, too, will have to come from Nicodemus.

Mr. Ages said to Justin: "What about the meeting? It can't be over already."

"It was temporarily adjourned," said Justin, "to wait for you. In fact, I came to find you."

"Then I suppose we had better go in."

Justin led the way through the arched entrance, with Mrs. Frisby and Mr. Ages following. Brutus remained outside at his post.

In the Library

The tunnel led gently downward, and after the first dozen steps they were in darkness. Mrs. Frisby could see nothing at all. Behind her Mr. Ages limped along; ahead she could hear the scuffle of Justin's footsteps. She followed the sound blindly. Then she heard his voice.

"Just walk straight forward, Mrs. Frisby. There's nothing to trip over, and nothing to bump into. If you get off course, you'll feel the wall." He added: "The dark part doesn't last long."

Now what did he mean by that? She thought it over for a minute or two as she walked and had just decided to ask him, when to her surprise she saw ahead of her a faint glow. A light! But how could there be a light down so far? "There, we're through it," said Justin cheerfully. "I know that blackout bit must be annoying the first time, but it's necessary."

"But aren't we under the ground?"

"Oh yes. About three feet down by now, I'd guess."

"Then how can it be light?"

"I could tell you," Justin said, "but if you'll wait fifteen seconds, you'll see for yourself."

In a few more steps the tunnel—Mrs. Frisby could now discern, dimly, its shape and direction—took a turn to the right, and she did see for herself. She stopped in astonishment.

Ahead of her stretched a long, well-lit hallway. Its ceiling and walls were a smoothly curved arch, its floor hard and flat, with a soft layer of carpet down the middle. The light came from the walls, where every foot or so on both sides a tiny light bulb had been recessed and the hole in which it stood, like a small window, had been covered with a square of colored glass— blue, green or yellow. The effect was that of stained-glass windows in sunlight.

Justin was watching her and smiling. "Do you like it? The carpet and the colored glass we don't really need. Some of the wives did that on their own, just for looks. They cut the glass, believe it or not, from old bottles. The carpet was a piece of trim they found somewhere."

"It's beautiful," Mrs. Frisby said. "But how . . ."

"We've had electricity for four years now."

"Five," said Mr. Ages.

"Five," said Justin agreeably. "The lights" — they were the very small, very bright twinkling kind — "we found on trees. In fact, most of our lights come from trees. Not until after Christmas, of course — about New Year's. The big light bulbs we have trouble handling."

Mrs. Frisby was familiar with electricity (her husband, who knew all kinds of things, had once explained it to her). At night she had seen the lamps shining in Mr. Fitzgibbon's house, and at Christmas time the lights that his sons strung on a pine tree outside.

"You mean you just took them?" she asked.

"We were careful to take only a few from each tree," said Mr. Ages.

"It was like picking fruit," Justin said rather dreamily. "The annual light bulb harvest. We had to go quite far up the road before we had enough. Even so, it took two Christmases."

"Justin," said Mr. Ages, "I think we'd better get on."

They continued along the corridor, which curved always slightly to the right, so Mrs. Frisby could never really tell how long it was, and which soon began to incline more steeply into the ground. Mrs. Frisby noticed that the air, which should have been dank and damp so deep underground, was on the contrary fresh and clean, and she thought she could even detect a very faint breeze blowing past her ears as she moved.

In a few more minutes the hall widened abruptly into a large oval chamber. Here the lights were set in the ceiling; at the far end, Mrs. Frisby could see, the long tunnel continued and looked as if it slanted upward again—perhaps to another entrance, a back door. Was this, then, their destination, the main hall of the rats? But if so, where were all the other rats? The room was entirely empty—not even a stick of furniture.

"A storeroom," said Justin. "Sometimes full. Now empty."

Then she saw that off one side of the chamber there was a stairway leading down, and beside it a small door. Justin led them to the door.

"For freight only," he said with a grin at Mr. Ages. "But considering your limp, I think we can make an exception. The stairs wouldn't be easy."

Mrs. Frisby looked at the stairway. It went down in a spiral and each step was neatly inlaid with a rectangular piece of slate. She could not tell how far down it led, since after the first turn of the spiral she could see no more, but she had a feeling it was a long way down. As Justin said, it would be hard for Mr. Ages.

Justin opened the door. It led into a square room that looked like a closet.

"After you," he said. Mrs. Frisby went in, the others followed, and the door swung shut. On the wall were two knobs. Justin pushed one of them, and Mrs. Frisby, who had never been in an elevator before, gasped and almost fell as she felt the floor suddenly sink beneath her feet. Justin reached out a hand to steady her.

"It's all right," he said. "I should have warned you."

"But we're falling!"

"Not quite. We're going down, but we've got two strong cables and an electric motor holding us."

Still, Mrs. Frisby held her breath during the rest of the descent, until finally the small elevator came to a gentle stop and Justin opened the door. Then she breathed again and looked out.

The room before her was at least three times as big as the one they had just left, and corridors radiated from it in as many directions as petals from a daisy. Directly opposite the elevator an open arch led into what looked like a still larger room — seemingly some kind of an assembly hall, for it had a raised platform at one end.

And now there were rats. Rats by dozens — rats standing and talking in groups of twos and threes and fours, rats walking slowly, rats hurrying, rats carrying papers. As Mrs. Frisby stepped from the elevator, it became obvious that strangers were a rarity down there, for the hubbub of a dozen conversations stopped abruptly, and all heads turned to look at her. They did not look hostile, nor were they alarmed — since her two companions were familiar to them — but merely curious. Then, as quickly as it had died out, the sound of talking began again, as if the rats were too polite to stand and stare. But one of them, a lean rat with a scarred face, left his group and walked toward them.

"Justin. Mr. Ages. And I see we have a guest." He spoke graciously, with an air of quiet dignity, and Mrs. Frisby noticed two more things about him. First, the scar on his face ran across his left eye, and over this eye he wore a black patch, fastened by a cord around his head. Second, he carried a satchel — rather like a handbag — by a strap over his shoulders.

"A guest whose name you will recognize," said Justin. "She is Mrs. Jonathan Frisby. Mrs. Frisby, this is Nicodemus."

"A name I recognize indeed," said the rat called Nicodemus. "Mrs. Frisby — are you perhaps aware of this? — your late husband was one of our greatest friends. You are welcome here."

"Thank you," said Mrs. Frisby, but she was more puzzled than ever. "In fact, I did not know that you knew my husband. But I'm glad to hear it, because I've come to ask your help."

"Mrs. Frisby has a problem," said Mr. Ages, "an urgent one."

"If we can help you, we will," said Nicodemus. He asked Mr. Ages: "Can it wait until after the meeting? An hour? We were just ready to begin again."

Mr. Ages considered. "An hour will make no difference, I think."

Nicodemus said: "Justin, show Mrs. Frisby to the library, where she can be comfortable until the meeting is over."

By this time the last of the other assembled rats had made their way into a large meeting hall, where they sat facing the raised platform. Nicodemus followed them, pulling some papers and a small reading glass from the satchel at his side as he walked to the front of the room.

Justin led Mrs. Frisby in another direction, down a corridor to their left, and again she had the impression of a faint, cool breeze against her face. She realized that the corridor she had walked up above was merely a long entranceway, and that the halls around her were the rats' real living quarters. The one down which Justin led her was lined with doors, one of which he opened.

"In here," he said.

The room they entered was big, square, well lit, and had a faint musty smell. "It's reasonably comfortable, and if you like to read . . ." he gestured at the walls. They were lined with shelves from floor to ceiling, and on the shelves stood — Mrs. Frisby dredged in her memory. "Books," she said. "They're books."

"Yes," said Justin. "Do you read much?"

"Only a little," said Mrs. Frisby. "My husband taught me. And the children . . ." She started to tell him how. Laboriously scratching letters in the earth with a stick — it seemed so long ago. But Justin was leaving.

"Excuse me — I've got to go to the meeting. I hate meetings, but this one's important. We're finishing up the schedule for the Plan." He pronounced it with a capital P.

"The Plan?"

But he was out the door, closing it gently behind him.

Mrs. Frisby looked around her. The room — the library, Nicodemus had called it — had, in addition to its shelves of books, several tables with benches beside them, and on these were stacked more books, some of them open.

Books. Her husband, Jonathan, had told her about them. He had taught her and the children to read (the children had mastered it quickly, but she herself could barely manage the simplest words; she had thought perhaps it was because she was older). He had also told her about electricity. He had known these things — and so, it emerged, did the rats. It had never occurred to her until now to wonder *how* he knew them. He had always known so many things, and she had accepted that as a matter of course. But who had taught him to read? Strangely, it also emerged that he had known the rats. Had they taught him? What had been his connection with them? She remembered his long visits with Mr. Ages. And Mr. Ages knew the rats, too.

She sighed. Perhaps when the meeting was over and she had had a chance to talk to Nicodemus — and had told him about Timothy and Moving Day — perhaps when that was settled, he could explain all this to her.

She noticed at the far end of the room a section of wall where there were no bookshelves. There was, instead, a blackboard, covered with words and numbers written in white chalk. There were pieces of chalk and an eraser in a rack at the bottom of it. The blackboard stood near the end of the longest of the tables. Was the library also used as a classroom? When she looked at the blackboard and, rather laboriously, read what was written on it, she saw that it was not. It was, rather, a conference room.

At the top of the board, in large letters, were printed the words:

THE PLAN OF THE RATS OF NIMH.

Isabella

Mrs. Frisby spelled it out slowly: The Plan of the Rats of Nimh. What, or where, was Nimh? The name had a strange and faraway sound. Had these rats, then, come here from someplace else? Did that explain why they had books and electric lights and wires and an electric motor? Yet they had been here—or at least there had been rats here—for as long as she could remember. Still, that was not so very long.

She wondered what other things they had. Suddenly she had an almost overwhelming desire to look around—to see what was behind the other doors and down the other corridors. She went to the door, opened it, and looked out into the hall. It was entirely deserted and silent, except that when she listened carefully she could hear a faint humming in the distance, as if something were running—another motor?

She started out into the hall, and then changed

her mind. Better not. Nicodemus had been
friendly—they had all been friendly—but ex-
plicit. He had said she was to wait in the library.
And she was not there to pry but to get help. She
went back into the library, closed the door, and
sat on one of the benches. The books on the table
were mostly paperbacks—small enough so that
the rats could handle them easily enough, but
too big for her; so she sat in front of the blackboard and looked at it again.

Beneath the title across the top, in neatly
chalked handwriting, were columns of words
and figures:

Schedule

January:

Group 1 (10):	Oats.	30 loads = 2 bu.
Group 2 (10):	Wheat.	30 loads = 2 bu.
Group 3 (10):	Corn.	20 loads = 1½ bu.
Group 4 (10):	Misc. seeds	Est. 10 loads total

The rest of the blackboard was filled with
more rows of figures, each headed by the name
of a month: February, March, April, May, and so
on through July. At the bottom a separate square
was ruled off:

Plows (Arthur's group) (14)
Plow No. 2. Complete: Jan. 1
Plow No. 3. Complete: Feb. 10
Plow No. 4. Complete: Mar. 20

Mrs. Frisby stared at all this, trying to make head or tail of it, but she could not. It was quite incomprehensible.

She was still puzzling over it when the door opened and a rat came in. It was a girl-rat, small and quite young, judging by her looks. She was carrying a pencil and some papers and looking at the papers as she walked, so that she did not see Mrs. Frisby at first. When she did she gasped and dropped the papers, scattering them on the floor. Her eyes opened wide.

"Who are you?" she asked. "I don't know you. How did you get in?" She backed toward the door.

"It's all right," said Mrs. Frisby. "I'm a friend of Mr. Ages." The rat was very young indeed, only a child.

"But why are you in here? Who let you in?"

"Nicodemus. He told me to wait here."

The girl-rat looked doubtful. "You might be a spy."

"A spy! How could I be? A spy from where?"

"I don't know. From outside. Maybe from Nimh?"

"I don't even know what Nimh is."

"That's what you *say*."

"But I don't. What is it?" asked Mrs. Frisby, feeling slightly annoyed.

"It's a place." The girl-rat, her alarm apparently subsiding, began picking up her scattered papers. "I'm supposed to be practicing my reading."

"What kind of a place?"

"It's where we came from. I don't know too much about it. I've never been there."

"How can you come from there if you've never been there?"

"My father and mother did. I was born afterward. I think it's white. Anyway, I know one thing. We don't want to go back. We don't want to get caught."

So, Mrs. Frisby thought—that sounds as if, whatever Nimh was, the rats had escaped from it to come here. But she realized that she was not likely to get very clear information from such a child. Again, she hoped that Nicodemus would explain it.

"Did Nicodemus come from Nimh, too?"

"Yes."

"And Justin?"

"Yes. You know Justin?"

"Yes."

"I guess you're not a spy," said the girl-rat. She sounded mildly disappointed. Then she added irrelevantly: "Justin's not married." She climbed on one of the benches and opened a book. "He's the best one of all. He's not even afraid of Dragon." She read in the book for perhaps thirty seconds, picked up her pencil, then put it down again. "I'm too young to get married."

"I suppose so," said Mrs. Frisby. "For a while yet. But that won't last long."

"That's what my mother says. But it seems long. And Justin might marry somebody else."

"Maybe not," said Mrs. Frisby, who could see beyond the tip of her nose. "He's pretty young himself yet. What's your name?"

"Isabella."

"It's a pretty name."

"It's all right. Only my brother calls me Izzy. I don't like that."

"I don't wonder. Where's your brother?"

"At the meeting. He's older. All the men are at the meeting. But my mother didn't go. The mothers don't always go. She's in the grain room, packing grain."

"Packing grain?"

"For the Plan. She doesn't like the Plan, though."

The Plan again.

"What is the Plan? Why doesn't she like it?"

"It's just — the Plan. For where we're going to live and all that. She doesn't like it because she says it's too hard — no more electric lights, no more refrigerator, no more running water. But she isn't deserting or anything. Not like Jenner. We didn't like Jenner."

"Who's Jenner?"

"He was in the group, but he quit. Maybe he went back to Nimh. We don't know."

Mrs. Frisby was gradually getting a picture of life in the rat colony — a somewhat confusing one because Isabella was a child, but nonetheless certain things were apparent: They had a grain room (presumably for food storage); the females sometimes went to meetings and sometimes not;

Nicodemus seemed to be the leader; they had a Plan for the future that some rats did not like; and one, named Jenner, had deserted. Or had others gone with him? She was about to ask Isabella when the library door opened and Nicodemus, Justin, and Mr. Ages entered. Another rat came with them, a stranger.

A Powder for Dragon

The strange rat was named Arthur. He was stocky, square and muscular, with bright, hard eyes. He looked efficient.

"You might call him our chief engineer," said Nicodemus to Mrs. Frisby, "as, indeed, you might call Justin the captain of the guard — if we had any such titles, but we don't. Mr. Ages thought Arthur should come along, though he didn't say why. So we still don't know what your problem is."

Isabella was gone. She had dropped her papers on the floor again when the others had entered, and Justin, to her intense confusion and visible delight, had helped her pick them up.

"Hello, Izzy," he had said. "How's the reading coming?"

"It's fine," she said. "I finished the Third Reader last week. Now I'm on the Fourth."

"The Fourth Reader already! You're getting

quite grown up!" At that she had almost dropped the papers a third time and made a dash for the door. It did not matter, Mrs. Frisby noticed, if Justin called her Izzy—just so he called her something.

Nicodemus closed the door behind her, then sat down on one of the benches, facing Mrs. Frisby; the others sat down, too, Mr. Ages stretching his splinted leg in front of him. Nicodemus took the reading glass from his satchel, opened it, and through it gravely examined Mrs. Frisby's face. "You will forgive the glass and the scrutiny," he said. "When I lost my left eye, I also damaged the right one; I can see little close-up without the glass—indeed, not very much even with it." At length he folded the glass and put it on the table.

"Now," he said, "what is it we can do to help you?"

So Mrs. Frisby recounted once more the events that had led to her coming there, and at the end repeated what the owl had advised her to say—"move the house into the lee of the stone."

She added: "I don't understand just what he meant by that. Jeremy—the crow—says it means the side where there's no wind. But what good would that do?"

"I think I know what he meant," said Nicodemus. "In a broad sense, lee means the sheltered side. A bird, flying over Mr. Fitzgibbon's garden, would notice something most of us would miss."

He reached into his satchel and took out a sheet of paper and a pencil; he opened the reading glass again. As he talked, he drew a sketch:

"When a farmer plows a field with a big rock in it, he plows around the rock—close on each side, but leaving a triangle of unplowed land on each end.

"Mrs. Frisby's house is beside the rock, and will get plowed up—and probably crushed, as the owl said. But if we can move it a few feet—so that it lies buried behind the rock—in the lee—

then she and her children can stay in it as long as they need to.

"From the air, the way the owl sees it, the garden would look like this." He inspected the sketch through the reading glass and then placed it on the table.

Mrs. Frisby climbed up on the bench and looked at it. It was a rough map, showing the garden, the big stone near the middle, and the way the furrows made by the plow would curve around it, rather like waves around a boat.

"Show me where your house is buried," said Nicodemus. Mrs. Frisby pointed to the spot on the sketch.

"I know where that cinder block is," said the rat named Arthur. "In fact, I thought about bringing it in, but I decided it was too long a haul. They had it tied on top of the harrow for weight, and it fell off just as they were finishing the garden."

"Can you move it," asked Nicodemus, pointing at the sketch, "to this spot right here, and bury it again?"

"Yes," said Arthur. "That shouldn't be hard."

Mrs. Frisby was delighted; looking at the map, it all became clear, and she could see what a beautifully simple idea it was. When Mr. Fitzgibbon plowed, he would go right past their house; they would not have to move until Timothy was well and until the weather was truly warm. She remembered again what her husband had said—how easy to unlock a door when you have the key. She had found the key. Or rather, the owl had found it.

Nicodemus asked Arthur: "How long will it take?"

"Depends. With a party of ten, a couple of hours. With twenty, maybe an hour."

"We can spare twenty. But it's still too long." He looked worried.

So did Arthur. "Yes," he said. "We'll have to work at night—but even so . . . There's just no cover at all. It's wide open."

"We'll have to take care of Dragon," said Justin.

"Yes," said Mr. Ages, "and with this leg, I can't do it. I'd never make it to the bowl, much less get back again."

Mrs. Frisby, looking at their baffled faces, felt her delight subsiding. Obviously something was wrong.

"I don't understand," she said. "I know about Dragon, of course, but . . ."

"At night," said Justin, "Dragon prowls the farmyard like a tiger. And you don't see him until he's on top of you."

"Then you can't move my house after all."

"Well," Justin said, "ordinarily . . ." He turned to Nicodemus. "Should I explain it to her?"

"Yes," said Nicodemus.

"Ordinarily," said Justin, "when we have a long project to do at night — sometimes even by day — we make sure Dragon won't bother us: We put sleeping powder in his food. Mr. Ages makes it. It doesn't do the cat any harm; but he stays extremely drowsy for the next eight hours or so. We station a sentry to watch him, and we're free to work."

"You did it yesterday!" cried Mrs. Frisby, remembering the figures toiling the wire through the grass, remembering how strangely disinterested Dragon had seemed when he saw her. "I saw the cat sleeping in the yard."

"Yes," said Justin, "but today Mr. Ages has a broken leg."

"Then he can't make the powder?"

"It isn't that," said Mr. Ages. "I've plenty of the powder."

"The trouble is," said Justin, "it's Mr. Ages who puts it in Dragon's dinner bowl, inside the farm kitchen. With his leg broken, he can't move fast enough."

"But why Mr. Ages?" said Mrs. Frisby. "Can't someone else do it?"

"I'd be glad to do it myself," said Justin, "but I'm too big."

"You see," Nicodemus explained, "Mrs. Fitzgibbon feeds the cat in the morning and in the evening, and his bowl is always kept in the same place—next to a cabinet in one corner of the kitchen. There's a very shallow space between the floor and the bottom of the cabinet. A few years ago when we conceived the idea of putting Dragon to sleep, we cut a hole in the floor just behind the cabinet—if we put it anywhere else they'd see it. To reach the bowl, Mr. Ages crawls under the cabinet. When he gets to the edge, he makes a quick dash to the bowl, drops in the powder, and dashes back out of sight. But with a broken leg, he can't dash."

"We might try leaving some bait outside the house," said Justin. "That worked once."

"Once out of a dozen tries," said Nicodemus. "It isn't dependable, and we don't have much time. To be safe, we ought to move that block tonight."

"If we had some catfood . . ." said Justin, thinking aloud. "He might eat that, even on the porch, because he knows it's his. Maybe tonight I could go in through the attic and down to the kitchen . . ."

"No use," said Mr. Ages. "They keep it in a

metal cabinet up on the wall. You couldn't get it without a crew. And that would make too much noise."

"Anyway," said Nicodemus, "it would put off moving the block until tomorrow night."

"Then," Justin said, "I guess what we do is stake out scouts wherever we can, try to keep track of Dragon, and hope for the best. Some nights he doesn't go near the garden at all. We might be lucky."

"Or we might not," said Arthur. "I don't like it. We can't dig that block out without some noise, you know."

Mrs. Frisby interrupted quietly. "There is another way," she said. "If Mr. Ages can get into the kitchen, so can I. If you will give me the powder and show me the way, I will try to put it in Dragon's bowl."

Justin said quickly: "No. It's no job for a lady."

"You forget," Mrs. Frisby said, "I'm Timothy's mother. If you, and Arthur, and others in your group can take risks to save him, surely I can, too. And consider this: I don't want any of you to be hurt—maybe even killed—by Dragon. But even more, I don't want the attempt to fail. Perhaps the worst that will happen to you, with luck, is that you will have to scatter and run, and leave my house unmoved. But then what will happen to us? Timothy, at least, will die. So if there is no one else to put the cat to sleep, I must do it."

Nicodemus considered, and then spoke:

"She's right, of course. If she chooses to take the risk, we can't deny her the right." To Mrs. Frisby he added: "But you should know that the danger is great. It was in the same kitchen, yesterday, running from Dragon's bowl, that Mr. Ages got his leg broken. And it was in doing the same thing, last year, that your husband died."

The Marketplace

Mrs. Frisby's head was buried in her arms. "I never knew," she said. "All I knew was that he didn't come back. But I never knew what happened. I didn't even know he knew you. Why didn't he ever tell me?"

Justin touched her shoulder gently. "It's hard for you to learn it this way, so suddenly," he said. "We thought about telling you when it happened, but we decided we shouldn't. It wouldn't have done any good."

"You ask why Jonathan never told you about us," Nicodemus added. "He had a reason, a good one. Still he worried about it a lot, and he might have told you in the end. But then it was too late."

"What was the reason?" Mrs. Frisby raised her face. There were tears on her cheeks, but she had stopped crying.

"To answer that I would have to tell you quite

a long story—the whole story about us, and Nimh, and Jonathan, and how we came here. He came with us, you see. I don't mind doing that, but I don't know if there is time now."

"I think there is," said Justin, "if Mr. Ages and I go to get the powder while you're telling it."

"With this leg," said Mr. Ages glumly, "that will take long enough to tell it twice."

"I had forgotten," said Justin contritely. "Would it be better if I went alone?"

"No," said Mr. Ages. "There are so many different powders in my storeroom. You wouldn't know which to bring back. I'll go with you. But we'll go slowly."

"And I," said Arthur, "will see about the equipment for tonight. We'll need shovels, crowbars, block and tackle, rollers . . ." He left, still listing tools.

Nicodemus said to Mrs. Frisby, "I think that we, too, should leave the library. There will be others coming in, like Isabella, to practice reading, and some to do research."

"Research?"

"We've got some new books on agriculture—farming, gardening, fertilizing, things like that—and we're studying them. It's part of the Plan."

"I don't know what the Plan is."

"No," agreed Nicodemus, "but when I've told

you our story, you'll understand that, too."

He opened the door and led Mrs. Frisby down the corridor past several more doors, all closed. He stopped before one, which he opened.

"My office," he said. "Please come in."

The room she entered was smaller than the library, but much more comfortably—almost elegantly—furnished. There was a rug on the floor (the same pattern, she noticed, as the carpet in the hallway above), a light recessed in the ceiling and another in the wall next to a table. There were bookshelves; on one shelf an electric clock hummed quietly to itself. A book lay open on the table, with a chair in front of it; against the opposite wall stood a small sofa, neatly upholstered in cloth. But what attracted Mrs. Frisby's attention most was a box in one corner of the room, a box with dials and a small light shining on the front; from this box came the soft sound of music. She listened entranced.

"You like music?" said Nicodemus. "So do I."

"That must be a radio." Again, something vaguely remembered from what Jonathan had once told her. Music. She had heard it only two or three times in her life, when the Fitzgibbons had left a window open and someone was playing inside. And never up close. It was a lovely sound.

"Yes," said Nicodemus. "We didn't get it for music, of course, but to hear the news. Still as long as it's here — why not use it?"

He sat down, and so did Mrs. Frisby.

"Now," he said, "I will tell you about Nimh. You'll be interested, I think, because your husband was part of it. And when I'm finished, I think you will see why he felt he could not tell you himself."

The story begins (Nicodemus continued) not at Nimh, but at a marketplace on the edge of a big city. It was called the Farmers' Market, a great square of a place with a roof over part of it and no walls to speak of. There early every morning the farmers arrived from all over the surrounding countryside, with trucks full of tomatoes, corn, cabbages, potatoes, eggs, chickens, hams, food for the city. One part of it was reserved for the fishermen who brought crabs and oysters and bass and flounders. It was a fine place, noisy and full of smells.

We lived near this market — my father, my mother, my nine sisters and brothers, and I — underground in a big pipe that had once been part of a storm sewer, but was no longer used. There were hundreds of other rats in the neighborhood. It was a rough life, but not so hard as you might think, because of the market.

Every evening at five o'clock the farmers and the fishermen would close up their stalls, pack their trucks, and go home. At night, hours later, the cleanup men would arrive with brooms and hoses. But in between, the market was ours. The food the farmers left behind! Peas and beans that fell from the trucks, tomatoes and squashes, pieces of meat and fish trimmed as waste—they lay on the sidewalks and in the gutters; they filled great cans that were supposed to be covered but seldom were. There was always ten times more than we could eat, and so there was never any need for fighting over it.

Fighting? Quite the contrary, the marketplace was a perfect place for playing, and so we did, the young rats at least, as soon as we had finished eating. There were empty boxes for hide-and-seek, there were walls to climb, tin cans to roll, and pieces of twine to tie and swing on. There was even, in the middle of the square, a fountain to swim in when the weather was hot. Then, at the first clang of the cleanup men in the distance, one of the older rats would sound a warning, and everyone would pick up as much food as he could to carry home. All of us kept a reserve supply, because some days—Sundays and holidays—the market would be closed, and we were never quite sure when this would happen.

When I went to the market, it was usually with two companions, my older brother Gerald and a friend of ours named Jenner. These were my two closest friends; we liked the same games, the same jokes, the same topics of conversation — even the same kinds of food. I particularly admired Jenner, who was extremely quick and intelligent.

One evening in early fall Jenner and I set out for the marketplace. It must have been September, for the leaves were just turning yellow and some children were throwing a football in a vacant lot. Gerald had to stay home that night; he had caught a cold, and since the air was chilly, my mother thought he should not go out. So Jenner and I went without him. I remember we promised to bring him back some of his favorite food, beef liver, if we could find any.

We took our usual route to the market, not along the streets but through the narrow walkways between the buildings, mostly commercial warehouses and garages, that bordered the square. As we walked, we were joined by more rats; at that time of day they converged on the marketplace from all directions. When we reached the square, I noticed there was a white truck of an odd, square shape parked on the street bordering it, perhaps a block away. I say I noticed it — I did not pay any particular attention to it, for trucks were common enough in that part of town; but if I had, I would have noticed that printed on each side of it were four small letters: NIMH. I would not have known what they were, of course, for at that time neither I nor any of the other rats knew how to read.

It was growing dark when we reached the market, but through the dusk we could see that there was an unusually large supply of food — a great mound of it — near the center of the square, away from the roofed-over portion. I suppose that should have served as a warning, but it didn't. I remember Jenner's saying, "They must have had a really busy day," and we ran joyfully toward the pile along with several dozen other rats.

Just as we reached the food it happened. All around us suddenly there was shouting. Bright, blinding search lights flashed on, aimed at us and at the mound of food, so that when we tried to run away from it, we could not see where we were going. Between and behind the lights there were shadows moving swiftly, and as they came toward us I could see that they were men — men in white uniforms carrying nets, round nets with long handles.

"Look out!" cried Jenner. "They're trying to catch us." He darted in one direction, I in another, and I lost sight of him.

We all ran — straight toward the men with the

nets. There was no other way to run; they had us encircled. The nets flailed down, scooped, flailed again. I suppose some rats made it through, slipping between the men and past the lights. I felt a swish—a net just missed me. I turned and ran back toward the mound, thinking I might hide myself in it. But then came another swish, and that time I felt the enveloping fibers fall over me. They entangled my legs, then my neck. I was lifted from the ground along with three other rats, and the net closed around us.

In the Cage

Mrs. Frisby said: "But why did they want to catch you? And how did you ever get away again?"

"At first," said Nicodemus, "I thought it must be because they didn't like our stealing the food. And yet you could hardly even call it stealing — it was waste food, and all they did with it was haul it away to the city incinerator. So what harm if we ate some of it? Of course, there are people who just dislike rats, whether they're doing any harm or not."

"And mice too," said Mrs. Frisby.

"True," said Nicodemus. "Though not so much as rats, I think. Anyway, that wasn't the reason at all; but what the real reason was, I didn't find out for a while. As to getting away — that, too, didn't happen until much later."

No, I was firmly and inextricably caught,

snared in the net and helpless (Nicodemus continued). When the man who held it saw that he had four rats, he pulled a draw string that closed it up. He put the net down and picked up another, an empty one. He moved on into the square, leaving us to lie there. I tried gnawing my way out, but the strands were made of some kind of plastic, as hard as wire.

The noise and movement began to die down eventually; I supposed the rats in the square had all either been caught or had escaped. I heard one man call to another: "I guess that's the lot." Someone else was turning a light this way and that, searching the rest of the market area.

"Not a one to be seen."

"We could hide and wait for another wave."

"There won't be another wave. Not tonight. Probably not for four or five nights."

"Word gets around."

"You mean they communicate?" A third voice.

"You bet they communicate. And the next time they do come, you can be sure they'll case the place carefully. We were lucky. These rats hadn't been bothered for years. They'd grown careless."

"How many did the lab order?" Someone was turning out the lights one at a time.

"Five dozen. How many have we got?"

"About that. Maybe more."

"Let's load the truck."

In a minute or so I felt myself being lifted up; and swinging back and forth in the net, I was carried with my three companions to the white truck I had seen earlier. Its back doors were open, and it was lighted inside. I could see that its whole interior was a large wire cage. Into this our net was thrust; the man then opened the draw string and we were dumped onto the floor, which was covered with sawdust. The other nets were emptied one at a time the same way; and in a few minutes there was a good-sized crowd of us on the floor, all more or less dazed and all (if I was typical) terrified. The cage was locked, the doors clanged shut, and the lights went out. I heard the truck motor start; a second later the floor lurched beneath me. We were moving. Where were they taking us? For what purpose?

Then, in the dark, I heard a voice beside me.

"Nicodemus?" It was Jenner. You can imagine how glad I was to hear him. But I was sorry too.

"Jenner. I thought maybe you got away."

"I was in the last net. I thought I saw you across the floor."

"Where are we going?"

"I don't know."

"What's a lab?"

"A laboratory."

"Yes, but what is it?"

"I don't know. I've just heard the word somewhere."

"Well, I think that's where we're going. Whatever it is."

The truck rumbled along through the dark, over bumpy streets at first, then, at a higher speed, over a smooth highway. There were no windows in the back, so it was impossible to see where we were going—not that I would have known anyway, never before having been more than a half a dozen blocks from home. I think we drove for about two hours, but it might have been less, before the truck slowed, and turned, and finally came to a stop.

The back doors were opened again, and through the wire wall of the cage I saw that we had come to a building, very modern, of white cement and glass. It was square and big, about ten stories tall. Night had fallen, and most of its windows were dark, but the platform to which our truck drove us was lighted, and there were people waiting for us.

A door opened, and three men came out. One of them pushed a cart, a hand truck piled with small wire cages. The man beside him was dressed in a heavy coat, boots, and thick leather gloves. The third man wore heavy horn-rimmed glasses and a white coat. He was obviously the leader.

The men from the truck, the ones who had caught us, now joined the men from the building.

"How many did you get?" asked the man in the white coat.

"Hard to count — they keep moving around. But I make it between sixty and seventy."

"Good. Any trouble?"

"No. It was easy. They acted almost tame."

"I hope not. I've got enough tame ones."

"Oh, they're lively enough. And they look healthy."

"Let's get them out."

The man with the gloves and the boots then donned a wire face-mask as well, and climbed in among us. He opened a small sliding trapdoor at the back of our cage; a man outside held one of the small cages up to the opening, and one at a time we were pushed out into our individual little prisons. A few of the rats snarled and tried to bite; I did not, and neither did Jenner; it was too obviously futile. When it was finished, the man in the white coat said, "Sixty-three — good work." A man from the truck said, "Thanks, Dr.

Schultz." And we were racked on the hand truck and wheeled into the building.

Dr. Schultz. I did not know it then, but I was to be his prisoner (and his pupil) for the next three years.

We spent the rest of that night in a long white room. It was, in fact, a laboratory, with a lot of equipment at one end that I didn't understand at all then—bottles and shiny metal things and black boxes with wires trailing from them. But our end held only rows of cages on shelves, each cage with a tag on it, and each separated from its neighbors by wooden partitions on both sides. Someone came around with a stack of small jars and fastened one to my cage; a little pipe led through the bars like a sipping straw—drinking water. Then the lights were dimmed and we were left alone.

That cage was my home for a long time. It was not uncomfortable; it had a floor of some kind of plastic, medium soft and warm to the touch; with wire walls and ceiling, it was airy enough. Yet just the fact that it was a cage made it horrible. I, who had always run where I wanted, could go three hops forward, three hops back again, and that was all. But worse was the dreadful feeling—I know we all had it—that we were completely at the mercy of someone we knew not at all, for some purpose we could not guess. What were their plans for us?

As it turned out, the uncertainty itself was the worst suffering we had to undergo. We were treated well enough, except for some very small, very quick flashes of pain, which were part of our training. And we were always well fed, though the food, scientifically compiled pellets, was not what you'd call delicious.

But of course we didn't know that when we arrived, and I doubt that any of us got much sleep that first night. I know I didn't. So, in a way, it was relief when early the next morning the lights snapped on and Dr. Schultz entered. There were two other people with him, a young man and a young woman. Like him, they were dressed in white laboratory coats. He was talking to them as they entered the room and walked toward our cages.

" . . . three groups. Twenty for training on injection series A, twenty on series B. That will leave twenty three for the control group. They get no injections at all — except, to keep the test exactly even, we will prick them with a plain needle. Let's call the groups A, B, and C for control; tag them and number them A-1 through A-20, B-1 through B-20, and so on. Number the cages the same way, and keep each rat in the same cage throughout. Diet will be the same for all."

"When do we start the injections?"

"As soon as we're through with the tagging. We'll do that now. George, you number the tags and the cages. Julie, you tie them on. I'll hold."

So the young woman's name was Julie; the young man was George. They all put gloves on, long, tough plastic ones that came to their elbows. One by one we were taken from our cages, held gently but firmly by Dr. Schultz while Julie fastened around each of our necks a narrow ribbon of yellow plastic bearing a number. I learned eventually that mine was number A-10.

They were kind, especially Julie. I remember that when one rat was being tagged, she looked at it and said, "Poor little thing, he's frightened. Look how he's trembling."

"What kind of biologist are you?" said Dr. Schultz. "The 'poor little thing' is a she, not a he."

When my turn came, the door of my cage slid open just enough for Dr. Schultz to put his gloved hand through. I cowered to the back of the cage, which was just what he expected me to do; one hand pressed me flat against the wire wall; then his fingers gripped my shoulders. The other hand held my head just behind the ears,

and I was powerless. I was lifted from the cage and felt the plastic collar clipped around my neck. I was back inside with the door closed in less than a minute. The collar was not tight, but by no amount of tugging, twisting, or shaking was I ever able to get it off.

I watched through the wire front of my cage as the others were caught and tagged. About six cages down from me, on the same shelf, I saw them put a collar on Jenner; but once he was back in his cage, I could see him no longer.

A little later in the morning they came around again, this time pushing a table on wheels. It was loaded with a bottle of some clear liquid, a long rack of sharp needles, and a plunger. Once more I was lifted from the cage. This time George did the holding while Dr. Schultz fastened one of the needles to the plunger. I felt a sharp pain in my hip; then it was over. We all got used to that, for from then on we got injections at least twice a week. What they were injecting and why, I did not know. Yet for twenty of us those injections were to change our whole lives.

The Maze

During the days that followed, our lives fell into a pattern, and the reason for our captivity gradually became clear. Dr. Schultz was a neurologist—that is, an expert on brains, nerves, intelligence, and how people learn things. He hoped, by experimenting on us, to find out whether certain injections could help us to learn more and faster. The two younger people working with him, George and Julie, were graduate students in biology.

"Watch always," he told them, "for signs of improvement, faster learning, quicker reaction in group A as compared to group B, and both as compared to the control group."

My own training began on the day after the first injections. It was George who did it; I suppose Julie and Dr. Schultz were doing the same test on other rats. He took my cage from the shelf and carried it to another room, similar to the first one but with more equipment in it, and no shelves of cages. He placed the cage in a slot against a wall, slid open the end, opened a matching door in the wall — and I was free.

Or so I thought. The small doorway in the wall led into a short corridor, which opened, or seemed to, directly onto a green lawn. I could see it clearly, and behind it some bushes, and behind them a street — all outdoors, and nothing but air between me and them. Furthermore, I could smell the fresh outdoor breeze blowing in. Were they letting me go?

I made a dash toward the open end of the corridor — and then jumped back. I could not go on. About two feet from my cage (still open behind me) there was something dreadfully wrong with the floor. When I touched my feet to it, a terrible, prickling feeling came over my skin, my muscles cramped, my eyes blurred and I got instantly dizzy. I never got used to that feeling — no one ever does — but I did experience it many times, and eventually learned what it was: electric shock. It is not exactly a pain, but it is unbearable.

Yet I was in a frenzy to reach that open lawn, to run for the bushes, to get away from the cage. I tried again — and jumped back again. No use. Then I saw, leading off to the left, another corridor. I had not noticed it at first because I had been looking so eagerly at the open end of the one I was in. The second one seemed to stop about five feet away in a blank wall. Yet there was light there: it must turn a corner. I ran down it, cautiously, not trusting the floor. At the end it turned right—and there was the lawn again, another opening. I got closer that time; then, just as I thought I was going to make it—another shock. I pulled back and saw that there was still another corridor, leading off to the right. Again I ran, again I saw the open escape hole, and again I was stopped by shock. This was repeated over and over; yet each time I seemed to get a little closer to freedom.

But when finally I reached it and the grass was only a step away, a wire wall snapped down in front of me, another behind me; the ceiling opened above me and a gloved hand reached in and picked me up.

A voice said: "Four minutes, thirty-seven seconds."

It was George.

I had, after all my running through the corridors, emerged into a trap only a few feet from where I had started, and through a concealed opening up above, George had been watching everything I did.

I had been in what is called a maze, a device to test intelligence and memory. I was put in it many times again, and so were the others. The second time I got through it a little faster, because I remembered — to some extent — which corridors had electric floors and which did not. The third time I was still faster; and after each trial George (or sometimes Julie, sometimes Dr. Schultz) would write down how long it took. You might ask: Why would I bother to run through it at all, if I knew it was only a trick? The answer is I couldn't help it. When you've lived in a cage, you can't bear not to run, even if what you're running toward is an illusion.

There were more injections, and other kinds of tests, and some of these were more important than the maze, because the maze was designed only to find out how quickly we could learn, while some of the others actually taught us things — or at least led up to actual teaching.

One was what Dr. Schultz called "shape recognition." We would be put into a small room with three doors leading out — one round, one square, and one triangular. These doors were on hinges, with springs that held them shut, but they were easy to push open, and each door led into another room with three more doors like the first one. But the trick was this: If you went through the wrong door, the room you entered had an electric floor, and you got a shock. So you had to learn: In the first room, you used the round door; second room, triangle, and so on.

All of these activities helped to pass the time, and the weeks went by quickly, but they did not lessen our longing to get away. I wished for my old home in the storm sewer; I wished I could see my mother and father, and run with my brother to the marketplace. I know all the others felt the same way; yet it seemed a hopeless thing. Still there was one rat who decided to try it anyway.

He was a young rat, probably the youngest of all that had been caught, and by chance he was in the cage next to mine; I might mention that like Jenner and me, he was in the group Dr. Schultz called A. His name was Justin.

It was late one night that I heard him calling to me, speaking softly, around the wooden partition between our cages. Those partitions generally kept all of us from getting to know each other as well as we might have done, and discouraged us from talking much to one another; it was quite hard to hear around them, and of course you could never see the one you were talking to. I think Dr. Schultz had purposely had them made of some soundproof material. But

131

you could hear, if you and your neighbor got in the corners of these cages nearest each other and spoke out through the wire front.

"Nicodemus?"

"Yes?" I went over to the corner.

"How long have we been here?"

"You mean since the beginning? Since we were caught?"

"Yes."

"I don't know. Several months—I think, but I have no way to keep track."

"I know. I don't either. Do you suppose it's winter outside now?"

"Probably. Or late fall."

"It will be cold."

"But not in here."

"No. But I'm going to try to get out."

"Get out? But how? Your cage is shut."

"Tomorrow we get injections, so they'll open it. When they do, I'm going to run."

"Run where?"

"I don't know. At least I'll get a look around. There might be some way out. What can I lose?"

"You might get hurt."

"I don't think so. Anyway they won't hurt me."

By they he meant Dr. Schultz and the other two. He added confidently:

"All those shots, all the time they've spent— we're too valuable to them now. They'll be careful."

That idea had not occurred to me before, but when I thought about it, I decided he was right. Dr. Schultz, Julie, and George had spent most of their working hours with us for months; they could not afford to let any harm come to us. On the other hand, neither could they afford to allow any of us to escape.

Justin made his attempt the next morning. And it did cause a certain amount of excitement, but not at all what we expected. It was Julie who opened Justin's cage with a hypodermic in her hand. Justin was out with a mighty leap, hit the floor (about four feet down) with a thump, shook himself, and ran, disappearing from my view heading toward the other end of the room.

Julie seemed not at all alarmed. She calmly placed the needle on a shelf, then walked to the door of the laboratory and pushed a button on the wall near it. A red light came on over the door. She picked up a notebook and pencil from a desk near the door and followed Justin out of my sight.

A few minutes later Dr. Schultz and George entered. They opened the door cautiously and closed it behind them. "The outer door is shut, too," said Dr. Schultz. "Where is it?"

"Down here," said Julie, "inspecting the air ducts."

"Really? Which one is it?"

"It's one of the A group, just as you expected. Number nine. I'm keeping notes on it."

Obviously the red light was some kind of a warning signal, both outside the door and in—"laboratory animal at large." And not only had Dr. Schultz known one of us was out, but he had expected it to happen.

" . . . a few days sooner than I thought," he was saying, "but so much the better. Do you realize . . . "

"Look," said Julie. "He's doing the whole baseboard—but he's studying the windows, too. See how he steps back to look up?"

"Of course," said Dr. Schultz. "And at the same time he's watching us, too. Can't you see?"

"He's pretty cool about it." said George.

"Can you imagine one of the lab rats doing that? Or even one of the controls? We've got to try to grasp what we have on our hands. The A group is now three hundred per cent ahead of the control group in learning, and getting smarter all the time. B group is only twenty per cent ahead. It's the new DNA that's doing it. We have a real breakthrough, and since it is DNA, we may very well have a true mutation, a brand new species of rat. But we've got to be careful with it. I think we should go ahead now with the next injection series."

"The steroids?"

(Whatever that meant.)

"Yes. It may slow them up a little—though I doubt it. But even if it does, it will be worth it, because I'm betting it will increase their life span by double at least. Maybe more. Maybe much more."

"Look," said Julie, "A-9 has made a discovery. He's found the mice."

George said: "See how he's studying them."

"Probably," said Dr. Schultz wryly, "he's wondering if they're ready for their steroid injections, too. As a matter of fact, I think the G group is. They're doing almost as well as A group."

"Should I get the net and put him back?" George asked.

"I doubt that you'll need it," Dr. Schultz said, "now that he's learned he can't get out."

But they were underestimating Justin. He had learned no such thing.

A Lesson in Reading

Of course, Justin did not escape that day, nor even that year. When they — Julie — put on a glove and went to pick him up, he submitted meekly enough, and in a short time he was back in his cage.

Yet he had learned some things. He had, as Julie noticed, examined the air ducts — the openings along the wall through which warm air flowed in winter, cool air in summer — and he had studied the windows. Mainly he had learned that he could, occasionally at least, jump from his cage and wander around without incurring any anger or injury. All of this, eventually, was important. For it was Justin, along with Jenner, who finally figured out how to get away. I had a part in it, too. But all that came later.

I won't go into details about the rest of our training except for one part of it that was the most useful of all. But in general, during the months that followed, two things were happening:

First, we were learning more than any rats ever had before, and were becoming more intelligent than any rats had ever been.

The second thing could be considered, from some points of view, even more important—and certainly more astonishing—than the first. Dr. Schultz (you will recall) had said that the new series of injections might increase our life span by double or more. Yet even he was not prepared for what happened. Perhaps it was the odd combination of both types of injections working together—I don't know, and neither did he. But the result was that as far as he could detect, in the A group the aging process seemed to stop almost completely.

For example—during the years we were in the laboratory, most of the rats in the control group grew old and sickly, and finally died; so did those in B group, for though they were getting injections, too, the formula was not the same as ours. But among the twenty of us in A group, no one could see any signs that we were growing older at all. Apparently (though we seldom saw them) the same thing was happening with the G group, the mice who were getting the same injections we were.

Dr. Schultz was greatly excited about this. "The short life span has always been a prime limiting factor in education," he told George and Julie. "If we can double it, and speed up the learning process at the same time, the possibilities are enormous." Double it! Even now, years later, years after the injections were stopped, we seem scarcely any older than we were then.

We could not detect either of these things ourselves. That is, we didn't *feel* any different, and since we had no contact with the other groups, we had no basis for comparison. All we had to go by was what Dr. Schultz said. He and the others were preparing a research paper about us — to be published in some scientific journal — so each morning he dictated the results of the previous day's tests into a tape recorder. We heard all of it, though there was a lot of technical stuff we couldn't understand, especially at first. Until the paper was published (he kept reminding George and Julie of this) the whole experiment was to be kept secret.

The one important phase of training began one day after weeks of really hard work at the "shape recognition" that I mentioned before. But this was different. For the first time they used sounds along with the shapes, and pictures, real pictures we could recognize. For example, one of the first and simplest of these exercises was a picture, a clear photograph, of a rat. I suppose they felt sure we would know what that was. This picture was shown on a screen, with a light behind it. Then, after I had looked at the picture and recognized it, a shape flashed on the screen under it—a sort of half circle and two straight lines, not like anything I had seen before. Then the voice began:

"Are."

"Are."

"Are."

It was Julie's voice, speaking very clearly, but it had a tinny sound—it was a record. After repeating "are" a dozen times or so, that particular shape disappeared and another one came on the screen, still under the picture of the rat. It was a triangle, with legs on it. And Julie's voice began again:

"Aiee."

"Aiee."

"Aiee."

When that shape disappeared a third one came on the screen. This one was a cross. Julie's voice said:

"Tea."

"Tea."

"Tea."

Then all three shapes appeared at once, and the record said:

"Are."

"Aiee."

"Tea."

"Rat."

You will already have recognized what was going on: they were teaching us to read. The symbols under the picture were the letters R-A-T. But the idea did not become clear to me, nor to any of us, for quite a long time. Because, of course, we didn't know what reading *was*.

Oh, we learned to recognize the shapes easily enough, and when I saw the rat picture I knew straight away what symbols would appear beneath it. In the same way, when the picture showed a cat, I knew the same shapes would appear, except the first one would be a half-circle, and Julie's voice would repeat: "See—see—see." I even learned that when the photograph showed not one but several rats, a fourth shape would appear under it—a snaky line—and the sound with that one was "ess—ess—ess." But as to what all this was *for*, none of us had any inkling.

It was Jenner who finally figured it out. By this time we had developed a sort of system of communication, a simple enough thing, just passing spoken messages from one cage to the next, like passing notes in school. Justin, who was still next to me, called to me one day:

"Message for Nicodemus from Jenner. He says important."

"All right," I said, "what's the message?"

"Look at the shapes on the wall next to the door. He says to look carefully."

My cage, like Jenner's and those of the rest of A group, was close enough to the door so I could see what he meant. Near the doorway there was a large, square piece of white cardboard fastened to the wall—a sign. It was covered with an assortment of black markings to which I had never paid any attention (though they had been there ever since we arrived).

Now, for the first time, I looked at them carefully, and I grasped what Jenner had discovered.

The top line of black marks on the wall were instantly familiar: R-A-T-S; as soon as I saw them I thought of the picture that went with them; and as soon as I did that I was, for the first time, reading. Because, of course, that's what reading is: using symbols to suggest a picture or an idea. From that time on it gradually became clear to me what all these lessons were for, and once I understood the idea, I was eager to learn more. I could scarcely wait for the next lesson, and the next. The whole concept of reading was, to me at least, fascinating. I remember how proud I was when, months later, I was able to read and understand that whole sign. I read it hundreds of times, and I'll never forget it:

RATS MAY NOT BE REMOVED FROM THE LABORATORY WITHOUT WRITTEN PER-MISSION. And at the bottom, in smaller letters, the word NIMH.

But then a puzzling thing came up, a thing we're still not sure about even now. Apparently Dr. Schultz, who was running the lessons, did not realize how well they were succeeding. He continued the training, with new words and new pictures every day; but the fact is, once we had grasped the idea and learned the different sounds each letter stood for, we leaped way ahead of him. I remember well, during one of the lessons, looking at a picture of a tree. Under it the letters flashed on: T-R-E-E. But in the photo-graph, though the tree was in the foreground, there was a building in the background, and a sign near it. I scarcely glanced at T-R-E-E, but concentrated instead on reading the sign. It said:

NIMH. PRIVATE PARKING BY PERMIT ONLY. RESERVED FOR DOCTORS AND STAFF. NO VISITOR PARKING. The building behind it, tall and white, looked very much like the building we were in.

I'm sure Dr. Schultz had plans for testing our reading ability. I could even guess, from the words he was teaching us, what the tests were going to be like. For example, he taught us "left," "right," "door," "food," "open," and so on. It was not hard to imagine the test: I would be placed in one chamber, my food in another. There would be two doors, and a sign saying: "For food, open door at right." Or something like that. Then if I—if all of us—moved unerringly toward the proper door, he would know we understood the sign.

As I said, I'm sure he planned to do this, but apparently he did not think we were ready for it yet. I think maybe he was even a little afraid to try it; because if he did it too soon, or if for any other reason it did not work, his experiment would be a failure. He wanted to be sure, and his caution was his undoing.

Justin announced one evening around the partition:

"I'm going to get out of my cage tonight and wander around a bit."

"How can you? It's locked."

"Yes. But did you notice, along the bottom edge there's a printed strip?"

I had not noticed it. I should perhaps explain that when Dr. Schultz and the others opened our cages we could never quite see how they did it;

143

they manipulated something under the plastic floor, something we couldn't see.

"What does it say?"

"I've been trying to read it the last three times they brought me back from training. It's very small print. But I think I've finally made it out. It says: To release door, pull knob forward and slide right."

"Knob?"

"Under the floor, about an inch back, there's a metal thing just in front of the shelf. I think that's the knob, and I think I can reach it through the wire. Anyway, I'm going to try."

"Now?"

"Not until they close up."

"Closing up" was a ritual Dr. Schultz, George, and Julie went through each night. For about an hour they sat at their desks, wrote notes in books, filed papers in cabinets, and finally locked the cabinets. Then they checked all the cages, dimmed the lights, locked the doors and went home, leaving us alone in the still laboratory.

About half an hour after they left that night, Justin said: "I'm going to try now." I heard a scuffling noise, a click and scrape of metal, and in a matter of seconds I saw his door swing open. It was as simple as that—when you could read.

"Wait," I said.

"What's the matter?"

"If you jump down, you won't be able to get back in. Then they'll know."

"I thought of that. I'm not going to jump down. I'm going to climb up the outside of the cage. It's easy. I've climbed up the inside a thousand times. Above these cages there's another shelf, and it's empty. I'm going to walk along there and see what I can see. I think there's a way to climb to the floor and up again."

"Why don't I go with you?" My door would open the same way as his.

"Better not this time, don't you think? If something goes wrong and I can't get back, they'll say: It's just A-9 again. But if two of us are found outside, they'll take it seriously. They might put new locks on the cages."

He was right, and you can see that already we both had the same idea in mind: that this might be the first step toward escape for all of us.

The Air Ducts

And so it was.

By teaching us how to read, they had taught us how to get away.

Justin climbed easily up the open door of his cage and vanished over the top with a flick of his tail. He came back an hour later, greatly excited and full of information. Yet it was typical of Justin that even excited as he was, he stayed calm, he thought clearly. He climbed down the front of my cage rather than his own, and spoke softly; we both assumed that by now the other rats were asleep.

"Nicodemus? Come on out. I'll show you how." He directed me as I reached through the wire bars of the door and felt beneath it. I found the small metal knob, slid it forward and sideward, and felt the door swing loose against my shoulder. I followed him up the side of the cage to the shelf above. There we stopped. It was the first time I had met Justin face to face.

He said: "It's better talking here than around that partition."

"Yes. Did you get down?"

"Yes."

"How did you get back up?"

"At the end of this shelf there's a big cabinet—they keep the mouse cages in it. It has wire mesh doors. You can climb up and down them like a ladder."

"Of course," I said. "I remember now." I had seen that cabinet many times when my cage was carried past it. For some reason—perhaps because they were smaller—the mice were kept in the cages-within-a-cage.

Justin said: "Nicodemus, I think I've found the way to get out."

"You have! How?"

"At each end of the room there's an opening in the baseboard at the bottom of the wall. Air blows in through one of them and out the other. Each one has a metal grid covering it, and on the grid there's a sign that says: Lift to adjust air flow. I lifted one of them; it hangs on hinges, like a trapdoor. Behind it there is a thing like a metal window—when you slide it wide open, more air blows in.

"But the main thing is, it's easily big enough to walk through and get out."

"But what's on the other side? Where does it lead?"

"On the other side there's a duct, a thing like a square metal pipe built right into the wall. I walked along it, not very far, but I can figure out where it must go. There's bound to be a duct like it leading to every room in the building, and they must all branch off one main central pipe—and that one has to lead, somewhere, to the outside. Because that's where our air comes from. That's why they never open the windows. I don't think those windows *can* open."

He was right, of course. The building had central air conditioning; what we had to do was find the main air shaft and explore it. There would have to be an intake at one end and an outlet at the other. But that was easier said than done, and before it was done there were questions to be answered. What about the rest of the rats? There were twenty of us in the laboratory, and we had to let the others know.

So, one by one, we woke them and showed them how to open their cages. It was an odd assembly that gathered that night, under the dimmed lights in the echoing laboratory, on the shelf where Justin and I had talked. We all knew each other in a way, from the passing of messages over the preceding months; yet except for

Jenner and me, none of us had ever really met. We were strangers—though, as you can imagine, it did not take long for us to develop a feeling of comradeship, for we twenty were alone in a strange world. Just how alone and how strange none of us really understood at first; yet in a way we sensed it from the beginning. The group looked to me as leader, probably because it was Justin and I who first set them free, and because Justin was obviously younger than I.

We did not attempt to leave that night, but went together and looked at the metal grid Justin had discovered, and made plans for exploring the air ducts. Jenner was astute at that sort of thing; he could foresee problems.

"With a vent like this leading to every room," he said, "it will be easy to get lost. When we explore, we're going to need some way of finding our way back here."

"Why should we come back?" someone asked.

"Because it may take more than one night to find the way out. If it does, whoever is doing the exploring must be back in his cage by morning. Otherwise Dr. Schultz will find out."

Jenner was right. It took us about a week. What we did, after some more discussion, was to find some equipment: first, a large spool of thread in one of the cabinets where some of us had seen

Julie place it one day. Second, a screwdriver that was kept on a shelf near the electric equipment—because, as Jenner pointed out, there would probably be a screen over the end of the airshaft to keep out debris, and we might have to pry it loose. What we really needed was a light, for the ducts, at night, were completely dark. But there was none to be had, not even a box of matches. The thread and the screwdriver we hid in the duct, a few feet from the entrance. We could only hope they would not be missed, or that if they were, we wouldn't be suspected.

Justin and two others were chosen as the exploration party (one of the others was Arthur, whom you've met). They had a terrible time at first: Here was a maze to end all mazes; and in the dark they quickly lost their sense of direction. Still they kept at it, night after night, exploring the network of shafts that laced like a cubical spiderweb through the walls and ceilings of the building. They would tie the end of their thread to the grid in our laboratory and unroll it from the spool as they went. Time and time again they reached the end of the thread and had to come back.

"It just isn't long enough," Justin would complain. "Every time I come to the end, I think: if I could just go ten feet farther . . . "

And finally, that's what he did. On the seventh night, just as the thread ran out, he and the other two reached a shaft that was wider than any they had found before, and it seemed, as they walked along it, to be slanting gently upward. But the spool was empty.

"You wait here," Justin said to the others. "I'm going just a little way farther. Hang on to the spool, and if I call, call back." (They had tied the end of the thread around the spool so they would not lose it in the dark.)

Justin had a hunch. The air coming through the shaft had a fresher smell where they were, and seemed to be blowing harder than in the other shafts. Up ahead he thought he could hear the whir of a machine running quietly and there was a faint vibration in the metal under his feet. He went on. The shaft turned upward at a sharp angle—and then, straight ahead, he saw it: a patch of lighter-colored darkness than the pitch black around him, and in the middle of it, three stars twinkling. It was the open sky. Across the opening there was, as Jenner had predicted, a coarse screen of heavy wire.

He ran toward it for a few seconds longer, and then stopped. The sound of the machine had grown suddenly louder, changing from a whir to a roar. It had, obviously, shifted speed; an automatic switch somewhere in the building had turned it from low to high, and the air blowing past Justin came on so hard it made him gasp. He braced his feet against the metal and held on. In a minute, as suddenly as it had roared, the machine returned to a whisper. He looked around and realized he was lucky to have stopped; by the dim light from the sky he could see that he had reached a point where perhaps two dozen air shafts came together like branches into the trunk of a tree. If he had gone a few steps farther he would never have been able to distinguish which shaft was his. He turned in his tracks, and in a few minutes he rejoined his friends.

We had a meeting that night, and Justin told all of us what he had found. He had left the thread, anchored by the screwdriver, to guide us out. Some were for leaving immediately, but it was late, and Jenner and I argued against it. We did not know how long it would take us to break through the screen at the end. If it should take more than an hour or two, daylight would be upon us. We would then be unable to risk returning to the laboratory, and would have to spend the day in the shaft — or try to get away by broad daylight. Dr. Schultz might even figure out how we had gone and trap us in the air shaft.

Finally, reluctantly, everyone agreed to spend

one more day in the laboratory and leave early the next night. But it was a hard decision, with freedom so near and everyone thinking as I did: "Suppose . . . " Suppose Dr. Schultz grew suspicious and put locks on our cages? Suppose some-one found our thread and pulled it out? (This was unlikely—the near end, tied to the spool, was six feet up the shaft, well hidden.) Just the same, we were uneasy.

Then, just as we were ending our meeting, a new complication arose. We had been standing in a rough circle on the floor of the laboratory, just outside the two screen doors that enclosed the mice cages. Now, from inside the cabinet, came a voice:

"Nicodemus." It was a clear but plaintive call, the voice of a mouse. We had almost forgotten the mice were there, and I was startled to hear that one of them knew my name. We all grew quiet.

"Who's calling me?" I asked.

"My name is Jonathan," said the voice. "We have been listening to your talk about going out. We would like to go, too, but we cannot open our cages."

As you can imagine, this caused a certain con-sternation, coming at the last minute. None of us knew much about the mice, except what we had heard Dr. Schultz dictate into his tape recorder. From that, we had learned only that they had been getting the same injections we were getting, and that the treatment had worked about as well on them as on us. They were a sort of side experiment, without a control group.

Justin was studying the cabinet.

"Why not?" he said. "If we can get the doors open."

Someone muttered: "They'll slow us down."

"No," said the mouse Jonathan. "We will not. Only open our cages when you go, and we will make our own way. We won't even stay with you, if you prefer."

"How many are you?" I asked.

"Only eight. And the cabinet doors are easy to open. There's just a simple hook, half way up."

But Justin and Arthur had already figured that out. They climbed up the screen, unhooked the hook, and the doors swung open.

"The cages open the same way as yours," said another mouse, "but we can't reach far enough to unlatch them."

"All right," I said. "Tomorrow night, as soon as Dr. Schultz and the others leave, we'll open your cages, and you can follow the thread with us to get out. After that you're on your own."

"Agreed," said Jonathan, "and thank you."

"And now," I said, "we should all get back to the cages. Justin, please hook the doors again."

I had latched myself into my cage and was getting ready for sleep when I heard a scratching noise on the door, and there was Jenner, climbing down from above.

"Nicodemus," he said, "can I come in?"

"Of course. But it's getting on toward morning."

"I won't stay long." He unlatched the door and entered. "There's something we've got to decide."

"I know," I said. "I've been thinking about it, too."

"When we do get out, where are we going to go?"

I could not see Jenner's face in the dark of the cage, but I knew from his voice that he was worrying. I said:

"At first I thought, home, of course. But then, when I began remembering, I realized that won't work. We could find the way, I suppose, now that we can read. But if we did—what then? We wouldn't find anyone we know."

"And yet," Jenner said, "you know that's not the real point."

"No."

"The real point is this: We don't know where

to go because we don't know what we are. Do you want to go back to living in a sewer-pipe? And eating other people's garbage? Because that's what rats do. But the fact is, we aren't rats anymore. We're something Dr. Schultz has made. Something new. Dr. Schultz says our intelligence has increased more than one thousand percent. I suspect he's underestimated; I think we're probably as intelligent as he is—maybe more. We can read, and with a little practice, we'll be able to write, too. I mean to do both. I think we can learn to do anything we want. But where do we do it? Where does a group of civilized rats fit in?"

"I don't know," I said. "We're going to have to find out. It won't be easy. But even so, the first step must be to get out of here. We're lucky to have a chance, but it won't last. We're a jump ahead of Dr. Schultz; if he knew what we know, he wouldn't leave us alone in here another night. And he's sure to find out soon."

"Another thing to worry about," Jenner said. "If we do get away, when he finds we're gone—won't he figure out how we did it? And won't he realize that we must have learned to read?"

"Probably."

"And then what? What will happen when he announces that there's a group of civilized rats roaming loose—rats that can read, and think, and figure things out?"

I said: "Let's wait until we're free before we worry about that."

But Jenner was right. It was a thing to worry about, and maybe it still is.

The next day was terrible. I kept expecting to hear Dr. Schultz say: "Who took my screw-driver?" And then to hear Julie add: "My thread is missing, too." That could have happened and set them to thinking—but it didn't, and that night, an hour after Julie, George, and Dr. Schultz left the laboratory, we were out of our cages and gathered, the whole group of us, before the mouse cabinet. Justin opened its doors, un-latched their cages, and the mice came out. They looked very small and frightened, but one strode bravely forward.

"You are Nicodemus?" he said to me. "I'm Jonathan. Thank you for taking us out with you."

"We're not out yet," I said, "but you're wel-come."

We had no time for chatting. The light coming in the windows was turning gray; in less than an hour it would be dark, and we would need light to figure out how to open the screen at the end of the shaft.

We went to the opening in the baseboard.

"Justin," I said, "take the lead. Roll up the thread as you go. I'll bring up in the rear. No noise. There's sure to be somebody awake somewhere in the building. We don't want them to hear us." I did not want to leave the thread where it might be found: the more I thought about it, the more I felt sure Dr. Schultz would try to track us down, for quite a few reasons.

Justin lifted the grid, pushed open the sliding panel, and one by one we went through. As I watched the others go ahead of me, I noticed for the first time that one of the mice was white. Then I went in myself, closing the grid behind me and pushing the panel half shut again, its normal position.

With Justin leading the way, we moved through the dark passage quickly and easily. In only fifteen or twenty minutes we had reached the end of the thread; then, as Justin had told us it would, the shaft widened; we could hear the whir of the machine ahead, and almost immediately we saw a square of gray daylight. We had reached the end of the shaft, and there a terrible thing happened.

Justin—you will recall—had told us that the machine, the pump that pulled air through the shaft, had switched from low speed to high when he had first explored through there. So we were forewarned. The trouble was, the fore-warning was no use at all, not so far as the mice were concerned.

We were approaching the lighted square of the opening when the roar began. The blast of air came like a sudden whistling gale; it took my breath and flattened my ears against my head, and I closed my eyes instinctively. I was still in the rear, and when I opened my eyes again I saw one of the mice sliding past me, clawing uselessly with his small nails at the smooth metal beneath him. Another followed him, and still another, as one by one they were blown backward into the dark maze of tunnels we had just left. I braced myself in the corner of the shaft and grabbed at one as he slid by. It was the white mouse. I caught him by one leg, pulled him around behind me and held on. Another blew face-on into the rat ahead of me and stopped there—it was Jonathan, who had been near the lead. But the rest were lost, six in all. They were simply too light; they blew away like dead leaves, and we never saw them again.

In another minute the roar stopped, the rush of air slowed from a gale to a breeze, and we were able to go forward again.

I said to the white mouse: "You'd better hold on to me. That might happen again."

He looked at me in dismay. "But what about the others? Six are lost! I've got to go back and look for them."

Jonathan quickly joined him: "I'll go with you."

"No," I said. "That would be useless and foolish. You have no idea which shaft they were blown into, nor even if they all went the same way. And if you should find them — how would you find your way out again? And suppose the wind comes again? Then there would be eight lost instead of six."

The wind did come again, half a dozen times more, while we worked with the screwdriver to pry open the screen. Each time we had to stop work and hang on. The two mice clung to the screen itself; some of us braced ourselves behind them, in case they should slip. And Justin, taking the thread with him as a guideline, went back to search for the other six. He explored shaft after shaft to the end of the spool, calling softly as he went—but it was futile. To this day we don't know what became of those six mice. They may have found their way out eventually, or they may have died in there. We left an opening in the screen for them, just in case.

The screen. It was heavy wire, with holes about the size of an acorn, and it was set in a steel frame. We pried and hammered at it with the screwdriver, but we could not move it. It was fastened on the outside—we couldn't see how. Finally the white mouse had an idea.

"Push the screwdriver through the wire near the bottom," he said, "and pry up," We did, and the wire bent a fraction of an inch. We did it again, prying down, then left, then right. The hole in the wire grew slowly bigger, until the white mouse said: "I think that's enough." He climbed to the small opening and by squirming and twisting, he got through. Jonathan followed him; they both fell out of sight, but in a minute Jonathan's head came back in view on the outside.

"It's a sliding bolt," he said. "We're working on it." Inside we could hear the faint rasping as the two mice tugged on the bolt handle, working it back. Then the crack at the base of the screen widened; we pushed it open, and we were standing on the roof of Nimh, free.

The Boniface Estate

Mrs. Frisby said: "Jonathan and Mr. Ages got the screen open."

"Yes," Nicodemus said, "and without them I doubt that we could have done it. The steel frame was strong, the bolt was secure, and the wire so stiff we could not have bent it enough for one of us to go through. So we were glad they were with us and asked them if they would, after all, like to stay with us. Since there were only two of them, they said they would, for the time being at least."

And now began a journey that was to last, with some interruptions, for almost two years. Parts of it were pleasant (it was a joyful feeling, at first, just to be free again and to get those laboratory collars off), and parts of it were terrible. I have made notes about all of it, and if the time ever comes when rats publish books of their own, I intend to write a book about it. It would be a long book, full of trouble and danger, too much to tell now. It was in one of the dangerous times that I lost my eye and got the scar you see on my face.

But we did have some happy times, and some pieces of great good luck, two in particular, that help to explain how we got here and what our plans are now.

It was early summer when we got out. We had known that beforehand—we could tell by the lateness of the light through the windows, though it was dark when we finally stood on the roof. We had no trouble getting down the side of the building, however. There were downspouts in the corners with plenty of toeholds (we dropped the screwdriver and the spool of thread into one of these); a little lower there was ivy; we were all good climbers, and there was moonlight to see by. In less than fifteen minutes we were on the ground. Staying in the darkest shadows, under the bushes when we could, we sped away from Nimh, not knowing or caring at first what direction we were going. Nobody saw us.

During the next few weeks we lived as we could. We had, in a way, to learn all over again how to get along, for although the world outside the laboratory was the same, we ourselves were different. We were, a couple of times, reduced to eating from dumps and garbage cans. But knowing how to read, we quickly learned to recognize signs on buildings: Groceries, Supermarket, Meats & Vegetables, for instance, let us know that there was food inside for the taking. And once inside a supermarket at night (they always leave a few lights on) we could even read the signs on the wall directing us to Section 8 for Dairy Products (cheese), Section 3 for Baked Goods, and so on. In the country there were barns and silos stocked with grain and corn, and chicken houses full of eggs.

Occasionally we came upon other rats, and a few times we talked with them, but not for long. Because after just a few words they would begin to look at us strangely, and edge away. Somehow they could tell that we were different. I think we even looked different; either the diet or the injections at Nimh had made us bigger and stronger than other rats, and all the strange rats we saw looked, to us, surprisingly weak and puny. So we were set apart from even our own kind.

It was while we were in the country that we had our first important stroke of luck. We had just about decided, after nearly four months of freedom and constant roving, to find a place to

164

settle down—if not permanently, at least for the winter. We thought that it should be in the country, but not too far from a town, so that we would have access to grocery stores as well as barns and gardens.

(It was about this time, too, that I began to wonder, and worry somewhat, about the fact that whatever we ate, whatever we needed, must always be stolen. Rats had always lived that way. And yet—why? I talked to some of the others about this. It was the beginning of a discontent and an idea that kept growing although slowly.)

The season was autumn. We were walking one evening down a winding country road. We never walked really on the road, but along the edge, so that we could vanish into the bushes or a ditch if anyone came along. You can imagine that twenty rats and two mice traveling in procession would cause some comment, and we did not want that.

As we walked, we reached a very high fence of wrought iron, the kind that looks like a row of black iron spears fastened together, with pointed tops—an expensive fence, surrounding a large estate with a big, expensive-looking house in the middle, and well kept grounds and gardens. We walked along past this fence until we reached a gate.

"There's nobody living in there," said Justin.

"How do you know?"

"The gate's padlocked. And look. Dead weeds standing outside of it, not even bent. Nobody's driven in here for a while."

The house had a quiet, deserted look. There was a mail box in front, hanging open, empty.

"I wonder if we could get in," Jenner said.

"Why should we?"

"It's a big place. It would have a big pantry, big cupboard, big freezer. If it's as empty as it looks . . ."

We turned into the grounds, moving cautiously, and from beneath some bushes we watched the windows. As dusk fell, lights came on in several of them, both upstairs and down.

Jenner said: "That's supposed to make us think there's someone there."

"Yes," said Justin, "but there isn't. I could see one of the lamps when it came on. There was nobody near it. And they all came on at the same time."

"Automatic switches. To keep burglars away."

"Well, they're not keeping me away," said Justin. He ran to the house, climbed to one of the windowsills, and looked in. He tried another. Then he came back. "Nobody," he said.

So we went in. We found a small window in the back with a cracked pane, knocked out one corner of the glass, and climbed through. At first, we planned just to look for food. We found it, too, enough to last us for a year or more. As Jenner had predicted, there was a big freezer, well stocked—bread, meat, vegetables, everything—and a whole room full of shelves covered with canned food. The cans baffled us at first, as they had in the grocery stores. We could read what was in them, but we couldn't get it out. Then Arthur found a machine on the kitchen counter. He read the instructions on the side of it: Slide can under cutter and press switch. We tried it. The can turned slowly around in the machine, and when we pulled it out, the top had been cut free. I'll always remember what was in that first can— clam chowder, delicious.

After we had eaten, we wandered around the house. It was a rich man's mansion, with beautiful furniture and fine rugs and carpeting on the floor. There was a crystal chandelier in the dining room, and a big stone fireplace in the living room.

But the greatest treasure of all, for us, was in the study. This was a large rectangular room, with walnut paneling, a walnut desk, leather chairs, and walls lined to the ceiling with books. Thousands of books, about every subject you could think of. There were shelves of paperbacks; there were encyclopedias, histories, novels, philosophies, and textbooks of physics, chemistry, electrical engineering, and others, more than I can name. Luckily, there was even one of those small ladders-on-wheels they use in some libraries to get to the top shelves.

Well, we fell on those books with even more appetite than on the food, and in the end, we moved into the house and stayed all winter. We could do that, it turned out, without much fear of discovery. We learned that from some newspaper cuttings I found on the desk in the study: They were about a wedding, and most of them showed pictures of a newly married couple leaving a house to begin their honeymoon. The groom was a Mr. Gordon Boniface—"heir to the Gould-Stetson fortune"—and the house they were leaving was the house we were in. According to the clippings, they were going on a trip all the way around the world. They were coming back to the Boniface Estate in May. Until then, it was our estate.

Oh, there was a caretaker-gardener who came three times a week, and once in a while he would check the house in a cursory sort of way. That is, he would unlock the front door, glance around to see that everything looked all right, and then lock it and leave. But he didn't live there; he lived in a small house down the road. And we were expecting him when he came; we had figured out, from the way the place was kept up, the lawns mowed, leaves raked, gardens weeded and watered, that there had to be somebody working on it. So we posted a watch, saw him coming, and kept watching him all the time he was there. And we made sure, when he looked in the house, that everything *did* look all right.

This involved a certain amount of work. We had to haul all our empty tin cans and other trash at night out into a hidden place in the woods quite far from the house. We cleaned up after ourselves carefully; we learned to use the water taps and the dusting cloths we found in the kitchen closet. If the caretaker had looked more closely, in fact, he would have seen that the kitchen counters were somewhat shinier than they should have been in an empty house. But he didn't. He never even noticed the small corner of glass missing from the back window.

And all winter, far into the night, we read books and we practiced writing.

The Main Hall

There came a knock on Nicodemus's office door; it opened, and Justin and Mr. Ages entered.

"Back so soon?" said Nicodemus.

"Soon?" said Justin. "It's past noon. It's lunchtime."

"Past noon!" Mrs. Frisby stood up, remembering her children waiting at home. Down in the rats' home, in the artificial light, it was hard to tell the passage of time, and she had been so engrossed in Nicodemus's story that she had not glanced at the clock.

Justin was wearing a satchel like Nicodemus's, and from it he took a small paper package. "Here's Dragon's medicine," he said, putting it on the table. He asked Mrs. Frisby: "Did he tell you about the Toy Tinker?"

Nicodemus said: "No. I was just coming to that."

"But I can't stay to hear it now," said Mrs. Frisby. "My children will be waiting for their lunch."

A plan was worked out. Mrs. Frisby would go home to take care of her children. Nicodemus, Justin, Arthur, and the other rats involved would work out the details of moving her house, which would be done that night at about eleven o'clock—"after the Fitzgibbons are asleep and we're sure Dragon is, too," said Nicodemus. Mrs. Frisby would return in mid-afternoon to the rosebush.

Mr. Ages said: "And I'm going to lie down. After making that trip with this cast, I'm tired."

"You can have your choice of rooms," said Nicodemus. "Now that Jenner and his friends are gone, we have seven empty."

"Thank you," said Mr. Ages. "Mrs. Frisby, when you return I will tell you as well as I can exactly how to put the powder in Dragon's food."

As she hurried home, Mrs. Frisby considered just how much she should tell her children about all that had happened—and all that was going to happen. She decided at that stage, at least, she would not tell them about their father's connection with the rats. Also that she would not say she had volunteered to put the sleeping powder into Dragon's bowl. That would worry them; she could tell them, perhaps, when it was safely done—when, among other things, there would be no chance for Martin to volunteer in her place.

She would tell them simply that as the owl had suggested, she had gone to the rats and asked for help. She had found them friendly and intelligent, and a group of them was coming that night to move the house to a place where it would be safe from the plow. That would be enough. She could tell them the whole story later—when she knew it all herself.

But it was not enough. The children were skeptical at first, then intensely curious, especially Timothy (who was looking stronger and feeling more energetic, but still staying in bed, primarily because Teresa and Martin had made him).

"But why should the rats do that?" said Timothy. "We don't know them at all. Nobody does. They keep to themselves."

"Maybe it's because the owl sent me," said Mrs. Frisby, searching for an answer that would satisfy him. "They seem to be impressed by the owl."

"For that matter," said Timothy, "I don't even see why the owl wanted to help. He's no friend of ours, either."

"Maybe they thought someday we could do them a favor in return."

"Oh, Mother!" said Cynthia. "How could *we* ever do *them* a favor?"

"You forget. I did do Jeremy a favor. That's what started the whole thing."

"That, and my getting sick," said Timothy. "I wish I could get up. I'm tired of bed."

"Not yet," said Mrs. Frisby, glad to change the subject. "You must save your strength, because tonight you will have to get up for a little while, when they move the house. We must be sure you're well wrapped up and hope that the night is warm."

"It will be," said Martin. "It's turned quite hot outside."

They ate lunch.

That afternoon Mrs. Frisby told the children that she must leave them to confer again with the rats about moving the house. When she thought of the danger she would face in just a few more hours, she wanted to kiss them all goodbye. But knowing that Timothy, at least, was already suspicious, she did not dare; but told them only that they should not worry if she was a little late getting home for supper.

On her way back to the rosebush she felt quite relieved, almost cheerful. Her problem was nearly solved, and the final solution was in sight. If all went well, Timothy would be saved.

If all went well. Then the thought of what she had to do came back to her like the clanging of an alarm bell. What worried her most was not so much putting the powder into Dragon's bowl, but the fear that at the last minute she might lose her nerve and bungle it somehow. That could wreck the plan.

She looked toward the Fitzgibbons' farmhouse, and there, on the back porch, lying in the sun, was Dragon. He was watching a pair of sparrows playing in the grass halfway to the chicken yard; the tip of his tail barely twitched as he debated whether or not they were near enough to spring for. He looked very big and very dangerous.

At least he was not looking in her direction, and Mrs. Frisby hurried on to the bush, directly to the hidden entrance, and slipped inside. When she reached the arched portal, Brutus was standing guard as before, but this time he greeted her politely.

"I've been expecting you," he said.

"May I go in?"

"If you'll wait just a minute, I'll get Justin." He went inside the arch and pressed a small button on the wall. Mrs. Frisby had not noticed it before.

"A doorbell," she said.

"It rings a buzzer down below. If I pushed it three times, you'd see some action."

"Action?"

"That's the alarm signal. A dozen rats would come out this door, ready to fight. All the rest, with the women and children, would be hurrying out the back door."

"I didn't know there was a back door."

"It comes out in the woods, in a blackberry bramble. It's got a longer tunnel than this one."

When Justin appeared, they went down the same hallway as before, but this time, when they reached the chamber where the elevator and the stairway led down, Justin paused.

"Nicodemus thought you might like to see our main hall—just a quick look. He said you asked about the Plan."

"I did," said Mrs. Frisby, "but he didn't tell me about it."

"It's more than just a plan now, but we're used to calling it that. If you see the main hall, you'll get an idea of what we're doing."

So instead of going down as they had before, Justin led the way across the chamber, where, as Mrs. Frisby had noticed, the tunnel continued. They walked along for what seemed like several more minutes.

"Somewhere right along here," Justin remarked, "we're entering the woods. You'll notice the tunnel runs a bit crooked. We had to bend it to go around tap roots — some as thick as fence posts."

They went on until they came to a fork in the tunnel. "Right fork leads out to the blackberry bramble," said Justin. "Left fork leads to the main hall." They took the left fork.

"Now brace yourself for a surprise."

From ahead came noises: the sound of many rats talking, a sound of hurrying and thumping and of machinery running. They stepped into a room as full of activity as a factory.

It was the biggest room Mrs. Frisby had ever seen, half the size of a house, with a ceiling and floor of hard gray rock. It was brightly lit with electric bulbs — here the large sized ones, strung unshaded — and beneath them were rats at work everywhere. Rats running electric motors that ran belts that ran small circular saws, lathes, drills, grindstones, and other tools Mrs. Frisby could not name; rats hammering, welding, cutting. But most of all, rats hauling.

There was a steady procession to and from the far end of the chamber, and each of these rats wore a harness to which was fastened a pair of large, sturdy sacks, one on each side, like a miniature pack horse. As the rats trooped in, their sacks were empty. They disappeared into a part of the room that was hidden by a high wall of wood. When they came out, the sacks were full and heavy.

As she watched, a troop of ten, their sacks bulging, went past her out the tunnel; they greeted Justin and nodded at her, but they did not pause. She noticed that just inside the entrance an electric fan whirred quietly, aiming inward, pulling fresh air into the room from somewhere out in the woods.

Mrs. Frisby stood beside Justin and gaped. She felt dizzy at the sight, the motion, the noise, and the size of the room, which must have measured twenty feet long and almost as wide.

"How could you ever dig out such a big room?" she asked.

"We didn't," said Justin. "We found it. It's a natural cave. You can see that the ceiling and floor are solid rock. That's the reason, or the main one, we chose this spot to live. Others had lived here before us. Probably, for centuries before there was a farmhouse, bears. Then wolves, then foxes, then ground hogs. We had quite a cleaning job to do, I can tell you.

"When we found it, there was a large hole, only a few feet long, leading straight in, but it was so full of sticks and leaves you could hardly see it. We closed that entrance entirely and dug another, longer and narrower—our back door. Then we dug our living quarters under the rose-bush, and the entrance you came in. But the cave is still our chief workshop. Let's go in."

As they entered some of the rats looked up, some waved and smiled, but all quickly turned back to the work they were doing, as if they were in a hurry.

"They're all on a schedule," Justin explained, talking close to Mrs. Frisby's ear to be heard above the noise, "so they can't stop working."

One group, especially busy, was gathered around an odd-shaped object of wood and metal about a foot long. It was curved and had a point at one end; it looked, Mrs. Frisby thought, rather like the side of a small boat. Could the rats be making a boat? Then she saw that they were fastening a strong metal ring to the top of it.

Justin led her to it.

"That," he said, "is our most important invention, the key to the whole Plan. We made a pilot model last fall. We tried it out, and it worked. So now we're making three more."

"But what is it?"

"It's a plow. Nicodemus designed it himself, after reading every book he could find about farm tools. It's light and sharp, especially made to be pulled by rats. It takes eight of us to pull it—more if the turf is tough. But with it we can turn over, in a day of hard work, a patch of earth about ten by fifteen feet."

"But why? What do you need it for?"

"Come over here, and I'll show you."

He led the way to the back of the cave where the high walls stood. He opened a door and beckoned her through. She stood in a large wooden bin; starting at her feet and rising in a slope to the wall of the cave was a small mountain of grain.

"Oats," said Justin.

He led her on, opened another door on another mountain. "Wheat," he said.

And others:

"Barley."

"Corn."

"Soy beans."

"We've been building these stockpiles for a long time," he said. "All from Mr. Fitzgibbon's barn. We now have a two-year supply for one hundred and eight rats, plus enough to plant for two crops, in case the first one fails. In there"— he gestured toward the last bin in the row—"we have boxes full of seeds. Seeds for tomatoes, beets, carrots, melons and a lot more."

All the time they stood there, the steady procession of rats continued. They entered the bins, took off their harness-sacks, filled the sacks with grain, put them on again, and left through the tunnel, out the back door. They looked, Mrs. Frisby thought, like very large ants endlessly toiling on an anthill.

Justin must have got the same impression, for he said:

"If the ants can do it, Nicodemus says, if the bees can do it, so can we."

"Do what?"

"Why, live without stealing, of course. That's the whole idea. That's the Plan."

The Toy Tinker

We left the Boniface Estate on the first of May," said Nicodemus. "We knew a lot more than when we went in. We had been there eight months."

"Then," said Justin, "we found the Toy Tinker."

They were back in Nicodemus's office; Mr. Ages, having rested, sat with them.

"Not quite yet," said Mr. Ages.

"No," said Nicodemus. "That was in late summer. When we first got out, we began searching for a place to live permanently, or at least a place where we could stay as long as we wanted. We had a pretty clear idea of what we were looking for. We had had plenty of time to talk about it, on the long winter evenings in the library between reading books."

The reading we did! We knew very little about the world, you see, and we were curious. We learned about astronomy, about electricity, biology and mathematics, about music and art. I even read quite a few books of poetry and got to like it pretty well.

But what I liked best was history. I read about the ancient Egyptians, the Greeks and Romans, and the Dark Ages, when the old civilizations fell apart and the only people who could read and write were the monks. They lived apart in monasteries. They led the simplest kind of lives, and studied and wrote; they grew their own food, built their own houses and furniture. They even made their own tools and their own paper. Reading about that, I began getting some ideas of how we might live.

Most of the books were about people; we tried to find some about rats, but there wasn't much.

We did find a few things. There were two sets of encyclopedias that had sections on rats. From them we learned that we were about the most hated animals on earth, except maybe snakes and germs.

That seemed strange to us, and unjust. Especially when we learned that some of our close cousins — squirrels, for instance, and rabbits — were well liked. But people think we spread diseases, and I suppose possibly we do, though never intentionally, and surely we never spread as many diseases as people themselves do.

Still, it seemed to us that the main reason we were hated must be that we always lived by stealing. From the earliest times, rats lived around the edges of human cities and farms, stowed away on men's ships, gnawed holes in their floors and stole their food. Sometimes we were accused of biting human children; I didn't believe that, nor did any of us—unless it was some kind of a subnormal rat, bred in the worst of city slums. And that, of course, can happen to people, too.

Had we, then, no use at all in the world? One encyclopedia had a sentence of praise for us: "The common rat is highly valued as an experimental animal in medical research due to his toughness, intelligence, versatility, and biological similarity to man." We knew quite a bit about *that* already.

But there was one book, written by a famous scientist, that had a chapter about rats. Millions of years ago, he said, rats seemed to be ahead of all the other animals, seemed to be making a civilization of their own. They were well organized and built quite complicated villages in the fields. Their descendants today are the rats known as prairie dogs.

But somehow it didn't work out. The scientist thought maybe it was because the rats' lives were too easy; while the other animals (especially the monkeys) were living in the woods and getting tougher and smarter, the prairie dogs grew soft and lazy and made no more progress. Eventually the monkeys came out of the woods, walking on their hind legs, and took over the prairies and almost everything else. It was then that the rats were driven to become scavengers and thieves, living on the fringes of a world run by men.

Still it was interesting to us that for a while, at least, the rats had been ahead. We wondered. If they had stayed ahead, if they had gone on and developed a real civilization—what would it have been like? Would rats, too, have shed their tails and learned to walk erect? Would they have made tools? Probably, though we thought not so soon and not so many; a rat has a natural set of tools that monkeys lack: sharp, pointed teeth that never stop growing. Consider what the beavers can build with no tools but their rodent teeth.

Surely rats would have developed reading and writing, judging by the way we took to it. But what about machines? What about cars and airplanes? Maybe not airplanes. After all, monkeys, living in trees, must have felt a need to fly, must have envied the birds around them. Rats may not have that instinct.

In the same way, a rat civilization would probably never have built skyscrapers, since rats prefer to live underground. But think of the endless subways-below-subways-below-subways they would have had.

We thought and talked quite a bit about all this, and we realized that a rat civilization, if one ever did grow up, would not necessarily turn out to be anything at all like human civilization. The fact was, after eight months in the Boniface Estate, none of us was sorry to move out of it. It had given us shelter, free food, and an education, but we were never really comfortable there. Everything in it was designed for animals who looked, moved, and thought differently from the way we did. Also, it was above ground, and that never felt quite natural to us.

So, when we left, we decided that our new home should be underground, preferably, if we could find it, a cave. But where? We thought hard, and studied maps and atlases—there were plenty of those in the study. Finally we reached some conclusions: To find a cave, we would have to go where there were mountains—there aren't many caves in flatlands. And for food, it would have to be near a town or better, a farm.

So we wanted to find a farm, preferably a big one, with a big barn and silos full of grain, near the mountains. We studied the maps some more, and it was Jenner, I think, who spotted this area as a good place to look. On the map, a big part of it was covered with the contour lines that show mountains, and across these were written the words, "Thorn Mountains National Forest." Beneath that, in smaller letters, it said, "Protected Wilderness Preserve." Bordering this, where the mountains turned to foothills, the map showed rolling country with quite a few roads but hardly any towns, which, we thought, ought to mean farmland.

We were right, as of course you know now. It took us two months of steady traveling to get to the Thorn Mountains National Forest, but we found it; we're under the edge of it right now. And there are plenty of caves, most of them never visited by people—because people aren't allowed to drive into a wilderness preserve. There aren't any roads in the forest, but only a few jeep trails used by rangers, and airplanes are not permitted to fly over it.

We looked at a lot of caves, some big, some small, some dry, but mostly damp. Before we chose this cave and this farm, however, we found the Toy Tinker.

It began as a sad sort of thing. We found an old man lying in the woods one morning, near one of the jeep trails not so far from here, and he was dead. We don't know what he died of; we guessed it must have been a heart attack. He was dressed in a black suit, old-fashioned in style but

186

neat, not ragged. His hair was white, and his face looked gentle.

"I wonder who he was, and where he was going," Justin said.

"Whoever he was," Jenner said, "he wasn't supposed to be in here at all."

"We ought to bury him," I said.

So we did, not by digging a grave, but by covering him with a high mound of leaves and stones and twigs and earth. It was in gathering material for this mound that Justin made the second discovery. He was back in the bushes, out of our sight.

"Look here," he called. "I found a truck."

It was a very ancient truck, with a small round hood, but it had been lovingly polished and was wonderfully shiny. The body, which was square and large, had been rebuilt and painted red and gold. It had little windows with white curtains, and between them, lettered in gold, were signs:

THE TOY TINKER
Toys
Repairs
Hobby Kits
Model Sets
Electrical Toys
All Work Guaranteed

Obviously the truck had belonged to the old

man. He was a peddler and mender of toys, the red and gold wagon was his shop and his home, and he had driven into the woods to camp for the night. It was against the law, of course, so he had concealed the truck behind some bushes, off the trail, under a big beech tree. We could see where he had made a campfire, carefully surrounding it with stones and clearing away the brush so he would not set the woods afire. Beyond the beech tree a brook flowed. It was a peaceful spot.

We could see what had probably caused the old man's death: one wheel of the truck had sunk into the soft earth and was stuck. A shovel lay near it—he had been trying to dig it out. The work had been too hard for him, and he had started to go for help when he collapsed.

This much we could figure out just by looking. Then somebody said:

"Whose truck is it now?"

"It belongs to his heirs," I said.

"Whoever they are," said Jenner. "He may not even have any. He seems to have been alone."

"Anyway," said someone else, "how would they ever find it?"

"That's true," I said. "We don't know who he was, and if we did, we have no way of notifying anyone. So I suppose, if we want it, the truck is ours."

"Why don't we see what's in it?"

Thorn Valley

It might almost be easier to tell what *wasn't* in it," Nicodemus continued. "That truck was as roomy as a small bus, and the old man hadn't wasted a square foot of it. Not that it was cluttered; on the contrary, everything was neatly in place on its shelf, or hook, or in its cabinet."

It took us a while to understand what a treasure we had found. The truck contained, as you might expect, a big stock of toys. It also contained the old man's simple living quarters: a cot, a lamp, a work table, a folding chair, a bucket for carrying water, a plate, pots, pans, and so on. There was a tiny refrigerator with food in it, and some canned stuff—peas, beans, peaches, things like that.

Most of the toys—we thought at first—we had no particular use for. There were toy automobiles and trucks, windmills and merry-go-rounds, airplanes, boats and a lot of others, mostly run on batteries. It was entertaining to look at them, and some of then we even tried out; for a while the floor looked like Christmas morning.

We tired of that and explored farther into the truck. Up near the front we found several large cardboard boxes, and when we opened them we found that they were full of electric motors of assorted sizes — replacement engines for broken or worn out toys. There were dozens of them, ranging from very small, no bigger than a spool of thread, up to some so heavy we could hardly move them.

Then, next to these, we found the real treasure: the old man's tools. They were neatly arranged in shining rows inside a steel cabinet as big as a trunk. There were screwdrivers, saws, hammers, clamps, vises, wrenches, pliers. There were welding tools, soldering irons, and electric drills. And the beauty of it was, since they were designed for working on toys, they were nearly all miniature, easily small enough for us to handle. Yet they were themselves not toys; they were made of the finest tempered steel, like the tools of a watchmaker or a dentist.

It was Arthur who said it first:

"Do you realize what we've got here? We could open our own machine shop. With these tools and all these motors, we could make anything we wanted."

"We could," said Jenner, "except you've forgotten one thing."

"What's that?"

"We have no electricity. The old man couldn't have run these tools off batteries. The small toy motors, yes, but not the real ones, not the power tools. He had to plug into house current to use those. See, there's his extension cord on the wall."

There was a long coil of heavy black cable hanging from a hook on the wall. It had a plug on one end and a socket on the other.

Now another rat spoke up, a rat named Sullivan. He was a great friend of Arthur's, and like him, had a particular interest in engines and electricity.

"Maybe," he said, "we could plug into a house current, too."

"How?" I said. "Who'd let us?"

"Do you remember that cave we looked at the other day? The one we decided was too close to the farmhouse?"

That was the beginning of it. The end you have seen yourself. He was speaking of the cave you saw today.

We all trooped back to it and examined it more carefully. It *was* too close, or at least closer than we had planned to live to a human habitation. But then we saw the huge rosebush near the tractor shed, where, with quite a lot of digging, we could put a concealed entrance. But most important, we noticed that there was an electric light in the tractor shed.

Mr. Fitzgibbon had an underground power cable leading out from his house to the shed. We dug a tunnel to it, tapped it, and we had all the electricity we needed. Near it ran a water pipe. We tapped that, too, and we had running water. Then, a few at a time, we moved the tools and the motors from the Toy Tinker's truck to the cave. We got nearly all of them before the truck disappeared. We went back one day and it was gone — only the hole remained, where its tire had been sunk. The forest rangers must have found it and hauled it away. But they never discovered or disturbed the mound where the old man lay buried.

So we built ourselves the life you see around you. Our colony thrived and grew to one hundred and fifteen. We taught our children to read and write. We had plenty to eat, running water, electricity, a fan to draw in fresh air, an elevator, a refrigerator. Deep underground, our home stayed warm in winter and cool in summer. It was a comfortable, almost luxurious existence.

And yet all was not well. After the first burst of energy, the moving in of the machines, the digging of tunnels and rooms—after that was done, a feeling of discontent settled upon us like some creeping disease.

We were reluctant to admit it at first. We tried to ignore the feeling or to fight it off by building more things—bigger rooms, fancier furniture, carpeted hallways, things we did not really need. I was reminded of a story I had read at the Boniface Estate when I was looking for things written about rats. It was about a woman in a small town who bought a vacuum cleaner. Her name was Mrs. Jones, and up until then she, like all of her neighbors, had kept her house spotlessly clean by using a broom and a mop. But the vacuum cleaner did it faster and better, and soon Mrs. Jones was the envy of all the other housewives in town—so they bought vacuum cleaners, too.

The vacuum cleaner business was so brisk, in fact, that the company that made them opened a branch factory in the town. The factory used a lot of electricity, of course, and so did the women with their vacuum cleaners, so the local electric power company had to put up a big new plant to keep them all running. In its furnaces the power plant burned coal, and out of its chinmeys black smoke poured day and night, blanketing the town with soot and making all the floors dirtier than ever. Still, by working twice as hard and twice as long the women of the town were able to keep their floors *almost* as clean as they had been before Mrs. Jones ever bought a vacuum cleaner in the first place.

The story was part of a book of essays, and the reason I had read it so eagerly was that it was called "The Rat Race" — which, I learned, means a race where, no matter how fast you run, you don't get anywhere. But there was nothing in the book about rats, and I felt bad about the title because, I thought, it wasn't a rat race at all, it was a People Race, and no sensible rats would ever do anything so foolish.

And yet here we were, rats getting caught up in something a lot like the People Race, and for no good reason. And the worst thing was that even with our make-work projects, we didn't really have enough to do. Our life was too easy. I thought of what the scientist had written about our prairie dog ancestors, and I was worried.

So were many of the others. We called a meeting — indeed, a whole series of meetings, extending over more than a year. We talked and argued and considered, and we remembered our evenings in the library at the Boniface Estate when we had wondered what a rat civilization would be like. Oddly enough, Jenner, my old and best friend, took little part in these discussions; he remained rather glumly silent and seemed disinterested. But most of the others felt as I did, and slowly some things became clear; we saw our problems and we figured out, as well as we could, what to do about them.

First, we realized that finding the Toy Tinker's truck, which had seemed like such an enormous stroke of luck, had in fact led us into the very trap we should have avoided. As a result we were now stealing more than ever before: not only food, but electricity and water. Even the air we breathed was drawn in by a stolen fan, run by stolen current.

It was this, of course, that made our life so easy that it seemed pointless. We did not have enough work to do because a thief's life is always based on somebody else's work.

Second, there was always the fear, in the back of all our minds, that we might get caught. Or perhaps not caught—we took precautions against that—so much as found out. Mr. Fitzgibbon was surely aware that some of his crops were being removed. And as our group grew larger, we would have to take more and more.

Already, he had begun lining some of his grain bins with sheet metal. That didn't bother us particularly, because we knew how to get the doors open. But suppose he should take to locking them? We could cut through the locks, of course, or even through the sheet metal walls; we have the tools for that. But it would be a dead giveaway. What would Mr. Fitzgibbon think about rats who could cut through metal?

All these things we worried about and talked about and puzzled over. But we could not find any easy answer—because there was none.

There was, however, a hard answer.

I began taking long walks into the forest. I had an idea in the back of my head. Sometimes I went alone, sometimes with some of the others.

On one particular day I went with Jenner. I had not yet told him about my idea, nor did I on the morning we set out, but merely proposed a direction. We took along enough food for lunch. I remember that it was autumn, a bright, cool day; the leaves made a rustling sound when the wind blew, and some were turning yellow.

In my walks I had been exploring the jeep trails, trying to find the wildest parts of the forest, places where not even the rangers ever went.

A few times I tried asking for information. I asked two squirrels, for instance, if they knew what lay on the other side of a mountain that rose before me. But they were silly, fearful creatures; and after looking at me in surprise, they both scurried up an oak tree and scolded senselessly in loud voices, shaking their tails, until I left. I asked some chipmunks, and they were more polite. They couldn't answer my question (never having been farther than a hundred yards from where they were born!), but advised me to ask the birds — more specifically, one bird, a very old owl who was famous throughout the forest. They even told me how to find the enormous tree in which he lived.

That was the beginning of my acquaintance with the owl. He knew every tree, every trail, every stone in the forest. He was (as you know) not naturally friendly toward rats, or mice either, but when I told him about our life at Nimh, and our escape, he grew interested. Though he did not say so, I think he had already been watching some of our activities from the air in the evenings. Anyway, he was curious and listened carefully when I told him about our problems and my ideas for solving them. I have talked to him many times since.

It was he who told me about Thorn Valley.

The valley lies deep in the forest, beyond the big tree. The jeep trails do not cross it, nor even go close to it, for the mountains around it are forbidding, too steep and rocky even for jeeps, and are covered with thorny thickets. The owl told me that in all the years he had been flying, he had never seen a human being near it.

Yet the bottom of the valley is level and broad and nearly a mile long; steep cliffs wall it in all around. There are three ponds or small lakes in it, and apparently these are fed by springs, for they never dry up. On clear days, the owl said, he sometimes saw small fish swimming in them. I thought: Could rats weave fish nets or make fish hooks?

It was this valley I was looking for the day I set out with Jenner. I had careful directions from the owl; yet it took us half a day, moving briskly, to reach the base of the mountains. Then up, up, very steeply, for more than an hour—not really difficult for us, since rats are better climbers than men; also, we are shorter, so we had little trouble with the spiney underbrush. From the top of the high ridge at last we looked down, and the valley lay before us.

It was beautiful and still, a wild and lonely place. Through the green and yellow treetops below us I could see the water of one of the ponds sparkling in the sun. I got the idea that my eyes — our eyes — were the first ever to see it. Yet that was not true, for as we descended into the valley, a deer suddenly appeared in the trees ahead and went bounding off down the slope. There were wild animals there, and I wondered if they even suspected that outside these walls of mountains there were cities and roads and people.

Most of the valley floor was in forest, great spreading oak and maple trees, but near one of the ponds I saw what I had hoped to find — a large natural clearing, a glade where only coarse grass and wild flowers grew, and some clumps of black raspberry bushes. This clearing was on the far side of the valley, beyond it the mountain wall rose again, a steep slope with big outcroppings of stone — granite ledges that thrust six or ten feet out of the earth.

"We could live here," I said to Jenner.

"I suppose we could," he said. "It's a beautiful place. But it's a long way from the barn. Think how far we'd have to carry food. And no electricity."

"We could grow our own food," I said. I started to add, but didn't: and maybe, someday, make our own electricity, if we decided we wanted to.

"We don't know how. Anyway, where would we grow it?"

"Right here. It would be easy to clear away these weeds and bushes. And if we dug into that mountainside, under those rock ledges, we'd have all the cave space we wanted, dry and warm, with a good roof. There could be room enough for a thousand of us."

"There aren't a thousand of us."

"There might be, someday."

"But why? Why move? We've got a better place to live right now. We've got all the food we want. We've got electricity, and lights, and running water. I can't understand why everybody talks about changing things."

"Because everything we have is stolen."

"That's silly. Is it stealing when farmers take milk from cows, or eggs from chickens? They're just smarter than the cows and chickens, that's all. Well, people are our cows. If we're smart enough, why shouldn't we get food from them?"

"It's not the same. Farmers feed the cows and chickens and take care of them. We don't do anything for what we take. Besides, if we keep it up, we're sure to be found out."

"What then? What if we are? People have been trying to exterminate rats for centuries, but they haven't succeeded. And we're smarter than the others. What are they going to do? Dynamite us? Let them try. We'll find out where they keep the dynamite and use it on them."

"Then we'd *really* be found out. Don't you see, Jenner, if we ever did anything like that, they'd figure out who we are and what we know? Then only two things could happen. Either they'd hunt us all down and kill us, or they'd capture us and put us in a sideshow, or maybe take us back to Nimh. And this time we'd never get away."

"I don't believe any of that," Jenner said. "You've got this idea stuck in your head. We've got to start from nothing and work hard and build a rat civilization. I say, why start from nothing if you can start with everything? We've already got a civilization."

"No. We haven't. We're just living on the edge of somebody else's, like fleas on a dog's back. If the dog drowns, the fleas drown, too."

That was the beginning of an argument that never had a satisfactory ending. Jenner would not yield to my point of view, nor I to his. It wasn't that he was lazy and didn't want to work. He was just more cynical than the rest of us; stealing did not bother him. And he was a pessimist. He never believed that we could really make it on our own. Maybe he was right. But I, and most of the others, felt that we must at least try. If we fail—well, then I suppose we must come back here, or find some other farm. Or eventually forget all we learned and go back to stealing garbage.

So we began working out the Plan. It has been a long time coming. Three years ago this spring we started watching Mr. Fitzgibbon to learn what he did, and how he did it, to bring food out of the earth. We collected books and magazines on farming. We discovered early that in order to stop stealing we would, for a while, have to steal more than ever. We've laid up a two-year food supply, so that even if we don't succeed in growing in a good crop the first year, we won't go hungry. We've got two-thirds of it moved to Thorn Valley already, and we've dug a dry cave to store it in, under one of the big rocks. We've got seeds; we have our plows; we've cleared and cultivated part of the land near the pond; and in a few days we'll begin our first planting. We've even dug some irrigation ditches, in case there's a drought.

We have a schedule worked out, sort of a countdown, and by early June we will be out of this cave, and out of Mr. Fitzgibbon's barn, I hope forever.

Captured

Speaking of schedules and countdowns"—Mr. Ages spoke suddenly—"we've got one for this evening. It's getting late."

The clock on Nicodemus's desk said five o'clock.

"Mrs. Fitzgibbon feeds Dragon at six p.m." He spoke gently, but his voice had a chilling sound to Mrs. Frisby. They all looked at her.

"I'm ready," she said quietly, "but there are still a few minutes, and one question you have not yet answered. Why did Jonathan never tell me anything about Nimh, or any of the rest?"

Mr. Ages said: "I'll try to explain. When Nicodemus and the others moved into the cave near the rosebush, they invited Jonathan and me to stay with them—after all, we had been with them for many months by that time—and at first we did. But after a few weeks we decided to move out. We were, you realize, different. We both felt strange, associating always and only with rats, even though they were our close and good friends. As for me, I wanted more solitude and less society; Jonathan, on the other hand, was younger than I and felt lonely.

"So we moved, at first together, to the basement of the old farmhouse where I still live. Then Jonathan met you, at a stream near the woods somewhere, I think he said . . ."

"Yes," Mrs. Frisby said, "I remember."

"From then on he worried. He didn't want to be secretive, but he didn't know how to tell you one thing. I'm sure Nicodemus has explained to you that the injections we got at Nimh had two effects. One of them was that none of us seemed to be growing any older at all—the children, yes, but not the adults. Apparently the injections had given us all a much longer life-span than even Dr. Schultz had anticipated.

"You can see why this would have been a dreadful thing for Jonathan to have to tell you. You never had the injections. That meant that while he stayed young, you would grow older, and older, and finally die. He loved you, and he could hardly stand that thought. Yet if it was distressing to him—he thought—how much more painful it would be to you! That is what he could not bring himself to tell you.

"He would have told you eventually; I know he intended to. Indeed, you would have found it out yourself, you would have seen it happening. But it was hard; he kept putting it off, and then, finally, it was too late."

"Poor Jonathan," said Mrs. Frisby. "He should have told me. I wouldn't have minded. But will my children . . ."

"Also have longer lives?" said Nicodemus. "We don't know yet. We think so, but our own children are not yet old enough to be certain. We do know they have inherited the ability to learn. They master reading almost without effort."

He stood up, took out his reading glass, and looked at the clock. But Mrs. Frisby interrupted again.

"One more thing," she said. "What happened to Jenner?"

Nicodemus said: "He left. He was against the Plan from the start. In our discussions, he tried to persuade others to oppose it, too. Only a few joined him; though there are some others who are still doubtful about it, they're going to stay with us and try it.

"The arguments stayed reasonably friendly, but the last straw, for Jenner, was when we decided to destroy the machines."

"Destroy them!"

"For two reasons. One, so that if anyone ever finds the cave, there won't be any evidence of what we've been doing—nothing but broken bits of metal, debris that will look like ordinary junk. We'll pull out our electric cable, our lights and our water pipes. We'll close up all the tunnels leading in.

"The other reason is more important. When we move to Thorn Valley, we're going to have some hard times. We know that, and we're braced for it. If this cave is still open, with the machines and lights, the carpets and running water still here, there will be a terrible temptation to give up and move back to the soft life. We want to remove that temptation.

"But when Jenner heard the decision—it was made at a meeting—he grew really angry. He denounced us all as idiots and dreamers. He stamped out of the meeting, and a few days later he left the group forever, taking six of his followers with him. We don't know where they went, but we think they will try to find someplace where they can set up a new life like this one.

"I wish them luck, but they'll have trouble. There won't be any Toy Tinker this time. They'll have to steal their machines—everything. That worries us some, because if they get caught, who knows what might happen? But there's nothing we can do about it. We're going ahead with the Plan; and once we get to Thorn Valley, I think we can stop worrying."

Justin stood up. "It's time to go." He picked up the paper with the sleeping draught in it.

Mrs. Frisby, Justin, and Mr. Ages walked together up the long corridor to the rosebush.

"Remember, when you come up through the hole in the kitchen floor," Mr. Ages said, "you'll be under a cabinet. It's low, but there's room to move. Go a few steps forward, and you'll be able to see out into the room.

"Mrs. Fitzgibbon will be there, getting dinner for her family. They eat at about six. When she's got their dinner ready, she'll feed Dragon. He won't be in the kitchen, but he'll be waiting just outside the kitchen door on the porch. She doesn't let him in while she's cooking because he makes such a pest of himself, rubbing against her ankles and getting between her feet.

"If you look to your right, you'll see his bowl. It's blue, and it has the word Kitty written over and over again around the side. She'll pick it up, fill it with catfood, and put it down again in the same place.

"Then watch closely. She'll walk over to the door to let him in, and that's your chance. Her back will be toward you. She's got to walk about twenty feet — it's a big kitchen. The bowl will be about two feet away from you. Be sure the paper packet is open — then dash out, dump the powder into the food, and dash back. You don't want to be in sight when Dragon comes in. I can tell you that from experience."

"Is that how you got hurt?"

"I got there a few seconds late. I decided there was still time. I was wrong."

At the arch in the rosebush Mr. Ages left them. With his cast, he would not be able to climb through the hole to the kitchen; there was no point in his going farther.

Mrs. Frisby and Justin moved out of the rosebush and looked around them. It was still light, though the sun was low on the horizon. Straight ahead of them, perhaps two hundred feet away, stood the big white farmhouse. Dragon was already on the porch, sitting just outside the door, looking at it expectantly. To their right was the tractor shed, and beyond that was the barnyard fence and the barn itself, casting a long shadow. Behind them rose the woods and the mountains; to the left Mrs. Frisby could see the big stone in the middle of the garden, near which her children waited. As soon as her task was done, she thought, she must hurry to them and get ready for the move.

"We go under the right side of the house," Justin said quietly. "Follow me." They made their way around the edge of the yard, staying in the shadows, keeping an eye on Dragon. Justin still wore his satchel and had put the powder package in it.

There was a basement under the main part of the Fitzgibbons' house, but the big kitchen had been added later and stood on a foundation of concrete blocks, with only a crawl space beneath. As they approached this gray foundation, Mrs. Frisby saw that near the middle of it, a few inches off the ground, there was a square patch of darker gray. It was a hole, left for ventilation, and there was a screen over it. When they reached it, Justin caught hold of the screen and pulled the corner. It swung open.

"We loosened it a bit," he explained, holding it open for her. Mrs. Frisby crept through.

"Careful," he said. "It's dark. There's a drop of about a foot. Just jump. We put some straw at the bottom, so it's soft."

Holding her breath, Mrs. Frisby jumped blindly into the blackness, and felt the cushion of straw under her feet. In a moment Justin landed beside her. They were under the Fitzgibbons' kitchen.

"Now," he said softly, "look to your left. See the patch of light? That's the hole. The light comes from the kitchen. We've piled dirt up under it, so it's easy to reach. Come on."

Mrs. Frisby followed him; as they got near the bright hole she could see around her a little. They were walking across bare earth, dry and cool to the touch; overhead there were heavy wooden beams holding up the floor, and above those the floorboards themselves. Under the hole rose a small round hill of dirt. They walked up this, and then Justin whispered:

"This is far as I can go. There's not room for me to get through. I'll wait here. Come back down as soon as you're finished. Here's the powder." He handed her the paper packet. "Remember to tear it open before you go out to Dragon's bowl. Hurry, now. I can hear Mrs. Fitzgibbon moving around. She's getting the dinner. Be careful, and good luck."

Mrs. Frisby first pushed the packet up through the hole. Then, as quietly as she could, grasping both sides, she pulled herself up and into the kitchen.

It was light there. But Mr. Ages had not been joking when he said the ceiling was low. There was less than an inch between the floor and the bottom of the cabinet, so that she could not walk properly but had to flatten herself out and crawl. She did, a few steps, and discovered that she was trembling. "Stay calm," she told herself. "Don't get panicky, or you'll do something foolish and spoil everything."

Thus admonished, she crept forward again until she was near the edge of the cabinet. She stopped. From there she could see out into the kitchen fairly well. Straight across from her stood a big white stove, and in front of it, putting the lid on a pot, was Mrs. Fitzgibbon. The edge of the cabinet was so low, Mrs. Frisby could not see her head, but only up to her shoulders.

"There," Mrs. Fitzgibbon said, as if to herself. "The stew is done, the bread's in the oven, the table is set."

Where was the cat's bowl? Mrs. Frisby looked to her right as Mr. Ages had said. There it was, blue, with words inscribed around the side. Yet something was wrong. It was not two feet from the cabinet, but more like four or five. In the corner, where it should have been, rose four round wooden legs. She realized that she was looking at the bottom of a kitchen stool.

No matter, she thought. The extra distance is just a couple of feet. Mr. Ages had not mentioned a stool, but perhaps they moved it around. She crawled to her right, as close to the bowl as she could get without showing herself, and tore open the package.

Just as she did this Mrs. Fitzgibbon walked over from the stove. Her hand appeared, picked up the bowl, and Mrs. Frisby heard it thump on the counter over her head. A cutting sound—a can opener—the scrape of a spoon, and the bowl was back on the floor. The strong fishy smell of catfood. Mrs. Fitzgibbon walked away.

Now.

Mrs. Frisby moved swiftly out into the room, across the open floor, holding the powder, her eyes intent only on the bowl. She was no longer trembling. She poured the powder, which instantly dissolved in the moist catfood. Still clutching the paper, she turned and sped toward the cabinet.

With a bang, the lights went dim. The ceiling, which had somehow become curved, was filled with little round moons. Mrs. Frisby kept running, and her face struck a cold, hard wall of metal.

A voice shouted:

"Mother! Don't let Dragon in yet. I've caught a mouse."

Billy, the younger Fitzgibbon son, had been sitting on the kitchen stool, his feet up on the rung, eating berries from a colander. The colander, upside down, was now over Mrs. Frisby.

Seven Dead Rats

From a birdcage, Mrs. Frisby watched the Fitz-gibbons eat dinner. There was dinner for her, too — breadcrumbs, cheese, and bits of carrot — on the floor of the cage, along with a small bowl of water. The cage had been occupied until a few months before by a yellow canary named Porgy, who had lived in it for five years 'and then died of old age.

To get her out from under the colander, Billy had slid a piece of cardboard beneath it, pinching her foot sharply in the process, so that it hurt when she walked. She had been transferred first to a shoebox.

"Can I keep it?" Billy had asked his mother.

"What for? It's just a field mouse."

"For a pet. I like it." Billy had tried to look at Mrs. Frisby through some holes he had punched in the top of the box, but it was dark inside.

"I suppose so. For a few days. You'll have to feed it."

"I think I'll put it in Porgy's cage. I can't see it in this box. It must be hungry. It was trying to eat Dragon's food. Dumb mouse. It might have been killed."

No one had noticed the small torn piece of paper at first; then Mrs. Fitzgibbon had absently picked it up and tossed it into the wastebasket.

A few days! Mrs. Frisby felt sick. And after a few days—then what? Would they let her go? Or would Billy plead for a few more? But even if they did set her free—her children were alone; the rats were coming tonight to move her house. Why had Billy picked today, of all days, to sit on the stool? She had not the heart to eat the food that lay on the cage floor. She felt like weeping.

Paul came in for dinner, followed by his father. He looked at her in the cage.

"Why don't you let it go?" he said to Billy. "Poor little thing. It's scared to death."

"No it's not. It's just not used to the cage."

"I bet it will die."

"I bet it won't."

"You can't just put wild animals in cages. You have to catch them when they're babies."

"They do it in zoos."

"Yes, but they know more about it. Anyway, a lot of those die, too."

"It's strange that it was in here at all," said

Mrs. Fitzgibbon. "I haven't seen any signs of mice. I didn't think we had any."

They sat at the table, and Mrs. Fitzgibbon served the stew. It was a long, square-cut farm table, big enough to feed, besides the family, the four hired hands who would be working with Mr. Fitzgibbon during the planting and harvesting. The Fitzgibbons sat together around one end of it.

Mrs. Frisby's cage hung from a metal stand in the corner on the opposite side of the room, quite high up, so that the floor where she crouched was above their heads. She could watch them, looking down; but if she retreated to the far side of the cage, they could not see her, nor she them. She kept hoping that Paul would resume the argument with Billy and win it, or at least convince Mr. or Mrs. Fitzgibbon that they should let her go.

But Paul was now busy eating. So, moving quietly, she crept to the back of the cage. There was a sliding door halfway up the side, which Billy had lifted to put her in. Remembering Nicodemus's story, she looked at it, wondering if she could climb to it, if she could get it open if she did. Not now, but later, when they had left the kitchen. Maybe. But it looked quite big and heavy.

She thought about her children again. Surely, when Justin had waited a little longer, he would realize that something had gone wrong. He would go and talk to them. But what could he tell them? "Children, your mother went into the kitchen with Dragon and she hasn't come out." No. But whatever he said, they would be dreadfully frightened and worried. Poor Cynthia! Poor Timothy—poor all of them.

She had one small satisfaction. Dragon, who had been admitted after she was safely caged, had eaten his bowl of catfood greedily, sleeping powder and all, purring as he licked the last scraps from the bottom.

Billy was looking at the cage.

"There," he cried. "It walked. I saw it. I told you it was all right." He started up from his chair.

"Billy, stay in your place and eat your stew," said Mrs. Fitzgibbon. "The mouse can wait."

"Speaking of mice," said Mr. Fitzgibbon, who had driven to town that afternoon, "there was quite a stir today at Henderson's hardware store."

"About mice?"

"No, but nearly. About rats. I went in to order the new linch pin, and there was quite a group there, talking about an odd thing that had happened.

"It seems that six or seven rats got themselves electrocuted there a few days ago. Very strange. Henderson sells motors — he has a whole shelf of them. The rats, for some reason, had got on the shelf. He says it looked as if they were fooling with one of the motors, trying to move it."

"That's a new one," said Paul. "Rats stealing motors."

"They weren't really, of course. Anyway, it happened during the night; when he — Henderson — came into the shop in the morning, he tried to turn on the lights, and the fuse was blown. He found the rats all grouped around the motor. It had been left plugged in, though it was turned off. They must have been gnawing at the insulation for some reason — at least that's what he thinks. They caused a short circuit, and all bunched together like that, the current went through them and killed the lot."

"Pretty good kind of a rat trap, I'd say," Mrs. Fitzgibbon remarked.

Mrs. Frisby was now listening to the conversation very closely. Dragon had stretched out on the floor, looking drowsy.

"Wait," said Mr. Fitzgibbon. "That's only the beginning. It seems that the local weekly was hard up for news. They heard about it and sent their reporter over."

"Fred Smith," said Mrs. Fitzgibbon.

"Yes. Fred wrote a little article about it, with a headline, MECHANIZED RATS INVADE HARDWARE STORE. Something like that. Well, it attracted more attention than he expected. The next thing they knew, believe it or not, the federal government got into it. They sent a squad over there from the Public Health Service with a truckload of equipment."

"Just on account of seven rats?" said Billy. "They should send the truck over here. We've got more than that."

"That's just what I said," Mr. Fitzgibbon went on. "And do you know? They're going to. I was joking, of course, but the man in charge of the group didn't take it as a joke at all. He wanted to know where the farm was, how far away, how many acres, what I raised, how many rats I thought there were. He acted really interested. It seems they wanted to examine the dead rats at Henderson's, but they couldn't. He'd already sent them to the town dump, and they were incinerated."

"I never heard of such a thing," said Mrs. Fitzgibbon. "All that fuss over a few dead rats."

"I have," said Paul. "And I bet I know what they're after."

"What?"

"They think the rats have rabies. They don't like to say so because it makes people panicky."

"What's rabies?" asked Billy.

"A disease," said Mr. Fitzgibbon. "A very bad one, spread by animals. You know, Paul, I think you're probably right. That would explain why the Public Health Service is in it. Epidemic control. Anyway, they're planning to check on the rats all over this area."

"Don't you remember," Paul said, "a few years ago when everybody had to lock up their dogs? And some people were shooting every dog they saw. That's why they keep it quiet until they're sure.

"And another thing. They taught us in the vet course in school that when an animal starts acting strange, it may be a sign of rabies. Well, chewing electric wires—that's strange enough."

"And they think some rats here might be infected?" Mrs. Fitzgibbon sounded worried.

"I suppose they must," said Mr. Fitzgibbon, "though they never mentioned rabies at all."

"When are they coming?"

"Day after tomorrow, Saturday morning. The man in charge, a Doctor somebody, said they had some more checking to do in town tomorrow. They're coming with an extermination truck—cyanide gas, I think."

"I can tell them where to look," Paul said.

"Me too," said Billy. "Under the rosebush."

"That's right," said Mr. Fitzgibbon. "In fact, they'll probably want to bulldoze that bush out of there. I can do that with the big tractor."

"Bulldoze my rosebush?" said Mrs. Fitzgibbon indignantly. "They will not!"

"Look at it this way," her husband said. "I've got to get rid of those rats anyway. I'd already decided to; they're stealing too much feed—seeds, too, more all the time. If I paid an exterminator to do it, he'd charge a couple of hundred dollars. If the government will do it free, why shouldn't we let them?"

"Well," said Mrs. Fitzgibbon, still not soothed, "then you can spend the money to buy me some new rosebushes."

"That's just what I had in mind," said Mr. Fitzgibbon with a smile. "And maybe some lilacs, too." Mrs. Fitzgibbon had always wanted a lilac bush; they were her favorite shrub.

Mrs. Frisby did not believe at all that it was rabies the men were looking for. She wished Mr. Fitzgibbon had been able to remember the name of the "Doctor somebody." And now she had another urgent reason to get out of the cage. Somehow, she had to warn Nicodemus.

Dragon slept on the kitchen floor.

Escape

At ten by the kitchen clock, the Fitzgibbons went to bed. Dragon was put out, the doors locked, the lights turned off. The first of these things was done by Billy, on instruction from his mother, not without some difficulty. He opened the door.

"Come on Dragon. Out."

"He won't get up."

"I never saw such a lazy cat. He gets worse every day."

Finally Dragon, protesting with only the sleepiest of whines, was picked up and deposited on the back porch. He scarcely opened his eyes.

By that time it was dark. Mrs. Frisby waited a few minutes until she was sure they were really gone and until her eyes adjusted so she could see the bars of her cage. They were vertical bars, smooth and no thicker than match sticks, which made them slippery to climb, but by turning more or less sideways, she was able to grip them fairly well. She inched her way up to the sliding door and tried to lift it.

She could tell from the first pull that it was no use. The door was stiff and it was heavy, and she could not get a good enough grip on either it or the cage wall to exert much pressure. Still she kept trying, first lifting on the middle of the door, then on one corner, then another, straining every muscle. In half an hour she admitted defeat, at least for the moment, and climbed back down to the bottom of the cage. She sat there, shaking from the effort, and thought.

Somehow, she had to get out. Her children, even now, would be alone in the dark house, alone at night for the first time. Martin and Teresa would be trying to reassure the younger ones; yet they themselves would be sadly frightened. What would they think? Since she had not told them about Dragon and the sleeping powder, she hoped that perhaps they would decide she had, for some reason, stayed with the rats.

But at eleven, which could not be far off (she could not read the kitchen clock in the dark), the rats would arrive to move the house. Or would they, knowing—since Justin must have told them—that she had not come out of the kitchen? She thought they would. She hoped they would, and that Justin would go with them and talk to the children and try to calm their fear. There was something about Justin, a kind of easy confidence, that would help them.

She no longer had any doubt, of course, that the rats could move her house. It was a generous thing to do, especially at a time when they were hurrying so in their Plan, their own move. And they had no idea yet how little time they really had, of the new danger that crowded upon them. If she could only get out! She would run and warn them, and it might still not be too late.

She thought: It's a good plan and a brave one. It would be the first time in all the world that intelligent beings, besides men, had ever tried to start a real civilization of their own. They ought to have a chance. It was not right that they should be killed at the last minute. Or captured. Could it be that they—the men who were coming—were somehow connected with Nimh? Or was it more likely, as Paul had guessed, that they were only worried about rabies? She decided it didn't really matter. The result would be the same. The day after next the truck would come with its poison gas, and that would be the end of all their plans. Unless they could be warned. Wearily, she got up to climb the wall and try the door again.

She heard a noise.

It was in the kitchen, near her cage, a small scuffling on the hard linoleum floor.

"Now what kind of a bird can that be, with no wings?"

It was Justin's voice, very soft, and he was laughing.

"Justin!"

"I thought you might like to come home. Your children are asking after you."

"Are they all right?"

"They're fine. They were worried, but I told them I'd bring you back. They seemed to believe me."

"But how did you know . . ."

"That you were here? You forget, I was waiting just under the cabinet. I heard what happened. I felt like biting Billy full of holes. But as soon as I heard that you were safely in the cage, I went and told the children you were all right, but that you'd be a little late. I didn't tell them exactly why.

"Now, let's get you out."

"I tried. I couldn't open the door."

"I'll get it open. I brought along a few tools—burglar's tools, you might say—in my back pack. Should I climb up the stand? No. It looks slippery. I think I'll try the curtain."

And in a matter of seconds Justin had swarmed up a window curtain a foot away, and she heard a thump as he leaped and landed on top of the cage, which swayed under the impact. The noise was slight, but they both listened intently for a moment to see if it produced another, from upstairs. All quiet.

"Now let me look at that door." Justin climbed easily down the side of the cage.

"Oh, I hope you can get it open."

"I can," Justin said, examining it, "easily enough. But I don't think I will."

"Why not?"

"Because you couldn't," Justin said, "and they'll know that. So they won't be curious, let's make it open itself. As I expected, it doesn't have real hinges." He had pulled a small metal bar out of his back pack, and was working as he talked. "Just little wire rings. Dime-store quality. Cheap, flimsy things. They're always coming apart." As he said that, one of them came apart; the door sagged and hung crazily by one corner. "There, you see? You couldn't help it if they put you in a defective cage. Come on out."

Mrs. Frisby climbed through and stood with Justin on the top of the cage.

"Now," he said, "we shinny down the stand like a fireman's pole. You go out the way you came in — under the cabinet and through the hole. I'll go out the way I came in through the attic. I'll meet you outside."

"Justin," Mrs. Frisby said, "there's something I've got to tell you, something I learned . . ."

"Wait till we're out," said Justin. "We've got to hurry. You see, we're having a little trouble moving your cinder block." He was off, running silently into the front of the house, from which the stairway led up two flights to the attic.

Mrs. Frisby crawled under the cabinet, searched in total darkness for the small hole, and finally felt one foot slip down. She dropped through. The square opening in the foundation was easier to find; it glowed palely ahead of her, lit with moonlight.

Justin was waiting for her as she came out of the corner of the screen. The night was warm, and a half-moon shone on the farmyard.

"Now," he said, "what was it you wanted to tell me?" He spoke seriously; he had heard the urgency in her voice. They hurried toward the garden, rounding the back porch. There, a dark heap in the moonlight, lay Dragon, no threat to anyone tonight.

"Some exterminators are coming to poison all of you." Mrs. Frisby told him, as briefly as she could, of the conversation she had heard at the Fitzgibbons' dinner table.

"Seven rats," Justin said. "Rabies. It might be.

227

But I'll bet it was Jenner. When are the men supposed to come?"

"The day after tomorrow."

To her surprise, Justin stopped. He looked at her in admiration.

"You know," he said, "I had a feeling the first time I clapped eyes on you that you'd bring us good luck."

"*Good* luck!" She was amazed.

"Oh, its bad news. It's serious. We'll have to change our plans, and quickly. But think how much worse it would be if you hadn't overheard it. We wouldn't have had a chance."

They came into the garden.

"Is Nicodemus here?" Mrs. Frisby asked.

"No. In a few minutes I'll go and tell him. But first we need your help to get started moving your house."

"My help? What can I do?"

"You can talk to your neighbor. She seems to think we're stealing your cinder block. She bit Arthur in the leg."

At one end of the big stone in the middle of the garden, ten rats were digging briskly, using scoops that looked more like teaspoons than shovels, piling the earth neatly beside a hole already almost big enough to hold Mrs. Frisby's house.

But on the other side of the stone there was an impasse.

Here another ten rats stood, baffled, in a semicircle. Behind them they had deposited a jumble of equipment: odd-shaped metal bars, pulleys, wooden structures that looked like ladders, other pieces of wood that resembled small logs. But between the rats and Mrs. Frisby's front door stood a small, defiant figure. The rats, looking enormous by comparison, remained a respectful distance away from her.

"Why," said Mrs. Frisby to Justin, "it's the shrew!"

"Yes," said Justin, "and acting shrewish."

One of the rats was speaking. Mrs. Frisby recognized Arthur.

". . . but I told you ma'am, we do have Mrs. Frisby's permission. She wants us to move her house. Ask the children. Call them out."

"Don't tell me that. What have you done with Mrs. Frisby? It's a good thing the children haven't heard you. They'd be frightened half to death! If Mrs. Frisby wanted you to move her house, she'd be here."

"It's all right," called Mrs. Frisby, running forward. "I'm here."

"Mrs. Frisby!" said the shrew. "You're just in time. I heard a noise, and came out and found these creatures—trying to dig up your house."

"I tried to explain it to her," said Arthur. "But she won't believe me."

"I certainly won't," said the shrew. "He said you asked him to dig up your house. Thieving rats!"

"It's true," Mrs. Frisby said. "I did ask them, and they said they would. It's very kind of them."

"Kind?" said the shrew. "Great hulking beasts. What do you mean?"

It took several more minutes of reassurance by Mrs. Frisby before the shrew grudingly moved aside, still muttering warnings. "I wouldn't trust them. How do you know they'll do what they say?" That, of course, Mrs. Frisby could not explain to her.

The rats now commenced to dig busily at the dirt on top of and around Mrs. Frisby's cinder block. Justin said: "I've got to go and talk to Nicodemus. You'd better get the children out." Mrs. Frisby hurried into her house.

She found them waiting in the living room, unaware of the small crisis that had been taking place outside. As Justin had said, they did not seem worried.

"We were scared at first," Teresa said. "But then one of the rats came to see us. He couldn't come in, but he called to us, and we came out, Martin and I. He said his name was Justin. Have you met him? He's very nice."

"I've met him," said Mrs. Frisby. "Now we'd better go outside. They're getting ready to move the house."

"I'm ready," said Timothy. "I'm all wrapped up like a scarecrow."

Martin and Teresa had taken pieces of warm cloth from the bed and tied them around him. Mrs. Frisby could not see him in the dark, but when she touched him she found they had even tied a piece like a bonnet around his head and ears.

"Good," she said. "And we're lucky—it's a warm night, and dry."

They went up the small tunnel to the garden and watched in the moonlight from a hillock a few feet away. The rats had finished digging the new hole, and all twenty of them were working near the house. It was a sight to see.

As soon as the earth had been cleared from the top and sides of the cinder block, so that it lay fully exposed in its hole, all of the rats turned to the pile of equipment. Under Arthur's direction the ladderlike structures became a scaffolding— four small towers standing one near each corner of the block. Across the tops of these the rats fastened strong, light bars of metal, probably, Mrs. Frisby thought, from the Toy Tinker's truck.

From these bars they now hung pulleys wound with strong, thin cord, and at the ends of the cords they fastened hooks, which they slipped into the oval shaped holes in the block and pulled taut. Five strong rats stood by each cord. One of them, Mrs. Frisby noticed, was bigger than the rest: her friend Brutus.

"Heave!" called Arthur.

The twenty rats strained on the cords, and the block rose an inch. Each rat stepped back a pace.

"Heave!" Another inch.

Slowly, the heavy block rose from the hole until it hung two inches above level ground.

"Steady," said Arthur. "Get the rollers."

Eight rats, two from each group, ran to the round pieces of wood Mrs. Frisby had noticed earlier; these resembled sawed-up pieces of broom handle, each about a foot long.

Two rats to a roller, they slipped four of these under the cinder block so that they lay athwart the hole, like bars across a window.

"Lower away," said Arthur, and the cinder block came to rest gently on the rollers.

"Let's see how it rolls."

They slipped the ropes free of the pulleys and rehooked two of them to the front of the block. Nine rats now manned each rope; two stayed behind, watching the rollers.

"Heave!"

The rollers turned and the heavy block slid forward easily, like a truck on wheels, in the direction of the new hole. When it moved off the hindmost of the rollers, as it did every few inches, the two rats in the rear would quickly pick that one up and replace it under the front of the block.

Almost like a game of leap-frog, Mrs. Frisby thought. But a well-rehearsed game; the rats had planned carefully; they knew exactly what they were doing; they moved with precision and never wasted a motion.

Within a very few minutes the first of the rollers lay across the new hole; then the second, and finally all four. The block was poised and in position; the hole was exactly the right size and shape. The rats had even dug out a new pantry-hole in one corner, and carved out the small tunnel that would connect the two rooms of the house.

The towers and the pulleys were put up again, and the whole process of lifting and lowering was done in reverse; the rollers were pulled away and the block was eased slowly into its new home.

"It's done!" cried Mrs. Frisby. She felt like applauding.

"Not quite yet," said Arthur over his shoulder. To the other rats he said: "Get the shovels and the backpacks."

Pausing a moment to rest, he explained to Mrs. Frisby: "We're going to cover it with turf, and then we've got to fill up the old hole with the dirt from the new one, or Mr. Fitzgibbon will wonder who's been digging up his garden. Also, we've still to dig you an entrance hole."

In her excitement Mrs. Frisby had forgotten this small detail. She could not get into her house. Now she watched in awe as Arthur and Brutus, using two small, sharp, long-handled shovels, dug the narrow tunnel down to her living room. It took them somewhat less than five minutes. It had taken her all day to dig the other one.

"Now," said Arthur, "you can put your children to bed. We'll take care of the rest."

At the Meeting

Mrs. Frisby slept well and soundly, the day just finished having been the longest and hardest she had ever known.

She awoke in the morning with a smile. Her house was warm, and it was safe at last. Her children slept peacefully beside her; Timothy's breathing was quiet and easy. They could stay in the house, now, as long as they needed to. On some warm day later in the spring, when Timothy was strong again, they would move to the summer house down by the brook. Another nice thing, she thought—when they left the house she would close up the entrance tunnel so that no one could find it; undisturbed by the plow, it would be ready and waiting for them in the fall. It could be theirs forever, thanks to the rats.

The rats! In her half-dreaming state she had forgotten. They were in terrible danger. What would they do? She felt as if she ought to go and offer to help them. But help how? She could think of nothing she could do.

At that moment she heard a voice calling her name from above.

"Mrs. Frisby."

She left the bed and went to the bottom of the entrance hole.

"Yes? Who's calling?"

"It's me, Brutus. Can you come up?"

Mrs. Frisby climbed up and out her front door, blinking in the early morning sunlight.

"Nicodemus wants to know if you can come with me. He's having a meeting."

"Just let me wake the children and tell them."

Two minutes later she was walking with Brutus toward the rosebush.

"What does Nicodemus want?"

"It's about the men. Justin told us last night. Nicodemus thinks they may be from Nimh. He wants to ask you more about what Mr. Fitzgibbon said."

That morning there were two rats on sentry duty—one just inside the entrance to the rosebush, watching Mr. Fitzgibbon's house, another at the arch where Brutus had stood. All of the rest were gathered in the large assembly room Mrs. Frisby had seen when she got off the elevator. Nicodemus, Justin, Arthur, and two other rats sat on the raised platform at the end. The rest sat facing them, filling every square inch of floor space except for an aisle up the center.

Mrs. Frisby had never seen so many rats. Even the young ones were present; she spotted Isabella, staring up at the platform with wide, round eyes. Some of the mothers held small babies at their sides. Most of them looked anxious; there was an air of tension, but none of panic.

Brutus led her up the center aisle to the raised platform. There was a table on it, covered with papers, and one vacant space, where a chair had been placed for Mrs. Frisby. The rats waited in complete silence while she sat down.

Then Nicodemus said, quite formally: "Justin has told us all that happened. Mrs. Frisby, it seems you have more than repaid us for the help we gave you in moving your house. Just as your husband did once, you have saved us from a disaster: Death or capture—we do not yet know which."

Justin gave her a wink. "Mrs. Frisby had a taste of capture herself last night."

"Would you tell us, as well as you can remember it, word for word what Mr. Fitzgibbon said—about the rats, about the men who were at the store?"

"As well as I can remember it." Mrs. Frisby's voice sounded small in the big room. "Mr. Fitzgibbon said a strange thing had happened in the hardware store—Henderson's, he called it."

Her memory was good; she had listened with great care to what Mr. Fitzgibbon had said, and she was able to recall the whole conversation word for word. The rats sat quietly while she told it.

Then Nicodemus went back over it, asking questions.

"You say that Mr. Fitzgibbon said six or seven rats. Did he ever say which number it really was?"

"No. I don't think he paid much attention to the number."

"Jenner's group was seven," said Justin. "But it could be a coincidence."

"Did he say how far away the town was where this happened? Or did he name it?"

"No. But it must not be very far. He'd been there and back that day."

"Did anyone see his car go out?" Nicodemus asked the others.

"I heard it," Brutus said. "I was on duty. It went after lunch."

"And he was back by dinner. But which direction? If we knew, we might send someone. You see," Nicodemus explained to Mrs. Frisby, "we need to know who those men are. If they're from Nimh, things are much worse for us."

"We'd never make it," said Arthur. "Driving at, say, forty or fifty miles an hour, Mr. Fitzgibbon might have gone fifteen or twenty miles in any direction, and returned easily the same afternoon. On the map"—there was a road map on the table—"you can see it could have been any one of a half a dozen small towns. And each of them might have a hardware store."

"You're right, of course," said Nicodemus. "Without the name, that idea is hopeless." He turned back to Mrs. Frisby. "Mr. Fitzgibbon said the rats were grouped around the motor 'as if they were trying to move it'?"

"That's what he said the store owner told him. He didn't see it himself."

"And that the motor was plugged in."

"'Had been left plugged in'," Mrs. Frisby quoted.

"But we don't know who plugged it in."

"I got the impression," Mrs. Frisby said, "from the way he said it, that the storeowner had left it plugged in. But I'm not sure."

"That would make sense," Arthur said. "If it was Jenner, and if they had plugged it in themselves, they'd have known better than to try to move it. So they must not have realized. It was probably pretty dark in the store."

"Poor Jenner," said Nicodemus. "I wish he had stayed with us."

"It will be poor us," said one of the rats at the table (Mrs. Frisby did not know his name), "if we don't get on with this."

"He did not mention the doctor's name," Nicodemus said. "Did he say even a word about what he looked like?"

"No."

"Did he describe the truck at all?"

"No. Only that it was full of equipment."

"Are you sure about the headline in the local paper: 'Mechanized Rats Invade Hardware Store'?"

"I'm sure that's what Mr. Fitzgibbon said. But I don't think he saw it. He didn't say so."

"In a way, that's the most puzzling thing about the whole story," Nicodemus said.

"Why is that? asked Justin.

"Because the headline doesn't really fit the facts. You don't call a bunch of dead rats mechanized just because you find them on a shelf near a motor."

"Maybe not," said the nameless rat. "But then why did the newspaper say that?"

"I'm wondering," Nicodemus said, "if perhaps there wasn't more to the story. Some stronger reason to think they were really taking the motor away, or that they knew how to use it."

"Maybe some other motors had been stolen," Justin said. "Or some tools. That would make them seem mechanized."

"It would," said Nicodemus. "And it would explain what the doctor meant when he said they had more checking to do in town."

"They're looking for the things that were missing," Arthur said, sounding suddenly worried. "They're looking for Jenner's headquarters. And if they find it . . ."

"We're just guessing, of course," Nicodemus said. "But it's a possibility."

"And a bad one."

"It means," Nicodemus continued, "that we

have no choice. We've got to assume they're from Nimh. We've also got to assume that by now they may have found Jenner's headquarters — whatever cave or cavern they were using."

"And," said Justin, "that now they're looking for us."

"Why for us?" asked one of the rats. "Why wouldn't they think Jenner's group are the only ones?"

"They might," Nicodemus admitted, "but I don't think so. After all, they know that there were twenty of us originally. Why should there be only seven now? And we already know that they're coming out here — in quite a hurry at that. So if they're from Nimh, obviously they *are* looking for us."

"I think," said Arthur, "that we've got to make some plans, and quickly."

"I agree," said Nicodemus. "It's a new situation, and a tricky one. We won't be able to do everything we hoped to. There isn't time. And somehow we have to convince the exterminators, when they come, that we aren't more of the mechanized rats they're looking for.

"We won't be able to move any more food to Thorn Valley," Nicodemus continued. "We'll have to get along on what we've already got stored there — about an eighteen-month supply, if we're careful. The seeds, I believe, are already moved."

"Yes," said Arthur. "The last load went yesterday."

"So with luck, we'll have our own first crops this summer and fall.

"We won't have time to destroy the motors, or the books, or the furniture as we planned. Instead, we'll move everything to the cave. And then we'll seal off all entrances to the cave as if it had never existed."

"That can be done," Arthur said.

"But there's more: We've got to pull all the wires and lights from the tunnel—they're likely to dig it up. And the carpet. We've got to tear down the arch.

"Then, when all that's done, when everything is hidden in the cave, we'll fill in the stairway and the elevator shaft. We'll seal off everything except the upper storage room and the tunnels leading in the front and out the back.

"When they dig, let them find that room. It's as big as an ordinary rat hole.

"Justin, tonight, take a group of a dozen or so. Go to the Fitzgibbons' garbage can. Bring back a load of the worst-smelling garbage you can find. The storage room is going to become an ordinary, typical rat hole, not in the least mechanized or civilized."

Nicodemus turned to Arthur: "What do you think?"

"I think we can do it all. We won't get much sleep, though."

Justin said: "But there's one more thing. Won't they think it's odd — especially if they're from Nimh — finding just an empty hole?"

Nicodemus said: "I was coming to that." He sounded suddenly very tired. "Tomorrow morning, as soon as it's light, the main group leaves for Thorn Valley. But some of us will have to stay behind. As Justin says, if they find just an empty hole, they're sure to be suspicious, and they'll keep on digging. So when they come with their gas truck, they've got to find some rats here. A rear guard. I'd say at least ten."

Mrs. Frisby walked slowly home, keeping to the edge of the woods, keeping out of sight.

Justin had instantly volunteered for the rear guard. Brutus was second, and behind him, eight more; there were fifty more waiting behind them. "Enough, enough," said Nicodemus. Isabella, in tears, had run forward. "I *want* to stay, *please*," she had pleaded, looking despairingly at Justin. "No children," said Nicodemus, and her mother led her away, still weeping.

Those ten, the ten who would remain, did not face certain death, nor certain capture. The exterminators (they presumed) would make noise, especially if they cleared away the rosebush. The rats would be alerted. When the men pumped gas (as expected) into the hole, the pump would also make a noise; the air below would move as the gas flowed in. When they felt that, the rats would scramble out the back exit, past the sealed off cave, emerge as noisily as possible in the blackberry bramble—indeed, show themselves—and dash off into the woods.

"But won't they block the rear exit?"

"Or put a net over it?"

"We'll give them another rear exit to block," Arthur had said cryptically. "One that's easier to find."

"Mother, why are you so quiet?" asked Teresa. They were sitting down to dinner for the first time in their newly moved house. "You seem sad."

"I suppose I am," Mrs. Frisby said. "Because the rats are all going away."

"But that's no reason. It's true, they moved our house and that was nice of them. But we didn't really know them."

"I was getting to know them pretty well."

"Where are they going?" Cynthia asked.

"To a new home, a long way away."

"When?"

"Tomorrow morning."

"Will you go to see them off?"

"I think I will."

"But why are they moving away?" asked Timothy.

"Because they want to," said Mrs. Frisby. Someday soon she would tell them the whole story. But not that night.

The Doctor

The next morning Mr. Fitzgibbon started the larger of his two tractors, the huge one he kept in the barn, the one that pulled the combine in the fall harvest. With help from Paul and Billy, he bolted the big bulldozer blade to the front of it, rumbled it up through the barnyard gate and stopped it near the rosebush.

"We'll wait until they come," he said, turning off the engine.

Mrs. Frisby could not bear to watch; and yet, even more, she could not bear not to watch. She knew there was nothing to be gained by it, nothing she could do. Yet how could she stay at home when the ten rats, including Justin and Brutus, were waiting bravely underground? She could not.

She thought at first of her watch-hole in the corner post. Then she decided against it. Nearer to the rosebush, on the edge of the woods, stood a hickory tree, its scaly bark like a ladder inviting her to climb. Ten feet up on this tree a large branch jutted straight out. On this branch, up close to the trunk, she had a vantage point from which, herself unseen, she could look down on the rosebush and also see into the woods to a blackberry bramble where, though she had never been in it, she was sure the rats' rear exit must be hidden. She settled down to wait. It was a chilly morning, with a damp breeze and a gray mist that blew by in patches.

Somewhere near the middle of the morning a square white truck came into the driveway. It went first to the house. A man in a white coverall uniform climbed out and knocked on the Fitzgibbons' door; it was too far away for Mrs. Frisby to hear the knock, or to hear what the man said when Mrs. Fitzgibbon came out on the porch. But ten seconds later Billy ran from the house to the barn, where Mr. Fitzgibbon was working. The man returned to the truck and waited, standing outside the open cab door. Through the windshield she could see that two more men sat in the front seat, and that one of them wore horn-rimmed glasses.

Now Mr. Fitzgibbon approached the truck, Billy dancing beside him, apparently in some ex-

citement. There was a conference, none of which
Mrs. Frisby could hear, accompanied by gestures
toward the rosebush and the waiting bulldozer.
The man in white climbed back into the driver's
seat and drove the truck across the grass. He
backed it up beside the bulldozer, stopping perhaps ten feet from the bush. Mrs. Frisby stared at
it. If there was anything printed on it, it must be
on the other side, away from her. Then three
men climbed out, and she could hear what they
said.

"It's a big one, all right," said one of the men.
"And look at those thorns. It's hard to see how
even a rat could get in there."

The man in the horn-rims walked around the
edge of the bush, examining it closely. He bent
over.

"Look at this," he said. "There's the entrance
hole, very neatly hidden. And look behind it — a
path leading in."

He turned to Mr. Fitzgibbon, who had walked
up with Billy.

"You were right. You'll need to bulldoze it. It
would take us all day to hack our way in there.
But cut it off just at the surface if you can. If you
dig too deep and open the hole, they'll get
away."

He added: "You better tell the boy to keep

back. We'll be using cyanide, and it's dangerous."

Billy, after some argument, was dispatched to the back porch, where Mrs. Fitzgibbon was also watching.

One of the men had walked around to the far side of the bush, the side near Mrs. Frisby's tree.

"Doc," he called, "here's another entrance in the bush, and there's a hole just inside it."

"Doc" was the man in the horn-rims. He was a doctor. Mrs. Frisby thought: Doctor Somebody. He was in charge.

"Can you get at it?" he asked.

"Not very well. Too many thorns."

The man who was a doctor walked around and looked at it. "No," he said. "Anyway, that would be the escape hatch. We'll find the main hole nearer the middle of the bush."

He turned to Mr. Fitzgibbon, who had mounted the tractor. "Okay," said the doctor. "Can you push it that way—away from the shed?"

Mr. Fitzgibbon nodded, and the motor started with a roar. He pulled a lever and flexed the heavy steel blade up and down, bringing the bottom edge to rest just even with the ground. The blade was fully eight feet across. He pulled another lever; the wheels, with cleated tires as tall as windows, dug in and the blade scraped forward.

The bush fought back, then yielded angrily, snapping and crackling before the inexorable thrust of steel. A single sweep, and a third of it lay, a writhing heap of thorns, in a pile twenty feet away. The ground trembled under the wheels, and Mrs. Frisby thought of the ten rats huddled below. Supposing the weight collapsed the earth, caved in the storage room and trapped them? Another sweep, and a third. Only a thorny stubble now stood where the bush has been. On the porch Mrs. Fitzgibbon covered her eyes with her hands, and Billy cheered in excitement.

Plainly exposed were two holes—simple, round rat holes. There was no trace of the small mound nor the elegant arched entrance. Arthur had done his work thoroughly. Mrs. Frisby wondered for a moment at the second hole. Then she remembered his saying: "We'll give them another rear exit to block." Of course! They had dug another hole, most likely, she thought, just a dummy, leading nowhere.

The men in the white suits went into action. The back doors of the truck were opened and a long, flexible pipe unrolled. It looked like a fire hose, except that at the end, instead of a nozzle, there was a round plunger like a big rubber ball cut in half. One of the men donned a mask with a glass visor and a tube that ran to a pack on his back. A gas mask.

The masked man pulled the hose over to the center rat hole and pressed the plunger over it, covering it completely.

From the back of the truck the other two took a large box made of wood and wire, almost a yard wide, and placed it over the second hole. It was a cage, but half of its bottom was a trapdoor, neatly mounted on hinges. This they raised, placing the open part directly over the opening in the earth. Then they backed away, one of them holding a trip cord which would close the trapdoor after the rats were inside.

"All set?" The doctor called to the man in the mask.

The mask nodded.

"Keep back, now," said the doctor to Mr. Fitzgibbon, who had left his tractor to watch. He walked to the truck, reached inside, and turned a switch. Mrs. Frisby heard the soft throb of a pump. Now.

She turned and watched the blackberry bramble in the woods. Would they hear the pump? Where were they? Oh, *let* them come out. Almost a minute passed. The men in white watched the trap. Nothing moved.

Then she saw it. Behind the bramble, half-hidden by a swirl of mist, a gray-brown shape, a rat, shaking dirt from his ears. Another. Then three more. They huddled in silence, waiting. More. How many? Ten? Seven. Only seven. Where were the other three? Still they waited.

Then, as if by agreement, they stopped waiting. They ran. All seven of them, not back into the woods to safety, but out of the woods, toward the stubble of the rosebush, toward the men. At the edge of the bush, they stopped as if in confusion, ran to the left, ran to the right, then fled back into the woods again. Now they were out of sight of the men, but not of Mrs. Frisby. Instantly they regrouped behind the blackberry bramble and charged out again—but this time in smaller numbers: first two, then three, then two again. She saw what they were up to. They were not in the least confused; they were making seven rats look like twenty rats, or forty, a steady stream of them. In the mist, in the hectic turning, running, turning, hiding, she could not tell whether or not she recognized any of them.

The men shouted:

"Look at that!"

"A pack of them!"

"How did they get out?"

"Get the nets!"

The doctor turned off the pump; the man with

the hose pulled off his mask. As a new wave of rats danced along the edge of the clearing all three men ran to the truck and from it pulled long-handled nets.

But Mrs. Frisby, up on her branch, was staring at the blackberry bush again. She saw something that all of the others, including the rats, did not see. An eighth rat had come out. He emerged running, but then he stumbled; he got up and ran again, this time more slowly, circling vaguely to the right. He did not seem to know where he was going. He reached a sparse thicket of saplings almost out of her sight, and there, abruptly, he fell over on his side and lay still.

Meanwhile all three men, holding their nets low, ran across the stubble toward the parade of rats. But as they approached the parade it vanished; the rats, their purpose accomplished, melted into the misty woods, and this time they did not reappear. Mrs. Frisby watched them as they loped away swiftly in single file and disappeared from her view, back into the deep forest and up the mountainside. The rear guard was gone, bound for Thorn Valley.

But the eighth rat still lay unmoving among the saplings. And two had never come out at all.

"They're gone," said the man who had worn the mask. "They fooled us."

"What happened?" asked Mr. Fitzgibbon.

"Simple enough," said the doctor. "They had two escape holes, and they used the other one." He walked back to the blackberry bramble and bent down, kicking the branches aside with his foot. "Here it is," he said. "Quite a long tunnel. One of the longest I've seen."

To the other two men he said: "Get the pick and the shovels."

For half an hour they dug, laying open a narrow trench along the tunnel. From her angle of view in the tree, Mrs. Frisby could see only the top of this trench, and not down into the bottom. Still she watched, saying to herself, perhaps, after all, there were only eight, maybe they decided that eight would be enough.

Then one of the shovels broke through into air; they had come to the rats' storage room.

"There's two of them," said one of the men, and her heart sank. Who were they? She wanted to run and look, but she did not dare.

"Careful," said the doctor. "There may still be some gas in there. Let the wind blow it out."

"Phew," said one of the men. "That's not gas, that's garbage."

"Open it up a little more," said the doctor.

One of the men wielded his shovel for another minute, and then the doctor peered in.

"Garbage," he said. "Last night's dinner. Garbage and two dead rats." Mrs. Frisby thought: He sounds disappointed.

"Only two?" said Mr. Fitzgibbon.

"Yes. It's easy to see what happened. In a hole this size there would have been a couple of dozen at least. But these two must have been up at the front, near the tunnel. They got a whiff of the gas, and it killed them. But before they died, they must have warned the others. So the rest ran out."

"Warned them?" said Mr. Fitzgibbon. "Could they do that?"

"Yes," said the doctor. "They're intelligent animals. Some can do a great deal more than that." But he did not elaborate; instead he turned to one of the men. "We might as well take these two back with us."

From the truck the man produced a white paper sack and a pair of plastic gloves. He pulled the gloves on, reached into the hole and placed the two dead rats into the sack. He did this with his back to Mrs. Frisby, so that she never got even a glimpse of them.

"All right," said the doctor. "Let's close it up." They shoveled the dirt back into the trench and returned to the truck.

"You'll let me know if they have rabies?" said Mr. Fitzgibbon.

"Rabies?" said the doctor. "Yes, of course. But I doubt it. They look perfectly healthy."

Perfectly healthy, thought Mrs. Frisby sadly, except for being dead. She looked into the woods, over toward the saplings where the other rat lay. Was he, too, now dead? To her surprise, she saw that he was moving. Or was he? In the mist it was hard to tell. But something had moved.

After the truck had left Mr. Fitzgibbon stood looking at the ruin of the rosebush. He seemed vaguely puzzled and disappointed; he must be wondering, she thought, whether it has been worth it, just to exterminate two rats. He had no way of knowing, of course, that all the rest were also gone and would not return, that his grain loft was safe. In a moment he turned and walked to the house.

As soon as he was safely gone Mrs. Frisby scurried down from her tree and into the woods. On the ground she could no longer see the rat or the thicket where he lay, but she knew the direction, and she ran. Around a stump, over a mound of leaves, past a cedar tree—there were the saplings and there lay the rat, still on his side.

It was Brutus. Beside him, futilely trying to move him, stood Mr. Ages.

She reached him, breathless from her run.

"Is he dead?"

"No. He's unconscious, but he's alive and breathing. I think he'll revive if I can just get him to swallow this." Mr. Ages indicated a small corked bottle, no bigger than a thimble, on the ground beside them.

"What is it?"

"An antidote for the poison. We thought this might happen, so we got it ready last night. He got just a little of the gas, made it this far, and then collapsed. Help me lift his head."

Mr. Ages had been unable to lift Brutus's head and the bottle at the same time. Now, with Mrs. Frisby's help, he forced open Brutus's mouth and poured in just a few drops of the smokey liquid the bottle contained. In a few seconds Brutus made a gulping noise, swallowed hard, and spoke.

"It's dark," he said. "I can't see."

"Open your eyes," said Mr. Ages.

Brutus opened them and looked around.

"I'm out," he said. "How did I get here?"

"Don't you remember?"

"No. Wait. Yes. I was in the hole. I smelled gas, an awful, choking, sweet smell. I tried to run, but I stumbled over somebody lying on the floor, and I fell down. I must have breathed some of the gas. I couldn't get up."

"And then?"

"I heard the others running past me. I couldn't see them. It was darker than night. Then one of them ran into me, and stopped. He pulled me up, and I tried to run again. But I was too dizzy. I kept falling. The other one helped me up again, and I went a few steps more. He kept pulling me, and then pushing, and somehow, finally, I got to the end of the tunnel. I saw daylight, and the air smelled better. But there was nobody else there; I thought the others must have left. So I ran a little farther, and that's all I remember."

Mrs. Frisby said: "What about the one who helped you?"

"I don't know who it was. I couldn't see, and he didn't speak at all. I suppose he was trying to hold his breath.

"When we got near the end, and I could see daylight, he gave me one last shove toward it, and then he turned back."

"He went back?"

"Yes. You see, there was still one rat back in there—the one I stumbled over. I think he went back to help that one."

"Whoever he was," said Mrs. Frisby, "he never came out. He died in there."

"Whoever he was," said Mr. Ages, "he was brave."

Epilogue

A few days later, in the morning, the plow
came through the garden. Mrs. Frisby heard the
chug of the tractor and the soft scrape of the steel
against the earth. She watched from just inside
her front door, fearfully at first, but then with
growing confidence. The owl and the rats had
calculated wisely, and the nearest furrow was
more than two feet from her house.

Behind the plow, in the moist and shining soil
the rudely-upturned red-brown earthworms
writhed in a frenzy to rebury themselves; hopping along each furrow a flock of spring robins
tried to catch them before they slid from sight.
And when the plowing was done and the worms
had all disappeared, either eaten or safely underground, Mr. Fitzgibbon came back with the harrow, breaking down the furrows, and turned
them all up again. It was a good day for the robins.

After the harrow; for the next two days came the Fitzgibbons themselves, all four of them with hoes and bags of seeds, planting lettuce, beans, spinach, potatoes, corn, and mustard greens. Mrs. Frisby and her family kept out of sight. Thoughtfully, Brutus and Arthur had dug their doorway behind a tuft of grass, so that not even Billy noticed it.

Brutus and Arthur. Mrs. Fitzgibbon did not suppose she would ever see either of them again, nor Nicodemus, nor any of the others. Brutus, after swallowing Mr. Ages' medicine and resting for half an hour, had gone on his way into the forest to join the colony in Thorn Valley. There was no talk of their coming back, unless their attempt to grow their own food should fail—and she did not believe that would happen; they were too smart. And even if they did fail, they would probably not come back to Mr. Fitzgibbon's farm.

She thought that it would be pleasant to visit them and see their new home, their small lake and their crops growing. But she had no idea where the valley was, and it would be, in any case, too long a journey for her and the children. So she could only wonder about them: Were they, at that moment, like the Fitzgibbons, planting seeds behind their own plow? Some (like Isabella's mother) might grumble about the hardness of the new life they had chosen. Yet the story of what had happened to Jenner and his friends (if it *was* Jenner and his friends), to say nothing of the destruction of their own home, would surely help to convince them that Nicodemus's ideas were right.

The Fitzgibbons finished their planting, and for a week or two all was quiet. But it would not stay that way. The crops would appear, the asparagus was ready to sprout, and for the rest of the spring and summer the garden would be too busy a place for mice to live in comfortably.

So on a day in May as warm as summer, early in the morning, Mrs. Frisby and her children laid a patchwork of sticks, grass, and leaves over the top of the entrance to their cinder block house, and then carefully scraped earth over it so that it would not show. With luck, they would not have to dig a new one in the fall.

They walked to their summer house, taking half a day to do it, strolling slowly and enjoying the fine weather, stopping on the way to eat some new spring leaves of field cress, some young poke greens and a crisp, spicy mushroom that had sprouted by the edge of the woods. For their main course, a little farther on, there was a whole field of winter wheat, its kernels newly ripe and soft.

As they approached the brook, toward the big

tree in the hollow of whose roots they would make their summer home, the children ran ahead, shouting and laughing. Timothy ran with them, and Mrs. Frisby was glad to see that he showed no trace of his sickness. It was an exciting time for them. In the garden they were always alone with themselves, but along the bank of the brook in summer lived five other mice families, all with children. Within a few minutes of arrival, her four had gone with a group of the others down to the water to see the tadpoles swim.

Mrs. Frisby set about the job of tidying up the house, which had acquired a carpet of dead leaves during the winter, and then bringing in a pile of soft green moss to serve as bedding for them all. The house was a roomy chamber with a pleasant, earthy smell. Its floor was hard-packed dirt, and its wooden roof was an arched intertwining of roots, above which rose the tree itself, an oak.

On her way to get the moss she saw one of her neighbors, a lady mouse named Janice who, like herself, had four children. Janice ran over to talk to her.

"You're so late getting here," she said. "We all thought something must have happened to you."

"No," said Mrs. Frisby, "we're all fine."

"But don't you live in the garden?" Janice persisted. "I should have thought you'd be afraid of the plowing."

"As a matter of fact," Mrs. Frisby explained, "they didn't plow the particular spot in the garden where we live. It's behind a boulder."

"You were lucky."

"That's true." More than that Mrs. Frisby did not tell; she had agreed to keep a secret, and she would do as she had said.

Still, she thought after quite a long deliberation, it was probably all right to tell her children, first making them promise to keep it secret. They were, after all, the children of Jonathan Frisby. For all she knew, and for all Nicodemus knew, they were likely to turn out to be quite different from other mice, and they had a right to know the reason.

The following evening, therefore, when they

had finished an early supper, she gathered them around her.

"Children, I have a story to tell you. A long one."

"Oh, good!" cried Cynthia. "What kind of story?"

"A true one. About your father and about the rats."

"How can it be about Father *and* the rats?" Teresa asked.

"Because he was a friend of theirs."

"He was?" said Martin incredulously. "I never knew that."

"It was mostly before you were born."

To everyone's surprise, Timothy said, "I thought he might be. I think Mr. Ages was, too."

"How did you know that?"

"I didn't know it. I just thought it. A couple of times I saw Mr. Ages leaving their rosebush. And I knew that Father used to visit him a lot. But I never saw him near the rosebush."

Probably, Mrs. Frisby thought, because he would have been careful always to leave through the blackberry bramble, just so we would not see him.

They sat down outside the entrance to the house, and beginning at the beginning, with her first visit to the rats, she told them all that she had seen and done, and all that Nicodemus had told her. It took a long time to tell it, and as she talked the sun sank low, turning the sky red and lighting the tops of the mountains, beyond which, somewhere, the rats of Nimh were living.

The children's eyes grew round when she told them about the escape from Nimh, and even rounder when she described her own capture and escape from the birdcage. But in the end the eyes of Teresa and Cynthia were filled with tears, and Martin and Timothy looked sad.

Teresa said: "But Mother, that's terrible. It must have been Justin. He saved Brutus and then went back. And he was so nice."

Mrs. Frisby said: "It may have been Justin. We can't be sure. It could have been one of the others."

Martin said: "I'm going to find out. I'm going to go to the Thorn Valley, somehow, someday."

"But it's too far. And you don't know where it is."

"No. But I'll bet Jeremy knows. Remember, he told you the rats had a clearing back in the hills. That must be in Thorn Valley." He thought about this for a minute. Then he added: "He might even fly me there on his back, the way he did you."

"But we don't know where Jeremy is, either.

267

We don't see the crows down here," Mrs. Frisby reminded him.

"No, but in the fall, when we go back to the garden—I could find him then. If I got something shiny and put it out in the sun, he'd come to get it." Martin was growing excited at his idea. "Oh, Mother, *may* I?"

"I don't know. I doubt that the rats will want visitors from the outside."

"They wouldn't mind. After all, you helped them, and so did Father. And I wouldn't do any harm."

"It's not something we have to decide tonight," said Mrs. Frisby. "I'll think about it. And now it's late. It's time for bed."

The sun had set. They went into the house and lay down on the soft moss Mrs. Frisby had placed on the floor of their room under the roots. Outside, the brook swam quietly through the woods, and up above them the warm wind blew through the newly opened leaves of the big oak tree. They went to sleep.

THE PLOT
AGAINST AMERICA

In 1998 Philip Roth won the Pulitzer Prize for *American Pastoral* and received the National Medal of Arts at the White House. In 2002 he received the highest award of the American Academy of Arts and Letters, the Gold Medal in Fiction, previously awarded to John Dos Passos, William Faulkner, and Saul Bellow, among others. He has twice won the National Book Award, the PEN/Faulkner Award, and the National Book Critics Circle Award.

In 2005 Philip Roth will become the third living American writer to have his work published in a comprehensive, definitive edition by the Library of America. The last of the eight volumes is scheduled for publication in 2013.

ALSO BY PHILIP ROTH

Zuckerman Books

The Ghost Writer
Zuckerman Unbound
The Anatomy Lesson
The Prague Orgy

The Counterlife

American Pastoral
I Married a Communist
The Human Stain

Roth Books

The Facts
Deception
Patrimony
Operation Shylock

Kepesh Books

The Breast
The Professor of Desire
The Dying Animal

Miscellany

Reading Myself and Others
Shop Talk

Other Books

Goodbye, Columbus
Letting Go
When She Was Good
Portnoy's Complaint
Our Gang
The Great American Novel
My Life as a Man
Sabbath's Theater

Philip Roth

THE PLOT
AGAINST AMERICA

V

VINTAGE

Published by Vintage 2005

2 4 6 8 10 9 7 5 3 1

Copyright © Philip Roth 2004

Philip Roth has asserted his right under the Copyright, Designs and
Patents Act, 1988 to be identified as the author of this work

First published in Great Britain in 2004 by
Jonathan Cape

Speech by Charles Lindberg, 'Who Are the War Agitators?',
copyright 1941, reprinted with permission of
The Des Moines Register

Vintage
Random House, 20 Vauxhall Bridge Road,
London SW1V 2SA

Random House Australia (Pty) Limited
20 Alfred Street, Milsons Point, Sydney
New South Wales 2061, Australia

Random House New Zealand Limited
18 Poland Road, Glenfield, Auckland 10,
New Zealand

Random House South Africa (Pty) Limited
Endulini, 5A Jubilee Road, Parktown 2193,
South Africa

The Random House Group Limited Reg. No. 954009
www.randomhouse.co.uk/vintage

A CIP catalogue record for this book
is available from the British Library

ISBN 0 09 947856 0

Papers used by Random House are natural, recyclable products
made from wood grown in sustainable forests. The manufacturing
processes conform to the environ-mental regulations of the country
of origin

Book design by Robert Overholtzer

Printed and bound in Great Britain by
Bookmarque Ltd, Croydon, Surrey

To S.F.R.

CONTENTS

8

October 1942
Bad Days · 287

9

October 1942
Perpetual Fear · 328

Postscript

1

June 1940–October 1940

Vote for Lindbergh
or Vote for War

EAR PRESIDES over these memories, a perpetual fear. Of course no childhood is without its terrors, yet I wonder if I would have been a less frightened boy if Lindbergh hadn't been president or if I hadn't been the offspring of Jews.

When the first shock came in June of 1940—the nomination for the presidency of Charles A. Lindbergh, America's international aviation hero, by the Republican Convention at Philadelphia—my father was thirty-nine, an insurance agent with a grade school education, earning a little under fifty dollars a week, enough for the basic bills to be paid on time but for little more. My mother—who'd wanted to go to teachers' college but couldn't because of the expense, who'd lived at home working as an office secretary after finishing high school, who'd kept us from feeling poor during the worst of the Depression by budgeting the earnings my father turned over to her each Friday as efficiently as she ran the household—was thirty-six. My brother, Sandy, a seventh-grader with a prodigy's talent for drawing, was twelve, and I, a third-grader a term ahead of himself—and an embryonic stamp collector inspired like millions of kids by the country's foremost philatelist, President Roosevelt—was seven.

We lived in the second-floor flat of a small two-and-a-half-family house on a tree-lined street of frame wooden houses with red-brick stoops, each stoop topped with a gable roof and fronted by a tiny yard boxed in with a low-cut hedge. The Weequahic neighborhood had been built on farm lots at the undeveloped southwest edge of Newark just after World War One, some half dozen of the streets named, imperially, for victorious naval commanders in the Spanish-American War and the local movie house called, after FDR's fifth cousin—and the country's twenty-sixth president—the Roosevelt. Our street, Summit Avenue, sat at the crest of the neighborhood hill, an elevation as high as any in a port city that rarely rises a hundred feet above the level of the tidal salt marsh to the city's north and east and the deep bay due east of the airport that bends around the oil tanks of the Bayonne peninsula and merges there with New York Bay to flow past the Statue of Liberty and into the Atlantic. Looking west from our bedroom's rear window we could sometimes see inland as far as the dark treeline of the Watchungs, a low-lying mountain range fringed by great estates and affluent, sparsely populated suburbs, the extreme edge of the known world—and about eight miles from our house. A block to the south was the working-class town of Hillside, whose population was predominantly Gentile. The boundary with Hillside marked the beginning of Union County, another New Jersey entirely.

We were a happy family in 1940. My parents were outgoing, hospitable people, their friends culled from among my father's associates at the office and from the women who along with my mother had helped to organize the Parent-Teacher Association at newly built Chancellor Avenue School, where my brother and I were pupils. All were Jews. The neighborhood men either were in business for themselves—the owners of the local candy store, grocery store, jewelry store, dress shop, furniture shop, service station, and delicatessen, or the proprietors of tiny industrial job shops over by the Newark-Irvington line, or self-employed plumbers, electricians, housepainters, and boilermen—or were foot-soldier salesmen like my father, out every day in the city streets and in people's

houses, peddling their wares on commission. The Jewish doctors
and lawyers and the successful merchants who owned big stores
downtown lived in one-family houses on streets branching off
the eastern slope of the Chancellor Avenue hill, closer to grassy,
wooded Weequahic Park, a landscaped three hundred acres whose
boating lake, golf course, and harness-racing track separated the
Weequahic section from the industrial plants and shipping termi-
nals lining Route 27 and the Pennsylvania Railroad viaduct east of
that and the burgeoning airport east of that and the very edge of
America east of that—the depots and docks of Newark Bay, where
they unloaded cargo from around the world. At the western end of
the neighborhood, the parkless end where we lived, there resided
an occasional schoolteacher or pharmacist but otherwise few professionals were among our immediate neighbors and certainly
none of the prosperous entrepreneurial or manufacturing families.
The men worked fifty, sixty, even seventy or more hours a week;
the women worked all the time, with little assistance from labor-
saving devices, washing laundry, ironing shirts, mending socks,
turning collars, sewing on buttons, mothproofing woolens, polish-
ing furniture, sweeping and washing floors, washing windows,
cleaning sinks, tubs, toilets, and stoves, vacuuming rugs, nursing
the sick, shopping for food, cooking meals, feeding relatives, tidying closets and drawers, overseeing paint jobs and household repairs, arranging for religious observances, paying bills and keeping the family's books while simultaneously attending to their
children's health, clothing, cleanliness, schooling, nutrition, conduct, birthdays, discipline, and morale. A few women labored
alongside their husbands in the family-owned stores on the nearby
shopping streets, assisted after school and on Saturdays by their
older children, who delivered orders and tended stock and did the
cleaning up.

It was work that identified and distinguished our neighbors for
me far more than religion. Nobody in the neighborhood had a
beard or dressed in the antiquated Old World style or wore a skull-
cap either outdoors or in the houses I routinely floated through

with my boyhood friends. The adults were no longer observant in the outward, recognizable ways, if they were seriously observant at all, and aside from older shopkeepers like the tailor and the kosher butcher—and the ailing or decrepit grandparents living of necessity with their adult offspring—hardly anyone in the vicinity spoke with an accent. By 1940 Jewish parents and their children at the southwestern corner of New Jersey's largest city talked to one another in an American English that sounded more like the language spoken in Altoona or Binghamton than like the dialects famously spoken across the Hudson by our Jewish counterparts in the five boroughs. Hebrew lettering was stenciled on the butcher shop window and engraved on the lintels of the small neighborhood synagogues, but nowhere else (other than at the cemetery) did one's eye chance to land on the alphabet of the prayer book rather than on the familiar letters of the native tongue employed all the time by practically everyone for every conceivable purpose, high or low. At the newsstand out front of the corner candy store, ten times more customers bought the *Racing Form* than the Yiddish daily, the *Forvertz.*

Israel didn't yet exist, six million European Jews hadn't yet ceased to exist, and the local relevance of distant Palestine (under British mandate since the 1918 dissolution by the victorious Allies of the last far-flung provinces of the defunct Ottoman Empire) was a mystery to me. When a stranger who did wear a beard and who never once was seen hatless appeared every few months after dark to ask in broken English for a contribution toward the establishment of a Jewish national homeland in Palestine, I, who wasn't an ignorant child, didn't quite know what he was doing on our landing. My parents would give me or Sandy a couple of coins to drop into his collection box, largess, I always thought, dispensed out of kindness so as not to hurt the feelings of a poor old man who, from one year to the next, seemed unable to get it through his head that we'd already had a homeland for three generations. I pledged allegiance to the flag of our homeland every morning at school. I sang of its marvels with my classmates at assembly programs. I eagerly observed its national holidays, and without giving a second thought to my affinity for the Fourth of July fireworks or the Thanksgiving turkey or the Decoration Day double-header. Our homeland was America.

Then the Republicans nominated Lindbergh and everything changed.

For nearly a decade Lindbergh was as great a hero in our neighborhood as he was everywhere else. The completion of his thirty-three-and-a-half-hour nonstop solo flight from Long Island to Paris in the tiny monoplane the *Spirit of St. Louis* even happened to coincide with the day in the spring of 1927 that my mother discovered herself to be pregnant with my older brother. As a consequence, the young aviator whose daring had thrilled America and the world and whose achievement bespoke a future of unimaginable aeronautical progress came to occupy a special niche in the gallery of family anecdotes that generate a child's first cohesive mythology. The mystery of pregnancy and the heroism of Lindbergh combined to give a distinction bordering on the divine to my very own mother, for whom nothing less than a global annunciation had accompanied the incarnation of her first child. Sandy would later record this moment with a drawing illustrating the juxtaposition of those two splendid events. In the drawing—completed at the age of nine and smacking inadvertently of Soviet poster art—Sandy envisioned her miles from our house, amid a joyous crowd on the corner of Broad and Market. A slender young woman of twenty-three with dark hair and a smile that is all robust delight, she is surprisingly on her own and wearing her floral-patterned kitchen apron at the intersection of the city's two busiest thoroughfares, one hand spread wide across the front of the apron, where the span of her hips is still deceptively girlish, while with the other she alone in the crowd is pointing skyward to the *Spirit of St. Louis,* passing visibly above downtown Newark at precisely the moment she comes to realize that, in a feat no less triumphant for a mortal than Lindbergh's, she has conceived Sanford Roth.

Sandy was four and I, Philip, wasn't yet born when in March 1932, Charles and Anne Morrow Lindbergh's own first child, a boy whose arrival twenty months earlier had been an occasion for national rejoicing, was kidnapped from his family's secluded new house in rural Hopewell, New Jersey. Some ten weeks later the decomposing body of the baby was discovered by chance in woods a few miles away. The baby had been either murdered or killed accidentally after being snatched from his crib and, in the dark, still in bedclothes, carried out a window of the second-story nursery and down a makeshift ladder to the ground while the nurse and mother were occupied in their ordinary evening activities in another part of the house. By the time the kidnapping and murder trial in Flemington, New Jersey, concluded in February 1935 with the conviction of Bruno Hauptmann—a German ex-con of thirty-five living in the Bronx with his German wife—the boldness of the world's first transatlantic solo pilot had been permeated with a pathos that transformed him into a martyred titan comparable to Lincoln.

Following the trial, the Lindberghs left America, hoping through a temporary expatriation to protect a new Lindbergh infant from harm and to recover some measure of the privacy they coveted. The family moved to a small village in England, and from there, as a private citizen, Lindbergh began taking the trips to Nazi Germany that would transform him into a villain for most American Jews. In the course of five visits, during which he was able to familiarize himself at first hand with the magnitude of the German war machine, he was ostentatiously entertained by Air Marshal Göring, he was ceremoniously decorated in the name of the Führer, and he expressed quite openly his high regard for Hitler, calling Germany the world's "most interesting nation" and its leader "a great man." And all this interest and admiration *after* Hitler's 1935 racial laws had denied Germany's Jews their civil, social, and property rights, nullified their citizenship, and forbidden intermarriage with Aryans.

By the time I began school in 1938, Lindbergh's was a name that provoked the same sort of indignation in our house as did the weekly Sunday radio broadcasts of Father Coughlin, the Detroit-area priest who edited a right-wing weekly called *Social Justice* and whose anti-Semitic virulence aroused the passions of a sizable audience during the country's hard times. It was in November 1938—the darkest, most ominous year for the Jews of Europe in eighteen centuries—that the worst pogrom in modern history, *Kristall-nacht*, was instigated by the Nazis all across Germany: synagogues incinerated, the residences and businesses of Jews destroyed, and, throughout a night presaging the monstrous future, Jews by the thousands forcibly taken from their homes and transported to concentration camps. When it was suggested to Lindbergh that in response to this unprecedented savagery, perpetrated by a state on its own native-born, he might consider returning the gold cross decorated with four swastikas bestowed on him in behalf of the Führer by Air Marshal Göring, he declined on the grounds that for him to publicly surrender the Service Cross of the German Eagle would constitute "an unnecessary insult" to the Nazi leadership.

Lindbergh was the first famous living American whom I learned to hate—just as President Roosevelt was the first famous living American whom I was taught to love—and so his nomination by the Republicans to run against Roosevelt in 1940 assaulted, as nothing ever had before, that huge endowment of personal security that I had taken for granted as an American child of American parents in an American school in an American city in an America at peace with the world.

The only comparable threat had come some thirteen months earlier when, on the basis of consistently high sales through the worst of the Depression as an agent with the Newark office of Metropolitan Life, my father had been offered a promotion to assistant manager in charge of agents at the company's office six miles west of our house in Union, a town whose only distinction I knew of was a drive-in theater where movies were shown even when it rained, and where the company expected my father and his family to live if he took the job. As an assistant manager, my father could soon be making seventy-five dollars a week and over the coming years as much as a hundred a week, a fortune in 1939 to people with our expectations. And since there were one-family houses selling in Union for a Depression low of a few thousand dollars, he would be able to realize an ambition he had nurtured growing up penniless in a Newark tenement flat: to become an American homeowner. "Pride of ownership" was a favorite phrase of my father's, embodying an idea real as bread to a man of his background, one having to do not with social competitiveness or conspicuous consumption but with his standing as a manly provider.

The single drawback was that because Union, like Hillside, was a Gentile working-class town, my father would most likely be the only Jew in an office of some thirty-five people, my mother the only Jewish woman on our street, and Sandy and I the only Jewish kids in our school.

On the Saturday after my father was offered the promotion—a promotion that, above all, would answer a Depression family's yearning for a tiny margin of financial security—the four of us headed off after lunch to look around Union. But once we were there and driving up and down the residential streets peering out at the two-story houses—not quite identical but each, nonetheless, with a screened front porch and a mown lawn and a piece of shrubbery and a cinder drive leading to a one-car garage, very modest houses but still roomier than our two-bedroom flat and looking a lot like the little white houses in the movies about small-town salt-of-the-earth America—once we were there our innocent buoyancy about the family ascent into the home-owning class was supplanted, predictably enough, by our anxieties about the scope of Christian charity. My ordinarily energetic mother responded to my father's "What do you think, Bess?" with enthusiasm that even a child understood to be feigned. And young as I was, I was able to surmise why: because she was thinking, "Ours will be the house 'where the Jews live.' It'll be Elizabeth all over again."

Elizabeth, New Jersey, when my mother was being raised there in a flat over her father's grocery store, was an industrial port a quarter the size of Newark, dominated by the Irish working class and their politicians and the tightly knit parish life that revolved around the town's many churches, and though I never heard her complain of having been pointedly ill-treated in Elizabeth as a girl, it was not until she married and moved to Newark's new Jewish neighborhood that she discovered the confidence that led her to become first a PTA "grade mother," then a PTA vice president in charge of establishing a Kindergarten Mothers' Club, and finally the PTA president, who, after attending a conference in Trenton on infantile paralysis, proposed an annual March of Dimes dance on January 30—President Roosevelt's birthday—that was accepted by most Newark schools. In the spring of 1939 she was in her second successful year as a leader with progressive ideas—already supporting a young social studies teacher keen on bringing "visual education" into Chancellor's classrooms—and now she couldn't help but envision herself bereft of all that had been achieved by her becoming a wife and a mother on Summit Avenue. Should we have the good fortune to buy and move into a house on any of the Union streets we were seeing at their springtime best, not only would her status slip back to what it had been when she was growing up the daughter of a Jewish immigrant grocer in Irish Catholic Elizabeth, but, worse than that, Sandy and I would be obliged to relive her own circumscribed youth as a neighborhood outsider.

Despite my mother's mood, my father did everything he could to keep up our spirits, remarking on how clean and well-kept everything looked, reminding Sandy and me that living in one of these houses the two of us would no longer have to share a small bedroom and a single closet, and explaining the benefits to be derived from paying off a mortgage rather than paying rent, a lesson in elementary economics that abruptly ended when it was necessary for him to stop the car at a red light beside a parklike drinking establishment dominating one corner of the intersection. There were green picnic tables set out beneath the shade trees full with foliage, and on this sunny weekend afternoon there were waiters in braided white coats moving swiftly about, balancing trays laden with bottles and pitchers and plates, and men of every age gathered at each of the tables, smoking cigarettes and pipes and cigars and drinking deeply from tall beakers and earthenware mugs. There was music, too—an accordion being played by a stout little man in short pants and high socks who wore a hat ornamented with a long feather.

"Sons of bitches!" my father said. "Fascist bastards!" and then the light changed and we drove on in silence to look at the office building where he was about to get his chance to earn more than fifty dollars a week.

It was my brother who, when we went to bed that night, explained why my father had lost control and cursed aloud in front of his children: the homey acre of open-air merriment smack in the middle of town was called a beer garden, the beer garden had something to do with the German-American Bund, the German-American Bund had something to do with Hitler, and Hitler, as I hadn't to be told, had everything to do with persecuting Jews.

The intoxicant of anti-Semitism. That's what I came to imagine them all so cheerfully drinking in their beer garden that day—like all the Nazis everywhere, downing pint after pint of anti-Semitism as though imbibing the universal remedy.

My father had to take off a morning of work to go over to the home office in New York—to the tall building whose uppermost tower was crowned with the beacon his company proudly designated "The Light That Never Fails"—and inform the superintendent of agencies that he couldn't accept the promotion he longed for.

"It's my fault," announced my mother as soon as he began to recount at the dinner table what had transpired there on the eighteenth floor of 1 Madison Avenue.

"It's nobody's fault," my father said. "I explained before I left what I was going to tell him, and I went over and I told him, and that's it. We're not moving to Union, boys. We're staying right here."

"What did he do?" my mother asked.

"He heard me out."

"And then?" she asked.

"He stood up and he shook my hand."

"He didn't say anything?"

"He said, 'Good luck, Roth.'"

"He was angry with you."

"Hatcher is a gentleman of the old school. Big six-foot goy. Looks like a movie star. Sixty years old and fit as a fiddle. These are the people who run things, Bess—they don't waste their time getting angry at someone like me."

"So now what?" she asked, implying that whatever happened as a result of his meeting with Hatcher was not going to be good and could be dire. And I thought I understood why. Apply yourself and you can do it—that was the axiom in which we had been schooled by both parents. At the dinner table, my father would reiterate to his young sons time and again, "If anybody asks 'Can you do this job? Can you handle it?' you tell 'em 'Absolutely.' By the time they find out that you can't, you'll already have learned, and the job'll be yours. And who knows, it just might turn out to be the opportunity of a lifetime." Yet over in New York he had done nothing like that.

"What did the Boss say?" she asked him. The Boss was how the four of us referred to the manager of my father's Newark office, Sam Peterfreund. In those days of unadvertised quotas to keep Jewish admissions to a minimum in colleges and professional schools and of unchallenged discrimination that denied Jews significant promotions in the big corporations and of rigid restrictions against Jewish membership in thousands of social organizations and communal institutions, Peterfreund was one of the first of the small handful of Jews ever to achieve a managerial position with Metropolitan Life. "He's the one who put you up for it," my mother said. "How must *he* feel?"

"Know what he said to me when I got back? Know what he told me about the Union office? It's full of drunks. *Famous* for drunks. Beforehand he didn't want to influence my decision. He didn't want to stand in my way if this was what I wanted. Famous for agents who work two hours in the morning and spend the rest of their time in the tavern or worse. And I was supposed to go in there, the new Jew, the big new sheeny boss the goyim are all dying to work for, and I was supposed to go in there and pick 'em up off the barroom floor. I was supposed to go in there and remind them of their obligation to their wives and their children. Oh, how they would have loved me, boys, for doing them the favor. You can imagine what they would have called me behind my back. No, I'm better off where I am. We're all better off."

"But can the company fire you for turning them down?"

"Honey, I did what I did. That's the end of it."

But she didn't believe what he'd told her the Boss had said; she believed that he was making up what the Boss had said to get her to stop blaming herself for refusing to move her children to a Gentile town that was a haven for the German-American Bund and by doing so denying him the opportunity of *his* lifetime.

The Lindberghs returned to resume their family life in America in April 1939. Only months later, in September, having already annexed Austria and overrun Czechoslovakia, Hitler invaded and conquered Poland, and France and Great Britain responded by declaring war on Germany. Lindbergh had by then been activated as a colonel in the Army Air Corps, and he now began traveling around the country for the U.S. government, lobbying for the development of American aviation and for expanding and modernizing the air wing of the armed forces. When Hitler quickly occupied Denmark, Norway, Holland, and Belgium, and all but defeated France, and the second great European war of the century was well under way, the Air Corps colonel made himself the idol of the isolationists—and the enemy of FDR—by adding to his mission the goal of preventing America from being drawn into the war or offering any aid to the British or the French. There was already strong animosity between him and Roosevelt, but now that he was declaring openly at large public meetings and on network radio and in popular magazines that the president was misleading the country with promises of peace while secretly agitating and planning for our entry into the armed struggle, some in the Republican Party began to talk up Lindbergh as the man with the magic to beat "the warmonger in the White House" out of a third term.

The more pressure Roosevelt put on Congress to repeal the arms embargo and loosen the strictures on the country's neutrality so as to prevent the British from being defeated, the more forthright Lindbergh became, until finally he made the famous radio speech before a hall full of cheering supporters in Des Moines that named among the "most important groups who have been pressing this country toward war" a group constituting less than three percent of the population and referred to alternately as "the Jewish people" and "the Jewish race."

"No person of honesty and vision," Lindbergh said, "can look on their pro-war policy here today without seeing the dangers involved in such a policy both for us and for them." And then, with remarkable candor, he added:

> A few far-sighted Jewish people realize this and stand opposed to intervention. But the majority still do not ... We cannot blame them for looking out for what they believe to be their own interests, but we must also look out for ours. We cannot allow the natural passions and prejudices of other peoples to lead our country to destruction.

The next day the very accusations that had elicited roars of approval from Lindbergh's Iowa audience were vigorously denounced by liberal journalists, by Roosevelt's press secretary, by Jewish agencies and organizations, even from within the Republican Party by New York's District Attorney Dewey and the Wall Street utilities lawyer Wendell Willkie, both potential presidential nominees. So severe was the criticism from Democratic cabinet members like Interior Secretary Harold Ickes that Lindbergh resigned his reserve commission as an Army colonel rather than serve under FDR as his commander in chief. But the America First

Committee, the broadest-based organization leading the battle against intervention, continued to support him, and he remained the most popular proselytizer of its argument for neutrality. For many America Firsters there was no debating (even with the facts) Lindbergh's contention that the Jews' "greatest danger to this country lies in their large ownership and influence in our motion pictures, our press, our radio, and our government." When Lindbergh wrote proudly of "our inheritance of European blood," when he warned against "dilution by foreign races" and "the infiltration of inferior blood" (all phrases that turn up in diary entries from those years), he was recording personal convictions shared by a sizable portion of America First's rank-and-file membership as well as by a rabid constituency even more extensive than a Jew like my father, with his bitter hatred of anti-Semitism—or like my mother, with her deeply ingrained mistrust of Christians—could ever imagine to be flourishing all across America.

The 1940 Republican Convention. My brother and I went to sleep that night—Thursday, June 27—while the radio was on in the living room, and our father, our mother, and our older cousin Alvin sat listening together to the live coverage from Philadelphia. After six ballots, the Republicans still hadn't selected a candidate. Lindbergh's name was yet to be uttered by a single delegate, and because of an engineering conclave at a midwestern factory where he'd been advising on the design of a new fighter plane, he wasn't present or expected to be. When Sandy and I went to bed the convention remained divided among Dewey, Willkie, and two powerful Republican senators, Vandenberg of Michigan and Taft of Ohio, and it didn't look as though a backroom deal was about to be brokered anytime soon by party bigwigs like former president Hoover, who'd been ousted from office by FDR's overwhelming 1932 victory, or by Governor Alf Landon, whom FDR had defeated even more ignominiously four years later in the biggest landslide in history.

Because it was the first muggy evening of the summer, the windows were open in every room and Sandy and I couldn't help but continue to follow from bed the proceedings being aired over our own living room radio and the radio playing in the flat downstairs and—since an alleyway only barely wide enough for a single car separated one house from the next—the radios of our neighbors to either side and across the way. As this was long before window air conditioners bested the noises of a neighborhood's tropical nights, the broadcast blanketed the block from Keer to Chancellor—a block on which not a single Republican lived in any of the thirty-odd two-and-a-half-family houses or in the small new apartment building at the Chancellor Avenue corner. On streets like ours the Jews voted straight Democratic for as long as FDR was at the top of the ticket.

But we were two kids and fell asleep despite everything and probably wouldn't have awakened till morning had not Lindbergh —with the Republicans deadlocked on the twentieth ballot—made his unanticipated entrance onto the convention floor at 3:18 A.M. The lean, tall, handsome hero, a lithe, athletic-looking man not yet forty years old, arrived in his flying attire, having landed his own plane at the Philadelphia airport only minutes earlier, and at the sight of him, a surge of redemptive excitement brought the wilted conventioneers up onto their feet to cry "Lindy! Lindy! Lindy!" for thirty glorious minutes, and without interruption from the chair. Behind the successful execution of this spontaneous pseudo-religious drama lay the machinations of Senator Gerald P. Nye of North Dakota, a right-wing isolationist who quickly placed in nomination the name of Charles A. Lindbergh of Little Falls, Minnesota, whereupon two of the most reactionary members of Congress—Congressman Thorkelson of Montana and Congressman Mundt of South Dakota—seconded the nomination, and at precisely four A.M. on Friday, June 28, the Republican Party, by acclamation, chose as its candidate the bigot who had denounced Jews over the airwaves to a national audience as "other peoples" employing their enormous "influence . . . to lead our country to destruction," rather than truthfully acknowledging us to be a small minority of citizens vastly outnumbered by our Christian countrymen, by and large obstructed by religious prejudice from attaining public power, and surely no less loyal to the principles of American democracy than an admirer of Adolf Hitler.

"No!" was the word that awakened us, "No!" being shouted in a man's loud voice from every house on the block. It can't be. No. Not for president of the United States.

Within seconds, my brother and I were once more at the radio with the rest of the family, and nobody bothered telling us to go back to bed. Hot as it was, my decorous mother had pulled a robe over her thin nightdress—she too had been asleep and roused by the noise—and she sat now on the sofa beside my father, her fingers over her mouth as though she were trying to keep from being sick. Meanwhile my cousin Alvin, able no longer to remain in his seat, set about pacing a room eighteen-by-twelve with a force in his gait befitting an avenger out searching the city to dispose of his nemesis.

The anger that night was the real roaring forge, the furnace that takes you and twists you like steel. And it didn't subside—not while Lindbergh stood silently at the Philadelphia rostrum and heard himself being cheered once again as the nation's savior, nor when he gave the speech accepting his party's nomination and with it the mandate to keep America out of the European war. We all waited in terror to hear him repeat to the convention his malicious vilification of the Jews, but that he didn't made no difference to the mood that carried every last family on the block out into the street at nearly five in the morning. Entire families known to me previously only fully dressed in daytime clothing were wearing pajamas and nightdresses under their bathrobes and milling around in their slippers at dawn as if driven from their homes by an earthquake. But what shocked a child most was the anger, the anger of men whom I knew as lighthearted kibbitzers or silent, dutiful breadwinners who all day long unclogged drainpipes or serviced furnaces or sold apples by the pound and then in the evening looked at the paper and listened to the radio and fell asleep in the living room chair, plain people who happened to be Jews now storming about the street and cursing with no concern for propriety, abruptly thrust back into the miserable struggle from which they had believed their families extricated by the providential migration of the generation before.

I would have imagined Lindbergh's not mentioning the Jews in his acceptance speech to be a promising omen, an indication that he had been chastened by the outcry that had caused him to relinquish his Army commission or that he had changed his mind since the Des Moines speech or that he had already forgotten about us or that secretly he knew full well that we were committed irrevocably to America—that though Ireland still mattered to the Irish and Poland to the Poles and Italy to the Italians, we retained no allegiance, sentimental or otherwise, to those Old World countries that we had never been welcome in and that we had no intention of ever returning to. If I could have thought through the meaning of the moment in so many words, this is probably what I would have been thinking. But the men out on the street thought differently. Lindbergh's not mentioning the Jews was to them a trick and no more, the initiation of a campaign of deceit intended both to shut us up and to catch us off guard. "Hitler in America!" the neighbors cried. "Fascism in America! Storm troopers in America!" After their having gone without sleep all night long, there was nothing that these bewildered elders of ours didn't think and nothing that they didn't say aloud, within our hearing, before they started to drift back to their houses (where all the radios still blared away), the men to shave and dress and grab a cup of coffee before heading for work and the women to get their children clothed and fed and ready for the day.

Roosevelt raised everyone's spirits by his robust response on learning that his opponent was to be Lindbergh rather than a senator of the stature of Taft or a prosecutor as aggressive as Dewey or a big-time lawyer as smooth and handsome as Willkie. When awakened at four A.M. to be told the news, he was said to have predicted from his White House bed, "By the time this is over, the young man will be sorry not only that he entered politics but that he ever learned to fly." Whereupon he fell immediately back into a sound sleep—or so went the story that brought us such solace the next day. Out on the street, when all anyone could think about was the menace posed to our safety by this transparently unjust affront, people had oddly forgotten about FDR and the bulwark he was against oppression. The sheer surprise of the Lindbergh nomination had activated an atavistic sense of being undefended that had more to do with Kishinev and the pogroms of 1903 than with New Jersey thirty-seven years later, and as a consequence, they had forgotten about Roosevelt's appointment to the Supreme Court of Felix Frankfurter and his selection as Treasury secretary of Henry Morgenthau, and about the close presidential adviser, financier Bernard Baruch, and about Mrs. Roosevelt and Ickes and Agriculture Secretary Wallace, all three of whom, like the president, were known to be friends of the Jews. There was Roosevelt, there was the U.S. Constitution, there was the Bill of Rights, and there were the papers, America's free press. Even the Republican *Newark Evening News* published an editorial reminding readers of the Des Moines speech and openly challenging the wisdom of Lindbergh's nomination, and *PM*, the new left-wing New York tabloid that cost a nickel and that my father had begun bringing home with him after work along with the *Newark News*—and whose slogan read, "*PM* is against people who push other people around"—leveled its assault on the Republicans in a lengthy editorial as well as in news stories and columns on virtually every one of its thirty-two pages, including anti-Lindbergh columns in the sports section by Tom Meany and Joe Cummiskey. On the front page the paper featured a large photo of Lindbergh's Nazi medal and, in its Daily Picture Magazine, where it claimed to run photographs that other papers suppressed—controversial photos of lynch mobs and chain gangs, of strikebreakers wielding clubs, of inhuman conditions in America's penitentiaries—there was page after page showing the Republican candidate touring Nazi Germany in 1938, culminating in the full-page picture of him, the notorious medal around his neck, shaking the hand of Hermann Göring, the Nazi leader second only to Hitler.

On Sunday night we waited through the lineup of comedy programs for Walter Winchell to come on at nine. And when he did and proceeded to say what we had hoped he would say just as contemptuously as we wanted him to say it, applause erupted from across the alleyway, as though the famous newsman weren't walled off in a radio studio on the far side of the great divide that was the Hudson but were here among us and fighting mad, his tie pulled down, his collar unbuttoned, his gray fedora angled back on his head, lambasting Lindbergh from a microphone atop the oilcloth covering on the kitchen table of our next-door neighbor.

It was the last night of June 1940. After a warm day, it had grown cool enough to sit comfortably indoors without perspiring, but when Winchell signed off at nine-fifteen, our parents were moved to go outside for the four of us to take in the lovely evening together. We were just going to walk to the corner and back—after which my brother and I would go to sleep—but it was nearly midnight before we got to bed and by then sleep was out of the question for kids so overcome by their parents' excitement. Because Winchell's fearless bellicosity had propelled all of our neighbors outdoors as well, what had begun for us as a cheerful little evening stroll ended as an impromptu block party for everyone. The men dragged beach chairs from the garages and unfolded them at the foot of the alleyways, the women carried pitchers of lemonade from the houses, the youngest of the children ran wildly from stoop to stoop, and the older ones sat laughing and talking off by themselves, and all because war had been declared on Lindbergh by America's best-known Jew after Albert Einstein.

It was Winchell, after all, whose column had famously ushered in the three dots separating—and somehow magically validating— each hot news item ever so tenuously grounded in fact, and it was Winchell who'd more or less originated the idea of firing into the face of the credulous masses buckshot pellets of insinuating gossip—ruining reputations, compromising celebrities, bestowing fame, making and breaking showbiz careers. It was his column alone that was syndicated in hundreds of papers all across the country and his Sunday-night quarter of an hour that was the country's most popular news program, the rapid-fire Winchell delivery and the pugnacious Winchell cynicism lending every scoop the sensational air of an exposé. We admired him as a fearless outsider and a cunning insider, a pal of J. Edgar Hoover, director of the FBI, as well as a neighbor of the mobster Frank Costello and a confidant of Roosevelt's inner circle, even a sometimes guest invited to the White House to amuse the president over a drink—the in-the-know street fighter and hardboiled man about town whom his enemies feared and who was on our side. Manhattan-born Walter Winschel (a.k.a. Weinschel) had transformed himself from a New York vaudeville dancer into a callow Broadway columnist earning big money by embodying the passions of the cheesiest of the new subliterate dailies, though ever since the rise of Hitler, and long before anyone else in the press had the foresight or the wrath to take them on, fascists and anti-Semites had become his number one enemy. He'd already labeled as "ratzis" the German-American Bund and hounded its leader, Fritz Kuhn, over the air and in print as a secret foreign agent, and now—after FDR's joke, the *Newark News* editorial, and the thoroughgoing denunciation by *PM*—Walter Winchell had only to disclose Lindbergh's "pro-Nazi philosophy" to his thirty million Sunday-evening listeners and to call Lindbergh's presidential candidacy the greatest threat ever to American democracy for all the Jewish families on block-long little Summit Avenue to resemble once again Americans enjoying the vitality and high spirits of a secure, free, protected citizenry instead of casting themselves about outdoors in their nightclothes like inmates escaped from a lunatic asylum.

My brother was known throughout the neighborhood for being able to draw "anything"—a bike, a tree, a dog, a chair, a cartoon character like Li'l Abner—though his interest of late was in real faces. Kids were always gathering around to watch him wherever he would park himself after school with his large spiral pad and his mechanical pencil and begin to sketch the people nearby. Inevitably the onlookers would start to shout, "Draw him, draw her, draw me," and Sandy would take up the exhortation, if only to stop them from screaming in his ear. All the while his hand was working away, he'd look up, down, up, down—and behold, there lived so-and-so on a sheet of paper. What's the trick, they all asked him, how'd you do it, as if tracing—as if outright magic—might have played some part in the feat. Sandy's answer to all this pestering was a shrug or a smile: the trick to doing it was his being the quiet, serious, unostentatious boy that he was. Compelling attention wherever he went by turning out the likenesses people requested had seemingly no effect on the impersonal element at the core of his strength, the inborn modesty that was his toughness and that he later sidestepped at his peril.

At home, he was no longer copying illustrations from *Collier's* or photos from *Look* but studying from an art manual on the figure. He'd won the book in an Arbor Day poster contest for schoolkids that had coincided with a citywide tree-planting program administered by the Department of Parks and Public Property. There'd even been a ceremony where he'd shaken the hand of a Mr. Bannwart, who was superintendent of the Bureau of Shade Trees. The design of his winning poster was based on a red two-cent stamp in my collection commemorating the sixtieth anniversary of Arbor Day. The stamp seemed to me especially beautiful because visible within each of its narrow, vertical white borders was a slender tree whose branches arched at the top to meet and form an arbor—and until the stamp became mine and I was able to examine through my magnifying glass its distinguishing marks, the meaning of "arbor" had been swallowed up in the familiar name of the holiday. (The small magnifying glass—along with an album for twenty-five hundred stamps, a stamp tweezers, a perforation gauge, gummed stamp hinges, and a black rubber dish called a watermark detector—had been a gift from my parents for my seventh birthday. For an additional ten cents they'd also bought me a small book of ninety-odd pages called *The Stamp Collector's Handbook,* where, under "How to Start a Stamp Collection," I'd read with fascination this sentence: "Old business files or private correspondence often contain stamps of discontinued issues which are of great value, so if you have any friends living in old houses who have accumulated material of this sort in their attics, try to obtain their old stamped envelopes and wrappers." We didn't have an attic, none of our friends living in flats and apartments had attics, but there'd been attics just beneath the roofs of the one-family houses in Union— from my seat in the back of the car I could see little attic windows at either end of each of the houses as we'd driven around the town on that terrible Saturday the year before, and so all I could think of when we got home in the afternoon were the old stamped envelopes and the embossed stamps on the prepaid newspaper wrappers secreted up in those attics and how I would now have no chance "to obtain" them because I was a Jew.)

The appeal of the Arbor Day commemorative stamp was greatly enhanced by its representing a human activity as opposed to a famous person's portrait or a picture of an important place—an activity, what's more, being performed by children: in the center of the stamp, a boy and a girl looking to be about ten or eleven are planting a young tree, the boy digging with a spade while the girl, supporting the trunk of the tree with one hand, holds it steadily in place over the hole. In Sandy's poster the boy and the girl are repositioned and stand on opposite sides of the tree, the boy is pictured as right-handed rather than left-handed, he wears long pants instead of knickers, and one of his feet is atop the blade pressing it into the ground. There is also a third child in Sandy's poster, a boy about my age, who is now the one wearing the knickers. He stands back and to the side of the sapling and holds ready a watering can—as I held one when I modeled for Sandy, clad in my best school knickers and high socks. Adding this child was my mother's idea, to help distinguish Sandy's artwork from that on the Arbor

Day stamp—and protect him from the charge of "copying"—but also to provide the poster with a social content that implied a theme by no means common in 1940, not in poster art or anywhere else either, and that for reasons of "taste" might even have proved unacceptable to the judges.

The third child planting the tree was a Negro, and what encouraged my mother to suggest including him—aside from the desire to instill in her children the civic virtue of tolerance—was another stamp of mine, a brand-new ten-cent issue in the "educators group," five stamps that I'd purchased at the post office for a total of twenty-one cents and paid for over the month of March out of my weekly allowance of a nickel. Above the central portrait, each stamp featured a picture of a lamp that the U.S. Post Office Department identified as the "Lamp of Knowledge" but that I thought of as Aladdin's lamp because of the boy in the *Arabian Nights* with the magic lamp and the ring and the two genies who give him whatever he asks for. What I would have asked for from a genie were the most coveted of all American stamps: first, the celebrated 1918 twenty-four-cent airmail, a stamp said to be worth $3,400, where the plane pictured at the center, the Army's Flying Jenny, is inverted; and after that, the three famous stamps in the Pan-American Exposition issue of 1901 that had also been mistakenly printed with inverted centers and were worth over a thousand dollars apiece.

On the green one-cent stamp in the educators group, just above the picture of the Lamp of Knowledge, was Horace Mann; on the red two-cent, Mark Hopkins; on the purple three-cent, Charles W. Eliot; on the blue four-cent, Frances E. Willard; on the brown ten-cent was Booker T. Washington, the first Negro to appear on an American stamp. I remember that after placing the Booker T. Washington in my album and showing my mother how it completed the set of five, I had asked her, "Do you think there'll ever be a Jew on a stamp?" and she replied, "Probably—someday, yes. I hope so, anyway." In fact, another twenty-six years had to pass, and it took Einstein to do it.

Sandy saved his weekly allowance of twenty-five cents—and what change he earned shoveling snow and raking leaves and washing the family car—until he had enough to bicycle to the stationery store on Clinton Avenue that carried art supplies and, over a period of months, to buy a charcoal pencil, then sandpaper blocks to sharpen the pencil, then charcoal paper, then the little tubular metal contraption he blew into to apply the fine fixative mist that prevented the charcoal from smudging. He had big bulldog clips, a masonite board, yellow Ticonderoga pencils, erasers, sketchpads, drawing paper—equipment that he stored in a grocery carton at the bottom of our bedroom closet and that my mother, when she was cleaning, wasn't permitted to disturb. His energetic meticulousness (passed on from our mother) and his breathtaking perseverance (passed on from our father) served only to magnify my awe of an older brother who everyone agreed was intended for great things, while most boys his age didn't look as though they were intended even to eat at a table with another human being. I was then the good child, obedient both at home and at school—the willfulness largely inactive and the attack set to go off at a later date—as yet altogether too young to know the potential of a rage of one's own. And nowhere was I less intransigent than with him.

For his twelfth birthday, Sandy had gotten a large, flat black portfolio made of hard cardboard that folded along a sewn seam and was secured at the top edge with two attached lengths of ribbon that he tied in a bow in order to fasten the leaves. The portfolio measured about two feet by a foot and a half, too big to fit into the drawers of our bedroom dresser or to be stacked upright against the wall in the crowded bedroom closet he and I shared. He was allowed to store it—along with his spiral sketchpads—laid out flat beneath his bed, and in it he saved the drawings he considered his best, beginning with his compositional masterwork of 1936, the ambitious picture of our mother pointing overhead at the Paris-bound *Spirit of St. Louis*. Sandy had several large portraits of the heroic aviator, in both pencil and charcoal, stowed away in his portfolio. They were part of a series he was assembling of prominent Americans that concentrated primarily on those living eminences most revered by our parents, such as President and Mrs. Roosevelt, New York mayor Fiorello La Guardia, United Mine Workers president John L. Lewis, and the novelist Pearl Buck, who'd won the Nobel Prize in 1938 and whose picture he copied from the jacket of one of her bestsellers. A number of drawings in the portfolio were of family members, and of those at least half were of our sole surviving grandparent, our paternal grandmother, who, on the Sundays when my uncle Monty brought her around to visit, would sometimes serve Sandy as a model. Under the sway of the word "venerable," he drew every wrinkle he could find in her face and every gnarl in her arthritic fingers while—as dutifully as she'd scrubbed floors on her knees all her life and cooked for a family of nine on a coal stove—tiny, sturdy Grandma sat in the kitchen and "posed."

We were alone together in the house only a few days after the Winchell broadcast when Sandy removed the portfolio from under his bed and carried it into the dining room. There he opened it out on the table (reserved for entertaining the Boss and celebrating special family occasions) and carefully lifted the Lindbergh portraits from the tracing paper protecting each drawing and lined them up on the tabletop. In the first, Lindbergh was wearing his leather flying cap with the loose straps dangling over each ear; in the second, the cap was partially hidden beneath large heavy goggles pushed up from his eyes and onto his forehead; in the third, he was bareheaded, nothing to mark him as an aviator other than the uncompromising gaze out to the distant horizon. To gauge the value of this man, as Sandy had rendered him, wasn't difficult. A virile hero. A courageous adventurer. A natural person of gigantic strength and rectitude combined with a powerful blandness. Anything but a frightening villain or a menace to mankind.

"He's going to be president," Sandy told me. "Alvin says Lindbergh's going to win."

He so confused and frightened me that I pretended he was making a joke and laughed.

"Alvin's going to go to Canada and join the Canadian army," he said. "He's going to fight for the British against Hitler."

"But nobody can beat Roosevelt," I said.

"Lindbergh's going to. America's going to go fascist."

Then we just stood there together under the intimidating spell of the three portraits. Never before had being seven felt like such a serious deficiency.

"Don't tell anybody I've got these," he said.

"But Mom and Dad saw them already," I said. "They've seen them all. Everybody has."

"I told them I tore them up."

There was nobody more truthful than my brother. He wasn't quiet because he was secretive and deceitful but because he never bothered to behave badly and so had nothing to hide. But now something external had transformed the meaning of these drawings, making them into what they were not, and so he'd told our parents that he'd destroyed them, making himself into what he was not.

"Suppose they find them," I said.

"How will they do that?" he asked.

"I don't know."

"Right," he said. "You don't. Just keep your little trap shut and nobody'll find anything."

I did as he told me for many reasons, one being that the third-oldest U.S. postage stamp I owned—which I couldn't possibly tear up and throw away—was a ten-cent airmail issued in 1927 to commemorate Lindbergh's transatlantic flight. It was a blue stamp, about twice as long as it was high, whose central design, a picture of the *Spirit of St. Louis* flying eastward over the ocean, had provided Sandy with the model for the plane in the drawing celebrating his conception. Adjacent to the white border at the left of the stamp is the coastline of North America, with the words "New York" jutting out into the Atlantic, and adjacent to the border at the right the coastlines of Ireland, Great Britain, and France, with the word "Paris" at the end of a dotted arc that charts the flight path between the two cities. At the top of the stamp, directly beneath the white letters that boldly spell out UNITED STATES POSTAGE are the words LINDBERGH—AIR MAIL in slightly smaller type but large enough certainly to be read by a seven-year-old with perfect vision. The stamp was already valued at twenty cents by Scott's *Standard Postage Stamp Catalogue,* and what I immediately realized was that its worth would only continue increasing (and so rapidly as to become my single most valuable possession) if Alvin was right and the worst happened.

On the sidewalk during the long vacation months we played a new game called "I Declare War," using a cheap rubber ball and a piece of chalk. With the chalk you drew a circle some five or six feet in diameter, partitioned it into as many pielike segments as there were players, and chalked into each the name of one of various foreign countries that had been in the news throughout the year. Next, each player picked "his" country and stood straddling the edge of the circle, one foot inside and one out, so that when the time came he could flee in a hurry. Meanwhile a designated player, holding the ball aloft in his hand, announced slowly, in an ominous cadence, "I—declare—war—on—" There was a suspenseful pause, and then the kid declaring war would slam the ball down, in the same instant shouting "Germany!" or "Japan!" or "Holland!" or "Italy!" or "Belgium!" or "England!" or "China!"—sometimes even shouting "America!"—and everybody would take off except the one on whom the surprise attack had been launched. His job was to catch the ball on the bounce as quickly as he could and call "Stop!" Everybody now allied against him would have to freeze in place, and the victim country would begin the counterattack, trying to eliminate one aggressor country at a time by walloping each as hard as he could with the ball, beginning by throwing at those closest to him and advancing his position with each murderous thwack.

We played this game incessantly. Until it rained and temporarily the names of the countries were washed away, people had to either step on them or step over them when they made their way down the street. In our neighborhood there was no other graffiti to speak of in those days, just this, the remnants of the hieroglyphics of our simple street games. Harmless enough, and yet it drove some of the mothers crazy who had to hear us at it for hours on end through their open windows. "Can't you kids do something else? Can't you find another game to play?" But we couldn't—declaring war was all we thought about too.

On July 18, 1940, the Democratic Convention meeting in Chicago overwhelmingly nominated FDR for a third term on the first ballot. We listened on the radio to his acceptance speech, delivered with the confidently intoned upper-class enunciation that, for close to eight years now, had inspired millions of ordinary families like ours to remain hopeful in the midst of hardship. There was something about the inherent decorum of the delivery that, alien though it was, not only calmed our anxiety but bestowed on our family a historical significance, authoritatively merging our lives with his as well as with that of the entire nation when he addressed us in our living room as his "fellow citizens." That Americans could choose Lindbergh—that Americans could choose *anybody*—rather than the two-term president whose voice alone conveyed mastery over the tumult of human affairs . . . well, that was unthinkable, and certainly so for a little American like me who'd never known a presidential voice other than his.

Some six weeks later, on the Saturday before Labor Day, Lindbergh surprised the country by failing to appear at the Detroit Labor Day parade, where he had been scheduled to launch his campaign with a motorcade through the working-class heartland of isolationist America (and the anti-Semitic stronghold of Father Coughlin and Henry Ford), and by arriving unannounced instead at the Long Island airfield from which his spectacular transatlantic flight had begun thirteen years before. The *Spirit of St. Louis* had been secretly trucked in under a tarp and stored overnight in a remote hangar, though by the time Lindbergh taxied the plane onto the field the next morning, every wire service in America and every radio station and newspaper in New York had a reporter on hand to witness the takeoff, westward this time across America to California rather than eastward across the Atlantic to Europe. Of course, by 1940, commercial air service had been hauling transcontinental freight, passengers, and mail for more than a decade, and doing so largely as a result of the incentive of Lindbergh's solo feat and his industrious efforts as a million-dollar-a-year consultant to the newly organized airlines. But it wasn't the wealthy advocate of commercial aviation who was launching his campaign that day, nor was it the Lindbergh who had been decorated in Berlin by the Nazis, nor the Lindbergh who, in a nationwide radio broadcast, had blamed overly influential Jews for attempting to drive the country into war, nor was it even the stoical father of the infant kidnapped and killed by Bruno Hauptmann in 1932. It was rather the unknown airmail pilot who'd dared to do what had never been done by any aviator before him, the adored Lone Eagle, boyish and unspoiled still, despite the years of phenomenal fame. On the holiday weekend that closed out the summer of 1940, Lindbergh came nowhere near besting the record time for a coast-to-coast nonstop flight that he'd himself set a decade back with an aircraft more advanced than the old *Spirit of St. Louis*. Nonetheless, when he arrived at Los Angeles Airport, a crowd consisting largely of aircraft workers—tens of thousands of them, employed by the big new manufacturers in and around L.A.—was as overcome with enthusiasm as any ever to greet him anywhere.

The Democrats called the flight a publicity gimmick stage-managed by Lindbergh's staff, when in fact the decision to fly to California had been made only hours earlier by Lindbergh alone and not by the professionals who had been assigned by the Republican Party to steer the political novice through his first political campaign and who, like everyone else, had been expecting him to turn up in Detroit.

His speech was unadorned and to the point, delivered in a high-pitched, flat, midwestern, decidedly un-Rooseveltian American voice. His flight outfit of high boots and jodhpurs and a light-weight jumper worn over a shirt and tie was a replica of the one in which he'd crossed the Atlantic, and he spoke without removing his leather headgear or flight goggles, which were pushed up onto his forehead exactly as Sandy had them positioned in the charcoal drawing hidden beneath his bed.

"My intention in running for the presidency," he told the raucous crowd, once they had stopped chanting his name, "is to preserve American democracy by preventing America from taking part in another world war. Your choice is simple. It's not between Charles A. Lindbergh and Franklin Delano Roosevelt. It's between Lindbergh and war."

That was the whole of it—forty-one words, if you included the A for Augustus.

After a shower and a snack and an hour's nap there at the L.A. airport, the candidate climbed back into the *Spirit of St. Louis* and flew to San Francisco. By nightfall he was in Sacramento. And wherever he landed in California that day, it was as though the country hadn't known the stock market crash and the miseries of the Depression (or the triumphs of FDR, for that matter), as though even the war he was there to prevent us from entering hadn't so much as crossed anyone's mind. Lindy flew down out of the sky in his famous plane, and it was 1927 all over again. It was Lindy all over again, straight-talking Lindy, who had never to look or to sound superior, who simply *was* superior—fearless Lindy, at once youthful and gravely mature, the rugged individualist, the legendary American man's man who gets the impossible done by relying solely on himself.

Over the next month and a half he proceeded to spend one full day in each of the forty-eight states, until in late October he made his way back to the Long Island runway from which he'd taken off on Labor Day weekend. Throughout the daylight hours he would hop from one city, town, or village to the next, landing on highways if there was no nearby airstrip and setting down and taking off from a stretch of pasture when he flew to talk with farmers and their families in the remotest of America's rural counties. His airfield remarks were broadcast over local and regional radio stations, and several times a week, from the state capital where he was spending the night, he broadcast a message to the nation. It was always succinct and went like this: To prevent a war in Europe is now too late. But it is not too late to prevent America from taking part in that war. FDR is misleading the nation. America will be carried to war by a president who falsely promises peace. The choice is simple. Vote for Lindbergh or vote for war.

As a young pilot in aviation's early, novelty days, Lindbergh, along with an older, more experienced sidekick, had entertained crowds throughout the Midwest by skydiving in a parachute or walking out parachuteless onto the plane's wing, and the Democrats were now quick to belittle his barnstorming in the *Spirit of St. Louis* by likening it to these stunts. At press conferences, Roosevelt no longer bothered to make a derisive quip when questioned by newsmen about the unorthodox Lindbergh campaign, but simply moved on to discuss Churchill's fear of an imminent German invasion of Britain or to announce that he would be asking Congress to fund the first American peacetime draft or to remind Hitler that the United States would not tolerate any interference with the transatlantic aid our merchant vessels were supplying to the British war effort. It was clear from the start that the president's campaign was to consist of remaining in the White House, where, in contrast to what Secretary Ickes labeled Lindbergh's "carnival antics," he planned to address the hazards of the international situation with all the authority at his command, working round the clock if necessary.

Twice during the state-by-state tour, Lindbergh was lost in bad weather and each time several hours passed before radio contact with him was reestablished and he was able to let the country know that all was well. But then in October, on the very day Americans were stunned to learn that in the latest of the destructive night raids on London the Germans had bombed St. Paul's Cathedral, a news flash at dinnertime reported that the *Spirit of St. Louis* had been seen to explode in the air over the Alleghenies and plummet to the earth in flames. This time it was six long hours before a second flash corrected the first with the news that it was engine trouble and not a midair explosion that had forced Lindbergh to make an emergency landing on treacherous terrain in the mountains of western Pennsylvania. Before the emendation was aired, however, our phone rang continuously—friends and relatives calling to speculate with our parents on the initial account of the fiery and probably fatal accident. In front of Sandy and me our parents said nothing to indicate relief at the prospect of Lindbergh's death, though neither did they say that they hoped it wasn't so nor were they among the jubilant when, around eleven that night, word came through that, far from having gone down in flames, the Lone Eagle had emerged safely from the undamaged plane and was waiting only for a replacement part so as to take off and resume his campaign.

On the October morning that Lindbergh landed at Newark Airport, among the entourage waiting to welcome him to New Jersey was Rabbi Lionel Bengelsdorf of B'nai Moshe, the first of the city's Conservative temples, organized by Polish Jews. B'nai Moshe was a few blocks from the heart of the old pushcart ghetto, still the city's poorest district though home no longer to B'nai Moshe's congregants but to a community of impoverished Negroes, recent migrants from the South. For years B'nai Moshe had been losing out in the competition for the well-to-do; by 1940, these families had either left Conservatism and affiliated themselves to the Reform congregations of B'nai Jeshurun and Oheb Shalom—each planted impressively amid the old mansions on High Street—or joined the other long-established Conservative temple, B'nai Abraham, located several miles west of where it had been originally housed in a former Baptist church and adjacent now to the homes of the Jewish doctors and lawyers living in Clinton Hill. The new B'nai Abraham was the most splendid of the city's temples, a circular building austerely designed in what was called "the Greek style" and vast enough to hold a thousand worshipers on the High Holidays. Joachim Prinz, an émigré expelled from Berlin by Hitler's Gestapo, had replaced the retiring Julius Silberfeld as the temple's rabbi the year before and was already emerging as a forceful man with a broad social outlook who offered his prosperous congregants a perspective on Jewish history marked strongly by his own recent experience at the bloody scene of the Nazi crime.

Rabbi Bengelsdorf's sermons were broadcast weekly over station WNJR to the hoi polloi he called his "radio congregation," and he was the author of several books of inspirational poetry routinely given as gifts to bar mitzvah boys and newlyweds. He'd been born in South Carolina in 1879, the son of an immigrant dry goods merchant, and whenever he addressed a Jewish audience, whether from the pulpit or over the air, his courtly southern accent, along with his sonorous cadences—and the cadences of his own multisyllabic name—left an impression of dignified profundity. On the subject, for instance, of his friendship with Rabbi Silberfeld of B'nai Abraham and Rabbi Foster of B'nai Jeshurun, he once told his radio audience, "It was fated: just as Socrates, Plato, and Aristotle belonged together in the ancient world, so we belong together in the religious world." And the homily on selflessness that he proffered to explain to radio listeners why a rabbi of his standing was content to stay on at the head of a waning congregation, he introduced by saying, "Perhaps you will be interested in my answer to questions that have been asked of me by literally thousands of people. Why do you renounce the commercial benefits of a peripatetic ministry? Why do you choose to remain in Newark, at Temple B'nai Moshe, as your only pulpit, when you have six opportunities every day to leave it for other congregations?" He had studied at the great institutions of learning in Europe as well as at American universities and was reputed to speak ten languages; to be versed in classical philosophy, theology, art history, and ancient and modern history; to never compromise on questions of principle; to never refer to notes at the lectern or on a lecture platform; to never be without a set of index cards pertaining to the topics most engaging him at the moment, to which he added new reflections and impressions every day. He was also an excellent equestrian, known to bring his horse to a halt so as to jot down a thought, employing his saddle as a makeshift desk. Early each morning, he exercised by riding out along the bridle paths of Weequahic Park, accompanied—until her death from cancer in 1936—by his wife, the heiress to Newark's wealthiest jewelry manufacturer. Her family mansion on Elizabeth Avenue, where the couple had been living just across from the park since their marriage in 1907, housed a treasury of Judaica said to be among the most valuable private collections in the world.

By 1940 Lionel Bengelsdorf claimed the longest record of service at his own temple of any rabbi in America. The newspapers referred to him as the religious leader of New Jersey Jewry and, in reporting on his numerous public appearances, invariably mentioned his "gift for oratory" along with the ten languages. In 1915, at the 250th anniversary celebration of the founding of Newark, he had sat at the side of Mayor Raymond and delivered the invocation just as he delivered invocations annually at the parades for Memorial Day and the Fourth of July: RABBI EXALTS DECLARATION OF INDEPENDENCE was a headline that appeared annually in the *Star-Ledger* every July fifth. In his sermons and talks calling "the development of American ideals" the first priority of Jews and "the Americanization of Americans" the best means to preserve our democracy against "Bolshevism, radicalism, and anarchism," he frequently quoted from Theodore Roosevelt's final message to the nation, in which the late president said, "There can be no divided allegiance here. Any man who says he is an American, but something else also, isn't an American at all. We have room for but one flag, the American flag." Rabbi Bengelsdorf had spoken on the Americanization of Americans in every Newark church and public school, before most every fraternal, civic, historical, and cultural group in the state, and news articles in the Newark papers about his speeches were datelined with the names of scores of cities around the country to which he'd been called to address conferences and conventions on that theme as well as on issues ranging from crime and the prison reform movement—"The prison reform movement is saturated with the highest ethical principles and religious ideals"—to the causes of the World War—"The war is the result of the worldly ambitions of the European peoples and their effort to reach the goals of military greatness, power, and wealth" —to the importance of day nurseries—"The nurseries are life gardens of human flowers in which each child is helped to grow in an atmosphere of joy and gladness"—to the evils of the industrial age—"We believe that the worth of the workingman is not to be computed by the material value of his production"—to the suffrage movement, whose proposal to extend to women the franchise to vote he strongly opposed, arguing that "if men are not capable of handling the business of the state, why not help them become so. No evil has ever been cured by doubling it." My uncle Monty, who hated all rabbis but had an especially venomous loathing of Bengelsdorf dating back to his childhood as a charity student in the B'nai Moshe religious school, liked to say of him, "The pompous son of a bitch knows everything—it's too bad he doesn't know anything else."

Rabbi Bengelsdorf's appearance at the airport—where, according to the caption beneath the photograph on the front page of the *Newark News*, he stood first in line to shake Lindbergh's hand when he emerged from the cockpit of the *Spirit of St. Louis*—was a source of consternation to great numbers of the city's Jews, my parents among them, as was the quotation attributed to him in the paper's account of Lindbergh's brief visit. "I am here," Rabbi Bengelsdorf told the *News*, "to crush all doubt of the unadulterated loyalty of the American Jews to the United States of America. I offer my support to the candidacy of Colonel Lindbergh because the political objectives of my people are identical with his. America is our beloved homeland. America is our only homeland. Our religion is independent of any piece of land other than this great country, to which, now as always, we commit our total devotion and allegiance as the proudest of citizens. I want Charles Lindbergh to be my president not in spite of my being a Jew but because I am a Jew—an *American* Jew."

Three days later, Bengelsdorf participated in the huge rally held at Madison Square Garden to mark the end of Lindbergh's flying tour. By then the election was but two weeks away, and though there appeared to be growing Lindbergh support among voters throughout the traditionally Democratic South, and close contests were predicted in the most conservative midwestern states, national polls showed the president comfortably ahead in the popular vote and well ahead in electoral votes. Republican Party leaders were reported to be in despair over their candidate's stubborn refusal to allow anyone other than himself to determine the strategy of his campaign, and so, to draw him out of the repetitious austerity of his interminable barnstorming and envelop him in an atmosphere more like that of the boisterous Philadelphia nominating convention, the Madison Square Garden rally was organized and broadcast nationwide on the evening of the second Monday in October.

The fifteen speakers introducing Lindbergh that night were described as "prominent Americans from all walks of life." Among them was a farm leader to talk about the harm a war would do to American farming, which was in crisis still from the First World War and the Depression; a labor leader to talk about the disaster a war would represent for American workers, whose lives would be regimented by government agencies; a manufacturer to talk about the catastrophic long-term consequences for American industry of wartime overexpansion and onerous taxation; a Protestant clergyman to talk about the brutalizing effect of modern warfare on the young men who would be doing the fighting; and a Catholic priest to talk about the inevitable deterioration of the spiritual life of a peace-loving nation like our own and the destruction of decency and kindness because of the hatred bred by war. Lastly there was a rabbi, New Jersey's Lionel Bengelsdorf, who received an especially hearty welcome from the full house of Lindbergh supporters when his turn came to take the lectern and who was there to expatiate on how Lindbergh's association with the Nazis was anything but complicitous.

"Yep," Alvin said, "they bought him. The fix is in. They slipped a gold ring through his big Jew nose, and now they can lead him anywhere."

"You don't know that," my father said, but not because he wasn't himself steamed up by Bengelsdorf's behavior. "Listen to the man," he told Alvin, "give the man a hearing. It's only fair"—words uttered largely for Sandy's benefit and mine, to keep the startling turn of events from seeming as terrible to the two of us as it did to the adults. The night before, I had fallen onto the floor in my sleep, something that hadn't happened since I'd first graduated from a crib to a bed and to prevent me from rolling out of it my parents had to set a pair of kitchen chairs at the side of the mattress. When it was assumed automatically that my falling like that after all these years could only have had to do with Lindbergh's showing up at Newark Airport, I insisted that I didn't remember a bad dream about Lindbergh, that I just remembered waking up on the floor between my brother's bed and mine, even though I happened to know that I virtually never got to sleep any longer without envisioning the Lindbergh drawings stashed away in my brother's portfolio. I kept wanting to ask Sandy if he couldn't hide them in our cellar storage bin instead of under the bed beside mine, but because I'd sworn not to speak about the drawings to anyone—and because I couldn't bring myself to part with my own Lindbergh stamp—I didn't dare to raise them as an issue, though they were indeed haunting me and rendering unapproachable the brother whose reassurance I'd never needed more.

It was a cold evening. The heat was on and the windows were closed, but even without being able to hear them you knew that radios were playing up and down the block and that families who wouldn't otherwise consider listening to a Lindbergh rally were tuned in because of the scheduled appearance there of Rabbi Bengelsdorf. Among his own congregants, a few important people had already begun to call for his resignation, if not for his immediate removal by the temple's board of trustees, while the majority continuing to support him tried to believe that their rabbi was merely exercising his democratic right of free speech and that, horrified though they were by his public endorsement of Lindbergh, to attempt to silence a conscience as renowned as his did not fall within their rights.

That night Rabbi Bengelsdorf disclosed to America what he claimed to be the true motive behind Lindbergh's personal flying missions to Germany in the 1930s. "Contrary to the propaganda disseminated by his critics," the rabbi informed us, "he did not once visit Germany as a sympathizer or a supporter of Hitler's but rather he traveled each and every time as a secret adviser to the U.S. government. Far from his betraying America, as the misguided and the ill-intentioned continue to charge, Colonel Lindbergh has almost single-handedly served to strengthen America's military preparedness by imparting his knowledge to our own military and by doing everything within his power to advance the cause of American aviation and to expand America's air defenses."

"Jesus!" cried my father. "Everybody *knows*—"

"Shhh," whispered Alvin, "shhh—let the great orator speak."

"Yes, in 1936, long before the beginning of the European hostilities, the Nazis awarded Colonel Lindbergh a medal, and, yes," continued Bengelsdorf, "yes, the colonel accepted their medal. But all the while, my friends, all the while secretly exploiting their admiration in order better to protect and preserve our democracy and to preserve our neutrality through strength."

"I cannot *believe*—" my father began.

"Try," muttered Alvin evilly.

"This is not America's war," Bengelsdorf announced, and the crowd at Madison Square Garden responded with a full minute of applause. "This," the rabbi told them, "is Europe's war." Again sustained applause. "It is one of a thousand-year-long sequence of European wars dating back to the time of Charlemagne. It is their second devastating war in less than half a century. And can anyone forget the tragic cost to America of their last great war? Forty thousand Americans killed in action. A hundred and ninety-two thousand Americans wounded. Seventy-six thousand Americans dead of disease. Three hundred and fifty thousand Americans on disability today because of their participation in that war. And just how astronomical will the price be this time? The number of our dead—tell me, President Roosevelt, will it be merely doubled or tripled or will it perhaps be quadrupled? Tell me, Mr. President, what sort of America will the massive slaughter of innocent American boys leave in its wake? Of course, the Nazi harassment and persecution of its German Jewish population is a cause of enormous anguish to me as it is to every Jew. During the years I was studying theology with the faculties of the great German universities in Heidelberg and in Bonn, I made many distinguished friends there, great men of learning who, today, simply because they are Germans of Jewish extraction, have been dismissed from long-held scholarly positions and are being ruthlessly persecuted by the Nazi hoodlums who have taken command of their homeland. I oppose their treatment with every ounce of my strength, and so too does Colonel Lindbergh oppose their treatment. But how will this cruel fate that has befallen them in their own land be alleviated by our great country going to war with their tormentors? If anything, the predicament of *all* of Germany's Jews would only worsen immeasurably—worsen, I fear, tragically. Yes, I am a Jew, and as a Jew I feel their suffering with a familial sharpness. But I am an American citizen, my friends"—again the applause—"I am an American born and raised, and so I ask you, how would my pain be lessened if America were now to enter the war and, along with the sons of our Protestant families and the sons of our Catholic families, the sons of our Jewish families were to fight and die by the tens of thousands on a blood-soaked European battleground? How would my pain be diminished by my having to console my very own congregants—"

It was my mother, usually the least ardent member of our family, the one ordinarily quieting the rest of us when we turned demonstrative, who all at once found the sound of Bengelsdorf's southern accent so intolerable that she had to leave the room. But until he finished his speech and was loudly cheered off the stage by the Garden audience, no one else moved or said another word. I wouldn't dare to, and my brother was preoccupied—as he often was in such a setting—with sketching what we all looked like, now while listening to the radio. Alvin's was the silence of murderous loathing, and my father—divested for perhaps the first time in his life of that relentless passion he brought to the struggle against set-back and disappointment—was too stirred up to speak.

Pandemonium. Unspeakable delight. Lindbergh had at last stepped onto the Garden stage, and like someone half demented, my father leaped from the sofa and snapped off the radio just as my mother came back into the living room and asked, "Who would like something? Alvin," she said, with tears in her eyes, "a cup of tea?"

Her job was to hold our world together as calmly and as sensi-bly as she could; that was what gave her life fullness and that was all she was trying to do, and yet never had any of us seen her ren-dered so ridiculous by this commonplace maternal ambition.

"What the hell is going on!" my father began to shout. "What the hell did he do *that* for? That stupid speech! Does he think that one single Jew is now going to go out and vote for this anti-Semite be-cause of that stupid, lying speech? Has he completely lost his mind? What does this man think he is *doing?*"

"Koshering Lindbergh," Alvin said. "Koshering Lindbergh for the goyim."

"Koshering what?" my father said, exasperated with Alvin's seemingly speaking sarcastic nonsense at a moment of so much confusion. "Doing *what?*"

"They didn't get him up there to talk to Jews. They didn't buy him off for that. Don't you understand?" Alvin asked, fiery now with what he took to be the underlying truth. "He's up there talk-ing to the goyim—he's giving the goyim all over the country his personal rabbi's permission to vote for Lindy on Election Day.

Don't you see, Uncle Herman, what they got the great Bengelsdorf to do? He just guaranteed Roosevelt's defeat!"

At about two A.M. that night, while soundly asleep, I again rolled out of my bed, but this time I remembered afterward what I'd been dreaming before I hit the floor. It was a nightmare all right, and it was about my stamp collection. Something had happened to it. The design on two sets of my stamps had changed in a dreadful way without my knowing when or how. In the dream, I'd gotten the album out of my dresser drawer to take with me to my friend Earl's and I was walking with it toward his house as I'd done dozens of times before. Earl Axman was ten and in the fifth grade. He lived with his mother in the new four-story yellow-brick apartment house built three years earlier on the large empty lot near the corner of Chancellor and Summit, diagonally across from the grade school. Before that he'd lived in New York. His father was a musician with the Glen Gray Casa Loma Orchestra—Sy Axman, who played tenor saxophone beside Glen Gray's alto. Mr. Axman was divorced from Earl's mother, a theatrically good-looking blonde who'd briefly been a singer with the band before Earl was born and, according to my parents, was originally from Newark and a brunette, a Jewish girl named Louise Swig who'd gone to South Side and became famous locally in musical revues at the YMHA. Among all the boys I knew, Earl was the only child with divorced parents, and the only one whose mother wore heavy makeup and off-the-shoulder blouses and billowing ruffled skirts with a big petticoat underneath. She'd also made a record of the song "Gotta Be This or That" when she was with Glen Gray, and Earl played it for me often. I never came upon another mother like her. Earl didn't call her Ma or Mom—he called her, scandalously, Louise. She had a closet in her bedroom full of those petticoats, and when Earl and I were alone together at his house, he'd show them to me. He even let me touch one once, whispering, while I waited to decide whether to do it, "Wherever you want." Then he opened a drawer and showed me her brassieres and offered to let me touch one of those, but that I declined. I was still young enough to admire a brassiere from afar. His parents each gave him a full dollar a week to spend on stamps, and when the Casa Loma Orchestra wasn't playing in New York and was out touring, Mr. Axman sent Earl envelopes with airmail stamps postmarked from cities everywhere. There was even one from "Honolulu, Oahu," where Earl, who wasn't above cloaking his absent father in splendor—as though to the son of an insurance agent having a saxophonist with a famous swing band for a father (and a peroxide-blond singer for a mother) weren't amazing enough—claimed that Mr. Axman had been taken to a "private home" to see the canceled two-cent Hawaiian "Missionary" stamp of 1851, issued forty-seven full years before Hawaii was annexed to the United States as a territory, an unimaginable treasure valued at $100,000 whose central design was just the numeral 2.

Earl owned the best stamp collection around. He taught me everything practical and everything esoteric that I learned as a small kid about stamps—about their history, about collecting mint versus used, about technical matters like paper, printing, color, gum, overprints, grills, and special printing, about the great forgeries and design errors—and, prodigious pedant that he was, had begun my education by telling me about the French collector Monsieur Herpin, who coined the word "philately," explaining its derivation from two Greek words, the second of which, *ateleia*, meaning freedom from tax, never quite made sense to me. And whenever we'd finished up in his kitchen with our stamps and he was momentarily done with his domineering, he'd giggle and say, "Now let's do something awful," which was how I got to see his mother's underwear.

In the dream, I was walking to Earl's with my stamp album clutched to my chest when someone shouted my name and began chasing me. I ducked into an alleyway and scurried back into one of the garages to hide and to check the album for stamps that might have come loose from their hinges when, while fleeing my pursuer, I'd stumbled and dropped the album at the very spot on the sidewalk where we regularly played "I Declare War." When I opened to my 1932 Washington Bicentennials—twelve stamps ranging in denomination from the half-cent dark brown to the ten-cent yellow—I was stunned. Washington wasn't on the stamps anymore. Unchanged at the top of each stamp—lettered in what I'd learned to recognize as white-faced roman and spaced out on either one or two lines—was the legend "United States Postage." The colors of the stamps were unchanged as well—the two-cent red, the five-cent blue, the eight-cent olive green, and so on—all the stamps were the same regulation size, and the frames for the portraits remained individually designed as they were in the original set, but instead of a different portrait of Washington on each of the twelve stamps, the portraits were now the same and no longer of Washington but of Hitler. And on the ribbon beneath each portrait, there was no longer the name "Washington" either. Whether the ribbon was curved downward as on the one-half-cent stamp and the six, or curved upward as on the four, the five, the seven, and the ten, or straight with raised ends as on the one, the one and a half, the two, the three, the eight, and the nine, the name lettered across the ribbon was "Hitler."

It was when I looked next at the album's facing page to see what, if anything, had happened to my 1934 National Parks set of ten that I fell out of the bed and woke up on the floor, this time screaming. Yosemite in California, Grand Canyon in Arizona, Mesa Verde in Colorado, Crater Lake in Oregon, Acadia in Maine, Mount Rainier in Washington, Yellowstone in Wyoming, Zion in Utah, Glacier in Montana, the Great Smoky Mountains in Tennessee—and across the face of each, across the cliffs, the woods, the rivers, the peaks, the geyser, the gorges, the granite coastline, across the deep blue water and the high waterfalls, across everything in America that was the bluest and the greenest and the whitest and to be preserved forever in these pristine reservations, was printed a black swastika.

2

November 1940–June 1941

Loudmouth Jew

IN JUNE 1941, just six months after Lindbergh's inauguration, our family drove the three hundred miles to Washington, D.C., to visit the historic sites and the famous government buildings. My mother had been saving in a Christmas Club account at the Howard Savings Bank for close to two years, a dollar a week out of the household budget to cover the bulk of our prospective travel expenses. The trip had been planned back when FDR was a second-term president and the Democrats controlled both Houses, but now with the Republicans in power and the new man in the White House considered a treacherous enemy, there was a brief family discussion about our driving north instead to see Niagara Falls and to take the boat cruise in rain slickers through the St. Lawrence Seaway's Thousand Islands and then to cross over in our car into Canada to visit Ottawa. Some among our friends and neighbors had already begun talking about leaving the country and migrating to Canada should the Lindbergh administration openly turn against the Jews, and so a trip to Canada would also familiarize us with a potential haven from persecution. Back in February, my cousin Alvin had already left for Canada to join the Canadian armed forces, just as he said he would, and fight on the British side against Hitler.

* * *

Till his departure Alvin had been my family's ward for close to seven years. His late father was my father's oldest brother; he died when Alvin was six, and Alvin's mother—a second cousin of my mother's and the one who'd introduced my parents to each other —died when Alvin was thirteen, and so he'd come to live with us during the four years he attended Weequahic High, a quick-witted boy who gambled and stole and whom my father was dedicated to saving. Alvin was twenty-one in 1940, renting a furnished room upstairs from a Wright Street shoeshine parlor just around the corner from the produce market, and by then working almost two years for Steinheim & Sons, one of the city's two biggest Jewish construction firms—the other was run by the Rachlin brothers. Alvin got the job through the elder Steinheim, the founder of the company and an insurance customer of my father's.

Old man Steinheim, who had a heavy accent and couldn't read English but who was, in my father's words, "made of steel," still attended High Holiday services at our local synagogue. On a Yom Kippur several years back, when the old man saw my father outside the synagogue with Alvin, he mistook my cousin for my older brother and asked, "What does the boy do? Let him come over and work for us." There Abe Steinheim, who'd turned his immigrant father's little building company into a multimillion-dollar operation—though only after a major family war had put his two brothers out on the street—took a liking to solid, stocky Alvin and the cocksure way he carried himself, and instead of sticking him in the mailroom or using him as an office boy, he made Alvin his driver: to run errands, to deliver messages, to whisk him back and forth to the construction sites to check on the subcontractors (whom Abe called "the chiselers," though it was he, Alvin said, who chiseled them and took advantage of everyone). On Saturdays during the summer, Alvin drove him down to Freehold, where Abe owned half a dozen trotters that he raced at the old harness track, horses he liked to refer to as "hamburgers." "We got a hamburger running today at Freehold," and down they'd shoot in the Caddy to watch his horse lose every time. He never made any money at it, but that wasn't the idea. He raced horses on Saturdays for the Road Horse Association at the pretty trotting track in Weequahic Park, and he talked to the papers about restoring the flat track at Mount Holly, whose glory days were long past, and this was how Abe Steinheim managed to become commissioner of racing for the state of New Jersey and got a shield on his car that enabled him to drive up on the sidewalk and sound a siren and park anywhere. And it was how he became friendly with the Monmouth County officials and insinuated himself into the horsy set at the shore—Wall Township and Spring Lake goyim who would take him to their fancy clubs for lunch, where, as Abe told Alvin, "Everybody sees me and all they're doing is whispering, can't wait to whisper, 'Look at what's here,' but they don't mind drinking my booze and getting treated to great dinners and so in the end it pays off." He had his deep-sea-fishing boat docked at the Shark River Inlet and he would take them out on it and liquor them up and hire guys to catch the fish for them, so that whenever a new hotel went up anywhere from Long Branch to Point Pleasant, it was on a site the Steinheims got for next to nothing—Abe, like his father, having the great wisdom of buying things only at discount.

Every three days Alvin would drive him the four blocks from the office to 744 Broad Street for a quick trim in the lobby barber shop behind the cigar stand, where Abe Steinheim bought his Trojans and his dollar-fifty cigars. Now, 744 Broad was one of the two tallest office buildings in the state, where the National Newark and Essex Bank occupied the top twenty floors and the city's prestigious lawyers and financiers occupied the rest and where New Jersey's biggest moneymen regularly frequented the barber shop—and yet a part of Alvin's job was to call immediately beforehand to tell the barber to get ready, Abe was coming, and whoever was in the chair, to throw him out. At dinner the night that Alvin got the job, my father told us that Abe Steinheim was the most colorful, the most exciting, the greatest builder Newark had ever seen. "And a genius," my father said. "He didn't get there without being a genius. Brilliant. And a handsome man. Blond. Husky, but not fat. Always looks nice. Camelhair coats. Black-and-white shoes. Beautiful shirts. Impeccably dressed. And a beautiful wife—polished, classy, a Freilich by birth, a New York Freilich, a very wealthy woman in her own right. Abe's shrewd as they come. And the man has guts. Ask anybody in Newark: the riskiest project and Steinheim takes it on. He does buildings where no one else will take a chance. Alvin will learn from him. He'll watch him and see what it is to work round the clock for something that's yours. He could be an important inspiration in Alvin's life."

Largely so my father could keep tabs on him and my mother could know that he wasn't surviving on hotdogs alone, Alvin came to our house a couple of times a week to eat a good meal, and miraculously, instead of his getting stern lectures about honesty and responsibility and hard work at the dinner table every night— as in the days after he'd been caught with his hand in the till at the Esso station where he worked after school and, until my father prevailed on Simkowitz, the owner, to drop the charges and himself made good with the money, looked to be headed for the Rahway reformatory—Alvin conversed heatedly with my father about politics, about capitalism particularly, a system that, ever since my father had gotten him to take an interest in reading the paper and talking about the news, Alvin deplored but that my father defended, patiently reasoning with his rehabilitated nephew, and not like a member of the National Association of Manufacturers but as a devotee of Roosevelt's New Deal. He'd warn Alvin, "You don't have to tell Mr. Steinheim about Karl Marx. Because the man won't hesitate—you'll be out on your keister. Learn from him. That's why you're there. Learn from him and be respectful, and this could be the opportunity of a lifetime."

But Alvin couldn't bear Steinheim and reviled him constantly— he's a fake, he's a bully, he's a cheapskate, he's a screamer, he's a shouter, he's a swindler, he's a man without a friend in the world, people cannot stand to be anywhere near him, and I, said Alvin, have to chauffeur him around. He's cruel to his sons, is uninterested even in looking at a grandchild, and his skinny wife, who never dares to say or do anything to displease him, he humiliates whenever the mood takes him. Everybody in the family has to live in apartments in the same luxury building that Abe built on a street of big oaks and maples near Upsala College in East Orange—from dawn to dusk the sons work for him in Newark and he's screaming and yelling at them, then at night he's on the house phone with them in East Orange and he's still screaming and yelling. Money is everything, though not to buy things but so as to be able always to weather the storm: to protect his position and insure his holdings and buy anything he wants in real estate at a discount, which is how he made a killing after the crash. Money, money, money—to be in the middle of the chaos and in the middle of the deals and make all the money in the world.

"Some guy retires at the age of forty-five with five million bucks. Five million in the bank, which is as good as a zillion, and you know what Abe says?" Alvin is asking this of my twelve-year-old brother and me. Supper is over and he's with us in the bedroom—all of us lying shoeless atop the covers, Sandy on his bed, Alvin on mine, and I beside Alvin, in the crook between his strong arm and his strong chest. And it's bliss: stories about man's avarice, his zealousness, his unbounded vitality and staggering arrogance, and to tell these stories, a cousin himself unbounded, even after all my father's work, a captivating cousin still emotionally among the rawest of the raw, who at twenty-one already has to shave his black stubble twice a day in order not to look like a hardened criminal. Stories of the carnivore descendants of the giant apes who once inhabited the ancient forests and have left the trees, where all day long they nibbled on leaves, to come to Newark and work downtown.

"What does Mr. Steinheim say?" Sandy asks him.

"He says, 'The guy has five million. That's all he has. Still young and in his prime, with a chance someday to be worth fifty, sixty, maybe as much as a hundred million, and he tells me, "I'm taking it all off the table. I'm not you, Abe. I'm not hanging around for the heart attack. I have enough to call it a day and spend the rest of my life playing golf."' And what does Abe say? 'This is a man who is a total schmuck.' Every subcontractor when he comes into the office on Friday to collect money for the lumber, the glass, the brick, Abe says, 'Look, we're out of money, this is the best I can do,' and he pays them a half, a third—if he can get away with it, a quarter—and these people need the money to survive, but this is the method that Abe learned from his father. He's doing so much building that he gets away with it and nobody tries to kill him."

"*Would* somebody try to kill him?" Sandy asks.

"Yeah," Alvin says, "me."

"Tell us about the wedding anniversary," I say.

"The wedding anniversary," he repeats. "Yeah, he sang fifty songs. He hires a piano player," Alvin tells us, exactly the way he tells the tale of Abe at the piano every time I ask to hear it, "and no one gets a word in, no one knows what is going on, all the guests spend the whole night eating his food, and he is standing in his tux by the piano singing one song after another, and when they leave he's still at the piano, still singing songs, every popular song you can think of, and he doesn't even listen when they say goodbye."

"Does he scream and yell at you?" I ask Alvin.

"At me? At everybody. He screams and yells wherever he goes. I drive him to Tabatchnick's on Sunday mornings. The people are lined up to buy their bagels and lox. We walk in and he's screaming—and there's a line of six hundred people, but he's yelling, 'Abe is here!' and they move him to the front of the line. Tabatchnick comes running out of the back, they push everyone aside, and Abe must order five thousand dollars' worth of stuff, and we drive home and there is Mrs. Steinheim, who weighs ninety-two pounds and knows when to get the hell out of the way, and he phones the three sons and they're there in five seconds flat, and the four of them eat a meal for four hundred people. The one thing he spends on is food. Food and cigars. You mention Tabatchnick's, Kartzman's, he doesn't care who is there, how many people—he gets there and buys out the whole store. They eat up every single slice of everything every Sunday morning, sturgeon, herring, sable, bagels, pickles, and then I drive him over to the renting office to see how many apartments are vacant, how many are rented, how many are being fixed up. Seven days a week. Never stops. Never takes a vacation. No mañana—that's his slogan. It drives him crazy if anybody misses a minute of work. He cannot go to sleep without knowing that the next day there are more deals that will bring more money—and the whole damn thing makes me sick. The man to me is one thing only—a walking advertisement for the overthrow of capitalism."

My father called Alvin's complaints kid stuff, and to be kept to himself on the job, especially after Abe decided that he was going to send Alvin to Rutgers. You're too smart, Abe told Alvin, to be so dumb, and then something happened beyond anything that my father could realistically have hoped for. Abe gets on the phone to the president of Rutgers and starts shouting at *him*. "You're going to take this boy, where he finished in high school is not the issue, the boy is an orphan, potentially a genius, you're going to give him a full scholarship, and I'll build you a college building, the most beautiful in the world—but not so much as a shithouse goes up unless this orphan boy goes to Rutgers all expenses paid!" To Alvin he explains, "I've never liked to have a formal chauffeur who was a chauffeur who was an idiot. I like kids like you with something going for them. You're going to Rutgers, and you'll come home and drive me in the summers, and when you graduate Phi Beta Kappa, then the two of us sit down and talk."

Abe would have had Alvin beginning as a freshman in New Brunswick in September 1941 and, after four years of college, coming back as a somebody into the business, but instead, in February, Alvin left for Canada. My father was furious with him. They argued for weeks before finally, without telling us, Alvin took the express train from Newark's Penn Station straight up to Montreal. "I don't get your morality, Uncle Herman. You don't want me to be a thief but it's okay with you if I work for a thief." "Steinheim's not a thief. Steinheim's a builder. What he's doing is what they do," my father said, "what they all have to do because the building trade is a cutthroat business. But his buildings don't fall down, do they? Does he break the law, Alvin? Does he?" "No, he just screws the workingman every chance he gets. I didn't know your morality was also for that." "My morality stinks," said my father, "everybody in this city knows about my morality. But the issue isn't me. It's your future. It's going to college. A four-year free college education." "Free because he browbeats the president of Rutgers the way he browbeats the whole goddamn world." "Let the president of Rutgers worry about that! What is the matter with you? You really want to sit there and tell me that the worst human being ever born is a man who wants to make you an educated person and find you a place in his building company?" "No, no, the worst human being ever born is Hitler, and frankly I'd rather be fighting that son of a bitch than waste my time with a Jew like Steinheim, who only brings shame on the rest of us Jews by his goddamn—" "Oh, don't talk to me like a child—and the 'goddamn's I can live without too. The man doesn't bring shame on anyone. You think if you worked for an Irish builder it would be better? Try it—go work for Shanley, you'll see what a lovely fellow he is. And the Italians, would they be better, you think? Steinheim shoots his mouth off—the Italians shoot guns." "And Longy Zwillman doesn't shoot guns?" "Please, I know all about Longy—I grew up on the same street with Longy. What does any of this have to do with Rutgers?" "It has to do with *me*, Uncle Herman, and being indebted to Steinheim for the rest of my life. Isn't it enough that he has three sons that he's already destroying? Isn't it enough that they have to attend every Jewish holiday with him and every Thanksgiving with him and every New Year's Eve with him—I have to be there to be shouted at too? All of them working in the same office and living in the same building and waiting around for only one thing—to split it all up on the day he dies. I can assure you, Uncle Herman, their grief won't last long." "You're wrong. Dead wrong. There is more to these people than just money." "*You're* wrong! He holds them in his hand with the money! The man is totally berserk, and they stay and take it for fear of losing the money!" "They stay because they're a family. All families go through a lot. A family is both peace and war. We're going through a little war right now. I understand it. I accept it. But that's no reason to give up the college you missed out on and that now you can have and to run off half-cocked to fight Hitler instead." "So," said Alvin, as though at last he had the goods not only on his employer but on his family protector as well, "you're an isolationist after all. You and Bengelsdorf. Bengelsdorf, Steinheim— they make a good couple." "Of what?" my father asked sourly, having finally run out of patience. "Of Jewish fakes." "Oh," said my father, "against the Jews now too?" "Those Jews. The Jews who are a disgrace to the Jews—yes, absolutely!"

The argument went on for four consecutive nights, and then, on the fifth, a Friday, Alvin didn't report to eat, though the idea had been to keep him showing up regularly for dinner until my father wore him down and the boy came to his senses—the boy whom my father had single-handedly changed from a callow good-for-nothing into the family's conscience.

The next morning we learned from Billy Steinheim, who was closest to Alvin of any of the sons and concerned enough about him to telephone us first thing Saturday, that after having received his Friday pay packet Alvin had thrown the keys to the Caddy in Billy's father's face and walked out, and when my father rushed off in our car to Wright Street to talk to Alvin in his room and get the whole story and gauge just how much damage he had done to his chances, the shoeshine parlor proprietor who was Alvin's landlord told him that the tenant had paid the rent and packed his things and was off to fight against the very worst human being ever born. Given the magnitude of Alvin's seething, no one less nefarious would do.

The November election hadn't even been close. Lindbergh got fifty-seven percent of the popular vote and, in an electoral sweep, carried forty-six states, losing only FDR's home state of New York and, by a mere two thousand votes, Maryland, where the large population of federal office workers had voted overwhelmingly for Roosevelt while the president was able to retain—as he could nowhere else below the Mason-Dixon Line—the loyalty of nearly half the Democrats' old southern constituency. Though on the morning after the election disbelief prevailed, especially among the pollsters, by the day after that everybody seemed to understand everything, and the radio commentators and the news columnists made it sound as if Roosevelt's defeat had been preordained. What had happened, they explained, was that Americans had shown themselves unwilling to break the tradition of the two-term presidency that George Washington had instituted and that no president before Roosevelt had dared to challenge. Moreover, in the aftermath of the Depression, the resurgent confidence of young and old alike had been quickened by Lindbergh's relative youth and by the graceful athleticism that contrasted so starkly with the serious physical impediments under which FDR labored as a polio victim. And there was the wonder of aviation and the new way of life it promised: Lindbergh, already the record-breaking master of long-distance flight, could knowledgeably lead his countrymen into the unknown of the aeronautical future while assuring them, by his strait-laced, old-fashioned demeanor, that modern engineering achievements need not erode the values of the past. It turned out, the experts concluded, that twentieth-century Americans, weary of confronting a new crisis in every decade, were starving for normalcy, and what Charles A. Lindbergh represented was normalcy raised to heroic proportions, a decent man with an honest face and an undistinguished voice who had resoundingly demonstrated to the entire planet the courage to take charge and the fortitude to shape history and, of course, the power to transcend personal tragedy. If Lindbergh promised no war, then there would be no war—for the great majority it was as simple as that.

Even worse for us than the election were the weeks following the inauguration, when the new American president traveled to Iceland to meet personally with Adolf Hitler and after two days of "cordial" talks to sign "an understanding" guaranteeing peaceful relations between Germany and the United States. There were demonstrations against the Iceland Understanding in a dozen American cities, and impassioned speeches on the floor of the House and the Senate by Democratic congressmen who'd survived the Republican landslide and who condemned Lindbergh for dealing with a murderous fascist tyrant as his equal and for accepting as their meeting place an island kingdom whose historic allegiance was to a democratic monarchy whose conquest the Nazis had already achieved—a national tragedy for Denmark, plainly deplorable to the people and their king, but one that Lindbergh's Reykjavík visit appeared tacitly to condone.

When the president returned from Iceland to Washington—a flight formation of ten large Navy patrol planes escorting the new two-engine Lockheed Interceptor that he himself piloted home—his address to the nation was a mere five sentences long. "It is now guaranteed that this great country will take no part in the war in Europe." That was how the historic message began, and this is how it was elaborated and concluded: "We will join no warring party anywhere on this globe. At the same time we will continue to arm America and to train our young men in the armed forces in the use of the most advanced military technology. The key to our invulnerability is the development of American aviation, including rocket technology. This will make our continental borders unassailable to attack from without while maintaining our strict neutrality."

Ten days later the president signed the Hawaii Understanding in Honolulu with Prince Fumimaro Konoye, premier of the Japanese imperial government, and Foreign Minister Matsuoka. As emissaries of Emperor Hirohito, the two had already signed a triple alliance with the Germans and the Italians in Berlin in September of 1940, the Japanese endorsing the "new order in Europe" established under the leadership of Italy and Germany, who in turn endorsed the "New Order in Greater East Asia" established by Japan. The three countries further pledged to support one another militarily should any of them be attacked by a nation not engaged in the European or Sino-Japanese war. Like the Iceland Understanding, the Hawaii Understanding made the United States a party in all but name to the Axis triple alliance by extending American recognition to Japan's sovereignty in East Asia and guaranteeing that the United States would not oppose Japanese expansion on the Asian continent, including annexation of the Netherlands Indies and French Indochina. Japan pledged to recognize U.S. sovereignty on its own continent, to respect the political independence of the American commonwealth of the Philippines—scheduled to be enacted in 1946—and to accept the American territories of Hawaii, Guam, and Midway as permanent U.S. possessions in the Pacific.

In the aftermath of the Understandings, Americans everywhere went about declaiming, No war, no young men fighting and dying ever again! Lindbergh can deal with Hitler, they said, Hitler respects him because he's Lindbergh. Mussolini and Hirohito respect him because he's Lindbergh. The only ones against him, the people said, are the Jews. And certainly that was true in America. All the Jews could do was worry. Our elders on the street speculated incessantly about what they would do to us and whom we could rely on to protect us and how we might protect ourselves. The younger kids like me came home from school frightened and bewildered and even in tears because of what the older boys had been telling one another about what Lindbergh had said about us to Hitler and what Hitler had said about us to Lindbergh during their meals together in Iceland. One reason my parents decided to keep to our long-laid plans to visit Washington was to convince Sandy and me—whether or not they themselves believed it—that nothing had changed other than that FDR was no longer in office. America wasn't a fascist country and wasn't going to be, regardless of what Alvin had predicted. There was a new president and a new Congress but each was bound to follow the law as set down in the Constitution. They were Republican, they were isolationist, and among them, yes, there were anti-Semites—as indeed there were among the southerners in FDR's own party—but that was a long way from their being Nazis. Besides, one had only to listen on Sunday nights to Winchell lashing out at the new president and "his friend Joe Goebbels" or hear him listing the sites under consideration by the Department of the Interior for building concentration camps—sites mainly located in Montana, the home state of Lindbergh's "national unity" vice president, the isolationist Democrat Burton K. Wheeler—to be assured of the fervor with which the new administration was being scrutinized by favorite reporters of my father's, like Winchell and Dorothy Thompson and Quentin Reynolds and William L. Shirer, and, of course, by the staff of *PM*. Even I now took my turn with *PM* when my father brought it home at night, and not just to read the comic strip *Barnaby* or to flip through the pages of photographs but to have in my hands documentary proof that, despite the incredible speed with which our status as Americans appeared to be altering, we were still living in a free country.

After Lindbergh was sworn into office on January 20, 1941, FDR returned with his family to their estate at Hyde Park, New York, and hadn't been seen or heard from since. Because it was as a boy in the Hyde Park house that he had first become interested in collecting stamps—when his mother, as the story went, had passed on to him her own childhood albums—I imagined him there spending all of his time arranging the hundreds of specimens that he had accumulated during his eight years in the White House. As every collector knew, no president before him had ever commissioned his postmaster general to issue so many new stamps, nor had there been another American president so intimately involved with the Post Office Department. Practically my first goal when I got my album was to accumulate all the stamps that I knew FDR had a hand in designing or had personally suggested, beginning with the 1936 three-cent Susan B. Anthony stamp commemorating the sixteenth anniversary of the women's suffrage amendment and the 1937 five-cent Virginia Dare stamp marking the birth at Roanoke three hundred and fifty years earlier of the first English child born in America. The 1934 three-cent Mother's Day stamp designed originally by FDR—and displaying in the left-hand corner the legend "In Memory and in Honor of the Mothers of America" and to the right of center the artist Whistler's celebrated portrait of his mother—was given to me in a block of four by my own mother to help get my collection going. She'd also contributed to my purchasing the seven commemorative stamps Roosevelt had approved in his first year as president, which I wanted because prominently displayed on five of them was "1933," the year I was born.

Before we went to Washington, I asked permission to take my stamp album on the trip. Out of fear that I would lose it and be heartbroken afterward, my mother at first said no but then allowed herself to be won over when I insisted on the necessity of at least having with me my president stamps—the sixteen, that is, that I owned of the 1938 set that progressed sequentially and by denomination from George Washington to Calvin Coolidge. The 1922 Arlington National Cemetery stamp and the 1923 Lincoln Memorial and Capitol Buildings stamps were far too expensive for my budget, but I nonetheless offered as another reason for taking my collection along that the three famous sites were clearly pictured in black and white on the album page reserved for them. In fact, I was afraid to leave the album at home in our empty flat because of the nightmare I'd had, afraid that either because I'd done nothing about removing the ten-cent Lindbergh airmail stamp from my collection or because Sandy had lied to our parents and his Lindbergh drawings remained intact under his bed—or because of the one filial betrayal conspiring with the other—a malignant transformation would occur in my absence, causing my unguarded Washingtons to turn into Hitlers, and swastikas to be imprinted on my National Parks.

Immediately upon entering Washington, we made a wrong turn in the heavy traffic, and while my mother was trying to read the road map and direct my father to our hotel, there appeared before us the biggest white thing I had ever seen. Atop an incline at the end of the street stood the U.S. Capitol, the broad stairs sweeping upward to the colonnade and capped by the elaborate three-tiered dome. Inadvertently, we had driven right to the very heart of American history, and whether we knew it in so many words, it was American history, delineated in its most inspirational form, that we were counting on to protect us against Lindbergh.

"Look!" my mother said, turning to Sandy and me in the back seat. "Isn't it thrilling?"

The answer, of course, was yes, but Sandy appeared to have fallen into a patriotic stupor, and I took my cue from him and let silence register my awe as well.

Just then a motorcycle policeman pulled alongside us. "What's up, Jersey?" he called through the open window.

"We're looking for our hotel," answered my father. "What's it called, Bess?"

My mother, enthralled only a moment earlier by the dwarfing majesty of the Capitol, immediately went pale, and her voice was so feeble when she tried to speak that she couldn't be heard above the traffic.

"Gotta get you folks out of here," the cop shouted. "Speak up, missus."

"The Douglas Hotel!" It was my brother eagerly calling out to him and trying to get a good look at the motorcycle. "On K Street, Officer."

"Attaboy," and he raised his arm in the air, signaling the cars behind us to stop and for ours to follow him as he made a U-turn and started in the opposite direction up Pennsylvania Avenue.

Laughing, my father said, "We're getting the royal treatment."

"But how do you know where he's taking us?" my mother asked. "Herman, what's happening?"

With the cop out front, we were headed past one big federal building after another when Sandy excitedly pointed toward a rolling lawn just to our left. "Up there!" he shouted. "The White House!" whereupon my mother began to cry.

"It isn't," she tried to explain just before we reached the hotel and the cop waved goodbye and roared away, "it isn't like living in a normal country anymore. I'm terribly sorry, children—please forgive me." But then she began to cry again.

In a little room at the rear of the Douglas there was a double bed for my parents and cots for my brother and me, and no sooner had my father tipped the bellhop who'd unlocked our door and set our bags down inside the room than our mother was her old self—or pretended as much by arranging the contents of our suitcases in the dresser and noting appreciatively that the drawers were freshly laid with lining paper.

We'd been on the road since leaving home at four in the morning and it was after one in the afternoon when we got back down to the street to look for a place to have lunch. The car was parked across from the hotel, and standing beside it was a sharp-faced little man in a double-breasted gray suit who doffed his hat and said, "My name is Taylor, folks. I am a professional guide to the nation's capital. If you don't want to be wasting time, you might want to hire someone like me. I'll drive for you so you don't get lost, I'll take you to the sights, tell you all there is to know, I'll wait and pick you up, I'll make sure you eat where the price is right and the food is tasty, and all it will cost, using your own automobile, is nine dollars a day. Here's my authorization," he said, and he unfolded a document of several pages to show to my father. "Issued by the Chamber of Commerce," he explained. "Verlin M. Taylor, sir, official D.C. guide since 1937. January 5, 1937, to be exact—the very day the Seventy-fifth U.S. Congress convened."

The two shook hands, and in his insurance man's best businesslike manner my father flipped through the guide's papers before handing them back to him. "Looks good to me," my father said, "but I don't think nine bucks a day is in the cards, Mr. Taylor, not for this family anyway."

"I appreciate that. But on your own, sir, you doing the driving and not knowing your way around and then trying to find a parking space in this city—well, you and the family won't see a half of what you'll be able to see with me, and you won't enjoy it anywhere near as much either. Why, I could drive you to a nice place to have your lunch, wait for you with the car, and then we can start right off with the Washington Monument. After that, down the Mall to the Lincoln Memorial. Washington and Lincoln. Our two greatest presidents—that's how I always like to begin. You know that Washington never did live in Washington. President Washington chose the site, he signed the bill making it the permanent seat of the government, but it was his successor, John Adams, who was the first president to move into the White House in 1800. November 1, to be exact. His wife, Abigail, joined him there two weeks later. Among the many interesting curios in the White House, there is still a celery glass owned by John and Abigail Adams."

"Well, that's something that I did not know," my father replied, "but let me take this up with my wife." Quietly he asked her, "Can we afford this? He sure knows his oats." Our mother whispered, "But who sent him? How did he spot our car?" "That's his job, Bess—to find who's the tourists. That's how the man makes a living." My brother and I were huddled up beside them, hoping our mother would shut up and that the easy-talking guide with the pointy face and the short legs would be hired for the duration.

"What do you want?" my father said, turning to Sandy and me.

"Well, if it costs too much . . . ," Sandy began.

"Forget the cost," my father replied. "Do you like this guy or not?"

"He's a character, Dad," Sandy whispered. "He looks like one of those duck decoys. I like when he says 'to be exact.'"

"Bess," my father said, "the man is a bona fide guide to Washington, D.C. Don't believe he's ever cracked a smile but he's an alert little guy and he couldn't be more polite. Let me see if he'll take seven bucks." Here he stepped away from us, walked up to the guide, they spoke seriously for a few minutes and then, the deal struck, the two again shook hands, and my father said aloud, "Okay, let's eat!" as always teeming with energy even when there was nothing to do.

It was hard to say what was most unbelievable: my being out of New Jersey for the first time in my life, my being three hundred miles from home in the nation's capital, or our family's being chauffeured in our own automobile by a stranger called by the same surname as the twelfth president of the United States, whose profile adorned the twelve-cent red-violet stamp in the album in my lap, hinged between the blue eleven-cent Polk and the green thirteen-cent Fillmore.

"Washington," Mr. Taylor was telling us, "is divided into four sections: northwest, northeast, southeast, and southwest. With some few exceptions, the streets running north and south are numbered and the streets running east and west are lettered. Of all the existing capitals in the Western world, this city alone was developed solely to provide a home for the national government. That is what makes it different not only from London and Paris but from our own New York and Chicago."

"Did you hear that?" my father asked, looking over his shoulder at Sandy and me. "Did you hear that, Bess, what Mr. Taylor said about why Washington is so special?"

"Yes," she said, and took my hand in hers to assure herself by assuring me that everything was now going to be all right. But I had only my one concern from the time we entered Washington until we left—preserving my stamp collection from harm.

The cafeteria where Mr. Taylor dropped us off was clean and cheap and the food as good as he'd said it would be, and when we finished our meal and headed for the street, there was our car pulling up to double-park out front. "What timing!" my father cried.

"Over the years," Mr. Taylor said, "you learn to estimate how long it takes a family to eat their lunch. Was that okay, Mrs. Roth?" he asked our mother. "Everything to your taste?"

"Very nice, thank you."

"So's everybody ready for the Washington Monument," he said, and off we drove. "You know, of course, who the monument commemorates—our first president, and in the opinion of most, our best president alongside President Lincoln."

"I'd include FDR in that list, you know. A great man, and the people of this country turned him out of office," my father said. "And just look what we got instead."

Mr. Taylor listened courteously but offered no response. "Now," he resumed, "you've all seen photos of the Washington Monument. But they don't always communicate just how impressive it is. At five hundred fifty-five feet, five and one-eighth inches above ground, it is the tallest masonry structure in the world. The new electric elevator will carry you to the top in one and a quarter minutes. Otherwise you can take a winding staircase of eight hundred and ninety-three steps to the top by foot. The view from up there has a radius of some fifteen to twenty miles. It's worth a look. There—see it?" he said. "Straight ahead."

Minutes later Mr. Taylor found a parking spot on the monument grounds and, when we left the car, trotted bandy-legged alongside us, explaining, "The monument was cleaned just a few years back for the first time. Just imagine that for a cleaning job, Mrs. Roth. They used water mixed with sand and steel-bristled brushes. Took five months and cost a hundred thousand dollars."

"Under FDR?" my father asked.

"I believe so, yes."

"And do people know?" my father asked. "Do people care? No. They want an airmail pilot running the country instead. And that's not the worst of it."

Mr. Taylor remained outside while we entered the monument. At the elevator, our mother, who again had taken hold of my hand, drew close to our father and whispered, "You mustn't talk like that."

"Like what?"

"About Lindbergh."

"That? That's just expressing my opinion."

"But you don't know who this man *is*."

"I sure do. He's an authorized guide with the documents to prove it. This is the Washington Monument, Bess, and you're telling me to keep my thoughts to myself as though the Washington Monument is situated in Berlin."

His speaking so bluntly distressed her even more, especially as the others waiting for the elevator could overhear our conversation. Turning to another of the fathers, who was standing alongside his wife and two kids, my father asked him, "Where you folks from? We're from Jersey." "Maine," the man replied. "Hear that?" my father said to my brother and me. Altogether some twenty children and adults entered the elevator, filling it up about halfway, and as the car rose through the housing of iron pillars, my father used the minute and a quarter it took to get to the top to ask the remaining families where each was from.

Mr. Taylor was waiting outside when we finished our tour. He asked Sandy and me to describe what we'd seen from the windows five hundred feet up and then he guided us on a quick walking tour around the exterior of the monument, recounting the fitful history of its construction. Next he took some pictures of the family with our Brownie box camera; then my father, over Mr. Taylor's objections, insisted on taking a picture of him with my mother, Sandy, and me with the Washington Monument as the background, and finally we got into our car and, with Mr. Taylor again at the wheel, started down the Mall for the Lincoln Memorial.

This time, while he parked, Mr. Taylor warned us that the Lincoln Memorial was like no other edifice anywhere in the world and that we should prepare ourselves to be overwhelmed. Then he accompanied us from the parking area to the great pillared building with the wide marble stairs that led us up past the columns to the hall's interior and the raised statue of Lincoln in his capacious throne of thrones, the sculpted face looking to me like the most hallowed possible amalgamation—the face of God and the face of America all in one.

Gravely my father said, "And they shot him, the dirty dogs."

The four of us stood directly at the base of the statue, which was lit so as to make everything about Abraham Lincoln seem colossally grand. What ordinarily passed for great just paled away, and there was no defense, for either an adult or a child, against the solemn atmosphere of hyperbole.

"When you think of what this country does to its greatest presidents . . ."

"Herman," my mother pleaded, "don't start."

"I'm not starting anything. This was a great tragedy. Isn't that right, boys? The assassination of Lincoln?"

Mr. Taylor came over and quietly told us, "Tomorrow we'll go to Ford's Theatre, where he was shot, and across the street to the Petersen House, to see where he died."

"I was saying, Mr. Taylor, it is the damnedest thing what this country does to its great men."

"Thank goodness we have President Lindbergh," said the voice of a woman just a few feet away. She was elderly and she was standing apart, by herself, consulting a guidebook, and her remark seemed spoken to no one and yet prompted somehow by her overhearing my father.

"Compare Lincoln to Lindbergh? Boy oh boy," my father moaned.

In fact the elderly lady was not alone but with a group of tourists, among whom was a man of about my father's age who might have been her son.

"Something bothering you?" he asked my father, assertively stepping in our direction.

"Not me," my father told him.

"Something bothering you about what the lady just said?"

"No, sir. Free country."

The stranger took a long, gaping look at my father, then my mother, then Sandy, then me. And what did he see? A trim, neatly muscled, broad-chested man five feet nine inches tall, handsome in a minor key, with soft grayish-green eyes and thinning brown hair clipped close at the temples and presenting his two ears to the world a little more comically than was necessary. The woman was slender but strong and she was tidily dressed, with a lock of her wavy dark hair over one eyebrow and roundish cheeks a little rouged and a prominent nose and chunky arms and shapely legs and slim hips and the lively eyes of a girl half her age. In both adults a surfeit of prudence and a surfeit of energy, and with the couple two boys still pretty much all soft surfaces, young children of youthful parents, keenly attentive and in good health and incorrigible only in their optimism.

And the conclusion the stranger drew from his observations he demonstrated with a mocking movement of the head. Then, hissing noisily so as to mislead no one about his assessment of us, he returned to the elderly lady and their sightseeing party, walking slowly off with a rolling gait that seemed, along with the silhouette of his broad back, intended to register a warning. It was from there that we heard him refer to my father as "a loudmouth Jew," followed a moment later by the elderly lady declaring, "I'd give anything to slap his face."

Mr. Taylor led us quickly away to a smaller hall just off the main chamber where there was a tablet inscribed with the Gettysburg Address and a mural whose theme was the Emancipation.

"To hear words like that in a place like this," said my father, his choked voice quivering with indignation. "In a shrine to a man like this!"

Meanwhile Mr. Taylor, pointing to the painting, said, "See there? An angel of truth is freeing a slave."

But my father could see nothing. "You think you'd hear that here if Roosevelt was president? People wouldn't dare, they wouldn't dream, in Roosevelt's day . . . ," my father said. "But now that our great ally is Adolf Hitler, now that the best friend of the president of the United States is Adolf Hitler—why, now they think they can get away with anything. It's disgraceful. It starts with the White House . . ."

Whom was he talking to other than me? My brother was trailing after Mr. Taylor, asking about the mural, and my mother was trying to prevent herself from saying or doing anything, struggling against the very emotions that had overpowered her earlier in the car—and back then without anything like this much justification.

"Read that," my father said, alluding to the tablet bearing the Gettysburg Address. "Just read it. 'All men are created equal.'"

"Herman," gasped my mother, "I can't go on with this."

We came back out into the daylight and gathered together on the top step. The tall shaft of the Washington Monument was a half mile away, at the other end of the reflecting pool that lay at the base of the terraced approach to the Lincoln Memorial. There were elm trees planted all around. It was the most beautiful panorama I'd ever seen, a patriotic paradise, the American Garden of Eden spread before us, and we stood huddled together there, the family expelled.

"Listen," my father said, pulling my brother and me close to him, "I think it's time we all had a nap. It's been a long day for everybody. I say we go back to the hotel and get some rest for an hour or two. What do you say, Mr. Taylor?"

"Up to you, Mr. Roth. After supper I thought the family might enjoy a tour in the car of Washington by night, with the famous monuments all lit up."

"Now you're talkin'," my father told him. "Sound good, Bess?" But my mother wasn't so easy to cheer up as Sandy and I. "Honey," my father told her, "we ran into a screwball. Two screwballs. We might have gone up to Canada and run into somebody just as bad. We're not going to let that ruin our trip. Let's have a nice rest, all of us, and Mr. Taylor will wait for us, and we'll go on from there. Look," he then said, with a sweep of his outstretched arm. "This is something every American should see. Turn around, boys. Take one last look at Abraham Lincoln."

We did as he instructed but it was impossible any longer to feel the raptures of patriotism turning me inside out. As we began the long descent down the marble staircase, I heard some kids behind us asking their parents, "Is that really him? Is he buried there under all that stuff?" My mother was directly beside me on the stairs, trying to act like someone whose panic wasn't running wild within her, and suddenly I felt that it had fallen to me to hold her together, to become all at once a courageous new creature with something of Lincoln himself clinging to him. But all I could do when she offered me a hand was to take it and clutch it like the unripened being I was, a boy whose stamp collection still represented nine-tenths of his knowledge of the world.

In the car, Mr. Taylor plotted the rest of our day. We'd go back to the hotel, nap, and at quarter to six he'd come to pick us up and drive us to dinner. We could return to the cafeteria near Union Station where we'd had our lunch, or he could recommend a couple of other popular-priced restaurants whose quality he could vouch for. And after dinner, he'd take us on the tour of Washington by night.

"Nothing fazes you, does it, Mr. Taylor?" my father said.

He replied only with a noncommittal nod.

"Where you from?" my father asked him.

"Indiana, Mr. Roth."

"Indiana. Imagine that, boys. And what's your hometown out there?" my father asked him.

"Didn't have one. My father's a mechanic. Fixed farm machinery. Moved all the time."

"Well," said my father, for reasons that can't have been clear to Mr. Taylor, "I take my hat off to you, sir. You should be proud of yourself."

Again, Mr. Taylor gave only a nod: he was a no-nonsense man in a tight suit and with something decidedly military about his efficiency and his bearing—like a hidden person, except there was nothing to hide, everything impersonal about him being plainly visible. Voluble talking about Washington, D.C., close-mouthed about everything else.

When we got back to the hotel, Mr. Taylor parked the car and accompanied us in as though he were not just our guide but our chaperone, and a good thing it was, because inside the lobby of the small hotel we discovered our four suitcases standing beside the front desk.

The new man at the desk introduced himself as the manager.

When my father asked what our bags were doing downstairs, the manager said, "Folks, I have to apologize. Had to pack these up for you. Our afternoon clerk made a mistake. The room he gave you was being held for another family. Here's your deposit." And he handed my father an envelope containing a ten-dollar bill.

"But my wife wrote you people. You wrote us back. We had a reservation months ago. That's why we sent the deposit. Bess, where's the copies of the letters?"

She pointed to the bags.

"Sir," said the manager, "the room is occupied and there are no vacancies. We will not charge you for what use you all made of the room today or for the bar of soap that is missing."

"Missing?" Just the word to send him right off the rails. "Are you saying we *stole* it?"

"No, sir, I am not. Perhaps one of the children took the soap as a souvenir. No harm done. We're not going to haggle about something so small or start looking through their pockets for the soap."

"What is the meaning of this!" my father demanded to know, and under the manager's nose pounded his fist on the front desk.

"Mr. Roth, if you're going to make a scene here . . ."

"Yes," my father said, "I am going to make a scene till I find out what's up with that room!"

"Well, then," replied the manager, "I have no choice but to phone the police."

Here my mother—who was holding my brother and me around the shoulders, shielding us alongside her and at a safe distance from the desk—called my father's name, trying to prevent him from going further. But it was too late for that. It always had been. Never could he have consented to quietly occupying the place that the manager wished to assign him.

"This is that goddamn Lindbergh!" my father said. "All you little fascists are in the saddle now!"

"Shall I call the District police, sir, or will you take your bags and your family and leave immediately?"

"Call the police," my father replied. "You do that."

There were now five or six guests aside from us in the lobby. They'd entered while the argument was under way and they were lingering to find out what was going to come of it.

It was then that Mr. Taylor stepped up to my father's side and said, "Mr. Roth, you are perfectly in the right, but the police are the wrong solution."

"No, that is the *right* solution. Call the police," my father repeated to the manager. "There are laws in this country against people like you."

The manager reached for the phone, and while he dialed, Mr. Taylor went over to our bags, swept up two in either hand, and carried them out of the hotel.

My mother said, "Herman, it's over. Mr. Taylor took the bags."

"No, Bess," he said bitterly. "I've had enough of their guff. I want to talk to the police."

Mr. Taylor reentered the lobby on the run and without stopping bore down on the desk, where the manager was completing his call. In a lowered voice, he spoke only to my father. "There is a nice hotel not very far away. I telephoned them from the booth outside. They have a room for you. It's a nice hotel on a nice street. Let's drive over there and get the family registered."

"Thank you, Mr. Taylor. But right now we are waiting for the police. I want them to remind this man of the words in the Gettysburg Address that I read carved up there just today."

The people watching all smiled at one another when my father mentioned the Gettysburg Address.

I whispered to my brother, "What happened?"

"Anti-Semitism," he whispered back.

From where we were standing we saw the two policemen when they arrived on their motorcycles. We watched them cut their engines and come into the hotel. One of them stationed himself just inside the door, where he could keep an eye on everybody while the other approached the front desk and beckoned the manager over to where the two of them could speak confidentially.

"Officer—" my father said.

The policeman spun around and said, "I can attend to only one party to a dispute at a time, sir," and resumed talking with the manager, his chin cupped thoughtfully in one hand.

My father turned to us. "Got to be done, boys." To my mother he said, "There's nothing to worry about."

Having finished his discussion with the manager, the policeman now came around to talk to my father. He didn't smile as he had intermittently while standing and listening to the manager, but he spoke nonetheless without a trace of anger and in a tone that seemed friendly at first. "What's the problem, Roth?"

"We sent a deposit for a room at this hotel for three nights. We received a letter confirming everything. My wife has the paperwork in our bags. We get here today, we register, we occupy the room and unpack, we go out to sightsee, and when we come back we're evicted because the room was reserved for somebody else."

"And the problem?" the cop asked.

"We're a family of four, Officer. We drove all the way from New Jersey. You can't just throw us into the street."

"But," said the cop, "if somebody else reserves a room—"

"But there is nobody else! And if there was, why should we take a back seat to them?"

"But the manager returned your deposit. He even packed up your belongings for you."

"Officer, you're not understanding me. Why should our reservation take a back seat to theirs? I was with my family at the Lincoln Memorial. They have the Gettysburg Address up on the wall. You know what the words are that are written there? 'All men are created equal.'"

"But that doesn't mean all hotel reservations are created equal."

The policeman's voice carried to the bystanders at the edge of the lobby; unable any longer to control themselves, some of them laughed aloud.

My mother left Sandy and me standing alone in order to step forward now and intervene. She had been waiting for a moment when she wouldn't make things worse, and, despite her rapid breathing, seemed to believe this was it. "Dear, let's just go," she beseeched my father. "Mr. Taylor found us a room nearby."

"No!" my father cried, and he threw off the hand with which she had tried to snatch his arm. "This policeman knows why we were evicted. He knows, the manager knows, everybody in this lobby knows."

"I think you ought to listen to your wife," the cop said. "I think you ought to do what she tells you, Roth. Leave the premises." Jerking his head in the direction of the door, he said, "And before you wear out my patience."

There was more resistance in my father, but there was still some sanity in him as well, and he was able to understand that his argument had run out of interest to anyone other than himself. We left the hotel with everybody watching us. The only one to speak was the other cop. From where he'd stationed himself just beside the potted plant in the entranceway, he nodded amiably and, as we approached, put a hand out to muss my hair. "How you doin', young fella?" "Good," I replied. "Whattaya got there?" "My stamps," I said, but just kept going before he could ask to see my collection and I had to show it to him to avoid arrest.

Mr. Taylor was waiting on the sidewalk outside. My father said to him, "That has never happened to me before in my life. I'm out among people all the time, people from all backgrounds, from all walks of life, and never . . ."

"The Douglas has changed hands," Mr. Taylor said. "This is a new ownership."

"But we had friends who stayed there and were a hundred percent satisfied," my mother told him.

"Well, Mrs. Roth, it's changed hands. But I've got you a room at the Evergreen, and everything is going to work out fine."

Just then there was the loud roar of a low-flying plane passing over Washington. Down the street where some people were out walking, they stopped and one of the men raised his arms to the sky, as though, in June, it had begun to snow.

Sandy, who could recognize just about anything flying from its silhouette, knowledgeable Sandy pointed and cried, "It's the Lockheed Interceptor!"

"It's President Lindbergh," Mr. Taylor explained. "Every afternoon about this time he takes a little spin along the Potomac. Flies up to the Alleghenies, then down along the Blue Ridge Mountains, and on out to the Chesapeake Bay. People look forward to it."

"It's the world's fastest plane," my brother said. "The Germans' Messerschmitt 110 flies three hundred and sixty-five miles an hour —the Interceptor flies five hundred miles an hour. It can outmaneuver any fighter in the world."

We all watched along with Sandy, who was unable to conceal his enchantment with the very Interceptor that the president had flown to and from Iceland for his meeting with Hitler. The plane climbed steeply with tremendous force before disappearing into the sky. Down the street, the people out walking burst into applause, somebody shouted "Hurray for Lindy!" and then they continued on their way.

At the Evergreen, my mother and father slept together in one single bed and Sandy and I in the other. Twin beds were the best Mr. Taylor had been able to locate on such short notice, but after what had happened at the Douglas nobody complained—either that the beds weren't exactly made for rest or that the room was smaller even than our first accommodations or that the matchbox bathroom, heavily doused though it was with disinfectant, didn't smell right—especially as we were welcomed graciously when we arrived by a cheerful woman at the front desk and our suitcases stacked on a dolly by an elderly Negro in a bellhop's uniform, a lanky man the woman called Edward B., who upon unlocking the door to the ground-floor room at the nether end of an airshaft, humorously announced, "The Evergreen Hotel welcomes the Roth family to the nation's capital!" and ushered us in as though the dimly lit crypt were a boudoir at the Ritz. My brother hadn't stopped staring at Edward B. from the time he loaded our luggage, and the next morning, before anyone else was awake, he stealthily dressed, grabbed his sketchpad, and raced to the lobby to draw him. As it happened, a different Negro bellhop was on duty, one not picturesquely grooved and crannied quite like Edward B., though from an artistic point of view no less of a find—very dark with strongly African facial features of a kind Sandy had never before gotten to draw from anything other than a photo in a back issue of *National Geographic*.

We spent most of the morning with Mr. Taylor showing us around the Capitol and Congress, and later the Supreme Court and the Library of Congress. Mr. Taylor knew the height of every dome and the dimensions of every lobby and the geographic origins of all the marble flooring and the names of the subjects and the events commemorated in every painting and mural in every government building we entered. "You are something," my father told him. "A small-town boy from Indiana. You should be on *Information Please*."

After lunch, we drove south along the Potomac into Virginia to tour Mount Vernon. "Of course, Richmond, Virginia," Mr. Taylor explained, "was the capital of the eleven southern states that left the Union to form the Confederate States of America. Many of the great battles of the Civil War were fought in Virginia. Some twenty miles due west is the Manassas National Battlefield Park. The park includes both battlefields where the Confederates routed the Union forces near the little stream of Bull Run, first under General P.G.T. Beauregard and General J. E. Johnston in July 1861, and then under General Robert E. Lee and General Stonewall Jackson in August 1862. General Lee was in command of the Army of Virginia, and the president of the Confederacy, who governed from Richmond, was Jefferson Davis, if you remember your history. To the southwest a hundred and twenty-five miles from here is Appomattox, Virginia. You know what happened in the courthouse there in April 1865. April 9, to be exact. General Lee surrendered to General U. S. Grant, thus ending the Civil War. And you all know what happened to Lincoln six days later: he was shot."

"Those dirty dogs," my father said again.

"Well, there it is," said Mr. Taylor, just as Washington's house came into view.

"Oh, it's so beautiful," my mother said. "Look at the porch. Look at the tall windows. Children, this isn't a replica—this is the real house where George Washington lived."

"And his wife, Martha," Mr. Taylor reminded her, "and his two stepchildren, whom the general doted on."

"Did he?" my mother asked. "I didn't know that. My younger son has Martha Washington on a stamp," she told him. "Show Mr. Taylor your stamp," and I immediately found it, the brown 1938 one-and-a-half-cent stamp that pictured the first president's wife in profile, her hair covered with what my mother had identified for me, when I first got the stamp, as something between a bonnet and a snood.

"Yep, that's her all right," said Mr. Taylor. "And she is also, as I'm sure you know, on a four-cent nineteen hundred and twenty-three and on an eight-cent nineteen hundred and two. And that nineteen hundred and two stamp, Mrs. Roth, that is the first stamp ever to show an American woman."

"Did you know that?" my mother asked me.

"Yes," I said, and for me all the complications of our being a Jewish family in Lindbergh's Washington simply vanished and I felt the way I felt in school when, at the start of an assembly program, you rose to your feet and sang the national anthem, giving it everything you had.

"She was a great companion to General Washington," Mr. Taylor told us. "Martha Dandridge was her maiden name. The widow of Colonel Daniel Parke Custis. Her two children were Patsy and John Parke Custis. She brought to her marriage to Washington one of the largest fortunes in Virginia."

"That's what I always tell my boys," my father said, laughing as we hadn't heard him laugh all day. "Marry like President Washington. It's as easy to love 'em rich as poor."

The visit to Mount Vernon was the happiest time we had on that trip, perhaps because of the beauty of the grounds and the gardens and the trees and of the house, commandingly situated on a bluff overlooking the Potomac; perhaps because of the unusualness to us of the furnishings, the decoration, and the wallpaper—wallpaper about which Mr. Taylor knew a million things; perhaps because we got to see from only a few feet away the four-poster bed in which Washington slept, the desk where he wrote, the swords that he wore, and the books that he owned and read; or perhaps just because we were fifteen miles from Washington, D.C., and from Lindbergh's spirit hovering over everything.

Mount Vernon was open until four-thirty, so we had plenty of time to see all the rooms and the outbuildings and to wander the grounds and then to visit the souvenir shop, where I succumbed to the temptation of a letter opener that was a four-inch pewter replica of a Revolutionary musket and bayonet. I bought it with twelve of the fifteen cents I'd been saving for our visit the next day to the stamp division of the Bureau of Engraving and Printing, while Sandy prudently bought with his savings an illustrated history of Washington's life, a book whose pictures he could use to suggest more portraits for the patriotic series stored in the portfolio under his bed.

It was the end of the day and we were off to have a drink in the cafeteria just as a low-flying plane in the distance came zooming our way. As the roar grew louder, people shouted, "It's the president! It's Lindy!" Men, women, and children all ran out onto the great front lawn and began to wave at the approaching plane, which as it crossed over the Potomac tipped its wings. "Hurray!" people shouted. "Hurray for Lindy!" It was the same Lockheed fighter we'd seen in the air over the city the previous afternoon, and we had no choice but to stand there like patriots and watch with the rest of them as it banked and flew back over George Washington's home before it turned to follow the Potomac north.

"It wasn't him—it was her!" Someone claiming to have been able to see into the cockpit had begun to spread word that the pilot of the Interceptor was the president's wife. And it could have been true. Lindbergh had taught her to fly when she was still his young bride and she'd often flown alongside him on his air trips, and so now people began telling their children that it was Anne Morrow Lindbergh whom they'd just seen flying over Mount Vernon, a historical event they would never forget. By then her audacity as a pilot of the most advanced American aircraft, combined with her demure manner as a well-bred daughter of the privileged classes and her literary gifts as the author of two published books of lyric poetry, had established her in all the polls as the nation's most admired woman.

So our perfect outing was ruined—and not so much because a recreational flight piloted by one or another of the Lindberghs happened by chance to have passed over our heads for the second day in a row but because of what the stunt, as my father called it, had inspired in everyone except us. "We knew things were bad," my father told the friends he immediately sat down to phone when we got home, "but not like this. You had to be there to see what it looked like. They live in a dream, and we live in a nightmare."

It was the most eloquent line I'd ever heard him speak, and arguably distinguished by more precision than any ever written by Lindbergh's wife.

Mr. Taylor drove us back to the Evergreen so we could wash up and rest, and promptly at five forty-five returned to drive us to the inexpensive cafeteria near the railroad station; we'd all meet up afterward, he said, to start the night tour of Washington postponed from the day before.

"Why don't you come along tonight?" my father said to him. "It must get lonely eating by yourself all the time."

"I wouldn't want to invade your privacy, Mr. Roth."

"Listen here, you're a wonderful guide, and we would enjoy it. Treat's on us."

The cafeteria was even more popular at night than it was during the day, every chair occupied and customers standing in line waiting to have their selections spooned out by the three men in white aprons and white caps who were so busy serving they didn't have time to stop and dry their perspiring faces. At our table my mother took solace in resuming her motherly mealtime role—"Darling, try not to lower your chin to the plate when you take a bite"—and our having Mr. Taylor seated beside us as if he were a relative or family friend, though not so novel an adventure as being thrown out of the Douglas Hotel, provided the opportunity to watch someone eat who'd grown up in Indiana. My father was the only one of us paying attention to the other diners, all of them laughing and smoking and diligently digging into the Frenchified evening special—roast beef au jus and pecan pie à la mode—while he sat there fingering his water glass, seemingly trying to figure out how the problems in their lives could be so unlike his own.

When he got around to expressing his thoughts—which continued to take precedence over his eating—it wasn't to one of us but to Mr. Taylor, who was just starting in on the piece of pie topped with American cheese that he'd chosen for dessert. "We are a Jewish family, Mr. Taylor. You know that by now, if you didn't already, because that's the reason we were evicted yesterday. That was a big shock," he said. "That's hard to get over just like that. It's a shock because though it's something that could have happened without this man being president, he is the president and he is no friend of the Jews. He is the friend of Adolf Hitler."

"Herman," my mother whispered, "you'll frighten the little one."

"The little one knows everything already," he said, and resumed addressing Mr. Taylor. "You ever listen to Winchell? Let me quote you Walter Winchell: 'Was there any more to their diplomatic understanding, other things they talked about, other things they agreed on? Did they reach an understanding about America's Jews —and if so, what was it?' That's the kind of guts Winchell has. Those are the words he has the guts to speak to the entire country."

Surprisingly, someone had stepped up so close to our table that he was hanging half over it—a heavyset, mustached elderly man with a white paper napkin jammed into his belt who seemed inflamed with whatever he had in mind to say. He had been eating at a nearby table and his companions there were all leaning our way, eager to hear what was coming next.

"Hey, what's doin', bud?" my father said. "Back up, will ya?"

"Winchell is a Jew," the man announced, "in the pay of the British government."

What happened next was that my father's hands rose violently from the table, as though to drive his knife and his fork upward into the stranger's holiday-goose of a belly. He hadn't to elaborate further to communicate his abhorrence, and yet the man with the mustache did not budge. The mustache wasn't a dark close-clipped little square patch like Hitler's but one conceived of in a less officious, more whimsical spirit, a conspicuously substantial white walrus mustache of the type displayed by President Taft on the light red 1938 fifty-cent stamp.

"If ever there was a case of a loudmouth Jew with too much power—" the stranger said.

"That is enough!" Mr. Taylor cried and, jumping to his feet, placed himself—undersized as he was—between the large figure looming over us and my outraged father, pinned in below by all that ludicrous bulk.

Loudmouth Jew. And for the second time in less than forty-eight hours.

Two of the aproned men from behind the serving counter had rushed out onto the floor of the cafeteria and taken hold of our assailant from either side. "This is not your corner saloon," one of them told him, "and don't you forget it, mister." At his table, they pushed him down into his chair, and then the one who'd chastised him came over to us and said, "I want you folks to fill your coffee cups as much as you like. Let me bring the boys some more ice cream. You folks just stay and finish up your supper. I am the owner, my name is Wilbur, and all the desserts you want is on the house. Let's bring you fresh ice water while we're at it."

"Thank you," my father said, speaking with the eerie impersonality of a machine. "Thank you," he repeated. "Thank you."

"Herman, please," my mother whispered, "let's just go."

"Absolutely not. No. We're finishing our food." He cleared his throat to continue. "We're touring Washington by night. We are not going home till we tour Washington by night."

The evening, in other words, was to be seen through to the end without our being frightened away. For Sandy and me that meant consuming big new dishes of ice cream, delivered to our table by one of the countermen.

It took a few minutes for the cafeteria to come alive again with the squeaking of chairs and the rattle of cutlery and the light tinkle of plates, if not yet the full dinnertime clamor.

"Would you like more coffee?" my father said to my mother. "You heard the owner—he wants you to fill your cup."

"No," she murmured, "no more."

"And you, Mr. Taylor—coffee?"

"Nope, I'm fine."

"So," my father said to Mr. Taylor—stiffly, lamely, but beginning again to push back at everything awful that was surging in. "What kind of job did you do before this one? Or have you always been a guide in Washington?"

And it was here that we heard once again from the man who'd stepped up to inform us that, like Benedict Arnold before him, Walter Winchell had sold out to the British. "Oh, don't you worry," he was assuring his friends, "the Jews will find out soon enough."

In all that quiet there was no mistaking what he'd said, especially as he hadn't bothered to modulate the taunt in any way. Half the diners didn't even look up, pretending to have heard nothing, but more than a few twisted round to look right at the offending objects.

I'd seen tarring and feathering only once, in a Western movie, but I thought, "We are going to be tarred and feathered," envisioning all our humiliation sticking to the skin like a coat of thick filth that you could never get off.

My father was stalled for a moment, having to decide once again whether to attempt to control the event or give in to it. "I was asking Mr. Taylor," he suddenly said to my mother while taking her hands in both of his, "about what he did before being a guide." And he looked at her like someone casting a spell, someone whose art is to prevent your will from being free of his and keep you from acting on your own.

"Yes," she said, "I heard." And then, her anguish once again filling her with tears, she nonetheless drew herself up erect in her seat and said to Mr. Taylor, "Yes, please tell us."

"Keep eating your ice cream, boys," my father said, reaching out and patting our forearms until we looked him right in the eye. "Is it good?"

"Yes," we said.

"Well, you just keep eating and take your time." He smiled to make us smile, and then said to Mr. Taylor, "The job before this one, your old job—what was it you did again, sir?"

"I was a college teacher, Mr. Roth."

"Is that right?" my father said. "Hear that, boys? You're eating your dinner with a college teacher."

"A college history teacher," added Mr. Taylor for the sake of accuracy.

"Should have known," my father admitted.

"Little college in northwest Indiana," Mr. Taylor told the four of us. "When they shut half the place down in '32, that was it for me."

"And so what'd you do then?" my father asked.

"Well, you can imagine. What with unemployment and all the strikes, I did a little of everything. Harvested mint up in the Indiana mucklands. Packed meat for the slaughterhouse in Hammond. Packed soap for Cudahy in East Chicago. Worked a year for Real Silk Hosiery Mills in Indianapolis. Even worked a stint at Logansport, at the mental hospital there, worked as an orderly for people suffering mental diseases. Hard times finally washed me up here."

"And what was the name of that college where you taught?" my father asked.

"Wabash."

"Wabash? Well," said my father, soothed by the very sound of the word, "everybody has heard of that."

"Four hundred and twenty-six students? I'm not so sure they have. What everybody has heard of is something that one of our distinguished graduates once said, though they don't necessarily know him for being a Wabash man. They know him for being U.S. vice president, 1912 to 1920. That is our two-term vice president Thomas Riley Marshall."

"Sure," my father said. "Vice President Marshall, the Democratic governor of Indiana. Vice president under another great Democrat, Woodrow Wilson. Man of dignity, President Wilson. It was President Wilson," he said, after two days of tutelage under Mr. Taylor, himself in the mood now to elucidate, "who had the courage to appoint Louis D. Brandeis to the Supreme Court. First Jewish member ever of the Supreme Court. You know that, boys?"

We did—it was hardly the first time he'd told us. It was only the first time he'd told us in a booming voice in a cafeteria like this one in Washington, D.C.

Sailing on, Mr. Taylor said, "And what the vice president said has been famous nationwide ever since. One day, in the United States Senate—while he was presiding over a Senate debate—he said to the senators there, 'What this country needs,' he said, 'is a really good five-cent cigar.'"

My father laughed—that was indeed a folksy observation that had won the heart of his whole generation and that even Sandy and I knew through his repeating it to us. So he laughed genially, and then, to further astonish not only his family but probably everyone in the cafeteria, to whom he'd already extolled Woodrow Wilson for appointing a Jew to the Supreme Court, he proclaimed, "What this country needs now is a new president."

No riot ensued. Nothing. Indeed, by not quitting he appeared almost to have won the day.

"And isn't there a Wabash River?" my father next asked Mr. Taylor.

"Longest tributary of the Ohio. Runs four hundred and seventy-five miles clear across the state east to west."

"And there is a song, too," my father remembered almost dreamily.

"Right you are," replied Mr. Taylor. "A very famous song. Maybe as famous as 'Yankee Doodle' itself. Written by Paul Dresser in 1897. 'On the Banks of the Wabash, Far Away.'"

"Of course!" cried my father.

"The favorite song," said Mr. Taylor, "of our Spanish-American War soldiers in 1898 and adopted as the state song of Indiana in 1913. March 4, to be exact."

"Sure, sure, I know that one," my father told him.

"I expect every American does," Mr. Taylor said.

And all at once, in a brisk cadence, my father began to sing it, and strongly enough for everyone in the cafeteria to hear. "'Through the sycamores the candlelights are gleaming . . .'"

"Good," said our guide with admiration, "very good," and outright bewitched by my father's baritone bravura, the solemn little encyclopedia smiled at last.

"My husband," said my dry-eyed mother, "has a lovely singing voice."

"That he does," said Mr. Taylor, and though there was no applause—other than from Wilbur, back of the serving counter—here we abruptly got up to go before we outstayed our tiny triumph and the man with the presidential mustache went berserk.

3

June 1941–December 1941

Following Christians

O
N JUNE 22, 1941, the Hitler-Stalin Non-Aggression Pact
—signed two years earlier by the two dictators only days
before invading and dividing up Poland—was broken
without warning when Hitler, having already overrun continental
Europe, dared to undertake the conquest of the enormous land-
mass that stretched from Poland across Asia to the Pacific by staging a massive assault to the east against Stalin's troops. That evening, President Lindbergh addressed the nation from the White
House about Hitler's colossal expansion of the war and astonished
even my father by his candid praise for the German Führer. "With
this act," the president declared, "Adolf Hitler has established himself as the world's greatest safeguard against the spread of Communism and its evils. This is not to minimize the effort of imperial
Japan. Dedicated as the Japanese are to modernizing Chiang Kai-
shek's corrupt and feudal China, they are equally dedicated to
rooting out the fanatical Chinese Communist minority, whose aim
is to seize control of that vast country and, like the Bolsheviks in
Russia, to turn China into a Communist prison camp. But it is
Hitler to whom the entire world must be grateful tonight for striking at the Soviet Union. If the German army is successful in its
struggle against Soviet Bolshevism—and there is every reason to
believe that it will be—America will never have to face the threat
of a voracious Communist state imposing its pernicious system on

the rest of the world. I can only hope that the internationalists still serving in the United States Congress recognize that if we had allowed our nation to be dragged into this world war on the side of Great Britain and France, we would now find our great democracy allied with the evil regime of the USSR. Tonight the German army may well be waging the war that would otherwise have had to be fought by American troops."

Our troops were at the ready, however, and would be, the president reminded his countrymen, for a long time to come because of the peacetime draft established by Congress at his request, twenty-four months of compulsory military training for eighteen-year-olds, followed by eight years on call in the reserves which would contribute enormously to fulfilling his dual goal of "keeping America out of all foreign wars and of keeping all foreign wars out of America." "An independent destiny for America"—that was the phrase Lindbergh repeated some fifteen times in his State of the Union speech and again at the close of his address on the night of June 22. When I asked my father to explain what the words meant—absorbed by the headlines and weighed down by all my anxious thoughts, I was more and more asking what everything meant—he frowned and said, "It means turning our back on our friends. It means making friends with their enemies. You know what it means, son? It means destroying everything that America stands for."

Under the auspices of Just Folks—described by Lindbergh's newly created Office of American Absorption as "a volunteer work program introducing city youth to the traditional ways of heartland life"—my brother left on the last day of June 1941 for a summer "apprenticeship" with a Kentucky tobacco farmer. Because he'd never been away from home before, and because the family had never lived with such uncertainty before, and because my father objected strenuously to what the OAA's existence implied about our status as citizens—and also because Alvin, already off serving with the Canadian army, had become a perpetual source of concern—Sandy's was an emotional leave-taking. What had given Sandy strength to resist our parents' arguments against his participating in Just Folks—and planted the idea to apply in the first place—was the support he'd received from my mother's vivid younger sister, Evelyn, now executive assistant to Rabbi Lionel Bengelsdorf, who'd been appointed by the new administration to serve as the first director of the OAA office for the state of New Jersey. The announced purpose of the OAA was to implement programs "encouraging America's religious and national minorities to become further incorporated into the larger society," though by the spring of 1941 the only minority the OAA appeared to take a serious interest in encouraging was ours. It was the intention of Just Folks to remove hundreds of Jewish boys between the ages of twelve and eighteen from the cities where they lived and attended school and put them to work for eight weeks as field hands and day laborers with farm families hundreds of miles from their homes. Notices extolling the new summer program had been posted on bulletin boards at Chancellor and at Weequahic, the high school just next door, where the student population, like ours, was nearly one hundred percent Jewish. One day in April, a representative from the New Jersey OAA had come to talk to the boys twelve and over about the program's mission, and that evening Sandy showed up at the dinner table with an application blank that required a parent's signature.

"Do you understand what this program is actually trying to do?" my father asked Sandy. "Do you understand why Lindbergh wants to separate boys like you from their families and ship them out to the sticks? Do you have any idea what's behind all this?"

"But this doesn't have anything to do with anti-Semitism, if that's what you think. You have one thing on your mind and one thing only. This is just a great opportunity, that's all."

"Opportunity for what?"

"To live on a farm. To go to Kentucky. To draw all the things there. Tractors. Barns. Animals. All kinds of animals."

"But they're not sending you all that way to draw animals," my father told him. "They're sending you there to fetch the slops for the animals. They're sending you there to spread manure. You'll be so bushed by the end of the day that you won't be able to stand on your feet, let alone draw a picture of an animal."

"And your hands," my mother said. "There's barbed wire on farms. There are machines with sharp blades. You could injure your hands, and then where would you be? You'd never draw again. I thought you were going to take classes at Arts High this summer. You were going to take drawing with Mr. Leonard."

"I can always do that—this is seeing America!"

The next night Aunt Evelyn came to dinner, invited by my mother for the hours Sandy was planning to be at a friend's house doing his homework; that way he wouldn't be around to witness the argument that was certain to flare up between Aunt Evelyn and my father on the subject of Just Folks, and that did indeed erupt upon her entering the house to announce that she would be taking care of Sandy's application the moment it reached the office. "Don't do us any favors," said my unsmiling father.

"You mean to tell me you're not letting him go?"

"Why should I? Why would I?" he asked her.

"Why on earth wouldn't you," Aunt Evelyn replied, "unless you're another Jew afraid of his shadow."

Their disagreement only grew more passionate during dinner, my father maintaining that Just Folks was the first step in a Lindbergh plan to separate Jewish children from their parents, to erode the solidarity of the Jewish family, and Aunt Evelyn intimating none too gently that the greatest fear of a Jew like her brother-in-law was that his children might escape winding up as narrow-minded and frightened as he was.

Alvin was the renegade on my father's side, Evelyn was the maverick on my mother's, a substitute elementary school teacher in the Newark system who'd been active several years earlier in founding the left-wing, largely Jewish Newark Teachers Union, whose few hundred members were competing with a more staid, apolitical teachers' association to negotiate contracts with the city. Evelyn was just thirty in 1941, and until two years before, when my maternal grandmother died of heart failure after a decade as a coronary invalid, it was Evelyn who'd cared for her in the tiny top-floor apartment of a two-and-a-half-family house that mother and daughter shared on Dewey Street, not far from Hawthorne Avenue School, where Evelyn usually subbed. On the days when a neighbor wasn't free to stop by to keep an eye on our grandmother, my mother would take the bus over to Dewey Street and look after her until Evelyn got home from work, and when Evelyn went to New York to see a play with her intellectual friends on a Saturday night, either our grandmother would be driven to our house by my father to spend the evening with us or my mother would return to Dewey Street to tend to her there. Many nights Aunt Evelyn never made it home from New York—even when she'd planned to return before midnight—and so my mother would be forced to spend the night away from her husband and children. And then there were the afternoons Evelyn didn't get back until hours after school was over, because of a long-standing off-and-on love affair with a substitute teacher from North Newark, like Evelyn a forceful union advocate, and unlike Evelyn married, Italian, and the parent of three children.

My mother would always contend that if Evelyn hadn't got waylaid at home for all those years nursing their invalid mother, she would have settled down to marry after getting her teaching certificate and never have ended up falling in and out of "unsavory" relationships with married men who were her fellow teachers. Her large nose didn't prevent people from calling Aunt Evelyn "striking," and it was true, as my mother observed, that when tiny Evelyn walked into a room—a vivacious brunette with a perfect, if miniaturized, womanly silhouette, enormous dark eyes slanted like a cat's, and crimson lipstick guaranteed to dazzle—everyone turned to look, the women as well as the men. Her hair was lacquered to a metallic luster and pulled back in a chignon, her eyebrows were dramatically plucked, and when she went off to sub, she donned a brightly colored skirt with matching high-heeled shoes and a broad white belt and a semisheer, pastel-colored blouse. My father considered her apparel in poor taste for a school-teacher, and so did the principal at Hawthorne, but my mother, who, wrongly or not, reproached herself for Evelyn's having had to "sacrifice her youth" caring for their mother, was incapable of judging her sister's boldness harshly, even when Evelyn resigned from teaching, quit the union, and, seemingly without a qualm, abandoned her political loyalties to work for Rabbi Bengelsdorf in Lindbergh's OAA.

It would be several months before it occurred to my parents that Aunt Evelyn was the rabbi's mistress and had been ever since he'd met her at a reception following his speech to the Newark Teach-ers Union on "The Classroom Development of American Ideals"— and they realized it only then because, on leaving the New Jersey OAA to assume the job of federal director at the national head-quarters in Washington, Bengelsdorf announced to the Newark papers news of his engagement, at age sixty-three, to his thirty-one-year-old firebrand of an assistant.

When he first ran off to fight Hitler, Alvin imagined that the quick-est way to see action would be aboard one of the Canadian de-stroyers that were protecting the merchant marine ships carrying supplies to Great Britain. Stories in the newspaper regularly re-ported the sinking by German submarines of one or more of the Canadian ships in the North Atlantic, sometimes as close to the mainland as the coastal fishing waters of Newfoundland—an es-pecially ominous development for the British because Canada had become virtually their only source of arms, food, medicine, and machinery once the Lindbergh administration overturned the aid legislation enacted by the Roosevelt Congress. In Montreal Alvin met a young American defector who told him to forget about the navy—it was the Canadian commandos who were in the thick of things, carrying out nighttime raids on the Nazi-occupied conti-nent, sabotaging utilities vital to the Germans, blowing up ammu-nition arsenals, and, alongside British commandos and in concert with underground European resistance movements, destroying dock and shipyard facilities up and down the coastline of western Europe. When he recounted for Alvin all the many ways the commandos taught you to kill a man, Alvin dropped his original plans and went to join up. Like the rest of the Canadian armed forces, the commandos were eager to accept qualified American citizens into their ranks, and so, after sixteen weeks of training, Alvin was assigned to an active commando unit and shipped to a secret staging area in the British Isles. And that was when we heard from him finally, receiving a six-word letter that read, "Off to fight. See you soon."

It was just days after Sandy, all on his own, took the overnight train to Kentucky that my parents received a second letter, this one not from Alvin but from the War Department in Ottawa, advising Alvin's designated next of kin that their nephew had been wounded in action and was in a convalescent hospital in Dorset, England. After the dinner dishes were cleared that night, my mother sat back down at the kitchen table with a fountain pen and the box of monogrammed stationery reserved for important correspondence. My father seated himself across from her, and I stood looking over her shoulder to observe how her cursive script uniformly unfurled because of the handwriting mechanics she'd employed as a secretary and taught early on to Sandy and me—the third and fourth fingers positioned to support the hand, and the forefinger nearer the pen point than the thumb. She spoke each sentence aloud before writing it down in case my father wanted to change or add anything.

> Dearest Alvin,
>
> This morning we received a letter from the Canadian government telling us that you were wounded in action and that you're in a hospital in England. The letter contained nothing more specific other than a mailing address for you.
>
> Right now we are at the kitchen table, Uncle Herman, Philip, and Aunt Bess. We all want to know everything

about your condition. Sandy is away for the summer, but we'll write him about you immediately.

Is there any chance you will be sent back to Canada? If so, we would drive there to see you. In the meantime, we send you our love and hope you will write us from England. Please write or ask someone to write for you. Whatever you want us to do, we will do.

Again, we love you and we miss you.

To this message we appended our three signatures. It was nearly a month before we got a response.

Dear Mr. and Mrs. Roth:

Corporal Alvin Roth received your letter of July 5. I am the senior nurse on his unit and I read the letter to him several times to be sure he understood who it was from and what it said.

Right now Cpl. Roth is not communicative. He lost his left leg below the knee and was seriously wounded in his right foot. The right foot is healing and that wound should not leave him impaired. When his left leg is ready, he will be fitted with a prosthesis and taught to walk with it.

This is a dark moment for Cpl. Roth, but I wish to assure you that in time he should be able to resume his life as a civilian with no significant physical problems. This hospital is limited to amputees and burn cases. I have seen many men undergo the same psychological difficulties as Cpl. Roth, but most of them come through, and I strongly believe that Cpl. Roth will too.

Sincerely,
Lt. A. F. Cooper

Once a week, Sandy wrote saying he was fine and reporting how hot it was in Kentucky and concluding with a sentence about life on the farm—something like "There's a bumper crop of blackberries" or "The steer are being driven crazy by flies" or "Today they're cutting alfalfa" or "Topping began," whatever that might mean.

Then, below his signature—and perhaps to prove to his father that he had stamina enough to do his artwork even after working all day on the farm—he'd sketch a picture of a pig ("This pig," he noted, "weighs over three hundred pounds!") or a dog ("Suzie, Orin's dog —her specialty is scaring snakes") or a lamb ("Mr. Mawhinney took 30 lambs to the stockyards yesterday") or of a barn ("They just painted this place with creosote. P-U!"). Usually far more space was taken up by the drawing than by the message, and, to my mother's chagrin, the questions she would raise in her own weekly letter, asking if he needed clothes or medicine or money, rarely got answered. Of course I knew my mother cared for each of her children with equal devotion, but not till Sandy was gone to Kentucky did I learn how much he meant to her as someone distinct from his little brother. Though she wasn't about to grow despondent over being separated for eight weeks from a son already thirteen, all summer long there was an undercurrent of the forlorn noticeable in certain gestures and facial expressions, particularly at the kitchen table when the fourth chair drawn up for dinner remained empty night after night.

Aunt Evelyn was with us when we went to Penn Station to pick Sandy up on the late-August Saturday that he arrived back in Newark. She was the last one my father wanted coming along, but just as when, against his own inclinations, he'd eventually allowed Sandy to apply for Just Folks and accept the summer job in Kentucky, he had yielded to his sister-in-law's influence over his son to avoid making more difficult a predicament whose ultimate danger still wasn't entirely clear.

At the station, Aunt Evelyn was the first of us to recognize Sandy when he stepped from the train onto the platform, some ten pounds heavier than when he'd left and his brown hair blondish from his working in the fields under the summer sun. He'd grown a couple of inches as well, so that his pants were now nowhere near his shoe tops, and altogether my impression was of my brother in disguise.

"Hey, farmer," Aunt Evelyn called, "over here!" and Sandy came loping in our direction, swinging his bags at his sides and sporting an outdoorsy new walk to go with the new physique.

"Welcome home, stranger," my mother said, and, with the air of a young girl, happily threw her arms around his neck, and the words she murmured into his ear ("Was there ever a boy so handsome?") caused him to complain, "Ma! Cut it out!" which, of course, handed the rest of the family a big laugh. We all hugged him, and, standing beside the train he'd boarded seven hundred fifty miles away, he flexed his biceps so I could feel them. In the car, when he began answering our questions, we heard how husky his voice had become, and we heard for the first time the drawl and the twang.

Aunt Evelyn was triumphant. Sandy talked about the last job he'd had out in the fields—going around with Orin, one of the Mawhinneys' sons, picking up the tobacco leaves broken off during harvesting. They were usually the lowest on the plant, Sandy said, they were called "flyings," and it so happened they were top-grade tobacco and fetched the highest price at the market. But the men doing the cutting on a tobacco patch of twenty-five acres can't bother about the leaves on the ground, he told us, as they have to cut some three thousand sticks of tobacco a day in order to get everything housed in the curing barn in two weeks. "Whoa, whoa —what's a 'stick,' dear?" Aunt Evelyn asked, and gladly he obliged her with the lengthiest possible explanation. And so what's a curing barn, she asked, what's topping, what's suckering, what's worming —and the more questions Aunt Evelyn came up with, the more authoritative Sandy became, so that even when we got to Summit Avenue and my father pulled the car into the alleyway, he was still going on about raising tobacco as though expecting us all to head right for the backyard and start preparing the weedy patch of dirt next to the garbage cans for Newark's first crop ever of white burley. "It's the sweetened burley in Luckys," he informed us, "that gives 'em the taste," and meanwhile I was itching to feel his biceps again, which to me were no less extraordinary than the regional accent, if that's what it was—he said "cain't" for "can't" and "rimember" for "remember" and "fahr" for "fire" and "agin" for "again" and "awalkin'" and "atalkin'" for "walking" and "talking," and whatever you wanted to call that concoction of English, it wasn't what we natives of New Jersey spoke.

Aunt Evelyn was triumphant but my father was stymied, said almost nothing, and at the dinner table that evening looked especially glum when Sandy got around to reporting on what a paragon Mr. Mawhinney was. First off, Mr. Mawhinney had graduated from the College of Agriculture at the University of Kentucky, while my father, like most other Newark slum children before the World War, hadn't been educated beyond the eighth grade. Mr. Mawhinney owned not just one farm but three—the lesser two rented to tenants—land that had been in his family going back nearly to the days of Daniel Boone, and my father owned nothing more impressive than a six-year-old car. Mr. Mawhinney could saddle a horse, drive a tractor, operate a thresher, ride a fertilizer drill, work a field as easily with a team of mules as with a team of oxen; he could rotate crops and manage hired men, both white and Negro; he could repair tools, sharpen plow points and mowers, put up fences, string barbed wire, raise chickens, dip sheep, dehorn cattle, slaughter pigs, smoke bacon, sugar-cure ham—and he raised watermelons that were the sweetest and juiciest Sandy had ever eaten. By cultivating tobacco, corn, and potatoes, Mr. Mawhinney was able to make a living right out of the earth and then, at Sunday dinner (where the six-foot-three-inch, two-hundred-and-thirty-pound farmer consumed more fried chicken with cream gravy than everyone else at the table combined), eat only food that he himself had raised, and all my father could do was sell insurance. It went without saying that Mr. Mawhinney was a Christian, a long-standing member of the great overpowering majority that fought the Revolution and founded the nation and conquered the wilderness and subjugated the Indian and enslaved the Negro and emancipated the Negro and segregated the Negro, one of the good, clean, hard-working Christian millions who settled the frontier, tilled the farms, built the cities, governed the states, sat in Congress, occupied the White House, amassed the wealth, possessed the land, owned the steel mills and the ball clubs and the railroads and the banks, even owned and oversaw the language, one of those unassailable Nordic and Anglo-Saxon Protestants who ran America and would always run it—generals, dignitaries, magnates, tycoons, the men who laid down the law and called the shots and read the riot act when they chose to—while my father, of course, was only a Jew.

Sandy got the news about Alvin once Aunt Evelyn had gone home. My father was at the kitchen table working on his account books preparatory to going out to make his evening collections and my mother was in the cellar with Sandy sorting through the clothes he'd brought back from Kentucky, deciding what to repair and what to throw out before putting everything else in the washtub. My mother always did immediately whatever had to be done, and she was set on disposing of his dirty clothes before she went to bed. I was down there with them, unable to let my brother out of my sight. He'd always known everything I didn't know, and he'd come back from Kentucky knowing still more.

"I have to tell you about Alvin," my mother said to him. "I didn't want to write because . . . well, I didn't want to shock you, dear." Here, having gathered herself together to make certain she wouldn't cry, she said in a low voice, "Alvin was wounded. He's in a hospital in England. He's there recovering from his wounds."

Astonished, Sandy asked, "Who wounded him?" as though she were reporting an occurrence in our neighborhood rather than in Nazi-occupied Europe, where people were being maimed, wounded, and killed all the time.

"We don't know any details," my mother said. "But it wasn't a superficial wound. I have to tell you something very sad, Sanford." And despite her attempt to keep everyone's courage up, her voice began to waver when she said, "Alvin's lost a leg."

"A leg?" There aren't many words less abstruse than "leg," but it took some doing for him to comprehend it.

"Yes. According to a letter we got from one of his nurses, his left leg below the knee." As if it might somehow soothe him, she added, "If you'd like to read it, the letter's upstairs."

"But—how will he walk?"

"They're going to fit him with an artificial leg."

"But I don't understand who wounded him. How did he get wounded?"

"Well, they were there to fight the Germans," she said, "so it must have been one of them."

Still half staving off what was half sinking in, Sandy asked, "Which leg?"

As tenderly as she could, she repeated, "The left."

"The whole leg? The whole thing?"

"No, no, no," she rushed to reassure him. "I told you, dear—below the knee."

Suddenly Sandy began to cry, and because he was so much bigger across the shoulders and through the chest and around the wrists than he'd been just last spring, because his arms were now brawny like a man's rather than stringy like a child's, I was so startled to see tears running down his deeply tanned face that I started crying too.

"Dear, it's awful," my mother said. "But Alvin is not dead. He is still alive, and now at least he's out of the war."

"*What?*" Sandy erupted. "Did you hear what you just said to me?"

"What do you mean?" she asked.

"Didn't you hear yourself? You said, 'He's out of the war.'"

"And he is. Absolutely. And because he is, he'll now come home before anything more can possibly happen."

"But why was he even *in* the war, Ma?"

"Because—"

"Because of Dad!" Sandy shouted.

"Dear, no, this isn't true," and her hand flew up to cover her mouth as though it were she who had spoken those unpardonable words. "That is not *so*," she objected. "Alvin went off to Canada without telling us. He ran away on that Friday night. You remember how terrible it was. Nobody wanted Alvin to go to war—he just went, on his own."

"But Dad wants the whole country to go to war. Well, doesn't he? Isn't that why he voted for Roosevelt?"

"Lower your voice, please."

"First you say thank God that Alvin is out of the war—"

"Lower your *voice!*" and the tension of the day now so overwhelmed her that she lost her temper, and to the boy she had so painfully missed all summer long, she snapped, "You don't know what you're talking about!"

"But you won't *listen,*" he shouted. "If it wasn't for President Lindbergh—"

That name again! I would rather have heard a bomb go off than to have to hear one more time the name that was tormenting us all.

Just then my father appeared in the dim light of the landing at the top of the cellar stairs. It was probably a good thing that from where we were standing by the deep laundry sink, all we could see of him were trousers and shoes.

"He's upset about Alvin," my mother said, looking up to explain what the shouting was about. "I made a mistake." To Sandy she said, "I should never have told you tonight. It's not easy for a boy to come home from a big experience like that . . . it's never easy to go from one place to another . . . and anyway you're so tired . . . ," and then, helpless, giving herself up to her own exhaustion, she said, "The two of you, both of you, go upstairs now so I can do the wash."

And so we turned to mount the stairs and found, fortunately, that my father had already disappeared from the landing and was off in the car to make his evening collections.

In bed, one hour later. The lights are out all over the house. We whisper.

Did you really have a good time?

I had a great time.

What made it so great?

Being on a farm is great. You get to get up early in the morning, and you're outside all day, and there are all these animals. I drew a lot of animals, I'll show you my drawings. And we had ice cream every night. Mrs. Mawhinney makes it herself. There's fresh milk there.

All milk is fresh.

No, we got it right from the cow. It was still warm. We put it on the stove and we'd boil it and just take the cream off the top, and then we'd drink it.

You couldn't get sick from it?

That's why you boil it.

But you don't just drink it right out of the cow.

I tried that once but it doesn't taste so good. It's so creamy.

Did you milk a cow?

Orin showed me how to do it. It's hard to do. Orin would squirt it, and the cats would come around, and they'd try to catch the milk.

Did you have any friends?

Well, Orin's my best friend.

Orin Mawhinney?

Yeah. He's my age. He goes to school there. He works on the farm. He gets up at four o'clock in the morning. He does chores. It's not like us. He goes to school on the bus. It's about forty-five minutes on the bus, and then he comes back in the evening, and he does some more chores, and he does his homework, and he goes to bed. He gets up at four o'clock the next morning. It's hard work to be a farmer's son.

But they're rich, aren't they?

They're pretty rich.

How come you talk like that now?

Why shouldn't I? That's the way they talk in Kentucky. You should hear Mrs. Mawhinney. She's from Georgia. She makes pancakes for breakfast every morning. With bacon. Mr. Mawhinney smokes his own bacon. In a smokehouse. He knows how to.

You ate bacon every morning?

Every morning. It's delicious. And on Sundays when we got up we had pancakes and bacon and eggs. From their own chickens. The eggs—they're almost red in the middle, they're so fresh. You go and take 'em from the chickens and bring 'em in and you eat 'em right there.

Did you eat ham?

We had ham for dinner about two times a week. Mr. Mawhinney makes his own ham. He has a special family recipe. He says if a ham isn't hung up to be aged for a year he doesn't want to eat it.

Did you eat sausage?

Yeah. He makes the sausage, too. They grind it in a sausage grinder. We had sausage sometimes instead of bacon. It's good. Pork chops. They're good too. They're great. I don't really know why we don't eat it.

Because it's stuff from a pig.

So what? Why do you think farmers raise pigs? For people to look at 'em? It's like anything else you eat. You just eat it, and it's really good.

You going to keep eating it now?

Sure.

It was really hot there, though, huh?

During the day. But we'd come in at lunchtime, and we'd have tomato and mayonnaise sandwiches. With lemonade—with lots of lemonade. We'd rest inside and then we'd go back out into the fields and do whatever we had to. Weeding. Weed all afternoon. Weed the corn. Weed the tobacco. We had a vegetable garden, me and Orin, and we'd weed that. We'd work with the hired hands, and there were some Negroes, day laborers. And there's one Negro, Randolph, who is a tenant, and he rose from hired hand. He's a grade-A farmer, Mr. Mawhinney says.

Can you understand when the Negroes talk?

Sure.

Can you imitate one?

They say " 'bacca" for tobacco. They say "I 'clare." I 'clare this and I 'clare that. But they don't talk much. Mostly they work. At hog-killing time, Mr. Mawhinney has Clete and Old Henry who gut the hogs. They're Negroes, they're brothers, and they take the intestines home and eat 'em fried. Chitterlings.

Would you eat that?

Do I look like a Negro? Mr. Mawhinney says Negroes are starting to move away from the farm because they think they can earn more money in the city. Sometimes Old Henry got arrested on Saturday nights. For drinking. Mr. Mawhinney pays the fine to get him out because he needs him on Monday.

Do they have shoes?

Some. The kids are barefoot. The Mawhinneys give them their clothes when they're done with them. But they were happy.

Anybody say anything about anti-Semitism?

They don't even think about it, Philip. I was the first Jew they ever met. They told me that. But they never said anything mean. It's Kentucky. People there are really friendly.

So, are you glad to be home?

Sort of. I don't know.

You going to go back next year?

Sure.

What if Mom and Dad won't let you?

I'll go anyway.

Seemingly as a direct consequence of Sandy's having eaten bacon, ham, pork chops, and sausage, there was no containing the transformation of our lives. Rabbi Bengelsdorf was coming to dinner. Aunt Evelyn was bringing him.

"Why us?" my father said to my mother. Dinner was over, Sandy was on his bed writing to Orin Mawhinney, and I was alone with them in the living room, intent on seeing how my father was going to take the news now that everything around us was moving at once.

"She is my sister," said my mother, a touch belligerently, "he is her boss—I can't tell her no."

"I can," he said.

"You will do nothing of the sort."

"Then explain again why we deserve this great honor? The big shot has nothing more pressing than to come here?"

"Evelyn wants him to meet your son."

"That's ridiculous. Your sister has always been ridiculous. My son is in the eighth grade at Chancellor Avenue School. He spent the summer pulling weeds. This is *all* ridiculous."

"Herman, they're coming on Thursday night, and we're going to make them welcome. You may hate him, but he's not nobody."

"I know that," he said impatiently. "That's *why* I hate him."

When he walked about the house now a copy of *PM* was constantly in his hands, either rolled up like a weapon—as though he were preparing, if called upon, to go to war himself—or turned back to a page where there was something he wanted to read aloud to my mother. He was perplexed on this particular evening as to why the Germans continued to advance so easily into Russia, and so, rattling the paper in exasperation, he all at once exclaimed, "Why don't those Russians *fight*? They have planes—why don't they use them? Why doesn't anybody over there put up a fight? Hitler walks into a country, crosses the border and walks right in, and bingo, it's his. England," he announced, "is the only country in Europe to stand up to that dog. He pounds away at those English cities every single night, and they just come back and keep on fighting him with the RAF. Thank God for the men of the RAF."

"When is Hitler going to invade England?" I asked him. "Why doesn't he invade England now?"

"That was part of the deal he made with Mr. Lindbergh up in Iceland. Lindbergh wants to be the savior of mankind," my father explained to me, "and negotiate the peace that ends the war, and so after Hitler takes Russia, and after he takes the Middle East, and after he takes everything else he could possibly want, Lindbergh will call a phony peace conference—the kind that's right up the Germans' alley. The Germans will be there, and the price for world peace and no German invasion of Great Britain will be installing in England an English fascist government. Putting a fascist prime minister in Downing Street. And when the English say no, *then* Hitler will invade, and all with the consent of our president the peacemaker."

"Is that what Walter Winchell says?" I asked, thinking that all he had explained to me was just too smart for him.

"That's what *I* say," he told me, and probably that was true. The pressure of what was happening was accelerating everyone's education, my own included. "But thank God for Walter Winchell. Without him we'd be lost. He's the last person left on the radio to speak out against these dirty dogs. It's disgusting. It's worse than disgusting. Slowly but surely, there's nobody in America willing to speak out against Lindbergh's kissing Hitler's behind."

"What about the Democrats?" I asked.

"Son, don't ask me about the Democrats. I'm angry enough as it is."

My mother had me help her set the table in the dining room on Thursday evening, and then sent me to my bedroom to change into my good clothes. Aunt Evelyn and Rabbi Bengelsdorf were to arrive at seven, forty-five minutes later than we would ordinarily have finished eating in the kitchen, but seven was the earliest the rabbi could manage to get to our house because of all his official duties. This was the very traitor whom my father, usually so respectful of the Jewish clergy, had accused aloud of making "a stupid, lying speech" in behalf of Lindbergh at Madison Square Garden, the "Jewish fake," according to Alvin, who'd guaranteed Roosevelt's defeat by "koshering Lindbergh for the goyim," and so it was puzzling to witness the lengths to which we were going to feed him. I was myself instructed beforehand not to use the fresh towels in the bathroom or to go anywhere near my father's armchair, which was for the rabbi to occupy before we ate dinner.

First we all sat stiffly in the living room while my father offered the rabbi a highball or, if he preferred, a shot of schnapps, both of which Bengelsdorf declined in favor of a glass of tap water. "Newark has the best drinking water in the world," the rabbi said, and said it as he would say everything, with deep consideration. Graciously he received the glass, on a coaster, from my mother, whom I could still recall back in October running from the radio in order not to have to hear him praise Lindbergh. "You have a most agreeable house," he said to her. "Everything in its place and everything placed perfectly. It bespeaks the love of order which I myself share. I see you have a penchant for the color green."

"Forest green," said my mother, trying to smile and trying to please but speaking with difficulty and unable as yet to look his way.

"You should take great pride in your lovely home. I am honored to be a guest here."

The rabbi was quite tall, built on the order of Lindbergh, a thin, bald-headed man in a dark three-piece suit and gleaming black shoes; his erect posture alone seemed to me to express an allegiance to mankind's highest ideals. From the mellifluous southern accent I'd heard on the radio I had envisioned somebody looking far less severe, but just his eyeglasses were intimidating, in part because they were the owlish oval spectacles that pinched the nose to stay on the face, like the ones that Roosevelt wore, and in part because the very fact that he wore them—and examined you through them microscopically—made it clear that he was not a man with whom to disagree. Yet when he spoke his tone was warm, friendly, even confiding. I kept waiting for him to treat us with contempt or order us around, but all he did was to talk in that accent (which wasn't at all like Sandy's), and so softly that at times you had to hold your breath to hear how learned he was.

"And you must be the boy," he said to Sandy, "who's made us all so proud."

"I'm Sandy, sir," Sandy replied, flushing furiously. It was, to my mind, a brilliant retort to a question that another successful boy, trying to meet the sanctioned standard of modesty, might not have been able to handle with such dispatch. No, nothing could now undo Sandy, not with those muscles and that sun-bleached hair and the abundance of pig he'd stashed away without asking permission of anyone.

"And what was it like," the rabbi asked, "to work there in the Kentucky fields under the burning sun?" He said "wuhk" for "work" and "buhning" for "burning" and "theyuh" for "there," and pronounced "Kentucky" as it was spelled and not, as Sandy now did, as though the first three letters were K-i-n.

"I learned a lot, sir. I learned a lot about my country."

Aunt Evelyn visibly approved, as well she might have, since on the phone the evening before she'd fitted him out with the answer to just such a question. Since she had always to be superior to my father, there could be no greater delight than to shape the existence of his older son right in front of his nose.

"You were on a tobacco farm, your aunt Evelyn tells me."

"Yes, sir. White burley tobacco."

"Did you know, Sandy, that tobacco was the economic foundation of the first permanent English settlement in America, at Jamestown in Virginia?"

"I didn't," he admitted, but added, "Though I'm not surprised to hear it," and, in a flash, the worst was over.

"Many mishaps beset the Jamestown pioneers," the rabbi told him. "But what saved them from starvation and saved the settlement from extinction was the cultivation of tobacco. Think of it. Without tobacco, the first representative government in the New World would never have met at Jamestown, as it did in 1619. Without tobacco, the Jamestown colony would have collapsed, the colonization of Virginia would have failed, and the First Families of Virginia, whose wealth derived from their tobacco plantations, would themselves have never come to prominence. And when you remember that the First Families of Virginia were the forebears of the Virginia statesmen who were our country's Founding Fathers, you appreciate tobacco's vital importance to the history of our republic."

"You do," Sandy answered.

"I myself," said the rabbi, "was born in the American South. I was born fourteen years after the tragedy of the Civil War. My father as a young man fought for the Confederacy. His father came from Germany to settle in South Carolina in 1850. He was a peddler. He had a horse with a wagon and he wore a long beard and he sold to the Negroes and to the white people both. Did you ever hear of Judah Benjamin?" the rabbi asked Sandy.

"No, sir." But again he quickly righted himself, this time by replying, "May I ask who he was?"

"Well, he was a Jew and second only to Jefferson Davis in the government of the Confederacy. He was a Jewish lawyer who served Davis as attorney general, as secretary of war, and as secretary of state. Prior to the secession of the South he had served in the U.S. Senate as one of South Carolina's two senators. The cause for which the South went to war was neither legal nor moral in my judgment, yet I have always held Judah Benjamin in the highest regard. A Jew was a rarity in America in those days, in the North no less than the South, but don't think there wasn't anti-Semitism to contend with back then. Nonetheless Judah Benjamin came close to the very pinnacle of political success in the Confederate government. After the war was lost, he moved abroad to become a distinguished lawyer in England."

Here my mother removed herself to the kitchen—purportedly to check on the dinner—and Aunt Evelyn said to Sandy, "Maybe this is a good time for the rabbi to see the drawings you made on the farm."

Sandy got up and carried over to the rabbi's chair the several sketchbooks that he'd filled with drawings during the summer and that he'd been holding in his lap since we'd all gathered in the living room.

The rabbi took one of the books and began slowly turning the pages.

"Tell the rabbi a little something about each picture," Aunt Evelyn suggested.

"That's the barn," Sandy said. "That's where they hang the tobacco to cure after they harvest it."

"Well, that is a barn, all right, and a beautifully drawn barn. I very much like the pattern of light and dark. You're very talented, Sanford."

"And that's a tobacco plant growing. That's what they look like. See, it's shaped like a triangle. They're big. That one's still got the blossom on top. It's before they top it."

"And this tobacco plant," the rabbi said, turning to a new page, "with the bag on the top—that is something I've never seen before."

"That's how they get the seed. That's a seed plant. They cover the blossom with a paper bag and tie it tight. It keeps the blossom the way they want it."

"Very, very good," the rabbi said. "It isn't easy to draw a plant accurately and still make it into a work of art. Look how you've shadowed the undersides of the leaves. Very good indeed."

"And that's a plow, of course," Sandy said, "and that's a hoe.

That's a hand hoe. To do your weeding with. Though you can also use just your hands."

"And did you weed much?" the rabbi asked teasingly.

"Oh, boy," Sandy said, and Rabbi Bengelsdorf smiled, looking not at all now like a frightening figure. "And that's just the dog," Sandy went on, "Orin's dog. She's sleeping. And that's one of the Negroes, Old Henry, and those are his hands. I thought they had character."

"And who is this?"

"That's Old Henry's brother. That's Clete."

"I like the way you've rendered him. How weary the man looks, slouching like that. I know those Negroes—I grew up with them, and I respect them. And this? Just what would this be?" the rabbi asked. "Here, with the bellows."

"Well, a person's inside. That's how he sprays against tobacco worms. He has to dress like that from head to foot with big gloves and heavy clothes all buttoned up so he doesn't get burned. When he squirts the insecticide out through the bellows he can burn himself with it. It's green, the dust, and when he's finished his clothes are covered with it. I tried to get the look of the dust, I tried to make it lighter where the dust is, but I don't think it came out right."

"Well, I'm sure," said the rabbi, "that it's hard to draw dust," and began to progress a little more rapidly through the remaining pages until he came to the end and closed the book. "Kentucky was an experience that wasn't wasted on you, was it, young man?"

"I loved it," Sandy replied, and my father, who had been silent and unmoving on the sofa since yielding the rabbi his favorite chair, got up and said, "I have to help Bess," the way he might have said, "I'm now going to jump out the window and kill myself."

"The Jews of America," the rabbi told us at dinner, "are unlike any other community of Jews in the history of the world. They have the greatest opportunity accorded to our people in modern times. The Jews of America can participate fully in the national life of their country. They need no longer dwell apart, a pariah community separated from the rest. All that is required is the courage that your son Sandy displayed by going on his own into the unknown of Kentucky to work for the summer as a farm hand there. I believe that Sandy and the other Jewish boys like him in the Just Folks program should serve as models not only for every Jewish child growing up in this country but for every Jewish adult. And this is not merely a dream of mine; it is the dream of President Lindbergh."

Our ordeal had suddenly taken the worst possible turn. I'd not forgotten how in Washington my father had stood up to the hotel manager and the bullying policeman, and so now that Lindbergh's name had been spoken with deference in his house I thought the moment had come when he would stand up to Bengelsdorf.

But a rabbi was a rabbi, and he didn't.

My mother and Aunt Evelyn served the meal, three courses followed by a marble cake freshly baked in our oven that afternoon. We ate off the "good" dishes with the "good" silverware, and in the dining room no less, where we had our best rug and our best furniture and our best linens and where we ourselves ate only on special occasions. From my side of the table you could see the photographic portraits of the family dead arranged atop the breakfront that was our memorial shrine. Framed there were two grandfathers, our maternal grandmother, a maternal aunt, and two uncles, one of them Uncle Jack, Alvin's father and my father's beloved older brother. In the aftermath of Rabbi Bengelsdorf's invoking Lindbergh's name, I was more confused than ever. A rabbi was a rabbi, but Alvin meanwhile was in a Canadian army hospital in Montreal learning to walk on an artificial left leg after having lost his own left leg battling Hitler, and in my own house—where I was supposed to wear anything *except* my good clothes—I had to put on my one tie and my one jacket to impress the very rabbi who helped to elect the president whose friend was Hitler. How could I not be confused, when our disgrace and our glory were one and the same? Something essential had been destroyed and lost, we were being coerced to be other than the Americans we were, and yet, by the light of the cut-glass chandelier, amid the weighty, dark-stained suite of dining room furniture, we were eating my mother's pot roast in the company of the first famous visitor we had ever entertained.

To further confound me and make me pay the full price for my thoughts, Bengelsdorf began, all at once, to speak about Alvin, whom he'd learned about from Aunt Evelyn. "I am saddened by the casualty in your family. My heart goes out to all of you. Evelyn tells me that when your nephew is released from the hospital he will come to convalesce with you all. I'm sure you know the mental anguish that such a wound can provoke in someone still in the flower of his youth. It will require all the love and patience you can muster to bring him to where he can again resume a useful life. His story is particularly tragic because there was no necessity whatsoever for his having crossed over to Canada to join their armed forces. Alvin Roth was born a citizen of the United States, and the United States is not at war with anyone, has no intention of going to war with anyone, and doesn't require the sacrifice of life or limb in warfare from a single one of its young men. Some of us have gone to great lengths to make this so. I have encountered considerable hostility from members of the Jewish community for allying myself in the 1940 election with the Lindbergh campaign. But I have been sustained by my abhorrence of war. It is terrible enough that young Alvin should have lost his leg in a battle on the European continent having nothing to do with the security of America or the well-being of Americans . . ."

On he went, more or less repeating what he'd said at Madison Square Garden in support of America's remaining neutral, but my focus now was only on Alvin. He was coming to stay with us? I looked at my mother. She'd told us nothing about it. When would he arrive? Where would he sleep? It was bad enough, as my mother had said in Washington, that we weren't living in a normal country; now we would never again be living in a normal house. A life of even more suffering was taking shape around me, and I wanted to scream "No! Alvin can't stay here—he has only one leg!"

I was so upset that it was a while before I realized that the dining room reign of decorum had ended and my father was no longer allowing himself to be shoved aside. Somehow he had managed at last to overturn the obstacles posed by Bengelsdorf's credentials and by his own insufficiencies; he had ceased being intimidated by the rabbinical grandeur, and, urged on by his irrepressible sense of an impending disaster—and violently irritated by the condescension—he was letting Bengelsdorf have it, pince-nez and all.

"Hitler," I heard him saying, "Hitler is not business as usual, Rabbi! This madman is not making a war from a thousand years ago. He is making a war such as no one has ever seen on this planet. He has conquered Europe. He is at war with Russia. Every night he bombs London into rubble and kills hundreds of innocent British civilians. He is the worst anti-Semite in history. And yet his great friend our president takes him at his word when Hitler tells him that they have an 'understanding.' Hitler had an understanding with the Russians. Did he keep it? He had an understanding with Chamberlain. Did he keep it? Hitler's goal is to conquer the world, and that includes the United States of America. And since everywhere he goes he shoots the Jews, when the time is right he will come and shoot the Jews here. And what will our president do then? Protect us? Defend us? Our president will not lift a finger. *That* is the understanding that they reached at Iceland, and any adult who thinks otherwise is crazy."

Rabbi Bengelsdorf showed no impatience with my father but listened respectfully, as if in sympathy with at least some of what he was hearing. Only Sandy seemed to be having trouble keeping his feelings to himself, and when our father referred scornfully to Lindbergh as "our president," he turned to me and made a face that revealed how far he'd spun out of the family orbit merely by making the ordinary American's adjustment to the new administration. My mother was seated to my father's right and, when he had finished, gripped his hand in hers, though to communicate how proud she was of him or to signal him to be still wasn't clear. As for Aunt Evelyn, she took all her cues from the rabbi, concealing her thoughts behind a mask of benign sufferance while her shallow brother-in-law dared to oppose with his piddling vocabulary a scholar who could talk in ten languages.

Bengelsdorf did not immediately respond but instead created a portentous interval in which quietly to insert his rejoinder: "I was at the White House talking to the president just yesterday morning." Here he sipped from his glass of water, allowing time for us to regain self-possession. "I was congratulating him," he continued, "on the significant inroad he had made into allaying the Jewish suspiciousness that dated back to his trips to Germany in the late thirties, when he was secretly taking the measure of the German air force for the U.S. government. I informed him that any number of my own congregants who had voted for Roosevelt were now his strong supporters, grateful that he had established our neutrality and spared our country the agonies of yet another great war. I told him that Just Folks and programs like it were beginning to convince the Jews of America that he is anything but their enemy. Admittedly, before his becoming president he at times made public statements grounded in anti-Semitic clichés. But he spoke from ignorance then, and admits as much today. I am pleased to tell you that it took no more than two or three sessions alone with the president to get him to relinquish his misconceptions and to appreciate the manifold nature of Jewish life in America. This is not an evil man, not in any way. This is a man of enormous native intelligence and great probity who is rightly celebrated for his personal courage and who wants now to enlist my aid to help him raze those barriers of ignorance that continue to separate Christian from Jew and Jew from Christian. Because there is ignorance as well among Jews, unfortunately, many of whom persist in thinking of President Lindbergh as an American Hitler when they know full well that he is not a dictator who attained power in a putsch but a democratic leader who came to office through a landslide victory in a fair and free election and who has exhibited not a single inclination toward authoritarian rule. He does not glorify the state at the expense of the individual but, to the contrary, encourages entrepreneurial individualism and a free enterprise system unencumbered by interference from the federal government. Where is the fascist statism? Where is the fascist thuggery? Where are the Nazi Brown Shirts and the secret police? When have you observed a single manifestation of fascist anti-Semitism emanating from our government? What Hitler perpetrated on Germany's Jews with the passage in 1935 of the Nuremberg Laws is the absolute antithesis of what President Lindbergh has undertaken to do for America's Jews through the establishment of the Office of American Absorption. The Nuremberg Laws deprived Jews of their civil rights and did everything to exclude them from membership in their nation. What I have encouraged President Lindbergh to do is to initiate programs inviting Jews to enter as far into the national life as they like—a national life that I'm sure you would agree is no less ours to enjoy than anyone else's."

A pouring forth of sentences as informed as these had never before occurred at our dining table or probably anywhere on our block, and it was startling then—when the rabbi concluded by inquiring rather gently, even intimately, "Tell me, Herman, does what I've explained begin to address your fears?"—to hear my father respond flatly, "No. No. Not for a moment." And then, heedless of rendering an affront that would not only arouse the rabbi's displeasure but insult his dignity and provoke his vindictive contempt, my father added, "Hearing a person like you talk like that— frankly, it alarms me even more."

The following evening Aunt Evelyn phoned and bubblingly informed us that out of the one hundred New Jersey boys who'd gone west that summer under the sponsorship of Just Folks, Sandy had been selected as the statewide "recruiting officer" to speak as a veteran to eligible Jewish youngsters and their families about the OAA program's many benefits and to encourage them to apply.

Thus did the rabbi extract his revenge. Our father's older son was now an honorary member of the new administration.

It was shortly after Sandy began spending his afternoons downtown at Aunt Evelyn's OAA office that my mother put on her best suit—the tailored gray jacket and skirt with the pale pinstripe that she wore to preside over PTA meetings and as a poll watcher in the school basement at election time—and went off to look for a job. At dinner she announced that she had found work selling ladies' dresses at Hahne's, a big downtown department store. She had been hired early as holiday help to work six days a week and Wednesday evenings, but as she was an experienced office secretary she harbored the hope that over the coming weeks a job might open up on the store's administrative floor and she would be retained after Christmas as a permanent employee. She explained to Sandy and me that her paycheck would contribute toward meeting the larger household bills occasioned by Alvin's return while her real intention (known to no one other than her husband) was to deposit her paychecks by mail into a Montreal bank account in case we had to flee and start from scratch in Canada.

My mother was gone, my brother was gone, and Alvin would soon be on his way home. My father had driven to Montreal to visit him in the army hospital there. One Friday morning, hours before Sandy and I got up for school, my mother made his breakfast, filled his thermos, packed food—three paper bags marked with Sandy's shading crayon, *L* for lunch, *S* for snack, *D* for dinner—and away he headed for the international border three hundred and fifty miles to the north. Since his boss could give him only the Friday off, he'd have to drive all that day to see Alvin on Saturday and then drive all day Sunday to be back for the morning staff meeting on Monday. He had a flat tire going and two more coming home and to make it to his meeting had to bypass us and drive from the highway directly downtown. By the time we saw him at dinner he'd been sleepless for over a day and without a proper wash for longer than that. Alvin, he told us, looked like a corpse, his weight down to something around a hundred pounds. Hearing this, I wondered how much the leg weighed that he'd lost, and that evening, without success, tried to weigh mine on the bathroom scale. "He's got no appetite," my father said. "They put food in front of him and he pushes it away. That boy, tough as he is, doesn't want to live, doesn't want anything except to lie there emaciated with that terrible grim face. I said, 'Alvin, I've known you since you were born. You're a fighter. You don't give up. You've got your father's strength. Your father could take the hardest blow and still keep going. So could your mother.' I told him, 'When your father died, the woman had to bounce back—she had no choice, she had you.' But I don't know what sunk in. I hope something," he said, his voice growing husky, "because while I was there, with all those sick boys in those beds all around me, while I was sitting beside his bed in that hospital—" and that was as far as he got. It was the first time I saw my father cry. A childhood milestone, when another's tears are more unbearable than one's own.

"It's because you're so tired," my mother said to him. She got up from her chair and, trying to calm him, came around and began to stroke his head. "When you finish eating," she said, "you'll take a shower and go right to bed."

Pressing his skull firmly back into the grip of her hand, he started to sob uncontrollably. "They blew his leg off," he told her, and here my mother motioned for Sandy and me to leave her to comfort him alone.

A new life began for me. I'd watched my father fall apart, and I would never return to the same childhood. The mother at home was now away all day working for Hahne's, the brother on call was now off after school working for Lindbergh, and the father who'd defiantly serenaded all those callow cafeteria anti-Semites in Washington was crying aloud with his mouth wide open—crying like both a baby abandoned and a man being tortured—because he was powerless to stop the unforeseen. And as Lindbergh's election couldn't have made clearer to me, the unfolding of the unforeseen was everything. Turned wrong way round, the relentless unforeseen was what we schoolchildren studied as "History," harmless history, where everything unexpected in its own time is chronicled on the page as inevitable. The terror of the unforeseen is what the science of history hides, turning a disaster into an epic.

As I was on my own, I began to spend all my after-school hours with Earl Axman, my stamp mentor, and not just to pore over his collection with my magnifying glass or to look through his mother's bureau at her puzzling array of undergarments. Since my homework took no time and my only other chore was setting the table for dinner, I was now wholly available for mischief. And since, in the afternoons, Earl's mother seemed always to be off at the beauty parlor or over in New York shopping, Earl was free to provide it. He was nearly two years older than I, and because his glamorous parents were divorced—and because they were glamorous—he seemed never to have bothered being a model child. Of late, increasingly irritated by being one myself, I'd taken to mumbling in my bed, "Now let's do something awful," the suggestion with which Earl alternately thrilled and unnerved me whenever he got tired of what we were up to. Adventurousness was bound to assert its appeal sooner or later, but disillusioned by a sense that my family was slipping away from me right along with my country, I was ready to learn of the liberties a boy from an exemplary household could take when he stopped working to please everyone with his juvenile purity and discovered the guilty enjoyment of secretly acting on his own.

What I fell into with Earl was following people. He'd been doing it a couple of times a week for months now—traveling downtown alone after school and hanging around bus stops looking for men on their way home from work. When the one he settled on boarded his bus, Earl climbed aboard too, unobtrusively rode with him until he got off, got off right after him, and then from a safe distance followed him home. "Why?" I asked. "To see where they live." "But that's all? That's it?" "That's a lot. I go all over. I even leave Newark. I go anyplace I want. People live everywhere," Earl explained. "How do you get home before your mother?" "That's the trick—to go as far as I can and get back before she does." The money for the bus fares he readily confessed to stealing from his mother's handbags and then, as gleefully as if he were springing the lock on the vault at Fort Knox, opened wide a bedroom drawer where all kinds of handbags were piled haphazardly atop one another. On the weekends when he went to stay with his father in New York, he stole from the pockets of the suits hanging in his father's closet, and when four or five musicians from the Casa Loma Orchestra came over to his father's apartment to play poker on Sundays, he helpfully piled their overcoats on the bed, then went through *their* pockets and hid the change in a dirty sock at the bottom of his suitcase. Then he'd nonchalantly saunter into the living room to watch the card game all afternoon and listen to the funny stories they told about playing at the Paramount and the Essex House and the Glen Island Casino. In 1941 the band had just come back from Hollywood, where they'd been in a movie, and so between hands they talked about the stars and what they were like, inside information that Earl passed on to me and that I then repeated to Sandy, who invariably said, "That's bullshit," and warned me not to hang around with Earl Axman. "Your friend," he told me, "knows too much for a little kid." "He's got a great stamp collection." "Yeah, and he's got a mother," Sandy said, "who'll go out with anybody. She goes out with men who aren't even her age." "How do you know?" "Everybody on Summit Avenue knows." "I don't," I said. "Well," he told me, "that's not all you don't know," and, greatly pleased with myself, I thought, "Maybe there's something that you don't know either," but I nervously had to wonder if my best friend's mother wasn't what the older boys called "a whore."

It turned out to be far easier than I could have believed getting used to stealing from my mother and father, and easier than I would have thought following people, even though the first few times there wasn't a moment that didn't stun me, beginning with being downtown unwatched at three-thirty in the afternoon. Sometimes we'd go all the way to Penn Station to find someone, sometimes to Broad and Market, sometimes up Market to the courthouse to wait at the bus stop and catch our prey there. We never followed women. They didn't interest us, Earl said. We never followed anybody we thought was Jewish. They didn't interest us. Our curiosity was directed at men, the adult Christian men who worked all day in downtown Newark. Where did they go when they went home?

My apprehension was at its worst when we stepped up into the bus and paid. The fare money was stolen, we were where we shouldn't be, and where we were headed we had no idea—and by the time we got to wherever that was, I was too dizzy with emotion to understand what Earl told me when he whispered the name of the neighborhood into my ear. I was lost, a lost boy—that's what I pretended. What will I eat? Where will I sleep? Will dogs attack me? Will I be arrested and thrown in jail? Will some Christian take me in and adopt me? Or will I wind up being kidnapped like the Lindbergh child? I pretended either that I was lost in some far-off region unknown to me or that, with Lindbergh's connivance, Hitler had invaded America and Earl and I were fleeing the Nazis.

And all the while I assailed myself with my fears, we were surreptitiously turning corners and crossing streets and crouching behind trees to stay out of sight until the climactic moment when the man we were following reached his home and we watched him open the door and go in. Then we would stand off at a distance and look at the house—its door once again shut—and Earl would say something like, "That lawn's really big," or "Summer's over—why are there screens up?" or "See in the garage? That's the new Pontiac." And then, because trying to sneak up to the windows to peer in unobserved exceeded even Earl Axman's Peeping Jewism, he'd lead us back to the bus that would return us to Penn Station. Often at that hour, with everyone busy leaving work, the bus headed back downtown would be empty of passengers other than us, and so it was as though the driver were a chauffeur and the Public Service bus our private limousine and the two of us the most daring two boys alive. Earl was an extremely well-fed, white-skinned ten-year-old, already a bit of a vat, with full babyish cheeks and long dark lashes and tight black ringlets perfumed with his father's hair oil, and if the bus was empty, he would stretch himself out on the long rear seat in a pashalike posture perfectly embodying his swaggering mood, while sitting up beside him, lean and bony, I sported the half-ashamed little sidekick's smile of sublimity.

From Penn Station we'd catch the 14 home, taking our fourth bold bus ride of the afternoon. At dinner I'd think, "I followed a Christian, and nobody knows. I could have been kidnapped, and nobody knows. Using the money we've got between us, we could've, if we'd wanted . . ." and would sometimes all but give myself away to my sharp-eyed mother because beneath the kitchen table (and exactly like Earl when he was cooking up something) I couldn't stop jiggling my knee. And night after night I went to sleep under the exciting spell of the great new aim I'd unearthed for my eight-year-old life: to escape it. When at school I heard a bus through the open window climbing the Chancellor Avenue hill, all I could think about was being on board; the whole of the outside world had become a bus the way for a boy in South Dakota it was a pony—the pony that carries him to the limits of permissible flight.

I joined Earl as apprentice liar and thief in late October and, with no dwindling of the sense of momentousness, our secret jaunts continued as the weather grew colder in November and then on into December, when the Christmas decorations went up downtown and there was an excess of men to choose from at just about every bus stop. Christmas trees were for sale right on the downtown sidewalks, something I'd never seen before, and selling the trees for a buck apiece were kids who looked to be either hardship cases or toughs recently released from reform school. Money changing hands like that out in the open struck me at first as against the law and yet nobody appeared concerned with concealing the transaction. There were cops in profusion, cops with nightsticks walking the beat in their large blue overcoats, but they looked happy enough and seemed to be in on it—in on Christmas, that is. Big wind-driven blizzards had been whipping in twice a week since just after Thanksgiving, and so to either side of the freshly cleared streets grimy hillocks of snow were already banked as high as a car.

Unimpeded by the late-afternoon throngs, the vendors wrested one tree free from the others, carried it a ways onto the busy sidewalk, and propped it on its sawed-off trunk to be sized up by the customer. It was strange to see trees grown by some tree farmer miles from the city massed along the wrought-iron railings out front of the city's oldest churches and leaning in piles against the façades of the imposing banks and insurance buildings, and strange too, on a downtown street, to breathe in their rustic tang. There were no trees for sale in our neighborhood—because there was no one to buy them—and so the month of December, if it smelled at all, smelled of something a hissing alley cat had tugged from an overturned garbage can in somebody's yard, and of supper heating on the stove of a flat whose steamy kitchen window was open a crack to let in air from the alleyway, and of the bursts of noxious coal gas spewed from the furnace chimneys, and of the pail of ashes dragged up from the cellar to be emptied outdoors over slippery patches of sidewalk. Compared with the fragrances of North Jersey's damp spring and swampy summer and unsettled, moody fall, the smells of a bitter-cold winter were almost unnoticeable—or so I was convinced until I traveled downtown with Earl and saw the trees and took a whiff and discovered that, as with many things, for Christians December was otherwise. What with all of downtown strung with thousands of bulbs and the carolers singing and the Salvation Army band reveling and on every street corner another Santa Claus laughing, it was the month of the year when the heart of my birthplace was sublimely theirs and theirs alone. In Military Park there was a decorated Christmas tree forty feet tall, and from the face of the Public Service building hung a giant metal Christmas tree, illuminated by floodlights, that the *Newark News* said was eighty feet tall, while I was barely four and a half feet tall.

My final trip with Earl occurred one afternoon a few days before our Christmas vacation when we boarded the Linden bus behind a man who was carrying in either hand a department store shopping bag stuffed with gifts and decorated for the season in red and green; just ten days later Mrs. Axman would suffer a nervous breakdown and be taken away in an ambulance in the middle of the night, and soon after that, on New Year's Day 1942, Earl would be whisked off by his father, stamp collection and all. A mover's truck showed up later in January and, while I watched, took all the household furnishings away, including the bureau with Earl's mother's underwear, and no one on Summit Avenue saw the Axmans again.

Because the cold winter twilight now descended so quickly, following people home from the bus made us feel all the more satisfied with ourselves, as though we were about our business long after midnight, when other kids had been asleep for hours. The man with the shopping bags stayed on the bus past the Hillside line and over into Elizabeth and got off just past the big cemetery, not far from the corner where my mother had grown up, above her father's grocery store. We got off after him quietly enough, the two of us looking indistinguishable from a thousand other local schoolkids in the standard-issue winter camouflage of hooded mackinaw and thick woolen mittens and shapeless corduroy trousers tucked into ill-fitting rubber galoshes with half of their maddening toggles undone. But because we imagined ourselves more concealed than we were by the deepening shadows, or because our adroitness was losing its power to time, we must have tailed him less skillfully than we were practiced at doing, and thus compromised "the invincible duo," as Earl had vaingloriously dubbed the pair of Christian-trackers we'd become.

There were two long blocks to traverse, both of them lined with stately brick houses bright with Christmas lights that Earl identified in a whisper as "millionaires' mansions"; then there were two shorter blocks of much smaller, modest frame houses of the kind that by then we'd seen by the hundreds on the streets that we'd traveled, each with a Christmas wreath on the door. On the second of the two blocks the man turned onto a narrow brick pathway that curved up to a low shoebox of a shingled house that poked up prettily out of the banked snow like the edible adornment on a big frosted cake. Lamps were burning dimly upstairs and down, and the Christmas tree could be seen twinkling through one of the windows to the side of the front door. While the man set down his shopping bags to get his key out, we drew closer and closer to the undulating white lawn until, through the window, we were able to discern the ornaments decorating the tree.

"Look," Earl whispered. "See the top? At the very top of the tree—see that? It's Jesus!"

"No, it's an angel."

"What do you think Jesus is?"

I whispered back, "I thought he was their God."

"And chief of the angels—and there he is!"

This then was the culmination of our quest—Jesus Christ, who by their reasoning was everything and who by my reasoning had fucked everything up: because if it weren't for Christ there wouldn't be Christians, and if it weren't for Christians there wouldn't be anti-Semitism, and if it weren't for anti-Semitism there wouldn't be Hitler, and if it weren't for Hitler Lindbergh would never be president, and if Lindbergh weren't president . . .

Suddenly the man we'd followed, standing now in the open doorway with his shopping bags, twirled around and softly, as though exhaling a smoke ring, called, "Boys."

So flabbergasted were we by being caught that I, for one, felt summoned to step forward onto the path leading up to the house and, like the model child I'd been two months before, clear my conscience by telling him my name. Only Earl's arm held me back.

"Boys, don't hide. You don't have to," the man said.

"What now?" I whispered to Earl.

"Shhhhhh," he whispered back.

"Boys, I know you're there. Boys, it's getting awfully dark," he warned in a friendly voice. "Aren't you freezing out there? Wouldn't you like a nice cup of cocoa? Inside now, children, quickly inside now before it snows. There's hot cocoa, and I have spice cake and I have seed cake and gingerbread men, I have animal crackers frosted in all different colors, and there are marshmallows—there are marshmallows, boys, marshmallows in the cupboard that we can toast over a fire."

When I again looked at Earl to find out what to do, he was already on his way back to Newark. "Run for it," he shouted at me over his shoulder, "beat it, Phil—it's a fairy!"

4

January 1942–February 1942

The Stump

ALVIN WAS DISCHARGED in January 1942, after forsaking first the wheelchair and then the crutches and, over the course of a long hospital rehabilitation, having been trained by the Canadian army nurses to walk unassisted on his artificial limb. He would be receiving a monthly disability pension from the Canadian government of a hundred and twenty-five dollars, a little more than half of what my father earned each month from the Metropolitan, and an additional three hundred dollars in separation pay. As a handicapped veteran he was eligible for further benefits should he choose to remain in Canada, where foreign volunteers into the Canadian armed forces, if they wished, were granted citizenship immediately upon discharge. And why didn't he become a Canuck? asked Uncle Monty. Since he couldn't stand America anyway, why didn't he just stay up there and cash in?

Monty was the most overbearing of my uncles, which probably accounted for why he was also the richest. He'd made his fortune wholesaling fruit and vegetables down near the railroad tracks at the Miller Street market. Alvin's father, Uncle Jack, had begun the business and taken in Monty, and after Uncle Jack died Monty had taken in his youngest brother, my uncle Herbie; when he invited my father in as well—back when my parents were penniless newlyweds—my father said no, having already been sufficiently bullied by Monty while they were growing up. My father could keep pace with Monty's prodigious expenditure of energy, and his capacity to endure all manner of hardship was no less remarkable than Monty's, but he knew from the clashes of boyhood that he was no match for the innovator who'd first gambled on bringing ripe tomatoes to Newark in the wintertime by buying up carloads of green tomatoes from Cuba and ripening them in specially heated rooms on the creaky second floor of his Miller Street warehouse. When they were ready, Monty packed them four to a box, got top dollar, and was known thereafter as the Tomato King.

While we remained rent-paying tenants in a five-room second-story flat in Newark the uncles in the wholesale produce business lived in the Jewish section of suburban Maplewood, where each owned a large, white, shuttered Colonial with a green lawn out front and a polished Cadillac in the garage. For good or bad, the exalted egoism of an Abe Steinheim or an Uncle Monty or a Rabbi Bengelsdorf—conspicuously dynamic Jews all seemingly propelled by their embattled status as the offspring of greenhorns to play the biggest role that they could commandeer as American men—was not in the makeup of my father, nor was there the slightest longing for supremacy, and so though personal pride was a driving force and his blend of fortitude and combativeness was heavily fueled, like theirs, by the grievances attending his origins as an impover-ished kid other kids called a kike, it was enough for him to make something (rather than everything) of himself and to do so with-out wrecking the lives around him. My father was born to contend but also to protect, and to inflict damage on an enemy didn't make his spirits soar as it did his older brother's (not to mention all the rest of the brutal entrepreneurial *machers*). There were the bosses and there were the bossed, and the bosses usually were bosses for a reason—and in business for themselves for a reason, whether the business was construction or produce or the rabbinate or the rackets. It was the best they could come up with to remain unob-structed—and, in their own eyes, unhumiliated—not least by the discrimination of the Protestant hierarchy that kept ninety-nine

percent of the Jews employed by the dominant corporations un-
complainingly in their place.

"If Jack was alive," Monty said, "the kid wouldn't have got out
the front door. You should never have let him go, Herm. He runs
away to Canada to become a war hero and this is where it lands
him, a goddamn gimp for the rest of his life." It was the Sunday
before the Saturday of Alvin's return, and Uncle Monty, wearing
clean clothes instead of the badly stained windbreaker and splat-
tered old pants and filthy cloth cap that were his usual market attire, was leaning against our kitchen sink, a cigarette dangling out
of his mouth. My mother was not present. She had excused herself,
as she generally did when Monty was around, but I was a small boy
and mesmerized by him, as though he were indeed the gorilla that
she privately called him when her exasperation with his coarseness
got the upper hand.

"Alvin can't bear your president," my father replied, "that's why
he went to Canada. Not so long ago you couldn't bear the man either. But now this anti-Semite is your friend. The Depression is
over, all you rich Jews tell me, and thanks not to Roosevelt but to
Mr. Lindbergh. The stock market is up, profits are up, business is
booming—and why? Because we have Lindbergh's peace instead of
Roosevelt's war. And what else matters, what besides money counts
with you people?" "You sound like Alvin, Herman. You sound like
a kid. What counts besides money? Your two boys count. You want
Sandy to come home one day like Alvin? You want Phil," he said,
looking over to where I sat listening at the kitchen table, "to come
home one day like Alvin? We're out of the war, and we're staying
out of the war. Lindbergh's done me no harm that I can see." I expected my father to respond "Just you wait," but probably because
I was there and frightened enough already, he didn't.

As soon as Monty left, my father told me, "Your uncle doesn't
use his head. Coming home like Alvin—that's not something that's
going to happen." "But what if Roosevelt is president again? Then
there would be a war," I said. "Maybe and maybe not," my father
replied, "nobody can predict that in advance." "But if there was a

war," I said, "and if Sandy was old enough, then he would be drafted to fight in the war. And if he fought in the war, then what happened to Alvin *could* happen to him." "Son, anything can happen to anyone," my father told me, "but it usually doesn't." "Except when it does," I thought, but I didn't dare to say as much because he was already upset by my questions and might not even know how to answer if I kept on going. Since what Uncle Monty said to him about Lindbergh was exactly what Rabbi Bengelsdorf had told him—and also what Sandy was secretly saying to me—I began to wonder if my father knew what he was talking about.

It was close to a year after Lindbergh took office that Alvin returned to Newark on an overnight train from Montreal, accompanied by a Canadian Red Cross nurse and missing half of one of the legs that he'd left with. We drove downtown to Penn Station to meet him as we did to meet Sandy the summer before, only this time Sandy was with us. A few weeks earlier, in the interest of family harmony, I had been allowed to go off with Aunt Evelyn and him to sit in the audience and listen as he impressed the congregation of a synagogue some forty miles south of Newark, in New Brunswick, encouraging them to enroll their children in Just Folks with stories of his Kentucky adventure and an exhibition of his drawings. My parents had made it clear to me that Sandy's job with Just Folks was something I needn't mention to Alvin; they'd themselves explain everything, but only after Alvin had a chance to get used to being home and could better understand how America had changed since he'd gone to Canada. It was a matter not of hiding anything from Alvin or of lying to him but of protecting him from whatever could interfere with his recovery.

The Montreal train was late that morning, and to pass the time—and because the political situation was with him now every moment of the day—my father had bought a copy of the *Daily News*. Seated on a bench at Penn Station, he scanned the paper, a right-wing New York tabloid that he unfailingly referred to as a "rag," while the rest of us paced the platform, anxiously waiting for the next phase of our new life to begin. When the PA system announced that the Montreal train would be arriving even later than expected, my mother, linking arms with Sandy and me, walked us back to the bench to wait there together. My father had meanwhile finished as much of the *Daily News* as he could bear and thrown it into a trash basket. Since ours was a household where nickels and dimes mattered, I was as perplexed to see him discard the paper only minutes after buying it as I'd been to see him reading it in the first place. "Can you believe these people?" he said. "This fascist dog is *still* their hero." What he didn't say was that by making good on his campaign promise to keep America out of the worldwide war, the fascist dog had by now become the hero of virtually every paper in the country with the exception of *PM*.

"Well," said my mother as the train finally entered the station and began to pull to a stop, "here comes your cousin."

"What should we do?" I asked her, as she prompted us onto our feet and the four of us stepped toward the platform's edge.

"Say hello. It's Alvin. Welcome him home."

"What about his leg?" I whispered.

"What about it, dear?"

I shrugged.

Here my father took me by the shoulders. "Don't be afraid," he said to me. "Don't be afraid of Alvin and don't be afraid of his leg. Let him see how you've grown up."

It was Sandy who broke away from us and went racing toward the car that had come to a halt a couple of hundred feet down the track. Alvin was being pushed from the train in a wheelchair by a woman in a Red Cross uniform while the person who was barreling down on him shouting his name was the only one of us who'd been won over to the other side. I didn't know any longer what to make of my brother, but then I didn't know what to make of myself, so busy was I trying to remember to conceal everyone's secrets while doing my best to suppress my fears and trying not to stop believing in my father as well as in the Democrats and FDR and whoever else could keep me from teaming up with the rest of the country in adoring President Lindbergh.

"You're back!" Sandy cried. "You're home!" And then I watched as my brother, who'd only just turned fourteen but was as strong now as a young man of twenty, dropped to his knees on the platform's concrete floor, the better to be able to throw his arms around Alvin's neck. My mother began crying then, and my father quickly took me by the hand, either to try to prevent me from going to pieces or to protect himself from his own chaos of feelings.

I thought it must be my job to run to Alvin next, and so I pulled away from my parents and broke for the wheelchair and, once there, imitating Sandy, threw *my* arms around him, only to discover how rotten he smelled. I thought at first that the smell must be coming from his leg, but it was coming from his mouth. I held my breath and shut my eyes and only released my hold on Alvin when I felt him lean forward in the chair to shake my father's hand. I noticed then the wooden crutches strapped to one side of the wheelchair, and for the first time dared to look straight at him. I'd never before seen anyone so skeletal or so dejected. His eyes showed no fear, however, or any trace of weeping, and they surveyed my father with ferocity, as though it were the guardian who had committed the unpardonable act that had rendered the ward a cripple.

"Herman," he said, but that was all.

"You're here," my father said, "you're home. We're taking you home."

Then my mother bent forward to kiss him.

"Aunt Bess," Alvin said.

The left trouser leg dropped straight down from the knee, a sight generally familiar to adults but one that startled me, even though I already knew of a man with no legs at all, a man who began at the hips and was himself no more than a stump. I had seen him before, begging on the sidewalk outside my father's downtown office, but overwhelmed as I was by the colossal freakishness, I'd never had to think much about it since there was never any danger of his coming to live in our house. He did best with his begging in baseball season when, as the men working there left the building at the end of the day, he would run through the afternoon's final scores in his incongruously deep, declamatory voice, and each of them would drop a couple of coins into the battered laundry pail that was his alms box. He moved about on—appeared, in fact, to live on—a small platform of plywood fitted beneath with roller skates. Aside from my remembering the heavy, weatherbeaten work gloves he wore all year round—to protect the hands that were his means of ambulation—I'm unable to describe the rest of his outfit because the fear of gaping merged with the terror of seeing to prevent me from ever looking long enough to register what he wore. That he dressed at all seemed as miraculous as that he was somehow able to urinate and defecate, let alone remember the ball scores. Whenever I came along to the empty insurance office on a Saturday morning with my father—largely for the delight of twirling in his desk chair while he attended to the week's mail—he and the stump of a man would always greet each other with a friendly nod. I discovered then that the grotesque injustice of a man's being halved had not merely happened, which was incomprehensible enough, but happened to someone called Robert, as commonplace as a male name could be and six letters long, like my own. "How you doin', Little Robert?" my father said as we two passed together into the building. "How you, Herman?" Little Robert would reply. Eventually I asked my father, "Does he have a last name?" "Do you?" my father asked me. "Yes." "Well, so does he." "What is it? Little Robert what?" I asked. My father thought a moment, then laughed and said, "To tell you the truth, son, I don't know."

From the moment I found out that Alvin was returning to Newark to convalesce in our house, I would involuntarily envision Robert on his platform and wearing his work gloves whenever I lay stiffly in the dark trying to force myself asleep: first my stamps covered with swastikas, then Little Robert, the living stump.

"I thought you'd be up on the leg they gave you. I thought they couldn't discharge you otherwise," I heard my father saying to Alvin. "What's happened?"

Without bothering to look at him, Alvin snapped, "Stump broke down."

"What's that mean?" my father asked.

"It's nothing. Don't worry about it."

"Does he have luggage?" my father asked the nurse.

But before she could answer, Alvin said, "Sure I got luggage. Where do you think my leg is?"

Sandy and I were headed for the baggage counter on the main concourse with Alvin and his nurse while my father hurried off to get the car from the Raymond Boulevard lot, accompanied by my mother, who went along with him at the last minute, more than likely to talk over all they hadn't anticipated about Alvin's mental state. Out on the platform, the nurse had summoned a redcap, and together they helped Alvin to a standing position and then the redcap took charge of the wheelchair while the nurse walked at Alvin's side as he hopped to the head of the escalator. There she took up her place as a human shield, and he hopped after her, clutching the moving banister as the escalator descended. Sandy and I stood at Alvin's back, out of range at last of his unfragrant breath—and where Sandy instinctively braced himself to catch him should Alvin lose his balance. The redcap, carrying upside down and over his head the wheelchair with the crutches still strapped to one side, took the stairs parallel to the escalator and was already on the main concourse to greet us when Alvin hopped from the escalator and we stepped off behind him. The redcap placed the wheelchair right side up on the concourse floor and firmly positioned it for Alvin to sit back down, but Alvin turned on his one foot and began to hop vigorously away, leaving his nurse—to whom he'd said neither thank you nor goodbye—to watch him speed off along the crowded marble floor in the direction of the baggage room.

"Can't he fall?" Sandy asked the nurse. "He's going so fast. What if he slips and falls?"

"Him?" the nurse replied. "That boy can hop anywhere. That boy can hop a very long way. He won't fall. He's the world-champion hopper. He'd have been happier to hop from Montreal than to have me helping him down here by train." She then confided to us, two protected children entirely ignorant of the bitterness of loss, "I've seen 'em angry before," she said, "I've seen the ones without *any* limbs angry, but nobody before ever angry like him."

"Angry at what?" Sandy asked anxiously.

She was a strapping woman with stern gray eyes and hair short as a soldier's under her gray Red Cross cap, but it was in the softest maternal tones, with a gentleness that came as yet another of the day's surprises, as though Sandy were one of her very own charges, that she explained, "At what people get angry at—at how things turn out."

My mother and I had to take the bus home because there wasn't enough room in the little family Studebaker. Alvin's wheelchair went into the trunk, though as it was the old unwieldy uncollapsible type, the lid of the trunk had to be tied shut with heavy twine to accommodate it. His canvas overseas bag (with the artificial leg somewhere inside) was stuffed so full that Sandy was unable to lift it even with my help, and we had to drag it across the concourse floor and through the door to the street; there my father took charge and he and Sandy laid it flat out across the back seat. Practically doubled over at the waist, Sandy was perched atop the bag for the ride home, Alvin's crutches straddling his lap. The crutches' rubber-capped tips protruded from one of the rear side-windows, and my father tied his pocket handkerchief around the ends to warn off other drivers. My father and Alvin rode up front, and I was unhappily preparing to squeeze between them just to the right of the floor shift when my mother said she wanted my company on the ride home. What she wanted, it turned out, was to prevent me from having to witness any more of the misery.

"It's okay," she said as we headed around the corner for the underpass where the line formed for the 14 bus. "It's perfectly natural to be upset. We all are."

I denied being in any way upset but found myself looking around the bus stop for somebody to follow. Easily a dozen different routes started out from this one Penn Station stop, and it happened that a Vailsburg bus bound for distant North Newark was taking on passengers at the very moment that my mother and I stood at the curbside of the underpass waiting for a 14 to show up. I spotted just the man to follow, a businessman with a briefcase who seemed to me—with my admittedly imperfect grasp of the telling characteristics that Earl was so masterfully attuned to—not to be Jewish. Yet I could only look with longing as the bus door closed behind him and he rode off without my spying on him from a nearby seat.

Once we were alone together on the bus, my mother said, "Tell me what's bothering you."

When I didn't reply she began to explain Alvin's behavior at the train station. "Alvin is ashamed. He feels ashamed for us to be seeing him in a wheelchair. When he left he was strong and independent. Now he wants to hide and he wants to scream and he wants to lash out, and it's terrible for him. And it's terrible too for a boy like you to have to see your big cousin like this. But that's all going to change. Just as soon as he understands that there's nothing about the way he looks or about what happened for him to be ashamed of, he's going to gain back the weight he lost, and he'll start to walk everywhere on his artificial leg, and he's going to look just as you remember him before he left for Canada . . . Does that help any? Does what I'm telling you reassure you at all?"

"I don't need to be reassured," I said, but what I wanted to ask was: "His stump—what does it mean that it's broken down? Do I have to look at it? Will I ever have to touch it? Are they going to fix it?"

On a Saturday a couple of weeks earlier I'd gone into the cellar with my mother and helped her empty the cartons full of Alvin's belongings, rescued by my father from the Wright Street room after Alvin had run off to join the Canadian army. Everything washable my mother scrubbed on the washboard in the divided cellar tub, soaping in one sink, rinsing in the other, and then feeding a piece at a time into the wringer while I cranked the handle to force out the rinse water. I hated that wringer; each piece of wash emerged flattened out from between its two rollers, looking as if it had been run over by a truck, and whenever I was down in the cellar for whatever reason, I was always afraid to turn my back on the thing. But now I steeled myself to drop each wet, deformed item of mangled laundry into the laundry basket and carry the basket upstairs so that my mother could dry everything on the backyard clothesline. I fed her the clothespins as she leaned from the window to hang out the wash, and while she stood in the kitchen after dinner that evening ironing the shirts and pajamas that I had just helped her to reel in, I sat at the kitchen table folding Alvin's underwear and rolling each pair of socks into a ball, determined to make everything turn out right by being the best little boy imaginable, much, much better than Sandy and better even than myself.

After school the next day, it required two trips for me to carry Alvin's good clothes around the corner to the tailor shop where they did our dry cleaning. Later in the week I picked them up and at home placed everything—topcoat, suit, sport jacket, and two pairs of his pants—on wooden hangers in the half I'd apportioned him of my bedroom closet and stacked the rest of the clean apparel in the top two drawers that had formerly been Sandy's. Since Alvin was going to be sleeping in our bedroom—to provide him with the easiest possible access to the bathroom—Sandy had already gotten himself ready to move to the sun parlor at the front of the flat by arranging his own belongings in the breakfront in the dining room, beside the linen tablecloth and napkins. One evening a few days before Alvin's scheduled return I shined his pair of brown shoes and his pair of black shoes, ignoring as best I could any uncertainty I had as to whether shining all four of them was still necessary. To make those shoes gleam, to get his good clothes clean, to neatly pile the dresser drawers with his freshly washed things—and all of it simply a prayer, an improvised prayer imploring the household gods to protect our humble five rooms and all they contained from the vengeful fury of the missing leg.

I tried to gauge from what I saw beyond the bus window how much time remained before we got to Summit Avenue and it was too late to unseal my fate. We were on Clinton Avenue just passing the Riviera Hotel, where, as I never failed to remember, my mother and father had spent their wedding night. We were clear of downtown, about halfway home, and directly ahead was Temple B'nai Abraham, the great oval fortress built to serve the city's Jewish rich and no less foreign to me than if it had been the Vatican.

"I could move into your bed," my mother said, "if that's what's bothering you. For now, until everybody gets used to everybody else again, I could sleep in your bed next to Alvin's bed and you could go in and sleep with Daddy in our bed. Would that be better?"

I said that I'd rather sleep alone in my own bed.

"What if Sandy moved back from the sun parlor to his bed," my mother suggested, "and Alvin slept in yours and you slept where Sandy was going to sleep, on the daybed in the sun parlor? Would you be lonely up at the front of the house, or is that what you would really prefer?"

Would I prefer it? I'd have loved it. But how possibly could Sandy, who was now working for Lindbergh, share a room with someone who had lost his leg going to war against Lindbergh's Nazi friends?

We were turning onto Clinton Place from the Clinton Avenue stop, the familiar residential corner where—back before Sandy deserted me for Aunt Evelyn on Saturday afternoons—he and I used to disembark for the double feature at the Roosevelt Theater, whose black-lettered marquee was a block away. Soon the bus would be sailing past the narrow alleyways and the two-and-a-half-family houses lining the level length of Clinton Place—streets that looked much like our own but whose red-brick bank of gabled front stoops aroused not a one of the basic boyhood emotions that ours did—before arriving at the big final turn onto Chancellor Avenue. There the grinding pull up the hill would begin, past the elegant fluted piers of the spiffy new high school, on to the sturdy flagpole out front of my grade school, and through to the crest of the hill, where a band of Lenni Lenapes were said by our third-grade teacher to have lived in a tiny village, cooking their food over hot stones and drawing designs on their pots. This was our destination, the Summit Avenue stop, diagonally across from the platters of freshly dipped chocolates profligately displayed in the lace-trimmed windows of Anna Mae's, the sweetshop that had succeeded the Indians' tepees and whose tantalizing scent honeyed the air less than a two-minute walk from our house.

In other words, the time left to say yes to the sun parlor was precisely measurable and running out, movie theater by movie theater, candy store by candy store, stoop by stoop, and yet all I could say was no, no, I'll be fine where I am, until my mother had nothing soothing left to suggest and, despite herself, went gloomily silent in a very ominous, undisguised way, as though the eventfulness of the morning was at last working her over the way it had me. Meanwhile, since I didn't know how long I could go on concealing that I couldn't bear Alvin because of his missing limb and his empty trouser leg and his awful smell and his wheelchair and his crutches and the way he wouldn't look up at any of us when he talked, I began to pretend that I was following somebody on our bus who didn't look Jewish. It was then that I realized—employing all the criteria imparted to me by Earl—that my mother looked Jewish. Her hair, her nose, her eyes—my mother looked *unmistakably* Jewish. But then so must I, who so strongly resembled her. I hadn't known.

What made Alvin smell bad was all the decay in his mouth. "You lose your teeth when you've got problems," Dr. Lieberfarb explained after looking around with his little mirror and saying "Uh-oh" nineteen times, and that very afternoon he started drilling. He

was going to do all that work for nothing because Alvin had volunteered to fight the fascists and because, unlike "the rich Jews"
who astonished my father by imagining themselves secure in Lindbergh's America, Lieberfarb remained undeluded about what "the
many Hitlers of this world" might yet have in store for us. Nineteen
gold inlays was a big deal, but that's how he showed solidarity with
my father, my mother, me, and the Democrats, as opposed to Uncle
Monty, Aunt Evelyn, Sandy, and all the Republicans currently enjoying their countrymen's love. Nineteen inlays also took a long
time, particularly for a dentist who'd trained in night school while
working days packing cargo crates at Port Newark, and whose
touch was never that light. Lieberfarb was drilling away for months,
but within the first few weeks enough of the rot had been removed
so that it was no longer such a trial to be sleeping more or less next
to Alvin's mouth. The stump was something else. "Broken down"
means that the end of the stump goes bad: it opens up, it cracks, it
gets infected. There are boils, sores, edema, and you can't walk on
it with the prosthesis and so have to be without it and resort to
crutches until it heals and can take the pressure without breaking
down again. At fault was the fit of the artificial leg. The doctors
would tell him, "You've lost your fit," but he hadn't lost his fit, he
never *had* a fit, Alvin said, because the legmaker hadn't got the
measurements right to begin with.

"How long does it take to heal?" I asked him the night he finally
told me what "broken down" meant. Sandy up at the front of the
house and my parents in their bedroom had already been asleep
for hours, and so too were Alvin and I when he began to shout
"Dance! Dance!" and, with a frightening gasp, shot upright in his
bed, wide awake. When I flipped on the night lamp and saw him
covered with sweat, I got up and opened the bedroom door, and
though suddenly covered in sweat myself, I tiptoed across the little
back foyer, not to my parents' room, however, to report what had
happened, but into the bathroom to get Alvin a towel. He used it
to mop his face and his neck, then pulled off his pajama shirt to
wipe his chest and his underarms, and now at last I saw what had

become of the upper man since the lower man had been blown apart. No wounds, stitches, or disfiguring scars, but no strength either, just the pale skin of a sickly boy adhering to the knobs and ridges of bone.

This was our fourth night together. On the first three nights Alvin had been careful to change into his pajamas in the bathroom and then to hop back to hang his clothes in the closet, and since he used the bathroom again to dress in the mornings, I hadn't as yet had to look at the stump and could pretend I didn't know it was there. At night I turned to the wall and, fatigued by all my worries, fell right off to sleep and remained asleep until sometime in the early hours when Alvin got up and hopped to the bathroom and back to bed. He did all this without turning on the light and I lay there afraid he was going to bang into something and crash to the floor. At night, his every move made me want to run away, and not merely from the stump. It was on this fourth night, when Alvin had finished drying himself off with the towel and was lying there in just his pajama bottoms, that he pulled up the pajamas' left leg to take a look at the stump. I supposed this was a hopeful sign—that he was starting to be less crazily agitated, at least with me—but I still didn't want to look his way . . . and so I did, trying to be a soldier in my bed. What I saw extending down from his knee joint was something five or six inches long that resembled the elongated head of a featureless animal, something on which Sandy, with just a few well-placed strokes, could have crayoned eyes, a nose, a mouth, teeth, and ears, and turned it into the likeness of a rat. What I saw was what the word "stump" describes: the blunt remnant of something whole that belonged there and once had been there. If you didn't know what a leg looked like, this one might have seemed normal to you, given how the hairless skin was rounded off softly at the abbreviated end as though it were nature's handiwork and not the result of a trying sequence of medical amputations.

"Is it healed?" I asked him.

"Not yet."

"How long will it take?"

"Forever," he replied.

I was stunned. Then this is endless! I thought.

"Extremely frustrating," Alvin said. "You get on the leg they make for you and the stump breaks down. You get on crutches and it starts to swell up. The stump goes bad whatever you do. Get my bandages from the dresser."

I did as he told me. I was going to have to handle the beige elasticized wrappings he used to prevent his stump from swelling when the artificial leg was off. They were coiled up in a corner of the drawer beside his socks. Each was about three inches wide and had a large safety pin stuck through the end to keep it from unrolling. I no more wanted to plunge my hand into that drawer than to go down to the cellar and stick it into the wringer, but I did, and when I delivered the bandages to the bed, one in each fist, he said, "Good boy," and was able to make me laugh by petting my head like a dog's.

Afraid to see what came next, I sat on my bed and watched.

"You put this bandage on," he explained, "to keep it from blowing up." He held the stump in one hand and with the other undid the safety pin and began to unroll one of the bandages in a crisscrossing pattern over the stump and on up to the knee joint and then several inches beyond that. "You put this bandage on to keep it from blowing up"—he repeated the words wearily, with exaggerated patience—"but you don't want bandages over the breakdown because that won't let the breakdown heal. So you're just going back and forth until you're nuts." When he finished unrolling the bandage and inserted the safety pin to fasten the end, he showed me the results. "You have to pull it tight, you see?" He began a similar routine with the second bandage. The stump—when he was through with it—again reminded me of a small animal, this time one whose head had to be muzzled extra carefully to prevent it from sinking its razor-sharp teeth into the hand of its captor.

"How do you learn that?" I asked him.

"You don't have to learn. You just put it on. Except," he suddenly announced, "it's too goddamn tight. Maybe you *do* have to learn. Goddamn son of a bitch! It's either too fucking loose or too fucking tight. It makes you nuts—the whole goddamn thing." He removed the safety pin that fastened the second bandage and then undid both bandages in order to start again. "You can see," he told me, struggling now to suppress disgust with the futility of *everything*, "how good at doing this you get," and resumed the rewrapping, which, like the healing, appeared destined to go on in our bedroom forever.

The next day when school was over, I ran straight home to a house that I knew would be empty—Alvin was at the dentist, Sandy was off somewhere with Aunt Evelyn, the two of them inexplicably helping Lindbergh achieve his ends, and my parents wouldn't be back from work until suppertime. As Alvin had settled on using the daytime hours to allow the breakdown to heal unbandaged and the nights to wrap the stump to prevent the swelling, I readily found the two bandages in the corner of the top dresser drawer where he'd returned them rolled up that morning. I sat on the edge of my bed, turned up my left trouser leg, and, shocked to realize that what remained of Alvin's leg was not much bigger around than my own, set out to bandage myself. I'd spent the day at school mentally running through what I'd watched him do the night before, but at three-twenty, when I got home, I'd only just started to wrap the first bandage around an imaginary stump of my own when, against the flesh below my knee, I felt what turned out to be a ragged scab from the ulcerated underside of Alvin's stump. The scab must have come loose during the night—Alvin had either ignored it or failed to notice it—and now it was stuck to me and I was out way beyond what I could deal with. Though the heaves began in the bedroom, by racing for the back door and then down the back stairway to the cellar, I managed to position my head over the double sink seconds before the real puking began.

To find myself alone in the dank cavern of the cellar was an ordeal under any circumstances, and not only because of the wringer. With its smudged frieze of mold and mildew running along the cracking whitewashed walls—stains in every hue of the excremental rainbow and seepage blotches that looked as if they'd leaked from a corpse—the cellar was a ghoulish realm apart, extending beneath the whole of the house and deriving no light at all from the half-dozen slits of grime-clouded glass that looked onto the cement of the alleyways and the weedy front yard. There were several saucer-sized drains sunk into the bottom of a sloping concavity at the middle of the concrete floor. Secured in the mouth of each was a heavy black disc pierced by the concentric dime-sized perforations from which, with no difficulty, I imagined vaporous creatures spiraling malevolently up from the earth's innards into my life. The cellar was a place bereft not just of a sunny window but of every human assurance, and when I came to study Greek and Roman mythology in a freshman high school class and read in the textbook about Hades, Cerberus, and the River Styx, it was always our cellar that I was reminded of. One 30-watt bulb hung over the washtub into which I'd vomited, a second hung in the vicinity of the coal furnaces—ablaze and bulkily aligned together like the three-personed Pluto of our underworld—and another, almost always burned out, was suspended from an electrical cord inside each of the storage bins.

I could never accept that the wintertime responsibility would fall to me for shoveling coal into our family's furnace first thing each morning, then banking the fire before going to bed, and once a day carrying a pailful of cold ashes out to the ashcan in the backyard. Sandy had by now grown strong enough to take over from my father, and in a few more years, when he went off like every other eighteen-year-old American boy to receive his twenty-four months of military training in President Lindbergh's new citizen Army, I would inherit the job and relinquish it only when I too was conscripted. Imagining a future when I'd be in the cellar manning the furnace all alone was, at nine, as upsetting as thinking about the inevitability of dying, which had also begun tormenting me in bed every night.

But I mainly feared the cellar because of those who were already dead—my two grandfathers, my mother's mother, and the aunt and uncle who once constituted Alvin's family. Their bodies may have been interred just off Route 1 on the Newark-Elizabeth line, but in order to patrol our affairs and scrutinize our conduct their ghosts resided two stories beneath our flat. I had little or no recollection of any of them other than of the grandmother who'd died when I was six, and yet whenever I was headed for the cellar by myself, I took care to warn each in turn that I was on my way and to beg them to keep their distance and not to besiege me once I was in their midst. When Sandy was my age he used to arm himself against his brand of fear by barreling down the cellar stairs shouting, "Bad guys, I know you're down there—I've got a gun," while I would descend whispering, "I'm sorry for whatever I did that was wrong."

There was the wringer, the drains, the dead—the ghosts of the dead watching and judging and condemning as I vomited into the double sink where my mother and I had washed Alvin's clothes—and there were the alley cats who would disappear into the cellar when the outside back door was left ajar and then yowl from wherever in the dark they were crouched, and there was the agonized cough of our downstairs neighbor Mr. Wishnow, a cough that sounded from the cellar as though he were being ripped apart by the teeth of a two-man saw. Like my father, Mr. Wishnow was an insurance agent with the Metropolitan, but for over a year he had been on disability pay, too ill with cancer of the mouth and the throat to do anything but stay at home and listen to the daytime radio serials when he wasn't asleep or uncontrollably coughing. With the blessing of the home office, his wife had taken over for him—the first female insurance agent in the history of the Newark district—and now kept the same long hours as my father, who generally had to go back out after dinner to make his collections and canvassed for prospective customers most every Saturday or Sunday, weekends being the only time when he could hope to find a breadwinner at home to listen to his spiel. Before my mother had herself begun to work as a saleslady at Hahne's, she would stop downstairs a couple of times a day to see how Mr. Wishnow was doing; and now, when Mrs. Wishnow called to say she couldn't be home in time to cook a proper dinner, my mother would prepare a little more of whatever we were eating and Sandy and I, before we were allowed to sit down to our own meal, each carried a warm plateful of food to the first floor on a tray, one for Mr. Wishnow and one for Seldon, the Wishnows' only child. Seldon would open the door for us and we would maneuver our trays through the foyer and into the kitchen, absorbed in trying not to spill anything as we set them on the table where Mr. Wishnow was already waiting, a paper napkin tucked into the top of his pajamas but looking in no way able to feed himself, however desperately in need of nutrition. "You boys all right?" he would ask us in the shredded rag of a voice that was left to him. "How about a joke for me, Phillie? I could use a good joke," he allowed, but without bitterness, without sadness, merely demonstrating the soft, defensive joviality of someone still hanging on for no seeming reason. Seldon must have told his father that I could make the kids laugh at school, and so I would teasingly be asked to tell him a joke when just by his proximity he'd have obliterated my capacity to speak. The best I could do was to try to look at somebody whom I knew to be dying—and, worse, *resigned* to dying—without allowing my eyes to see in his the gruesome evidence of the bodily misery he was being made to pass through on the way to a spectral life in our cellar with all the other dead. Sometimes, when Mr. Wishnow's supply of medicine had to be refilled at the drugstore, Seldon would hurry up the stairs to ask if I wanted to go with him, and because I had learned from my parents that Seldon's father was doomed—and because Seldon himself acted as if he knew nothing about it—there was no way I could think of to refuse him, even though I'd never liked being with anyone so nakedly eager to be befriended. Seldon was a child transparently under the sway of his loneliness, undeservedly rich with sorrow and working much too hard to achieve the permanent smile, one of those skinny, pallid, gentle-faced boys who embarrass everyone by throwing a ball like a girl but also the smartest kid in our class and the schoolwide whiz at arithmetic. Oddly, there was nobody in gym class better than Seldon at scrambling up and down the ropes that dangled from the gymnasium's high ceiling, his aerial nimbleness integrally related—according to one of our teachers—to his unchallengeable adroitness with numbers. He was already a little champ at chess, which his father had taught him, and so whenever I accompanied him to the drugstore I knew there was no way to prevent my winding up later at the chessboard in his family's darkened living room—dark to save electricity and dark because the drapes were now drawn all the time to keep the neighborhood's morbidly curious from peering in at Seldon's step-by-step descent into fatherlessness. Undeterred by my stern resistance, Solitary Seldon (as he'd been nicknamed by Earl Axman, whose mother's overnight mental collapse had been a startling parental catastrophe of another order) would try to teach me for the millionth time how to move the pieces and play the game while, behind the back bedroom door, his father coughed so frequently and with so much force that there seemed to be not one father but four, five, six fathers in there coughing themselves to death.

In less than a week it was I and not Alvin who was bandaging his stump, and by then I'd practiced enough on myself—and without again throwing up—that he hadn't once to complain of the bandages being too loose or too tight. I did this nightly—even after the stump had healed and he was walking regularly on the artificial leg—to stave off a resurgence of the swelling. All the while the stump was healing, the artificial leg had been at the back of the clothes closet, largely hidden from sight by the shoes on the floor and by the trousers hanging down from the crossrod. It still took some doing not to notice it, but I was determined and didn't know what it was made of till the day Alvin took it out to put on. Except for its eerily replicating the shape of the lower half of a real lower limb, everything about it was horrible, but horrible and a wonder both, beginning with what Alvin called his harness: the dark leather thigh-corset that laced up the front and extended from just below the buttock to the top of the kneecap and that was attached to the prosthesis by hinged steel joints on either side of the knee. The stump, with a long white woolen sock pulled over it, fit snugly into a cushioned socket carved into the top of the prosthesis, which was fashioned of hollowed-out wood with air holes punched into it and not, as I'd been imagining, of a length of black rubber resembling a comic-book bludgeon. At the end of the leg was an artificial foot that flexed only a few degrees and was cushioned with a sponge sole. It screwed neatly into the leg without any of the hardware showing, and though it looked more like a wooden shoetree than a living foot with five separate toes, when Alvin slipped into his socks and shoes—the socks washed by my mother, the shoes shined by me—you'd have thought that the feet were both his own.

The first day back on his artificial leg Alvin exercised in the alleyway by walking back and forth from the garage at the far end to the scrawny hedge enclosing the tiny front yard, but never a step farther, to where he could be seen by someone out on the street. The second day he again exercised alone in the morning, but when I got home from school he took me outdoors with him for another session, this time not just concentrating on his walking but pretending that the soundness of his stump and the fit of his prosthesis—and the long future ahead as a one-legged man—weren't weighing on his mind. The following week Alvin was wearing the leg around the house all day, and the week after that, he said to me, "Go get the football." Only we didn't own a football—owning a football was as big a deal as owning cleats or shoulder pads, and no kid had one who wasn't "rich." And I couldn't just go and sign one out from the playground back of the school unless we were going to use it right there, so what I did—I who'd not stolen anything so far other than some change from my parents' pockets—what I did without a moment's hesitation was to stroll down Keer Avenue to where there were one-family houses with front and back lawns and case every driveway until I saw what I was after—a football to steal, a real leather Wilson football, scuffed from the pavement, with worn leather lacing and a bladder you inflated, that some kid with money had left unattended. I tucked it under my arm and took off, tearing all the way up the hill to Summit Avenue as if I were returning a kickoff for old Notre Dame.

That afternoon we practiced pass plays in the alleyway for close to an hour, and at night, when we examined the stump together behind our bedroom's closed door, we saw not one sign of its breaking down, even though while tossing me his perfect left-handed spirals Alvin had been taking practically the whole of his weight on the artificial limb. "I didn't have a choice" is the defense I would have formulated had I been caught in the act on Keer Avenue that day. My cousin Alvin wanted a football, Your Honor. He lost his leg fighting Hitler and now he's home and he wanted a football. What else could I possibly do?

By then a month had passed since the awful homecoming at Penn Station and, though it wasn't necessarily pleasant, I'd feel no revulsion to speak of when, while going for my shoes in the morning, I reached to the back of the closet for Alvin's prosthesis and handed it across to where he was seated on the bed in his undershorts, waiting his turn in the bathroom. The grimness was fading and he'd begun gaining weight, gorging himself between meals on fistfuls of whatever was in the refrigerator, and his eyes didn't look so enormous, and his hair had grown thick again, wavy hair so black it had a waxen sheen, and as he sat there semihelpless with his stump exposed, there was more each morning for a boy who worshiped him to worship, and what there was to pity was a little less impossible to bear.

Soon Alvin was no longer confining himself to the alleyway, and without having to rely on the crutches or the cane that it humiliated him to use in public, he was all over the place on his artificial leg, shopping for my mother at the butcher's, the bakery, and the vegetable store, buying a hotdog for himself down at the corner, taking the bus not only to the dentist on Clinton Avenue but all the way on to Market Street to buy a new shirt at Larkey's—and also, as I didn't yet know, dropping by the playing fields back of the high school with his separation pay in his pocket to see who might be hanging around wanting to play poker or shoot craps. After school one day, the two of us made room in the storage bin for the wheelchair, and that night after dinner I reported to my mother something that had dawned on me at school. Wherever I was and no matter what I was supposed to be doing, I found myself thinking about Alvin and how I could get him to forget about his prosthesis—and so I said to my mother, "If Alvin had a zipper on the side of his pant leg, it would be easier for him, wouldn't it, to get in and out of his pants when he's got his leg on?" The next morning, on her way to work, my mother dropped off a pair of Alvin's army trousers with a neighborhood seamstress who worked out of her house, and the seamstress was able to open the side seam and sew in a zipper that extended some six inches up the uncuffed left pant leg. That night when Alvin pulled on the trousers after having undone the zipper, the pant leg passed easily up over the prosthesis without his having to curse everyone on earth just because he was getting dressed. And when he closed the zipper, you couldn't see it. "You don't even know it's there!" I cried. In the morning, we put all his other trousers in a paper bag for my mother to take to the seamstress to fix. "I couldn't live without you," Alvin said to me when we went to bed that night. "I couldn't put my pants on without you," and he gave me to keep forever the Canadian medal that he'd been awarded "for performance under exceptional circumstances." It was a circular silver medal, on one side King George VI in profile and on the other a triumphant lion standing on the body of a dragon. I of course cherished it and began to wear it regularly, but with the narrow green ribbon from which it hung pinned to my undershirt so no one would see it and question my loyalty to the United States. I left it in my drawer at home only on days I had gym and we had to strip off our outer shirts to exercise.

And where did this leave Sandy? Because he was himself so busy, he seemed at first not to notice my breakneck transformation into personal valet to a decorated Canadian war hero who'd now gone ahead and decorated me; and when he did—and was made miserable at first not so much because of Alvin's involvement with me, which was bound to follow from our new sleeping arrangement, but because of the hostile indifference Alvin evinced toward him— it was too late to oust me from the great supporting role (with its nauseating duties) that I'd virtually been forced to undertake and that, to Sandy's surprise, had elicited such sublime recognition in the waning years of my long career as his little brother.

And all of this had been achieved without my once alluding to Sandy's affiliation, by way of Aunt Evelyn and Rabbi Bengelsdorf, with our present hateful administration. Everyone, including my brother, had avoided speaking of the OAA and Just Folks anywhere near Alvin, convinced that until he came to understand how the enormous popularity of Lindbergh's isolationist policies had begun to win even the support of many Jews—and how it was far less traitorous than it might appear for a Jewish boy Sandy's age to have been drawn to the adventure that Just Folks offered—there'd be nothing to mitigate the outrage of the most self-sacrificing and staunchest Lindbergh-hater of us all. But Alvin seemed already to have sensed that Sandy had let him down and, being Alvin, didn't bother disguising his feelings. I'd said nothing, my parents had said nothing, certainly Sandy hadn't said anything to incriminate himself in Alvin's eyes, and yet Alvin had come to know (or to behave as though he knew) that the first one to welcome him home at the train station had also been first to sign on with the fascists.

Nobody was sure what Alvin was going to do next. There would be problems finding a job because not everyone was going to hire somebody who was considered a cripple, a traitor, or both. However, it was essential, my parents said, to thwart any inclination Alvin might have to do nothing and just sulk and feel sorry for himself for the rest of his life while squeaking by on his pension. My mother wanted him to use his monthly disability check to put himself through college. She had asked around and been told that if he spent a year at Newark Academy, earning B's for the courses he'd got D's and F's in at Weequahic, more than likely he'd be able to get into the University of Newark the following year. But my father couldn't imagine Alvin voluntarily going back to the twelfth grade, even at a downtown private school; at twenty-two and after all he'd been through, he needed as quickly as possible to get a job with a future, and for this my father proposed Alvin's contacting Billy Steinheim. Billy was the son who'd befriended Alvin back when he was Abe's driver, and if Billy was willing to make the case to his father for giving Alvin a second chance, maybe they would agree to find a place for him in the firm, a lowly job for now but one in which he could redeem himself in Abe Steinheim's eyes. If need be, and only if need be, Alvin could get a start with Uncle Monty, who'd already come around to offer his nephew work at the produce market; that had been in those bad early days when Alvin's stump was seriously broken down and he was still in bed most of the time and wouldn't allow the shades to be raised in our room out of his dread of catching so much as a glimpse of the little world in which he'd once been whole. Driving home from Penn Station in the car with my father and Sandy, he'd shut his eyes once the high school came into view rather than be reminded of the innumerable times he'd come bounding out of that building at the end of the day unimpeded by bodily torment and equipped to pursue whatever he wanted.

It was on the very afternoon before Uncle Monty's visit that I was a little late returning from school—it had been my turn to stay to clean the blackboards—and got home to discover that Alvin was gone. I couldn't find him in his bed or in the bathroom or anywhere else in the flat, and so I ran outside to look for him in the backyard and then, bewildered, raced back into the house where, from the foot of the stairwell, I heard faint moaning sounds rising from below—ghosts, the suffering ghosts of Alvin's mother and father! When I edged down the cellar stairs to see if they could be seen there as well as heard, what I saw instead, up by the front wall of the cellar, was Alvin himself peering out of the horizontal little glass slit that looked at street level onto Summit Avenue. He was in his bathrobe, a hand to help him maintain his balance clutching the narrow sill. The other hand I couldn't see. He was using it for something that I was too young to know anything about. Through a little circle of window that had been cleared of grime, he was watching the high school girls who lived on Keer Avenue walk home from Weequahic along our street. Their legs scooting by the front hedge was about all that he could have possibly seen, but seeing that much was enough and caused him to moan with what I took to be anguish at his no longer himself having two legs to walk on. I retreated silently up the stairs and out the back door and squatted in the farthest corner of our garage, plotting to run away to New York to live with Earl Axman. Only because it was getting dark and I had homework to do, did I return to the house, stopping first to peek into the cellar to see if Alvin was still there. He wasn't, and so I dared to descend the stairs, dashing quickly past the wringer and around the drains, and once at the window and up on my toes—intending only to look out at the street the way he did—I discovered the whitewashed wall beneath the window slick and syrupy with an abundance of goo. Since I didn't know what masturbation was, I of course didn't know what ejaculate was. I thought it was pus. I thought it was phlegm. I didn't know what to think, except that it was something terrible. In the presence of a species of discharge as yet mysterious to me, I imagined it was something that festered in a man's body and then came spurting from his mouth when he was completely consumed by grief.

The afternoon Uncle Monty stopped by to see Alvin, he was on his way downtown to Miller Street, where, since he was fourteen years old, he'd been working all night long at the market, arriving at around five and getting home only at nine the next morning to eat his big meal and go to sleep for the day. That was the life lived by the richest member of our family. His two children fared better. Linda and Annette, who were a little older than Sandy and exhibited the painful shyness of girls who tiptoe around a tyrannical father, had lots of clothes and attended suburban Columbia High School in Maplewood, where there were more Jewish kids who had lots of clothes and whose fathers, like Monty, each owned a Caddy for themselves and had a second car in the garage for the convenience of the wife and the grown children. Living with them all in the big Maplewood house was my grandmother, who also had a lot of clothes, all bought for her by her most successful son and none of which she wore other than on the High Holidays and when Monty made her get dressed up to go out to eat with the family on Sundays. The restaurants weren't sufficiently kosher to meet her standards, so all she ever ordered was the à la carte prisoner's meal of bread and water, and then she never knew how to act in a restaurant anyway. Once when she saw a busboy carrying a staggering load of dishes back to the kitchen, she'd gotten up to go over and help him. Uncle Monty cried, "Ma! No! *Loz im tsu ru!* Let the boy be!" and when she slapped his hand away had to be pulled back to the table by the sleeve of her ridiculously sequined dress. There was a black woman, known as "the girl," who came by bus from Newark to clean two days a week, but that didn't stop Grandma from going down on her knees when no one was around to scrub the kitchen and bathroom floors or from doing her own wash on a washboard despite the presence in Monty's finished basement of a brand-new $99 Bendix Home Laundry. My aunt Tillie, Monty's wife, was endlessly complaining because her husband slept all day and was never home at night, though everyone else in the family considered that—far more than her own new Oldsmobile—to be her good luck.

Alvin was lying in bed and still in pajamas at four in the afternoon on that January day when Monty first dropped by to see him and to dare ask the question whose answer none of us exactly knew—"How the hell did you manage to lose a leg?" Since Alvin had been so uncompanionable when I got home from school, responding with a grunt of disgust to whatever I offered to cheer him up, I hardly expected our least lovable relative to elicit any response at all.

But the intimidating presence of Uncle Monty, with the ever-present cigarette dangling from the corner of his mouth, was such that not even Alvin, in those early days, could tell him to shut up and go away. On that particular afternoon Alvin couldn't begin to mimic the brash defiance that had enabled him to hop like a marvel across the Penn Station concourse upon arriving back home as an amputee.

"France," Alvin hollowly replied to the big question.

"Worst country in the world," Monty told him, and with no lack of certainty. As a twenty-one-year-old in the summer of 1918, Monty had himself fought in France against the Germans in the second bloody Battle of the Marne, and then in the Argonne Forest when the Allies broke through on the Germans' western front, and so, of course, he knew everything about France.

"I'm not asking you where," Monty said, "I'm asking you how."

"How," repeated Alvin.

"Spit it out, kid. It'll do you good."

He knew that too—what would do Alvin good.

"Where were you," he asked, "when you got hit? And don't tell me 'the wrong place.' All your life you been in the wrong place."

"We were waiting for the boat to get us out."

Here he closed his eyes as though hoping never to open them again. But instead of stopping right there, as I was praying for him to do—"Shot a German," he suddenly said.

"And?" said Monty.

"He was out there screaming for the rest of the night."

"So? So? Go on. So he was screaming. So what?"

"So near dawn, before the boat's due in, I crawled over to where he was. Maybe fifty yards away. By then he was already dead. But I crawled around to the top of him and I shot him twice in the head. Then I spit on the son of a bitch. And in that second they threw the grenade. I got it in both legs. On one of my legs the foot was twisted around. Broken and twisted. That one they could fix. They operated and fixed it. They put a cast on it. They straightened it out. But the other was gone. I looked down and I saw one foot backwards and one leg dangling. The left leg just about amputated already."

There it was, and nothing like the heroic reality that I had so shallowly imagined.

"Out in no man's land all alone," Monty told him, "could be you were hit by one of your own. It's not yet light, it's half-light, a guy hears gunfire, he panics—bingo, he yanks the pin."

As for that surmise, Alvin had nothing to say.

Anyone else might have understood and relented, if only because of the perspiration beading Alvin's forehead and the droplets pooled in the hollow of his throat and the fact that he still wouldn't open his eyes. But not my uncle—he understands and *doesn't* relent. "And how come you didn't get left there? After pulling that stunt, how come they didn't just leave you to die?"

"There was mud everywhere" was Alvin's vacant reply. "The ground was mud. All I remember is that there was mud."

"Who saved you, misfit?"

"They took me. I must have been out of it. Came and took me."

"I'm trying to picture your brain, Alvin, and I can't. Spits. He spits. And that's the story of how he loses a leg."

"Some things you don't know why you do them." It was I who was speaking. What did I know? But I was telling my uncle, "You just do them, Uncle Monty. You can't not."

"You can't not, Phillie, when you're a professional misfit." To Alvin he said, "So now what? You going to lay there living off disability checks? You going to live like a sharpie off your luck? Or would you maybe consider supporting yourself like the rest of us dumb mortals do? There's a job at the market for you when you're up out of bed. You start at the bottom, hosing down the floor and grading tomatoes, you start at the bottom with the buggy-luggers and the schleppers, but there's a job there working for me, and a paycheck every week. You pocket half the take at the Esso station, but I'll go with you anyway because you're still Jack's kid, and for my brother Jack I do anything. I wouldn't be where I am without Jack. Jack taught me the produce business and then he died. Just like Steinheim wanted to teach you the building business. But nobody can teach you, misfit. Throws the keys in Steinheim's face. Too big for Abe Steinheim. Only Hitler is big enough for Alvin Roth."

In the kitchen, in a drawer with the potholders and the oven thermometer, my mother kept a long stiff needle and heavy thread to truss up the Thanksgiving turkey after it was stuffed. It was the only instrument of torture, aside from the wringer, that I could think of that we owned, and I wanted to go in and get it and use it to shut my uncle's mouth.

At the bedroom door, before leaving for the market, Monty turned back to summarize. Bullies love to summarize. The redundant upbraiding summary—nothing to equal it outside the old-fashioned flogging. "Your buddies risked everything to save you. Went in and dragged you out under fire. Didn't they? And for what? So you could spend the rest of your life shooting craps with Margulis? So you can play seven-card stud up at the schoolyard? So you can go back and pump gas and steal Simkowitz blind? You make every mistake in the book. Everything you do you do wrong. Even shooting Germans you do wrong. Why is that? Why do you throw keys at people? Why do you spit? Someone who is already dead—and you spit? Why? Because life wasn't handed to you on a silver platter like it was handed to the rest of the Roths? If it wasn't for Jack, Alvin, I wouldn't be standing here wasting my breath. There is nothing you have earned. Let's be clear about that. Nothing. For twenty-two years you have remained a disaster. I'm doing this for your father, sonny, not for you. I'm doing it for your grandmother. 'Help the boy,' she tells me, so I'm helping you. Once you figure out how you want to make your fortune, come around on your pegleg and we'll talk."

Alvin didn't cry, didn't curse, didn't holler, even after Monty was out the back door and into his car and he could have unleashed his every evil thought. He was too far gone to roar that day. Or even to crack. Only I did, after he refused to open his eyes and look at me when I begged him to; only I cracked, alone later in the one place in our house where I knew I could go to be apart from the living and all that they cannot not do.

5

March 1942–June 1942

Never Before

Here's how Alvin came to have it in for Sandy.

Before leaving him alone on the morning of his first Monday back, my mother had made Alvin promise to use his crutches to get around on until one of us was home to fetch for him. But Alvin so despised being on crutches that he refused even by himself to submit to the stability they provided. At night, when we were in our beds and the lights were out, Alvin would get me laughing by explaining why crutching wasn't so simple as my mother thought. "You go to the bathroom," Alvin said, "and they're always falling. They're always clattering. They're always making a fucking noise. You go to the bathroom, you've got these crutches, you try to get your cock, and you can't get your cock because your crutches are in the way. You gotta get rid of the crutches. Then you're standing on one leg. That's not so good. You lean one way or another, you splatter all over the place. Your father tells me to sit down to piss. Know what I say? 'I'll sit when you do, Herman.' Fucking crutches. Standing on one leg. Taking your dick out. Jesus. Pissing is hard enough to do as it is." I'm laughing uncontrollably now not only because the story is especially funny as he half whispers it in the darkened room, but because never before has a man revealed himself to me this way, using the prohibited words so freely and openly cracking toilet jokes. "Come on," Alvin says, "own up to it, kiddo—pissing's not something that's as easy as it looks."

So it happened that on that first Monday morning alone, when the amputation was still a limitless loss that he assumed would impede and torment him forever, he took the fall that no one in the family knew about other than me. He was standing braced against the kitchen sink, where, without the aid of his crutches, he'd gone for a glass of water. When he turned to start back to the bedroom he forgot (for all possible reasons) that he had just the one leg and, instead of hopping, did what everyone else did in our house— began to walk and of course toppled over. The pain shooting up from the butt end of his stump was worse than the pain in the missing segment of his leg—pain, Alvin explained to me after I first watched him succumb to a siege in the bed beside me, "that grabs you and won't let you go," though no limb is left to cause it. "There's pain where you are," Alvin said when the time had come to reassure me with some kind of comical remark, "and there's pain where you ain't. I wonder who thought that up."

The English hospital gave the amputees morphine to control the pain. "You're always calling for it," Alvin told me. "And whenever you do they give it to you. You push a button for the nurse and when she gets to you, you tell her, 'Morphine, morphine,' and then you're pretty much out of it." "How much did it hurt in the hospital?" I asked him. "It was no fun, kiddo." "Was that the worst pain you ever had?" "Worst pain I ever had," he replied, "was when my father closed the door of the car on my finger when I was six years old." He laughed, and so I laughed. "My father said—when he saw me crying like hell, this little stinker about that high—my father said, 'Stop crying, that doesn't do any good.'" Quietly laughing again, Alvin said, "And that was probably worse than the pain. My last memory of him, too. Later that day he keeled over and died."

Writhing on the kitchen linoleum, Alvin had no one to call for help, let alone for a shot of morphine; everybody was off either at school or at work, and so, in time, it was necessary to grope his way across the kitchen and the foyer to his bed. But just as he was positioning himself to push up from the floor, he spotted Sandy's art portfolio. Sandy still used the portfolio to preserve his large pencil and charcoal drawings between tracing paper and to carry them with him when he had to take the drawings somewhere to show. It was too large to store in the sun parlor, and so he'd left it behind in our room. Mere curiosity impelled Alvin to fish the portfolio out a ways from beneath the bed, but because he was unable right off to determine its purpose—and because all he really wanted was to be back under the covers—he was ready to forget about it when he noticed the ribbon that held the two halves together. Existence was worthless, living was unendurable, he still throbbed with pain from the mindless accident at the kitchen sink, and so for no reason other than that he felt himself powerless to carry off a physical task any more formidable, he fiddled with the ribbons until he undid the bow.

What he found inside were the three portraits of Charles A. Lindbergh as an aviator that Sandy had told my parents he'd destroyed two years back as well as those that he'd drawn at the behest of Aunt Evelyn once Lindbergh became president. I'd only seen the new ones myself when Aunt Evelyn took me along to New Brunswick to hear Sandy give his Just Folks recruitment speech in the synagogue basement. "This shows President Lindbergh signing into law the Universal Conscription Act, designed to keep America at peace by teaching our youth the skills necessary to protect and defend the nation. This one shows the president at a draftsman's drawing board, adding his aeronautical suggestions to the design for the nation's newest fighter-bomber. Here I show President Lindbergh relaxing at the White House with the family dog."

Each of the new Lindbergh portraits exhibited as a prelude to Sandy's New Brunswick talk Alvin examined on the bedroom floor. Then, despite the destructive urge aroused by his registering the skill so meticulously expended on these beautiful likenesses, he placed them between the leaves of tracing paper and shoved the portfolio back under the bed.

Once Alvin was out and around in the neighborhood, he hadn't to rely only on Sandy's Lindbergh drawings to realize that, while he'd been making raids on ammo depots in France, Roosevelt's Republican successor had come to be, if not entirely trusted by the Jews, accepted as tolerable for the time being even among those of our neighbors who had started out hating him as passionately as my father did. Walter Winchell persisted in attacking the president on his Sunday-night radio show, and everybody on the block devotedly tuned him in to give credence, while they listened, to his alarming interpretations of the president's policies, but as nothing that they feared had come to pass since the inauguration, our neighbors slowly began putting more faith in Rabbi Bengelsdorf's optimistic assurances than in Winchell's dire prophecies. And not just the neighbors but Jewish leaders all over the country began openly to acknowledge that Newark's Lionel Bengelsdorf, far from having betrayed them by endorsing Lindy in the 1940 election, had been prescient enough to see where the nation was headed and that his elevation to the directorship of the Office of American Absorption —and the administration's foremost adviser on Jewish affairs— was the direct result of his having cleverly gained Lindbergh's confidence as an early supporter. If the president's anti-Semitism had somehow been neutralized (or, more remarkably, eradicated), Jews were willing to attribute the miracle to the influence of the venerable rabbi who was soon to become—another miracle—an uncle by marriage to Sandy and me.

One day early in March I wandered over, uninvited, to the dead-end street backing onto the school playground where Alvin had begun shooting craps and playing stud poker if the afternoon was warm enough and it wasn't raining. He was rarely in the house anymore when I got home after school, and though generally he made it back by five-thirty for dinner, after dessert he'd head out to the hotdog hangout a block from our house to meet up with his old high school friends, a few of whom used to pump gas at the Esso station owned by Simkowitz and had been fired along with him for stealing from the boss. I'd be asleep by the time he got in for the night, and only when he removed his leg and began hopping to and from the bathroom did I open my eyes and mumble his name before falling back to sleep. Some seven weeks after he'd moved into the bed beside mine, I ceased to be indispensable and abruptly found myself bereft of the mesmeric surrogate he'd been for Sandy, vanished now from my side into the stardom masterminded for him by Aunt Evelyn. The maimed and suffering American pariah who had come to loom larger for me than any man I'd ever known, including my father, whose passionate struggles had become my own, whose future I fretted over when I should have been listening to the teacher in class, had begun to buddy up with the same good-for-nothings who'd helped turn him into a petty thief at sixteen. What he appeared to have lost in combat, along with his leg, was every decent habit inculcated in him when he was living as my parents' ward. Nor did he display any interest in the fight against fascism, which, two years earlier, no one could restrain him from joining. In fact, why he went scooting out of the house on his artificial leg every night was, at the beginning anyway, largely to avoid having to sit in the living room while my father read the war news aloud from the paper.

There was no campaign against the Axis powers that my father didn't agonize about, particularly when things went badly for the Soviet Union and Great Britain and it was clear how urgently they needed the U.S. arms embargoed by Lindbergh and the Republican Congress. By this time my father could deploy the terminology of a war strategist quite proficiently when he expatiated on the need for the British, Australians, and Dutch to prevent the Japanese—who, in sweeping across Southeast Asia, exhibited all the righteous cruelty of the racially superior—from proceeding westward into India and southward into New Zealand and on to Australia. In the early months of 1942 the Pacific war news that he read to us was uniformly bad: there was the successful Japanese drive into Burma, the Japanese capture of Malaya, the Japanese bombing of New Guinea, and, after devastating attacks from the sea and air and the capturing of tens of thousands of British and Dutch troops on the ground, the fall of Singapore, Borneo, Sumatra, and Java. But it was the progress of the Russian campaign that upset my father most. The year before, when the Germans appeared to be on the verge of overrunning every major city in the western half of the Soviet Union (including Kiev, from whose environs my maternal grandparents had emigrated to America in the 1890s), the names of even lesser Russian cities, like Petrozavodsk, Novgorod, Dnepropetrovsk, and Taganrog, had become as familiar to me as the capitals of the forty-eight states. In the winter of 1941–42 the Russians had staged the impossible counterattacks that broke the sieges of Leningrad, Moscow, and Stalingrad, but by March the Germans had regrouped from their winter catastrophe and, as demonstrated by the troop movements mapped out in the *Newark News,* were reinforcing for a spring offensive to conquer the Caucasus. My father explained that what made the prospect of a Russian collapse so awful was that it would represent to the world the invincibility of the German war machine. The vast natural resources of the Soviet Union would fall into German hands and the Russian people would be forced to serve the Third Reich. Worst of all "for us" was that with Germany's eastward advance millions and millions of Russian Jews would come under the control of an occupying army equipped in every way to implement Hitler's messianic program to deliver humanity from the clutches of the Jews.

According to my father, the brutal triumph of antidemocratic militarism was imminent just about everywhere, the massacre of Russian Jewry, including members of my mother's extended family, was all but at hand, and Alvin didn't care one bit. No longer was he burdened by concern for anyone's suffering other than his own.

I found Alvin down on the good knee of the real leg, dice in hand and the pile of bills beside him secured by a jagged chunk of cement. With the prosthetic leg jutting straight out in front of him, he looked like a squatting Russian dancing one of those crazy Slavic jigs. There were six other gamblers tightly encircling him, three still in the game, clutching what was left of their dough, two who were broke and just standing around—whom I vaguely recognized as ex-Weequahic washouts now in their twenties—and the long-legged guy hovering over him, Alvin's "partner," as it turned out, Shushy Margulis, a skinny zoot-suiter with a sinewy build and a gliding gait, the hanger-on from Alvin's gas station days whom my father most despised. Shushy was known to us kids as the Pinball King because a racketeer uncle whom he boasted about *was* the pinball king—and king as well of all illegal slots down in Philadelphia, where he reigned—and also because of the hours he spent racking up scores by banging away at the pinball machines in the neighborhood candy stores, shoving the machine, cursing it, violently shaking it from side to side until play was terminated either by the colored lights flashing "Tilt" or by the store owner chasing him out. Shushy was the famous comedian who entertained his admirers by gleefully tossing lit matches into the mouth of the big green mailbox across from the high school, and who had once eaten a live praying mantis on a bet, and who, during his short-lived academic career, liked to hand the crowd a laugh outside the hotdog hangout by limping across Chancellor Avenue with one hand raised to stop the oncoming traffic—limping badly, tragically, though nothing was wrong with him. By this time he was already into his thirties and still living with his seamstress mother in one of the little flats at the top of a two-and-a-half-family house next door to the synagogue on Wainwright Street. It was to Shushy's mother, known sympathetically to one and all as "poor Mrs. Margulis," that my mother had taken Alvin's pants to have the zippers sewn in—poor Mrs. Margulis not merely because she survived as a widow by doing piecework at slave wages for a Down Neck dress manufacturer but because her sharpie son seemed never to have held a job other than as a runner for the bookie who worked out of the poolroom around the corner from their house and just down the street from the Catholic orphanage on Lyons Avenue.

The orphanage stood within the fenced-off grounds of St. Peter's, the parish church that oddly monopolized some three square blocks at the very heart of our unredeemable neighborhood. The church itself was topped by a tall bell tower and an even taller steeple that was capped by a cross that rose divinely above the tele-phone wires. Locally there was no building that high to be seen until you proceeded nearly a mile down the Lyons Avenue hill to my birthplace, the Beth Israel Hospital, where every boy I knew had been born as well and, at the age of eight days, ritually cir-cumcised in the hospital's sanctuary. Flanking the bell tower of the church were two smaller steeples that I never cared to examine be-cause the faces of Christian saints were said to be carved into the stone, and the church's high, narrow stained-glass windows told a story that I didn't want to know. Near the church was a small rec-tory; like most everything else situated within the black iron pal-ings of this alien world it had been built during the latter part of the previous century, several decades before the first of our houses went up and the western edge of the Weequahic neighborhood took shape as Newark's Jewish frontier. Behind the church was the grammar school serving the orphans—there were about a hundred of them—and a smaller number of local Catholic kids. The school and the orphanage were run by an order of nuns, German nuns, I remember being told. Jewish children raised even in tolerant households like mine would generally cross the street on the rare occasions we saw them swishing our way in their witchy attire, and family lore had it that when my brother, as a small child sitting alone on our front stoop one afternoon, spotted a pair of them ap-proaching from Chancellor Avenue, he had called excitedly to my mother, "Look, Ma—the nuts."

A convent stood next to the orphans' residence. Both were sim-ple red-brick buildings, and at the end of a summer's day you'd sometimes catch a glimpse of the orphans—white children, girls and boys, aged from about six to fourteen—sitting outdoors on the fire escape. I have no memory of seeing the orphans in a group anywhere else, certainly not running freely about the streets the way we did. A swarm of them would have discomfited me no less than did the unsettling appearance of the nuns, primarily because they were orphaned but also because they were said to be both "neglected" and "indigent."

Back of the residence hall, and unlike anything to be seen in our neighborhood—or anywhere else in an industrial city of close to half a million—was a truck farm of the kind that made New Jersey "the Garden State," back when compact family vegetable farms able to turn a small profit dotted the undeveloped rural reaches of the state. The food grown and harvested at St. Peter's went to feed the orphans, the dozen or so nuns, the old monsignor in charge, and the younger priest who was his assistant. With the help of the orphans, the land was worked by a resident German farmer called Thimmes—unless I'm remembering incorrectly and that was the name of St. Peter's monsignor, who'd been running the place for years.

At our public elementary school less than a mile away it was rumored that the nuns who instructed the orphans in class routinely smacked the stupidest of them across the hands with wooden rulers and that when a boy's offense was so gross as to be intolerable the monsignor's assistant was called in to beat him across the buttocks with the same whip the farmer used on the swaybacked pair of lumbering workhorses that pulled the plow for the spring planting. These horses we all knew and recognized because from time to time they'd wander together across the farm to the little wooded meadow at the southern boundary of St. Peter's domain and stick their heads inquisitively out above the gate that backed onto Goldsmith Avenue, where the crap game I'd come upon was taking place.

There was a chain-link fence about seven feet high at the edge of the playground on the near side of Goldsmith Avenue and a wire fence set in posts at the wooded edge of the truck farm on the far side, and since no houses had as yet gone up anywhere nearby and there was never much foot or automobile traffic to speak of, an almost sylvan seclusion was conveniently provided there for the neighborhood's tiny handful of losers to pursue their pleasures out of harm's way. The closest I'd ever come to one of these sinister conclaves before was when, during some playground game, I'd had to chase a ball that had rolled to where they all huddled together just beyond the fence, uttering imprecations at one another and saving their sweet talk for the dice.

Now, I was no righteous little foe of crapshooting, and I had begged Alvin to teach me how to play one afternoon when he was still on crutches and my mother had instructed me to accompany him to his dentist appointment and do things like drop his fare into the fare box and hold his crutches for him while he hopped onto the street from the bus's back door. That night, when everyone else had gone to sleep and we'd switched off table lamp on the stand between our beds, he watched with a smile as, by the beam of my flashlight, I whispered, "Dice be nice," and soundlessly rolled three consecutive sevens across my sheets. Yet as I watched him now in the clutches of his inferiors, and remembered all that my family had sacrificed to prevent him from turning himself into a replica of Shushy, every obscenity I'd learned as his roommate flooded foully into my mind. I cursed him in behalf of my father, my mother, and especially my ostracized brother—was it for this that all of us had agreed to endure Alvin's objectionable behavior toward Sandy? Was it for this that he'd run off to fight in the war? I thought, "Take your fucking medal, gimp, and shove it!" If only he would learn his lesson by losing every last penny of his disability pension, but in fact he couldn't stop himself from winning, any more than he could stop himself from abandoning the desire to ever again be anyone's hero, and, having already raked in a big wad of bills, he held the dice to my lips and, in a gravelly voice with which he intended to be funny for his friends, he instructed me, "Blow on 'em—baby." I blew, he rolled and won yet again. "Six and one—making what?" he asked. "Seven," I obediently answered, "the hard way."

Shushy reached down to muss my hair and began calling me Alvin's mascot, as though "mascot" could encompass what I'd resolved to be for Alvin since he'd come home, as though a word so hollow and childish could account for why Alvin's King George medal was pinned to my undershirt. Shushy was dressed in a

chocolate-colored double-breasted gabardine suit, with pegged
trousers and wide, padded shoulders and flamboyant lapels, his favored getup whenever he went bopping around the neighborhood
snapping his fingers—and, in my mother's words, "wasting his
life"—while back in their tiny attic flat his mother hemmed a hundred dresses a day to meet the family's bills.

When he missed his point, Alvin drew all his winnings together
and ostentatiously stuffed the bundle into his pocket—the man
who broke the bank behind the high school. Then, by grasping the
chain-link fence, he pulled himself to his feet. I knew (and not just
from observing the tortured way he began limping about to get
himself going) that a big boil had erupted on his stump the night
before and that he wasn't in the best of shape that day. But he refused any longer to be seen on crutches by anyone outside the
family, and before going off to team up with sleazy Shushy—and
spend another day blatantly repudiating all the ideals that had
made him a cripple—he harnessed the stump into the prosthesis
however much it hurt.

"Goddamn legmaker" was all he said by way of complaint as he
came up to put his hand on my shoulder.

"Can I go home now?" I whispered.

"Sure, why not?" and then he took two ten-dollar bills out of
his pocket—nearly half my father's weekly paycheck—and flattened them against the palm of my hand. Never before had money
seemed like something alive.

Instead of heading back across the playground, I took a slightly
longer route home, proceeding down the Goldsmith Avenue hill to
Hobson Street so that I could look up close at the orphanage
horses. I had never dared to reach over and touch them, and before
that day I'd never spoken to them the way other kids did, satirically
calling these mud-spattered beasts drooling gooey saliva "Omaha"
and "Whirlaway," which were the names of two of the greatest Kentucky Derby winners of our day.

I stopped a safe distance back from where the darkly gleaming high-relief eyes peered out above the orphanage fence, impassively monitoring through their long lashes the no man's land separating the stronghold of St. Peter's from the neighborhood of Jews beyond the pale. The chain was unlooped and hanging down off the gate. I had only to yank up on the latch and swing the gate open and the horses would be free to gallop away. The temptation was enormous—as was the spite.

"Fucking Lindbergh," I said to the horses, "Nazi fucking bastard Lindbergh!" and then, for fear that if I did fling open the gate, instead of the horses running free they'd use their big teeth to drag me into the orphanage, I darted down the street and, turning on Hobson, raced past the block-long row of four-family houses and out to the corner of Chancellor Avenue, where housewives I recognized were in and out of the grocery and the bakery and the butcher shop, and older boys whose names I knew were riding their bikes, and the tailor's son was carrying over either shoulder a load of newly pressed clothes for delivery, and where Italian singing issued onto the street through the shoemaker's doorway, his radio tuned as always to WEVD—the EVD to honor the persecuted socialist hero Eugene V. Debs—and where I was safe from Alvin, Shushy, the horses, the orphans, the priests, the nuns, and the parochial-school whip.

When I turned back up the hill toward home a man neatly dressed in a business suit fell in step beside me. It was still too early for the local workingmen to be getting home for dinner, and so I knew right off to be suspicious.

"Master Philip?" he inquired with a broad smile. "Do you ever listen to *Gangbusters* on the radio, Master Philip? About J. Edgar Hoover and the FBI?"

"Yes."

"Well, I work for Mr. Hoover. He's my boss. I'm an agent from the FBI. Here," he said, and he removed a billfold from an inside coat pocket and flipped it open to show me his badge. "If you wouldn't mind, I'd like to ask a few little questions."

"I don't mind, but I'm on my way home. I have to get home."

Immediately I thought about the two ten-dollar bills. If he searched me, if he had a warrant to search me, wasn't he going to find all that money and assume it was stolen? Wouldn't anybody? And until ten minutes earlier, for an entire lifetime, I'd been walking around with my pockets empty, out on the street without a penny to my name! My allowance of five cents a week I saved in a jelly jar with a slit Sandy chiseled into the lid with the can opener blade of his Boy Scout knife. Now I was walking around like a bank robber.

"Don't be frightened. Calm down, Master Philip. You've heard *Gangbusters.* We're on your side. We protect you. I just want to ask a few questions about your cousin Alvin. How's he doing?"

"He's fine."

"How's his leg coming along?"

"Good."

"He's able to walk okay?"

"Yes."

"Wasn't that him I saw over where you just came from? Wasn't that Alvin behind the playground? Out on the sidewalk, wasn't that Alvin with Shushy Margulis?"

I didn't reply, and so he said, "It's okay if they're shooting craps. That's no crime. That's just part of being a big man. Alvin must have shot craps a lot in the army hospital up in Montreal."

When I still wouldn't speak, he asked, "What were the fellas talking about?"

"Nothing."

"All afternoon they're out there, and they're talking about nothing?"

"They were just saying how much they were losing."

"Nothing else? Nothing about the president? You know who the president is, don't you?"

"Charles A. Lindbergh."

"Nothing about President Lindbergh, Master Philip?"

"Not that I heard," I answered truthfully.

But might he not have overheard *me* saying what I'd said to the horses? Impossible—and yet by now I was sure that he knew every move I'd made since Alvin came home from the war and gave me his medal. It was indisputable that he knew that I was wearing the medal. Why else was he looking me over from head to toe?

"Did they talk about Canada?" he asked. "About going to Canada?"

"No, sir."

"Call me Don, why don't you? And I'll call you Phil. You know what a fascist is, don't you, Phil?"

"I think so."

"Did they call anybody a fascist that you remember?"

"No."

"Don't rush yourself. Don't rush to answer. Take all the time you need. Try hard to remember. It's important. Did they call anybody a fascist? Did they say anything about Hitler? You know who Hitler is."

"Everybody does."

"He's a bad man, isn't he?"

"Yes," I said.

"He's against the Jews, isn't he?"

"Yes."

"Who else is against the Jews?"

"The Bund."

"Anyone else?" he asked.

I knew enough not to mention Henry Ford, America First, the southern Democrats, or the isolationist Republicans, let alone Lindbergh. Over the past few years, the list I heard at home of prominent Americans who hated Jews was far longer than that, and then there were the ordinary Americans, tens of thousands of them, maybe millions of them, like the beer drinkers we didn't want to live beside in Union and the owner of the hotel in Washington and the mustached diner who'd insulted us in the cafeteria near Union Station. "Don't talk," I told myself, as though a protected boy of nine were mixed up with criminals and had something to hide. But I must already have begun to think of myself as a little criminal because I was a Jew.

"And who else?" he repeated. "Mr. Hoover wants to know who else. Come clean, Phil."

"I *am*," I insisted.

"How's your aunt Evelyn doing?"

"She's fine."

"She's getting married. Isn't that right, that she's getting married? You can at least answer that."

"Yes."

"And do you know who she's marrying?"

"Yes."

"You're a smart boy. I think you know more—a lot more. But you're too smart to tell me, aren't you?"

"She's marrying Rabbi Bengelsdorf," I said. "He's head of the OAA."

My saying that made him laugh. "Okay," he told me, "you go on home. Go home and eat your matzohs. Isn't that what makes you so smart? Eating the matzohs?"

We were now at the corner of Chancellor and Summit, and I could see the stoop of our house down at the end of the block. "Bye!" I cried, and didn't wait for the light to change but ran for home before I fell into his trap, if I hadn't fallen into it already.

There were three police cars parked on the street in front of our house, our alleyway was blocked off by an ambulance, and a couple of cops stood on the stoop talking together while another was posted beside the back door. The women on the block, most of them still in their aprons, were on their front stoops trying to figure out what was going on, and all the kids were huddled on the sidewalk across the street from our house, peering out at the cops and the ambulance from between the row of parked cars. Never before could I remember them silently gathered together like that, looking so apprehensive.

Our downstairs neighbor was dead. Mr. Wishnow had committed suicide. That was why everything I could never have expected to see was now right outside the door of our house. Weighing barely eighty pounds, he had been able to strangulate himself by stringing the living room curtain cords over the wooden rod in the back-foyer coat closet, then looping them around his neck and falling forward off the edge of the kitchen chair where he'd seated himself inside the closet. When Seldon, home from school, went to put his coat away, he found his father, in his pajamas, hanging face-down on the closet floor amid the family's rubbers and galoshes. My first thought on learning the news was that I no longer had to be fearful of hearing a coughing fit emanating from the dying man in the first-floor flat whenever I was alone in the cellar, or of hearing him in my bed on the floor above when I was trying to fall asleep. But then I realized that the ghost of Mr. Wishnow would now join the circle of ghosts already inhabiting the cellar and that, just because I was relieved he was dead, he would go out of his way to haunt me for the rest of my life.

Since I didn't know what else to do, I at first kneeled at the side of the parked cars, hiding there with the other kids. None of them had a conception any larger than my own of the cataclysm that had befallen the Wishnows, but it was from their whisperings that I pieced together how Mr. Wishnow had died and how he'd been found and learned that Seldon and his mother were inside with one of the policemen and the medics. And with the corpse. The corpse was what the kids were all waiting to see. I waited with them rather than wind up entering the back hallway just as they were carrying Mr. Wishnow down the stairs. Nor did I want to get home and have to sit there alone until my mother, my father, or Sandy appeared. As for Alvin, I wanted never to see him again or to be questioned about him by anyone.

The woman who emerged from the house accompanying the medics wasn't Mrs. Wishnow but my mother. I couldn't understand why she was home from work until it dawned on me that the dead father they were carrying away was my own. Yes, of course—

my father had committed suicide. He couldn't take any more of Lindbergh and what Lindbergh was letting the Nazis do to the Jews of Russia and what Lindbergh had done to our family right here and so it was he who had hanged himself—in *our* closet.

I didn't have hundreds of memories of him then, I had just one, and it did not seem to me at all important enough to be the memory I ought to be having. Alvin's last memory of his father was of him closing the car door on his little boy's finger—mine of my father was of him greeting the stump of a man who begged every day outside his office building. "How you doin', Little Robert?" my father said, and the stump of a man replied, "How you, Herman?"

It was here that I edged myself between the closely parked cars and darted out across the street.

When I saw that the sheet covering my father's body and face couldn't possibly allow him to breathe, I began to wail.

"Don't, don't, darling," my mother said. "There's nothing to be frightened of." She put her arms around my head, held me to her, and repeated, "There's nothing to be frightened of. He was sick and he was suffering and he died. Now he's not suffering anymore."

"He was in the closet," I said.

"No, he wasn't. He was in his bed. He died in his bed. He was very, very sick. You knew that. That was why he coughed all the time."

By now the ambulance doors were swung open to receive the stretcher. The medics carefully maneuvered it inside and pulled the doors shut behind them. My mother stood next to me on the street, holding my hand in hers and to my amazement looking perfectly composed. Only when I made a move to break away from her and run after the ambulance, only when I cried, "He can't breathe!" did she finally realize what was torturing me.

"It's Mr. Wishnow—it's Mr. *Wishnow* who is dead." She shook me, gently shook me back and forth to bring me to my senses. "It's *Seldon's* father, dear—he died from his illness this afternoon."

I couldn't tell if she was lying to keep me from becoming more hysterical or if she was telling the wonderful truth.

"Seldon found him in the closet?"

"No. I told you—no. Seldon found his father in his bed. Seldon's mother wasn't home so he called the police. I came because Mrs. Wishnow called me at the store and asked me to help her. Do you understand? Daddy's at work. Daddy's working. Oh, what on earth have you been thinking? Daddy will be home for dinner very soon. So will Sandy. There's nothing to be afraid of. Everybody will be home, everybody is coming home, we'll have our dinner," she said reassuringly, "and everything is going to be fine."

But nothing was "fine." The FBI agent who'd grilled me about Alvin on Chancellor Avenue had earlier stopped by Hahne's dress department to question my mother, then by the Metropolitan's Newark office to question my father, and, just after Sandy left Aunt Evelyn's office for home, he had boarded my brother's bus and, from the seat alongside him, conducted yet another interrogation. Alvin wasn't at dinner to hear about any of this—just as we were sitting down to eat, he'd phoned and told my mother not to save anything for him. It seemed that every time he'd made a killing at poker or craps, Alvin took Shushy downtown with him to the Hickory Grill for a charcoal-broiled steak dinner. "Alvin's partner in crime," my father called Shushy. What he called Alvin that evening was ungrateful, stupid, reckless, ignorant, and incorrigible.

"And bitter," said my mother, sadly, "so bitter because of his leg."

"Well, I'm sick and tired of his leg," said my father. "He went to war. Who sent him? I didn't. You didn't. Abe Steinheim didn't. Abe Steinheim wanted to send him to college. He went to war on his own, and he's lucky he wasn't killed. He's lucky it was just his leg. This is it, Bess. I've had it with that boy. The FBI questions my children? Bad enough they harass you and me—and in my office, mind you, in front of the Boss! No," he told her. "This has to stop and stop now. This is a home. We are a family. He has dinner downtown with Shushy? Let him go live with Shushy."

"If only he would go to school," my mother said. "If only he would take a job."

"He has a job," my father replied. "Bum."

After we'd finished eating, my mother put a meal together for Seldon and Mrs. Wishnow, and my father helped her carry the plates downstairs while Sandy and I were left with the dinner dishes. We set to work at the sink as we did most nights, except that I couldn't shut up. I told him about the crap game. I told him about the FBI agent. I told him about Mr. Wishnow. "He didn't die in his bed," I said. "Mother's not telling us the truth. He committed suicide, only she doesn't want to say it. Seldon found him in the closet when he got home from school. He hung himself. That's why the police came."

"Did he turn colors?" my brother asked me.

"I only saw him under the sheet. Maybe it was colors—I don't know. I don't *want* to know. It was bad enough when they jiggled the stretcher that you could see him move." That I had thought at first it was my father under the sheet I didn't say aloud for fear that if I did it would turn out to be true. The fact that my father was alive, vividly alive—angry at Alvin and threatening to throw him out of the house—had no impact on my thinking.

"How do you know he was in the closet?" Sandy asked.

"That's what all the kids said."

"And you believe them?" Because of his fame, he was becoming a very hard boy whose tremendous confidence now sounded more and more like lordly arrogance whenever he spoke about me or my friends.

"Well, why were all the police here? Just because he died? People die all the time," I said, trying, however, not to believe it. "He killed himself. He had to."

"And is that against the law, killing yourself?" my brother asked me. "What were they going to do, put him in jail for killing himself?"

I didn't know. I didn't know any longer what the law was and so I didn't know what might or might not be against it. I didn't seem to know whether my own father—who'd just headed downstairs with my mother—was really alive or pretending to be alive or being driven around dead in the back of that ambulance. I didn't know anything. I didn't know why Alvin was bad now instead of good. I didn't know if I had dreamed that an FBI agent had questioned me on Chancellor Avenue. It had to be a dream and yet couldn't be if everybody else said they'd been questioned too. Unless that was the dream. I felt woozy and thought I was going to faint. I'd never before seen anyone faint, other than in a movie, and I'd never before fainted myself. I'd never before looked at my house from a hiding place across the street and wished that it was somebody else's. I'd never before had twenty dollars in my pocket. I'd never before known anyone who'd seen his father hanging in a closet. I'd never before had to grow up at a pace like this.

Never before—the great refrain of 1942.

"You better call Mom," I told my brother. "Call her—tell her to come home right away!" But before Sandy could reach the back door to rush down to the Wishnows, I was vomiting into the dishtowel still in my hand, and when I collapsed it was because my leg had been blown off and my blood was everywhere.

I remained in bed with a high fever for six days, so weak and lifeless that the family doctor stopped by every evening to check on the progress of my disease, that not uncommon childhood ailment called why-can't-it-be-the-way-it-was.

The next day for me was Sunday. It was late afternoon, and Uncle Monty was visiting. Alvin was there too, and from what I could overhear from my bed of what was being said in the kitchen, he hadn't been seen anywhere around since Mr. Wishnow had committed suicide on Friday and he'd walked away from that crap game with his bundle of fives, tens, and twenties. But since dinnertime Friday I'd been away myself, off with the horses and their hooves, enveloped by kaleidoscopic hallucinations of the orphanage workhorses pursuing me to the edge of the earth.

And now Uncle Monty again, again Uncle Monty attacking

Alvin, and with words I could not believe were being spoken in our house in the presence of my mother. But then, Uncle Monty knew how to subdue Alvin in ways that my father just couldn't employ.

By nightfall, after all the shouting had subsided into lamentations for my late uncle Jack and Monty's booming voice had gone hoarse, Alvin accepted the job at the produce market that he'd refused to consider when Monty had offered it first. As unmanned as he'd been by his mutilation on the morning he arrived at Penn Station in the care of that hulking Canadian nurse, as overridden by defeat as when, from his wheelchair, he wouldn't dare to look a one of us in the eye, Alvin consented to dissolve his partnership with Shushy and to give up gambling on the neighborhood streets. A hater no less of subservience than of weeping, he astonished everyone by breaking into guilty tears and begging forgiveness and agreeing to stop being a brute to my brother, an ingrate to my mother and father, and a bad influence on me, and to treat us with the appreciation we were due. Uncle Monty warned Alvin that if he didn't abide by his promises and continued instead to sabotage Herman's household, the Roths would be finished with him for good.

Though Alvin appeared to be trying hard to make a go of the menial donkeywork that was his first job, he didn't last long enough at the market to rise even a notch above sweeping and fetching. One day, when he'd been there little more than a week, the FBI came around to inquire about him, the same agent using the same menacingly innocuous questions he'd asked my family and me, only insinuating now to the other produce workers that Alvin was a self-declared traitor plotting with anti-American malcontents like himself to assassinate President Lindbergh. The charges were ludicrous, and yet tame as Alvin had been all that week—tame as he'd sworn and dedicated himself to remaining— he was fired on the spot and, on the way out, instructed by one of the goons in charge never to come anywhere near the market again. When my father got on the phone to his brother demanding to know what had happened, Monty replied that he'd had no choice—he'd been ordered to get rid of his nephew by Longy's boys. Newark's Longy Zwillman, who'd grown up like my father and his brothers a son of immigrants in the old Jewish slums, ran the Jersey rackets back then, the ruthless potentate of everything from bookmaking and strikebreaking to the trucking and hauling services foisted on merchants like Belmont Roth. Because the feds were the last people Longy needed snooping around, Alvin lost the job, cleared out of our house, and left the city in under twenty-four hours, this time not across the international border for Montreal and the Canadian commandos but just over the Delaware for Philadelphia and a job with Shushy's uncle the gambling-machine king, a racketeer seemingly more tolerant of traitors than his peerless counterpart up in North Jersey.

In the spring of 1942, to celebrate the success of the Iceland Understanding, a state dinner was given at the White House by President and Mrs. Lindbergh to honor Foreign Minister Joachim von Ribbentrop, who was known to have touted Lindbergh to his Nazi colleagues as Germany's ideal American presidential candidate long before the Republican Party drafted Lindbergh at its 1940 convention. Von Ribbentrop was the negotiator seated at Hitler's side throughout the Iceland meetings and the first Nazi leader to be invited to America by *any* government official or agency since the fascists had come to power nearly ten years before. No sooner was the announcement of the von Ribbentrop dinner made public than strong criticism was voiced by the liberal press, and rallies and demonstrations were staged all across the country protesting the White House decision. For the first time since he left office, former president Roosevelt emerged from seclusion to make a brief nationwide address from Hyde Park urging President Lindbergh to rescind the invitation "for the sake of all freedom-loving Americans, and particularly the tens of millions of Americans of European stock whose ancestral countries must live beneath the Nazis' crushing yoke."

Roosevelt was immediately attacked by Vice President Wheeler for "playing politics" with a sitting president's conduct of foreign affairs. It wasn't merely cynical, said the vice president, but utterly irresponsible of him to argue for the same dangerous policies that had all but dragged America into a bloody European war while the New Deal Democrats were running the country. Wheeler was himself a Democrat, a former three-term senator from Montana and the first and only member of the opposition party to be chosen to share a ticket with a presidential candidate since Lincoln picked Andrew Johnson as his second-term running mate in 1864. Early in his political career, Wheeler was so far to the left that he'd been the voice of Butte's radical labor leaders, the enemy of Anaconda Copper—the mining company that ran Montana pretty much like a company store—and, as an early supporter of FDR's, had been suggested as his vice presidential candidate in 1932. He'd first departed the Democratic Party in 1924 to team up with Wisconsin's reformist senator Robert La Follette on the union-supported Progressive Party presidential ticket, and then, after abandoning La Follette and his supporters in the non-Communist American left, he joined Lindbergh and the right-wing isolationists in helping to found America First, attacking Roosevelt with antiwar statements so extreme that they prompted the president to label his criticism "the most untruthful, dastardly, unpatriotic thing that has been said in public life in my generation." Wheeler had been chosen by the Republicans to be Lindbergh's running mate in part because his own political machine in Montana had helped to elect Republicans to Congress throughout the late thirties but mainly to persuade the American people of the strength of the bipartisan support for isolationism and to have on the ticket a combative, un-Lindbergh-like candidate whose job would be to attack and revile his own political party at every opportunity, as he did in the press conference from the vice president's office when he predicted that if the reckless "war-minded" rhetoric in Roosevelt's message from Hyde Park was any indication of the campaign the Democrats intended to wage in the forthcoming elections, they would suffer even greater congressional losses than they had in the 1940 Republican landslide.

The very next weekend, the German-American Bund filled Madison Square Garden with a near-capacity crowd, some twenty-five thousand people who had turned out to support President Lindbergh's invitation to the German foreign minister and to denounce the Democrats for their renewed "warmongering." During Roosevelt's second term, the FBI and congressional committees investigating the Bund's activities had immobilized the organization, designating it a Nazi front and bringing criminal charges against leaders in its high command. But under Lindbergh, government efforts at harassing or intimidating Bund members ceased and they were able to regain their strength by identifying themselves not only as American patriots of German extraction opposed to America's intervention in foreign wars but as staunch enemies of the Soviet Union. The deep fascist fellowship uniting the Bund was now masked by vociferous patriotic declamations on the peril of a worldwide Communist revolution.

As an anti-Communist rather than a pro-Nazi organization, the Bund was as anti-Semitic as before, openly equating Bolshevism with Judaism in propaganda handouts and harping on the number of "prowar" Jews—like Treasury Secretary Morgenthau and financier Bernard Baruch, who'd been Roosevelt confidants—and, of course, holding fast to the purposes enunciated in their official declaration on first organizing in 1936: "to combat the Moscow-directed madness of the Red world menace and its Jewish bacillus-carriers" and to promote "a free Gentile-ruled United States." Gone, however, from the 1942 Madison Square Garden rally were the Nazi flags, the swastika armbands, the straight-armed Hitler salute, the storm trooper uniforms, and the giant picture of the Führer that had been on display for the first rally, on February 20, 1939, an event promoted by the Bund as "George Washington Day Birthday Exercises." Gone were the wall banners proclaiming "Wake up America—Smash Jewish Communists!" and the references by speechmakers to Franklin D. Roosevelt as "Franklin D. Rosenfeld" and the big white buttons with the black lettering that had been distributed to Bund members to stick into their lapels, the buttons that read:

KEEP AMERICA

OUT OF

THE JEWISH WAR

Meanwhile, Walter Winchell continued to refer to the Bundists as "Bundits," and Dorothy Thompson, the prominent journalist and wife of novelist Sinclair Lewis, who'd been expelled from the 1939 Bund rally for exercising what she called her "constitutional right to laugh at ridiculous statements in a public hall," went on denouncing their propaganda in the same spirit she'd demonstrated three years earlier when she'd exited the rally shouting, "Bunk, bunk, bunk! *Mein Kampf,* word for word!" And on his Sunday-night program following the Bund rally, Winchell contended, with his usual cocksureness, that growing hostility to the von Ribbentrop state dinner marked the end of America's honeymoon with Charles A. Lindbergh. "The presidential blunder of the century," Winchell called it, "the blunder of blunders for which the reactionary Republican henchmen of our fascist-loving president will pay with their political lives in the November elections."

The White House, accustomed to nearly universal deification of Lindbergh, seemed stymied by the strong disapproval that the opposition was so rapidly able to muster against him, and though the administration sought to distance itself from the Bund's New York rally, the Democrats—determined to associate Lindbergh with the organization's ignominious reputation—held a Madison Square Garden rally of their own. Speaker after speaker scathingly denounced "the Lindbergh Bundists," until to everyone's astonished delight, FDR himself appeared on the platform. The ten-minute ovation his presence elicited would have gone on even longer had not the former president called out forcefully, above the roar, "My fellow Americans, my fellow Americans—I have a message for both Mr. Lindbergh and Mr. Hitler. The moment compels my stating with a candor they cannot misunderstand that it is we, and not they, who are the masters of America's destiny," words so stirring and dramatic that every human being in that crowd (and in our living room and in the living rooms up and down our street) was swept away by the joyous illusion that the nation's redemption was at hand.

"The only thing we have to fear," FDR told his audience—recalling the opening seven words of a sentence as renowned as any ever spoken at a first inaugural—"is the obsequious yielding to his Nazi friends by Charles A. Lindbergh, the shameless courting by the president of the world's greatest democracy of a despot responsible for innumerable criminal deeds and acts of savagery, a cruel and barbaric tyrant unparalleled in the chronicle of man's misdeeds. But we Americans will not accept a Hitler-dominated America. We Americans will not accept a Hitler-dominated world. Today the entire globe is divided between human slavery and human freedom. We—choose—freedom! We accept only an America consecrated to freedom! If there is a plot being hatched by antidemocratic forces here at home harboring a Quisling blueprint for a fascist America, or by foreign nations greedy for power and supremacy—a plot to suppress the great upsurge of human liberty of which the American Bill of Rights is the fundamental document, a plot to replace American democracy with the absolute authority of a despotic rule such as enslaves the conquered people of Europe—let those who would dare in secret to conspire against our freedom understand that Americans will not, under any threat or in the face of any danger, surrender the guarantees of liberty framed for us by our forefathers in the Constitution of the United States."

Lindbergh's response came a few days afterward—he donned his Lone Eagle flying gear and early one morning took off from Washington in his two-engine Lockheed Interceptor to meet with the American people face to face and reassure them that every decision he made was designed solely to increase their security and guarantee their well-being. That's what he did when the smallest crisis loomed, flew to cities in every region of the country, this time to as many as four and five in a single day owing to the Interceptor's phenomenal speed, and everywhere his plane set down the cluster of radio microphones was waiting for him as were the local bigwigs, the wire-service stringers, the city's reporters, and the thousands of citizens who had gathered to catch sight of their young president in his famous aviator's windbreaker and leather cap. And each time he landed, he made it clear that he was flying the country unescorted, without either Secret Service or Air Corps protection. This was how safe he considered the American skies to be; this was how secure the *country* was now that his administration, in little more than a year, had dispelled all threat of war. He reminded his audiences that the life of not a single American boy had been put at risk since he'd come to office and would not be put at risk so long as he remained in office. Americans had invested their faith in his leadership, and every promise he had made to them he had kept.

That was all he said or had to say. He never mentioned von Ribbentrop's name or FDR's or made reference to the German-American Bund or the Iceland Understanding. He said nothing in support of the Nazis, nothing to reveal an affinity with their leader and his aims, not even to note with approval that the German army had recovered from its winter losses and that all along the Russian front, the Soviet Communists were being pushed farther eastward toward their ultimate defeat. But then everyone in America knew that it was an unshakable conviction of the president's, as it was of his party's dominant right wing, that the best protection against the spread of Communism across Europe, into Asia and the Middle East, and as far as to our own hemisphere was the total destruction of Stalin's Soviet Union by the military might of the Third Reich.

In his low-key, taciturn, winning way, Lindbergh told the airfield crowds and the radio listeners who he was and what he'd done, and by the time he climbed back aboard his plane to take off for his next stop, he could have announced that, following the von Ribbentrop White House dinner, the First Lady would be inviting

Adolf Hitler and his girlfriend to spend the Fourth of July weekend as vacation guests in the Lincoln bedroom of the White House and still have been cheered by his countrymen as democracy's savior.

My father's boyhood friend Shepsie Tirschwell had been one of several projectionist-editors at the Newsreel Theater on Broad Street since its opening in 1935 as the city's only all-news movie house. The Newsreel's one-hour show comprised news clips, shorts, and "The March of Time," and it ran daily from early morning until midnight. Every Thursday, out of thousands of feet of news film supplied by companies like Pathé and Paramount, Mr. Tirschwell and the three other editors selected stories and spliced together an up-to-the-minute show so that regular customers like my father— whose office on Clinton Street was only a few blocks away—could keep pace with national news, important happenings worldwide, and exciting moments from championship sports matches that, back in the radio era, could be seen on film nowhere but at a movie theater. My father would try to find an hour each week to catch a complete show, and when he did, he'd recount over dinner what he'd seen and whom. Tojo. Pétain. Batista. De Valera. Arias. Quezon. Camacho. Litvinov. Zhukov. Hull. Welles. Harriman. Dies. Heydrich. Blum. Quisling. Gandhi. Rommel. Mountbatten. King George. La Guardia. Franco. Pope Pius. And that was but an abbreviated list of the tremendous cast of newsreel characters prominent in events that my father told us we would one day remember as history worthy of passing on to our own children.

"Because what's history?" he asked rhetorically when he was in his expansive dinnertime instructional mode. "History is everything that happens everywhere. Even here in Newark. Even here on Summit Avenue. Even what happens in his house to an ordinary man—that'll be history too someday."

On the weekends when Mr. Tirschwell was working, my father would take Sandy and me to be further educated at the Newsreel Theater. Mr. Tirschwell would leave free passes at the box office for us, and each time my father brought us up to the projection booth after the show would give the same civics lecture. He'd tell us that in a democracy, keeping abreast of current events was a citizen's most important duty and that you could never start too early to be informed about the news of the day. We'd gather close to the film projector, each of whose parts he'd name for us, and then we'd look at the framed photographs on the walls that had been taken at the theater's black-tie opening night, when Newark's first and only Jewish mayor, Meyer Ellenstein, had cut the ribbon strung across the lobby and welcomed the famous guests, among whom, as Mr. Tirschwell told us, pointing to their pictures, was the former U.S. ambassador to Spain and the founder of Bamberger's department store.

What I liked best about the Newsreel Theater was that the seats were constructed so that even an adult didn't have to get up to let others by, that the projection booth was said to be soundproof, and that on the carpet in the lobby was a design of motion picture reels that you could step on when you went in and out. Not until I think back to those consecutive Saturdays in 1942, when Sandy was fourteen and I was nine and we were taken by my father specifically to see the Bund rally one week and FDR addressing the anti-Ribbentrop Garden rally the next, am I able to remember anything much other than the narrating voice of Lowell Thomas, who introduced most of the political news, and of Bill Stern, who enthusiastically reported on sports. But the Bund rally I've not forgotten because of the hatred instilled in me by the Bundists up on their feet chanting von Ribbentrop's name as though it were he who was now president of the United States, and FDR's speech I've not forgotten because when he proclaimed to the anti-Ribbentrop rally, "The only thing we have to fear is the obsequious yielding to his Nazi friends by Charles A. Lindbergh," a good half of the movie audience booed and hissed while the rest, including my father, clapped as loudly as they could, and I wondered if a war might not break out right there on Broad Street in the middle of the day and if, when we left the darkened theater, we'd find downtown Newark a rubble heap of smoking ruins and fires burning everywhere.

It wasn't easy for Sandy to sit through those two Saturday-after-noon shows at the Newsreel Theater, and since he'd already under-stood beforehand that it wasn't going to be, he at first refused my father's invitation and agreed to come along with us only when he was ordered to do so. By the spring of 1942, Sandy was a few months from beginning high school, a lean, tall, good-looking boy whose attire was neat, whose hair was combed, and whose posture, standing or sitting, was as perfect as a West Point cadet's. His ex-perience as a leading young spokesman for Just Folks had endowed him, in addition, with an air of authority seldom seen in one so young. That Sandy should prove himself so adept at influencing adults and that he should have developed a reverential following among the younger neighborhood kids who were eager to emulate him and qualify for the Office of American Absorption's summer farm program had surprised my parents and made their older child more intimidating to have around the house than he was back when everyone thought of him as an affable, fairly ordinary boy with a gift for drawing people's likenesses. To me he'd always been the mighty one because of his seniority; now he seemed mightier than ever and easily aroused my admiration despite my having turned away from him because of what Alvin had described as his opportunism—though even the opportunism (if Alvin was correct and that was the word for it) seemed another remarkable attain-ment, the emblem of a calm, self-aware maturity knowingly wed-ded to the ways of the world.

Of course, the concept of opportunism was barely familiar to me at the age of nine, yet its ethical status Alvin communicated clearly enough by the disgust with which he'd pronounced his in-dictment and what he added by way of amplification. He was still fresh from the hospital then and far too miserable to show much restraint.

"Your brother's nothing," he informed me from his bed one night. "He's less than nothing." And that was when he labeled Sandy op-portunistic.

"Is he? Why?"

"Because people are, because they look for the advantage for themselves and the hell with everything else. Sandy's a fucking opportunist. So's your bitch aunt with the big pointy tits. So's the great rabbi. Aunt Bess and Uncle Herman are honest people. But Sandy—selling out to these bastards right off the bat? At his age? With his talent? A real fucking doozy, this brother of yours."

Selling out. Language also new to me, but now no more difficult to understand than "opportunist."

"He just drew some pictures," I explained.

But Alvin was in no mood to have me try to downplay the existence of those pictures, especially as he'd somehow come to know about Sandy's affiliation with Lindbergh's Just Folks. I didn't have the courage to ask how he'd found out what I'd determined never to tell him, though what I figured was that, after accidentally uncovering the artwork beneath the bed, he must have gone ahead to scavenge the drawers of the dining room breakfront, where Sandy stored his school notebooks and his writing paper, and found there all the evidence necessary to hate Sandy forever.

"It doesn't mean what you think," I said, but immediately I had to think what else it *could* mean. "He's doing it to protect us," I announced. "So we don't get in trouble."

"Because of me," Alvin said.

"No!" I protested.

"But that's what he told you. So the family won't get in trouble because of Alvin. That's how he justifies this shit he's up to."

"But why else *would* he be doing it?" I asked this as guilelessly as a child could and with all of a child's cunning—and with no idea of how to begin to extricate myself from a conflict I had only intensified by lying idiotically in my brother's defense. "What's wrong with what he's doing if he's trying to help?"

He merely replied, "I don't believe you, ace," and, because I was no match for Alvin, I gave up trying to believe myself. Though if only Sandy *had* told me he was leading a double existence! If only he *was* making the best of a terrible situation and masquerading as a Lindbergh loyalist to protect us! But having seen him lecturing an audience of Jewish adults in that New Brunswick synagogue basement, I knew how convinced he was of what he was saying and how he gorged on the attention it brought him. My brother had discovered in himself the uncommon gift to be somebody, and so while making speeches praising President Lindbergh and while exhibiting his drawings of him and while publicly extolling (in words written by Aunt Evelyn) the enriching benefits of his eight weeks as a Jewish farm hand in the Gentile heartland—while doing, if the truth be known, what I wouldn't have minded doing myself, by doing what was normal and patriotic all over America and aberrant and freakish only in his home—Sandy was having the time of his life.

Then came history's next outsized intrusion: an engraved invitation from President and Mrs. Charles A. Lindbergh for Rabbi Lionel Bengelsdorf and Miss Evelyn Finkel to attend a state dinner in honor of the German foreign minister on the evening of Saturday, April 4, 1942. The cross-country solo flying tour of thirty cities had raised Lindbergh's reputation as a no-nonsense realist and plaintalking man of the people higher even than it had been before Winchell had labeled the von Ribbentrop dinner "the political blunder of the century." Soon the editorial pages of the country's largely Republican press were crowing that it was FDR and the Democrats whose blunder it had been to deliberately misrepresent as a sinister conspiracy what was no more than a cordial White House dinner for a foreign dignitary.

Stunned as my parents were to learn of the invitation, there was nothing much for them to do about it. Months earlier they had registered with Evelyn their disappointment in her for having become another of the small band of misguided Jews to serve as underlings to those now in power. It made no sense to challenge yet again her remote administrative connection to the president of the United States, especially since they knew that it wasn't ideological conviction that animated her, as it appeared to have back in her union days, or just craven political ambition, but the exhilaration of having been rescued by Rabbi Bengelsdorf from her life as a substitute teacher living in an attic flat on Dewey Street and removed to a life at court as miraculously as Cinderella. However, when she phoned unexpectedly one evening to tell my mother that she and the rabbi had arranged for my brother to accompany them to the von Ribbentrop dinner . . . well, at first no one was willing to believe her. It was still barely possible to accept that Evelyn could herself have stepped overnight from our local little society into "March of Time" celebrity, but now Sandy as well? His preaching for Lindbergh in synagogue basements wasn't improbable enough? This simply could not be so, my father insisted—meaning that it mustn't be so, that, credibility aside, it was too repellent to be so. "It only proves," he told my brother, "that your aunt is nuts."

And maybe she was—driven temporarily nuts by an exaggerated sense of her newfound importance. How else could she have mustered the audacity to seek an invitation to such a great event for her fourteen-year-old nephew? How else could she have prevailed on Rabbi Bengelsdorf to make so outlandish a request of the White House other than by insisting with the uncompromising tenacity of a self-absorbed screwball on the way up? Over the phone my father spoke to her as calmly as he could. "Enough of this foolishness, Evelyn. We're not important people. Leave us alone, please. There's too much for an ordinary person to put up with as it is." But my aunt's commitment to liberating an exceptional nephew from the confines of an ignorant brother-in-law's insignificance (so that he could play a leading role in the world like her) was by now unassailable. Sandy was to attend the dinner as a testament to the success of Just Folks, he was to attend as nothing less than the nationwide representative of Just Folks, and no ghetto father was going to stop him—or her. She got in her car, and fifteen minutes later the reckoning came.

After he hung up, my father did nothing to conceal his outrage, and his voice rose and rose as if he were Uncle Monty. "In Germany Hitler has the decency at least to bar the Jews from the Nazi Party.

That and the armbands, that and the concentration camps, and at least it's clear that dirty Jews aren't welcome. But here the Nazis pretend to invite the Jews *in*. And why? To lull them to sleep. To lull them to sleep with the ridiculous dream that everything in America is hunky-dory. But *this?*" he cried. "*This?* Inviting them to shake the blood-stained hand of a Nazi criminal? Unbelievable! Their lying and their scheming do not stop for a minute! They find the best boy, the most talented boy, the hardest-working, most grown-up boy . . . No! They have mocked us enough with what they are doing to Sandy! He is not going anywhere! They have already stolen my country—they are not stealing my son!"

"But nobody," Sandy shouted, "is mocking *anybody*. This is a great *opportunity*." "For an opportunist," I thought, but kept my mouth shut.

"Be still," my father told him, just that, and the quiet sternness was more effective than the anger in causing Sandy to understand that he was on the brink of the worst hour of his life.

Aunt Evelyn was knocking and my mother got up to open the back door. "What is this woman doing *now?*" my father called after her. "I tell her to leave us alone—and so here she comes, crazy as a coot!"

My mother was by no means at odds with my father's resolve, but she did manage to look imploringly at him as she left the kitchen, hoping she might dispose him to be somewhat merciful however little mercy Evelyn deserved for the reckless stupidity with which she had exploited Sandy's zeal.

Aunt Evelyn was astonished (or pretended to be) by my parents' inability to grasp what it meant for a boy Sandy's age to be invited to the White House, what it would mean for his future to have been a dinner guest at the White House . . . "I am not impressed by *the White House!*" my father cried, hammering on the table to shut her up after she'd said "the White House" for the fifteenth time. "I am only impressed by who lives there. And the person who lives there is a Nazi." "He is not!" Evelyn insisted. "And do you want to tell me that Herr von Ribbentrop isn't a Nazi either?" In response, she called my father a frightened, provincial, uncultivated, narrow-minded . . . and he called her an unthinking, gullible, social-climbing . . . and the quarrel raged across the table, each hotly spitting out indictments to increase the fury of the other, until something Aunt Evelyn said—something relatively mild, as it turned out, about all the strings Rabbi Bengelsdorf had pulled for Sandy—was one absurdity too many for him, and he got up from the table and told her to leave. He walked out of the kitchen and into the rear foyer, where he opened the door to the stairwell, and from there he called to her, "Get out. Go. And don't come back. I never want to see you in this house again."

She couldn't believe it any more than the rest of us. It seemed to me to be a joke, a line tossed off in an Abbott and Costello movie. Get out, Costello. If you're going to carry on like that, leave this house and never come back.

My mother got up from where the three adults had been sitting with their tea and followed him out into the foyer.

"The woman is an idiot, Bess," my father said to her, "a childish idiot who understands nothing. A *dangerous* idiot."

"Close the door, please," my mother said to him.

"Evelyn," he called. "Now. Immediately. Leave."

"Don't do this," my mother whispered.

"I am waiting for your sister to get out of my house," he replied.

"Our house," my mother said, and she came back into the kitchen. "Ev, go home," she said softly, "so everything can quiet down." Aunt Evelyn's face was on the table, hidden in her hands. My mother took her by the arm and lifted her to her feet and walked her to the back door and out of the house, our assertive, effervescent aunt looking as though she had been hit by a bullet and was being carried off to die. Then we heard my father slam the door.

"The woman thinks it's a *party*," he said to Sandy and me when we stepped out into the foyer to view the aftermath of the battle. "She thinks it's a *game*. You've been to the Newsreel Theater. I took you boys. You know what you saw there."

"Yes," I said. I felt I had to say something since my brother was now refusing to speak. He had stoically endured Alvin's remorseless ostracism and he had stoically endured the Newsreel Theater and now he was stoically enduring the banishment of his favorite aunt—at fourteen already at one with the family's obstinate men, determined to stand up to anything.

"Well," my father said, "it's *not* a game. It's a fight. Remember that: a fight!"

Again I said yes.

"Outside in the world . . ." But here he stopped. My mother hadn't returned. I was nine and thought that she would never return. And it may have been that my father, at forty-one, thought so too: my father, who had been freed by hardship of many fears, was not free of the fear of losing his precious wife. Catastrophe was no longer far from anyone's mind, and he was looking at his children as though we were suddenly as bereft of a mother as Earl Axman was on the night of Mrs. Axman's nervous breakdown. When my father went to the living room to look out the front windows, Sandy and I trailed closely behind. Aunt Evelyn's car was no longer at the curb. And my mother wasn't standing on the sidewalk or on the stoop or out in the alleyway or even across the street—nor was she in the cellar when my father ran down the cellar stairs calling her name. Nor was she with Seldon and his mother. They were eating in their kitchen when my father knocked and the three of us were let in.

My father said to Mrs. Wishnow, "Did you see Bess?"

Mrs. Wishnow was a beefy woman, tall and ungainly, who walked around with her fists clenched and who, amazingly to me, was said to have been a laughing, lighthearted girl when my father knew her and her family down in the Third Ward before the Great War. Now that she was both mother and family breadwinner, my parents were constantly extolling her unstinting exertions in behalf of Seldon. That *her* life was a fight was indisputable: you had only to look at her fists.

"What's wrong?" she asked him.

"Isn't Bess here?"

Seldon left the kitchen table to come out and say hello to us. Since his father's suicide, my aversion to him had grown stronger, and at the end of the day I hid back of the school when I knew he was out front waiting to walk me home. And though we lived just one short block from the school, in the morning I'd tiptoe down the stairs and leave the house fifteen minutes before I had to in order to beat him out the door. But then late in the afternoon I would invariably run into him, even if I was at the other end of the Chancellor Avenue hill. I'd be on a household errand and there would be Seldon at my heels, acting as if he'd turned up by accident. And whenever he came by to try to teach me to play chess, I would pretend I wasn't home and not answer the door. If my mother was around she would try to persuade me to play with him by reminding me of the very thing that I wanted to forget. "His father was a wonderful chess player. Years ago he was champion at the Y. He taught Seldon, and now Seldon has no one to play with, and he wants to play with you." I'd tell her that I didn't like or understand the game or know how to play it, but finally there'd be no choice and Seldon would show up with the chess board and his chessmen and I'd sit down across from him at the kitchen table where he'd immediately begin to remind me how his father had made the board and found the chess pieces. "He went into New York, and he knew just the places to go to, and he found just the right pieces—aren't they beautiful? They're made of special wood. And he made this board. He found the wood, and he cut it —you see how the different colors are?" and the only way I found to stop him from perpetually going on about his terrifyingly dead father was to bombard him with the latest toilet jokes I'd heard at school.

When we were headed upstairs again I realized that my father was now going to marry Mrs. Wishnow, and that one evening soon the three of us would carry our belongings down the back stairway and move in with her and Seldon, and that on the way to school as on the way home there would be no way ever again of avoiding Seldon and his unceasing need to draw sustenance from me. And once back in the house, I would have to put my coat away in the closet where Seldon's father had hanged himself. Sandy would sleep in the Wishnow sun parlor, as he had in ours when Alvin lived with us, I'd sleep in the back bedroom beside Seldon, while in the other bedroom my father would sleep where Seldon's father used to sleep, alongside Seldon's mother and her clenched fists.

I wanted to go to the corner and get on a bus and disappear. I still had Alvin's twenty dollars hidden in the tip of a shoe at the bottom of my closet. I'd take the money and get on a bus and down at Penn Station buy a one-way ticket for the train to Philadelphia. There I would find Alvin, and never live with my family again. Instead I would stay with Alvin and look after his stump.

My mother called home after she had put Aunt Evelyn to bed. Rabbi Bengelsdorf was in Washington, but he had talked with Evelyn on the phone and afterward spoke to my mother, assuring her that he knew better than her dunce of a husband what was and was not in the interest of the Jews. How Herman had treated Evelyn would not be forgotten, he said, especially after all he himself had gone out of his way to do for her nephew at Evelyn's request. The rabbi concluded by telling my mother that appropriate action would be taken when the time came.

Around ten, my father went to pick my mother up and drive her home. Sandy and I were already in pajamas when she came into the room and sat down on my bed and took my hand. I'd never seen her so exhausted—not completely depleted like Mrs. Wishnow but hardly the untiring mother full of contentment who used to live so energetically inside her skin back when her worries were merely the ones of making do for her family on a husband's take-home pay of less than fifty dollars a week. A downtown job, a house to run, a tempestuous sister, a determined husband, a headstrong fourteen-year-old, an apprehensive nine-year-old—not even the simultaneous inundation of all these concerns with all their exacting demands need have been overly burdensome for a woman so resourceful, if only there weren't Lindbergh, too.

"Sandy," she said, "what shall we do? Should I explain to you why Daddy doesn't think you should go? Can we do that together quietly? At some point we have to talk everything through. Just you and me off by ourselves. Sometimes Daddy can fly off the handle, but I don't—you know that. You can trust me to listen to you. But we have to get some perspective on what is going on. Because maybe it really isn't a good thing for you to be drawn any further into something like this. Maybe Aunt Evelyn made a mistake. She's overexcited, darling. She's been like that all her life. Something out of the ordinary happens and she loses all perspective. Daddy thinks . . . Shall I continue, dear, or do you want to go to sleep?"

"Do what you want," Sandy said flatly.

"Continue," I said.

My mother smiled at me. "Why? What do you want to know?"

"What everyone's yelling for."

"Because everybody sees things differently." Kissing me goodnight, she said, "Because there's a lot on everyone's mind," but when she leaned toward Sandy's bed to kiss him, he turned his face into the pillow.

Usually my father was off to work before Sandy and I were awake, and my mother would be up early to eat breakfast with him and to make our lunch sandwiches and wrap them in wax paper and put them in the refrigerator and then would herself leave for work after seeing that we two were ready for school. The following day, however, my father didn't leave for his office until he'd had a chance to clarify for Sandy why he was not going to the White House and why he was no longer to participate in any of the programs sponsored by the OAA.

"These friends of von Ribbentrop," he explained to Sandy, "are no friends of ours. Every dirty scheme that Hitler has foisted on Europe, every filthy lie he has told other countries, has come through the mouth of Mr. von Ribbentrop. Someday you'll study what happened at Munich. You'll study the role that Mr. von Ribbentrop played in tricking Mr. Chamberlain into signing a treaty that wasn't worth the paper it was written on. Read *PM* about this man. Listen to Winchell about this man. Foreign Minister von Ribbensnob, Winchell calls him. You know what he did for a living before the war? Sold champagne. A liquor salesman, Sandy. A fake —a plutocrat and a thief and a fake. Even the 'von' in his name is a fake. But you know none of this. You know nothing about von Ribbentrop, you know nothing about Göring, you know nothing about Goebbels and Himmler and Hess—but I *do* know. Did you ever hear about the castle in Austria where Herr von Ribbentrop wines and dines the rest of the Nazi criminals? Know how he got it? He stole it. The nobleman who owned it Himmler threw into a concentration camp, and now it is the property of the liquor salesman! Do you know where Danzig is, Sandy, and what happened to it? Do you know what the Treaty of Versailles is? Did you hear of *Mein Kampf*? Ask Mr. von Ribbentrop—he'll tell you. And I will tell you too, though not from the Nazi point of view. I follow things, and I read things, and I know who these criminals are, son. And I am not allowing you anywhere near them."

"I'll never forgive you for this," Sandy replied.

"But you will," my mother said to him. "One day you'll understand that what Daddy wants for you is only what's in your best interest. He's right, dear, believe me—you have no business with such people. They are only making you their tool."

"Aunt Evelyn?" Sandy asked. "Aunt Evelyn is making me into a 'tool'? Getting me invited to the White House—that's making me into a 'tool'?"

"Yes," my mother said sadly.

"No! That isn't true!" he said. "I'm sorry but I can't let Aunt Evelyn down."

"Your aunt Evelyn," my father told him, "is the one who let *us* down. Just Folks," he said contemptuously. "The only purpose of this so-called Just Folks is to make Jewish children into a fifth column and turn them against their parents."

"Bullshit!" Sandy said.

"Stop that!" my mother said. "Stop that right now. Do you realize that we're the only family on the block going through anything like this? The only family in this entire neighborhood. Everybody else knows by now just to continue living as they were living before the election and to forget who the president is. And that's what we're doing too. Bad things have happened, but now they're over. Alvin is gone and now Aunt Evelyn is gone, and everything is going to get back to normal."

"And when are we moving to Canada," Sandy asked her, "because of your persecution complex?"

Pointing his finger, my father said, "Don't mimic your stupid aunt. Don't talk back like that ever again."

"You're a dictator," Sandy said to him, "you're a dictator *worse* than Hitler."

Because my parents had each been raised in a household where an old-country father had not hesitated to discipline his children in accordance with traditional methods of coercion, they were themselves incapable of ever hitting Sandy or me and disapproved of corporal punishment for anyone. Consequently, all my father did in response to being told by a child of his that he was worse than Hitler was to turn away in disgust and leave for work. But he was hardly out the back door when my mother raised her hand and, to my astonishment, smacked Sandy across the face. "Do you know what your father has just done for you?" she shouted at him. "Don't you understand yet what you were about to do to yourself? Finish your breakfast and go to school. And you be home when school is over. Your father laid down the law—you better obey it."

He didn't flinch when she hit him, and now, all resistance, he undertook to enlarge his heroism by brazenly telling her, "I'm going to the White House with Aunt Evelyn. I don't care whether you ghetto Jews like it or not."

To add to the morning's ugliness, to add to the nerve-shattering implausibility of all our disorder, she made him pay in full for his filial defiance by dealing him a second blow, and this time he burst into tears. And had he not, this prudent mother of ours would have raised her gentle, kindly mothering hand and hit him a third, a fourth, and a fifth time. "She doesn't know what she's doing," I thought, "she's somebody else—*everybody* is," and I grabbed my schoolbooks and ran down the back stairs to the alleyway and out to the street, and, as if the day weren't already gruesome enough, there was Seldon waiting on the front stoop to walk me to school.

On the way home from work a couple of weeks later my father stopped off at the Newsreel Theater to catch the filmed coverage of the von Ribbentrop dinner. It was then that he learned from Shepsie Tirschwell, whom he visited up in his booth after the show, that on the first of June his old boyhood friend was leaving for Winnipeg with his wife, his three children, his mother, and his wife's elderly parents. Representatives of Winnipeg's small Jewish community had helped Mr. Tirschwell to find work as a projectionist at a neighborhood movie house there and had located apartments for the entire family in a modest Jewish neighborhood much like our own. The Canadians had also arranged a low-interest loan to pay for the Tirschwells' move from America and to assist with the support of the in-laws until Mrs. Tirschwell found a job in Winnipeg that would enable her to cover her parents' living expenses. Mr. Tirschwell told my father that he hated parting from his native city and his dear old friends and that of course he regretted leaving his one-of-a-kind job at Newark's most important theater. There was much to leave and much to lose, but he was convinced by all the raw unedited film he'd been watching for the past several years from newsreel crews working around the world that the secret side of the pact reached in Iceland between Lindbergh and Hitler in 1941 provided for Hitler first to defeat the Soviet Union, then to invade and conquer England, and only after that (and after the Japanese had overrun China, India, and Australia, thus completing the creation of their "New Order in Greater East Asia") for America's president to establish the "American Fascist New Order," a totalitarian dictatorship modeled on Hitler's that would set the stage for the last great continental struggle—the German invasion, conquest, and Nazification of South America. Two years down the line, with Hitler's swastika flying from London's houses of Parliament, the Rising Sun flying over Sydney, New Delhi, and Peking, and Lindbergh having been elected to the presidency for another four years, the U.S. border with Canada would be closed, diplomatic relations between the two countries would be severed, and, so as to focus Americans on the grave internal danger that necessitated the curtailment of their constitutional rights, the onslaught would begin en masse against America's four and a half million Jews.

In the wake of von Ribbentrop's Washington visit—and the triumph it represented for the most dangerous of Lindbergh's American supporters—this was Mr. Tirschwell's forecast, and it was so much more pessimistic than anything my father was predicting that he decided not to repeat it to us or, when he got home from the Newsreel Theater for dinner early that evening, to say anything about the Tirschwells' imminent departure, certain that the news would terrify me, rile Sandy, and set my mother clamoring to emigrate at once. Since Lindbergh's inauguration a year and a half earlier, there were estimated to be only two to three hundred Jewish families who had taken up permanent residence in the haven of Canada; the Tirschwells were the first such fugitives that my father knew personally, and learning of their decision had left him shaken.

And then there was the shock of seeing on film the Nazi von Ribbentrop and his wife warmly greeted on the White House portico by the president and Mrs. Lindbergh. And the shock of seeing all the prominent guests stepping from their limousines and smiling with anticipation at the prospect of dining and dancing in von Ribbentrop's presence—and among the guests, seemingly no less thrilled than the others by the disgusting occasion, Rabbi Lionel Bengelsdorf and Miss Evelyn Finkel. "I could not believe it," my father said. "The smile on her face is a mile wide. And the husband-to-be? He looks like he thinks the dinner is for him. You should see this man—nodding at everyone as if he actually mattered!" "But why did you go," my mother asked him, "when it was bound to upset you like this?" "I went," he told her, "because every day I ask myself the same question: How can this be happening in America? How can people like these be in charge of our country? If I didn't see it with my own eyes, I'd think I was having a hallucination."

Though we had only just begun dinner, Sandy set down his silverware, mumbled "But nothing is happening in America, *nothing,*" and left the table—and not for the first time since the morning my mother had smacked him across the face. At meals now, should the smallest reference be made to the news, Sandy would get up and without explanation or apology disappear into our room, pulling the door shut behind him. The first few times my mother got up after him and went in to talk with him and to invite him back to the table, but Sandy would sit at his desk sharpening a charcoal pencil or doodling with it on his drawing pad until she let him be. My brother wouldn't even speak to me when, merely out of loneliness, I dared to ask how much longer he was going to act like this. I began to wonder if he might not pick up and leave home, and not for Aunt Evelyn's but to live with the Mawhinneys on their Kentucky farm. He'd change his name to Sandy Mawhinney and we'd never see him again, just as we were never going to see Alvin. And nobody need bother to kidnap him—he'd do it himself, hand himself over to the Christians so as never again to have anything to do with Jews. Nobody needed to kidnap him because Lindbergh had kidnapped him already, along with everyone else!

Sandy's behavior so unsettled me that, in the evenings, I took to doing my homework out of sight of him at the kitchen table. That was how I came to overhear my father—who was in the living room with my mother, reading the evening paper there while Sandy remained in contemptuous seclusion at the back of the flat—reminding her that our private turmoil was exactly the sort of dissension that the Lindbergh anti-Semites had hoped to stir up between Jewish parents and their children with programs like Just

Folks. Understanding this, however, had only hardened his resolve not to follow Shepsie Tirschwell's lead and leave.

"What are you talking about?" said my mother. "Are you telling me that the Tirschwells are going to Canada?" "In June, yes," he replied. "Why? Why June? What's happening in June? When did you find out? Why didn't you say something?" "Because I knew it would upset you." "And it has—why shouldn't it? Why," she demanded to know, "why, Herman, are they leaving in June?" "Because in Shepsie's judgment the time has come. Let's not discuss it," my father said softly. "The little one is in the kitchen, and he's frightened enough. If Shepsie feels it's time, that is his decision for himself and his family, and good luck to him. Shepsie sits and watches the latest news hour after hour. The news is Shepsie's life, and the news is terrible, and so it affects how he thinks, and this is the decision he came up with." "The man came up with the decision," my mother said, "because he is *informed*." "I am also informed," he said sharply. "I am no less informed—I have just reached a different conclusion. Don't you understand that these anti-Semitic bastards *want* us to run away? They want to get the Jews so fed up with everything," he told her, "that they leave for good, and then the goyim will have this wonderful country all to themselves. Well, I have a better idea. Why don't *they* leave? The whole bunch of them—why don't they all go live under their Führer in Nazi Germany? Then *we* will have a wonderful country! Look, Shepsie can do whatever he thinks is right, but we aren't going anywhere. There is still a Supreme Court in this country. Thanks to Franklin Roosevelt, it is a liberal Supreme Court, and it is there to look after our rights. There is Justice Douglas. There is Justice Frankfurter. There is Justice Murphy and Justice Black. They are there to uphold the law. There are still good men in this country. There is Roosevelt, there is Ickes, there is Mayor La Guardia. In November there is a congressional election. There is still the ballot box and people can still vote without anybody telling them what to do." "And what will they vote for?" my mother asked, and immediately answered herself. "The American people will vote," she said, "and the Republicans will be even *stronger*." "Quiet. Try to keep your voice down, will you? When November comes," he told her, "we'll find out the results, and there'll be time then to decide what to do." "And if there isn't time?" "There will be. Please, Bess," he said, "this cannot go on every night." And his was the last word, though it was probably only because of me doing my homework in the kitchen that my mother forced herself to say no more.

The next day, right after school, I walked down Chancellor Avenue and around to Clinton Place and then beyond the high school to where I figured chances were slight that anybody would recognize me and waited there for a bus downtown to the Newsreel Theater. I'd checked the newspaper timetable the night before. There was an hour-long show beginning at five minutes to four, which meant that I could catch a five o'clock 14 at the Broad Street stop across from the theater and be safely back in time for dinner, or even earlier, depending on when von Ribbentrop was slotted into the program. One way or another, I had to see Aunt Evelyn at the White House, and not because, like my parents, I was appalled and outraged by what she was doing but because her having gone there at all seemed to me more remarkable than anything that could possibly befall a member of our family—except for what had befallen Alvin.

NAZI BIGWIG WHITE HOUSE GUEST—that was the black-lettered headline spelled out across either side of the theater's triangular marquee, and along with my being downtown without my brother or Earl Axman or one of my parents, it made me feel powerfully delinquent when I stepped up to the box-office window and asked for a ticket.

"Unaccompanied by an adult? No, sir," the woman selling tickets told me. "I'm an orphan," I told her. "I live at the orphanage on Lyons Avenue. The sister sent me to do a report on President Lindbergh." "Where's her note?" I'd carefully written one out on the bus, using a blank page from my notebook, and handed it through the money slot. It was modeled after the notes of permission my mother wrote for school trips, only it was signed "Sister Mary Catherine, St. Peter's Orphanage." The woman looked at it without reading it, then beckoned for me to push my money over. I gave her one of Alvin's tens—a huge bill for a kid my size, let alone an orphan from St. Peter's—but she was busy and gave back nine-fifty in change and slipped me a ticket without any fuss. She failed, however, to return the note. "I need that," I said. "Let's go, sonny," she said impatiently, and motioned for me to make room for the people still lining up for the next show.

I got inside just as the lights went out and the martial music came on and the film began to roll. Because seemingly every man in Newark (the theater drew only a very few women) wanted to get a look at the unlikely White House guest, the place was filled to capacity for this late-Friday-afternoon show and the only empty seat I could find was in the far reaches of the balcony—anyone entering now would have to stand at the back of the orchestra's last row. A great excitement came over me, not only because of my having pulled off something that was not expected of me, but because enveloped by the fumes of the hundreds of cigarettes and the extravagant odor of the five-cent cigars, I felt deep in the virile magic of a boy masquerading as a man among men.

British land on Madagascar to take over French naval base.

Pierre Laval, chief of Vichy French government, denounces British move as "act of aggression."

RAF bombs Stuttgart third consecutive night.

British fighter planes in savage air battle over Malta.

German army resumes assault on USSR in the Kerch Peninsula.

Mandalay falls to Japanese army in Burma.

Japanese army launches new drive in jungles of New Guinea.

Japanese army marches into Yunnan province of China from Burma.

Chinese guerrillas raid city of Canton, killing five hundred Japanese troops.

A multitude of helmets, uniforms, weapons, buildings, harbors, beaches, flora, fauna—human faces of every race—but otherwise the same inferno again and again, the unsurpassable evil from whose horrors the United States, of all the great nations, was alone in being spared. Picture after picture of misery without end: the mortars bursting, the infantrymen doubled over and running, marines with raised rifles wading ashore, airplanes dropping bombs, airplanes blown apart and spiraling to earth, the mass graves, the kneeling chaplains, the improvised crosses, the sinking ships, the drowning sailors, the sea in flames, the shattered bridges, the tank bombardment, the targeted hospitals sheared in two, pillars of fire coiling upward from bombed-out oil tanks, prisoners corralled in a sea of mud, stretchers bearing living torsos, bayoneted civilians, dead babies, beheaded bodies bubbling blood . . .

And then the White House. A twilit spring evening. Shadows falling across the sprawl of lawn. Blooming bushes. Flowering trees. Limousines driven by liveried chauffeurs and everyone exiting them in formal attire. From the marble hallway beyond the open portico doors, a string ensemble playing last year's number one hit song, "Intermezzo," popularized from a theme in Wagner's *Tristan and Isolde.* Gracious smiles. Quiet laughter. The lean, beloved, handsome president. Beside him the talented poetess, daring aviatrix, and decorous socialite who is the mother of their murdered child. The loquacious, silver-haired honored guest. The elegant Nazi spouse in her long satin gown. Welcoming words, witticisms, and the Old World gallant, steeped in the theatrics of the royal court and looking in his evening clothes like a million bucks, charmingly kissing the First Lady's hand.

Had it not been for the Iron Cross, awarded to the foreign minister by his Führer and embellishing the pocket just inches below the impeccably arranged silk handkerchief, as persuasively civilized a sham as human cunning could devise.

And there! Aunt Evelyn, Rabbi Bengelsdorf—past the marine guards, through the doorway, and gone!

They couldn't have been on the screen for as long as three seconds, and yet the rest of the national news and the closing sports clips were incomprehensible to me and I kept hoping for the film to spin back to the moment where my aunt materialized asparkle with the gems previously the property of the rabbi's late wife. Among the many improbabilities that the cameras established as irrefutably real, Aunt Evelyn's disgraceful triumph was for me the least real of all.

When the show was over and the lights went up, a uniformed usher was standing in the aisle motioning with his flashlight. "You," he said. "You come with me."

He led me into the crowd that was emptying out of the lobby and through a door he unlocked with a key and then up a narrow stairway that I recognized from when Sandy and I had been brought here to see the Madison Square Garden von Ribbentrop rallies. "How old are you?" the usher asked me.

"Sixteen."

"That's a good one. Keep it up, kid. Get yourself in more hot water."

"I have to go home now," I told him. "I'm going to miss my bus."

"You're going to miss a lot more than that."

He rapped sharply on the famous soundproof door to the Newsreel's projection booth and Mr. Tirschwell let us in.

He was holding the note from Sister Mary Catherine.

"I don't see how I cannot show this to your parents," he told me.

"It was just a joke," I said.

"Your father's coming to pick you up. I telephoned his office to tell him you were here."

"Thank you," I said as politely as I had been taught to say it.

"Please sit down."

"But it was a joke," I repeated.

Mr. Tirschwell was preparing the reels for the new show. I saw when I got to looking around that many of the signed photos of the theater's renowned patrons had been removed from the walls, and realized that Mr. Tirschwell had begun to gather together the mementos he was taking to Winnipeg. And I realized too that the gravity of such a move might alone have been enough to account for the sternness with which he was treating me. Yet he also struck me as the exacting sort of adult whose sense of responsibility often extends to what is none of his business. It would have been hard to tell from either his looks or his speech that he'd grown up in a Newark tenement with my father. He was an understated, distinctly more polished and prideful version than my father of the scantily educated slum child who'd lifted himself out of his parents' immigrant poverty almost entirely by virtue of a vigilant, programmatic industriousness. Ardor, for these men, was all they had to go on. What their Gentile betters called pushiness was generally just this—the ardor that was everything.

"If I go outside," I said, "I can still get the bus and be home in time for dinner."

"Stay where you are, please."

"But what did I do wrong? I wanted to see my aunt. This isn't fair," I said, dangerously close to crying. "I wanted to see my aunt at the White House, that's all."

"Your aunt," he said, and he gritted his teeth so as to say no more.

Of all things, his disdain for Aunt Evelyn triggered my tears. Here Mr. Tirschwell lost his patience. "Are you suffering?" he asked sardonically. "What, what are you suffering? Do you have any idea what people are going through all over the world? Did you understand nothing of what you just saw? I only hope that in the future you're spared any real reason to cry. I hope and pray that in the days ahead your family—" He stopped abruptly, clearly unaccustomed to an undignified eruption of irrational emotion, particularly in the handling of an insignificant child. Even I could understand that his argument was with something other than me, but that didn't lessen the shock of my having to bear the brunt of it.

"What's going to happen in June?" I asked him. It was the unanswered question that I'd overheard my mother ask my father the night before.

Mr. Tirschwell continued scanning my face as though trying to determine how lacking in intelligence I was. "Pull yourself together," he finally said. "Here," and handed me his handkerchief. "Dry your eyes."

I did as he told me, but when I repeated, "What's going to happen? Why are you going to Canada?" the exasperation all at once disappeared from his voice and something emerged both stronger and milder—*his* intelligence.

"I have a new job there," he replied.

That he was sparing me terrified me, and I was again in tears.

My father arrived some twenty minutes later. Mr. Tirschwell handed him the note I'd written to get myself into the theater, but my father didn't take the time to read it until he had steered me by the elbow out of the theater and into the street. That's when he hit me. First my mother hits my brother, now my father reads the words of Sister Mary Catherine and, for the first time ever, wallops me, without restraint, across the face. As I am already overwrought —and nothing like as stoical as Sandy—I break down uncontrollably alongside the ticket booth, in plain view of all the Gentiles hurrying home from their downtown offices for a carefree spring weekend in Lindbergh's peacetime America, the autonomous fortress oceans away from the world's war zones where no one is in jeopardy except us.

6

May 1942–June 1942

Their Country

May 22, 1942

Dear Mr. Roth:

In compliance with a request from Homestead 42, Office of American Absorption, U.S. Department of the Interior, our company is offering relocation opportunities to senior employees like yourself, deemed qualified for inclusion in the OAA's bold new nationwide initiative.

It was exactly eighty years ago that the U.S. Congress passed the Homestead Act of 1862, the famous legislation, unique to America, which granted 160 acres of unoccupied public land virtually free to farmers willing to pull up stakes and settle the new American West. Nothing comparable has been undertaken since then to provide adventurous Americans with exciting new opportunities to expand their horizons and to strengthen their country.

Metropolitan Life is proud to be among the very first group of major American corporations and financial institutions selected to be participants in the new Homestead program, which is designed to give emerging American families a once-in-a-lifetime opportunity to move their households, at government expense, in order to strike roots in an inspiring region of America previously inaccessible to them. Homestead 42 will provide a challenging environment steeped in our country's oldest traditions where parents and children can enrich their Americanness over the generations.

Upon receipt of this announcement you should immediately contact Mr. Wilfred Kurth, the Homestead 42 representative in our Madison Avenue office. He will personally answer all your questions and his staff will courteously assist you in every way they can.

Congratulations to you and your family for having been chosen from among numerous deserving candidates at Metropolitan Life to be among the company's first pioneering "homesteaders" of 1942.

Sincerely yours,
Homer L. Kasson
Vice President for Employee Affairs

Several days had to pass before my father could summon the composure to show the company's letter to my mother and to break the news that as of September 1, 1942, he was being transferred from the Metropolitan's Newark district to a district office opening in Danville, Kentucky. On a map of Kentucky that had been included in the Homestead 42 packet presented to him by Mr. Kurth, he located Danville for us. Then he read aloud from a page in a Chamber of Commerce pamphlet entitled *The Blue Grass State.* "'Danville is the county seat of rural Boyle County. It sits in beautiful Kentucky countryside about sixty miles south of Lexington, the state's second-biggest city after Louisville.'" He began flipping through the pamphlet to find still more interesting facts to read aloud that would somehow mitigate the senselessness of this turn of events. "'Daniel Boone helped to blaze "the Wilderness Road," which opened the way to the settlement of Kentucky . . . In 1792, Kentucky became the first state west of the Appalachians to join the Union . . . The population of Kentucky in 1940 was 2,845,627.' The population of Danville—let me get it here—Danville's population was 6,700."

"And how many Jews in Danville," my mother asked, "of the

six thousand and seven hundred? How many in the whole state?"

"You already know, Bess. There are very few. All I can tell you is that it could be worse. It could be Montana, where the Gellers are going. It could be Kansas, where the Schwartzes are going. It could be Oklahoma, where the Brodys are going. Seven men are leaving from our office, and I am the luckiest, believe me. Kentucky is a beautiful place with a beautiful climate. It is not the end of the world. We will wind up living out there just about the way we live here. Maybe better, given that everything is cheaper and the climate's so nice. There's going to be school for the boys, there's going to be the job for me, there's going to be the house for you. Chances are we'll be able to afford to buy a place of our own where the boys can each have a separate room and a yard out back to play in."

"And just where do they get the gall to do this to people?" my mother asked. "I am dumbfounded, Herman. Our families are here. Our lifelong friends are here. The children's friends are here. We have lived in peace and harmony here all of our lives. We are only a block from the best elementary school in Newark. We are a block from the best high school in New Jersey. Our boys have been raised among Jews. They go to school with other Jewish children. There is no friction with the other children. There is no name-calling. There are no fights. They have never had to feel left out and lonely the way I did as a child. I cannot believe the company is doing this to you. The way you have worked for those people, the hours that you put in, the effort—and this," she said angrily, "is the reward."

"Boys," my father said, "ask me what you want to know. Mother is right. This is a big surprise for all of us. We are all a little dumbfounded. So ask whatever is on your mind. I don't want anybody to be confused about anything."

But Sandy wasn't confused, nor did he look dumbfounded in any way. Sandy was thrilled and barely able to hide his glee, and all because he knew exactly where to find Danville, Kentucky, on the map—fourteen miles from the Mawhinneys' tobacco farm. It could have been that he'd also known we would be moving there long before any of the rest of us did. My father and mother may not have said as much, but then, precisely because of what no one was saying, even I could understand that my father's being selected as one of his district's seven Jewish "homesteaders" was no more fortuitous than his assignment to the company's new Danville office. Once he'd opened the back door to our flat and told Aunt Evelyn to leave the house and never come back, our fate could have played out no other way.

It was after dinner and we were in the living room. Serenely unperturbed, Sandy was drawing something and had no questions to ask, and I—looking outside with my face pressed to the screen of the open window—I had no questions to ask either, and so my father, grimly absorbed in his thoughts, and knowing he'd been defeated, began to pace the floor, and my mother, on the sofa, murmured something under her breath, refusing to resign herself to what awaited us. In the drama of confrontation, in the struggle against we knew not what, each had taken on the role that the other had played in the lobby of the Washington hotel. I realized how far things had gone and how terribly confusing everything now was and how calamity, when it comes, comes in a rush.

Since about three it had been squalling steadily, but abruptly the wind-driven downpour stopped and the sun came blazing out as though the clocks had been turned ahead and, over in the west, tomorrow morning was now set to begin at six P.M. today. How could a street as modest as ours induce such rapture just because it glittered with rain? How could the sidewalk's impassable leaf-strewn lagoons and the grassy little yards oozing from the flood of the downspouts exude a smell that roused my delight as if I'd been born in a tropical rain forest? Tinged with the bright after-storm light, Summit Avenue was as agleam with life as a pet, my own silky, pulsating pet, washed clean by sheets of falling water and now stretched its full length to bask in the bliss.

Nothing would ever get me to leave here.

"And who will the boys play with?" my mother asked.

"There are plenty of children in Kentucky to play with," he assured her.

"And who will I talk to?" she asked. "Who will I have there like the friends I've had my whole life?"

"There are women there, too."

"Gentile women," she said. Ordinarily my mother drew no strength from scorn, but she spoke scornfully now—that's how perplexed she was and how endangered she felt. "Good Christian women," she said, "who will fall all over themselves to make me feel at home. They have no right to do this!" she proclaimed.

"Bess, please—this is what it is like to work for a big company. Big companies transfer people all the time. And when they do, you have to pick up and go."

"I'm talking about the government. The *government* cannot do this. They cannot force people to pick up and go—that is not in any constitution that I ever heard of."

"They aren't forcing us."

"Then why are we going?" she asked. "Of course they are forcing us. This is *illegal*. You cannot just take Jews because they're Jews and force them to live where you want them to. You cannot take a city and just do what you want with it. To get rid of Newark as it is, with Jews living here like everyone else? What business is it of theirs? This is against the law. Everyone *knows* it is against the law."

"Yeah," said Sandy without bothering to look up from what he was sketching, "why don't we sue the United States of America?"

"You *can* sue," I told him. "In the Supreme Court."

"Ignore him," my mother told me. "Until your brother learns to be civil, we just continue to ignore him."

Here Sandy got up and took his drawing materials into our bedroom. Unable any longer to witness the spectacle of my father's defenselessness and my mother's anguish, I unlocked the front door and raced down the front stairs and out into the street where the kids who'd finished their dinner were already dropping Popsicle sticks into the gutters and watching them cascade over the iron grate into the gurgling sewer along with the natural detritus shaken by the storm from the locust trees and the swirl of candy wrappers, beetles, bottle caps, earthworms, cigarette butts, and, mysteriously, inexplicably, predictably, the single mucilaginous rubber. Everybody was out having one last good time before they had to turn in for bed—and all of them still capable of having a good time because none had a parent working for any of the corporations collaborating with Homestead 42. Their fathers were men who worked for themselves or with a partner who was a brother or an in-law and so they weren't going to have to go anywhere. But I wasn't going anywhere either. I would not be driven by the United States government from a street whose very gutters gushed with the elixir of life.

Alvin was in the rackets in Philadelphia, Sandy lived in exile in our house, and my father's authority as a protector had been drastically compromised if not destroyed. Two years earlier, to preserve our chosen way of life, he had mustered his strength to drive over to the home office and, face to face with the big boss, to decline the promotion that would have advanced his career and increased his earnings but at the price of taking us to live in heavily Bundist New Jersey. Now he no longer had it in him to challenge an uprooting potentially no less hazardous, having concluded that confrontation was futile and our fate out of his hands. Shockingly enough, my father had been rendered impotent by his company's having obediently joined hands with the state. There was nobody left to protect us except me.

After school the next day, I covertly headed off again for the downtown bus, this time for the number 7 line, whose route ran some three-quarters of a mile from Summit Avenue, on the far side of the farmed acreage of the orphan asylum, out where St. Peter's Church fronted the thoroughfare of Lyons Avenue and where, in the shadow of its cross-capped steeple, I was even less likely to be spotted by a neighbor or a schoolmate or a family friend than when I made it my business to walk past the high school and down to Clinton Place to take the 14.

I waited at the bus stop outside the church beside two nuns identically buried within the coarse heavy cloth of those voluminous black habits that I'd never had a chance to study as I did that day. Back then, a nun's habit reached to her shoes, and that, along with the brilliant white, starched arc of cloth that starkly framed her facial features and obliterated all lateral vision—the stiffened wimple that hid scalp, ears, chin, and neck and was itself enfolded in an extensive white headcloth—made of the traditionally dressed Catholic nuns the most archaic-looking creatures I had ever seen, far more startling to behold in our neighborhood than even the creepily morticianlike priests. No buttons or pockets were visible, and thus there was no way to figure out how that sheath of thickly gathered curtaining got hooked up or how it was taken off or whether it ever was taken off, given that overlaying everything was a large metal cross suspended from a long cord necklace, and strung beads, big and shiny as "killer" marbles, that dangled several feet down from the front of a black leather belt, and, secured to the headcloth, a black veil that broadened at the back and fell straight to the waist. Other than within the naked little region that was the wimpled, plain, unornamented face, no nap, no softness, no fuzziness anywhere.

I assumed these were two of the nuns who supervised the lives of the orphans and taught in the parochial school. Neither looked my way and, on my own, without a wisecracking sidekick like Earl Axman, I didn't dare to look at them other than in stolen glances, though even while I stared at my own two feet, the clever child's capacity for self-censorship deserted me and I confronted the mysteries again and again, all the questions concerning their female bodies and its lowliest functions, and all tending toward depravity. Despite the seriousness of the afternoon's secret mission and everything that rode on its outcome, I couldn't manage to be anywhere near a nun, let alone a pair of them, without a mind awash in my none-too-pure Jewish thoughts.

The nuns took the two seats behind the driver and, though most of the seats farther to the rear were empty, I sat down across the narrow aisle from the two of them, in the seat just back from the turnstile and the fare box. I'd had no intention of sitting there, didn't understand why I was doing so, but instead of moving off to where I could be out from under the sway of unfettered curiosity, I opened my notebook to pretend to do my schoolwork, simultaneously hoping and dreading that I'd overhear them say something in Catholic. Alas, they were silent, praying I supposed, and no less spellbinding for doing it on a bus.

Some five minutes from downtown, there was a musical clacking of rosary beads as together they rose to disembark at the wide intersection of High Street and Clinton Avenue. On one side of the junction there was an auto dealer's lot and on the other the Hotel Riviera. As they passed, the taller of the nuns smiled down at me from the aisle and, with a vague sadness in her quiet voice—perhaps because the Messiah had come and gone without my knowing it—commented to her companion, "What a well-scrubbed, cute little boy."

She should have known what I'd been thinking. Then again, maybe she did.

A few minutes later, before the bus took the big final turn off Broad Street and started down Raymond Boulevard for its last stop outside Penn Station, I too got off and began running toward the Federal Office Building on Washington Street, where Aunt Evelyn had her office. Inside the lobby I was told by an elevator operator that the OAA was on the top floor, and when I got there I asked for Evelyn Finkel. "You're Sandy's brother," the receptionist announced. "You could be his little twin," she added appreciatively. "Sandy's five years older," I told her. "Sandy's a wonderful, wonderful boy," she said, "everybody loved having him around," and then she buzzed Aunt Evelyn's office. "Nephew Philip's here, Miss F.," she announced, and within seconds, Aunt Evelyn had swept me past the desks of some half-dozen men and women working at their typewriters and into her office overlooking the public library and the Newark Museum. She was kissing me and hugging me and telling me how much she had missed me, and, despite all my apprehensions—beginning, of course, with the fear that my meeting with our estranged aunt would be discovered by my parents—I proceeded as I had planned by confiding in Aunt Evelyn how I had secretly gone alone to the Newsreel Theater to see her at the White House. I sat in the chair at the side of her desk—a desk easily twice the size of my father's just over on Clinton Street—and asked her to tell me what it had been like to eat dinner with the president and Mrs. Lindbergh. When she began to answer in elaborate detail— and with an eagerness to impress that didn't quite make sense to a mere child already overwhelmed by the magnitude of her betrayal—I couldn't believe I was so easily tricking her into thinking that this was why I was here.

There were two big maps pierced with clumps of colored pins and fixed to an enormous cork bulletin board on the wall back of her desk. The larger map was of the forty-eight states and the smaller of just New Jersey, whose long inland river boundary with neighboring Pennsylvania we had been taught in school to identify as the uncanny outline of an Indian chief's profile, the brow up by Phillipsburg, the nostrils down by Stockton, and the chin narrowing into the neck in the vicinity of Trenton. The state's densely populated easternmost corner, encompassing Jersey City, Newark, Passaic, and Paterson, and extending northward to the ruler-straight border with the southernmost counties of the state of New York, denoted the upper back end of the Indian's feathered headdress. That was how I saw it then, and how I continue to see it; along with the five senses, a child of my background had a sixth sense in those days, the geographic sense, the sharp sense of where he lived and who and what surrounded him.

On Aunt Evelyn's spacious desktop, beside separately framed pictures of my dead grandmother and of Rabbi Bengelsdorf, there was a large autographed photo of President and Mrs. Lindbergh standing together in the Oval Office and a smaller photo of Aunt Evelyn in her evening gown shaking the president's hand. "That's

the reception line," she explained. "On the way into the state dining room, the guests each file past the president and the First Lady
and the evening's honored guest. You're introduced by name and
they take a photograph and the White House sends it to you."

"Did the president say anything?"

"He said, 'Nice to have you here.'"

"Are you allowed to say anything back?" I asked.

"I said, 'I'm honored, Mr. President.'" She made no effort to disguise how important that exchange had been to her and perhaps to
the president of the United States. As always with Aunt Evelyn,
there was something very winning about her enthusiasm, though
in the context of my household's confusion, I couldn't miss what
was diabolical about it as well. Never in my life had I so harshly
judged any adult—not my parents, not even Alvin or Uncle Monty
—nor had I understood till then how the shameless vanity of utter
fools can so strongly determine the fate of others.

"Did you meet Mr. von Ribbentrop?"

Now almost girlishly bashful, she replied, "I danced with Mr.
von Ribbentrop."

"Where?"

"There was dancing after dinner in a big tent on the White
House lawn. It was a beautiful night. An orchestra and dancing,
and Lionel and I were introduced to the foreign minister and his
wife, and we got to talking, and then he just bowed and asked me
to dance. He's known to be an excellent dancer, and he is, it's true
—a perfectly magical ballroom dancer. And his English is faultless.
He studied at the University of London and then lived for four
years as a young man in Canada. His great youthful adventure,
he calls it. I found him a very charming gentleman and *highly* intelligent."

"What'd he say?" I asked.

"Oh, we talked about the president, about the OAA, about our
lives—we talked about everything. He plays the violin, you know.
He's like Lionel, a man of the world who can talk knowledgeably
about anything. Here, look, darling—look at what I was wearing.

Do you see the bag I was carrying? It's gold mesh. See this? See the scarabs? Gold, enamel, and turquoise scarabs."

"What's a scarab?"

"It's a beetle. It's a gem that's cut to resemble a beetle. And it was made right here in Newark by the family of the first Mrs. Bengelsdorf. Their workshop was world famous. They made jewelry for the kings and queens of Europe and all of the wealthiest people in America. Look at my engagement ring," she said, placing her perfumed little hand so close to my face I felt like a dog suddenly and wanted to lick it. "See the stone? That is an emerald, my dearest dear child."

"A real one?"

She kissed me. "A real one! And in the photo, here—that's a link bracelet. It's gold with sapphires and pearls. *Real* ones!" she said, kissing me again. "The foreign minister said he'd never seen a bracelet more beautiful anywhere. And what do you think that is around my neck?"

"A necklace?"

"A festoon necklace."

"What's 'festoon'?"

"A chain of flowers, a garland of flowers. You know the word 'festival.' You know 'festivities.' And you know 'feast,' too, don't you? Well, they're all related. And look, the two brooches, see them? They're sapphires, darling—Montana sapphires set in gold. And do you see who is wearing them? Who? Who is that? It's Aunt Evelyn! It's Evelyn Finkel of Dewey Street! At the White House! Isn't it unbelievable?"

"I guess so," I said.

"Oh, sweetheart," she said, drawing me to her and kissing me now all over my face, "I guess so too. I'm so glad you came to see me. I've missed you so," and she stroked me then as if to find out if my pockets were stuffed with stolen goods. Only years later did I come to understand that her skillful way with her groping hands may well have been what accounted for the rapid renovation of Aunt Evelyn's life by a figure of the stature of Lionel Bengelsdorf.

Brilliant and erudite though the rabbi was, superior to everyone even in his egoism, Aunt Evelyn must never have been at a loss with him.

The paradise of envelopment that followed was, of course, unidentifiable at the time. Wherever I put my own two hands, there was the soft surface of her body. Wherever I moved my face, there was the thickness of her scent. Wherever I looked, there was her clothing, new spring wrappings so light and gauzy that they didn't even veil the sheen of her slip. And there were the eyes of another human being as I'd never quite seen them before. I had not reached the age of desire, was blinded, of course, by the word "aunt," still found the random little stiffening of my acorn of a penis the puzzling nuisance it had always been, and so the delight that I took nestling into the curvaceousness of my mother's thirty-one-year-old sister, a tiny, lively Thumbelina seemingly timid in no way and formed after the model of hills and apples, was a lifeless feeling of frenzy and nothing more, as though a rare, imperfectly printed treasure of a stamp that I knew to be priceless had accidentally turned up on an ordinary letter dropped by the postman into our Summit Avenue mailbox.

"Aunt Evelyn?"

"My darling."

"Do you know that we're moving to Kentucky?"

"Uh-huh."

"I don't want to go, Aunt Evelyn. I want to stay at my school."

She stepped sharply back from me, and with the air now of anything but a paramour, asked, "Who sent you here, Philip?"

"Sent me? Nobody."

"Who sent you to see me? Tell the truth."

"It is the truth. Nobody."

She returned to the chair behind the desk, and the look in her eyes made it necessary for me to do everything I could not to get up and run. But I wanted what I wanted too much to run.

"There's nothing to be afraid of in Kentucky," she said.

"I'm not afraid. I just don't want to have to move."

Even her silence was all-embracing and, if I had indeed been lying, would have forced from me the confession she wanted. Her life, poor woman, was a perpetual state of intensity.

"Can't Seldon and his mother go instead of us?" I asked.

"Who is Seldon?"

"The boy downstairs whose father died. His mother works for the Metropolitan now. How come we have to go and they don't?"

"Wasn't it your father who put you up to this, dear?"

"No. No. Nobody even knows I'm here."

But I saw she still didn't believe me—her aversion to my father was too precious to be dislodged by the obvious truth.

"Does Seldon want to go with you to Kentucky?" she asked me.

"I didn't ask him. I don't know. I just thought I'd ask you if they could go instead."

"My dear little boy, do you see the New Jersey map? Do you see these pins in the map? Each one represents a family chosen for relocation. Now look at the map of the whole country. See all the pins there? Those represent the location to which each New Jersey family has been assigned. Making these assignments involves the cooperation of many, many people, in this office, in the Washington headquarters, and in the state to which each family is moving. The biggest and most important corporations in New Jersey are relocating employees in a partnership with Homestead 42, and so much more planning, much, much more than you can begin to imagine, has gone into all of this. And, of course, no decision is made by any one person. But even if it was, and I were that person, and I could do something to keep you near your friends and your school, I would continue to think that you for one are going to benefit enormously by becoming something more than another Jewish child whose parents have made him too frightened ever to leave the ghetto. Look what your family has done to Sandy. You saw your brother in New Brunswick that night. You saw him talking to all those people about his adventure on the tobacco farm. Do you remember that night?" she asked me. "Weren't you proud of him?"

"Yes."

"And did it sound as though living in Kentucky was frightening and that Sandy was ever, for a moment, afraid?"

"No."

Here, having reached into her desk for something, she got up and came around again to where I was sitting. Her pretty face, with its large features and thickly applied makeup, suddenly looked to me preposterous—the carnal face of the ravenous mania to which, in my mother's judgment, her emotional younger sister had help-lessly fallen prey. To be sure, for a child in the court of Louis XIV the ambitions and satisfactions of such a relative would never have attained the same intimidating aura of significance that Aunt Eve-lyn's did for me, nor would the worldly advancement of a cleric like Rabbi Bengelsdorf have seemed the least bit scandalous to my parents were they themselves raised at court as a marquis and a marchioness. Probably I couldn't have done any worse—I might well have done a lot better—seeking solace from the two nuns on the Lyons Avenue bus than from someone reveling in the pleasures of the standard, petty corruptions that proliferate wherever people compete for even the tiniest advantages of rank.

"Be brave, darling. Be a brave boy. Do you want to sit on the front stoop of Summit Avenue for the rest of your life, or do you want to go out into the world like Sandy did and prove that you are as good as anyone? Suppose I'd been afraid to go to the White House and meet the president because people like your father say things about him and call him names. Suppose I'd been afraid to meet the foreign minister because they call *him* names. You cannot go around being afraid of everything that isn't familiar to you. You cannot grow up to be frightened like your parents. Promise me you won't."

"I promise."

"Here," she said, "I have a treat for you." And she handed me one of two little cardboard packets that she had been holding in her hand. "I got this for you at the White House. I love you, sweetheart, and I want you to have it."

"What is it?"

"An after-dinner chocolate. It's a chocolate wrapped in gold paper. And you know what's embossed right on the chocolate? The presidential seal. Here's one for you, and if I give you Sandy's, will you bring it to him for me?"

"Okay."

"This is what's on your table at the White House at the end of the meal. Chocolates in a silver dish. And the moment I saw them there I thought of the two boys in the world I most want to make happy."

I got up, clutching the chocolates in my hand, and Aunt Evelyn put her arm tightly around my shoulder and walked me out past all the people working for her and into the corridor, where she pressed the button for the elevator.

"What is Seldon's last name?" she asked me.

"Wishnow."

"And he's your best friend."

How could I explain that I couldn't bear him? And so at last I lied and said, "Yes, he is," and, since my aunt did indeed love me and was not herself lying when she said she wanted to make me happy, only a few days later, after I'd finally disposed of the White House chocolates by waiting until no one was around and throwing them over the orphanage fence, Mrs. Wishnow received a letter from the Metropolitan informing her that she and her family were fortunate enough to have been chosen to move to Kentucky as well.

On a Sunday afternoon at the end of May, a confidential meeting was convened in our living room for the Jewish insurance agents who, along with my father, were being relocated from the Metropolitan's Newark office under the auspices of Homestead 42. They all came with just their wives, having agreed that it would be best to leave the children at home. Earlier in the afternoon Sandy and I, joined by Seldon Wishnow, had arranged the chairs for the meeting, including a set of bridge chairs we'd carried upstairs from the Wishnows'. Afterward Mrs. Wishnow drove the three of us to the Mayfair Theater in Hillside, where we would catch a double feature and then be picked up by my father when the meeting was over.

The other guests were Shepsie and Estelle Tirschwell, who were only days from moving their family to Winnipeg, and Monroe Silverman, a distant cousin who'd recently opened a law office in Irvington, just above the haberdashery store owned by my father's second-older brother, Lenny, the uncle who supplied Sandy and me with new school clothes "at cost." When my mother suggested —out of her enduring respect for everything that one is taught to respect—that Hyman Resnick, our local rabbi, should be invited to attend the meeting, nobody else among the organizers who'd assembled in our kitchen the week before showed much enthusiasm for the idea and, after a deferential few minutes of discussion (during which my father said diplomatically what he always said diplomatically about Rabbi Resnick, "I like the man, like his wife, no doubt in my mind he does an excellent job, but he's really not very brilliant, you know"), my mother's proposal was tabled. Even though, to the delight of a small child, these intimate friends of our family spoke in as wide and entertaining a range of voices as the characters on *The Fred Allen Show* and were each as distinctively different-looking as the comic-strip figures in the evening paper— this was back when evolution's sly wit was still rampantly apparent, long before the youthful renovation of face and figure became a serious adult aspiration—they were very similar people at the core: they raised their families, budgeted their money, attended to their elderly parents, and cared for their modest homes alike, on most every public issue thought alike, in political elections voted alike. Rabbi Resnick presided over an unimposing yellow-brick synagogue at the edge of the neighborhood where everyone showed up in their High Holiday best for the three days each year of Rosh Hashanah and Yom Kippur observances but otherwise returned there for little else, except, when necessary, to dutifully recite the daily prayer for the dead during the period prescribed. A rabbi was to officiate at weddings and funerals, to bar mitzvah their sons, to visit the ill in the hospital, and to console the bereft at the shiva; beyond that he did not play a role of any importance in their day-to-day lives, nor did any of them—including my respectful mother—expect him to, and not just because Resnick wasn't that brilliant. Their being Jews didn't issue from the rabbinate or the synagogue or from their few formal religious practices, though over the years, largely for the sake of living parents who came once a week to visit and eat, several of the households, ours among them, were kosher. Their being Jews didn't even issue from on high. To be sure, each Friday at sundown, when my mother ritually (and touchingly, with the devotional delicacy she'd absorbed as a child from watching her own mother) lit the Sabbath candles, she invoked the Almighty by his Hebrew title but otherwise no one ever made mention of "Adonoy." These were Jews who needed no large terms of reference, no profession of faith or doctrinal creed, in order to be Jews, and they certainly needed no other language—they had one, their native tongue, whose vernacular expressiveness they wielded effortlessly and, whether at the card table or while making a sales pitch, with the easygoing command of the indigenous population. Neither was their being Jews a mishap or a misfortune or an achievement to be "proud" of. What they were was what they couldn't get rid of—what they couldn't even begin to want to get rid of. Their being Jews issued from their being themselves, as did their being American. It was as it was, in the nature of things, as fundamental as having arteries and veins, and they never manifested the slightest desire to change it or deny it, regardless of the consequences.

I'd known these people all my life. The women were close and reliable friends who exchanged confidences and swapped recipes, who commiserated with one another on the phone and looked after one another's children and regularly celebrated one another's birthdays by traveling the twelve miles to Manhattan to see a Broadway show. The men had not only worked for years in the same district office but met to play pinochle on the two evenings a month the women had their mahjong game, and from time to time, on a

Sunday morning, a group of them went off to the old sweatbaths on Mercer Street with their young sons in tow—the offspring of this set happened all to be boys somewhere between Sandy's age and mine. On Decoration Day, the Fourth of July, and Labor Day the families would usually organize a picnic some ten miles west of our neighborhood at the bucolic South Mountain Reservation, where the fathers and the sons tossed horseshoes and chose up sides for softball and listened to a ball game on somebody's static-ridden portable radio, the most magical technology known to our world. The boys weren't necessarily the best of friends but we felt connected through our fathers' affiliation. Of us all, Seldon was the least robust, least confident, and, most painfully for him, least lucky, and yet it was to Seldon that I had managed to contract myself for the remainder of boyhood and probably beyond. He'd begun to shadow me more doggedly since he and his mother had learned of their relocation, and I could only think that because we two were going to be the sole Jewish pupils in the Danville elementary school system, I'd be expected—by the Danville Gentiles no less than by our parents—to be his natural ally and closest companion. Seldon's omnipresence might not be the worst that was awaiting me in Kentucky, but to the imagination of a nine-year-old it registered as an unendurable ordeal and accelerated the urge to rebel.

How? I didn't know yet. All I'd felt so far was the pre-mutinous roiling, and all I'd done about it was to find a small, water-stained cardboard suitcase forgotten beneath the usable luggage in our cellar storage bin and, after cleaning it of mildew inside and out, hidden the clothing there that I surreptitiously took, piece by piece, from Seldon's room whenever my mother dragooned me into enduring my hour downstairs as a peevish student of chess. I would have taken my own clothes to stow away in the suitcase except that I knew my mother would discover what was missing and one day soon I'd have to come up with an explanation. She still did the wash on the weekends and put the laundered clothes back—as well as the dry cleaning that it was my job to collect from the tailor shop on Saturdays—and so mapped out in her head was an inventory of everyone's wardrobe that was complete down to the location of the last pair of socks. On the other hand, stealing clothes from Seldon was a snap, and—what with his having latched on to me as his other self—vengefully irresistible. Underclothes and socks were easy enough to get out of the Wishnow apartment—and down the cellar stairs to the suitcase—tucked beneath my undershirt. Stealing and hiding a pair of his trousers, a sport shirt, and a pair of his shoes posed a more difficult problem, but suffice it to say that Seldon was distractible enough for the theft to be accomplished and, for a time, to go unnoticed.

Once having gathered together everything of his I needed, I couldn't have said what I planned to do next. He and I were about the same size, and on the afternoon when I dared to secrete myself in the bin and change out of my clothes and into Seldon's, all I did was to stand there and whisper, "Hello. My name is Seldon Wishnow," and feel like a freak, and not just because Seldon had become such a freak to me and I was being him but because it was clear from all my transgressive sneaking around Newark—and culminating in this costume party in the dark cellar—that I had become a far bigger freak myself. A freak with a trousseau.

The $19.50 left from Alvin's $20 also went into the suitcase, under the clothes. I then hurriedly got back into my own clothes, shoved the cardboard suitcase beneath the other luggage, and, before the angry ghost of Seldon's father could strangle me to death with a hangman's rope, ran for the alleyway and the outdoors. Over the next few days I was able to forget what I'd hidden and the unspecified purpose it was meant to serve. I could even count this latest little escapade as nothing seriously aberrant and as harmless as following Christians with Earl, until the evening when my mother had to rush downstairs to sit and hold Mrs. Wishnow's hand and make her a cup of tea and put her to bed, so wretched and distraught was Seldon's overworked mother because of her son's inexplicably "losing his clothes."

Seldon meanwhile was up in our flat, where he'd been sent to do his homework with me. He was plenty distraught himself. "I didn't lose them," he said through his tears. "How could I lose a pair of shoes? How could I lose a pair of pants?"

"She'll get over it," I said.

"No, not her—she doesn't get over anything. 'You're going to send us to the poorhouse,' she told me. Everything to my mother is 'the last straw.'"

"Maybe you left them at gym class," I suggested.

"How could I? How could I get out of gym class without any clothes on?"

"Seldon, you had to leave them somewhere. Think."

The next morning, before I headed for school and my mother left for work, she suggested my making a gift to Seldon of a set of my own clothes to replace his that had disappeared. "There's the shirt that you never wear—the one from Uncle Lenny's that you say is too green. And the pair of Sandy's corduroy trousers, the brown ones that never fit you right—I'm sure they would fit Seldon just fine. Mrs. Wishnow is beside herself, and it would be such a thoughtful gesture on your part," she said.

"And underwear? Do you want to give him my underwear too? Should I take it off now, Ma?"

"That's not necessary," she said, smiling to soothe my irritation. "But the green shirt and the brown corduroys and maybe one of your old belts that you don't use. It's entirely up to you, but it would mean a lot to Mrs. Wishnow, and to Seldon it would mean the world. Seldon worships you. You know that."

I immediately thought, "She knows. She knows what I did. She knows everything."

"But I don't want him walking around in my clothes," I said. "I don't want him telling everyone in Kentucky, 'Look at me, I'm wearing Roth's clothes.'"

"Why don't you worry about Kentucky when and if we go to Kentucky."

"He'll wear them to school *here*, Ma."

"What is the *matter* with you?" she replied. "What is going on with you? You're turning into—"

"So are you!" and I ran off with my books to school, and when I got home for lunch at noon I pulled from the bedroom closet the green shirt I hated and the brown corduroy pants that never fit and brought them downstairs to Seldon, who was in his kitchen eating the sandwich his mother had left for him and playing chess with himself.

"Here," I said, throwing the clothes on the table. "I'm giving you these," and then I told him, for all the good it did in rerouting the direction of either of our lives, "Only stop following me around!"

There were leftover delicatessen sandwiches for our supper when Sandy, Seldon, and I got back from the movies. The adults, who'd eaten in the living room when their meeting was through, had by now all left for home, except for Mrs. Wishnow, who sat at the kitchen table with her fists clenched, still embattled, still grappling day in and day out with everything determined to crush her and her fatherless son. She listened, along with the three of us, to the Sunday-night comedy shows and, while we ate, watched Seldon the way an animal watches over her newborn when she's caught a whiff of something stealthily creeping their way. Mrs. Wishnow had washed and dried the dishes and put them away in the pantry cupboard, my mother was in the living room pushing the carpet sweeper over the rug, and my father had collected and put out the garbage and carried the Wishnows' set of bridge chairs downstairs to return them to the back of the closet where Mr. Wishnow had killed himself. The reek of tobacco smoke pervaded the house despite every window having been thrown open and the ashes and butts flushed down the toilet and the glass ashtrays rinsed clean and stacked away in the breakfront's liquor cabinet (from which not a bottle had been removed that afternoon nor—in keeping with the matter-of-fact temperance practiced in the bulk of the homes of that first industrious American-born generation—a drop requested by a single guest).

For the moment, our lives were intact, our households were in place, and the comfort of habitual rituals was almost powerful enough to preserve a child's peacetime illusion of an eternal, unhounded now. We had the radio going with our favorite programs, we had dripping corned beef sandwiches for supper and rich coffee cake for dessert, we had the resumption of the routines of the school week before us and a double feature under our belts. But because we had no idea what our parents had decided about the future—had as yet no way of telling whether Shepsie Tirschwell had persuaded them to immigrate to Canada, whether cousin Monroe had come through with an affordable legal maneuver to challenge the relocation plan without getting everyone fired, or whether, after poring over the ins and outs of their government-ordained displacement as unemotionally as it was in them to do, they'd found no alternative but to accept that the guarantees of citizenship no longer fully extended to them—the embrace of the totally familiar wasn't the Sunday-night debauch it would ordinarily have been.

Seldon had got mustard all over his face when he hungrily attacked his sandwich, and it surprised me to see his mother reach over to wipe it off with a paper napkin. His letting her do it surprised me even more. I thought, "It is because he has no father," and though by now I believed that about everything that concerned him, probably this time I was right. I thought, "This is the way it's going to be in Kentucky." The Roth family against the world, and Seldon and his mother for dinner forever.

Our voice of belligerent protest, Walter Winchell, came on at nine. Everyone had been waiting on successive Sunday evenings for Winchell to lay into Homestead 42, and when he failed to, my father attempted to rid himself of his agitation by sitting down to compose a letter to the one man aside from Roosevelt whom he considered America's last best hope. "This is an experiment, Mr. Winchell. This is the way Hitler did it. The Nazi criminals start with something small, and if they get away with it," he wrote, "if no one like you raises a cry of alarm . . ." but he never proceeded to list the horrors that could ensue, because my mother was sure that the letter would wind up in the office of the FBI. It is mailed to Walter Winchell, she reasoned, but it never reaches Walter Winchell—at the post office it's diverted to the FBI and placed in a folder labeled "Roth, Herman," to be filed beside the existing folder labeled "Roth, Alvin."

My father argued, "Never. Not the U.S. Mail," but my mother's commonsensical reply stripped him on the spot of what little remained of his certainty. "You're sitting there writing Winchell," she said, "you're predicting to him how these people will stop at nothing once they know what they can get away with. And now you're trying to tell me that they can't do what they want to the postal system? Let someone else write to Walter Winchell. Our children have been questioned by the FBI already. The FBI is already watching like a hawk because of what Alvin did." "But that," he told her, "is *why* I'm writing him. What else should I do? What more *can* I do? If you know, advise me. Should I just sit here waiting for the worst to happen?"

In his helpless bewilderment she saw her opportunity, and, not because she was callous but because she was desperate, she seized it and thereby humbled him further. "You don't see Shepsie sitting around writing letters and waiting for the worst to happen," she said. "No," he replied, "not Canada again!" as though Canada were the name of the disease insidiously debilitating us all. "I don't want to hear it. Canada," he told her firmly, "is not a solution." "It's the *only* solution," she pleaded. "I am not running away!" he shouted, startling everyone. "This is our country!" "No," my mother said sadly, "not anymore. It's Lindbergh's. It's the goyim's. It's their country," she said, and her breaking voice and the shocking words and the nightmare immediacy of what was mercilessly real forced my father, in the prime of his manhood, fit, focused, and undiscourageable as any forty-one-year-old could possibly be, to see himself with mortifying clarity: a devoted father of titanic energy no more capable of protecting his family from harm than was Mr. Wishnow hanging dead in the closet.

To Sandy—still silently enraged by the injustice of having been stripped of his precocious importance—neither of them sounded anything but stupid, and alone with me he didn't hesitate to speak of them in the language he'd picked up from Aunt Evelyn. "Ghetto Jews," Sandy told me, "frightened, paranoid ghetto Jews." At home he sneered at just about everything they said, on any subject, and then sneered at me when I appeared to be skeptical of his bitterness. He might anyway have begun by now to seriously enjoy sneering, and perhaps even in ordinary times our mother and father might have found themselves having to tolerate as best they could a restless adolescent's contemptuous derision, but back in 1942 what made it more than merely exasperating was the ambiguously menacing predicament throughout whose duration he would continue disparaging them right to their faces.

"What's 'paranoid'?" I asked him.

"Somebody afraid of his shadow. Somebody who thinks the whole world's against him. Somebody who thinks Kentucky is in Germany and that the president of the United States is a storm trooper. These people," he said, mimicking our captious aunt whenever she would superciliously distinguish herself from the Jewish rabble. "You offer to pay their moving expenses, you offer to throw open the gates for their children . . . Know what paranoid is?" Sandy said. "Paranoid is nuts. The two of them are bats—they're crazy. And you know what's made them crazy?"

The answer was Lindbergh, but I didn't dare say it to him. "What?" I asked.

"Living like a bunch of greenhorns in a goddamn ghetto. You know what Aunt Evelyn says Rabbi Bengelsdorf calls it?"

"Calls what?"

"The way these people live. He calls it 'Keeping faith with the certainty of Jewish travail.'"

"And what's that supposed to mean? I don't understand. Translate, please. What's 'travail'?"

"Travail? Travail is what you Jews call *tsuris*."

* * *

The Wishnows had gone back downstairs and Sandy had settled into the kitchen to finish his homework when my parents, at the front of the house, tuned the living room radio to Walter Winchell. I was in bed with the lights out: I didn't want to hear another panic-stricken word from anyone about Lindbergh, von Ribbentrop, or Danville, Kentucky, and I didn't want to think about my future with Seldon. I wanted only to disappear into forgetful sleep and to wake up in the morning somewhere else. But because it was a warm night and the windows were wide open, I couldn't help, at the stroke of nine, but be beset from virtually every quarter by the renowned Winchell radio trademark—the clatter of dots and dashes sounding over the telegraph ticker and signaling in Morse code (which Sandy had taught me) absolutely nothing. And then, above the ticker's dimming clatter, the red-hot blast of Winchell himself issuing from all the houses on the block. "Good evening, Mr. and Mrs. America . . ." followed by the staccato barrage of the long-hoped-for words—at last the purgative Winchell scourge that would change everything. In normal times, when it was generally within the power of my mother and father to set things right and explain away enough of the unknown to make existence appear to be rational, it wasn't at all like this, but because of the maddening here and now, Winchell, even to me, had become an out-and-out god and more important by far than Adonoy.

"Good evening, Mr. and Mrs. America and all the ships at sea. Let's go to press! Flash! To the glee of rat-faced Joe Goebbels and his boss, the Berlin Butcher, the targeting of America's Jews by the Lindbergh fascists is officially under way. The phony moniker for phase one of organized Jewish persecution in the land of the free is 'Homestead 42.' Homestead 42 is being aided and abetted by the most respectable of America's robber barons—but don't worry, they'll be rewarded in giveaway tax breaks by Lindbergh's Republican henchmen in the next pro-greed Congress.

"Item: Whether the Homestead 42 Jews end up in concentration camps à la Hitler's Buchenwald has yet to be decided by Lindbergh's two top swastinkers, Vice President Wheeler and Secretary of the Interior Henry Ford. Did I say 'whether'? Pardon my German. I meant when.

"Item: Two hundred and twenty-five Jewish families have already been told to vacate the cities of America's northeast in order to be shipped thousands of miles from family and friends. This first shipment has been kept strategically small in order to escape national attention. Why? Because it marks the beginning of the end for the four and a half million American citizens of Jewish descent. The Jews will be scattered far and wide to wherever Hitlerite America Firsters flourish. There the right-wing saboteurs of democracy—the so-called patriots and the so-called Christians—can be turned against these isolated Jewish families overnight.

"And who's next, Mr. and Mrs. America, now that the Bill of Rights is no longer the law of the land and the racial haters are running the show? Who's next under the Wheeler-Ford pogrom-plan for government-funded persecution? The long-suffering Negroes? The hard-working Italians? The last of the Mohicans? Who else among us is no longer welcome in Adolf Lindbergh's Aryan America?

"Scoop! This reporter has learned that Homestead 42 was in the works on January 20, 1941, the day the American Fascist New Order moved its mob into the White House, and was signed into the Iceland sellout between the American Führer and his Nazi partner in crime.

"Scoop! This reporter has learned that only in return for the gradual relocation—and eventual mass imprisonment—of America's Jews by the Lindbergh Aryans would Hitler agree to spare the British Isles from a massive armed invasion across the English Channel. The two beloved Führers agreed in Iceland that massacring blue-eyed, blond-haired bona fide Aryans didn't make sense unless you definitely had to. And it comes as no surprise that Hitler will most definitely have to if Oswald Mosley's British fascist party fails to take dictatorial control of 10 Downing Street before

1944. That's when the master race plans to wrap up the Nazi enslavement of three hundred million Russians and to raise the swastika over the Moscow Kremlin.

"And how long will the American people stand for this treachery perpetrated by their elected president? How long will Americans remain asleep while their cherished Constitution is torn to shreds by the fascist fifth column of the Republican right marching under the sign of the cross and the flag? Stay with me, your New York correspondent Walter Winchell, for my next big bombshell about Lindbergh's treasonous lies.

"I'll be back in a flash with a flash!"

Three things then happened at once: the calming voice of announcer Ben Grauer started hawking hand lotion for the program's sponsor; the phone began to ring in the hallway outside my bedroom as it never did after nine in the evening; and Sandy exploded. Addressing only the radio (but so passionately that my father was instantly roused from his living room chair), he began to shout, "You filthy liar! You lying prick!"

"Whoa," said my father, rushing into the kitchen. "Not in this house. Not that language. That is enough."

"But how can you *listen* to this crap? *What* concentration camps? There are no concentration camps! Every word is a lie—bullshit and more bullshit to get you people to tune in! The whole country knows Winchell's full of hot air—it's only you people who don't."

"And which people exactly is that?" I heard my father say.

"I lived in Kentucky! Kentucky is one of the forty-eight states! Human beings live there like they do everywhere else! It is not a concentration camp! This guy makes millions selling his shitty hand lotion—and *you* people believe him!"

"I told you already about the dirty words, and now I'm telling you about this 'you people' business. 'You people' one more time, son, and I am going to ask you to leave the house. If you want to go live in Kentucky instead of here, I'll drive you down to Penn Station and you can catch the next train out. Because I know very well what 'you people' means. And so do you. So does everyone. Don't you use those two words in this house ever again."

"Well, in my opinion Walter Winchell is full of it."

"Fine," he said. "That is your opinion and you are entitled to it. But other Americans hold a different opinion. It so happens that millions and millions of Americans listen to Walter Winchell every single Sunday night—and they are not just what you and your brilliant aunt call 'you people.' His program is still the highest-rated news show on the air. Franklin Roosevelt confided to Walter Winchell things he would never tell another newspaperman. And listen to me, will you—these are *facts*."

"But I *can't* listen to you. How can I listen to you when you tell me about 'millions' of people? Millions of people are nothing but idiots!"

Meanwhile my mother had answered the phone in the hall, and from my bed I could now hear her speaking as well. Yes, she said, of course they had Winchell on. Yes, it was terrible, it was worse than they thought, but at least now it was out in the open. Yes, Herman would call as soon as the Winchell show was over.

Four consecutive times she had this conversation, but when the phone rang a fifth time, she didn't jump to answer, even though the caller had to have been another of their friends shaken by Winchell's rapid-fire disclosures—she didn't answer because the commercial was finished and she and my father were back beside the radio in the living room. And Sandy was now in the bedroom, where I pretended to be asleep while he got himself ready for bed by the night light, the small lamp with the pump-handle switch that he had made from scratch in shop class back when he was merely an artistic boy engrossed by what he could fashion with his own skillful hands and blessedly uncontaminated by ideological battling.

Our phone hadn't been used so incessantly so late at night since the death of my grandmother a couple of years back. It was close to eleven before my father had returned everyone's call, and another hour before my parents left the kitchen, where they'd been quietly conversing together, and themselves went to bed. And it was another two hours after that before I could assure myself that they were sound asleep and that, in the bed beside mine, my brother was no longer glaring at the ceiling but was also asleep, and that I could safely get up without being discovered and make my way to the back door and undo the lock and slip out of the flat and pad down the stairs into the cellar and, in the dark, steer myself barefoot across the dank floor to our storage bin.

There was nothing impulsive or hysterical driving me, nothing melodramatic about my decision, nothing reckless that I could see. People said afterward that they'd had no idea that beneath the fourth-grade patina of obedience and good manners I could be such a surprisingly irresponsible, daydreaming child. But this was no shallow daydream. I wasn't playing at make-believe, and I wasn't making mischief for mischief's sake. As it turned out, the mischief-making with Earl Axman had been valuable training but undertaken for a purpose entirely different. I surely didn't feel as though I were rushing headlong into insanity, not even when I stood in the dark bin removing my pajamas and stepping into Seldon's pants while at the same time mentally warding off the ghost of his father and trying not to be terrified by Alvin's empty wheelchair. I wasn't being swallowed up by anything other than the determination to resist a disaster our family and our friends could no longer elude and might not survive. Later my parents said, "He didn't know what he was doing," and "sleepwalking" became the official explanation. But I was fully awake and my motivation never obscure to me. All that was obscure was whether I would succeed. One of my teachers suggested that I had been suffering from "delusions of grandeur" inspired by what I was learning in school about the Underground Railroad, organized before the Civil War to assist the slaves in making their way north to freedom. Not so. I wasn't at all like Sandy, in whom opportunity had quickened the desire to be a boy on the grand scale, riding the crest of history. I wanted nothing to do with history. I wanted to be a boy on the smallest scale possible. I wanted to be an orphan.

There was only one thing I couldn't leave behind—my stamp album. Perhaps if I could have been sure that it would be preserved undisturbed after I was gone, I wouldn't, at the last moment, on the way out of my bedroom, have stopped to open my dresser drawer and, as quietly as I could, lifted it from where it was stored beneath my socks and my underclothes. But it was intolerable to think of my album ever being broken up or thrown out or, worst of all, given away wholly intact to another boy, and so I took it under my arm, and along with it the musket-shaped letter opener I'd bought at Mount Vernon whose beak of a bayonet I used to neatly slice open the only mail ever addressed to me, other than birthday cards—the packets of "approvals" sent regularly from Boston 17, Massachusetts, by "the world's largest stamp firm," H. E. Harris & Co.

I remember nothing between my stealing out of the house and starting down the empty street toward the orphanage grounds and my waking up the next day to see my grim-faced parents at the foot of my bed and to be told by a doctor busily extracting some kind of tube from my nose that I was a patient in Beth Israel Hospital and that though I probably had a terrible headache, I was going to be all right. My head did hurt, excruciatingly, but it wasn't from a blood clot's putting pressure on the brain—a possibility they feared when I was found bleeding and unconscious—and not because there was brain damage. X-rays ruled out a skull fracture and the neurological examination showed no damage to the nerves. Other than a three-inch-long laceration requiring eighteen stitches that were removed the following week, and the fact that I had no memory of the blow itself, nothing serious was wrong with me. A routine concussion, the doctor said—that's all that was causing the pain as well as the amnesia. I'd probably never remember being kicked by the horse—or the series of events leading to that collision—but the doctor said that was routine, too. Otherwise my memory was intact. Luckily. He used that word several times and it sounded like ridicule in my aching head.

They kept me for observation all that day and overnight—rousing me just about every hour to be sure I didn't slip into unconsciousness again—and the next morning I was discharged and instructed only to go easy with physical activities for a week or two. My mother had taken off from work to be with me at the hospital and she was there to take me home on the bus. Because my head didn't stop hurting for some ten days, and because there was nothing to be done about it, I was kept home from school, but otherwise I was said to be fine, and fine thanks primarily to Seldon, who, from a distance, had witnessed almost everything that I was unable to remember. If Seldon hadn't sneaked out of bed when he heard me coming down the back stairs, hadn't followed me in the dark along Summit Avenue and across the high school playing field to the Goldsmith Avenue side of the orphanage and through the unlatched gate and into the orphanage woods, I probably would have lain there unconscious in his clothes until I bled to death. Seldon ran all the way back to our house, woke my parents, who immediately dialed the operator for help, and got in our car with them and directed them to the very spot where I was. It was by then close to three in the morning and pitch black; kneeling beside me on the damp ground, my mother pressed a towel she'd brought with her against my head to stanch the bleeding while my father covered me with an old picnic blanket that was in the trunk of the car and kept me warm until the ambulance arrived. My parents organized my rescue, but Seldon Wishnow saved my life.

I had apparently startled the two horses when, disoriented, I began stumbling about in the dark where the woods opened out into the farming field, and when I turned to try to escape the horses and make it back to the street through the woods one of them reared up, I tripped and fell, and the other horse, in fleeing, nicked me with a hoof high on the back of my skull. For weeks Seldon recounted excitedly to me (and, of course, to the entire school) every detail of my nocturnal attempt to run away from home and be taken in by the nuns as a familyless child—in his telling, savoring particularly the mishap with the workhorses as well as the fact that, outdoors in the middle of the night, barefoot and in just his pajamas, he had twice traversed the mile of abrasive terrain between the orphanage woods and our house.

Unlike his mother and my parents, Seldon couldn't get over the thrill of discovering that it wasn't he who had inexplicably "lost" his clothes but I who had stolen them to use for my getaway. This utter improbability established, as never before, a value to his own existence that had previously escaped his attention. Telling the story with all the prestige of savior and co-conspirator both—and showing everyone who'd look at them his scraped feet—seemed to make Seldon significant at last even in his own eyes, a daredevil of a boy able to compel a hero's attention for the first time in his life, while I was devastated, not only by the shame of it all, which was more unbearable and longer lasting than the headache, but because my stamp album, my greatest treasure, that which I could not live without, was gone. I didn't remember having taken it with me until the day after I got home from the hospital and got up in the morning to get dressed and saw that it was missing from beneath my socks and my underwear. The reason I stored it there in the first place was so as to see it first thing every morning when I dressed for school. And now the first thing I saw on my first morning home was that the biggest thing I had ever owned was gone. Gone and irreplaceable. Like—and utterly unlike—losing a leg.

"Ma!" I shouted. "Ma! Something terrible happened!"

"What is it?" she cried, and came running from the kitchen into my room. "What's wrong?"

She thought, of course, that I'd begun to bleed from my stitches or that I was about to faint or that the headache was more than I could stand.

"My stamps!" That was all I could say, and she was able to figure out the rest.

What she did then was to go looking for them. All alone she

went into the orphanage woods and searched the ground where I'd been discovered, but she was unable to find the album anywhere— found not so much as a single stamp.

"Are you sure you had them?" she asked when she got home.

"Yes! Yes! They're there! They have to be there! I can't lose my stamps!"

"But I looked and looked. I looked everywhere."

"But who could have taken them? Where could they be? They're mine! We've got to find them! They're my stamps!"

I was inconsolable. I envisioned a horde of orphans spotting the album in the woods and tearing it apart with their filthy hands. I saw them pulling out the stamps and eating them and stomping on them and flushing them by the handful down the toilet in their terrible bathroom. They hated the album because it wasn't theirs— they hated the album because nothing was theirs.

Because I asked her to, my mother told neither my father nor my brother what had become of my stamps or about the money in Seldon's pants. "In the pocket, when we found you, there were nineteen dollars and fifty cents. I don't know where it came from and I don't want to know. That episode is over and done with. I opened a savings account for you at the Howard Savings Bank. I deposited it for you there for your future." Here she handed me a little bankbook with my name written inside it and "$19.50" the first and only item stamped in black on the deposit page. "Thank you," I said. And then she made the judgment of her second son that I believed she carried with her to her grave. "You are the strangest child," she told me. "I had no idea," she said. "I didn't begin to know." And then she handed me my letter opener, the miniaturized pewter musket from Mount Vernon. The stock was scratched and dirty and the bayonet bent slightly out of shape. She had found it that afternoon when, unknown to me, she had raced back from work at lunch hour and returned for a second time to comb through the soil of the orphanage woods in search of the tiniest remnant of the stamp collection that had dissolved into thin air.

7

The Winchell Riots

THE DAY BEFORE I discovered that my stamps were gone, I'd learned of my father's decision to quit his job. Only minutes after I got home from the hospital on Tuesday morning, he drove up to our house and into the alley in Uncle Monty's truck with the slatted-wood sides and parked it there behind Mrs. Wishnow's car, having just finished his first night of work at the Miller Street market. From then on, Sunday night through Friday morning, he'd come home at nine, ten A.M., wash up, eat his big meal, go to bed and be asleep by eleven, and when I returned from school I had to be careful not to slam the back door and wake him. A little before five in the afternoon he'd be up and gone, because by about six or seven the farmers began arriving at the market with their produce, and then anywhere from ten P.M. to four in the morning the retail grocers would be coming in to buy, along with the restaurant owners and the hotelkeepers and the last of the city's horse-and-wagon peddlers. He'd survive through the long night on the thermos of coffee and the couple of sandwiches my mother had prepared for him to take to work. On Sunday mornings he'd visit his mother at Uncle Monty's or Monty would bring her to the house to see us, and he'd spend the rest of Sunday sleeping, and again we'd have to be quiet so as not to disturb him. It was a hard life, especially since on occasion he had to drive out well before dawn to farmers in Passaic and Union counties and bring their produce in all by himself if Uncle Monty could get a better deal that way.

I knew it was a hard life because when he got home in the morning he'd have a drink. Ordinarily in our house a bottle of Four Roses lasted for years. My mother, a caricature of a teetotaler, couldn't stand the look of a foaming glass of beer, let alone the smell of straight whiskey, and when did my father ever take a drink, other than on their anniversary or when his boss came for dinner and he served him Four Roses on the rocks? But now he would get home from the market and, before he changed out of his dirty clothes and took his shower, he'd pour the whiskey into a shot glass, tilt back his head, and take it down in one gulp, making the face of a man who'd just bit into a light bulb. "Good!" he'd say aloud. "Good!" Only then could he ease up enough to eat a full meal without getting indigestion.

I was dumbfounded, and not only by the abrupt decline in my father's vocational status—not only by the truck in the alleyway and the thick-soled boots on the feet of a man who had previously gone off to work in a suit and a tie and polished black shoes, not only by the preposterousness of his slugging down his shot and having his dinner alone at ten in the morning—but by my brother as well, by *his* unforeseen transformation.

Sandy wasn't angry any longer. He wasn't contemptuous. He wasn't superior-acting in any way. It was as though he too had taken a blow to the head, but one that, instead of bringing on amnesia, had rejuvenated the quiet, conscientious boy whose satisfactions emanated not from his being a precocious big shot full of contrary opinions but from that strong, even current of an interior life that carried him steadily along from morning to night and that, in my eyes, had always made him genuinely superior to the other kids his age. Or perhaps it was that the passion for stardom—along with the capacity for conflict—had been spent; perhaps he had never possessed the necessary egoism, and was secretly relieved no longer having to be publicly stupendous. Or perhaps he'd just never believed in what he was supposed to be promulgating. Or perhaps, while I lay unconscious in the hospital with a possibly life-threatening hematoma, my father had given him the talking-to that had done the trick. Or perhaps, in the wake of the crisis I'd precipitated, he was merely concealing the stupendous self *behind* the old Sandy, masquerading, calculating, cleverly waiting in hiding until . . . until who knew what befell us next. At any rate, for now the shock of circumstances had steered my brother back into the family fold.

And my mother was no longer a working woman. There wasn't nearly what she'd hoped to accumulate in the Montreal savings account, but enough to get us across the border and started in Canada if we should have to flee at a moment's notice. She'd left her job at Hahne's no less expeditiously than my father had jettisoned the security of his twelve-year affiliation with the Metropolitan to foil the government's plans for our transfer to Kentucky and safeguard us against the anti-Semitic subterfuge that he, along with Winchell, understood Homestead 42 to be. She was back running the household full time and would once again be there when we came home for lunch and got home from school, and during the summer vacation she'd be there to monitor Sandy and me so that we didn't again spin out of control owing to lack of supervision.

A father remodeled, a brother restored, a mother recovered, eighteen black silk sutures stitched in my head and my greatest treasure irretrievably lost, and all with a wondrous fairy-tale swiftness. A family both declassed and rerooted overnight, facing neither exile nor expulsion but entrenched still on Summit Avenue, whereas in three short months, Seldon—to whom I was helplessly yoked now that he was going around the neighborhood reveling in having prevented me from bleeding to death while disguised in his clothes—Seldon was shipping out. As of September 1, Seldon would be off living with his mother, the only Jewish kid in Danville, Kentucky.

My "sleepwalking" would likely have caused an even more humiliating scandal than it did in our immediate locale had not Walter

Winchell been fired by Jergens Lotion only hours after coming off the air on the Sunday night that I'd run away. There was the truly shocking news that nobody could believe and that Winchell wasn't about to let the country forget. After ten years as America's leading radio reporter, he was replaced at nine P.M. the following Sunday by yet another dance band broadcasting from yet another sophisticated supper club on the terrace of a midtown Manhattan hotel. Jergens's first charge against him was that a broadcaster with a weekly nationwide audience of more than twenty-five million had essentially "cried fire in a crowded theater"; the second was that he had slandered a president of the United States with malicious accusations "that only the most outrageous demagogue would contrive to arouse the passions of the mob."

Even the moderate *New York Times,* a paper founded and owned by Jews—and highly esteemed for that reason by my father—and by no means uncritical of Lindbergh's policy toward Hitler's Germany, announced its unqualified support of the action taken by Jergens Lotion in an editorial entitled "A Professional Disgrace." "A competition has been in progress for some time," wrote the *Times,*

> among anti-Lindbergh entrepreneurs to determine who can produce the most outrageous accounts of the motives of the Lindbergh administration. With one bombastic stride, Walter Winchell has moved to the head of the pack. The borderline scruples and questionable taste of Mr. Winchell have tumbled over into an outburst of vitriol that is as unpardonable as it is unethical. With accusations so far-fetched that even a lifelong Democrat may find himself feeling unexpected sympathy for the president, Winchell has disgraced himself irredeemably. Jergens Lotion is to be commended for the speed with which it has removed him from the airwaves. Journalism as it is practiced by the Walter Winchells of this country is an insult as much to our enlightened citizenry as to the journalistic standards of accuracy, fairness, and responsibility, toward which Mr. Win-

chell, his cynical tabloid cohorts, and their money-hungry
publishers have always displayed the utmost contempt.

In a subsequent attack delivered on behalf of the Lindbergh administration and published by the *Times* as the first and lengthiest
of the letters elicited by its editorial, one eminent correspondent,
after alluding gratefully to the editorial and reinforcing its argument by further examples of Winchell's ostentatious abuse of the
First Amendment, concluded: "The attempt to inflame and frighten
his fellow Jews is no less detestable than the disregard for the
norms of decency that your paper so forcefully condemns. Certainly nothing is so heinous as preying upon the historical fears of
a persecuted people, particularly when full participation in an
open society free of oppression is precisely what the present administration is working to achieve for this same group through the
efforts of the Office of American Absorption. For Walter Winchell
to characterize Homestead 42, a program designed to broaden and
enrich the involvement of America's proud Jewish citizens in the
national life, as a fascistic strategy to isolate Jews and exclude them
from the national life is the height of journalistic recklessness and
an illustration of the Big Lie technique that is today the greatest
threat to democratic freedom everywhere."

The letter was signed "Rabbi Lionel Bengelsdorf, Director, Office of American Absorption, Department of the Interior, Washington, D.C."

Winchell's response came in the column he wrote for the *Daily
Mirror*, the New York paper belonging to America's wealthiest publisher, William Randolph Hearst, who owned a chain of some thirty
right-wing papers and half a dozen popular magazines as well as
King Features, where Winchell was syndicated and read by many
millions more. Hearst despised Winchell's political allegiances,
particularly his glorification of FDR, and would have fired him
years earlier had it not been that the very New Yorkers for whose
nickels the *Mirror* competed against the *Daily News* found irresistible the gutter charm of the columnist's singular concoction of

muckraking contentiousness and cloying patriotism. According to Winchell, why Hearst finally did fire him had less to do with the long-standing animosity between the columnist and his publisher than with pressure from the White House that even a ruthless old tycoon as powerful as Hearst could not dare to resist for fear of the consequences.

"The Lindbergh fascists"—so began the characteristically brazen, unregenerate Winchell column published just days after he'd lost his radio contract—"have openly begun their Nazi assault on freedom of expression. Today Winchell's the enemy to be silenced . . . Winchell 'the warmonger,' 'the liar,' 'the alarmist,' 'the Commie,' 'the kike.' Today yours truly, tomorrow every newscaster and reporter who dares to tell the truth about the fascist plot to destroy American democracy. Honorary Aryans like the rabid rabbi Lyin' Lionel B. and the snooty Park Avenue proprietors of the gutless *New York Times* aren't the first ultracivilized Jewish Quislings to grovel before an anti-Semitic master because they're just too, too refined to fight like Winchell . . . and they won't be the last. The jerks at Jergens aren't the first corporate cowards to play ball with the dictatorial lying machine that is now ruining this country . . . and they won't be the last, either."

And that column—which proceeded to list some fifteen more of his personal enemies who qualified as America's leading fascist collaborators—was, in fact, to be *his* last.

Three days later, after visiting Hyde Park to make certain that FDR was still determined not to come out of political retirement to run for a third term, Winchell announced his candidacy for president of the United States in the next general election. Until then, those considered in the running were Roosevelt's secretary of state, Cordell Hull; the former secretary of agriculture and the vice presidential candidate on the 1940 ticket, Henry Wallace; Roosevelt's postmaster general and the chairman of the Democratic Party, James Farley; Supreme Court Justice William O. Douglas; and two middle-of-the-road Democrats, neither of them New Dealers, former Indiana governor Paul V. McNutt and Senator Scott W. Lucas of Illinois. There was also an unconfirmed report (circulated and perhaps originated by Winchell back when he was still making $800,000 a year circulating unconfirmed reports) that should the convention wind up deadlocked, as could easily happen with so unexciting a slate of candidates, Eleanor Roosevelt, a forceful political and diplomatic presence during her husband's two terms—and still a popular figure whose blend of outspokenness and aristocratic reserve had gained her an enormous following among the party's liberal constituency as well as numerous mocking enemies in the right-wing press—would appear on the convention floor the way Lindbergh did at the 1940 Republican Convention and sweep the nomination by acclamation. But once Walter Winchell became the first Democratic candidate to enter the race, and to do so almost thirty months in advance of the '44 election, in advance even of the midterm congressional elections—and to do so immediately after the noisy fracas that resulted from his having been "purged" from his profession by "the strong-arm putsch tactics of the fascist gang in the White House" (as Winchell described his enemies and their methods in announcing his candidacy)—the one-time gossip columnist became the man to beat, the only Democrat with a name known to everyone and audacious enough to assault with ferocity an incumbent as beloved as Lindy.

Republican leaders didn't deign to take Winchell seriously, assuming either that the irrepressible performer was putting on a self-glorifying sideshow to sucker funds out of a handful of rich diehard Democrats or that he was a flamboyant stalking horse for FDR (or perhaps for Roosevelt's ambitious wife), at once stirring up and measuring whatever underground anti-Lindbergh sentiment might possibly exist in a nation where polls showed that Lindbergh continued to be supported by a record eighty to ninety percent of every classification and category of voter, except the Jews. Winchell, in short, was the candidate of the Jews, and himself a Jew of the coarsest type, in no way resembling the inner circle of well-bred, dignified Jewish Democrats like Roosevelt's wealthy friend Bernard Baruch or the banker and New York governor Herbert Lehman or the recently retired Supreme Court justice Louis Brandeis. And as if being a Jew of no background who embodied just about every vulgar trait that made Jews less than welcome in the better strata of American social and business society weren't enough to render him an irrelevant impertinence on the political scene anywhere other than the heavily Jewish precincts of New York City, there was his reputation as an adulterous philanderer with a penchant for seducing long-legged showgirls and his profligate nightlife among the loose-living Hollywood and Broadway celebrities who drank to all hours at New York's Stork Club to make him anathema to the straitlaced multitude. His candidacy was a joke and the Republicans treated it as nothing more.

But on our street that week, in the immediate aftermath of the firing of Winchell and his instantaneous resurrection as a presidential candidate, the significance of the two events was almost all that neighbors could talk about among themselves. After nearly two years of never knowing whether to believe the worst, of trying to focus on the demands of their day-to-day lives and then helplessly absorbing every rumor about what the government had in store for them, of never being able to justify either their alarm or their composure with hard fact—after so much perplexity, they were so ripe for delusion that, when the parents gathered on their beach chairs to chat together in the alleyways at night, the guessing game that invariably started up could go on without letup for hours: Who would be vice president on the Winchell ticket? Whom would he appoint to his cabinet? Whom would he appoint to the Supreme Court? Who would turn out to be the greater leader, FDR or Walter Winchell? They plunged headlong into a thousand fantasies, and the very small children also caught the spirit and went skipping and dancing about, chanting, "Wind-shield for pres-i-dent . . . Wind-shield for pres-i-dent." Of course, that no Jew could ever be elected to the presidency—least of all a Jew with a mouth as unstoppable as Winchell's—even a kid as young as I was already accepted, as if the proscription were laid out in so many words in the U.S. Constitution. Yet not even that ironclad certainty could stop the adults from abandoning common sense and, for a night or two, imagining themselves and their children as native-born citizens of Paradise.

The wedding of Rabbi Bengelsdorf and Aunt Evelyn took place on a Sunday in the middle of June. My parents were not invited, nor did they expect or want to be, and yet nothing could be done to ease my mother's distress. I'd overheard her crying from behind her bedroom door before, and though it wasn't a usual occurrence or one I liked, in all the months during which my parents struggled to assess the menace posed by the Lindbergh administration and to determine the response sensible for a Jewish family to take, I'd never known her to be so inconsolable. "Why does this have to happen too?" she asked my father. "They're only getting married," he told her. "It isn't the end of the world." "But I can't stop thinking about my father," she said. "Your father died," he said, "my father died. They weren't young men, they got sick and they died." It would have been hard to imagine a tone any more sympathetic than his, but her misery was such that the gentler his voice, the worse she suffered. "And I think," she said, "about my mother, how Momma wouldn't know what to make of anything anymore." "Honey, it could all be a lot more terrible—you know that." "And it will be," my mother said. "Maybe not, maybe not. Maybe everything is starting to change. Winchell—" "Oh, please, Walter Winchell won't—" "Shhh, shhh," he said to her, "the little one."

And so I understood that Walter Winchell wasn't, in fact, the candidate of the Jews—he was the candidate of the children of the Jews, something we were being given to clutch at, the way not too many years before we'd been given the breast not merely for nutrients but for the alleviation of babyhood's fears.

The wedding ceremony was held at the rabbi's temple and the reception afterward in the ballroom of the Essex House, Newark's most luxurious hotel. The notables who attended, each accompanied by a wife or a husband, were listed inside a box separate from the wedding story itself and directly beside photographs of the bride and groom that appeared in the *Newark Sunday Call.* The list was surprisingly long and impressive, and I present it here to explain why I, for one, had to wonder if my parents and their Metropolitan friends weren't completely out of touch with reality to imagine that any harm could befall them because of a government program being administered by a luminary of the stature of Rabbi Bengelsdorf.

To begin with, there were Jews in abundance at the wedding ceremony, among them family and friends, congregants from Rabbi Bengelsdorf's temple, admirers and colleagues from around New Jersey, and others who had traveled from all over the country to be present. And many Christians were there as well. And, according to the article in the *Sunday Call*—which took up one and a half of the two society pages that day—among the several invited guests who were unable to attend but who sent their best wishes through Western Union, was the wife of the president, the First Lady, Anne Morrow Lindbergh, identified as a close friend of the rabbi's, "a fellow New Jerseyite and a fellow poet" with whom he shared "cultural and intellectual interests" and met frequently "over afternoon tea for a White House tête-à-tête to discuss philosophy, literature, religion, and ethics."

Representing the city were the two highest-ranking Jews ever in Newark's government, the two-term ex-mayor, Meyer Ellenstein, and the city clerk, Harry S. Reichenstein, and five of the slew of Irishmen currently most prominent in the city, the director of Public Safety, the director of the Department of Revenue and Finance, the director of Parks and Public Property, the city's chief engineer, and the corporation counsel. Newark's federal postmaster was there, and the head librarian of the Newark Public Library as well as the president of the library's board of trustees. Among the distinguished educators attending the wedding were the president of the University of Newark, the president of Newark College of Engineering, the superintendent of schools, and the headmaster of

St. Benedict's Prep. And an array of distinguished clergymen—
Protestant, Catholic, and Jewish—were also among those present.
From the First Baptist Peddie Memorial Church, the city's largest
Negro congregation, there was Reverend George E. Dawkins; from
Trinity Cathedral, Reverend Arthur Dumper; from Grace Episco-
pal Church, Reverend Charles L. Gomph; from St. Nicholas Greek
Orthodox Church, on High Street, Reverend George E. Spyridakis;
and from St. Patrick's Cathedral, the Very Reverend John Delaney.

Absent—and glaringly so to my parents, though nowhere al-
luded to in the newspaper story—was Rabbi Bengelsdorf's an-
tagonist and the foremost of Newark's rabbis, Joachim Prinz of
Congregation B'nai Abraham. Before Rabbi Bengelsdorf's rise to national prominence, Rabbi Prinz's authority among Jews throughout the city, in the wider Jewish community, and among scholars
and theologians of every religion had far exceeded his elder col-
league's, and it was he alone of the Conservative rabbis leading the
city's three wealthiest congregations who had never flinched in his
opposition to Lindbergh. The other two, Charles I. Hoffman of
Oheb Shalom and Solomon Foster of B'nai Jeshurun, were in attendance, however, and Rabbi Foster presided over the wedding
ceremony.

Present as well were the presidents of Newark's four major
banks, the presidents of two of its largest insurance companies, the
president of its biggest architecture firm, the two founding part-
ners of its most prestigious law firm, the president of the Newark
Athletic Club, the owner of three of the big downtown movie
houses, the president of the Chamber of Commerce, the president
of New Jersey Bell Telephone, the editors in chief of the two daily
papers, and the president of P. Ballantine, Newark's most famous
brewery. From the Essex County government there was the supervisor of the Board of Freeholders and three members of the board,
and from the New Jersey judiciary were the vice chancellor of the
Court of Chancery and an associate justice from the state's Supreme Court. From the State Assembly there was the majority
speaker and three of the four assemblymen from Essex County,

and from the State Senate a representative from Essex County. The ranking state official was a Jew, Attorney General David T. Wilentz, who had successfully led the prosecution of Bruno Hauptmann, but the state official whose presence most impressed me was Abe J. Greene, another Jew but more importantly New Jersey's boxing commissioner. One of Jersey's two U.S. senators was there, the Republican W. Warren Barbour, as was our congressman Robert W. Kean. From the District Court of the United States for the District of New Jersey there was a circuit judge, two district judges, and the district attorney (whose name I recognized from listening to *Gangbusters*), John J. Quinn.

A number of close associates of the rabbi at the national headquarters of the OAA and several officials representing the Department of the Interior had come up from Washington, and though there was nobody at the wedding from the very highest echelons of the federal government, there was an eloquent proxy representing no less a personage than the president himself: the telegram from the First Lady that was read aloud by Rabbi Foster at the reception, after which reading the wedding guests rose spontaneously to applaud the First Lady's sentiments and were then asked by the groom to remain standing and to join with him and his bride in singing the National Anthem.

The lengthy text of the telegram was carried in full by the *Sunday Call*. It went as follows:

My dear Rabbi Bengelsdorf and Evelyn:

My husband and I send you our heartfelt best wishes, and we join in wishing you the most blissful happiness.

We were delighted to have an opportunity to meet Evelyn at the White House State Dinner for the German Foreign Minister. She is an enchanting, energetic young woman, clearly a most worthy and upright person, and it took no more than the few moments I spent chatting with her for me to recognize the gifts of personality and intellect that won her the devotion of a man as extraordinary as Lionel Bengelsdorf.

I recall today the splendidly succinct lines of poetry my meeting with Evelyn brought to mind that evening. The poet is Elizabeth Barrett Browning, and the words with which she begins the fourteenth of her *Sonnets from the Portuguese* embody just such womanly wisdom as I saw emanating from Evelyn's astonishingly dark and beautiful eyes. "If thou must love me," wrote Mrs. Browning, "let it be for naught/ Except for love's sake only . . ."

Rabbi Bengelsdorf, you have been more than a friend since we met here in the White House after the ceremony establishing the Office of American Absorption; since your moving to Washington to become the OAA director, you have been an invaluable mentor. Our engrossing conversations, along with the enlightening books you have generously given me to read, have taught me much, not just about the Jewish faith but about the tribulations of the Jewish people and the sources of the great spiritual strength which has been the mainspring of their survival for three thousand years. I am all the richer for having discovered through you how profoundly rooted my own religious heritage is in yours.

Our greatest mission as Americans is to live in harmony and brotherhood as a united people. I know from the excellent work you are both doing for the OAA how dedicated the two of you are to helping us achieve this precious goal. Of the many blessings bestowed upon our nation by God, none is more valuable than our having among us citizens like yourselves, proud, vital champions of an indomitable race whose ancient concepts of justice and freedom have sustained our American democracy since 1776.

> With every best wish,
> Anne Morrow Lindbergh

The second time the FBI entered our lives, it was my father who was under surveillance. The same agent who'd stopped to question me about Alvin, on the day that Mr. Wishnow hanged himself (and who'd questioned Sandy on the bus, my mother at the store, and my father at the office), showed up at the produce market and hung around the diner where the men would go to eat and get coffee in the middle of the night and, behaving as he'd done when Alvin began working for Uncle Monty, started asking around now about Alvin's uncle Herman and what he was saying to people about America and our president. Word got back to Uncle Monty through one of Longy Zwillman's henchmen, who passed on to Uncle Monty what Agent McCorkle had reported to him—namely, that after having housed and fed a traitor who'd fought for a foreign country, my father had now quit a good job with Metropolitan Life rather than participate in a government program designed to unify and strengthen the American people. Uncle Monty told Longy's guy that his brother was a poor schnook with no education who had two kids and a wife to support and couldn't do much harm to America by schlepping produce crates six nights a week. And Longy's guy listened sympathetically, according to Uncle Monty, who, with none of the decorum ordinarily practiced in our house, told us the whole story in our kitchen one Saturday afternoon—"and still the guy says to me, 'Your brother's gotta go.' So I told him, 'This is all bullshit. Tell Longy this is all part of the bullshit against Jews.' And the guy is himself a Jew, Niggy Apfelbaum, but what I say does not make a dent. Niggy goes back to Longy, and he tells him Roth don't do as he's told. What happens next? The Long One himself shows up, right there in my stinky little office and wearing a silk handmade suit. Tall, soft-spoken, dressed to kill—you see how he gets the movie stars. I said to him, 'I remember you from grade school, Longy. I could see even then you were going places.' So Longy says to me, 'I remember you, too. I could see even then you were going nowhere.' We started to laugh, and I told him, 'My brother needs a job, Longy. Can I not give my own brother a job?' 'And can I not have the FBI snooping around?' he asks me. 'I know all this,' I say, 'and didn't I get rid of my nephew Alvin because of the FBI? But with my own brother, it's not the

same, is it? Look,' I tell him, 'twenty-four hours and I'll fix everything. If I don't, if I can't, Herman goes.' So I wait till after we close
up the next morning, and I walk over to Sammy Eagle's, and sitting
at the bar is the mick shmegeggy from the FBI. 'Let me buy your
breakfast,' I tell him, and I order him a boilermaker, and I sit down
next to him and I say, 'What do you got against Jews, McCorkle?'
'Nothing,' he says. 'Then why are you after my brother like this?
What did he do to anybody?' 'Look, if I had something against
Jews, would I be sitting here in Eagle's, would Sammy Eagle be my
friend if I did?' He calls down the bar for Eagle to come over. 'Tell
him,' McCorkle says, 'do I have anything against Jews?' 'Not that I
know,' Eagle says. 'When your boy had the bar mitzvah, didn't I
come and give him a tie clasp?' 'He still wears it,' Eagle tells me.
'See?' McCorkle says. 'I'm just doing my job, the way Sammy does
his and you do yours.' 'And that's all my brother is doing,' I tell him.
'Fine. Good. So don't say I'm against the Jews.' 'My error,' I tell him,
'I apologize.' And meantime I slip him the envelope, the little
brown envelope, and that's that."

Here my uncle turned to me and said, "I understand you're a
horse thief. I understand you stole a horse from the church. Smart
boy. Let me see." I leaned over and showed him where the horse's
hoof had opened up my head. He laughed when he ran his finger
lightly over the length of the scar and around the shaved patch
where the hair was just growing in. "May you have many more," he
told me—and then, as he'd been doing for as long as I could remember, he lifted me roughly onto one of his knees so that I could
straddle it like, of all things, a horse. "You been to a bris, ain't you?"
he asked, and began to give me the up-and-down ride by raising
and lowering his thigh. "You know when they circumcise the baby
at the bris, you know what they do, don't you?" "They cut off the
foreskin," I said. "And what do they do with the little foreskin? After
it's off—do you know what they do?" "No," I told him. "Well," said
Uncle Monty, "they save them up, and when they got enough they
give them to the FBI to make agents out of." I couldn't help myself,
and even though I knew I wasn't supposed to—and even though

last time he'd told me the joke, he'd said, "They send them to Ireland to make priests out of"—I began to laugh. "What was in the envelope?" I asked him. "Take a guess," he said. "I don't know. Money?" "Money is right. You're a bright little horse thief. The money that makes all trouble go away."

Only later did I learn from my brother, who'd overheard my parents talking in their bedroom, that the full amount of the bribe given to McCorkle was to be repaid to Uncle Monty, out of my father's already paltry paycheck, at the rate of ten dollars per week over the next six months. And my father could do nothing about it. About the laboriousness of the work, about the mortifications attendant upon serving his brother, all he ever said was "He's been this way since he's ten years old, he'll be this way till he dies."

Aside from Saturdays and Sunday mornings, my father was hardly to be seen that summer. My mother, on the other hand, was now around all the time, and since Sandy and I had to be home at noon for lunch and again in the midafternoon to check in with her and be accounted for, neither of us could stray very far, and in the evenings we were forbidden to go anywhere beyond the school playing field a block from the house. Either my mother was keeping a very strict vigil over herself or she'd managed temporarily to make peace with all her chagrin, because though my father had taken a steep pay cut and the household budget required some difficult trimming, she showed no disabling signs of the improbabilities she'd confronted over the past year. Her resilience had a lot to do with her being back at a job whose compensations mattered more to her than those derived from selling dresses, work she hadn't shrunk from doing but that seemed to her meaningless measured against her normal pursuits. Just how troubling her worries continued to be would only be clear to me when a letter arrived from Estelle Tirschwell, reporting on the family's progress in Winnipeg. Every lunchtime I brought the mail upstairs with me from our mailbox in the front entryway, and if there was an envelope bearing Canadian postage, she immediately sat down at the

kitchen table and, while Sandy and I ate our sandwiches, read the
letter to herself twice over, then folded it up to carry around in her
apron pocket to look at another ten times before passing it on to
my father to read when he got up to go to the market—the letter
for my father, the canceled Canadian stamps for me, to help get me
started on a new collection.

Sandy's friends were suddenly the girls his age, the teenage girls
whom he knew from school but had never examined so covetously
before. He went to find them at the playground where the organized summer activities took place all day and into the early evening. I was there too, accompanied regularly now by Seldon. I'd
watch Sandy with fluctuating feelings of trepidation and delight, as
though my own brother had become a pickpocket or a professional
shill. He'd park himself on a bench near the ping-pong table, where
the girls tended to congregate, and he'd start making pencil drawings in his sketchpad of the cutest around; invariably they'd want
to see the drawings, and so before the day was over, chances were
good he'd be walking dreamily out of the playground hand in hand
with one of them. Sandy's strong proclivity for infatuation was no
longer galvanized by propagandizing for Just Folks or topping tobacco for the Mawhinneys but fomented by these girls. Either the
fresh excitement of desire had transformed his existence with the
same incredible swiftness that Kentucky had and, at fourteen and
a half, he'd been recast anew in a single hormonal blast or, as I believed—with my own proclivity to grant him omnipotence—getting girls to go off with him was simply an amusing ruse, how he
was biding his time until . . . Always with Sandy I thought there
must be a great deal more going on than I could begin to understand, when in fact, despite the handsome boy's air of self-assur-
ance, he had no more idea than anyone else why he took the bait.
Lindbergh's Jewish tobacco farmer discovers breasts, and suddenly
he turns up as just another teenager.

My parents ascribed the girl-craziness to defiance, to "rebel-
liousness," to a compensatory display of independence following
his forced retirement from the Lindbergh cause, and seemed will-

ing to consider it relatively harmless. One of the girls' mothers felt otherwise evidently, and called to say so. When my father got home from work, there was a long conversation between my mother and father behind their bedroom door, and then another between my brother and my father behind the bedroom door, and for the rest of the week Sandy was not allowed to leave the vicinity of the house. But they couldn't, of course, keep him cooped up on Summit Avenue for the whole of the summer, and soon he was back at the playground confidently drawing pictures of the pretty ones, and whatever these girls allowed him to do with his hands when they went off by themselves—which couldn't have been much for eighth-graders as ignorant of sex as kids that young were back in those years—they didn't rush home to report, and so there were no more excited phone calls for my parents to contend with in the midst of all their other troubles.

Seldon. Seldon was *my* summer. Seldon's muzzle in my face like a dog's, and kids I'd known all my life laughing and calling me Sleepy, kids with their arms raised stiffly out in front of them and walking with slow, clumpy, zombie steps, supposedly in imitation of me lurching toward the orphanage in my sleep, and the team in the field all chanting "Hi ho Silver!" whenever I came to bat in a choose-up game.

There would be no big end-of-summer picnic up at the South Mountain Reservation on Labor Day that year because all of my parents' Metropolitan friends had left Newark with their boys by September to settle in around the country before the start of the school year. One by one, throughout that summer, each of the families drove up on a Saturday to visit and say goodbye. It was awful for my parents, who alone of the group from the local Metropolitan district designated for relocation by Homestead 42 had chosen to stay where we were. These were their dearest friends, and the hot Saturday afternoons with the tearful adults embracing out on the street while all the children forlornly looked on—afternoons that ended with the four of us who were remaining behind waving goodbye from the curb as my mother called after the departing car, "Don't forget to write!"—were the most harrowing moments so far, when our defenselessness became real to me and I sensed the beginning of the destruction of our world. And when I realized that my father, of all these men, was the most obstinate, helplessly bonded to his better instincts and their excessive demands. I only then understood that he had quit his job not merely because he was fearful of what awaited us down the line should we agree like the others to be relocated but because, for better or worse, when he was bullied by superior forces that he deemed corrupt it was his nature not to yield—in this instance, to resist either running away to Canada, as my mother urged our doing, or bowing to a government directive that was patently unjust. There were two types of strong men: those like Uncle Monty and Abe Steinheim, remorseless about their making money, and those like my father, ruthlessly obedient to their idea of fair play.

"Come," my father said, trying to perk us up on the Saturday when the last of the six homesteading families had seemingly vanished forever. "Come on, boys. We're going out for ice cream." The four of us walked down Chancellor to the drugstore, where the pharmacist was one of his oldest insurance customers and where in summertime it was generally more pleasant than it was out on the street, what with the awnings unfurled to prevent the sun's rays from piercing the plate glass window and the paddle blades of the three ceiling fans creaking softly as they revolved overhead. We slipped into a booth and ordered sundaes, and though my mother could not bring herself to eat despite my father's prompting, she was able eventually to stop the tears from running down her face. We, after all, were no less enjoined to an unknowable future than were our exiled friends, and so we sat spooning our sundaes in the awninged semidarkness of the cool pharmacy, everyone speechless and completely spent, until my mother at last looked up from the paper napkin she was neatly shredding and, with that wry, stripped-down smile that comes when one is entirely cried out, said to my father, "Well, like it or not, Lindbergh is teaching us what it is to be

Jews." Then she added, "We only think we're Americans." "Nonsense. No!" my father replied. "*They* think we only think we're Americans. It is not up for discussion, Bess. It is not up for negotiation. These people are not understanding that I take this for *granted,* goddamnit! Others? He dares to call us *others? He's* the other. The one who looks most American—and he's the one who is least American! The man is unfit. He shouldn't be there. He shouldn't be there, and it's as simple as that!"

For me the hardest departure to stomach was Seldon's. Of course I was delighted to see him go. All summer long I'd been counting the days. Yet that early morning in the last week of August when the Wishnows drove off with two mattresses strapped to the car roof (lifted there and tied down beneath a tarp the night before by my father and Sandy) and clothing jammed to the top of the old Plymouth's back seat (stacks of clothing, including several items of my own, that my mother and I had helped them to carry from the house), I was the one, grotesquely enough, who couldn't stop crying. I was remembering an afternoon when Seldon and I were just six years old, and Mr. Wishnow was alive and seemingly well and still working every day for the Metropolitan, and Mrs. Wishnow was still a housewife like my mother, absorbed by her family's everyday needs and even, on occasion, looking after me if my mother had to be off doing her PTA work and Sandy wasn't around and I was home by myself after school. I was remembering the generic maternalism that she shared with my mother—the succoring warmth I wallowed in as a matter of course—and that I experienced so strikingly on the afternoon that I got stuck in their bathroom and couldn't get out. I was remembering how kind she'd been to me while I repeatedly tried and failed to open the door, spontaneously caring for me as though, regardless of differences in appearance and temperament and immediate circumstance, the four of us—Seldon and Selma, Philip and Bess—were all one and the same. I was remembering Mrs. Wishnow when what was uppermost in her mind was what was uppermost in my mother's mind—back when she was just another watchful member of the local matriarchy whose overriding task was to establish a domestic way of life for the next generation. I was remembering Mrs. Wishnow unperturbed, when her fists weren't clenched and her face full of pain.

It was a small bathroom, exactly like ours, quite confining, the door next to a toilet and the toilet abutting a sink and a bathtub squeezed in beside that. I pulled on the door but it didn't open. At home I would just have closed it behind me, but at the Wishnows' I locked it—something I'd never done before in my life. I locked it and I peed and I flushed and I washed my hands and, because I didn't want to touch their towel, wiped them dry on the back of the legs of my corduroys—everything was fine, and then I went to exit the bathroom, and I couldn't undo the lock above the doorknob. I could turn it a little ways but then it would catch and stop. I didn't bang on the door or rattle the doorknob, I just kept trying to turn the lock as quietly as I could. But it wouldn't go, and so I sat back down on the toilet and I thought that maybe it would somehow work itself out. I sat there for a while but then I got lonesome and stood up and tried the lock again. It still wouldn't uncatch, and I started to knock lightly on the door, and Mrs. Wishnow came and said, "Oh, the lock on the door does that sometimes. You have to turn it like this." She explained how to do it, but I still couldn't get it open, and so very calmly she said, "No, Philip, while you're turn-ing it you have to pull it *back*," and though I tried to do as she told me it still didn't work. "Dear," she said, "turn and back simultane-ously—turn and back at the same time." "Which way is back?" I said. "Back. Back towards the wall." "Oh, the wall. Okay," I said, but I couldn't get it right no matter what I did. "It won't work," I said, and I began to sweat, and then I heard Seldon. "Philip? It's Seldon. Why did you lock it? We weren't going to come in." "I didn't say you were," I said. "Then why did you lock it?" "I don't know," I said. "Do you think we should call the fire department, Mom? They can get him out with a ladder." "No, no, no," Mrs. Wishnow said. "Come on, Philip," Seldon said, "it's not that hard." "But it is. It's stuck." "How's he gonna get out, Ma?" "Seldon, be still. Philip?"

"Yes." "Are you all right?" "Well, it's hot in here. It's getting hot." "Take a glass of cold water, dear. There's a glass in the medicine cabinet. Take a glass of water and slowly drink it and you'll be fine." "Okay." But the glass had something slimy at the bottom, and though I took it out, I only pretended to drink from it and drank instead from my cupped hands. "Ma," Seldon said, "what's he doing wrong? Philip, what are you doing wrong?" "How do I know?" I said. "Mrs. Wishnow? Mrs. Wishnow?" "Yes, dear." "It's getting too hot in here. I'm really starting to sweat." "Then open the window. Open the little window in the shower. Are you tall enough to do that?" "I think so." I took off my shoes and stepped into the shower in just my socks, and standing on my tiptoes I was able to reach the window—a smallish window of pebbled glass that looked onto the alleyway—but when I tried to open it, it was stuck too. "It won't go," I said. "Bang it a little, dear. Bang the frame at the bottom, but not too hard, and I'm sure it will open." I did as she told me but couldn't get it to budge. By now my shirt was saturated with sweat, and so I angled myself to be able to give the window a good strong shove upwards, but in turning I must have struck the shower handle with my elbow because suddenly the water was on. "Oh, no!" I said, and ice-cold water was pouring over my head and down the back of my shirt, and I jumped out of the shower and onto the tile floor. "What happened, dear?" "The shower started." "How?" Seldon said. "How could the shower start?" "I don't know!" "Are you very wet?" she asked me. "Sort of." "Get a towel," she told me. "Get a towel out of the closet. The towels are in the closet." We had the same narrow little bathroom closet directly upstairs over the Wishnows' bathroom closet, and we used it for towels too, but when I went to open theirs, I couldn't—the door was stuck. I yanked but it wouldn't open. "What is it now, Philip?" "Nothing." I couldn't tell her. "Did you take a towel?" "Yes." "Then dry yourself off. And you must stay calm. There's nothing to worry about." "I am calm." "Sit down. Sit down and dry yourself off." I was soaking wet, and now the floor was getting wet, and I sat on the toilet seat, and that's when I saw a bathroom for what it is—the upper end of a sewer—

and that's when I felt the tears begin to well up. "Don't worry," Seldon called in to me, "your mother and father will be home soon." "But how will I get *out?*" And all at once the door was open—and there was Seldon and behind him his mother. "How'd you do that?" I said. "I opened the door," he said. "But how?" He shrugged. "I pushed. I just pushed. It was open all the time." And that was when I began to bawl and Mrs. Wishnow took me in her arms and said, "That's okay. Things like this happen. They can happen to anyone." "It was open, Ma," Seldon said to her. "Shhh," she told him. "Shhh. It doesn't matter," and then she came into the bathroom and turned off the cold water—which was still streaming into the tub—and, without any problem she opened the closet door and took out a fresh towel and began to dry my hair and my face and my neck, all the while gently telling me that it didn't matter and that these things happened to people all the time.

But that was long before everything else went wrong.

The congressional campaign began at eight A.M. the Tuesday after Labor Day, with Walter Winchell up on a soapbox at Broadway and 42nd Street—the celebrated crossroads where he'd announced his presidential candidacy from atop the very same genuine wooden soapbox—and looking in broad daylight exactly as press photos pictured him broadcasting from the NBC studio Sunday nights at nine: jacketless, in his shirtsleeves, with the cuffs rolled up and his tie yanked down and, pushed back from his forehead, the hard-boiled newsman's fedora. Within only minutes some half-dozen mounted New York City policemen were already needed to divert traffic away from the eager stream of working people charging onto the street to hear and see him in the flesh. And once word spread that the orator with the bullhorn wasn't just another Bible bore prophesying doom for sinful America but the Stork Club habitué only recently the country's most influential radio broadcaster and the city's most nefarious tabloid journalist, the number of onlookers grew from the hundreds to the thousands—nearly ten thousand people all told, said the papers, up from the subways and emptying out of the buses, drawn by the maverick and his immoderation.

"The broadcasting cowards," he told them, "and the billionaire publishing hooligans controlled from the White House by the Lindbergh gang say Winchell was canned for crying 'Fire!' in a crowded theater. Mr. and Mrs. New York City, the word wasn't 'fire.' It was 'fascism' Winchell cried—and it still is. Fascism! Fascism! And I will continue crying 'fascism' to every crowd of Americans I can find until Herr Lindbergh's pro-Hitler party of treason is driven from the Congress on Election Day. The Hitlerites can take away my radio microphone, and they've done just that, as you know. They can take away my newspaper column, and they have done that, as you know. And when, God forbid, America goes fascist, Lindbergh's storm troopers can lock me away in a concentration camp to shut me up—and they will do that too, as you know. They can even lock *you* away in a concentration camp to shut *you* up. And I hope by now that you damn well know that. But what our homegrown Hitlerites cannot take away is my love for America and yours. My love for democracy and yours. My love for freedom and yours. What they cannot take away—unless the gullible and the sheepish and the terrified are patsies enough to return them to Washington one more time—is the power of the ballot box. The Hitlerite plot against America must be stopped—and stopped by you! By you, Mr. and Mrs. New York! By the voting power of the freedom-loving people of this great city on Tuesday, November 3, nineteen hundred and forty-two!"

All that day—September 8, 1942—and into the evening, Winchell climbed atop his soapbox in every neighborhood in Manhattan, from Wall Street, where he was largely ignored, to Little Italy, where he was shouted down, to Greenwich Village, where he was ridiculed, to the Garment District, where he was intermittently cheered, to the Upper West Side, where he was welcomed as their savior by the Roosevelt Jews, and eventually north to Harlem, where, in the crowd of several hundred Negroes who gathered at dusk to hear him speak at the corner of Lenox Avenue and 125th

Street, a few laughed and a handful applauded but most remained respectfully dissatisfied, as though to work his way into their antipathies would require his delivering a very different spiel.

It was difficult to ascertain the impact Winchell made on the voting public that day. To Winchell's former paper, Hearst's *Daily Mirror,* the ostensible effort to gather local grass-roots support for routing the Republican Party from Congress nationwide looked more like a publicity stunt than anything else—a predictably egomaniacal publicity stunt by an unemployed gossip columnist who could not bear being out of the spotlight—and especially so since not a single Democratic congressional candidate running for election in Manhattan chose to appear anywhere within hearing distance of the Winchell bullhorn. If any candidates were out campaigning, they stayed far from wherever Winchell repeatedly committed the political blunder of associating the name of Adolf Hitler with that of an American president whose heroics the world still idolized, whose achievement even the Führer respected, and whom an overwhelming majority of his countrymen continued to adore as their nation's godlike catalyst of peace and prosperity. In a brief, sardonic editorial, "At It Again," the *New York Times* was able to reach but one conclusion about the latest of Winchell's "self-serving shenanigans": "There is nothing Walter Winchell has more talent for," wrote the *Times,* "than himself."

Winchell spent a full day in each of the other four boroughs of the city, and the following week headed north to Connecticut. Though still in want of a Democratic candidate willing to wed a fledgling congressional campaign to his inflammatory rhetoric, Winchell went ahead to set up his soapbox outside the gates to the factories of Bridgeport and at the entrance to the shipyards in New London, where he pushed back his fedora, pulled down his tie, and cried "Fascism! Fascism!" into the face of the crowd. From Connecticut's industrial coast he traveled north again to the working-class enclaves of Providence and then crossed from Rhode Island into the factory towns of southeastern Massachusetts, addressing tiny street-corner gatherings in Fall River, Brockton, and Quincy with no less fervor than he'd expended in his maiden speech in Times Square. From Quincy he went on to Boston, where he planned to spend three days moving through Irish Dorchester and South Boston into the Italian North End. However, on his first afternoon at South Boston's busy Perkins Square the few jeering hecklers who'd been baiting him as a Jew ever since his departing his native New York—and his leaving behind there the police protection guaranteed him by Fiorello La Guardia, the city's anti-Lindbergh Republican mayor—burgeoned into a mob waving handmade placards reminiscent of the banners and signs beautifying the Bund rallies in Madison Square Garden. And the moment Winchell opened his mouth to speak, somebody brandishing a burning cross rushed toward the soapbox to set him aflame and a gun was fired twice into the air, either as a signal from the organizers to the rioters or as a warning to the marked man from "Jew York," or as both. There in the old brick cityscape of little family-run shops and streetcars and shade trees and small houses, each topped back then, before TV, only by the appendage of a towering chimney, in the Boston where the Depression had never ended, amid the storefronts sacred to the American main street—the ice cream parlor, the barber shop, the pharmacy—and just up the way from the dark, spiky outline of St. Augustine's Church, thugs with clubs surged forward screaming "Kill him!" and, two weeks from its inception in New York's five boroughs, the Winchell campaign, as Winchell had imagined it, was under way. He had at last brought the Lindbergh grotesquery to the surface, the underside of Lindbergh's affable blandness, raw and undisguised.

Though the Boston police did nothing to restrain the rioters—the gunshots had sounded a full hour before a squad car drove up to survey the scene—the plainclothes team of armed professional bodyguards who'd been stationed at Winchell's side throughout the trip managed to douse the flames consuming one of his trouser legs and, having freed him from the first wave of the crowd after only a few blows had fallen, to lift him into a car parked just yards from the soapbox and drive him to Carney Hospital on Telegraph

Hill, where he was treated for facial wounds and minor burns.

His first visitor at the hospital wasn't the mayor, Maurice Tobin, or Tobin's defeated mayoral rival, ex-governor James M. Curley (another FDR Democrat who, like the Democrat Tobin, wanted no part of Walter Winchell). Nor was it the local congressman, John W. McCormack, whose roughneck brother, a bartender known as Knocko, presided over the neighborhood with as much authority as the popular Democratic representative. To everyone's surprise, beginning with Winchell himself, his first visitor was a patrician Republican of distinguished New England lineage, the two-term Massachusetts governor, Leverett Saltonstall. On hearing of Winchell's hospitalization, Governor Saltonstall had left his State House office to communicate his concern directly to Winchell (whom privately he could only have despised), and to promise a thorough investigation into the well-plotted, obviously premeditated pandemonium that, by a mere fluke, had produced no fatalities. He also assured Winchell of protection by the state police—and, if need be, by the National Guard—for as long as Winchell campaigned in Massachusetts. And before the governor left the hospital, he saw to it that two armed troopers were stationed at the door only feet from Winchell's bed.

The *Boston Herald* interpreted Saltonstall's intervention as a political maneuver to gain him recognition as a courageous, honorable, fair-minded conservative who could serve his party as a dignified replacement in 1944 for the Democratic vice president, Burton K. Wheeler, who'd done the job required in the 1940 campaign but whose imprudence as an orator many Republicans now believed might compromise their president the second time around. In a hospital press conference where Winchell appeared before the photographers in his robe, with surgical dressings half covering his face and a heavily bandaged left foot, he welcomed Governor Saltonstall's offer but declined assistance in a message (cast, now that he was under assault, in language more statesmanlike than his standard feverish patter) that was distributed to the two dozen reporters from the radio and the press who had converged on his room. The statement began, "On the day when a candidate for the presidency of the United States requires a phalanx of armed police officers and National Guardsmen to protect his right to free speech, this great country will have passed over into fascist barbarism. I cannot accept that the religious intolerance emanating from the White House has already so corrupted the ordinary citizen that he has lost all respect for fellow Americans of a creed or faith different from his own. I cannot accept that the abhorrence for my religion shared by Adolf Hitler and Charles A. Lindbergh can already have corroded . . ."

From then on, anti-Semitic agitators hunted Winchell down at every crossing, though without success in Boston, where Saltonstall had ignored Winchell's grandstanding and directed his troops to impose order, employing force if need be, and to carry the violent off to jail, a command that they undertook to execute, however reluctantly. Meanwhile—using a cane to support himself because of his burned foot and with his jaw and forehead still bandaged—Winchell proceeded to draw an angry mob chanting "Kike go home!" in every single parish where he displayed his stigmata to the faithful, from Gate of Heaven Church in South Boston to St. Gabriel's Monastery in Brighton. Beyond Massachusetts, in communities in upper New York State, in Pennsylvania, and throughout the Midwest that were already notorious for their bigotry—and to which Winchell's explosive strategy inevitably pointed him—most of the local authorities did not share Saltonstall's unwillingness to tolerate civil unrest, and so, despite the doubling of his entourage of plainclothes bodyguards, the candidate came close to getting himself mauled each time he stepped onto the soapbox to denounce "the fascist in the White House" and to assign responsibility directly to the president's "religious hatred" for "fostering unheard-of Nazi barbarism in the American streets."

The worst and most widespread violence occurred in Detroit, the midwestern headquarters of the "Radio Priest" Father Coughlin and his Jew-hating Christian Front and of the crowd-pleasing minister known as "the dean of anti-Semites," Reverend Gerald

L. K. Smith, who preached that "Christian character is the true basis of real Americanism." Detroit, of course, was also home to the American automobile industry and to Lindbergh's elderly secretary of the interior, Henry Ford, whose avowedly anti-Semitic newspaper, the *Dearborn Independent,* published in the 1920s, addressed itself to "an investigation of the Jewish Question" that Ford ultimately reprinted in four volumes, totaling nearly one thousand pages, entitled *The International Jew,* in which he directed that in the cleansing of America "the International Jew and his satellites, as the conscious enemies of all that Anglo-Saxons mean by civilization, are not spared."

It was to be expected that organizations like the American Civil Liberties Union and eminent liberal journalists like John Gunther and Dorothy Thompson would be outraged by the Detroit riots and immediately make public their disgust, but so too were many conventional middle-class Americans, who, even if they found Walter Winchell and his rhetoric repugnant and understood him to be "asking for trouble," were also appalled by the eyewitness reports of how the rioting that had begun at Winchell's first stop in Hamtramck (the residential section inhabited chiefly by auto workers and their families and said to contain the world's largest Polish population outside Warsaw) had suspiciously spread within minutes to 12th Street, to Linwood and then to Dexter Boulevard. There, in the city's biggest Jewish neighborhoods, shops were looted and windows broken, Jews trapped outdoors were set upon and beaten, and kerosene-soaked crosses were ignited on the lawns of the fancy houses along Chicago Boulevard and out front of the modest two-family dwellings of the housepainters, plumbers, butchers, bakers, junk dealers, and grocers who lived on Webb and Tuxedo and in the little dirt yards of the poorest Jews on Pingry and Euclid. In midafternoon, only moments before the school day ended, a firebomb was thrown into the front foyer of Winterhalter Elementary School, where half the students were Jewish, another into the foyer of Central High, whose student body was ninety-five percent Jewish, another through a window at the Sholem Aleichem

Institute—a cultural organization Coughlin had ridiculously identified as Communist—and a fourth outside another of Couglin's
"Communist" targets, the Jewish Workers' Alliance. Next came the
attack on houses of worship. Not only were windows broken and
walls defaced on some half of the city's thirty-odd Orthodox synagogues, but as evening services were scheduled to begin an explosion went off on the steps of the prestigious Chicago Boulevard
temple Shaarey Zedek. The explosion there caused extensive damage to the exotic centerpiece of architect Albert Kahn's Moorish design—the three massive arched doorways that conspicuously exhibited to a working-class populace a distinctively un-American
style. Five passersby, none of whom happened to be Jews, were injured by flying debris from the façade, but no casualties were otherwise reported.

By nightfall, several hundred of the city's thirty thousand Jews
had fled and taken refuge across the Detroit River in Windsor,
Ontario, and American history had recorded its first large-scale pogrom, one clearly modeled on the "spontaneous demonstrations"
against Germany's Jews known as *Kristallnacht,* "the Night of Broken Glass," whose atrocities had been planned and perpetrated
by the Nazis four years earlier and which Father Coughlin in his
weekly tabloid, *Social Justice,* had defended at the time as a reaction
by the Germans against "Jewish-inspired Communism." Detroit's
Kristallnacht was similarly justified on the editorial page of the
Detroit Times as the unfortunate but inevitable and altogether understandable backlash to the activities of the troublemaking in-
terloper the paper identified as "the Jewish demagogue whose aim
from the outset had been to incite the rage of patriotic Americans
with his treasonous rabble-rousing."

The week after the September assault on Detroit's Jews—which
was addressed with dispatch by neither Michigan's governor nor
the city's mayor—new violence was directed at homes, shops, and
synagogues in Jewish neighborhoods in Cleveland, Cincinnati, Indianapolis, and St. Louis, violence that Winchell's enemies attributed to his deliberately challenging appearances in those cities after

the cataclysm that he'd instigated in Detroit, and that Winchell himself—who, in Indianapolis, barely escaped being crushed by a paving stone hurled from a rooftop that had broken the neck of the bodyguard stationed beside him—explained by the "climate of hate" emanating from the White House.

Our own street in Newark was many hundreds of miles from Dexter Boulevard in Detroit, nobody around had ever been to Detroit, and before September 1942 all that the boys on the block knew about Detroit was that organized baseball's only Jewish player was the Tigers' star first baseman, Hank Greenberg. But then came the Winchell riots, and suddenly even the children could recite the names of the Detroit neighborhoods that had been shaken by violence. Parroting what they heard from their parents, they would argue back and forth as to whether Walter Winchell was courageous or foolish, self-sacrificing or self-serving, and whether or not he was playing right into Lindbergh's hands by allowing the Gentiles to tell themselves that the Jews had brought their misery on themselves. They argued over whether it would be better if— before Winchell set off a nationwide pogrom—he desisted and allowed "normal" relations to be restored between the Jews and their fellow Americans or whether in the long run it would be better for him to continue to raise the alarm among the country's more complacent Jews—and to arouse the conscience of Christians—by exposing the menace of anti-Semitism from one end of America to the other. On the way to school, on the playground after school, between classes in the school corridors, you would see the smartest kids standing toe to toe, kids Sandy's age as well as a few no older than me, heatedly debating whether Walter Winchell's crisscrossing the country with his soapbox to flush into the open the German-American Bundists and the Coughlinites and the Ku Klux Klanners and the Silver Shirts and the America Firsters and the Black Legion and the American Nazi Party, whether getting these organized anti-Semites and their thousands of unseen sympathizers to reveal themselves for what they were—and to reveal the president for what *he* was, a chief executive and commander in chief who hadn't yet bothered to acknowledge that anything like a state of emergency existed, let alone called in federal troops to prevent further rioting—was good for the Jews or bad for the Jews.

After Detroit, the Jews of Newark—numbering some fifty thousand in a city of well over half a million—began to ready themselves for serious violence erupting on their own streets, either because of a Winchell visit to New Jersey when he swung back east or because of the riots inevitably spilling over into cities where, as in Newark, there was a heavily Jewish neighborhood abutting large communities of working-class Irish, Italians, Germans, and Slavs that were already home to a goodly number of bigots. The assumption was that these people wouldn't require much encouragement to be molded into a mindless, destructive mob by the pro-Nazi conspiracy that had successfully plotted the riot in Detroit.

Almost overnight, Rabbi Joachim Prinz, along with five other eminent Newark Jews—including Meyer Ellenstein—established the Newark Committee of Concerned Jewish Citizens. Quickly the group became a model for similar ad hoc Jewish citizens' groups in other big cities that were determined to ensure their communities' safety by enlisting the authorities to draw up contingency plans to prepare for the worst possibility. The Newark committee arranged first for a City Hall meeting—presided over by Mayor Murphy, whose election had ended Ellenstein's eight-year tenure—with Newark's police chief, fire chief, and director of the Department of Public Safety. The next day the committee met at the State House in Trenton with Democratic governor Charles Edison, the superintendent of the New Jersey State Police, and the commanding officer of the New Jersey National Guard. Attorney General Wilentz, an acquaintance of all six committee members, also attended, and, in the bulletin the Newark committee issued to the Jersey papers, he was reported to have assured Rabbi Prinz that anyone attempting an assault on the Jews of Newark would be prosecuted to the full extent of the law. The committee next telegrammed Rabbi Bengelsdorf, requesting a meeting with him in Washington, but was informed that theirs was a local and not a federal issue and advised to address their concern, as they were doing, to state and city officials.

Partisans of Rabbi Bengelsdorf lauded him for keeping himself aloof from the sordid Walter Winchell affair while quietly, in private White House conversations with Mrs. Lindbergh, urging assistance to those innocent Jews throughout the country who were tragically paying for the iniquitous conduct of the renegade candidate, a provocateur cynically encouraging American citizens who needed in no way to feel besieged to cling to their oldest, most crippling anxieties. The Bengelsdorf supporters constituted an influential clique drawn from the highly assimilated upper echelon of German Jewish society. A good many of them had been born to wealth and were among the first Jewish generation to attend elite secondary schools and Ivy League colleges, where, because their numbers were minute, they had mingled with the non-Jews, whom they subsequently associated with in communal, political, and business endeavors and who sometimes appeared to accept them as equals. To these privileged Jews there was nothing suspicious about the programs designed by Rabbi Bengelsdorf's agency to assist poorer, less cultivated Jews in learning to live in closer harmony with the nation's Christians. What was unfortunate, in their opinion, was that Jews like us continued to huddle together in cities like Newark out of a xenophobia fostered by historical pressures that no longer existed. The status conferred by economic and vocational advantage inclined them to believe that those who lacked their prestige were rebuffed by the larger society more because of insular clannishness than because of any pronounced taste for exclusiveness on the part of the Christian majority, and that neighborhoods like ours were less the result of discrimination than its breeding grounds. They recognized, of course, that there were pockets of backward people in America among whom virulent anti-Semitism was still their strongest, most obsessive passion, but that seemed only another reason for the director of the OAA to encourage Jews handicapped by the limitations of a segregated exis-

tence to at least permit their children to enter the American main-
stream and show themselves there to be nothing like the caricature
of the Jew disseminated by our enemies. Why these wealthy, ur-
bane, self-assured Jews particularly abhorred the self-caricaturing
Winchell was because he so deliberately reinforced the very hostility that they imagined themselves to have propitiated by their exemplary behavior toward their Christian colleagues and friends.

Aside from Rabbi Prinz and ex-mayor Ellenstein, the four remaining members of the Newark committee were the elderly civic
leader responsible for the success of the Americanization programs
for immigrant children in the Newark school system—and the
wife of Beth Israel Hospital's leading surgeon—Jenny Danzis; the
department store executive and son of the founder of S. Plaut &
Co., as well as ten-time president of the Broad Street Association,
Moses Plaut; the prominent city property owner and past president of the Newark Conference of Jewish Charities, community
leader Michael Stavitsky; and the chief of Beth Israel's medical
staff, Dr. Eugene Parsonette. That Newark's leading mobster, Longy
Zwillman, hadn't been enlisted to join a group of local Jews as distinguished as this was no surprise to anyone, even though Longy
was a wealthy man of enormous influence and hardly less distressed than Rabbi Prinz by the menace posed by the anti-Semites
who, under the pretext of being provoked by Walter Winchell, had
ushered in what looked to many like stage one of the resolution of
Henry Ford's "Jewish Question."

Longy set out separately, apart from the many civil authorities
who had promised Rabbi Prinz their fullest cooperation, to ensure that if and when the Newark cops and the New Jersey state
troopers failed to respond any more vigorously than the police had
to the disorder in Boston and Detroit, the city's Jews would not
be left unprotected. Bullet Apfelbaum, the close associate known
throughout the city as Longy's chief enforcer—and the older
brother of Niggy Apfelbaum—was assigned by Longy to supple-
ment the good work of the Newark Committee of Concerned Jewish Citizens by recruiting that scattering of incorrigible Jewish kids

who had failed to graduate from high school and training them as cadre for a hastily assembled volunteer corps to be called the Provisional Jewish Police. These were the local boys without any of the ideals that were embedded in the rest of us, who'd already begun to emanate an aura of lawlessness as far back as the fifth grade, inflating condoms in the school toilet and breaking into fistfights on the 14 bus and wrestling till they bled onto the concrete sidewalk outside the movies, the ones who, during their years in school, parents directed their children to have nothing to do with and who were now in their twenties and occupied running numbers and shooting pool and washing dishes in the kitchens of one or another of the neighborhood's delicatessen restaurants. To most of us they were known, if at all, only by the hoodlum magic of their supercharged nicknames—Leo "the Lion" Nusbaum, Knuckles Kimmelman, Big Gerry Schwartz, Dummy Breitbart, Duke "Duke-it-out" Glick—and by their double-digit IQ scores.

And now they were stationed on every second street corner, our neighborhood's handful of flops, spitting expertly into the gutter from between their teeth and signaling back and forth by whistling with their fingers angled deep in their mouths. Here they were, the callous and the obtuse and the mentally deficient, the Jews' very own deviants strolling the streets like sailors on shore leave looking for a fight. Here they were, the brainless few we had been raised to pity and fear, the Stone Age oafs and the seething runts and the ominous, swaggering weightlifters, buttonholing kids like me out on Chancellor Avenue and telling us to keep our baseball bats at the ready in case we were called in the night to take to the streets and going around to the Y in the evenings and to the ball fields on Sundays and to the local stores during the week, shanghaiing the able-bodied from among the neighborhood's grown men so as to bring to a total of three on each block a squad they could count on in an emergency. They embodied everything crude and despicable that our parents had hoped to leave behind, along with their childhood pennilessness, in the Third Ward slums, and yet here were our demons got up as our guardians, each with a loaded revolver strapped to his calf, a gun on loan from the collection of Bullet Apfelbaum, who was known by everyone to have devoted his existence to loyally intimidating folks on Longy's behalf, threatening them, beating them, torturing them, and—despite the fact that, in imitation of a boss easily thirty pounds leaner and a foot taller, Bullet was never to be seen other than in a three-piece suit adorned with a neatly folded silk pocket handkerchief the color of his tie and wearing an expensive Borsalino debonairly angled only inches above what was admittedly the ungenerous glower of an extremely severe judge of human nature—ending their lives for them, should that be the boss's pleasure.

What made the death of Walter Winchell worthy of instantaneous nationwide coverage wasn't only that his unorthodox campaign had touched off the century's worst anti-Semitic rioting outside Nazi Germany, but that the murder of a mere candidate for the presidency was unprecedented in America. Though Presidents Lincoln and Garfield had been shot and killed in the second half of the nineteenth century and McKinley at the start of the twentieth, and though in 1933 FDR had survived an assassination attempt that had instead taken the life of his Democratic supporter Chicago's Mayor Cermak, it wasn't until twenty-six years after Winchell's assassination that a second presidential candidate would be gunned down —that was New York's Democratic senator Robert Kennedy, fatally shot in the head after winning his party's California primary on Tuesday, June 4, 1968.

On Monday, October 5, 1942, I was home alone after school listening on our living room radio to the final innings of the fifth game of the World Series between the Cardinals and the Yankees, when, in the top of the ninth, with the Cardinals coming to bat in a 2–2 tie—and leading the Series three games to one—the play-by-play broadcast was halted by a voice with that finely articulated, faintly Anglicized diction prized in a network news announcer back in radio's earlier days: "We interrupt this program to bring you an important bulletin. Presidential candidate Walter Winchell has been shot and killed. We repeat: Walter Winchell is dead. He has been assassinated in Louisville, Kentucky, while addressing an open-air political rally. That is all that is known at this time of the Louisville assassination of Democratic presidential candidate Walter Winchell. We return to our regularly scheduled program."

It wasn't quite five P.M. My father had just left for the market in Uncle Monty's truck, my mother had gone out to Chancellor Avenue a few minutes earlier to buy something for dinner, and my single-minded brother was off in search of a trysting place to resume importuning one of his after-school girls to grant him access to her chest. I heard shouting in the street, then a scream from a nearby house, but the game had come back on and the suspense was tremendous: Red Ruffing pitching to the Cardinals' rookie third baseman Whitey Kurowski, Cardinals catcher Walker Cooper on first base with his sixth hit in five games, and the Cardinals needing only this victory to take the Series. Rizzuto had homered for the Yankees, the portentously surnamed Enos Slaughter had homered for the Cardinals, and, as histrionic little fans like to tell one another, I "knew" before Ruffing had even fired his first pitch that Kurowski was about to hit a second Cardinal home run and give the Cards their fourth straight victory after an opening-day loss. I couldn't wait to run outside crying, "I knew it! I called it! Kurowski was due!" But when Kurowski homered and the game was over and I was out the door and headed at top speed down our alleyway, I saw two members of the Jewish police—Big Gerry and Duke Glick—running from one side of the street to the other to bang on doors and shout into hallways, "They shot Winchell! Winchell is dead!"

Meanwhile more kids were rushing out of their houses, delirious with World Series excitement. But no sooner did they hit the street howling Kurowski's name than Big Gerry began barking at them, "Go get your bats! The war is on!" And he didn't mean the war against Germany.

By evening there wasn't a Jewish family on our street that wasn't barricaded behind double-locked doors, their radios playing non-

stop to catch the latest bulletin and everyone phoning to tell everyone else that Winchell had said nothing remotely inflammatory to
the Louisville crowd, that he had, in fact, begun his speech in what
could only have been intended as an open appeal to civic self-
esteem—"Mr. and Mrs. Louisville, Kentucky, proud citizens of the
unique American city that is home to the greatest horse race in the
world and birthplace of the very first Jewish justice of the United
States Supreme Court—" and yet before he could speak aloud the
name of Louis D. Brandeis, he'd been brought down by three bul-
lets to the back of the head. A second report, aired just moments
later, identified the spot where the murder occurred as only a few
yards from one of the most elegant municipal buildings constructed in the Greek Revival style in the whole of Kentucky, the
Jefferson County Courthouse, with its commanding statue of Thomas Jefferson facing the street and a long, wide staircase leading up
to the grandly columned portico. The shots that killed Winchell
appeared to have been fired from one of the courthouse's large,
austere, beautifully proportioned front windows.

My mother began making her first calls immediately upon coming in from shopping. I had stationed myself just inside the door
to tell her about Walter Winchell the instant she got home, but by
then she already knew the little there was to be known, first because the butcher's wife had phoned the store to repeat the news
bulletin to her husband just as he was wrapping my mother's order, and then because of the bewilderment apparent among the
people out on the street, who were already scurrying for the safety
of their homes. Failing to reach my father, whose truck hadn't yet
pulled up at the market, she of course began to worry about my
brother, who was cutting it close once again and probably wouldn't
come rushing up the back stairs until seconds before he was due at
the kitchen table with his hands washed of the day's dirt and his
face scrubbed clean of lipstick. It was the worst moment imaginable for either of them to be away and their precise whereabouts unknown, but without taking time to unbag the groceries or to regis-

ter her alarm, my mother said to me, "Get me the map. Get your map of America."

There was a large folding map of the North American continent squared away in a pocket inside volume one of the encyclopedia set sold to us by a door-to-door salesman the year I started school. I rushed into the sun parlor, where, shelved between the brass George Washington bookends bought at Mount Vernon by my father, was the whole of our library: the six-volume encyclopedia, a leather-bound copy of the United States Constitution awarded by Metropolitan Life, and the unabridged Webster's dictionary that Aunt Evelyn had given Sandy for his tenth birthday. I opened the map and spread it across the kitchen table's oilcloth covering, whereupon my mother—using the magnifying glass that I'd received from my parents for a seventh-birthday gift along with my irreplaceable, unforgotten stamp album—searched for the speck in north-central Kentucky that was the city of Danville.

In only seconds the two of us were back at the telephone table in the foyer, above which hung yet another of my father's awards for selling insurance, a framed copper engraving replicating the Declaration of Independence. Local dial service within Essex County was barely ten years old and probably a good third of the people in Newark didn't as yet have any phone service at all—and most who did were, like us, on a party line—and so the long-distance call was still a wondrous phenomenon, not only because making one was far from an ordinary household experience for a family of our means but because no technological explanation, however basic, could remove it entirely from the realm of magic.

My mother spoke to the operator very precisely to be sure that nothing went wrong and we weren't charged by mistake for anything extra. "I want to make a long-distance person-to-person call, operator. To Danville, Kentucky. Person-to-person to Mrs. Selma Wishnow. And please, operator, when my three minutes are up, don't forget to tell me."

There was a long pause while the operator got the number from the directory operator. When my mother finally heard the call being placed, she signaled for me to put my ear beside hers but not to speak.

"Hello!" Answering enthusiastically is Seldon.

Operator: "This is long distance. I have a person-to-person call for Mrs. Selma Wistful."

"Uh-uh," Seldon mumbles.

"Is this Mrs. Wistful?"

"Hello? My mother's not home right now."

Operator: "I'm calling for Mrs. Selma Wistful—"

"Wishnow," my mother shouts. "*Wish-now.*"

"Who's that?" Seldon says. "Who's calling?"

Operator: "Young lady, is your mother home?"

"I'm a boy," Seldon says. Taken aback. Another blow. They won't stop coming. Yet he does sound girlish, his voice higher-pitched even than when he'd been living downstairs. "My mother's not home from work yet," Seldon says.

Operator: "Mrs. Wishnow is not at home, madam."

My mother looks at me and says, "What could have happened? The boy is alone. Where could she be? He's all by himself. Operator, I'll talk to anyone."

Operator: "Go ahead, sir."

"Who's this?" Seldon asks.

"Seldon, it's Mrs. Roth. From Newark."

"Mrs. Roth?"

"Yes. I'm calling long distance to speak to your mother."

"From Newark?"

"You know who I am."

"But it sounds like you're just down the street."

"Well, I'm not. This is a long-distance call. Seldon, where's your mother?"

"I'm just having a snack. I'm waiting for her to come home from work. I'm having some Fig Newtons. And some milk."

"Seldon—"

"I'm waiting for her to come home from work—she works late.

She always works late. I just sit here. Sometimes I have a snack—"

"Seldon, stop right there. Be still a moment."

"And then she comes home and she makes dinner. But she's late every night."

Here my mother turns to me and makes to hand me the phone. "Talk to him. He won't listen when I speak."

"Talk to him about what?" I say, waving the phone away.

"Is Philip there?" Seldon asks.

"Just a moment, Seldon," my mother says.

"Is Philip there?" Seldon repeats.

To me, my mother says, "Take the phone, please."

"But what am I supposed to say?" I ask.

"Just get on the phone," and she places the receiver in my one hand and lifts the speaker for me to hold in the other.

"Hello, Seldon?" I say.

Softly tentative, unbelieving, he replies, "Philip?"

"Yes. Hi, Seldon."

"Hey, you know, I don't have any friends in school."

I tell him, "We want to speak to your mother."

"My mother's at work. She works late every night. I'm having a snack. I'm having some Fig Newtons and a glass of milk. It's going to be my birthday in about a week and my mother said I could have a party—"

"Seldon, wait a minute."

"But I don't have any friends."

"Seldon, I have to ask my mother a question. Just wait." I muzzle the speaker and whisper to her, "What am I supposed to say to him?"

My mother whispers, "Ask him if he knows what happened today in Louisville."

"Seldon, my mother wants to know if you know what happened today in Louisville."

"I live in Danville. I live in Danville, Kentucky. I'm just waiting for my mom to come home. I'm having a snack. Did something happen in Louisville?"

"Just a minute, Seldon," I say. "Now what?" I whisper to my mother.

"Just talk to him, please. Keep talking to him. And if the operator says the three minutes are up, you tell me."

"Why are you calling?" Seldon asks. "Are you going to come visit?"

"No."

"Remember when I saved your life?" he says.

"Yes, I do. I remember."

"Hey, what time is it there? Are you in Newark? Are you on Summit Avenue?"

"We told you we were. Yes."

"It's really clear, isn't it? It sounds like you're just down the block. I wish you could come over and have a snack with me, and then you could be here for my birthday party next week. I don't have any friends to invite to my birthday party. I don't have anybody to play chess with. I'm sitting here now practicing my opening move. Remember my opening move? I move out the pawn that's just in front of the king. Remember when I tried to teach you? I move out the king's pawn, remember? Then I put out the bishop, then I move the knight, and then the other knight—and remember the move when there's no pieces between the king and one of the rooks? When I move my king over two spaces to protect him?"

"Seldon—"

My mother whispers, "Tell him you miss him."

"Ma!" I say to her.

"Tell him, Philip."

"I miss you, Seldon."

"Do you want to come over for a snack then? I mean it sounds like—are you really just down the street?"

"No, this is a long-distance phone call."

"What time is it there?"

"It's, uh—about ten to six."

"Oh, it's ten to six here. My mom should already be home

around five. Five-thirty the latest. One night she came home at *nine*."

"Seldon," I say, "do you know that Walter Winchell was killed?"

"Who's that?" he asks.

"Let me finish. Walter Winchell was killed in Louisville, Kentucky. In your state. Today."

"I'm sorry to hear that. Who is that?"

Operator: "Your three minutes are up, sir."

"Is that your uncle?" Seldon asks. "Is that your uncle who came to see you? Is he dead?"

"No, no," I say, and I'm thinking that, alone now out in Kentucky, he sounds as though *he* were the one who was kicked in the head. He sounds stunned. Stunted. He sounds *stopped*. And yet he was the smartest kid in our class.

My mother takes the phone. "Seldon, this is Mrs. Roth. I want you to write something down."

"Okay. I have to go find a piece of paper. And a pencil."

Waiting. Waiting. "Seldon?" my mother says.

More waiting.

"Okay," he says.

"Seldon, write this down. This is now costing a lot of money."

"I'm sorry, Mrs. Roth. I just couldn't find a pencil in the house. I was at the kitchen table. I was having a snack."

"Seldon, write down that Mrs. Roth—"

"Okay."

"—called from Newark."

"From Newark. Gosh. I wish I was still in Newark, living downstairs. You know, I saved Philip's life."

"Mrs. Roth called from Newark to be sure—"

"Just a minute. I'm writing."

"—to be sure everything is okay."

"Is something supposed to not be okay? I mean Philip's all right. And you're okay. Is Mr. Roth okay?"

"Yes, thank you for asking, Seldon. Tell your mother that's why I called. There's nothing to worry about here."

"Should I be worried about something?"

"No. Just eat your snack—"

"I think I've had enough Fig Newtons now, but thanks anyway."

"Goodbye, Seldon."

"I like Fig Newtons, though."

"Goodbye, Seldon."

"Mrs. Roth?"

"Yes?"

"Is Philip going to come visit me? It's my birthday next week and I don't have anybody to invite for my birthday party. I don't have any friends in Danville. The kids here call me Saltine. I have to play chess with a kid who's six years old. He lives next door. He's the only one I can play with. One kid. I taught him chess. Sometimes he makes moves you can't do. Or he moves his queen and I have to tell him not to. I win all the time but it's really no fun. But I have nobody else to play with."

"Seldon, it's hard for everyone. It's hard for everyone now. Goodbye, Seldon." And she placed the receiver onto the hook and began to sob.

Only days before, on October first, the two Summit Avenue flats vacated in September by the "homesteaders of 1942"—the one beneath ours and another across the street, three doors down—were occupied by Italian families up from the First Ward. Essentially their new living quarters had been assigned to them by outright government edict, though with the sweetening incentive of a rent discount of fifteen percent (or $6.37 on their monthly $42.50) over a five-year period, that money to be paid directly to the landlord by the Department of the Interior over the life of the initial three-year lease and for the first two years of a lease's three-year renewal. Such arrangements derived from a previously unpublicized section of the homesteading plan called the Good Neighbor Project, designed to introduce a steadily increasing number of non-Jewish residents into predominantly Jewish neighborhoods and in this way "enrich" the "Americanness" of everyone involved. What one heard at

home, however—and sometimes even at school from our teachers—was that the underlying goal of the Good Neighbor Project,
like that of Just Folks, was to weaken the solidarity of the Jewish social structure as well as to diminish whatever electoral strength a
Jewish community might have in local and congressional elections.
If the displacing of Jewish families and their replacement by the
conscripting of Gentile families followed the timetable of the
agency's master plan, a Christian majority might well be dominant
in at least half of America's twenty most heavily populated Jewish
neighborhoods as early as the start of Lindbergh's second term and
a resolution of America's Jewish Question close at hand, by one
means or another.

The family conscripted to move in downstairs from us—a
mother, a father, a son, and a grandmother—were the Cucuzzas.
Because of my father's years of canvassing the First Ward, where
the customers whose tiny premiums he collected each month were
by and large Italians, he was already familiar with the new tenants,
and consequently, when he got home from work on the morning
after Mr. Cucuzza, a night watchman, had trucked the family's possessions up from their cold-water flat in a tenement building on
a side street not far from Holy Sepulchre Cemetery, my father
stopped off first at the downstairs door to see if, despite his ap-
pearing there without a coat and a tie and with dirty hands, the
elderly grandmother would recognize him as the insurance man
who'd sold her husband the policy that had provided the family
with the means to bury him.

The "other" Cucuzzas (relatives of "our" Cucuzzas, who'd moved
from their own First Ward cold-water flat to the house three doors
away) were a much larger family—three sons, a daughter, the two
parents, and a grandfather—and potentially noisier, more disrup-
tive neighbors. They were associated through the grandfather and
the father with Ritchie "the Boot" Boiardo, the mobster who ruled
Newark's Italian precincts and constituted the city's only serious
competitor to Longy's underworld monopoly. To be sure, the father, Tommy, was but one of a bevy of underlings and, like his own

retired father, doubled as a waiter at Boiardo's popular restaurant, the Vittorio Castle, when he wasn't making the rounds of the taverns, barber shops, brothels, schoolyards, and candy stores of the Third Ward slums to extract their pocket change from the Negroes who faithfully played the daily numbers game. Regardless of religion, the other Cucuzzas were hardly the sort of neighbors my parents wanted anywhere near their impressionable young sons, and to comfort us at breakfast on Sunday morning my father explained how much worse off we would have been if we'd gotten the numbers runner and his three boys instead of the night watchman and his son, Joey, an eleven-year-old recently enrolled at St. Peter's and, by my father's report, a good-natured kid with a hearing problem who had little in common with his roughneck cousins. Whereas down in the First Ward all four of Tommy Cucuzza's kids had gone to the local public school, here they'd been enrolled along with Joey at St. Peter's rather than at a public school like ours, brimming with brainy little Jews.

Since my father had left work only a few hours after the Winchell assassination and, over Uncle Monty's angry objections, driven back home to spend the remainder of that tense evening beside his wife and his children, the four of us were seated together at the kitchen table waiting for the radio to bring fresh news when Mr. Cucuzza and Joey came up the back stairway to pay a visit. They knocked on the door and then had to wait on the landing until my father was sure who was there.

Mr. Cucuzza was a bald, hulking man, six and a half feet tall, weighing over two hundred and fifty pounds, and he was dressed for work in his night watchman's uniform, a dark blue shirt, freshly pressed dark blue trousers, and a wide black belt that along with holding up his trousers supported several pounds of the most extraordinary collection of equipment I'd ever been close enough to reach out and touch. There were keys in bunches each the size of a hand grenade hanging to the side of either pants pocket, there was a set of real handcuffs, and a night watchman's clock in its black case dangled by a strap from the polished belt buckle. At first glance, I took the clock for a bomb, but there was no mistaking for other than what it was the pistol in a holster at his waist. A longish flashlight that had to have doubled as a blackjack was stuck lamp upward into his back pocket, and high on one sleeve of his starched workshirt was a triangular white patch whose blue lettering read "Special Guard."

Joey was also big—only two years my senior and already twice my weight—and to me the equipment he sported was nearly as intriguing as his father's. Looking like a wad of molded bubble gum plugging the hole of his right ear was a hearing aid attached by a thin wire to a round black case with a dial on the front that he wore clipped to his shirt pocket; another wire attached to a battery about the size of a large cigarette lighter that he carried around in his pants pocket. And in his hands he carried a cake, a gift from his mother to mine.

Joey's gift was the cake, Mr. Cucuzza's was a pistol. He owned two, one that he wore for work and the other that he kept hidden away at home. He'd come to offer my father the spare.

"Nice of you," my father said to him, "but I really don't know how to shoot."

"You pulla the trig'." Mr. Cucuzza had a surprisingly soft voice for someone so enormous, though with a raspy edge to it, as if it had been exposed too long to the weather during his hours of walking the watchman's beat. And his accent was so enjoyable to hear that when I was alone I sometimes pretended that the way he talked was the way I talked too. How many times did I entertain myself by saying aloud "You pulla the trig'"? With the exception of Joey's American-born mother, our Cucuzzas all had oddish voices, the bewhiskered grandmother's being oddest of all, odder even than Joey's, which sounded less like a voice than like the uninflected echo of a voice. And odd not just because she went around speaking only Italian, whether to others (including me) or to herself while she swept the back stairway or kneeled in the dirt planting her vegetables in our minute backyard or just stood muttering in the dark doorway. Hers was oddest because it sounded like a man's—she looked like a tiny old man in a long black dress and she sounded like one too, particularly when barking the commands and decrees and injunctions that Joey never dared disobey. The playful half of him, the soul that the nuns and the priests never saw enough of to save, was virtually all that I ever encountered when we two were alone. Why it was hard to feel too sorry about his hearing was because Joey was himself a very jolly, prankish boy with his own brand of hooting laughter, a talkative, curious, monumentally gullible boy whose mind moved quickly if unpredictably. It was hard to feel sorry for him, yet when he was around his family Joey's obedience was so painstakingly thorough that I found it almost as astonishing to contemplate as the painstakingly thorough lawlessness of a Shushy Margulis. There couldn't have been a better son in all of Italian Newark, which was why my own mother soon found him irresistible—his faultless filial devotion and his long dark eyelashes, the way he imploringly looked at adults, waiting to be told what to do, allowed her to set aside the uneasy aloofness that was her inbuilt defense against Gentiles. The old-country grandmother, however, gave her—and me—the willies.

"You aim," Mr. Cucuzza explained to my father, using a finger and a thumb to demonstrate, "and uhyou shoot. You aim and uhyou shoot and that's it."

"I don't need it," my father said.

"But ifuh they come roun'," Mr. Cucuzza said, "how you gonna protect?"

"Cucuzza, I was born in the city of Newark in the year nineteen hundred and one," my father told him. "All my life I have paid my rent on time, I have paid my taxes on time, and I have paid my bills on time. I've never cheated on an employer for as much as a dime. I have never tried to cheat the United States government. I believe in this country. I love this country."

"Me too," said our massive new downstairs neighbor, whose wide black belt might have been hung with shrunken heads, given the enchantment that it continued to cast over me. "I come-uh here I was uhten. Best country anyplace. No Mussolini here."

"I'm glad you feel that way, Cucuzza. It's a tragedy for Italy, it's a human tragedy for people like you."

"Mussolini, Hitler—make-uh me sick."

"You know what I love, Cucuzza? Election Day," my father told him. "I love to vote. Since I was old enough, I have not missed an election. In 1924 I voted against Mr. Coolidge and for Mr. Davis, and Mr. Coolidge won. And we all know what Mr. Coolidge did for the poor people of this country. In 1928 I voted against Mr. Hoover and for Mr. Smith, and Mr. Hoover won. And we know what *he* did for the poor people of this country. In 1932 I voted against Mr. Hoover for the second time and for Mr. Roosevelt for the first time, and, thank God, Mr. Roosevelt won, and he put America back on its feet. He took this country out of the Depression and he gave the people what he promised—a new deal. In 1936 I voted against Mr. Landon and for Mr. Roosevelt, and again Mr. Roosevelt won—two states, Maine and Vermont, that is all Mr. Landon is able to carry. Can't even carry Kansas. Mr. Roosevelt sweeps the country by the biggest presidential vote there has ever been, and once again he keeps every promise to the working people that he made in that campaign. And so what do the voters up and do in nineteen hundred and forty? They elect a fascist instead. Not just an idiot like Coolidge, not just a fool like Hoover, but an out-and-out fascist with a medal to prove it. They put in a fascist and a fascist rabble-rouser, Mr. Wheeler, as his sidekick, and they put Mr. Ford into the cabinet, not only an anti-Semite right up there with Hitler but a slave driver who has turned the workingman into a human machine. And so tonight you come to me, sir, in my own home, and you offer me a pistol. In America in the year nineteen hundred and forty-two, a brand-new neighbor, a man I do not even know yet, has to come here and offer me a pistol in order for me to protect my family from Mr. Lindbergh's anti-Semitic mob. Well, don't you think I'm not grateful, Cucuzza. I will never forget your concern.

But I am a citizen of the United States of America, and so is my wife, and so are my children, and so," he said, his voice catching, "and so was Mr. Walter Winchell—"

But now, suddenly, there is a radio bulletin *about* Walter Winchell. "Shhh!" my father says. "Shhh!" as though in the kitchen someone other than himself had been the orator holding forth. We all listen—even Joey appears to listen—the way birds flock to migrate and fish swim in a school.

The body of Walter Winchell, slain that day at a political rally in Louisville, Kentucky, by a suspected American Nazi Party assassin working in collaboration with the Ku Klux Klan, will be carried overnight by train from Louisville to Pennsylvania Station in New York City. There, by order of Mayor Fiorello La Guardia and under the protection of the New York City police, the body will lie in state in the great hall of the train station throughout the morning. According to Jewish custom, a funeral service will be held that same day, at two P.M. in Temple Emanu-El, New York's largest synagogue. A public-address system will broadcast the proceedings beyond the temple to a gathering of mourners on Fifth Avenue expected to number in the tens of thousands. Along with Mayor La Guardia, speakers will include Democratic senator James Mead, New York's Jewish governor, Herbert Lehman, and the former president of the United States, Franklin D. Roosevelt.

"It's happening!" my father cries. "He's back! FDR is back!"

"We need him bad," Mr. Cucuzza says.

"Boys," he asks, "do you understand what is happening?" and here he throws his arms around Sandy and me. "It's the beginning of the end of fascism in America! No Mussolini here, Cucuzza—no more Mussolini here!"

8

October 1942

Bad Days

A LVIN APPEARED at our house the next night, driving a
brand-new green Buick and with a fiancée named Minna
Schapp. "Fiancée" always got me when I heard the word
spoken as a kid. It made whoever she was sound like somebody
special—then she showed up and she was just some girl who, when
she met the family, was afraid to say the wrong thing. The special
one here wasn't the intended wife anyway but the intended father-
in-law, a masterful deal-maker prepared to deliver Alvin from the
game-machine business—where, assisted by two strong-arm thugs
who lifted the freight and fended off evildoers, my cousin was employed trucking and setting up the illegal machines—and into a
hand-tailored Hong Kong silk suit and a white-on-white monogrammed shirt as an Atlantic City restaurateur. Though Mr. Schapp
had himself started out in the twenties as Pinball Billy Schapiro, a
two-bit hustler associated with the worst hoods from the most
rundown row houses on the most violent streets of the South
Philly badlands—among them the uncle of Shushy Margulis—by
1942 the return on the pinballs and the slots amounted to upward
of fifteen thousand unreported dollars each week, and Pinball Billy
had been regenerated as William F. Schapp II, highly esteemed
member of the Green Valley Country Club, of the Jewish fraternal
organization Brith Achim (where on Saturday nights he took his
dynamic wife in her gigantic jewels to dance to the music of Jackie

Jacobs and his Jolly Jazzers), and of Har Zion Synagogue (through whose burial society he purchased a family plot in a beautifully landscaped corner of the synagogue's cemetery), as well as the maharajah of an eighteen-room mansion in suburban Merion and wintertime occupant of a poor boy's dream of a penthouse suite annually reserved for him at the Miami Beach Eden Roc.

At thirty-one, Minna was eight years Alvin's senior, a buttery-complexioned woman with a browbeaten look who, when she even dared to speak in her babyish voice, enunciated each word as though she had only just learned to tell time. She was every inch the child of overbearing parents, but because the father owned, in addition to the Intercity Carting Company—the public face of the gaming-machine operation—half an acre of lobster house across from the Steel Pier where people lined up twice around the block to get in on weekends, and because back in the early thirties, when Prohibition ended and Pinball Billy's lucrative side interest in Waxey Gordon's interstate bootlegging syndicate suddenly dried up, he'd established Philadelphia's "Original Schapp's"—the steak house popular with what in Philly they called the Jew Mob—Pinball Billy figured strongly with Alvin as Minna's advocate. "The contract goes like this," Schapp told him when he handed Alvin the cash to buy his daughter's engagement ring. "Minna takes care of your leg, you take care of Minna, and I take care of you."

That's how my cousin came to don the hand-tailored suits and to arrogate to himself the glamorous responsibility for ushering to their tables big-name customers such as Jersey City's crooked mayor, Frank Hague; New Jersey's light-heavyweight champion, Gus Lesnevich; and racket tycoons like Cleveland's Moe Dalitz, Boston's King Solomon, L.A.'s Mickey Cohen, and even "the Brain" himself, Meyer Lansky, when they were in town for a gangland convention. And regularly, every September, to welcome fresh from her pageant triumph, the newly crowned Miss America with all her befuddled relatives in tow. Once everyone was lavishly complimented and into their silly lobster bibs, it was Alvin's pleasure to signal to the waiter, by a snap of his fingers, that the house would pick up the tab.

Pinball Billy's one-legged future son-in-law soon gained a nick-name of his own, Showy, bestowed on him, as Alvin told everyone, by Allie Stolz, the contender for the world lightweight title. Alvin was up from Philly to visit with Stolz—like Gus Lesnevich, a New-ark boy—the day he and Minna wound up at our house for dinner. Stolz had fought and lost a fifteen-round decision against the light-weight champion in Madison Square Garden the previous May and was training that fall at Marsillo's Market Street gym for a November fight against Beau Jack that would gain him a shot at Tippy Larkin if he won. "Once Allie gets past Beau Jack," Alvin said, "there's just Larkin between him and the title, and Larkin's got a glass jaw."

Glass jaw. Phony-baloney. A going-over. A hard guy. What's his beef? I'll take the grunt. The oldest dodge in the world. Alvin had a new vocabulary and a whole new ostentatious way of talking that it clearly pained my parents to hear. Yet when he said adoringly of Stolz's generosity, "Allie's a guy who is rapid with the dollar," I couldn't wait to sound like a hard guy myself by repeating the amazing expression at school along with the extensive medley of slang that Alvin now used just for the word "money."

Minna was silent during the meal—though my mother tried mightily to draw her out—I was overcome by shyness, and my fa-ther could think of nothing but the synagogue bombing that had taken place in Cincinnati the previous night and the looting of Jewish-owned stores in American cities scattered across two time zones. This was the second night in a row that he'd walked out on Uncle Monty rather than leave the family alone on Summit Av-enue, but he couldn't worry about his brother's wrath at a time like this, and instead all through dinner kept getting up to go into the living room to turn on the radio and hear what news there was in the aftermath of the Winchell funeral. Alvin, meanwhile, was able to talk only about "Allie" and his quest for the world boxing crown as though the lightweight contender native to Newark embodied Alvin's profoundest conception of the human race. Could the abandonment have been any more complete of the moral code that had cost him his leg? He had disposed of whatever once stood between him and the aspirations of a Shushy Margulis—he had disposed of us.

I wondered, when I met her, if Alvin had even told Minna that he was an amputee. It didn't occur to me that her subjugated personality was precisely what made her the first and only woman Alvin *could* tell, nor did I understand that Minna was the evidence of his incapacity with women. His stump, in fact, constituted Alvin's greatest *success* with Minna, particularly after Schapp died in 1960 and Minna's worthless brother took over the slots, while Alvin was content just to acquire the restaurants and to begin running with the best-looking hookers in two states. Whenever the stump cracked and got sore and bloody and infected—which it did as a result of his many follies—Minna immediately stepped in and wouldn't allow him to wear his prosthesis. Alvin would say to her, "For Christ's sake, don't worry about it, it'll be all right," but here alone Minna prevailed. "You can't put a load on that leg," she'd tell him, "till you get it fixed"—meaning the artificial leg, which was always, in the legmaker's phrase that Alvin had taught me back when I, not yet nine, was the mothering Minna, "losing its fit." When Alvin got older and his stump broke down all the time from bearing all the weight he'd gained, when he had to be without the prosthesis for weeks on end until it healed, Minna would drive him to the public beach in the summertime and watch fully clothed from under a big umbrella while he played for hours in the all-healing surf, bobbing in the waves and floating on his back and spouting saltwater geysers into the air and then, to throw a scare into the tourists crowding the beach, emerging from the water screaming "Shark! Shark!" while pointing in horror at his stump.

Alvin showed up with Minna for dinner after phoning that morning to tell my mother that he was going to be in North Jersey and wanted to stop by to thank his aunt and uncle for all they had done for him when he'd come home from the commandos and given everyone a hard time. He had a lot to be grateful for, he said, and he wanted to make peace with the two of them and to see the two boys, and to introduce his fiancée. That's what he said and that may even have been what he had in mind before he came face to face with my father and the memory of my father's reforming instincts—and the fact of their innate antipathy, the antipathy as human types that was really there from the start—and it was why, when I got home from school and heard the news, I dug down into my drawer and found his medal and, for the first time since he'd left for Philly, pinned it back on my undershirt.

Of course it was hardly an ideal day for a conciliatory visit from the family's black sheep. There'd been no anti-Semitic violence reported in Newark or in the other major New Jersey cities during the night, but the firebombing of the synagogue that subsequently burned to the ground some hundred miles up the Ohio River from Louisville, in Cincinnati, and the random window-smashing and looting of Jewish-owned stores in eight other cities (St. Louis, Buffalo, and Pittsburgh the three largest) did nothing to diminish fear that the spectacle of Walter Winchell's Jewish funeral just across the Hudson in New York—and the demonstrations and counter-demonstrations coinciding with all the solemn observances—could easily provoke an outbreak of violence a lot closer to home. At school, first thing in the morning, a special half-hour assembly program had been called for grades four through eight. Along with a representative from the Board of Education, a deputy from Mayor Murphy's office, and the current president of the PTA, the principal spelled out the measures being taken to ensure our safety during the day and offered ten rules that would protect us from harm on our way to and from school. While no mention was made of Bullet Apfelbaum's Jewish police—who'd been on the streets all night long and were still there in the morning, drinking hot coffee out of thermoses and eating powdered doughnuts donated by Lehrhoff's bakery when Sandy and I started off for school—we were assured by the mayor's deputy that "until normal conditions are restored," extra details of city police would be patrolling the neighborhood and we were instructed not to be alarmed if we found a uniformed policeman stationed at each of the school doors and a policeman in the corridors. Two mimeographed sheets were then distributed to every pupil, one listing the rules to obey on the street, which our teachers would go over with us when we returned to our homerooms, and the other to take to our parents to advise them of the new safety procedures. If there were questions, our parents should direct them to Mrs. Sisselman, the PTA president who'd succeeded my mother.

We ate in the dining room, where we last had a meal when Aunt Evelyn had brought Rabbi Bengelsdorf to meet us. After Alvin's call, my mother (whose inability to hold a personal grudge Alvin would have known he could count on the moment he heard her answer the phone) went off to buy food for a dinner that would especially please him, and this despite the anxiety aroused in her each time she had to unlock the door and go back out on the street. That armed Newark cops were now walking the beat and cruising the local streets in squad cars gave her only slightly more assurance than did the glimpses of Bullet Apfelbaum's Jewish police, and so, like anyone else shopping in a city under siege, she wound up all but running back and forth to Chancellor Avenue to pick up everything she needed. In the kitchen she proceeded to bake the chocolate layer cake with chocolate icing and chopped walnuts that had been Alvin's favorite and to peel the potatoes and chop the onions for the latkes that Alvin could devour by the batch, and the house still smelled of the baking and frying and broiling that had been touched off by the unexpected homecoming when Alvin drove his new Buick into the alleyway. There (where we'd run pass plays together with the football I stole) Alvin pulled up behind the little Ford pickup that Mr. Cucuzza used to move people's furniture as a second job and that happened to be parked in the garage because it was the night watchman's day off, and on his day off he slept round the clock.

Alvin arrived wearing a pearl-gray sharkskin suit padded heavily at the shoulders, perforated two-tone wingtip shoes with taps on the toes, and bearing gifts for all: Aunt Bess's was a white apron decorated with red roses, Sandy's a sketchpad, mine a Phillies cap, and Uncle Herman's a certificate entitling a family of four to a free lobster dinner at the Atlantic City restaurant. His giving us all presents reassured me that just because he'd run off to Philadelphia, he hadn't forgotten all the good stuff he'd found in our house in the years preceding his losing his leg. It certainly did not look then and there as though we were a divided family or that when dinner was over—and Minna already in the kitchen taking a lesson in latke-making from my mother—a battle royal could possibly break out between my father and Alvin. Perhaps if Alvin hadn't shown up in his flashy clothes and his snazzy car all but seething with the raw carnality of Marsillo's gym and exuberant with the imminent acquisition of undreamed-of wealth . . . perhaps if Winchell hadn't been assassinated twenty-four hours earlier and the worst that had been feared when Lindbergh first took office hadn't seemed closer to befalling us than ever before . . . perhaps then the two grown men who mattered most to me throughout my childhood might never have come so close to murdering each other.

Before that night, I'd had no idea my father was so well suited for wreaking havoc or equipped to make that lightning-quick transformation from sanity to lunacy that is indispensable in enacting the unbridled urge to destroy. Unlike Uncle Monty he preferred never to speak of the ordeal of a Jewish tenement kid on Runyon Street before World War One, when the Irish, armed with sticks and rocks and iron pipes, regularly came streaming up through the viaduct underpasses of the Ironbound section seeking vengeance against the Christ-killers of the Jewish Third Ward, and much as he enjoyed taking Sandy and me to Laurel Garden on Springfield Avenue when tickets to a good match came his way, men fighting each other outside a boxing ring appalled him. That he'd always had a muscular physique I knew from a snapshot taken when he was eighteen and pasted by my mother into the family photo album alongside the only other photograph surviving from his youth, a picture of him at the age of six standing next to Uncle Monty, three years older and close to a foot and a half taller—two ragtag kids stiffly posing in their ancient overalls and their dirty shirts and with their caps pushed back just far enough to reveal the cruelty of their haircuts. In that sepia photo of him at eighteen he's already a million miles from childhood, a full-fledged force of nature standing cross-armed in his bathing suit on the sunny beach at Spring Lake, New Jersey, the immovable keystone at the base of a human pyramid of six raffish hotel waiters enjoying their afternoon off. As evidenced in that 1919 photo, he'd been powerful through the chest right from the start, and the yoke-bearing shoulders and brawny arms he had somehow retained even through his years knocking on doors for Metropolitan Life, so that now, at forty-one, after having worked hauling heavy crates and lifting hundred-pound sacks six nights a week all through September, there was probably more explosive strength stored up in that body than ever before in his life.

Prior to that night, it would have been as impossible for me to envision him beating somebody up—let alone battering bloody his beloved older brother's fatherless son—as to imagine him atop my mother, especially as there was no taboo stronger among Jews with our impoverished European origins and our tenaciously held American ambitions than the pervasive, unwritten prohibition against settling disputes by force. In that era, the common Jewish propensity was by and large nonviolent as well as nonalcoholic, a virtue whose shortcoming was the failure to educate the bulk of the young of my generation in the combative aggression that was the first law of other ethnic educations and indisputably of great practical value when you couldn't negotiate your way out of violence or manage to run away. Among, say, the several hundred boys in my elementary school between the ages of five and fourteen who were not chromosomally preordained to be top-flight lightweights like Allie Stolz or successful racketeers like Longy Zwillman, surely far fewer fistfights broke out than in any of the other neighborhood schools in industrial Newark, where the ethical obligations of a child were differently defined and schoolmates demonstrated their belligerence by means not readily available to us.

So then, for every reason imaginable it was a devastating night. I didn't have the capacity in 1942 to begin to decipher all the awful implications, but just the sight of my father's and Alvin's blood was stunning enough. Blood spattered the length and breadth of our imitation Oriental rug, blood dripping from the splintered remains of our coffee table, blood smeared like a sign across my father's forehead, blood spurting from my cousin's nose—and the two of them not so much fistfighting, not so much wrestling as caroming, with a terrible bony thwack colliding, rearing back and charging in like men with antlers branching from their brows, fantastical, cross-species creatures sprung from mythology into our living room and pulping each other's flesh with their massive, snaggletoothed horns. Inside a house you usually scale down your movements, you scale down your speed, but here the scale of things was reversed and terrifying to behold. The South Boston riots, the Detroit riots, the Louisville assassination, the Cincinnati firebombing, the mayhem in St. Louis, Pittsburgh, Buffalo, Akron, Youngstown, Peoria, Scranton, and Syracuse . . . and now this: in an ordinary family living room—traditionally the staging area for the collective effort to hold the line *against* the intrusions of a hostile world—the anti-Semites were about to be abetted in their exhilarating solution to America's worst problem by our taking up the cudgels and hysterically destroying ourselves.

The horror ended with Mr. Cucuzza, in his nightshirt and his nightcap (attire I'd never before seen on anyone, man or boy, other than in a funny movie), crashing into our flat with his pistol drawn. A frantic wail rose from Joey's Old World grandmother, appropriately swathed like the Calabrian Queen of the Shades at the foot of our landing—and from within our own flat came a noise equally hair-raising the instant the splintered back door flew open and my mother saw that the nightshirted intruder was armed. Minna began bringing up into her hands everything she'd just swallowed at dinner, I couldn't help myself and promptly urinated, while Sandy, who alone among us was able to find the right words and the vocal strength to utter them, cried, "Don't shoot! It's Alvin!" But Mr. Cucuzza was a professional guardian of private property trained to act now and draw distinctions later and—without pausing to ask "Who's Alvin?"—immobilized my father's assailant in a strangulating half nelson with one arm while holding the pistol to his head with the hand of the other.

Alvin's prosthesis had cracked in two, his stump was torn to shreds, and one of his wrists was broken. Three of my father's front teeth were shattered, two ribs were fractured, a gash was opened along his right cheekbone that had to be sutured with almost twice as many stitches as were needed to close the wound inflicted on me by the orphanage horse, and his neck was so badly wrenched that he had to go around in a high steel collar for months afterward. The glass-topped coffee table with the dark mahogany frame that my mother had saved over the years to buy at Bam's (and where, at the conclusion of a pleasant hour of evening reading, she would set down, with its ribboned bookmark in place, the new novel by Pearl Buck or Fannie Hurst or Edna Ferber borrowed from the local pharmacy's tiny rental library) lay in fragments all across the room, and microscopic crumbs of glass were embedded in my father's hands. The rug, the walls, and the furniture were speckled with chocolate icing (from the slices of layer cake they had been eating when they sat down over dessert to talk together in the living room) as well as with their blood, and then there was the smell of it—the airless, gag-inducing slaughterhouse smell.

It's so heartbreaking, violence, when it's in a house—like seeing the clothes in a tree after an explosion. You may be prepared to see death but not the clothes in the tree.

And all of it the result of my father's failing to understand that Alvin's nature was never really reformable, despite the lecturing and the hectoring love—all of it the result of having taken him in to save him from what it was simply in his nature to become. All of it the result of my father's looking Alvin over and remembering the tragically evanescent life of Alvin's late father, and, in his despair, sadly shaking his head and saying, "A Buick automobile, a sharpie's suits, the scum of the earth for your friends—but do you know, do you care, does it bother you at all, Alvin, what's happening in this country tonight? It did years ago, damn it. I can remember clear as day when it did. But now no. Now it's big cigars and motor cars. But do you have any idea at all what is happening to the Jews even while we sit here?"

And Alvin, whose lot had finally come to something, whose prospects never before had been so hopeful, could not bear and would not endure being informed by the custodian whose tutelage had once meant everything—by the relative who, when no one else would have him, had twice taken him to live in a homey little Wee-quahic flat amid a kindly family and their benign concerns—that he had come to nothing. His voice husky with the grievance of the injured party, his delivery staccato and without a single caesura to let anything in that wasn't retaliatory, all calumny, all castigation, all coercion and fatuous bluff, Alvin shouted at my father, "The *Jews?* I wrecked my *life* for the Jews! I lost my fuckin' *leg* for the Jews! I lost my fuckin' leg for *you!* What did I give a shit either way about Lindbergh? But you send me to go fuckin' fight him, and the stupid fuckin' kid I am, I *go.* And look, *look,* Uncle Fucking Disaster—*I have no fucking leg!*"

Here he hiked up a handful of the pearl-gray fabric in which he was so lustrously clad to reveal where there was indeed no longer a lower limb of flesh and blood and muscle and bone. And then, insulted, negated, inwardly once again the unmanned man (and the bum kid), he added his final heroic touch by spitting into my father's face. A family, my father liked to say, is both peace and war, but this was family war as I could never have imagined it. Spitting into my father's face the way he'd spit into the face of that dead German soldier!

If only he had been allowed to go along unrehabilitated, on his own stinking trajectory, but that hadn't happened, and so this was how the great menace undid us and the abomination of violence entered our house, and I saw how bitterness blinds a man and the defilement it spawns.

And why, why did he go to fight in the first place? Why did he fight and why did he fall? Because there is a war going on, he chooses that way—the raging, rebellious instinct historically trapped! If only the times were different, if only he had been smarter . . . But he wants to fight. He's like the very fathers he wants to be rid of. That's the tyranny of the problem. Trying to be faithful to what he's trying to be rid of. Trying to be faithful and to get rid of what he's faithful to at the same time. And that's why he went to fight in the first place, as best I can figure it out.

Later that night, after a pair of Alvin's buddies had pulled up in a Caddy with Pennsylvania plates (one of them to get Alvin and Minna over to Allie Stolz's doctor's office on Elizabeth Avenue, the other to drive their Buick back to Philly); after my father was home from the Beth Israel emergency room (where they'd plucked the glass out of his hands and stitched up his face and x-rayed his neck and taped his ribcage and, on his way out, handed him codeine tablets to take for the pain); after Mr. Cucuzza, who'd rushed my father to the hospital in his pickup, had returned him safely to the befouled and littered battlefield that was now our flat, the gunshots erupted on Chancellor Avenue. Shots, screaming, shouting, sirens —the pogrom had begun, and it was only seconds before Mr. Cucuzza charged back up the stairs he'd only just descended and banged once on our broken back door before rushing in.

Desperate for sleep, I was dragged from bed by my brother, but when my legs wouldn't work and kept collapsing from uncontrollable fear, I had to be carried off in his arms by my father. My mother—who instead of going to bed and trying to sleep had donned her apron and a pair of rubber gloves and set about to purge the house of its filth with a bucket and a broom and a mop —my meticulous mother, weeping amid the wreckage of her living room, was guided to the door by Mr. Cucuzza, and the four of us were herded down the stairs and into the Wishnows' old flat to take cover there.

This time when Mr. Cucuzza offered a pistol, my father accepted it. His poor human body was black-and-blue and bandaged just about everywhere, his mouth was full of broken teeth, and still he sat with us on the floor in the Cucuzzas' windowless back foyer, regarding the weapon in his hands with all his concentration, as though it were no longer just a weapon but the most serious thing entrusted to him since he'd first been given his infant babies to hold. My mother sat straight up between Sandy's self-conscious stoicism and my stupefied inertness, gripping us each by the arm closest to her and doing all she could to keep a thin layer of courage from revealing her terror to the children. Meanwhile the biggest man I'd ever seen moved with a pistol through the darkened flat, stealthily advancing from window to window to ascertain with the eagle-eyed thoroughness of the veteran night watchman whether anyone lurked anywhere nearby with an ax, a gun, a rope, or a can of kerosene.

Joey, his mother, and his grandmother had been directed by Mr. Cucuzza to remain in their beds, though the old lady could not resist the magnetism of all that turbulence and the picture we four presented of sheer plight. Snarling in tiny bursts of raw Italian that could not have been complimentary to her guests, she peered out from the doorway of the dark kitchen—where she customarily slept in her clothes on a cot next to the stove—fixing us in the crosshairs of her madness (because mad she was) as if she were the patron saint of anti-Semitism whose silver crucifix had engendered it all.

The firing went on for less than an hour but we didn't head back upstairs until dawn, and didn't learn, until after Mr. Cucuzza bravely ventured forth as a scout to where Chancellor Avenue was cordoned off, that the gun battle had been not between the city police and the anti-Semites but between the city police and the Jewish police. There'd been no pogrom in Newark that night, just a shootout, extraordinary for having occurred within earshot of our house but otherwise not much different from the disorder that could erupt in any large city after dark. And though three Jews had been killed—Duke Glick, Big Gerry, and Bullet himself—it wasn't necessarily because they were Jews ("though it didn't hurt," my Uncle Monty said) but because they were exactly the sort of thugs that the new mayor wanted off the streets, primarily to signal to Longy that he was no longer an honorary member of the city's Board of Commissioners (a position he was rumored—by Meyer Ellenstein's enemies—to have held under Murphy's Jewish predecessor). Nobody bothered taking the police commissioner too seriously when he explained to the *Newark News* that it was the "trigger-happy vigilantes" who, without provocation, had opened fire a little before midnight on two foot patrolmen walking their beat, nor, among our neighbors, was there any noticeable expression of grief because of how the three—dangerous people in their own right whose protection nobody decent would have dreamed of requesting—had been unceremoniously mowed down. Of course, it was awful that the blood of violent men should stain the pavement where the neighborhood children wended their way to school every day, but at least it wasn't blood shed in a clash with the Klan or the Silver Shirts or the Bund.

No pogrom, and yet at seven that morning my father was on the phone long-distance to Winnipeg to admit to Shepsie Tirschwell that the Jews were so frightened and the anti-Semites so emboldened that it was no longer possible in Newark—where fortunately the prestige of Rabbi Prinz had continued to exert an influence over the powers that be and nothing worse than relocation had as yet been forced on a single Jewish family—to live as normal people. Whether outright government-sanctioned persecution was inevitable, nobody could say for sure, but the fear of persecution was such that not even a practical man grounded in his everyday tasks, a ˌˌˌ son who tried his best to contain the uncertainty and the anx-

ˌˌd the anger and operate according to the dictates of reason, ˌˌhope to preserve his equilibrium any longer.

Yes, my father admitted, he had been wrong all along and Bess and the Tirschwells had been right—and then, as best he could, he shook off his abashment over everything he'd mismanaged and badly misjudged, including the improbable violence that had smashed to bits, along with our coffee table, that lifelong barrier of rigid rectitude that had stood between his harsh upbringing and his mature ideals. "That's it," he told Shepsie Tirschwell, "I can't live any longer not knowing what will happen tomorrow," and their phone conversation moved on to emigration and the steps to be taken and the arrangements to be made, so that by the time Sandy and I left the house, there was no misunderstanding that, quite incredibly, we'd been overpowered by the forces arrayed against us and were about to flee and become foreigners. I wept all the way to school. Our incomparable American childhood was ended. Soon my homeland would be nothing more than my birthplace. Even Seldon in Kentucky was better off now.

But then it was over. The nightmare was over. Lindbergh was gone and we were safe, though never would I be able to revive that unfazed sense of security first fostered in a little child by a big, protective republic and his ferociously responsible parents.

Drawn from the
Archives of Newark's Newsreel Theater

Tuesday, October 6, 1942

Thirty thousand mourners stream through the great hall of Pennsylvania Station to view Walter Winchell's flag-draped coffin. The turnout exceeds even the expectations of New York mayor Fiorello La Guardia, whose decision it was to transform the assassination into the occasion for a citywide day of mourning for "American victims of Nazi violence," culminating in a funeral oration to be delivered by FDR. Outside the station (as at numerous other locations throughout the city), silent men and women dressed in somber clothing distribute half-dollar-sized black buttons whose white lettering poses the question "Where is Lindbergh?" Just before noon, Mayor La Guardia arrives at the studio of the city radio station, where he removes his wide-brimmed black Stetson (a memento of his boyhood roots in the Arizona Territory as the son of a U.S. Army bandmaster) to recite the Lord's Prayer; then he puts the hat back on to read aloud, in Hebrew, the Jewish prayer for the dead. At the stroke of noon, by decree of the City Council, a minute of silence is observed in the five boroughs. The New York police are in evidence everywhere, chiefly to oversee the protest demonstrations organized by the array of right-wing groups located in preponderantly German Yorkville—the Manhattan neighborhood north of the Upper East Side and south of Harlem that is the main headquarters for the American Nazi movement—and that militantly endorse the president and his policies. At one P.M. an honor guard of motorcycles manned by policemen wearing black armbands aligns itself with the funeral cortege forming outside Penn Station and, with the mayor leading the way from a motorcycle sidecar, escorts the cortege slowly northward up Eighth Avenue, eastward along 57th Street, northward again on Fifth Avenue to 65th Street and Temple Emanu-El. There, among the dignitaries summoned by La Guardia to fill the temple's every last seat, are the ten members of Roosevelt's 1940 cabinet, Roosevelt's four Supreme Court appointees, President Philip Murray of the CIO, President William Green of the AFL, President John L. Lewis of the United Mine Workers, Roger Baldwin of the American Civil Liberties Union, as well as past and current Democratic governors, senators, and congressmen from New York, New Jersey, Pennsylvania, and Connecticut, among them the Democrats' defeated 1928 presidential aspirant, former New York governor Al Smith. Loudspeakers installed overnight by municipal laborers and wired to telephone poles and barber poles and door lintels throughout the city carry the memorial service to the New Yorkers who've assembled on the streets of every Manhattan neighborhood (except Yorkville) and to the thousands of out-of-towners who have congregated alongside them—all those Mr. and Mrs. Americas who'd been listening to Walter Winchell weekly since he first came on the air and who have journeyed to his hometown to pay their respects. And virtually every man, woman, and child among them wears that now ubiquitous badge of defiant solidarity, the black-and-white "Where is Lindbergh?" button.

Fiorello H. La Guardia—the down-to-earth idol of the city's working people; the flamboyant ex-congressman who'd belligerently represented a congested East Harlem district of poor Italians and Jews for five terms, who as early as 1933 described Hitler as a "perverted maniac" and called for a boycott of German goods; the tenacious spokesman for the unions, the needy, and the unemployed who'd battled almost single-handedly against Hoover's do-nothing congressional Republicans during the first dark year of the Depression and, to the dismay of his own party, called for taxation to "soak the rich"; the liberal anti-Tammany reform Republican who has been the three-term Fusion mayor of the country's most populous city, the metropolis that is home to the largest concentration of Jews in the hemisphere—La Guardia is alone among the members of his party in displaying his contempt for Lindbergh and for the Nazi dogma of Aryan superiority that he (himself the son of an unobservant Jewish mother from Austrian Trieste and a freethinker Italian father who came to America as a ship's musician) has identified as the precept at the heart of Lindbergh's credo and of the huge American cult that worships the president.

La Guardia stands beside the coffin and addresses the dignitaries with that same excitable, high-pitched voice in which he famously narrated the Sunday comic strips over the city's radio station to the city's children every Sunday morning during a New York newspaper strike, like the best of uncles proceeding patiently, panel by panel, balloon by balloon, from Dick Tracy to Little Orphan Annie and on through the rest of the serialized funnies.

"We can dispense with the cant at the start," says the mayor. "Everybody knows that Walter was not a lovely human being. Walter was not the strong, silent type who hides everything but the muckraker who hates everything hidden. As anybody who ever turned up in his column can tell you, Walter was not always as accurate as he might have been. He was not shy, he was not modest, he was not decorous, discreet, kindly, et cetera. My friends, if I were to list for you everything lovely that W.W. was not, we'd be here till next Yom Kippur. I'm afraid that the late Walter Winchell was just one more doozy of a specimen of the imperfect man. In declaring himself a candidate for the presidency of the United States were his motives pure as Ivory soap? Walter Winchell's motives? Was his preposterous candidacy uncontaminated by a raving ego? My friends, only a Charles A. Lindbergh has motives pure as Ivory soap when he runs for the American presidency. Only a Charles A. Lindbergh is decorous, discreet, et cetera—oh, and accurate too, wholly accurate always when every few months he summons up the gregariousness to address his ten favorite platitudes to the nation. Only a Charles A. Lindbergh is a selfless ruler and a strong, silent saint. Walter, on the other hand, was Mr. Gossip Columnist. Walter, on the other hand, was Mr. Broadway: liked the ponies, liked the late hours, liked Sherman Billingsley—somebody once told me that he even liked the girls. And the repeal of that 'noble experiment,' as Mr. Herbert Hoover called it, the repeal of the hypocritical, expensive, stupid, unenforceable Eighteenth Amendment, was no more ignoble to Walter Winchell than it was to the rest of us here in New York. In short, Walter lacked every gleaming virtue demonstrated daily by the incorruptible test pilot ensconced in the White House.

"Oh yes, several more differences that are perhaps worth noting between fallible Walter and infallible Lindy. Our president is a fascist sympathizer, more than likely an outright fascist—and Walter Winchell was the enemy of the fascist. Our president is no lover of Jews and more than likely a dyed-in-the-wool anti-Semite while Walter Winchell was a Jew and the unwavering, vociferous enemy of the anti-Semite. Our president is an admirer of Adolf Hitler and more than likely a Nazi himself—and Walter Winchell was Hitler's first American enemy and his worst American enemy. There's where our imperfect Walter was incorruptible—where it mattered. Walter is too loud, Walter talks too fast, Walter says too much, and yet, by comparison, Walter's vulgarity is something great, and Lindbergh's decorum is hideous. Walter Winchell, my friends, was the enemy of Nazis *everywhere,* not excluding the Dieses and the Bilbos and the Parnell Thomases who serve their Führer in the United States Congress, not excluding the Hitlerites who write for the *New York Journal-American* and the *New York Daily News,* not excluding those who royally fete Nazi murderers in our American White House at the taxpayer's expense. And it was *because* he was Hitler's enemy and it was *because* he was the Nazis' enemy that Walter Winchell was gunned down yesterday in the shadow of the statue of Thomas Jefferson in gracious old Louisville's most historic and beautiful public square. For speaking his mind in the state of Kentucky, W.W. was assassinated by the Nazis of America, who, thanks to the silence of our strong, silent, selfless president, today run rampant throughout this great land. It can't happen here? My friends, it *is* happening here—and where is Lindbergh? *Where is Lindbergh?*"

Out in the streets, those listening together around the loudspeakers take up the mayor's cry, and soon their chant is cascading eerily across the entire city—"Where is *Lind*-bergh? Where is *Lind*-bergh?"—while inside the synagogue the mayor repeats and repeats his four irate syllables, angrily banging the pulpit not like an orator theatrically emphasizing a point but like an outraged citizen demanding the truth. "Where is Lindbergh?" This is the snarling peroration with which the red-faced La Guardia readies the assembled mourners for the climactic appearance of Franklin D. Roosevelt, who stuns even his closest political cronies (Hopkins, Morgenthau, Farley, Berle, Baruch, all sitting behatted only feet from the coffin of the martyred candidate, whose brand of megalomania was never to the taste of the White House inner circle, however useful a mouthpiece he may have been to their boss) by ordaining as Winchell's successor the cunning, contemptuous, short-tempered, bullheaded, roly-poly politico standing five feet two inches tall and known affectionately to his devoted constituents as the Little Flower. From the pulpit of Temple Emanu-El, the nominal head of the Democratic Party pledges his support to New York's Republican mayor as a "national unity" candidate to oppose Lindbergh's quest for a second term in 1944.

Wednesday, October 7, 1942

Piloted by President Lindbergh, the *Spirit of St. Louis* departs from Long Island in the morning, lifting off from the runway that served as the point of embarkation for the transatlantic solo flight of May 20, 1927. With no protective escort, the plane speeds through a cloudless autumn sky across New Jersey, Pennsylvania, Ohio, and down to Kentucky. Only an hour before he is to set down in the midday sunshine at the Louisville commercial airport is the White House notified by the president of his destination. His timing allows just enough notice for Louisville mayor Wilson Wyatt and the city and its citizens to prepare for the president's arrival. A mechanic is at the ready on the ground to check over the plane and tune and equip it for the return flight.

Of Louisville's 320,000 residents, the police estimate that at least a third have made the five-mile trek out from the city and are already packing the fields and the roads adjacent to Bowman Field when the president lands and smoothly taxies his plane to a platform where a microphone has been hooked up for him to address the vast crowd. When finally the great din of their greeting begins to diminish and his voice can be heard, the president makes no mention of Walter Winchell, does not allude to the assassination two days earlier or to the funeral the day before or to the speech made by Mayor La Guardia on the occasion of his anointment as Winchell's successor by Franklin Roosevelt in a New York synagogue. He does not have to. That La Guardia is, like Winchell before him, no more than a stalking horse for FDR in his dictatorial quest for an unprecedented third presidential term, and that those behind the "vicious La Guardia libel of our president" are the very same people who would have forced America to go to war in 1940, has already been colorfully explained to the nation by Vice President Wheeler in an impromptu Washington speech before the American Legion convention the previous evening.

All that the president says to the crowd is "Our country is at peace. Our people are at work. Our children are at school. I flew down here to remind you of that. Now I'm going back to Washington so as to keep things that way." An innocuous enough string of sentences, but to these tens of thousands of Kentuckians who've been the subject of national interest for two full days it is as though he has announced the end of all hardship on earth. Pandemonium once again, while the president, as laconic as ever and bidding farewell with just a single wave, squeezes his lanky frame back into the plane's cockpit, and from the airstrip a smiling mechanic signals with his wrench that everything's checked out and ready to go. The engine turns, the Lone Eagle waves a final goodbye, and with a rush and a roar the *Spirit of St. Louis* lifts free of Daniel Boone's gorgeous wilderness state, inch by inch, foot by foot, until at last (like the barnstorming, skydiving, wing-walking stunt pilot he'd been as a kid, flying low over the farming towns of the West—and to the delight of the delirious crowd) Lindy clears by no more than a hairsbreadth the telephone wires strung from the poles along Route 58. Rising steadily into the stream of a warm, gentle tailwind, the most famous small plane in aviation history—the modern-day counterpart of Columbus's *Santa María* and the Pilgrims' *Mayflower*—disappears eastward, never to be seen again.

Thursday, October 8, 1942

Ground searches of the regular flight path between Louisville and Washington yield no evidence of wreckage despite the perfect fall weather that makes it possible for local search parties to penetrate deep into the rugged mountains of West Virginia and to range over the harvested farmlands of Maryland and for state authorities to dispatch police launches up and down the Maryland and Delaware coastlines throughout the daylight hours. In the afternoon the Army, Coast Guard, and Navy join the search, along with hundreds of men and boys in every county from every state east of the Mississippi who have volunteered to assist the National Guard units called out by the state governors. Yet by dinnertime in Washington there is still no reported sighting of the plane or its wreckage, and so at eight P.M. the cabinet is summoned to an emergency meeting at the vice president's home. There Burton K. Wheeler announces that, after consulting with the First Lady and the majority leaders of the House and the Senate and the chief justice of the Supreme Court, he has deemed it in the country's best interest to assume the duties of acting president in accordance with Article II, Section 1 of the U.S. Constitution.

In dozens of newspapers, the evening headline, printed in the boldest, blackest type seen on America's front pages since the stock market crash of 1929 (and intended to shame Fiorello La Guardia), somberly reads: WHERE IS LINDBERGH?

Friday, October 9, 1942

By the time Americans awaken to begin their day, martial law has been imposed throughout the continental United States and in the territories and possessions. At noon Acting President Wheeler travels under military guard to the Capitol, where he announces to an emergency closed-door session of Congress that the FBI has received information establishing that the president has been kidnapped and is being held by parties unknown at a location somewhere in North America. The acting president assures the Congress that all steps are being taken to secure the president's release and to bring the perpetrators of the crime to justice. In the meantime the country's borders with Canada and Mexico have been sealed, airports and seaports have been shut down, and law and order, says the acting president, is to be maintained in the District of Columbia by the U.S. armed forces and elsewhere by the National Guard in cooperation with the FBI and local police authorities.

AGAIN!

So reads the one-word headline carried on every Hearst paper in the country and printed above pictures of the little Lindbergh baby, last photographed alive in 1932, only days before his kidnapping at the age of twenty months.

Saturday, October 10, 1942

German state radio announces that the kidnapping of Charles A. Lindbergh, thirty-third president of the United States and signatory to America's historic Iceland Understanding with the Third Reich, has been discovered to have been perpetrated by a conspiracy of "Jewish interests." Top-secret Wehrmacht intelligence data are cited to corroborate initial reports from the Ministry of State that the plot was masterminded by the warmonger Roosevelt—in collusion with his Jewish Treasury secretary, Morgenthau, his Jewish Supreme Court justice, Frankfurter, and the Jewish investment banker Baruch—and that it is being financed by the international Jewish usurers Warburg and Rothschild and carried out under the command of Roosevelt's mongrel henchman, the half-Jew gangster La Guardia, mayor of Jewish New York City, along with the powerful Jewish governor of New York State, the financier Lehman, in order to return Roosevelt to the White House and launch of an all-out Jewish war against the non-Jewish world. The intelligence data, which have been turned over to the FBI by the German embassy in Washington, allege that the assassination of Walter Winchell was planned and executed by the same cabal of Roosevelt Jews—and responsibility for the crime predictably attributed by them to Americans of German descent—so as to foster the vicious "Where is Lindbergh?" campaign, which in turn moved the president to take to the air and fly to the scene of the assassination to reassure the citizens of Louisville, Kentucky, who were justifiably fearful of organized Jewish retaliation. But there—according to the Wehrmacht reports—as the president addressed the crowd, an airport mechanic bribed by the Jewish conspiracy (who has himself vanished and is believed to have been murdered by order of La Guardia) rendered the aircraft's radio inoperative. No sooner had the president taken off for Washington than he was unable to make contact with the ground or with other aircraft and had no choice but to capitulate when the *Spirit of St. Louis* was corralled by high-flying British fighter planes, which forced him to deviate from his course and to land, some hours later, at an airstrip secretly maintained by international Jewish interests across the Canadian border from Lehman's state of New York.

In America, the German announcement prompts Mayor La Guardia to tell City Hall reporters, "Any American who can believe that lollapalooza of a Nazi lie has sunk to the lowest possible level." Nonetheless, both the mayor and the governor are said by informed sources to have been interviewed at length by agents of the FBI, and Secretary of the Interior Ford is demanding that Mackenzie King, prime minister of Canada, conduct an intensive search on Canadian soil for President Lindbergh and his captors. Acting President Wheeler is reported to be examining the German documentation with White House aides but will make no comment about the allegations until the search for the president's plane has been completed. Navy destroyers along with Coast Guard PT boats are now looking for signs of an air crash as far north as Cape May, New Jersey, and as far south as Cape Hatteras, North Carolina, while ground units of the Army, Marine Corps, and National Guard continue to search in twenty states for clues to the missing plane's whereabouts.

The National Guard units enforcing the nationwide curfew report no incidents of violence prompted by the president's disappearance. Under martial law, America remains calm, though the Grand Wizard of the Ku Klux Klan and the leader of the American Nazi Party have jointly called upon the acting president "to implement extreme measures to protect America from a Jewish coup d'état."

Meanwhile a committee of American Jewish clergymen led by Rabbi Stephen Wise of New York telegrams the First Lady expressing their deepest sympathy in her family's hour of need. Rabbi Lionel Bengelsdorf is seen entering the White House in the early evening, reportedly there at Mrs. Lindbergh's request to offer spiritual guidance to the family during what is now the third day of their vigil. The White House invitation to Rabbi Bengelsdorf is widely interpreted to indicate the First Lady's refusal to accept that "Jewish interests" have had anything to do with her husband's disappearance.

Sunday, October 11, 1942

At church services around the country, prayers are offered in behalf of the Lindbergh family. The three major radio networks cancel regularly scheduled programs to broadcast the services conducted at Washington's National Cathedral, where the First Lady and her children are in attendance, and for the remainder of the day and into the evening, programming is devoted exclusively to inspirational music. At eight P.M. Acting President Wheeler addresses the nation, assuring his fellow Americans that he has no plans to abandon the search. He reports that at the invitation of the Canadian prime minister representatives from American law enforcement agencies will assist the Royal Canadian Mounted Police in scouring the eastern half of the U.S.-Canada border and the southernmost counties of the easterly Canadian provinces.

Having emerged as official spokesman for the First Lady, Rabbi Lionel Bengelsdorf tells a large group of reporters waiting on the White House portico that Mrs. Lindbergh urges the American people to ignore speculation emanating from any foreign government concerning the circumstances of her husband's disappearance. She would remind the public, the rabbi says, that in 1926, as an airmail pilot on the St. Louis–Chicago run, the president twice survived, without injury, crashes that demolished his aircraft, and that as of the moment it is the First Lady's belief that the president will once again be found to have survived should there have been another crash. The First Lady remains unconvinced, says the rabbi, by the evidence of a kidnapping that has been presented to her by the acting president. When Rabbi Bengelsdorf is asked why Mrs. Lindbergh cannot speak for herself and why the press is being prevented from questioning her directly, he replies, "Bear in mind that this is not the first time in her thirty-six years that Mrs. Lindbergh has been required to deal with inquiries from the press while enduring the gravest of family crises. I would think that Americans are altogether willing to accept whatever arrangement the First Lady decides will best protect her and her children's privacy for however long the search continues." When he is asked if there is any truth to rumors that Mrs. Lindbergh is too distraught to make her own decisions and that it is Lionel Bengelsdorf who is reaching her decisions for her, the rabbi replies, "Anyone who observed the demeanor of the First Lady at the cathedral this morning is able to see for himself that she is wholly competent intellectually, in complete possession of all her faculties, and that, despite the magnitude of the situation, neither her reason nor her judgment has been in any way impaired."

Despite the rabbi's assurances, stories go out over the wire services reporting on suspicions voiced by a "highly placed government official"—believed to be Secretary Ford—that the First Lady has become the captive of "Rabbi Rasputin," the Jewish spokesman considered comparable in his influence over the president's wife to the lunatic Siberian peasant monk who insidiously controlled the minds of the czar and czarina of Russia and all but ruled the imperial palace in the days leading up to the Russian Revolution and whose mad reign ended only when he was murdered by a conspiracy of patriotic Russian aristocrats.

Monday, October 12, 1942

The London morning papers report that British intelligence has forwarded to the FBI German coded communications proving beyond a doubt that President Lindbergh is alive and in Berlin. British intelligence ascertains that on October 7, in keeping with a long-standing plan conceived by Air Marshal Hermann Göring, the president of the United States succeeded in ditching the *Spirit of St. Louis* at predetermined coordinates in the Atlantic approximately three hundred miles east of Washington. There he reconnoitered with a waiting German U-boat whose crew transferred him to a German naval vessel waiting off the coast of Portugal to take him to Italian-occupied Cotor in Montenegro, on the Adriatic Sea. The wreckage of the president's plane was commandeered and taken on board by a German military freighter, dismantled, crated, and transported to a Gestapo warehouse in Bremen. The president himself was flown from a Cotor airstrip to Germany in a camouflaged Luftwaffe plane, accompanied by Air Marshal Göring, and upon his arrival at a Luftwaffe airbase was driven to Hitler's Berchtesgaden hideaway to confer with the Führer.

Serbian resistance groups in Yugoslavia confirm the British intelligence reports on the basis of information supplied by sources within the German-instituted Belgrade government of General Milan Nedich, whose interior ministry directed the naval operation at the port of Cotor.

In New York, Mayor La Guardia tells reporters, "If it is true that our president has voluntarily fled to Nazi Germany, if it is true that, since his taking the oath of office, he has been working from the White House as a Nazi agent, if it is true that our domestic and foreign policies have been dictated to the president by the Nazi regime that today tyrannizes the entire European continent, then I lack the words to describe a treason whose wickedness is without equal in human history."

Despite the imposition of martial law and a nationwide curfew, and despite the presence of heavily armed National Guard troops patrolling the streets of every major American city, anti-Semitic riots begin just after sundown in Alabama, Illinois, Indiana, Iowa, Kentucky, Missouri, Ohio, South Carolina, Tennessee, North Carolina, and Virginia, and continue throughout the night and into the early morning. Not until approximately eight A.M. are federal troops—dispatched by Acting President Wheeler to support the National Guard units—able to quell these disturbances and to bring under control the worst of the fires the rioters have set. By then 122 American citizens have lost their lives.

Tuesday, October 13, 1942

In a noontime radio address, Acting President Wheeler places responsibility for the riots on "the British government and their warmongering American supporters."

"Having falsely disseminated the vilest charges that could possibly be leveled against a patriot of the stature of Charles A. Lindbergh, just what did these people expect from a nation already grieving over the disappearance of a beloved leader? To advance their own economic and racial interests," says the acting president, "these people choose to try to the limit the conscience of a heartsick nation, and just what do they then expect will occur? I can report that order has been restored to our ravaged cities throughout the South and the Midwest, but at what cost to the equanimity of our nation?"

A statement from the president's wife is subsequently delivered by Rabbi Lionel Bengelsdorf. Once again the First Lady counsels her countrymen to ignore all unverifiable hypotheses about her husband's disappearance emanating from foreign capitals, and she requests of the U.S. government the immediate termination of the weeklong search for her husband's plane. The First Lady wishes the country to recall the tragic plight of Amelia Earhart, the greatest of woman aviators, who, following the lead of President Lindbergh, made her heralded solo flight across the Atlantic in 1932, only to disappear without a trace in 1937 while attempting a solo flight across the Pacific. "As an experienced aviator in her own right," Rabbi Bengelsdorf tells the press, "the First Lady has concluded that something very like what happened to Amelia Earhart appears now to have overtaken the president. Life is not without risk, and aviation, of course, is not without risk, particularly for those like Amelia Earhart and Charles A. Lindbergh, whose daring and courage as solo aviators launched the aeronautical age in which we now live."

Requests by reporters to meet with the First Lady are once again politely declined by her official spokesman, prompting Secretary Ford to demand the arrest of Rabbi Rasputin.

Wednesday, October 14, 1942

In the early evening Mayor La Guardia calls a press conference to point in particular to three manifestations of the "sheer derangement that is threatening the nation's sanity."

First, a front-page *Chicago Tribune* article, datelined Berlin, reports that the twelve-year-old son of President and Mrs. Lindbergh —the child believed to have been kidnapped and murdered in New Jersey in 1932—has been reunited with his father at Berchtesgaden after having been rescued by the Nazis from a dungeon in Kraków, Poland, where he had been held prisoner in the city's Jewish ghetto ever since his disappearance and where, each year, blood was drawn from the captive boy to be used in the ritual preparation of the community's Passover matzohs.

Second, House Republicans introduce a bill calling for a declaration of war against the Commonwealth of Canada should Prime Minister King fail to reveal the whereabouts of America's missing president within forty-eight hours.

Third, law enforcement agencies in the South and the Midwest report that the "so-called anti-Semitic riots" of October 12 were instigated by "local Jewish elements" working as part of "a far-reaching Jewish conspiracy intent on undermining the country's morale." Of the 122 killed in the rioting, 97 have already been identified as "Jewish provocateurs" seeking to deflect suspicion from the very group responsible for the disorder and plotting to take control of the federal government.

Mayor La Guardia says, "There's a plot afoot all right, and I'll gladly name the forces propelling it—hysteria, ignorance, malice, stupidity, hatred, and fear. What a repugnant spectacle our country has become! Falsehood, cruelty, and madness everywhere, and brute force in the wings waiting to finish us off. Now we read in the *Chicago Tribune* that all these years clever Jewish bakers have been using the blood of the kidnapped Lindbergh child for making Passover matzohs in Poland—a story just as nutty today as when it was first concocted by anti-Semitic maniacs five hundred years ago. How it must please the Führer to be poisoning our country with this sinister nonsense. Jewish interests. Jewish elements. Jewish usurers. Jewish retaliation. Jewish conspiracies. A Jewish war against the world. To have enslaved America with this hocus-pocus! To have captured the mind of the world's greatest nation without uttering a single word of truth! Oh, the pleasure we must be affording the most malevolent man on earth!"

Thursday, October 15, 1942

Just before dawn Rabbi Lionel Bengelsdorf is taken into custody by the FBI under suspicion of being "among the ringleaders of the Jewish conspiratorial plot against America." At the same time the First Lady, said to be suffering from "extreme nervous exhaustion," is transferred by ambulance from the White House to Walter Reed Army Hospital. Others arrested in the early-morning roundup include Governor Lehman, Bernard Baruch, Justice Frankfurter, Frankfurter protégé and Roosevelt administrator David Lilienthal, New Deal advisers Adolf Berle and Sam Rosenman, labor leaders David Dubinsky and Sidney Hillman, economist Isador Lubin, leftist journalists I. F. Stone and James Wechsler, and socialist Louis Waldman. More arrests are said to be imminent, but the FBI has not disclosed whether the charge of conspiring to kidnap the president will be brought against any or all of the suspects.

Tank and infantry units of the U.S. Army enter New York to assist the National Guard in putting down sporadic antigovernment street violence. In Chicago, Philadelphia, and Boston attempts to mount protest demonstrations against the FBI—demonstrations in violation of martial law—result only in minor injuries, though arrests numbering in the hundreds are reported by police.

In Congress, leading Republicans praise the FBI for thwarting the conspirators' plot. In New York, Mayor La Guardia is joined at a press conference by Eleanor Roosevelt and Roger Baldwin of the ACLU. They demand the immediate release of Governor Lehman along with his alleged co-conspirators. La Guardia is subsequently arrested at the mayor's mansion.

To address an emergency protest rally convened by a New York citizens' committee, former president Roosevelt travels from his home at Hyde Park to New York; "for his own protection" he is promptly taken into custody by the police. The U.S. Army shuts down all newspaper offices and radio stations in New York, where the after-dark martial-law curfew will be enforced round the clock until further notice. Tanks close off all bridges and tunnels into the city.

In Buffalo the mayor announces his intention to distribute gas masks to the city's citizens, and the mayor of nearby Rochester initiates a bomb shelter program "to protect our residents in the event of a surprise Canadian attack." An exchange of small-arms fire is reported by the Canadian Broadcasting Company on the border between Maine and the province of New Brunswick, not far from Roosevelt's summer home on Campobello Island in the Bay of Fundy. From London, Prime Minister Churchill warns of an imminent German invasion of Mexico, purportedly to protect America's southern flank while the United States sets about to wrest control of Canada from the British. "It is no longer a matter," says Churchill, "of the great American democracy taking military action to save us. The time has come for American citizens to take civil action to save themselves. There are not two isolated historical dramas, the American and the British, and there never were. There is only one ordeal, and now as in the past we face it in common."

Friday, October 16, 1942
Beginning at nine A.M., a radio transmitter secreted somewhere in the nation's capital broadcasts the voice of the First Lady, who, with the assistance of Lindbergh loyalists inside the Secret Service, has managed to escape from Walter Reed, where—alleged by authorities to be a mental patient in the care of Army psychiatrists—she has been straitjacketed and held prisoner for nearly twenty-four hours. The tone is appealingly gentle, the words uttered without a trace of harshness or righteous contempt—altogether the evenly paced voice of someone entirely respectable who is ed-

ucated to face down sorrow and disappointment without ever losing her self-restraint. She is no cyclone, yet the undertaking is extraordinary and she shows no fear.

"My fellow Americans, unlawfulness on the part of America's law enforcement agencies cannot and will not be allowed to prevail. In my husband's name, I ask all National Guard units to disarm and disband and for our guardsmen to return to civilian life. I ask all members of the United States armed forces to leave our cities and to regroup at their home bases under the command of their authorized senior officers. I ask the FBI to release all of those arrested on charges of conspiring to harm my husband and to restore immediately their full rights as citizens. I ask law enforcement authorities throughout the nation to do the same with those who have been detained in local and state jails. There is not a shred of evidence that a single detainee is in any way responsible for whatever befell my husband and his plane on or after Wednesday, October 7, 1942. I ask the New York City police to vacate the illegally occupied premises of government-sequestered newspapers, magazines, and radio stations and that these facilities resume their normal activities as guaranteed under the First Amendment to the Constitution. I ask the Congress of the United States to initiate proceedings to remove from office the current acting president of the United States and to appoint a new president in accordance with the Presidential Succession Act of 1886, which designates the secretary of state as next in line for the presidency should the vice presidency be vacant. The Succession Act of 1886 also states that, under the circumstances described, Congress shall decide whether to call a special presidential election, and so I ask the Congress to do just that and to authorize a presidential election that will coincide with the congressional election scheduled for the first Tuesday after the first Monday of November."

Her morning broadcast is repeated by the First Lady every half hour until, at noon, she announces that, in defiance of the acting president—whom she charges by name with having ordered her illegal abduction and confinement—she is returning to take up residence with her children at the White House. Deliberately appropriating for her peroration echoes of American democracy's most revered text, she concludes, "I will not yield to or be intimidated by the illegal representatives of a seditious administration, and I ask no more of the American people than that they follow my example and refuse to accept or support government conduct that is indefensible. The history of the present administration is a history of repeated injuries and usurpations, all having in direct object the establishment of an absolute tyranny over these states. This government has been deaf to the voice of justice and has extended over us an unwarrantable jurisdiction. Consequently, in defense of those same inalienable rights claimed in July of 1776 by Jefferson of Virginia and Franklin of Pennsylvania and Adams of Massachusetts Bay, and by the authority of the same good people of these United States, and appealing to the same supreme judge of the world for the rectitude of our intentions, I, Anne Morrow Lindbergh, a native of the state of New Jersey, a resident of the District of Columbia, and the spouse of the thirty-third president of the United States, declare that injurious history of usurpation to be ended. Our enemies' plot has failed, liberty and justice are restored, and those who have violated the Constitution of the United States shall now be addressed by the judicial branch of government, in strict keeping with the law of the land."

"Our Lady of the White House"—as Harold Ickes grudgingly christens Mrs. Lindbergh—returns to the presidential living quarters early that evening, and from there, marshaling the power of her mystique as sorrowing mother of the martyred infant and resolute widow of the vanished god, engineers the speedy dismantling by Congress and the courts of the unconstitutional Wheeler administration, whose criminality, in a mere eight days in office, has far exceeded that of Warren Harding's Republican administration twenty years earlier.

The restoration of orderly democratic procedures initiated by Mrs. Lindbergh culminates two and a half weeks later, on Tuesday, November 3, 1942, in a sweep by the Democrats of the House and the Senate and the landslide victory of Franklin Delano Roosevelt for a third presidential term.

The next month—following the devastating surprise attack on Pearl Harbor by the Japanese and, four days later, the declaration of war on the United States by Germany and Italy—America enters the global conflict that had begun in Europe some three years earlier with the German invasion of Poland and had since expanded to encompass two-thirds of the world's population. Disgraced by their collusion with the acting president and demoralized by their colossal electoral defeat, the few Republicans remaining in Congress pledge their support to the Democratic president and his fight to the finish against the Axis powers. The House and the Senate approve America's going to war without a dissenting vote in either chamber, and the day following his inauguration, President Roosevelt issues Proclamation No. 2568, "Granting a Pardon to Burton Wheeler." In part it reads:

> As a result of certain acts occurring before his removal from the Office of Acting President, Burton K. Wheeler has become liable to possible indictment and trial for offenses against the United States. To spare the country the ordeal of such a criminal prosecution against a former Acting President of the United States and to protect against the disruptive distraction of such a spectacle during a time of war, I, Franklin Delano Roosevelt, President of the United States, pursuant to the pardon power conferred upon me by Article II, Section 2 of the Constitution, have granted and by these presents do grant a full, free, and absolute pardon unto Burton Wheeler for all offenses against the United States which he, Burton Wheeler, has committed or may have committed or taken part in during the period from October 8, 1942, through October 16, 1942.

As everyone knows, President Lindbergh was not found or heard from again, though stories circulated throughout the war and for a decade afterward, along with the rumors about other prominent missing persons of that turbulent era, like Martin Bormann, Hitler's private secretary, who was thought to have eluded the Allied armies by escaping to Juan Peron's Argentina—but who more likely perished during the last days of Nazi Berlin—and Raoul Wallenberg, the Swedish diplomat whose distribution of Swedish passports saved some twenty thousand Hungarian Jews from extermination by the Nazis, although he himself disappeared, probably into a Soviet jail, when the Russians occupied Budapest in 1945. Among the dwindling number of Lindbergh conspiracy scholars, reports on clues and sightings have continued to appear in intermittently published newsletters devoted to speculation on the unexplained fate of America's thirty-third president.

The most elaborate story, the most unbelievable story—though not necessarily the least convincing—was first made known to our family by Aunt Evelyn after Rabbi Bengelsdorf's arrest, her source none other than Anne Morrow Lindbergh, who allegedly confided the details to the rabbi just days before she was removed from the White House against her will and held prisoner in the psychiatric wing of Walter Reed.

Mrs. Lindbergh, reported Rabbi Bengelsdorf, traced everything to the 1932 kidnapping of her infant son Charles, secretly plotted and financed, she maintained, by the Nazi Party shortly before Hitler came to power. According to the rabbi's recapitulation of the First Lady's story, the baby had been passed on for safekeeping by Bruno Hauptmann to a friend living near him in the Bronx—a fellow German immigrant who in actuality was a Nazi espionage agent—and only hours after having been lifted from the Hopewell, New Jersey, crib and carried down the makeshift ladder in Hauptmann's arms, Charles Jr. had already been smuggled out of the country and was en route to Germany. The corpse found and identified as the Lindbergh baby ten weeks later was another child, selected by the Nazis to be murdered because of its resemblance to the Lindbergh baby and then, when the body was already decomposing, planted in the woods near the Lindbergh home to ensure

Hauptmann's conviction and execution and to keep secret the true circumstances of the kidnapping from everyone but the Lindberghs themselves. Through a Nazi spy stationed as a foreign newspaper correspondent in New York, the couple had been informed early on of Charles's arrival, healthy and unharmed, on German soil and assured that the best of care would be given him by a specially selected team of Nazi doctors, nurses, teachers, and military personnel—care merited by his status as firstborn son of the world's greatest aviator—provided that the Lindberghs cooperated fully with Berlin.

As a result of this threat, for the next ten years the lot of the Lindberghs and their kidnapped child—and, gradually, the destiny of the United States of America—was determined by Adolf Hitler. Through the skill and efficiency of his agents in New York and Washington—and in London and Paris after the celebrated couple, complying with orders, "fled" to live as expatriates in Europe, where Lindbergh began regularly to visit Nazi Germany and extol the achievements of its military machine—the Nazis set about to exploit Lindbergh's fame in behalf of the Third Reich and at the expense of America, dictating where the couple would reside, whom they would befriend, and, above all, what opinions they would espouse in their public utterances and published writings. In 1938, as a reward for Lindbergh's graciously accepting a prestigious medal from Hermann Göring at a Berlin dinner in the aviator's honor, and after numerous pleading letters that were secretly channeled from Anne Morrow Lindbergh to the Führer himself, the Lindberghs were at last allowed to visit their child, by then a handsome fair-haired boy of almost eight who, from the day he'd arrived in Germany, had been raised as a model Hitler youth. The German-speaking cadet did not understand, nor was he told, that the famous Americans to whom he and his classmates were introduced following parade exercises at their elite military academy were his mother and father, nor were the Lindberghs permitted to speak to him or to be photographed with him. The visit came at just the moment when Anne Morrow Lindbergh had concluded that the Nazis' kidnapping story was an unspeakably cruel hoax and that the time was long overdue for the Lindberghs to free themselves from their bondage to Adolf Hitler. Instead, after seeing Charles alive for the first time since his disappearance in 1932, the Lindberghs left Germany irreversibly in thrall to their country's worst enemy.

They were ordered to end their expatriation and return to America, where Colonel Lindbergh was to take up the cause of America First. Speeches were provided, written in English, denouncing the British, Roosevelt, and the Jews and supporting America's neutrality in the European war; detailed instructions specified where and when speeches were to be delivered, even the type of apparel to be donned for each public appearance. Every political stratagem originating in Berlin Lindbergh enacted with the same meticulous perfectionism that distinguished his aeronautical pursuits, right down to the night that he arrived in aviator attire at the Republican Convention and accepted the nomination for the presidency with words written for the occasion by Nazi propaganda minister Joseph Goebbels. The Nazis plotted every maneuver of the election campaign that followed, and once Lindbergh had defeated FDR, it was Hitler himself who took charge, proceeding to prepare—in weekly meetings with Göring, his designated successor and director of the German economy, and Heinrich Himmler, overlord of Germany's internal affairs and chief of the Gestapo, the police agency charged with Charles Lindbergh Jr.'s custody—a foreign policy for the United States that would best serve Germany's wartime objectives and his grand imperial design.

Soon Himmler began to interfere directly in U.S. domestic affairs by bringing pressure on President Lindbergh—humorously belittled in the Gestapo chief's memos as "our American Gauleiter"—to institute repressive measures against the four and a half million American Jews, and it was here, according to Mrs. Lindbergh, that the president undertook, if only passively at the start, to assert his resistance. To begin with, he ordered the establishment of the Office of American Absorption, in his judgment an agency inconsequential enough to leave the Jews essentially unharmed while seemingly meeting—with token programs like Just Folks and Homestead 42—Himmler's directive "to inaugurate in America a systematic process of marginalization that will lead in the foreseeable future to the confiscation of all Jewish wealth and the total disappearance of the Jewish population, their appurtenances, and their property."

Heinrich Himmler was hardly one to be misled by such a transparent deception or to bother to disguise his disappointment when Lindbergh dared to justify himself—through von Ribbentrop, whom Himmler dispatched to Washington, supposedly on a ceremonial state visit, to assist the president in formulating more stringent anti-Jewish measures—by explaining to the supreme commandant of Hitler's concentration camps that guarantees embedded in the U.S. Constitution, combined with long-standing American democratic traditions, made it impossible for a final solution to the Jewish problem to be executed in America as rapidly or efficiently as on a continent where there was a thousand-year history of anti-Semitism deeply rooted in the common people and where Nazi rule was absolute. During the state dinner given in von Ribbentrop's honor, the president was taken aside by his esteemed guest and handed a cablegram, decoded moments earlier at the German embassy, that constituted in its entirety Himmler's reply. "Think of the child," the cablegram read, "before you again respond with such poppycock. Think of brave young Charles, an outstanding German military cadet who already at the age of twelve knows better than his celebrated father the value assigned by our Führer to constitutional guarantees and democratic traditions, especially where the rights of parasites are concerned."

The dressing-down by Himmler of "the Lone Eagle with the chicken heart" (as Lindbergh was described in Himmler's internal m___) marked the beginning of Lindbergh's repudiation as a ___ useful to the Third Reich. By defeating Roosevelt and the ___ interventionists in Roosevelt's party he had provided the ___ rmy with additional time to quell the continuing and unexpected resistance from the Soviet Union without Germany's running the risk of having simultaneously to confront the industrial and military might of the United States. Even more important, Lindbergh's presidency furnished German industry and the German scientific establishment—already secretly developing a bomb of unparalleled explosive force powered by atomic fission, as well as a rocket engine capable of conveying this weapon across the Atlantic—with a further two years in which to complete preparation for the apocalyptic struggle with the United States whose outcome, as envisioned by Hitler, would determine the course of Western civilization and the progress of mankind for the next millennium. Had Himmler found in Lindbergh the visionary Jew-hater the German high command had been led to expect from intelligence reports, rather than what Himmler contemptuously dubbed "a dinner-party anti-Semite," perhaps the president would have been permitted to complete his term in office and to serve a second four years before retiring and ceding the government to Henry Ford, whom Hitler had already settled on as Lindbergh's successor, despite Ford's advanced age. Had Himmler been able to rely on an American president of unimpeachable American credentials to implement the final solution to America's Jewish problem, it would, of course, have been preferable to the employment at a later date of German resources and personnel to fulfill that mission in North America, and Lindbergh's plane would not have had to disappear from the skies, as was deemed necessary by Berlin, on Wednesday, October 7, 1942—nor would Acting President Wheeler have assumed power the following evening and, to the astonished delight of those who'd considered him till then nothing more than a buffoon, proved himself a genuine leader in a matter of days by spontaneously implementing the very measures that von Ribbentrop had proposed to Lindbergh and that, as Himmler believed, the American hero had failed to carry out because of the puerile moral objections of his wife.

Within an hour of Lindbergh's disappearance, Mrs. Lindbergh had been informed by the German embassy that responsibility for her child's well-being was now hers alone and that, should she do anything other than vacate the White House and withdraw in silence from public life, Charles Jr. would be removed from his military academy and dispatched to the Russian front for the November offensive on Stalingrad and remain on duty there as the Third Reich's youngest combat infantryman until he valiantly expired on the field of battle for the greater glory of the German people.

This is the story whose gist Aunt Evelyn conveyed to my mother when she appeared at our house in the hours after Rabbi Bengelsdorf was taken in handcuffs from their Washington hotel by agents of the FBI. More fully elaborated, it is the story told in *My Life Under Lindbergh*, the 550-page apologia published as an insider's diary just after the war by Rabbi Bengelsdorf and dismissed then in a press statement by a spokesman for the Lindbergh family as "a reprehensible calumny with no basis in fact, motivated by vengeance and greed, sustained by egomaniacal delusion, invented for the sake of crass commercial exploitation, and one that Mrs. Lindbergh will not dignify with a further response." When my mother first heard the story it seemed to her conclusive evidence that the shock of witnessing Rabbi Bengelsdorf's arrest had temporarily caused her sister to lose her mind.

The day after Aunt Evelyn's surprise visit was Friday, October 16, 1942, when Mrs. Lindbergh, before returning to the White House, went on the air from a secret Washington location and, based solely on her authority as "spouse of the thirty-third president of the United States," pronounced the "injurious history of usurpation" implemented by the administration of the acting president "to be ended." Whether any harm befell her kidnapped child as a consequence of the First Lady's bravery, whether Charles Jr. had ever even survived his infancy to suffer the dreadful fate that Himmler had promised, let alone to endure the childhood of a privileged ward and treasured hostage of the German state, whether Himmler, Göring, and Hitler had anything of importance to do with fostering Lindbergh's rise to political eminence as an

America Firster or shaping U.S. policy during the twenty-two-month Lindbergh presidency or implementing Lindbergh's mysterious disappearance—have been matters of controversy for over half a century, though by now a far less impassioned and widespread controversy than when, for some thirty-odd weeks in 1946 (and despite its oft-quoted characterization by Westbrook Pegler, the dean of America's Roosevelt-hating right-wing journalists, as "the crackpot diary of a certifiable mythomaniac"), *My Life Under Lindbergh* remained at the top of the American bestseller lists along with two personal biographies of FDR, who had died in office the previous year, only weeks before the unconditional surrender of Nazi Germany to the Allies marked the end of World War Two in Europe.

9

October 1942

Perpetual Fear

THE CALL FROM Seldon came when my mother, Sandy, and I were already in bed. This was Monday, the twelfth of October, and at dinnertime we had heard the reports on the radio of the rioting that had broken out in the Midwest and the South following the announcement by British intelligence that President Lindbergh had deliberately ditched his plane three hundred miles out to sea and from there had been whisked by the navy and air corps of Nazi Germany to a secret rendezvous with Hitler. Not until the next day were the morning papers able to furnish details of the riots sparked by this dispatch, though barely minutes after the news had reached us at our kitchen table, my mother had guessed correctly whom the rioters had targeted and why. It was by then three days since the border to Canada had been closed, and even to me, who found leaving America an unbearable prospect, it was clear that my father's refusal to listen to my mother and get us out of the country months before was the gravest mistake he'd ever made. He was now back working nights at the market, my mother went into the streets every day to shop for groceries—quixotically, she had attended a meeting at school one afternoon for the prospective poll watchers in the November election—Sandy and I went off to school each morning with our friends, but nonetheless, by the beginning of the second week of Acting President Wheeler's administration, the fear was everywhere, and this despite Mrs.

Lindbergh's advising Americans to dismiss the reports emanating from foreign countries about the president's whereabouts, despite the ascendancy as a newsworthy figure of Rabbi Bengelsdorf, a member now of our family, an uncle by marriage who'd even eaten dinner once in our house but who couldn't do a thing to help us and wouldn't if he could because of the contempt he and my father harbored each for the other. The fear was everywhere, the *look* was everywhere, in the eyes of our protectors especially, the look that comes in the split second after you have locked the door and realize you don't have the key. We had never before observed the adults all helplessly thinking the same thoughts. The strongest among them did their best to be calm and brave and to sound realistic when they told us that our worries would soon be over and the regular round of life restored, but when they turned on the news they were devastated by the speed with which everything dreadful was happening.

Then, on the evening of the twelfth—while each of us lay in bed unable to sleep—the phone rang: Seldon calling collect from Kentucky. It was ten at night and his mother still wasn't home, and since he knew our number by heart (and didn't know whom else to call), he cranked the phone, got the operator, and, in a rush, trying to articulate all the necessary words before the power of speech deserted him, said to her, "Collect, please. Newark, New Jersey. 81 Summit Avenue. Waverley 3–4827. My name is Sheldon Wishnow. I want to speak person-to-person to Mr. or Mrs. Roth. Or Philip. Or Sandy. Anyone, operator. My mother's not home. I'm ten. I haven't eaten and she's not here. Operator, please—Waverley 3–4827! I'll talk to anybody!"

That morning Mrs. Wishnow had driven to Louisville, to the Metropolitan regional office, to report at the company's request to her district supervisor. Louisville was more than a hundred miles from Danville, and the roads were so bad most of the way that it was going to take practically all day just to get there and back. Why the district supervisor couldn't have written a letter or picked up the phone to tell her what he had to say nobody ever understood, nor was the man himself ever asked to explain. My father's guess was that the company intended to fire her that day—to have her turn in her ledger with its handwritten record of collections and then to send her on her way, unemployed after a mere six weeks on the job and seven hundred miles from home. She'd done no business to speak of in those first weeks out in the rural reaches of Boyle County, though not for lack of hard work—primarily it was because there wasn't the business there to do. In fact, every last one of the transfers made by the Metropolitan under the auspices of Homestead 42 were turning into catastrophes for the agents formerly from the Newark district. In the barely inhabited corners of those distant states to which they and their families had been relocated, none of them were ever going to be able to earn a quarter of the amount of commissions they were accustomed to making in metropolitan North Jersey—and so, if only for that reason, my father had been wonderfully prescient in quitting his job and going to work instead for Uncle Monty. He hadn't been quite so prescient about getting us over the Canadian border before it closed down and martial law was declared.

"If she was alive . . ." Seldon told my mother, after she'd accepted the charges and taken his call, "if she was alive . . ." In the beginning, because of his crying, that was all he was able to say, and even those four words were barely comprehensible.

"Seldon, that's enough of that. You're doing this to yourself. You're making yourself hysterical. Of course your mother's alive. She's just late getting home—that's all that has happened."

"But if she was alive she would *call!*"

"Seldon, what if she's only caught in traffic? What if something happened to the car and she's had to pull over to get it fixed? Didn't that happen before, when you were here in Newark? Remember that night when it was raining and she had a flat and you came upstairs to stay with us? It's probably nothing more than a flat tire, so please, dear, calm down. You must stop crying. Your mother is fine. It only upsets you to say what you're saying, and it is not true, so please, please, right now, just make an effort and try to calm down."

"But she's dead, Mrs. Roth! Just like my father! Now *both* my parents are dead!" And, of course, he was right. Seldon knew nothing about the riots way off in Louisville and little about what was going on in the rest of America. Since there was no room left in Mrs. Wishnow's life for anything other than the child and the job, there was never a newspaper to read in the Danville house, and when the two of them sat down to dinner in Danville they didn't have the news on the way we did in Newark. More than likely she was too exhausted in Danville to listen to it, by now too benumbed to register any misfortune other than her own.

But Seldon had it perfectly right: Mrs. Wishnow was dead, though no one would know until the following day, when the burnt-out car containing his mother's remains was found smoldering in a drainage ditch alongside a potato field in the flat country just south of Louisville. Apparently she had been beaten and robbed and the car set ablaze within the first minutes of the evening's violence, which had not been restricted to the downtown Louisville streets where there were Jewish-owned shops or to the residential streets where the handful of Louisville's Jewish citizens lived. The Klansmen knew that once the torches were lit and the crosses burning, the vermin were going to try to get out, and so they were ready for them, not only on the main road leading north to Ohio but along the narrow country roads heading south, which was where Mrs. Wishnow paid with her life for the slander of Lindbergh's good name, first by the late Walter Winchell and now by the Jewish-controlled propaganda machine of Prime Minister Churchill and King George VI.

My mother said, "Seldon, you must take something to eat. That will help calm you down. Go to the refrigerator and get something to eat."

"I ate the Fig Newtons. There's none left."

"Seldon, I'm talking about your eating a meal. Your mother will be home very soon, but meanwhile you can't sit there waiting for her to feed you—you have to feed yourself, and not on cookies. Put the phone down and go look in the refrigerator and then come back and tell me what's in there that you could eat."

"But it's long distance."

"Seldon, do as I say."

To Sandy and me, gathered closely around her in the back foyer, my mother said, "She's very late, and he hasn't eaten, and he's all alone, and she hasn't phoned, and the poor child is frantic and starving to death."

"Mrs. Roth?"

"Yes, Seldon."

"There's pot cheese. It's old, though. It doesn't look too good."

"What else is in there?"

"Beets. In a bowl. Leftovers. They're cold."

"And anything else?"

"I'll look again—just a minute."

This time when Seldon put down the phone, my mother said to Sandy, "How far from Danville are the Mawhinneys?"

"With the truck about twenty minutes."

"In my dresser," my mother said to my brother, "in the top, in my change purse—their number is there. It's on a piece of paper in my little brown change purse. Get it for me, please."

"Mrs. Roth?" Seldon said.

"Yes. I'm here."

"There's butter."

"That's all? Isn't there any milk? Isn't there juice?"

"But that's breakfast. That's not dinner."

"Are there Rice Krispies, Seldon? Are there Corn Flakes?"

"Sure," he said.

"Then get whichever cereal you like best."

"Rice Krispies."

"Get the Rice Krispies, take out the milk and the juice, and I want you to make yourself breakfast."

"Now?"

"Do as I say, please," she told him. "I want you to eat breakfast."

"Is Philip there?"

"He's here, but you cannot talk to him. You have to eat first. I'm going to call you back in half an hour, after you've eaten. It's ten after ten, Seldon."

"In Newark it's ten after ten?"

"In Newark and Danville both. It's exactly the same time in both places. I'm going to call you back at quarter to eleven," she told him.

"Can I talk to Philip then?"

"Yes, but I want you to sit down first with everything you need at the kitchen table. I want you to use a spoon and a fork and a napkin and a knife. Eat slowly. Use dishes. Use a bowl. Is there any bread?"

"It's stale. It's just a couple of slices."

"Do you have a toaster?"

"Sure. We brought it here in the car. Remember the morning when we all packed the car?"

"Listen to me, Seldon. Concentrate. Make yourself some toast, with the cereal. And use the butter. Butter it. And pour yourself a big glass of milk. I want you to eat a good breakfast, and when your mother comes in, I want you to tell her to call us immediately. She can call here collect. Tell her not to worry about the charges. It's important for us to know when she's home. But either way, in half an hour I'm calling you back, so don't you go anywhere."

"It's dark out. Where would I go?"

"Seldon, eat your breakfast."

"Okay."

"Goodbye," she said. "Goodbye, for now. I'll call you back at quarter to eleven. You stay where you are."

Next she phoned the Mawhinneys. My brother handed her the piece of paper with the number and she asked the operator to put through the call and when somebody answered at the other end, she said, "Is this Mrs. Mawhinney? This is Mrs. Roth. I'm Sandy Roth's mother. I'm calling you from Newark, New Jersey, Mrs. Mawhinney. I'm sorry if I woke you up, but we need you to help us with a little boy who's alone in Danville. What? Yes, of course, yes."

To us she said, "She's getting her husband."

"Oh, no," my brother moaned.

"Sanford, this is not the time for that. I don't like what I'm doing either. I realize I don't know these people. I realize they're not like us. I know farmers go to bed early and get up early and that they work very hard. But you tell me what else I should do. That little boy is going to go crazy if he's left alone any longer. He doesn't know where his mother is. Somebody has to be there. He's had too many shocks for someone his age already. He lost his father. Now his mother is missing. Can't you understand what this means?"

"Sure I can," said my brother indignantly. "Sure I understand."

"Good. Then you understand that somebody has to go to him. Somebody—" but then Mr. Mawhinney got on the phone, and my mother explained to him why she was calling, and he immediately agreed to do all she asked. When she hung up she said, "At least there's some decency left in this country. At least there's some decency *somewhere*."

"I told you," my brother whispered.

Never would she seem more remarkable to me than she did that night, and not merely for the abandon with which she was accepting and making phone calls to and from Kentucky. There was more, much more. There was, to begin with, Alvin's assault on my father the week before. There was my father's explosive response. There was the wreckage of our living room. There was my father's broken teeth and broken ribs, the stitches in his face and the brace on his neck. There was the shootout on Chancellor Avenue. There was our certainty that it was a pogrom. There were the sirens all night long. There was the screaming and the shouting in the streets all night long. There was our hiding in the Cucuzzas' foyer, the loaded pistol in my father's lap, the loaded pistol in Mr. Cucuzza's fist—and that was just the week before. There was also the month before, the year before, and the year before that—all those blows, insults, and surprises intent on weakening and frightening the Jews that still hadn't managed to shatter my mother's strength. Before I heard her telling Seldon, from more than seven hundred miles away, to make himself something to eat and to sit down and eat it, before I heard her calling the Mawhinneys—churchgoing Gentiles whom she'd never laid eyes on—to enlist them in saving Seldon from going mad, before I heard her asking to speak to Mr. Mawhinney and then telling him that if something serious had happened to Mrs. Wishnow the Mawhinneys needn't worry they'd be stuck with Seldon, that my father was prepared to get in the car and drive to Kentucky to bring Seldon back to Newark (and promising Mr. Mawhinney this even while no one knew just how far the Wheelers and the Fords intended to allow the American mob to go), I hadn't understood anything of the story that was her life in those years. Till Seldon's frantic phone call from Kentucky, I'd never totted up the cost to my mother and father of the Lindbergh presidency—till that moment, I'd been unable to add that high.

When my mother phoned Seldon at quarter to eleven she explained the plan worked out with the Mawhinneys. He was to put his toothbrush, pajamas, underwear, and a pair of clean socks into a paper bag, and he was to get on a heavy sweater and his warm coat and his flannel cap, and he was to wait in the house for Mr. Mawhinney to come for him in his truck. Mr. Mawhinney was a very kind man, my mother told Seldon, a kind, generous man with a nice wife and four children whom Sandy knew from the summer he lived at the Mawhinney farm.

"Then she *is* dead!" Seldon screamed.

No, no, no, absolutely not—his mother would be coming to pick him up at the Mawhinneys' the next morning and to drive him from there to school. Mr. and Mrs. Mawhinney would arrange all that for him and he wasn't to worry about a thing. But meanwhile there was work to do: in his best handwriting Seldon was to write a note for his mother and leave it on the kitchen table, a note telling her that he was going to be at the Mawhinneys' for the night and leaving the Mawhinneys' phone number for her. He was also to tell her in the note to call Mrs. Roth collect in Newark the moment that she got in. Then Seldon was to sit in the living room and wait there until he heard Mr. Mawhinney outside blowing the horn, then he was to turn off all the lights in the house . . .

She took him through each stage of his departure and then, at what financial expense I couldn't begin to calculate, she continued to stay on the line until he'd done what she'd directed him to do and had come back to the phone to tell her that he'd done it, and still she didn't hang up or stop reassuring him about everything until at last Seldon shouted, "It's him, Mrs. Roth! He's blowing the horn!" and my mother said, "Okay, good, but calmly now, Seldon, calmly—take your bag, turn out the lights, don't forget to lock the door on the way out, and tomorrow morning, bright and early, you're going to see your mother. Now, good luck, dear, and don't run, and—Seldon? Seldon, hang up the phone!" But this he neglected to do. In his hurry to flee as fast as he could that frightening, lonely, parentless house, he left the phone dangling, though it hardly mattered. The house could have burned to the ground and it wouldn't have mattered because Seldon was never to set foot inside it again.

On Sunday, October 18, he arrived back on Summit Avenue. My father, accompanied by Sandy, drove out to Kentucky to get him. The casket containing Mrs. Wishnow's remains followed after them by train. I knew that in her car she had been burned beyond recognition, yet I kept envisioning her inside the casket with her fists still clenched. And alternately envisioning myself locked in their bathroom with Mrs. Wishnow just outside telling me how to open the door. How patient she'd been! How like my own mother! And now she was inside a casket, and I was the one who had put her there.

That was all I could think on the night that my mother, like a combat officer, led Seldon to organize his dinner and to organize his departure and to get himself safely into the Mawhinneys' hands. I did it. That was all I could think then and all I can think now. I did this to Seldon and I did this to her. Rabbi Bengelsdorf had done what he had done, Aunt Evelyn had done what she had done, but I was the one who had started it off—this devastation had been done by me.

On Thursday, October 15—the day the Wheeler putsch reached the heights of illegality—our phone rang at quarter to six in the morning. My mother thought it was my father and Sandy calling with bad news from Kentucky, or worse, someone calling about the two of them, but for now the bad news was from my aunt. Only minutes earlier FBI agents had knocked at the door of the Washington hotel room where Rabbi Bengelsdorf was living. Aunt Evelyn had traveled down just the day before from Newark and so happened to be there for the night—otherwise she might not have known the circumstances of his disappearance. The agents didn't bother to wait for anyone inside to open the door; the hotel manager's master key obligingly opened it for them, and after presenting a warrant for Rabbi Bengelsdorf's arrest and waiting silently while he dressed, they escorted him in handcuffs from the room without a word of explanation to Aunt Evelyn, who immediately after watching them drive off with him in an unmarked car called my mother to ask for help. But this was hardly the time when my mother was going to leave me in somebody else's care to travel for five hours by train so as to assist a sister from whom she'd been estranged now for months. A hundred and twenty-two Jews had been murdered three days earlier—among them, as we had only just learned, Mrs. Wishnow—my father and Sandy were still off on their perilous journey to rescue Seldon, and nobody knew what was in store even for those of us at home on Summit Avenue. The shootout with the city police that had resulted in the deaths of three local thugs was the worst that had happened in Newark so far; nonetheless, its having happened around the corner on Chancellor Avenue had left everyone on the street feeling as though a wall had been pulled down that previously protected their families—not the wall of the ghetto (which had protected no one, certainly not from fear and the pathologies of exclusion), not a wall intended to shut them out or to seal them in, but a sheltering wall of legal assurances standing between them and the derangements of a ghetto.

At five that afternoon, Aunt Evelyn showed up at our door, more crazed than she'd been on the phone in the wake of Rabbi Bengelsdorf's arrest. No one in Washington was either willing or able to tell her where her husband was being held, or if he was even alive any longer, and then when she heard of the arrests of seemingly impregnable figures like Mayor La Guardia, Governor Lehman, and Justice Frankfurter, she had succumbed to her panic and taken the train up from Washington. Fearful of returning alone to the rabbi's Elizabeth Avenue mansion—fearful too that if she called first she'd be told by my mother that she was to stay away—she'd taken a taxi from Penn Station directly to Summit Avenue to beg to be let in. Only a couple of hours earlier a shocking bulletin had come over the air—the news that President Roosevelt, upon entering New York to attend an evening protest rally at Madison Square Garden, had been "detained" by the New York police—and it was this that had prompted my mother to leave the house and, for the first time since I'd started kindergarten in 1938, to come pick me up at the end of the school day. Till then she had been as willing as everyone else on the street to abide by Rabbi Prinz's instructions for the community to carry on as usual and to leave security matters to his committee, but that afternoon she decided that events had now overtaken the rabbi's wisdom, and alongside a hundred other mothers who had reached a similar conclusion, she had turned up looking to retrieve her child when the last bell sounded and kids began pouring out of the exit doors for home.

"They're after me, Bess! I have to hide—you have to hide me!"

As if enough of our world hadn't been turned upside down in little over a week, there was my vibrant, haughty aunt, the wife (or perhaps by now the widow) of the most significant personage any of us had ever laid eyes on—there was tiny Aunt Evelyn, without her makeup, her hair in disarray, an ogress suddenly, made as ugly and vulnerable-looking by disaster as by her own theatricality. And there was my mother blocking our doorway and looking angrier than I could ever have imagined her. Never had I seen her in such a fury, nor had I heard her utter a curse word. I didn't even know she knew how to.

"Why don't you go to the von Ribbentrops' to hide?" my mother said. "Why don't you go to your friend Herr von Ribbentrop for protection? Stupid girl! What about *my* family? Don't you think that we're afraid too? Don't you think that we're in danger too? Selfish little bitch—we're *all* afraid!"

"But they're going to arrest me! They'll torture me, Bessie, because I know the truth!"

"You cannot stay here! That's out of the question!" my mother said. "You have a house, money, servants—you have everything to protect you. We have nothing like that, nothing at all like that. Leave, Evelyn! Go! Get out of this house!"

Astonishingly, my aunt turned to me to plead for sanctuary. "Darling boy, sweetheart—"

"How dare you!" my mother shouted, and slammed the door shut, barely missing the hand that Aunt Evelyn had helplessly extended toward mine.

The next moment she threw her arms so tightly around me that against my forehead I could feel her heart thump.

"How will she get home?" I asked.

"The bus. It's not our concern. She'll take the bus like everyone else."

"But what did she mean about the truth, Ma?"

"Nothing. Forget what she meant. Your aunt is not our concern anymore."

Back in the kitchen, she buried her face in her hands and was all at once convulsed with weeping. The responsible parental scruples gave way, and with it the strength she rigorously employed to hide her weaknesses and hold things together.

"How can Selma Wishnow be dead?" she asked. "How can they arrest President Roosevelt? How can any of this be happening?"

"Because Lindbergh disappeared?" I asked.

"Because he *appeared*," she replied. "Because he appeared in the first place, a goyisch idiot flying a stupid plane! Oh, I should never have let them go to get Seldon! Where is your brother? Where is your father?" Where too, she seemed to be asking, is that orderly existence once so full of purpose, where is the great, great enterprise of our being the four of us? "We don't even know where they are," she said, but sounding as though it were she who was lost. "To send them off like that . . . What was I thinking? To let them go when the entire country . . . when . . ."

Deliberately she stopped herself there, but the trend of her thought was clear enough: when the goyim are killing Jews in the street.

There was nothing for me to do except watch until the weeping had drained her to the dregs, whereupon my whole idea of her underwent a startling change: my mother was a fellow creature. I was shocked by the revelation, and too young to comprehend that there was the strongest attachment of all.

"How could I turn her away?" she said. "Oh, darling, what, oh what, would Grandma say now?"

Remorse, predictably, was the form taken by her distress, the merciless whipping that is self-condemnation, as if in times as bizarre as these there were a right way and a wrong way that would have been clear to somebody else, as if in confronting such predicaments the hand of stupidity is ever far from guiding anyone. Yet she reproached herself for errors of judgment that were not only natural when there was no longer a logical explanation for anything but generated by emotions she had no reason to doubt. The worst of it was how convinced she was of her catastrophic blunder, though, had she gone against her instincts, she would have had no less reason to deplore what she'd done. What it came down to for the child who was watching her being battered about by the most anguishing confusion (and who was himself quaking with fear) was the discovery that one could do nothing right without also doing something wrong, so wrong, in fact, that especially where chaos reigned and everything was at stake, one might be better off to wait and do nothing—except that to do nothing was also to do something . . . in such circumstances to do nothing was to do quite a lot—and that even for the mother who performed each day in methodical opposition to life's unruly flux, there was no system for managing so sinister a mess.

In light of the day's drastic developments (which not even passage of the Alien and Sedition Acts of 1798, not even what Jefferson called the Federalist "reign of witches," remotely equaled for tyrannical intolerance or treachery) there were emergency meetings called for that evening at the four local schools that together enrolled nearly all the Jewish pupils in Newark's elementary education system. Each meeting was to be presided over by a member of the Committee of Concerned Jewish Citizens. A sound truck had come by late in the afternoon asking everyone to spread word of the meeting among their neighbors. People were invited to bring their children if they did not wish to leave them home alone, and they were assured that a full-scale police mobilization throughout the South Ward—police protection extending as far east as Frelinghuysen Avenue and as far north as Springfield Avenue—had been promised to Rabbi Prinz by Mayor Murphy. The department's entire complement of mounted police—two platoons of twelve divided up and stabled in four different precincts—was to be called out specifically to patrol the streets to the west of the Weequahic section bordering Irvington (where, the previous night, a Jewish-owned liquor store on the main shopping street had been burned to the ground after being broken into and looted) and the streets to the south bordering Union County and the towns of Hillside (in my eyes renowned for the sizable Bristol-Myers plant along Route 22 that manufactured the Ipana tooth powder we used, where, the day before, a synagogue's windows had been smashed) and Elizabeth (where my mother's immigrant parents had settled at the turn of the century—where, most intriguingly to a nine-year-old, the New Jersey Pretzel Factory on Livingston Street was said to hire deaf-mutes from the state to do the pretzel bending—and where graves had been desecrated in the Temple B'nai Jeshurun cemetery, just a few blocks from the Weequahic Park golf course).

Shortly before six-thirty, my mother headed quickly down the street for the emergency meeting at Chancellor Avenue School. I remained at home, delegated by her to answer the phone and to accept the charges should my father call from the road. The Cucuzzas had promised her that they would look after me until she returned home, and, indeed, even as she was descending the stairs, Joey was climbing them, three at a time, dispatched by Mrs. Cucuzza to keep me company while I waited—in vain, as it turned out—for the long-distance call informing us that my father and my brother were both all right and would soon be arriving home with Seldon. Because under martial law the Army had commandeered the facilities of Bell Telephone for military use, the long-distance services still open to civilians were jammed, and forty-eight hours had passed since we'd last heard anything from my father.

As the Newark–Hillside line ran only a couple of hundred yards south of our house, it was possible that night, even with the windows closed, to find reassurance of sorts in the loud clattering of the police horses as they paraded up and down the Keer Avenue hill just around the corner. And when I threw open my bedroom window and leaned out over the darkening alleyway to listen, I could manage to hear them, if only faintly, when they sauntered on a ways to where Summit Avenue petered out and became Hillside's Liberty Avenue. Liberty ran through Hillside to Route 22, which proceeded westward into Union and from there swept southward into the vast Christian unknown of those authentically Anglo-Saxon-sounding towns of Kenilworth, Middlesex, and Scotch Plains.

These weren't the suburbs of Louisville, but they were farther west than I'd ever been, and though you had to traverse another three New Jersey counties just to reach the eastern border of Pennsylvania, on the night of October 15 I was able to alarm myself with

a nightmarish vision of America's anti-Semitic fury roaring eastward through the pipeline of 22 and surging from 22 into Liberty
Avenue and pouring from Liberty Avenue straight into our Summit Avenue alleyway and on up our back stairs like the waters of a
flood had it not been for the sturdy barrier presented by the gleaming bay haunches of the horses of the Newark police force, whose
strength and speed and beauty Newark's preeminent rabbi, the
nobly named Prinz, had caused to materialize at the end of our
street.

As was to be expected, Joey could hear next to nothing of what
was going on outdoors, and so took to running from room to
room, peering out of windows at either end of the house to try to
get a glimpse of the anatomy of at least one of the horses—horses
of a bloodline with limbs much longer, muscled torsos much slim-
mer, skulls elongated and much more exquisite than those of the
inelegant orphanage plowhorse that had kicked my head in—and
also to catch sight of the uniformed cops, each with two rows of
brass buttons shining down the length of his double-breasted,
snug-fitting tunic and a holstered pistol riding one hip.

Several years earlier my father had taken Sandy and me to Weequahic Park one Sunday morning to toss horseshoes at the public
pitch, and a mounted policeman went racing across the park in
pursuit of somebody who'd snatched a woman's purse—a moment
in Newark out of the court of King Arthur. It was days before the
thrill wore off and I could stop being stirred up by the gallantry of
it all. They recruited the most supple and athletic of the cops to
train as mounted policemen, and a small kid could be mesmerized
just watching one who'd been lazing majestically down the street
stop to write a parking ticket and then lean way over in the saddle
so as to place the ticket under the car's windshield wiper, a physical gesture, if ever there was one, of magnificent condescension to
the machine age. At the city's famous Four Corners there were
mounted patrol posts each facing a different point of the compass,
and on a Saturday lots of kids were taken downtown to see the
horses on duty there and to pet their noseless noses and to feed

them sugar cubes and to learn that each policeman up on a horse was worth four men on foot and, of course, to ask the usual questions of the mounted cops, such as "What's his name?" and "Is the horse real?" and "What's his foot made out of?" Sometimes you might see a police horse tied up at the side of a busy downtown street, undisturbed and calm as could be beneath the blue and white saddlecloth marked with the insignia *NP*, a gelding well over six feet high and weighing a thousand pounds, with a menacingly long nightstick belted to his flank and looking as blasé as the most gorgeous movie star while the policeman who had just dismounted stood nearby in his deep blue jodhpurs and high black boots, his pornographic leather holster molded perfectly in the engorged shape of the male genitalia, indifferent to injury amid the pandemonium of honking cars and trucks and buses and smartly signaling with his arms so as to restore a smooth flow of traffic to the city. These were the cops with a talent for everything—even, to my father's chagrin, for galloping into a strike crowd and sending picketers flying—and that they were so very close by looking so glamorously heroic helped to shore up my nerves for the calamity to come.

In the living room Joey took off his hearing aid and presented it to me, gave it to me, incomprehensibly *shoved* it at me—the earpiece along with the black microphone case, the battery, and all its wires. I didn't know why he thought I should want it, particularly on a night like this, but there the whole contraption was, cradled in the palms of my two hands and, if possible, looking more gruesome than it did when he wore it. I didn't know whether he expected me now to interrogate him about it or to admire it or to try to disassemble and fix it. It turned out that he wanted me to wear it.

"Put it on," he told me in his hollow, honking voice.

"Why?" I shouted. "It's not going to fit me."

"It don't fit nobody," he said. "Put it on."

"I don't know how," I complained in my loudest voice, and so

Joey clipped the microphone case to my shirt and dropped the battery into my pants pocket and, after he checked all the wiring, left it to me to insert the molded earpiece. I did so by closing my eyes and pretending it was a seashell and that we were down the shore and he wanted me to listen to the roar of the ocean . . . but I had to suppress the heaves when I managed to jiggle it into place, still stickily warm from the interior of his ear.

"Okay, now what?"

Whereupon he reached over and, as though it were the switch to the electric chair he was throwing and I were Public Enemy Number One, he gleefully turned the dial at the center of the microphone case.

"I don't hear anything," I told him.

"Wait'll I louden it."

"Is wearing this thing going to make me deaf?" and I saw myself made both deaf *and* dumb, and trapped in Elizabeth for the rest of my life bending pretzels in the New Jersey Pretzel Factory.

He laughed heartily at my saying that, though I hadn't meant it as a joke.

"Look," I said, "I don't want to do this. Not now. There's a lot going on outside that's not so great, you know."

But he was oblivious of what was not so great, either because he was Catholic and had nothing to worry about or simply because he was irrepressible Joey.

"You know what the crook said who sold it? He ain't even a doctor," Joey told me, "but he gives me the bullshit test anyway. He takes his pocket watch out and he holds it right up to my ear and he says to me, 'Can you hear the watch tick, Joey?' and I can hear a little, and so he starts backing away, and he says, 'Can you hear it now, Joey?' and I can't, I can't hear nothing, and so he writes some numbers down on a piece of paper. Then he takes two half-dollars out of his pocket and it's the same thing. He clicks them by my ear, clicks them together, and he says, 'Can you hear the coins click, Joey?' and then he starts walking away again, and I see him clicking them, but I can't hear nothing no more. 'The same,' I tell him—and so he writes that down. Then he looks at what he wrote down, looks real real hard, then he takes this tin piece of shit out of a drawer. He puts it on me, all the pieces, and he tells my father, 'Your boy is going to hear the grass growing, that's how good this model is,'" and with that Joey began to turn the dial again until what I heard was water running into a bathtub—and I was the bathtub. Then he spun it vigorously—and there was thunder.

"Cut it out!" I cried. "That's enough!" but Joey was joyfully leaping about, and so I reached up and yanked the earpiece out of my ear and was derailed for the moment thinking that, on top of Mayor La Guardia's being under arrest and President Roosevelt's being under arrest and even Rabbi Bengelsdorf's being under arrest, the new boy downstairs wasn't going to be any more of a picnic than the one before him had been, and this was when I determined to run away again. I was still too much of a fledgling with people to understand that, in the long run, nobody is a picnic and that I was no picnic myself. First I couldn't stand Seldon downstairs and now I couldn't stand Joey downstairs, and I determined then and there to run away from both of them. I would run away before Seldon got here, I would run away before the anti-Semites got here, I would run away before Mrs. Wishnow's body got here and there was a funeral that I had to go to. Under the protection of the mounted police, I would run away that very night from everything that was after me and everything that hated me and wanted to kill me. I would run away from everything I'd done and everything I hadn't done, and start out fresh as a boy nobody knew. And I realized, all at once, where to run away to—to Elizabeth, to the pretzel factory. I'd tell them in writing that I was a deaf-mute. They'd give me a job making pretzels, and I'd never speak and I'd pretend not to hear, and nobody would find out who I was.

Joey said, "You know about the kid who drank the horse's blood?"

"What horse's blood?"

"St. Peter's horse. This kid, he got in at night, into the farm, and drank the horse's blood. They're looking for him."

"Who is?"

"The guys. Nick. Those guys. The older guys."

"Who's Nick?"

"One of the orphans. He's eighteen. The kid that did it's a Jew like you. They know for sure he's a Jew, and they're going to find him."

"How come he drank the horse's blood?"

"Jews drink blood."

"You don't know what you're talking about. I don't drink blood. Sandy doesn't drink blood. My parents don't drink blood. Nobody I *know* drinks blood."

"This kid does."

"Yeah? And what's his name?"

"Nick don't know yet. But they're looking for him. Don't worry, they'll get him."

"And what will they do then, Joey? Drink *his* blood? *Jews don't drink blood.* Saying that is *crazy.*" I handed his hearing aid back to him—thinking that I could now add Nick to everything else I was having to flee—and soon Joey began racing from window to window again, trying to get a look at the horses, until, when he could no longer bear being out of range of a spectacle comparable in his mind to Buffalo Bill's Wild West Show coming to town and raising the big top in front of our house, he upped and flew out the door and that was the last I saw of him that night. There was rumored to be a police horse in Newark who munched on chewing tobacco, like the cop who rode him, and who was able to add numbers by tapping his right front hoof, and Joey later claimed that he'd seen him there on our block, a horse from the Eighth Precinct called Ned, who let kids swing from his tail without kicking out at them with his hind legs. And maybe he did meet the fabled Ned, and maybe that had made it all worth it. Nonetheless, for deserting me that night, for never returning, for succumbing to his love of excitement rather than obeying his mother's orders, Joey was soundly punished when his father got home from work the following morning, *his* horselike haunches thrashed mercilessly with the black strap off the night watchman's time clock.

Once Joey had disappeared, I double-locked the door behind him and would have turned on the radio to distract me from my worries if I hadn't been afraid of yet another bulletin interrupting a regularly scheduled program and relaying to me, all by myself, even more horrible news than had been coming at us throughout the day. It wasn't long before I started thinking again about running away to the pretzel factory. I remembered the article about the factory that had appeared in the *Sunday Call* about a year before and that I'd cut out to bring to school for a report I had to make on a New Jersey industry. In the article the owner, a Mr. Kuenze, had been quoted as debunking the idea, prevalent apparently throughout the world, that it took years to teach somebody to become a pretzel maker. "I can teach them overnight," he said, "if they can be taught." A lot of the article had been about a controversy over the need for salt on a pretzel. Mr. Kuenze claimed that salt on the outside was unnecessary and that he put it on only "to satisfy the trade." The important thing, he said, was to put salt in the dough, which he alone did, of all the pretzel makers in the state. The article said that Mr. Kuenze had one hundred employees, a good many deaf-mutes among them but also "boys and girls who work after school."

I knew which bus went by the pretzel factory—it was the same one that Earl and I had taken on the afternoon we'd followed home to Elizabeth the Christian who Earl had spotted as a fairy just in the nick of time. I'd have to pray that the fairy wouldn't be on the same bus—if by chance he was, I'd get off and take the next one. What I'd have to have with me was a note, a note this time not from Sister Mary Catherine but from a deaf-mute. "Dear Mr. Kuenze. I read about you in the *Sunday Call*. I want to learn to make pretzels. I'm sure I can be taught overnight. I am deaf and dumb. I am an orphan. Will you give me a job?" And I signed it

"Seldon Wishnow." I couldn't for the life of me think of another name.

I needed a note, and I needed clothes. I had to look to Mr. Kuenze like a kid he could trust, and I couldn't turn up without clothes. And this time I needed a plan, what my father called "a long-range plan." It came to me immediately: my long-range plan would be to save enough of the money I earned at the pretzel factory to buy a one-way train ticket to Omaha, Nebraska, where Father Flanagan ran Boys Town. I knew about Boys Town and Father Flanagan—as did every boy in America—from the movie with Spencer Tracy, who won an Academy Award for playing the famous priest and then donated his Oscar to the real Boys Town. I was five when I saw it at the Roosevelt with Sandy on a Saturday afternoon. Father Flanagan took in boys from the street, some of them already thieves and little gangsters, and brought them out to his farm, where they were fed and clothed and received an education and where they played baseball and sang in a choir and learned to become good citizens. Father Flanagan was father to all of them, regardless of race or creed. Most of the boys were Catholic, some Protestant, but a few needy Jewish boys lived on the farm as well— this I knew from my parents, who, like thousands of other American families who'd seen the movie and wept, made an annual ecumenical contribution to Boys Town. Not that I'd identify myself as Jewish once I reached Omaha. I'd say—speaking aloud at long last—that I didn't know what I was or who. That I was nothing and nobody—just a boy and nothing more, and hardly the person responsible for the death of Mrs. Wishnow and the orphaning of her son. Let my family raise her son as their son from here on out. He could have my bed. He could have my brother. He could have my future. I'd make my life with Father Flanagan in Nebraska, which was even farther from Newark than Kentucky.

Suddenly I thought of another name and rewrote the note, signing it "Philip Flanagan." Then I started for the cellar to get the cardboard suitcase in which I'd hidden Seldon's stolen clothes before running away the first time. This time I'd pack the suitcase with my own clothes and in my pocket carry the miniature pewter musket that I had bought at Mount Vernon and used to slice open the envelopes from the stamp company back when I still owned a serious collection and was getting mail. Its bayonet measured barely an inch in length, but leaving home for good I would need something for protection, and a letter opener was all I had.

Minutes later, descending the stairs with a flashlight, I was able to derive the strength to keep my legs from collapsing by realizing that this was the last occasion I'd ever have to go down into that cellar and confront the wringer or the alley cats or the drains or the dead. Or that dank, befouled wall facing the street on which one-legged Alvin had once spattered his grief.

It wasn't cold enough yet for us to start burning coal, and when, from the foot of the cellar stairs, I turned my flashlight on the ash-colored hulk of the fireless furnaces they looked to me like those ostentatious burial vaults where, for all the good it does them, the rich and mighty inter themselves. I stood there hoping that the ghost of Seldon's father would have gone off to Kentucky (perhaps unseen in the trunk of my father's car) to fetch his dead wife but understanding full well that he hadn't, that his business as a ghost was here with me—that his spectral heart seethed with curses, and all of them for me. "I didn't mean for them to move," I whispered. "That was a mistake. I'm not who's really responsible. I didn't mean to make Seldon the target."

I was prepared, of course, for the silence that inevitably surrounded my pleading utterances to the merciless dead, and instead heard my name pronounced in response—and by a woman! From beyond the furnaces, a woman moaning my name! Dead only hours and already back to begin haunting me for the rest of my life!

"I know the truth," she said, and there, emerging like an oracular priestess out of the Delphi of our storage bin, came my aunt. "They're after me, Philip," Aunt Evelyn said. "I know the truth, and they're going to kill me!"

*　*　*

Because she had to use the toilet and to eat something—because I didn't know what I could do other than to give my aunt whatever she needed—I had no choice but to bring her back upstairs with me. I sliced a piece of bread from the half a loaf that was left from dinner, buttered it, poured her a glass of milk, and, after she'd gone to the bathroom—and I'd pulled the kitchen shades so that nobody could see in from across the way—she came into the kitchen and feverishly gobbled everything down. Her coat and her purse were in her lap and she was still wearing her hat, and I hoped that as soon as she'd had enough to eat, she'd get up and go home so that I could go down and get the suitcase, pack it, and run away before my mother returned from the meeting. But once she'd eaten she began to babble, repeating again and again that she knew the truth and because of that they were going to kill her. They'd called out the mounted police, she informed me, to find where she was hiding.

In the silence that followed that startling remark—which, in those circumstances, when suddenly there were no longer any predictable happenings, I was enough of a child to almost believe—we followed the audible progress of a single horse prancing up the block toward Chancellor Avenue. "They know I'm here," she said.

"They don't, Aunt Evelyn," but the words had no hold on me as I spoke them. "*I* didn't know you were here."

"Then why did you come looking for me?"

"I didn't. I was looking for something else. The police are outside," I told her, convinced that I was deliberately lying even while speaking as earnestly as I could, "the police are outside because of the anti-Semitism. They're patrolling the streets to protect us."

She smiled the smile reserved for trusting souls. "Tell me another one, Philip."

Now *nothing* that I knew coincided with anything either of us was saying. The shadow of her madness had crept over me without my as yet understanding that while hiding in our storage bin —or perhaps earlier than that, while watching the FBI take the rabbi away in handcuffs—she had indeed lost her mind. Unless, of course, she'd already begun hopelessly slipping into insanity the night at the White House when she danced with von Ribbentrop. That was to be my father's theory—that long before the rabbi's arrest, when Bengelsdorf was astonishing all of Jewish Newark with the unseemliness of how high he had climbed in the president's esteem, she'd abandoned herself to the same credulity that had transformed the entire country into a madhouse: the worship of Lindbergh and his conception of the world.

"Do you want to lie down?" I asked, dreading that she would say yes. "Do you need to rest? Do you want me to call the doctor?"

Here she took my hand so firmly that her fingernails bit into my flesh. "Philip dearest, I know *everything*."

"Do you know what happened to President Lindbergh? Is that what you mean?"

"Where is your mother?"

"At school. At a meeting."

"You'll bring me food and water, darling boy."

"I will? Sure. Where?"

"To the cellar. I can't drink from the laundry sink. Someone will find me."

"You don't want that," I said, thinking immediately of Joey's grandmother and the fiery breath of madness that wafted from *her*. "I'll bring everything." But having promised her that, I couldn't possibly run away.

"Would you happen to have an apple?" asked Aunt Evelyn.

I opened the refrigerator. "No, no apple. We're out of apples. My mother hasn't been able to do much shopping. But there's a pear, Aunt Evelyn. You want that?"

"Yes. And another piece of bread. Make another piece of bread."

Her voice kept changing. Now she sounded as though we were doing nothing more than getting ready for a picnic, making the best of what we had on hand to take to Weequahic Park to eat by the lake under a tree, as though the events of the day were as unimportant to us as probably they were to everybody else in America: a minor nuisance to the Christians, if that. As there were more than thirty million Christian families in America and only about a million Jewish families, why, really, should it bother them?

I cut a second slice from the loaf for her to take down to the cellar and smeared it extra heavily with butter. If asked later about the bread missing from the loaf, I'd say that Joey ate it, that and the pear, before he ran off to see the horses.

When she got home to learn that my father hadn't called, my mother was unable to hide her response. Forlornly she looked at the kitchen clock, remembering perhaps the time that it used to be at this hour: bedtime, when all that was required was for the children to wash their faces and brush their teeth for the day dense with fulfillable duties to be rounded off to the satisfaction of all. Now *that* was nine o'clock—or so we'd been led to believe by that wholly convincing, immutable lifelikeness that now turned out to have been a sham.

And the day in, day out routine of school—was that a sham too, a cunning deception perpetrated to soften us up with rational expectations and foster nonsensical feelings of trust? "Why no school?" I asked when she told me that tomorrow we'd have the day off. "Because," my mother replied, making recourse to the colorless formulation suggested to the parents in order for them to be truthful without frightening the children unduly, "the situation has further deteriorated." "What situation?" I asked. "Our situation." "Why? What happened now?" "Nothing happened. It's just better that you children stay home tomorrow. Where is Joey? Where is your friend?" "He ate some bread, and he took the pear, and he left. He took the pear out of the refrigerator and ran outside. He went to see the horses." "And you're sure that no one phoned?" she asked, simply too exhausted to be angry with Joey for letting her down at a moment like this. "I want to know why there's no school, Ma." "Must you know tonight?" "Yes. Why can't I go to school?" "Well . . . it's because there may be a war with Canada." "With *Canada?* When?" "No one knows. But it's best if you all stay home until we see what's going on." "But why are we going to war with Canada?"

"Please, Philip, I can't take much more tonight. I've told you every-thing I know. You insisted and I told you. Now we just have to wait. We have to wait and see like everyone else." And then, as if the un-known whereabouts of my father and brother hadn't given rein to her worst imaginings—which was that we two were now, like the Wishnows, just a widow and her son—she said (trying doggedly to follow the protocol of the old nine o'clock), "I want you to wash up and go to bed."

Bed—as though as a place of warmth and comfort, rather than an incubator for dread, bed still existed.

War with Canada was far less of an enigma to me than what Aunt Evelyn was going to use for a toilet during the night. As best I could understand, the United States was at last entering into the worldwide war, not on the side of England and the British Com-monwealth, whom everyone had expected we would support while FDR was president, but on the side of Hitler and Hitler's allies, Italy and Japan. Moreover, two full days had passed since we had heard from my father and Sandy, and for all we knew they had been killed as horribly as Seldon's mother by the rioting anti-Sem-ites; there was, in addition, to be no school tomorrow, suggesting to me that there might never be school again if President Wheeler was now to inflict on us the laws we knew to have been imposed by the Nazis on the Jewish children of Germany. A political catastro-phe of unimaginable proportions was transforming a free society into a police state, but a child is a child, and all I could think about in my bed was that when the time came to move her bowels, Aunt Evelyn would have to do it on our storage bin floor. This was the uncontrollable event that weighed on me in lieu of everything else, that loomed over me like the embodiment of everything else, and that blotted out everything else. The most negligible danger of all, and it came to assume such momentous significance that around midnight I tiptoed into the bathroom and at the back of the bot-tom shelf of the towel closet I found the bedpan we had bought for Alvin to use in an emergency when he first got home from Canada. I was already at the back door and ready to carry the bedpan down to Aunt Evelyn when my mother confronted me in her nightgown, aghast at the picture I presented of a small boy so overwhelmed he was going out of his mind.

Minutes later Aunt Evelyn was being led by my mother up the stairwell and into our apartment. There's no need to describe the disturbance this caused in the Cucuzza household or the antagonistic response to the frightful figure of my aunt by that frightful figure who was Joey's grandmother—the farcical edge of suffering is familiar to everyone. I was sent to sleep in my parents' bed, and my mother and Aunt Evelyn took over my room, where my mother's next great task was to prevent her sister from getting up out of Sandy's bed and stealing into the kitchen to turn on the gas and kill us all.

The round trip of fifteen hundred miles was the adventure of Sandy's lifetime. It was something more fateful for my father. His Guadalcanal, I suppose, his Battle of the Bulge. At forty-one he was too old to be drafted when, that December, with Lindbergh's policies discredited and Wheeler disgraced and Roosevelt back in the White House, America finally went to war against the Axis powers, so this was as close as he would ever come to the fear, fatigue, and physical suffering of the frontline soldier. Wearing his high steel neck brace and nursing two broken ribs and a sutured facial wound and exhibiting a mouthful of broken teeth—and carrying Mr. Cucuzza's extra pistol in the glove compartment for protection against the people who'd already murdered 122 Jews in those very regions of the country toward which the car was headed—he drove the seven hundred and fifty miles to Kentucky stopping only to get gas and go to the toilet. And after sleeping at the Mawhinneys' for five hours and eating something, turned around and started back, though now with a painful infection simmering along the length of his suture and with Seldon, sick to his stomach and feverish in the back seat, hallucinating about his mother and all but performing feats of magic to do what he could to bring her back.

The trip out had taken just over twenty-four hours, but the one back took three times as long because of the many times they had to stop for Seldon to vomit by the side of the road or to pull down his pants and squat in a ditch, and because, in just a twenty-mile radius of Charleston, West Virginia (where they went round in circles, hopelessly lost, instead of proceeding east and north toward Maryland), the car broke down on six separate occasions in little over a day: once in the midst of the railroad tracks, power lines, and massive conveyors of Alloy, a town of two hundred where enormous mounds of ore and silica surrounded the factory buildings of the Electro-Metallurgical Company plant; once in the nearby little town of Boomer, where flames from the coke ovens reached so high my father, standing after sundown in the middle of the unlighted street, could read (or misread) the road map by the incandescence; once in Belle, yet another of those tiny, hellish industrial hamlets, where the fumes from the Du Pont ammonia plant almost knocked them flat when they got out of the car to lift the hood and try to figure out what was wrong; again in South Charleston, the city that looked to Seldon like "a monster" because of the steam and the smoke wreathing the freight yards and the warehouses and the long dark roofs of the soot-blackened factories; and twice on the very outskirts of the state capital, Charleston. There, around midnight, in order to call a tow truck, my father had to cross a railroad embankment on foot and then descend a hill of junk to a bridge that spanned a river lined with coal barges and dredging barges and tugboats to go looking for a riverfront dive with a pay phone, meanwhile leaving the two boys alone together in the car just across the river road from an endless jumble of a plant—sheds and shanties, sheet-iron buildings and open coal cars, cranes and loading booms and steel-frame towers, electric ovens and roaring forges, squat storage tanks and high cyclone fences—a plant that was, if you believed the sign the size of a billboard, "The World's Biggest Manufacturer of Axes, Hatchets, and Scythes."

That factory brimming with sharpened blades dealt the final

blow to the little that was left of Seldon's equilibrium—by morning he was screaming that he was going to be scalped by the Indians. And oddly he was on to something: an analogy could be made, even if one weren't delirious, to the uninvited white settlers who first poured through the Appalachian barrier into the favorite hunting grounds of the Delaware and Algonquin tribes, except that instead of alien, strange-looking whites affronting the local inhabitants with their rapaciousness, these were alien, strange-looking Jews provocative merely by their presence. This time around, though, those violently defending their lands from usurpation and their way of life from destruction weren't Indians led by the great Tecumseh but upright American Christians unleashed by the acting president of the United States.

It was by then October 15—the very Thursday when Mayor La Guardia was arrested in New York, when the First Lady was incarcerated at Walter Reed, when FDR was "detained" along with the "Roosevelt Jews" alleged to have masterminded the kidnapping of Lindbergh *père*, when Rabbi Bengelsdorf was arrested in Washington and Aunt Evelyn went to pieces in our storage bin. On that same day my father and Sandy were searching the West Virginia mountains for the county's one licensed physician (as opposed to the licensed barber, who'd already offered his services), to try to get him to give Seldon something to quiet him down. The man they found on a rural dirt road was over seventy and reeking of whiskey, a good, kind, spry old "Doc" who ran a country clinic out of a little frame house where the patients who lined up waiting their turn on the front porch were, as Sandy later described them to me, the raggediest-looking bunch of white people he had ever seen. The doc figured Seldon's delirium stemmed mainly from dehydration and directed Seldon to spend an hour taking down ladle after ladle of water from the well out near the creekbed behind the house. He also drained the pus from my father's infected face to prevent blood poisoning, which in those days, when antibiotics were just discovered and not widely available, would probably have spread through his system and killed him before he made it home. The old guy displayed less talent stitching the wound back up than he had in diagnosing the incipient septicemia, with the result that for the rest of his life my father looked as though he'd sustained a dueling scar while a student at Heidelberg. Afterward it seemed not simply a sign of the contingencies of that trip but, to me, the imprint of his insane stoicism. When finally he reached Newark he was so depleted by fever and chills—and a racking cough no less alarming than Mr. Wishnow's—that Mr. Cucuzza took him straight from our kitchen, where he'd fainted at the dinner table, and once again to the Beth Israel Hospital, where he very nearly died from pneumonia. But there was no way of stopping him until Seldon was saved. My father was a rescuer and orphans were his specialty. A displacement even greater than having to move to Union or to leave for Kentucky was to lose one's parents and be orphaned. Witness, he would tell you, what had happened to Alvin. Witness what had happened to his sister-in-law after Grandma had died. No one should be motherless and fatherless. Motherless and fatherless you are vulnerable to manipulation, to influences—you are rootless and you are vulnerable to everything.

Sandy in the meantime perched on the railing of the clinic's front porch sketching the patients, one of them a thirteen-year-old girl named Cecile. These were the years when my precocious brother was three different boys in the course of twenty-four months, the years when, for all his unflappability, he could seem to do nothing satisfactory even by excelling: my parents didn't like it when he went to work for Lindbergh and became Aunt Evelyn's oratorical boy wonder and New Jersey's leading authority on tobacco farming, they didn't like it when he left Lindbergh for the girls and overnight became the neighborhood's youngest Don Juan, and now, having volunteered to guide my father a quarter of the way across the continent to the Mawhinney farm—and hoping by an exhibition of genuine bravery to recapture his prestige as the older son and reenter the family from which he'd been torn away—he virtually subverted his cause by an amusement that must have seemed to him wholly harmless for being "artistic": drawing nubile Cecile. When my father—with a new bandage covering his cheek—came out of the doctor's office and saw what Sandy was up to, he took him by the belt of his trousers and dragged him, sketchpad and all, clear off the side of the porch and out to the road and into the car. "Are you crazy," my father whispered, peering furiously down at him over his neck brace, "are you nuts, drawing her?" "It's only her face," Sandy tried to explain, holding the sketchpad to his chest—and lying. "I don't care what it is! You never heard of Leo Frank? You never heard of the Jew they lynched in Georgia because of that little factory girl? Stop *drawing* her, damn it! Stop drawing *any* of them! These people don't *like* being drawn—can't you see that? We came out to Kentucky to get this boy because they have burned his mother to death in her car! For Christ's sake, put those drawing things away, and don't draw any more girls!"

Finally back on the road again, they had no idea that Philadelphia (which my father was hoping to reach by dawn of the seventeenth) had been occupied by tanks and troops of the U.S. Army, nor did my father know that Uncle Monty, indifferent to my mother's pleading and impervious to any hardship not his own, had fired him for not showing up at work a second week in a row. My father chooses resistance, Rabbi Bengelsdorf chooses collaboration, and Uncle Monty chooses himself.

To get to Boyle County and the Mawhinneys' they had traveled diagonally south across New Jersey to Camden, across the Delaware to Philadelphia, south from there to Baltimore, west and south across the length of West Virginia, and then into Kentucky until, a hundred or so miles on, they reached Lexington and, near a place called Versailles, turned south again for Boyle County's rolling hills. My mother tracked their trip on my encyclopedia's foldout map of the forty-eight states and the ten Canadian provinces, which she spread across the dining room table to look at whenever her anxiety overtook her, while out on the road Sandy, armed with a flashlight for the dark hours, charted their course on an Esso road map and kept an eye out for suspicious-looking characters, especially when they were passing through some grim one-street town whose name he couldn't even find on the map. Excluding the six times that the car broke down on the way back, Sandy counted at least another six in West Virginia when my father—who didn't like the look of a battered truck that was following behind them or of the pickups parked haphazardly by some roadside saloon or of the overalled kid in the gas station who'd pumped their gas and checked the car's front end and then spat on the ground when he took their money—had asked Sandy to open the glove compartment and pass him Mr. Cucuzza's spare pistol to hold in his lap while he drove, and each time sounding as though he, who'd never fired a shot in his life, wouldn't hesitate, if he had to, to pulla the trig'.

Sandy, who once he got home drew from memory his boyhood masterpiece—the illustrated history of their great descent into the hard American world—admitted to having been frightened just about all the time: frightened when they passed through cities where Ku Klux Klansmen had to be lying in wait for any Jew foolhardy enough to be driving through, but no less frightened when they were out beyond the ominous cities, beyond the faded billboards and the tiny filling stations and the last of the shacks where the poorest of people in their threadbare clothes lived—dilapidated timber shacks that Sandy rendered meticulously, underpinned at the four corners by rickety stone piles, with cutout holes for windows and a crudely built chimney crumbling at one end and, on the weather-worn roof, a few scattered rocks holding down the loose shingles—and into what my father called "the wilds." Frightened, said Sandy, speeding past the cows and the horses and the barns and the silos without another car in sight, frightened making hairpin turns up in the mountains without either a shoulder or a guardrail at the side of the road, and frightened when the paved road turned to gravel and the forest closed around them as though they were Lewis and Clark. And especially frightened because our car had no radio, and they didn't know whether the killing of Jews had stopped or whether they might be driving right into the thick of the country's murderous rage against people like us.

Seemingly the sole interlude that *hadn't* frightened my brother was what had so scared my father out front of the doctor's house: Sandy's drawing a picture of the West Virginia mountain girl whose looks had clearly gotten him all worked up. As it turned out, she'd been exactly the age of "the little factory girl" (as the whole country came to know her) murdered in Atlanta some thirty years earlier by her Jewish supervisor, a married businessman of twenty-nine named Leo Frank. The famous 1913 case of poor Mary Phagan—found dead with a noose around her neck on the floor of the pencil factory basement after going to Frank's office on the day of the murder to collect her pay envelope—had been all over the front pages, North *and* South, at about the time my father, an impressionable boy of twelve who'd only recently left school to help support the family, was at work in an East Orange hat factory, obtaining a first-class education there in the commonplace libel that linked him inextricably to the crucifiers of Christ. After Frank's conviction (on not entirely reliable circumstantial evidence that is all but discredited today), a fellow prison inmate became a statewide hero by slashing his throat and nearly killing him. One month later, a lynch mob of respectable citizens finished the job by abducting Frank from his jail cell and—much to the satisfaction of my father's co-workers on the factory floor—hanging "the sodomite" from a tree in Marietta, Georgia (Mary Phagan's hometown), as public warning to other "Jewish libertines" to stay the hell out of the South and away from their women.

To be sure, the Frank case was only a part of the history that fed my father's sense of danger in rural West Virginia on the afternoon of October 15, 1942. It all goes further back than that.

This was how Seldon came to live with us. After their safe return to Newark from Kentucky, Sandy moved into the sun parlor and Seldon took over where Alvin and Aunt Evelyn had left off—as the person in the twin bed next to mine shattered by the malicious indignities of Lindbergh's America. There was no stump for me to care for this time. The boy himself was the stump, and until he was taken to live with his mother's married sister in Brooklyn ten months later, I was the prosthesis.

Postscript

Note to the Reader

A True Chronology of the Major Figures

Other Historical Figures in the Work

Some Documentation

Note to the Reader

The Plot Against America is a work of fiction. This postscript is intended as a reference for readers interested in tracking where historical fact ends and historical imagining begins. The facts presented below are drawn from the following sources: John Thomas Anderson, *Senator Burton K. Wheeler and United States Foreign Relations* (dissertation presented to the graduate faculty, University of Virginia), 1982; Neil Baldwin, *Henry Ford and the Jews: The Mass Production of Hate*, 2001; A. Scott Berg, *Lindbergh*, 1998; Biography Resource Center, *Newark Evening News* and *Newark Star-Ledger*; Allen Bodner, *When Boxing Was a Jewish Sport*, 1997; William Bridgwater and Seymour Kurtz, eds., *The Columbia Encyclopedia*, 1963; James MacGregor Burns, *Roosevelt: The Soldier of Freedom*, 1970, and *Roosevelt: The Lion and the Fox*, 1984; Wayne S. Cole, *America First: The Battle Against Intervention, 1940–41*, 1953; Sander A. Diamond, *The Nazi Movement in the United States, 1924–1941*, 1974; John Drexel, ed., *The Facts on File Encyclopedia of the Twentieth Century*, 1991; Henry Ford, *The International Jew: The World's Foremost Problem*, vol. 3, *Jewish Influences in American Life, 1920–1922*; Neal Gabler, *Winchell: Gossip, Power, and the Culture of Celebrity*, 1994; Gale Group Publishing, *Contemporary Authors*, vol. 182, 2000; John A. Garraty and Mark C. Carnes, eds., *American National Biography*, 1999; Susan Hertog, *Anne Morrow Lindbergh: Her Life*, 1999; Richard Hofstadter and Beatrice K. Hofstadter, eds., *Great Issues in American History: From Reconstruction to the Present Day, 1864–1981*, vol. 3, 1982; Joseph G. E. Hopkins, ed., *Dictionary of American Biography*, supplements 3–9, 1974–1994; Joseph K. Howard, "The Decline and Fall of Burton K. Wheeler," *Harper's Magazine*, March 1947; Harold L. Ickes, *The Secret Diary of Harold L. Ickes, 1939–1941*, 1974; Thomas Kessner, *Fiorello H. La Guardia and the Making of Modern New York,* 1989; Herman Klurfeld, *Winchell: His Life and Times,* 1976; Anne Morrow Lindbergh, *The Wave of the Future: A Confession of Faith,* 1940; Albert S. Lindemann, *The Jew Accused: Three Anti-Semitic Affairs (Dreyfus, Beilis, Frank), 1894–1915,* 1991; Arthur Mann, *La Guardia: A Fighter Against His Times, 1882–1933,* 1959; Samuel Eliot Morison and Henry Steele Commager, *The Growth of the American Republic,* vol. 2, 1962; Charles Moritz, ed., *Current Biography Yearbook, 1988,* 1988; John Morrison and Catherine Wright Morrison, *Mavericks: The Lives and Battles of Montana's Political Legends,* 1997; *Random House Dictionary of the English Language,* 1983; Arthur M. Schlesinger, Jr., *The Coming of the New Deal, 1933–1935,* 1958, and *The Politics of Upheaval, 1935–1936,* 1960 (vols. 2 and 3 of *The Age of Roosevelt*); Peter Teed, *A Dictionary of Twentieth-Century History, 1914–1990,* 1992; Walter Yust, ed., *Britannica Book of the Year Omnibus, 1937–1942,* and *Britannica Book of the Year, 1943;* Ben D. Zevin, ed., *Nothing to Fear: The Selected Addresses of Franklin D. Roosevelt, 1932–1945,* 1961.

A True Chronology of the Major Figures

FRANKLIN DELANO ROOSEVELT
1882–1945

NOVEMBER 1920. After serving as assistant secretary of the navy under Wilson, Roosevelt runs as vice president on Democratic ticket with Governor James M. Cox of Ohio; Democrats defeated in Harding landslide.

AUGUST 1921. Stricken with polio, which leaves him badly crippled for life.

NOVEMBER 1928. Elected to first of two two-year terms as Democratic governor of New York, while national ticket, headed by ex-governor Alfred E. Smith, loses to Herbert Hoover. As governor, Roosevelt strongly establishes himself as a progressive liberal, an advocate of government relief for Depression victims, including unemployment insurance, and a foe of Prohibition. After landslide 1930 gubernatorial victory, becomes Democratic presidential front-runner.

JULY–NOVEMBER 1932. Selected as presidential candidate by Democrats at July convention; in November, defeats President Hoover with 57.4 percent of vote, and Democrats sweep both houses of Congress.

MARCH 1933. Inaugurated as president March 4; with nation paralyzed by Depression, proclaims in inaugural address that "the only thing we have to fear is fear itself." Quickly proposes New Deal recovery legislation for agriculture, industry, labor, and business, and relief programs for mortgage holders and the unemployed. Cabinet includes Harold L. Ickes, secretary of the interior; Henry A. Wallace, secretary of agriculture; Frances Perkins —first ever woman cabinet appointee—secretary of labor; and Henry Morgenthau, Jr.—the country's second Jew ever to be a cabinet member—secretary of the Treasury (to replace the ill secretary, William Woodin, on November 17, 1933). Begins brief national radio broadcasts from White House, known as fireside chats, and engages reporters in informative press conferences.

NOVEMBER 1933–DECEMBER 1934. Recognizes Soviet Union and soon starts rebuilding the U.S. fleet, in part owing to Japanese activities in Far East. By '34 black voters have shifted political loyalty from Lincoln's Republican Party to Roosevelt's Democratic Party in response to president's programs for the underprivileged.

1935. Burst of reform initiatives, referred to as "second New Deal," results in the Social Security Act, the National Labor Relations Act, as well as the WPA (Works Progress Administration), which employs two million workers a month. Signs first of several neutrality measures in response to unsettled European situation.

NOVEMBER 1936. Defeats Kansas Republican governor Alfred M. Landon, winning every state except Maine and Vermont; Democrats enlarge congressional lead. In inaugural address asserts, "Here is a challenge to our democracy . . . I see one-third of a nation ill-housed, ill-clad, ill-nourished." By 1937, economic recovery well under way, but economic crisis follows and, along with labor unrest, leads to Republican congressional victories in 1938.

SEPTEMBER–NOVEMBER 1938. Apprehensive over Hitler's intentions in Europe, appeals to Nazi leader to accept negotiated settlement in dispute with Czechoslovakia. At September 30 Munich conference, Britain and France capitulate to German demand for Czech Sudetenland and the dismemberment of Czechoslovakia; German troops, led by Hitler, enter in October (and, five months later, conquer the entire country, granting Slovakia independence as a German-backed fascist republic). In November Roosevelt orders enormous increase in production of combat airplanes.

APRIL 1939. Asks Hitler and Mussolini to agree for a period of ten years to refrain from attacking weaker European nations; Hitler replies in a Reichstag speech by heaping scorn on Roosevelt and boasting of German military might.

AUGUST–SEPTEMBER 1939. Telegrams Hitler asking him to negotiate settlement with Poland over territorial dispute; Hitler responds by invading Poland on September 1. England and France declare war on Hitler, and World War Two begins.

SEPTEMBER 1939. European war prompts Roosevelt to seek changes in Neutrality Act to allow Britain and France to obtain arms from U.S. When Hitler invades Denmark, Norway, Belgium, the Netherlands, Luxembourg, and France in first half of 1940, Roosevelt significantly increases U.S. arms production.

MAY 1940. Establishes Council of National Defense and, later, Office of Production Management, to prepare industry and armed forces for possible war.

SEPTEMBER 1940. Japan, at war with China and having invaded French Indochina (and having already annexed Korea in 1910 and occupied Manchuria in 1931), signs triple alliance with Italy and Germany in Berlin. At Roosevelt's urging, Congress passes first peacetime conscription bill in U.S. history, requiring all men between twenty-one and thirty-five to register for the draft and arranging for the induction into armed services of 800,000 draftees.

NOVEMBER 1940. Denounced by right-wing Republicans as a "warmonger," and campaigning as an avowed enemy of Hitler and fascism pledged to do everything possible to keep America out of the European war, Roosevelt wins unprecedented third term, by 449 to 82 electoral votes, defeating the Republican Wendell L. Willkie in an election in which national defense and U.S. relationship to the war are major issues; Willkie carries only Maine, Vermont, and the isolationist Midwest.

JANUARY–MARCH 1941. Inaugurated January 20. In March Congress passes his Lend-Lease Act, authorizing president to "sell, transfer, lend, lease" armaments, foodstuffs, and services to countries whose defense he deems vital to the defense of the U.S.

APRIL–JUNE 1941. After German army invades Yugoslavia and then Greece, Hitler breaks joint non-aggression pact and invades Russia. In April U.S. takes Greenland under protection; in June Roosevelt authorizes landing of U.S. forces in Iceland and extends Lend-Lease to Russia.

AUGUST 1941. Meeting at sea, Roosevelt and Churchill draw up Atlantic Charter of "common principles," containing eight-point declaration of peace aims.

SEPTEMBER 1941. Announces that Navy has been ordered to destroy any German or Italian submarines entering U.S. waters and threatening U.S. defense; asks Japan to begin military evacuation of China and Indochina, but war minister, General Tojo, refuses.

OCTOBER 1941. Asks Congress to amend Neutrality Act to allow arming of U.S. merchant ships and to permit them to enter combat zones.

NOVEMBER 1941. Massive Japanese striking force secretly assembles in Pacific while negotiations with U.S. on military and economic issues appear to continue with arrival in U.S. of Japanese envoys for "peace talks."

DECEMBER 1941. Japan launches surprise attack on U.S. possessions in the Pacific and far eastern possessions of Great Britain; after emergency address by president, Congress unanimously declares war on Japan the next day. On December 11 Germany and Italy declare war on the U.S.; Congress, in response, declares war on Germany and Italy. (Casualty figures for Japanese attack on Pearl Harbor: 2,403 American sailors, soldiers, marines, and civilians killed; 1,178 wounded.)

1942. Directing the war effort occupies president almost entirely. In his annual message to Congress he stresses increased war production, declares that "our objectives are clear—smashing the militarism imposed by the warlords on their enslaved peoples." Proposes record $58,927,000,000 budget to accommodate war expenses. With Churchill, announces creation of unified military command in Southeast Asia. Strategy conference with Churchill in June results in November invasion of French North Africa by Allied troops under command of General Dwight D. Eisenhower (German army driven from Africa seven months later); president assures France, Portugal, and Spain that Allies have no designs on their territories. In June asks Congress to recognize existence of state of war against fascist regimes of Romania, Bulgaria, and Hungary, allied with Axis powers. In July appoints commission to try eight Nazi saboteurs arrested by federal agents after landing on U.S. shores from enemy submarine; following secret trial, two are imprisoned and six are executed in Washington. In September, president's emissary Wendell Willkie received by Stalin in Moscow, where he urges second military front in Western Europe. In October president makes secret two-week tour of war production facilities and announces objectives are being met. Asks Congress to expand draft to eighteen- and nineteen-year-olds.

JANUARY 1943–AUGUST 1945. European war (and Hitler's concurrent massacre of Europe's Jews and the expropriation of their property) lasts until 1945. In April Mussolini executed by Italian partisans, and Italy surrenders. Germany surrenders unconditionally on May 7, a week after the suicide of Adolf Hitler in his Berlin bunker and less than a month after the sudden death, from a cerebral hemorrhage, of President Roosevelt—then in the first year of a fourth presidential term—and the swearing in of his successor, Vice President Harry S. Truman. War ends in Far East when Japan surrenders unconditionally on August 14. World War Two is over.

CHARLES A. LINDBERGH
1902–1974

MAY 1927. Charles A. Lindbergh, a twenty-five-year-old Minnesota-born stunt flier and airmail pilot, flies the monoplane *Spirit of St. Louis* from New York to Paris in thirty-three hours and thirty minutes; his completing first nonstop transatlantic solo flight makes him a celebrity around the globe. President Coolidge awards Lindbergh Distinguished Flying Cross and commissions him colonel in U.S. Army Air Corps Reserve.

MAY 1929. Lindbergh marries Anne Morrow, the twenty-three-year-old daughter of U.S. ambassador to Mexico.

JUNE 1930. Charles A. Lindbergh, Jr., born to Charles and Anne Lindbergh in New Jersey.

MARCH–MAY 1932. Charles Jr. kidnapped from family's secluded new house on 435 acres in rural Hopewell, New Jersey; some ten weeks later, decomposing corpse of baby discovered by chance in nearby woods.

SEPTEMBER 1934–MARCH 1935. A poor German immigrant carpenter and ex-convict, Bruno R. Hauptmann, arrested in Bronx, New York, for kidnap and murder of Lindbergh baby. Six-week trial in Flemington, New Jersey, characterized by press as "trial of the century." Hauptmann found guilty and executed in electric chair April 1936.

APRIL 1935. Anne Morrow Lindbergh publishes first book, *North to the Orient*, an account of her 1931 air adventures with Lindbergh; becomes a top bestseller and receives the National Booksellers Award as the most distinguished nonfiction book of the year.

DECEMBER 1935–DECEMBER 1936. Seeking privacy, Lindberghs leave America with their two small children and, until their return in spring 1939, reside mainly in small village in Kent, England. At the invitation of U.S. military, Lindbergh travels to Germany to report on Nazi aircraft development; makes repeated visits for this purpose over the next three years. Attends 1936 Berlin Olympics, where Hitler is in attendance, and later writes of Hitler to a friend, "He is undoubtedly a great man, and I believe has done much for the German people." Anne Morrow Lindbergh accompanies her husband to Germany and afterward writes critically of the "strictly puritanical view at home that dictatorships are of necessity wrong, evil, unstable and no good can come of them—combined with our funny-paper view of Hitler as a clown—combined with the very strong (naturally) Jewish propaganda in the Jewish-owned papers."

OCTOBER 1938. Service Cross of the German Eagle—a gold medallion

with four small swastikas, conferred on foreigners for service to the Reich
—presented to Lindbergh, "by order of the Führer," by Air Marshal Hermann Göring at American embassy dinner in Berlin. Anne Morrow Lindbergh publishes second account of her flying adventures, *Listen! the Wind*, a nonfiction bestseller despite her husband's growing unpopularity among American antifascists and the refusal by some Jewish booksellers to stock the book.

APRIL 1939. After Hitler invades Czechoslovakia, Lindbergh writes in his journal, "Much as I disapprove of many things Germany has done, I believe she has pursued the only consistent policy in Europe in recent years." At request of Air Corps chief, General "Hap" Arnold, and with approval of President Roosevelt—who dislikes and distrusts him—goes on active duty as colonel in U.S. Army Air Corps.

SEPTEMBER 1939. In journal entries after Germany invades Poland on September 1, Lindbergh notes the need to "guard ourselves against attack by foreign armies and dilution by foreign races . . . and the infiltration of inferior blood." Aviation, he writes, is "one of those priceless possessions which permit the White race to live at all in a pressing sea of Yellow, Black, and Brown." Earlier in year he notes, of a private conversation with a high-ranking member of the Republican National Committee and the conservative newsman Fulton Lewis, Jr., "We are disturbed about the effect of the Jewish influence in our press, radio, and motion pictures . . . It is too bad because a few Jews of the right type are, I believe, an asset to any country." In an April 1939 diary entry (omitted in 1970 from his published *Wartime Journals*) he writes, "There are too many Jews in places like New York already. A few Jews add strength and character to a country, but too many create chaos. And we are getting too many." In April 1940, speaking over the Columbia Broadcasting System, he says, "The only reason that we are in danger of becoming involved in this war is because there are powerful elements in America who desire us to take part. They represent a small minority of the American people, but they control much of the machinery of influence and propaganda. They seize every opportunity to push us closer to the edge." When Idaho Republican senator William E. Borah encourages Lindbergh to run for president, Lindbergh says he prefers to take political positions as a private citizen.

OCTOBER 1940. In spring America First Committee founded at Yale University Law School to oppose FDR's interventionist policies and promote American isolationism; in October Lindbergh addresses meeting of three thousand at Yale, advocating that America recognize "the new powers in Europe." Anne Morrow Lindbergh publishes third book, *The Wave of the Future*, a brief anti-interventionist tract subtitled "A Confession of Faith," which arouses enormous controversy and immediately becomes top nonfiction bestseller despite denunciation by Secretary of the Interior Harold Ickes as "the Bible of every American Nazi."

APRIL–AUGUST 1941. Addresses ten thousand at America First Committee rally in Chicago, another ten thousand at New York rally, prompting his bitter enemy Secretary Ickes to call him "the No. 1 United States Nazi fellow traveler." When Lindbergh writes to President Roosevelt complaining about Ickes's attacks on him, particularly for accepting the German medal, Ickes writes, "If Mr. Lindbergh feels like cringing when he is correctly referred to as a knight of the German Eagle, why doesn't he send back the disgraceful decoration and be done with it?" (Earlier, Lindbergh had declined returning the medal on grounds that it would constitute "an unnecessary insult" to the Nazi leadership.) President openly questions Lindbergh's loyalty, prompting Lindbergh to tender his resignation as Army colonel to Roosevelt's secretary of war. Ickes notes that while Lindbergh is swift in renouncing his Army commission, he remains adamant in refusing to return the medal received from Nazi Germany. In May, along with Senator Burton K. Wheeler of Montana, who is seated on the platform beside Anne Morrow Lindbergh, Lindbergh addresses twenty-five thousand at America First rally at Madison Square Garden; his appearance greeted with cries from the audience of "Our next president!" and his speech followed by a four-minute ovation. Speaks against American intervention in European war to large audiences across the country throughout spring and summer.

SEPTEMBER–DECEMBER 1941. Delivers his "Who Are the War Agitators?" radio speech to an America First rally in Des Moines on September 11; audience of eight thousand cheers when he names "the Jewish race" as among those most powerful and effective in pushing the U.S.—"for reasons which are not American"—toward involvement in the war. Adds that "we cannot blame them for looking out for what they believe to be their own interests, but we also must look out for ours. We cannot allow the natural passions and prejudices of other peoples to lead our country to destruction." Des Moines speech is attacked the next day by both Democrats and Republicans, but Senator Gerald P. Nye, Republican from North Dakota and staunch America Firster, defends Lindbergh from critics and reiterates charge against the Jews, as do other supporters. December 10 address, scheduled for Boston America First rally, canceled by Lindbergh after Japanese attack on Pearl Harbor and U.S. declaration of war on Japan, Germany, and Italy. Activities of America First Committee terminated by leadership, and organization disbands.

JANUARY–DECEMBER 1942. Travels to Washington to seek reinstatement in Air Corps, but key Roosevelt cabinet members strongly oppose, as does much of the press, and Roosevelt says no. Repeated attempts to find position in aviation industry also fail, despite a lucrative association during the late twenties and early thirties with Transcontinental Air Transport ("the Lindbergh Line") and as highly paid consultant with Pan American Airways. In spring finally finds work, with government approval, as consultant to Ford's bomber development program, outside Detroit at Willow Run, and family moves to Detroit suburb. (The September afternoon President Roosevelt visits Willow Run to inspect war production projects, Lindbergh makes it his business to be away.) Participates in experiments at Mayo Clinic aeromedical laboratory to decrease physical dangers of high-altitude flying; later participates as test pilot in experiments with oxygen equipment at high altitudes.

DECEMBER 1942–JULY 1943. Takes active role in training pilots for Navy/Marine Corps Corsair, fighter plane that he helps develop for United Aircraft in Connecticut.

AUGUST 1943. Anne Morrow Lindbergh, now mother of four children, publishes *The Steep Ascent,* a novella about a dangerous flying adventure; her first publishing failure, largely owing to hostility of reviewers and readers toward the prewar politics of the Lindbergh family.

JANUARY–SEPTEMBER 1944. After stint in Florida testing a variety of warplanes, including Boeing's new B-29 bomber, receives government permission to go to South Pacific to study Corsairs in action; once there, begins to fly combat and bombing runs against Japanese targets from New Guinea base, at first as observer but soon, with great success, as enthusiastic participant. Teaches pilots how to increase combat range by conserving fuel in flight. Having flown fifty missions—and downed a Japanese fighter plane—returns to America in September to resume work with United Aircraft's fighter program, and family moves from Michigan to Westport, Connecticut.

FIORELLO H. LA GUARDIA
1882–1947

NOVEMBER 1922. Having served congressional terms representing Lower East Side of Manhattan just before and after World War One, La Guardia is returned to Congress and serves five consecutive terms as Republican representative for the Italian and Jewish constituency of East Harlem.

Leads House in opposing President Hoover's sales tax and denouncing his failure to address Depression suffering; also opposes Prohibition.

NOVEMBER 1924. In presidential election, outspokenly supports Progressive Party candidate Robert M. La Follette rather than the Republican, President Coolidge.

JANUARY 1931. New York governor Franklin D. Roosevelt calls governors' conference to deal with Depression problems of unemployment; La Guardia praises him for promoting inquiry leading to labor and unemployment legislation that he himself had urged unsuccessfully on President Hoover.

1932. As a maverick Republican—and defeated lame-duck congressman—is chosen by president-elect Roosevelt to introduce New Deal legislation in lame-duck Seventy-second Congress after Democrats' 1932 landslide victory.

NOVEMBER 1933. Running as anti-Tammany candidate, elected Republican-Fusion (and later, in addition, American Labor Party) mayor of New York for first of three consecutive terms; sets out as activist mayor to bring economic recovery to Depression New York by fostering public works projects and establishing and increasing public services. Denounces fascism and American Nazis; in response to Nazis labeling him "Jew Mayor of New York," quips, "I never thought I had enough Jewish blood in my veins to justify boasting of it."

SEPTEMBER 1938. After Hitler dismembers Czechoslovakia, La Guardia attacks Republican isolationists and takes side of FDR in growing interventionist controversy.

SEPTEMBER 1940. Though Wendell Willkie is said to be considering him for vice presidential running mate, La Guardia again deserts Republicans, as he did in 1924; with Senator George Norris forms Independents for Roosevelt and openly campaigns for Roosevelt third term.

AUGUST–NOVEMBER 1940. With war looming, Roosevelt favors La Guardia for secretary of war but chooses Republican Henry Stimson instead, appointing La Guardia chairman of the American side of the U.S.-Canadian Defense Board.

APRIL 1941. Accepts unpaid position as FDR's director of civilian defense while continuing to hold office as mayor of New York.

FEBRUARY–APRIL 1943. Presses Roosevelt to return him to active Army duty as brigadier general, but Roosevelt, having failed to grant him a cabinet position or consider him for a running mate, declines, on advice of intimates who consider La Guardia too provocative; the disappointed mayor returns to his "street-cleaner's uniform."

AUGUST 1943. Wartime racial strife that previously struck Beaumont, Mobile, Los Angeles, and Detroit—where there are thirty-four deaths in June 21 riots—erupts in New York's Harlem. After nearly three days of vandalism, looting, and bloodshed, La Guardia praised by black leaders for strong, compassionate leadership during riots that leave 6 dead, 185 injured, and $5 million in property damage.

MAY 1945. A month after FDR's death, announces he will not run for a fourth term; famously, before his retirement, he reads the funnies over the radio to New York youngsters during a newspaper strike. After leaving office, accepts directorship of UNRRA (United Nations Relief and Rehabilitation Administration).

WALTER WINCHELL
1897–1972

1924. Ex-vaudevillian Walter Winchell hired by *New York Evening Graphic* and soon gains popularity as Broadway reporter and columnist.

JUNE 1929. Goes to work as columnist for William Randolph Hearst's *New York Daily Mirror,* a job he will keep for over thirty years. Hearst's King Features syndicates Winchell column nationwide; it eventually appears in more than two thousand papers. Inventor of modern gossip column naturally becomes regular at New York celebrity night spot the Stork Club.

MAY 1930. Makes radio debut as Broadway gossip newscaster; moves on to great popularity with *Lucky Strike Dance Hour* program and, in December 1932, on Sundays at nine P.M., the program for Jergens Lotion on the NBC Blue Network. Weekly Winchell quarter hour of insider gossip and general news soon claims radio's largest audience, and his opening gambit—"Good evening, Mr. and Mrs. America and all the ships at sea, let's go to press!"— becomes part of American parlance.

MARCH 1932. Begins covering Lindbergh kidnapping case, aided in his coverage by tips from FBI chief J. Edgar Hoover; continues to cover the case through the arrest of Bruno Hauptmann in 1934 and the trial in 1935.

FEBRUARY 1933. Almost alone among public commentators and among well-known Jews, begins public attack on Hitler and American Nazis, including Bund leader Fritz Kuhn; continues attack on radio and in column until outbreak of World War Two; coins neologisms "razis" and "swastinkers" to ridicule the Nazi movement.

JANUARY–MARCH 1935. Lauded for his work covering Hauptmann trial by J. Edgar Hoover. Hoover and Winchell subsequently trade information about American Nazis that winds up in Winchell's column.

1937. Support in column for Roosevelt and New Deal leads to May White House invitation and regular communication between the president and Winchell. Feud grows between Hearst and Winchell over Winchell's public support of FDR. Friendship develops between Winchell and New York neighbor, mobster Frank Costello.

1940. Winchell's combined audience for column and newscast estimated at fifty million, more than a third of America's population; his annual salary of $800,000 places him among highest-paid Americans. Winchell steps up attack on pro-Nazi activities with features in his column such as "The Winchell Column vs. The Fifth Column." Strongly endorses FDR for unprecedented third term; writes pseudonymous columns for *PM* attacking Republican candidate Willkie after Hearst censors Winchell's criticism of Willkie in *Daily Mirror.*

APRIL–MAY 1941. Attacks Lindbergh for isolationist and pro-German statements; warns Nazi foreign minister von Ribbentrop that America has the will to fight, and is then attacked by Senator Burton K. Wheeler for "blitzkrieging the American people into this war."

SEPTEMBER 1941. After Lindbergh's Des Moines speech charging Jews with pushing America toward war, writes that Lindbergh's "halo has become his noose" and repeatedly attacks Lindbergh as well as Senators Wheeler, Nye, Rankin, and others he identifies as pro-Nazi.

DECEMBER 1941–FEBRUARY 1972. After America's entrance into World War Two, Winchell's newscasts and columns deal predominantly with war news; as lieutenant commander in naval reserve, presses FDR for assignment and is called to active duty in November 1942. With end of war, turns to far right; becomes fierce foe of Soviet Union and anti-Communist supporter of Senator Joseph McCarthy. Fades into near obscurity in mid-1950s; at his death in 1972, funeral attended only by his daughter.

BURTON K. WHEELER
1882–1975

NOVEMBER 1920–NOVEMBER 1922. After defying Montana's powerful giant, Anaconda Copper Mining Company, as Montana state legislator and after opposing human rights violations committed during postwar Red Scare, Wheeler is badly defeated in 1920 run for governor, but in 1922 elected as Democrat to U.S. Senate for the first of four terms with the strong backing of farmers and labor. Over the years, converts Montana state government into bipartisan Wheeler machine.

FEBRUARY–NOVEMBER 1924. Chosen to head Senate inquiry into Teapot Dome graft scandal, which leads to resignation of President Coolidge's attorney general, Harry M. Dougherty, and humiliation of Coolidge's Justice Department. Abandons Democrats—and Democratic ticket headed by John W. Davis—to run for vice president on Progressive Party ticket with Wisconsin senator Robert M. La Follette. Coolidge overwhelmingly defeats both Democrats and Progressives, though latter party polls six million votes nationwide and nearly forty percent of vote in Montana.

1932–1937. Prior to Democratic Convention in 1932, visits sixteen states to promote Roosevelt nomination. Despite being the first national figure to endorse Democratic candidate and by and large sympathetic to New Deal social reform, in 1937 Wheeler bitterly opposes the president over his legislative proposal to enlarge Supreme Court and "pack" it with New Deal supporters; Wheeler's leadership leads to controversial bill's defeat, and aggravates personal enmity between him and the president.

1938. Wheeler's Montana machine works to undermine his Democratic rival, Congressman Jerry O'Connell, aiding election to the House of Jacob Thorkelson, a right-wing Republican labeled by Walter Winchell the "mouthpiece of the Nazi movement in Congress." Thorkelson calls Winchell a "Jewish vilifier" and files suit against him after Winchell includes Thorkelson in *Liberty* magazine series of articles called "Americans We Can Do Without." Congressman O'Connell, commenting on electoral activities of Wheeler Democrats, describes Wheeler as a "Benedict Arnold to his party and a traitor to his president."

1940–1941. Wheeler for President club formed in Montana by influential Democrats; in his home state and elsewhere, considered a formidable contender for Democratic nomination until Roosevelt announces his candidacy for a third term. In Senate, Wheeler increasingly aligned with Republicans and southern Democrats against liberal Roosevelt wing of Democratic Party. Vociferously opposes American intervention in European war. In June 1940 threatens to bolt Democratic Party "if it is going to be a war party." Meets that month to make plans "for countering war agitation and propaganda" with Charles A. Lindbergh and a group of isolationist senators; on Senate floor, defends Lindbergh against accusations of being pro-Nazi, and some months later, after Roosevelt publicly compares Lindbergh to a Civil

War "Copperhead" (a northerner who sympathized with the South), calls the remark "shocking and appalling to every right-thinking American." Speaking over NBC radio network, proposes an eight-point peace proposal for negotiating with Hitler and receives congratulatory telegram from Lindbergh. Meets with Yale students planning to organize America First Committee and assumes role of unofficial adviser; along with Lindbergh, becomes most popular speaker at AFC rallies. Speaks out against draft, calling Roosevelt's peacetime conscription proposal "a step toward totalitarianism." On Senate floor, arguing against Lend-Lease bill, says, "If the American people want a dictatorship—if they want a totalitarian form of government and if they want war—this bill should be steam-rollered through Congress, as is the wont of President Roosevelt." Claims Lend-Lease, if passed, "will plow under every fourth American boy," prompting Roosevelt to label Wheeler's remark "the most untruthful . . . most dastardly, unpatriotic thing . . . that has been said in public life in my generation." Publicly—and prematurely—reveals that U.S. is sending troops to Iceland; White House, along with Prime Minister Churchill, accuses Wheeler of endangering American and British lives. Again charged with compromising military secrecy when, in November 1941, he leaks to isolationist *Chicago Tribune* a classified War Department document disclosing U.S. strategy in the event of war.

DECEMBER 1941–DECEMBER 1946. Following Pearl Harbor, supports war effort, arguing, however, that America's alliance with Soviet Union aids survival of Communist government. In 1944, claiming "Communists are behind MVA," sides against liberals and with Montana Power Company and Anaconda Copper Company in helping defeat Missouri Valley counterpart to Tennessee Valley Authority (TVA). Subsequently loses last of Montana Democratic support and is defeated in 1946 Senate primary campaign by young Montana liberal Leif Erickson.

1950s. Practices law in Washington, D.C. Allies himself ideologically and politically with Senator Joseph McCarthy.

HENRY FORD
1863–1947

1903–1905. First Ford automobile, the two-cylinder, eight-horsepower Model A, designed by Henry Ford and manufactured by his newly incorporated Ford Motor Company, appears in 1903, selling for $850. Higher-priced models appear over next few years.

1908. Designed for rural America, Model T Ford is introduced and, until 1927, is the only model built by the company. Makes Ford the country's premier auto manufacturer, fulfilling his plan to "build a motorcar for the great multitude."

1910–1916. With his automotive associates, establishes a manufacturing process of sequential production and division of labor that evolves into the continuously moving assembly line—considered the greatest industrial advance since the advent of the Industrial Revolution—which leads to mass production of Model T. In 1914 Ford announces a basic wage of $5 for an eight-hour day; offer extends, in fact, to only a portion of Ford work force. Nonetheless his advocating the "Five Dollar Day" brings Ford much praise and fame as an enlightened businessman, if not as an enlightened thinker. "I don't like to read books," he explains. "They muss up my mind." "History," he declares, "is more or less bunk."

1916–1919. Name put into nomination for presidency at Republican National Convention and gains thirty-two first-ballot votes. Moves successfully to wield absolute power over all Ford enterprises. By 1916, company producing two thousand cars a day, with a production total to date of one million Model T's. At outbreak of World War One becomes active as pacifist opponent of war and attacks war profiteering. Announces to meeting of Ford officials, "I know who caused the war. The German-Jewish bankers. I have the evidence here. Facts. The German-Jewish bankers caused the war." With American entry into war, pledges to "operate without one cent of profit" in fulfilling government contracts, but neglects to do so. At urging of President Wilson, runs for Senate as a Democrat—though formerly identified as a Republican—and is defeated in close election. Attributes his losing to Wall Street "interests" and "the Jews."

1920. In May, *Dearborn Independent*—local weekly bought by Ford in 1918—prints first of ninety-one detailed articles devoted to exposing "The International Jew: The World's Problem"; in ensuing issues, serializes the text of the fraudulent *Protocols of the Learned Elders of Zion* while claiming the document—and its revelation of a Jewish plan for world domination—to be authentic. Circulation rises to close to 300,000 by second year of publication; subscriptions to paper are forced upon Ford dealers as a company product, and the strongly anti-Semitic articles are collected in a four-volume edition, *The International Jew: The World's Foremost Problem*.

1920s. Five millionth Ford car produced in 1921; more than half of cars sold in America are Model T's. Develops huge River Rouge plant and industrial city in Dearborn. Acquires forests, iron mines, and coal mines to supply auto company with raw materials. Diversifies Ford line of cars. His 1922 autobiography, *My Life and Work,* is a nonfiction bestseller, and the Ford name and legend are known throughout the world. Polls show him running ahead of President Harding in popularity, and is spoken of as potential Republican presidential candidate; in the fall of 1922 considers presidential run. Adolf Hitler, in 1923 interview, says, "We look to Heinrich Ford as the leader of the growing fascist movement in America." In mid-twenties, a suit for defamation filed against him by a Chicago Jewish lawyer is settled out of court, and in 1927, he retracts his attacks on Jews, agrees to discontinue anti-Semitic publications, and shuts down *Dearborn Independent,* a deficit enterprise that had cost him close to $5 million. When Lindbergh flies the *Spirit of St. Louis* to Detroit in August 1927, he meets Ford at Ford Airport and takes him in the famous plane for his first flight. Lindbergh interests Ford in aviation manufacturing. The two meet afterward numerous times, and in a 1940 Detroit interview Ford explains, "When Charles comes out here, we only talk about the Jews."

1931–1937. Competition from Chevrolet and Plymouth and impact of Depression produce large company losses despite innovation of Ford V-8 engine. Poor labor relations at River Rouge plant caused by speedup, job insecurity, and labor espionage. Efforts by United Auto Workers to organize Ford, along with General Motors and Chrysler, meet with violence and intimidation by Ford; Detroit vigilante group beats up labor organizers at River Rouge. Ford Company's labor policies condemned by National Labor Relations Board and considered worst in auto industry.

1938. In July, on his seventy-fifth birthday, accepts Service Cross of the German Eagle from Hitler's Nazi government at a birthday dinner in Detroit for fifteen hundred prominent citizens. (Same medal awarded to Lindbergh in October ceremony in Germany, causing Interior Secretary Ickes to tell a December meeting of the Cleveland Zionist Society, "Henry Ford and Charles A. Lindbergh are the only two free citizens of a free country who obsequiously have accepted tokens of contemptuous distinction at a time when the bestower of them counts that day lost when he can commit no new crimes against humanity.") Suffers first of two strokes.

1939–1940. With outbreak of World War Two joins his friend Lindbergh in supporting isolationism and America First Committee. Shortly after Ford is appointed to America First executive committee, Lessing J. Rosenwald, Jewish director of Sears, Roebuck and Company, resigns because of Ford's anti-Semitic reputation. For a while meets regularly with anti-Semitic radio priest Father Coughlin, whose activities Roosevelt and Ickes believe Ford is financing. Lends financial support to the anti-Semitic demagogue Gerald L. K. Smith for his weekly radio broadcast and his living expenses. (Some years later, Smith reprints Ford's *International Jew* in a new edition and maintains into the 1960s that Ford "never changed his opinion of Jews.")

1941–1947. Suffers second stroke. Company converts to defense production as war approaches; during war, produces B-24 bomber at huge Willow Run facility, where Lindbergh is hired as consulting adviser. Because of illness, Ford no longer able to run company and resigns in 1945. Dies April 1947, and 100,000 mourners view the body. Vast fortune in company stock goes mainly to Ford Foundation, soon the world's wealthiest private foundation.

Other Historical Figures in the Work

BERNARD BARUCH (1870–1965) Financier and government adviser. As director of War Industries Board under Woodrow Wilson, mobilized nation's industrial resources for World War One. Member of the White House circle during Roosevelt administrations. Appointed by Truman as U.S. representative to U.N. Atomic Energy Commission in 1946.

RUGGIERO "RITCHIE THE BOOT" BOIARDO (1890–1984) Newark crime figure and local rival to racketeer Longy Zwillman; his influence strongest in the city's Italian First Ward, where he owned a popular restaurant.

LOUIS D. BRANDEIS (1856–1941) Born in Louisville, Kentucky, to cultivated immigrant Jewish family from Prague. Public interest and labor attorney in Boston. Early organizer of Zionist movement in America. Appointed by President Wilson as associate justice of Supreme Court, but only after intense four-month controversy in Senate Judiciary Committee and around the country, which Brandeis attributed to his being first Jew nominated to the court. Served twenty-three years, until 1939.

CHARLES E. COUGHLIN (1891–1979) Roman Catholic priest and pastor of the Shrine of the Little Flower in Royal Oak, Michigan. Regarded Roosevelt as a Communist and fervently admired Lindbergh. In the 1930s, disseminated strongly anti-Semitic ideas in a weekly nationwide radio broadcast and his periodical *Social Justice,* which was barred from the U.S. Mail during the war for violating the Espionage Act and ceased publication in 1942.

AMELIA EARHART (1897–1937) In 1932, set transatlantic record of fourteen hours and fifty-six minutes for flight from Newfoundland to Ireland; first woman to make unaccompanied flights across Atlantic and across

Pacific from Honolulu to California. Her plane lost somewhere over the Pacific in 1937 attempt to fly around the world with navigator Frederick J. Noonan.

MEYER ELLENSTEIN (1885–1963) After careers as a dentist and a lawyer, chosen by fellow Newark city commissioners in 1933 to be mayor of Newark. The city's first and only Jewish mayor, served two terms, 1933–1941.

EDWARD FLANAGAN (1886–1948) In 1904, emigrated from Ireland to the U.S., where he began studies for priesthood; ordained 1912. In 1917, to provide for the welfare of homeless boys of all races and religions, founded Father Flanagan's Home for Boys in Omaha. Became national figure in 1938 because of popular film about Boys Town, starring Spencer Tracy as Father Flanagan.

LEO FRANK (1884–1915) Manager of Atlanta pencil factory, found guilty of murdering Mary Phagan, a thirteen-year-old employee, on April 26, 1913; assaulted with a knife while prisoner and later forcibly removed from jail by local citizens and lynched, August 1915. Anti-Semitism believed to have played important part in dubious conviction.

FELIX FRANKFURTER (1882–1965) Roosevelt-appointed associate justice of U.S. Supreme Court, 1939–1962.

JOSEPH GOEBBELS (1897–1945) An early member of the Nazi Party, in 1933 became Hitler's propaganda minister and culture czar, responsible for overseeing the press, radio, movies, and theater, and mounting public spectacles such as parades and mass rallies. Among the most devoted and brutal of Hitler's associates. In April 1945, with Germany destroyed and the Russians entering Berlin, he and his wife killed their six young children and together committed suicide.

HERMANN GÖRING (1893–1946) Founder and first head of the Gestapo, or secret police, and responsible for creation of the German air force. In 1940 Hitler named him as his successor, but dismissed him near war's end. Convicted at Nuremberg for war crimes and sentenced to death, he committed suicide two hours before execution.

HENRY (HANK) GREENBERG (1911–1986) Slugging first baseman for Detroit Tigers in 1930s and 1940s; fell two home runs short of Babe Ruth's record in 1938. Hero to Jewish baseball fans, he was first of two Jewish players elected to baseball's Hall of Fame.

WILLIAM RANDOLPH HEARST (1863–1951) American publisher, considered the foremost proponent of the sensational, jingoistic "yellow journalism" addressed to a mass audience; his newspaper empire flourished into the 1930s. Originally aligned with Democratic populists, became increasingly right wing and a bitter enemy of FDR's.

HEINRICH HIMMLER (1900–1945) Nazi leader, commander of the SS, which controlled concentration camps, and chief of the Gestapo; in charge of racial "purification" programs, and second in power only to Hitler. Poisoned himself and died after being captured by British troops in May 1945.

J(OHN) EDGAR HOOVER (1895–1972) Director of the Federal Bureau of Investigation (originally the Bureau of Investigation, a subsidiary of the Department of Justice), 1924–1972.

HAROLD L. ICKES (1874–1952) A progressive Republican turned Democrat, served nearly thirteen years as Roosevelt's secretary of the interior, making his the second-longest tenure of any Roosevelt cabinet member. A dedicated conservationist and an active foe of fascism.

FRITZ KUHN (1886–1951) German-born veteran of World War One, emigrated to America in 1927, and by 1938, as Bundesleiter who considered himself the American Führer, had established the German-American Bund as most powerful, most active, and richest Nazi group in U.S., with membership of twenty-five thousand. Convicted of larceny in 1939, denaturalized in 1943, deported to Germany in 1945. In 1948, convicted by German denazification court of attempting to transplant Nazism to U.S. and of having close ties to Hitler; sentenced to ten years at hard labor.

HERBERT H. LEHMAN (1878–1963) A partner in Lehman Brothers, banking house founded by his family. Lieutenant governor of New York under Governor Roosevelt; succeeded Roosevelt as governor, 1932–1942. New Deal supporter and strong interventionist. As Democratic senator from New York (1949–1957), early opponent of Senator Joseph McCarthy.

JOHN L. LEWIS (1880–1969) American labor leader. In 1935, as president of the United Mine Workers, broke with the American Federation of Labor (AFL) to form the new Committee for Industrial Organization, which became the Congress of Industrial Organizations in 1938. Initially a supporter of Roosevelt's, backed Republican Willkie in 1940 election and resigned CIO presidency after Willkie's defeat. Strikes by UMW during the war led to further enmity between Lewis and the administration.

ANNE SPENCER MORROW LINDBERGH (1906–2001) American author and aviator. Born to wealth and privilege in Englewood, New Jersey; her father, Dwight Morrow, a partner in the investment firm of J. P. Morgan and Co., the U.S. ambassador to Mexico during the Hoover administration, and a Republican senator from New Jersey; and her mother, Elizabeth Reeve Cutter Morrow, a writer, an educator, and, briefly, the acting president of Smith College, where Morrow received an A.B. in literature in 1928. Introduced to Charles Lindbergh the year before, while visiting her family at the ambassador's residence in Mexico City. For details of Morrow's life after that meeting, see True Chronology, Charles A. Lindbergh.

HENRY MORGENTHAU, JR. (1891–1967) Roosevelt-appointed secretary of the Treasury, 1934–1945.

VINCENT MURPHY (1888–1976) Meyer Ellenstein's successor as mayor of Newark, 1941–1949. Democratic nominee for governor of New Jersey in 1943 and dominant figure in New Jersey labor for thirty-five years after his 1933 election as secretary-treasurer of state Federation of Labor.

GERALD P. NYE (1892–1971) Ardently isolationist Republican senator from North Dakota, 1925–1945.

WESTBROOK PEGLER (1894–1969) Right-wing journalist whose column "As Pegler Sees It" appeared in Hearst newspapers from 1944 to 1962. In 1941 won Pulitzer Prize for exposé of labor racketeering. Fierce critic of the Roosevelts and the New Deal, which he characterized as Communist-inspired, and openly hostile toward the Jews. Close supporter and friend of Senator Joseph McCarthy, and adviser to McCarthy's investigating committee.

JOACHIM PRINZ (1902–1988) Rabbi, author, and civil rights activist, served as rabbi of Temple B'nai Abraham, Newark, 1939–1977.

JOACHIM VON RIBBENTROP (1893–1946) Hitler's chief foreign policy adviser in 1933 and minister for foreign affairs, 1938–1945. With Soviet foreign minister Molotov signed 1939 non-aggression pact that included secret agreement to partition Poland. Pact opened way for World War Two. Found guilty of war crimes at Nuremberg and, on October 16, 1946, became first of condemned Nazis to be hanged.

ELEANOR ROOSEVELT (1884–1962) Niece of Theodore Roosevelt, wife of her distant cousin FDR, and mother of their daughter and five sons. As First Lady, made speeches for liberal social causes, lectured on the status of minorities, the underprivileged, and women, spoke out against fascism, wrote daily syndicated column for sixty newspapers, and during World War Two was cochair of the Office of Civilian Defense. As U.N. delegate appointed by President Truman, supported establishment of a Jewish state, and in 1952 and 1956 campaigned for Adlai Stevenson for president. Appointed again as delegate to U.N. by President Kennedy, whose Bay of Pigs invasion she opposed.

LEVERETT SALTONSTALL (1892–1979) Descendant of Sir Richard Saltonstall, an original member of the Massachusetts Bay Company who arrived in America in 1630. Republican governor of Massachusetts, 1939–1944; Republican senator, 1944–1967.

GERALD L. K. SMITH (1898–1976) Minister and famous orator, allied first with Huey Long and later with Father Coughlin and Henry Ford, both of whom supported him in his unrelenting hatred of Jews. His anti-Semitic magazine, *The Cross and the Flag,* blamed the Jews for causing the Depression and World War Two. In 1942, polled 100,000 votes in Michigan as Republican nominee for Senate. Maintained that Roosevelt was a Jew, that *The Protocols of the Learned Elders of Zion* was an authentic document, and, after the war, that the Holocaust had never taken place.

ALLIE STOLZ (1918–2000) Lightweight boxer from Jewish Newark. Won 73 of 85 fights, losing two title fights in the 1940s; the first, a controversial fifteen-round decision, to champion Sammy Angott; the second—leading to his retirement in 1946—a thirteenth-round knockout, to champion Bob Montgomery.

DOROTHY THOMPSON (1893–1961) Journalist, political activist, and columnist syndicated in 170 newspapers during the 1930s. Early foe of Nazism and Hitler and bitter critic of Lindbergh's politics. Married to novelist Sinclair Lewis in 1928 and divorced in 1942. Opposed Zionism and supported Palestinian Arabs in 1940s and 1950s.

DAVID T. WILENTZ (1894–1988) New Jersey attorney general (1934–1944) whose prosecution of the Lindbergh baby kidnapping case led to the conviction and execution of Bruno Hauptmann. Later, influential in New Jersey Democratic organization and adviser to three Democratic governors of the state.

ABNER "LONGY" ZWILLMAN (1904–1959) Newark-born Prohibition era bootlegger who was leading New Jersey mobster from 1920s to 1940s. Member of East Coast racketeering's "Big Six," among them Lucky Luciano, Meyer

Lansky, and Frank Costello. Extensive criminal activities exposed by Senate Crime Committee's televised hearings in 1951. Committed suicide eight years later.

Some Documentation

Speech by Charles Lindbergh, "Who Are the War Agitators?," delivered at the America First Committee's rally in Des Moines on September 11, 1941. The text that follows appears at www.pbs.org/wgbh/amex/lindbergh/filmmore/reference/primary/desmoinesspeech.html.

It is now two years since this latest European war began. From that day in September, 1939, until the present moment, there has been an ever-increasing effort to force the United States into the conflict.

That effort has been carried on by foreign interests, and by a small minority of our own people; but it has been so successful that, today, our country stands on the verge of war.

At this time, as the war is about to enter its third winter, it seems appropriate to review the circumstances that have led us to our present position. Why are we on the verge of war? Was it necessary for us to become so deeply involved? Who is responsible for changing our national policy from one of neutrality and independence to one of entanglement in European affairs?

Personally, I believe there is no better argument against our intervention than a study of the causes and developments of the present war. I have often said that if the true facts and issues were placed before the American people, there would be no danger of our involvement.

Here, I would like to point out to you a fundamental difference between the groups who advocate foreign war, and those who believe in an independent destiny for America.

If you will look back over the record, you will find that those of us who oppose intervention have constantly tried to clarify facts and issues; while the interventionists have tried to hide facts and confuse issues.

We ask you to read what we said last month, last year, and even before the war began. Our record is open and clear, and we are proud of it.

We have not led you on by subterfuge and propaganda. We have not resorted to steps short of anything, in order to take the American people where they did not want to go.

What we said before the elections, we say again and again, and again today. And we will not tell you tomorrow that it was just campaign oratory.

Have you ever heard an interventionist, or a British agent, or a member of the administration in Washington ask you to go back and study a record of what they have said since the war started? Are their self-styled defenders of democracy willing to put the issue of war to a vote of our people? Do you find these crusaders for foreign freedom of speech, or the removal of censorship here in our own country?

The subterfuge and propaganda that exists in our country is obvious on every side. Tonight, I shall try to pierce through a portion of it, to the naked facts which lie beneath.

When this war started in Europe, it was clear that the American people were solidly opposed to entering it. Why shouldn't we be? We had the best defensive position in the world; we had a tradition of independence from Europe; and the one time we did take part in a European war left European problems unsolved, and debts to America unpaid.

National polls showed that when England and France declared war on Germany, in 1939, less than 10 percent of our population favored a similar course for America.

But there were various groups of people, here and abroad, whose interests and beliefs necessitated the involvement of the United States in the war. I shall point out some of these groups tonight, and outline their methods of procedure. In doing this, I must speak with the utmost frankness, for in order to counteract their efforts, we must know exactly who they are.

The three most important groups who have been pressing this country toward war are the British, the Jewish and the Roosevelt administration.

Behind these groups, but of lesser importance, are a number of capitalists, Anglophiles, and intellectuals who believe that the future of mankind depends upon the domination of the British empire. Add to these the Communistic groups who were opposed to intervention until a few weeks ago, and I believe I have named the major war agitators in this country.

I am speaking here only of war agitators, not of those sincere but misguided men and women who, confused by misinformation and frightened by propaganda, follow the lead of the war agitators.

As I have said, these war agitators comprise only a small minority of our people; but they control a tremendous influence. Against the determination of the American people to stay out of war, they have marshaled the power of their propaganda, their money, their patronage.

Let us consider these groups, one at a time.

First, the British: It is obvious and perfectly understandable that Great Britain wants the United States in the war on her side. England is now in a desperate position. Her population is not large enough and her armies are not strong enough to invade the continent of Europe and win the war she declared against Germany.

Her geographical position is such that she cannot win the war by the use of aviation alone, regardless of how many planes we send her. Even if America entered the war, it is improbable that the Allied armies could invade Europe and overwhelm the Axis powers. But one thing is certain. If England can draw this country into the war, she can shift to our shoulders a large portion of the responsibility for waging it and for paying its cost.

As you all know, we were left with the debts of the last European war; and unless we are more cautious in the future than we have been in the past, we will be left with the debts of the present case. If it were not for her hope that she can make us responsible for the war financially, as well as militarily, I believe England would have negotiated a peace in Europe many months ago, and be better off for doing so.

England has devoted, and will continue to devote every effort to get us into the war. We know that she spent huge sums of money in this country during the last war in order to involve us. Englishmen have written books about the cleverness of its use.

We know that England is spending great sums of money for propaganda in America during the present war. If we were Englishmen, we would do the same. But our interest is first in America; and as Americans, it is essential for us to realize the effort that British interests are making to draw us into their war.

The second major group I mentioned is the Jewish.

It is not difficult to understand why Jewish people desire the overthrow of Nazi Germany. The persecution they suffered in Germany would be sufficient to make bitter enemies of any race.

No person with a sense of the dignity of mankind can condone the persecution of the Jewish race in Germany. But no person of honesty and vision can look on their pro-war policy here today without seeing the dangers involved in such a policy, both for us and for them. Instead of agitating for war, the Jewish groups in this country should be opposing it in every possible way for they will be among the first to feel its consequences.

Tolerance is a virtue that depends upon peace and strength. History shows that it cannot survive war and devastation. A few far-sighted Jewish people realize this and stand opposed to intervention. But the majority still do not.

Their greatest danger to this country lies in their large ownership and influence in our motion pictures, our press, our radio and our government.

I am not attacking either the Jewish or the British people. Both races, I admire. But I am saying that the leaders of both the British and the Jewish races, for reasons which are as understandable from their viewpoint as they are inadvisable from ours, for reasons which are not American, wish to involve us in the war.

We cannot blame them for looking out for what they believe to be their own interests, but we also must look out for ours. We cannot allow the natural passions and prejudices of other peoples to lead our country to destruction.

The Roosevelt administration is the third powerful group which has been carrying this country toward war. Its members have used the war emergency to obtain a third presidential term for the first time in American history. They have used the war to add unlimited billions to a debt which was already the highest we have ever known. And they have just used the war to justify the restriction of congressional power, and the assumption of dictatorial procedures on the part of the president and his appointees.

The power of the Roosevelt administration depends upon the maintenance of a wartime emergency. The prestige of the Roosevelt administration depends upon the success of Great Britain to whom the president attached his political future at a time when most people thought that England and France would easily win the war. The danger of the Roosevelt administration lies in its subterfuge. While its members have promised us peace, they have led us to war heedless of the platform upon which they were elected.

In selecting these three groups as the major agitators for war, I have included only those whose support is essential to the war party. If any one of these groups—the British, the Jewish, or the administration—stops agitating for war, I believe there will be little danger of our involvement.

I do not believe that any two of them are powerful enough to carry this country to war without the support of the third. And to these three, as I have said, all other war groups are of secondary importance.

When hostilities commenced in Europe, in 1939, it was realized by these groups that the American people had no intention of entering the war. They knew it would be worse than useless to ask us for a declaration of war at that time. But they believed that this country could be entered into the war in very much the same way we were entered into the last one.

They planned: first, to prepare the United States for foreign war under the guise of American defense; second, to involve us in the war, step by step, without our realization; third, to create a series of incidents which would force us into the actual conflict. These plans were, of course, to be covered and assisted by the full power of their propaganda.

Our theaters soon became filled with plays portraying the glory of war. Newsreels lost all semblance of objectivity. Newspapers and magazines began to lose advertising if they carried anti-war articles. A smear campaign was instituted against individuals who opposed intervention. The terms "fifth columnist," "traitor," "Nazi," "anti-Semitic" were thrown ceaselessly at any one who dared to suggest that it was not to the best interests of the United States to enter the war. Men lost their jobs if they were frankly anti-war. Many others dared no longer speak.

Before long, lecture halls that were open to the advocates of war were closed to speakers who opposed it. A fear campaign was inaugurated. We were told that aviation, which has held the British fleet off the continent of Europe, made America more vulnerable than ever before to invasion. Propaganda was in full swing.

There was no difficulty in obtaining billions of dollars for arms under the guise of defending America. Our people stood united on a program of defense. Congress passed appropriation after appropriation for guns and planes and battleships, with the approval of the overwhelming majority of our citizens. That a large portion of these appropriations was to be used to build arms for Europe, we did not learn until later. That was another step.

To use a specific example; in 1939, we were told that we should increase our air corps to a total of 5,000 planes. Congress passed the necessary legislation. A few months later, the administration told us that the United States should have at least 50,000 planes for our national safety. But almost as fast as fighting planes were turned out from our factories, they were sent abroad, although our own air corps was in the utmost need of new equipment; so that today, two years after the start of war, the American army has a few hundred thoroughly modern bombers and fighters—less in fact, than Germany is able to produce in a single month.

Ever since its inception, our arms program has been laid out for the purpose of carrying on the war in Europe, far more than for the purpose of building an adequate defense for America.

Now at the same time we were being prepared for a foreign war, it was necessary, as I have said, to involve us in the war. This was accomplished under that now famous phrase "steps short of war."

England and France would win if the United States would only repeal its arms embargo and sell munitions for cash, we were told. And then a familiar refrain began, a refrain that marked every step we took toward war for many months—"the best way to defend America and keep out of war," we were told, was "by aiding the Allies."

First, we agreed to sell arms to Europe; next, we agreed to loan arms to Europe; then we agreed to patrol the ocean for Europe; then we occupied a European island in the war zone. Now, we have reached the verge of war.

The war groups have succeeded in the first two of their three major steps into war. The greatest armament program in our history is under way.

We have become involved in the war from practically every standpoint except actual shooting. Only the creation of sufficient "incidents" yet remains; and you see the first of these already taking place, according to plan—a plan that was never laid before the American people for their approval.

Men and women of Iowa: only one thing holds this country from war today. That is the rising opposition of the American people. Our system of democracy and representative government is on test today as it has never been before. We are on the verge of a war in which the only victor would be chaos and prostration.

We are on the verge of a war for which we are still unprepared, and for which no one has offered a feasible plan for victory—a war which cannot be won without sending our soldiers across the ocean to force a landing on a hostile coast against armies stronger than our own.

We are on the verge of war, but it is not yet too late to stay out. It is not too late to show that no amount of money, or propaganda, or patronage can force a free and independent people into war against its will. It is not yet too late to retrieve and to maintain the independent American destiny that our forefathers established in this new world.

The entire future rests upon our shoulders. It depends upon our action, our courage, and our intelligence. If you oppose our intervention in the war, now is the time to make your voice heard.

Help us to organize these meetings; and write to your representatives in Washington. I tell you that the last stronghold of democracy and representative government in this country is in our house of representatives and our senate.

There, we can still make our will known. And if we, the American people, do that, independence and freedom will continue to live among us, and there will be no foreign war.

From Lindbergh *by A. Scott Berg,* 1998

Peace, Lindbergh felt, could exist only so long as "we band together to preserve that most priceless possession, our inheritance of European blood, only
so long as we guard ourselves against attack by foreign armies and dilution
by foreign races." He viewed aviation as "a gift from heaven to those Western
nations who were already the leaders of their era . . . a tool specially shaped
for Western hands, a scientific art which others only copy in a mediocre fashion, another barrier between the teeming millions of Asia and the Grecian
inheritance of Europe—one of those priceless possessions which permit the
White race to live at all in a pressing sea of Yellow, Black, and Brown."

Lindbergh believed the Soviet Union had become the most evil empire on
earth and that Western civilization depended on repelling it and the Asiatic
powers that lay beyond its borders—the "Mongol and Persian and Moor." He
wrote that it also depended on "a united strength among ourselves; on a
strength too great for foreign armies to challenge; on a Western Wall of race
and arms which can hold back either a Genghis Khan or an infiltration of inferior blood . . ." (page 394)

www.randomhouse.co.uk/vintage